"Don't worry, I've done this very thing many times before,"

she said as she reached for the button on the waistband of his jeans.

He sucked in a hard breath. "I'll bet."

Nevada looked up at him with hard brown eyes. "That's the second time you've implied that I'm promiscuous. What gave you that idea?"

"You. You said you had boyfriends. Or did I misunderstand you?"

With a shake of her head, she focused her gaze on the fly of his jeans. "No. You didn't misunderstand. And aren't you glad I've got experience? Otherwise I might just get you all tangled up in this zipper."

Linc started to growl a warning to her but the loud sound of the zipper peeling open caused his mouth to snap shut. Now wasn't the time to press his luck. But if she didn't step away from him soon, he was going to do something crazy. Like grab her and kiss her until she couldn't say one more sassy word to him.

Dear Reader,

Well, it's September, which always sounds like a fresh start to me, no matter how old I get. And evidently we have six women this month who agree. In *Home Again* by Joan Elliott Pickart, a woman who can't have children has decided to work with them in a professional capacity—but when she is assigned an orphaned little boy, she fears she's in over her head. Then she meets his gorgeous guardian—and she's *sure* of it!

In the next installment of MOST LIKELY TO..., *The Measure of a Man* by Marie Ferrarella, a single mother attempting to help her beloved former professor joins forces with a former campus golden boy, now the college…custodian. What could have happened? Allison Leigh's *The Tycoon's Marriage Bid* pits a pregnant secretary against her ex-boss who, unbeknownst to him, has a real connection to her baby's father. In *The Other Side of Paradise* by Laurie Paige, next up in her SEVEN DEVILS miniseries, a mysterious woman seeking refuge as a ranch hand learns that she may have more ties to the community than she could have ever suspected. When a beautiful nurse is assigned to care for a devastatingly handsome, if cantankerous, cowboy, the results are…well, you get the picture—but you can have it spelled out for you in Stella Bagwell's next MEN OF THE WEST book, *Taming a Dark Horse*. And in *Undercover Nanny* by Wendy Warren, a domestically challenged female detective decides it's necessary to penetrate the lair of single father and heir to a grocery fortune by pretending to be…his nanny. Hmm. It *could* work….

So enjoy, and snuggle up. Fall weather is just around the corner….

Happy reading!

Gail Chasan
Senior Editor

Please address questions and book requests to:
Silhouette Reader Service
U.S.: 3010 Walden Ave., P.O. Box 1325, Buffalo, NY 14269
Canadian: P.O. Box 609, Fort Erie, Ont. L2A 5X3

TAMING A
DARK HORSE

Stella
Bagwell

Silhouette

SPECIAL EDITION

Published by Silhouette Books

America's Publisher of Contemporary Romance

To our own beloved horses:
Thunder, Trouble, Spider John, Diamond,
Rooster, Topper, Shy Girl, Badger, Miss Kitty,
Potion, Major Bob, Festus, Newly, Doll Brown,
Sante Fe Solid, Maggie and the baby on the way.

And also, in loving memory of Gus, my brother's great trail horse.

 SILHOUETTE BOOKS

ISBN 0-373-24709-5

TAMING A DARK HORSE

Copyright © 2005 by Stella Bagwell

Visit Silhouette Books at www.eHarlequin.com

Printed in U.S.A.

Books by Stella Bagwell

Silhouette Special Edition

Found: One Runaway Bride #1049
†*Penny Parker's Pregnant!* #1258
White Dove's Promise #1478
††*Should Have Been Her Child* #1570
††*His Defender* #1582
††*Her Texas Ranger* #1622
††*A Baby on the Ranch* #1648
In a Texas Minute #1677
††*Redwing's Lady* #1695
††*From Here to Texas* #1700
††*Taming a Dark Horse* #1709

Silhouette Books

The Fortunes of Texas
The Heiress and the Sheriff

Maitland Maternity
Just for Christmas

A Bouquet of Babies
†"Baby on Her Doorstep"

Midnight Clear
†"Twins under the Tree"

Going to the Chapel
"The Bride's Big Adventure"

Silhouette Romance

Golden Glory #469
Moonlight Bandit #485
A Mist on the Mountain #510
Madeline's Song #543
The Outsider #560
The New Kid in Town #587
Cactus Rose #621
Hillbilly Heart #634
Teach Me #657
The White Night #674
No Horsing Around #699
That Southern Touch #723
Gentle as a Lamb #748
A Practical Man #789
Precious Pretender #812
Done to Perfection #836
Rodeo Rider #878
**Their First Thanksgiving* #903
**The Best Christmas Ever* #909
**New Year's Baby* #915

Hero in Disguise #954
Corporate Cowgirl #991
Daniel's Daddy #1020
A Cowboy for Christmas #1052
Daddy Lessons #1085
Wanted: Wife #1140
†*The Sheriff's Son* #1218
†*The Rancher's Bride* #1224
†*The Tycoon's Tots* #1228
†*The Rancher's Blessed Event* #1296
†*The Ranger and the Widow Woman* #1314
†*The Cowboy and the Debutante* #1334
†*Millionaire on Her Doorstep* #1368
The Bridal Bargain #1414
Falling for Grace #1456
The Expectant Princess #1504
The Missing Maitland #1546
Because of the Ring #1589

††Men of the West
*Heartland Holidays
†Twins on the Doorstep

STELLA BAGWELL

sold her first book to Silhouette in November 1985. More than fifty novels later, she still loves her job and says she isn't completely content unless she's writing. Recently, she and her husband of more than thirty years moved from the hills of Oklahoma to Seadrift, Texas, a sleepy little fishing town located on the coastal bend. Stella says the water, the tropical climate and the seabirds make it a lovely place to let her imagination soar and to put the stories in her head down on paper.

She and her husband have one son, Jason, who lives and teaches high school math in nearby Port Lavaca.

HOW TO TAME A DARK HORSE:

1. Approach him with caution—he's an animal of flight.

2. Don't try to rope him too quickly—let him run until he tires.

3. When he starts to show interest, give him your shoulder—he'll want what he thinks he can't have.

4. When he decides to get close, talk to him—sweet whispered words in his ear will calm his fearful heart.

5. Once he allows you to touch him, show him you'll never hurt him—stroke him gently on his cheek and along his neck.

6. And finally, when he surrenders to you, give him a sugary treat—he'll love you for a lifetime.

Chapter One

"A nurse! Hell no! I don't need a nurse! I just need to get out of here!"

Linc Ketchum's loud protest rattled around the small hospital room. Normally he considered himself a quiet, unobtrusive guy, but since the terrible fire at the T Bar K horse barn two weeks ago he'd turned into a growling bear.

His tall, graying doctor gave him a stern look. "Sorry, Mr. Ketchum, but your hands and arms were badly burned and unless I'm assured that a nurse will be with you at all times, I cannot release you from this hospital. And that means round the clock.

You're still highly susceptible to infection and I don't want any sort of pressure placed on your hands before they heal completely. Your bandages will have to be changed routinely and your skin dressed. I want to know that it's done correctly."

Linc looked up at Dr. Olstead. "Hell, doc, if you're going to force me to have a nurse underfoot, I might as well stay in the hospital."

"I can certainly arrange that. As far as I'm concerned I'd rather have you here. But your family seems to think you'll heal better at home."

Grimacing, Linc glanced down at the sheets covering the lower half of his body. Except for short walks down the hall and sitting for brief spells in an armchair, he'd been stuck in this bed for too long. His whole body was beginning to ache. And that was just the physical side of things. Staring at the close, pale-green walls and the small television screen hanging in one corner of the room was enough to send him to the psychiatric ward. If he didn't get out of here soon he was going to start yelling and never stop.

"All right, doc. Whatever you say. If I have to have a nurse—well, guess there's not much I can do about it. At least I'll be getting out of here." He lifted his heavily bundled hands and arms. The stiff white objects reminded him of a couple of pesky tree stumps in an otherwise clean pasture. If he had to button his jeans without assistance, or walk out of the hospital naked, he'd be forced to choose the latter. "I want to get out of this mess, doc. I want to get back to work."

"I'm going to cut the bandaging down soon," the doctor assured him, "but it will be at least two or three more weeks before I'll even consider allowing you to go back to work."

Linc opened his mouth to protest, but the doctor jumped in before he could say a word and went on to discuss the do's and don'ts he wanted Linc to stick to once he was released from the hospital.

When the man finally left the room, Linc was overwhelmed and just a little angry at being put in such a vulnerable state. He was a man who had never needed or asked for anything. He took care of himself and had done so from the time he was a teenager. He didn't like depending on other people for anything. But it appeared as though in the coming days he was going to have to do a lot of things he didn't like.

The memories of the fire that had brought him here suddenly welled up in Linc's head. He saw flames ripping at the walls of the horse barn and licking at the gates to each stable, the terrified horses rearing and pawing as they tried to escape the fire closing in around them. Their frightened squeals and whinnies had mixed with the loud roar of the crackling flames and the horrible sound still continued to wake Linc from his sleep. And though he tried to forget, he couldn't get anything about that nightmarish night out of his mind.

Time after time, he'd run back into the burning barn, grabbing every mare that he could and opening stall gates that were being eaten up by the creeping fire. The only thing he had to be thankful for was that all his beloved horses had gotten out safely. Only one had been slightly burned and his cousin Ross had assured him that she was well on the mend. As for Linc, the ordeal had pretty much cooked his hands and arms. But when he thought of his mares and colts and stallion, he knew saving them was worth every second of the pain he was going through now.

"Well, we've finally gotten some good news," Ross said now as he and his sister Victoria entered the room. "At least you're getting out of here tomorrow. That's something to look forward to."

Ross Ketchum was Linc's cousin. The two of them were almost the same age and had grown up together on the Ketchum's T Bar K ranch. They shared the responsibilities of running the multi-million-dollar operation. In spite of Ross being talkative and outgoing and Linc liking his privacy, the two of them were more like brothers than anything else. They even shared the same physical characteristics: long legs, a lean torso full of muscles, dark-brown hair and green eyes. Only, Linc's hair was lighter than Ross's and his eyes a much darker, muddier green.

"Yeah," Linc mumbled. "But where the hell am I going to go? I'd drive the boys in the bunkhouse crazy and I can't have a nurse wandering around a bunch of naked cowboys in the mornings. Unless it was a male nurse."

Victoria Hastings, Ross's sister and a practicing medical doctor, looked at him and laughed. "I don't think any nurse would be welcome in the bunkhouse."

"Only if it was Nurse Goodbody," Ross jokingly interjected.

Victoria rolled her eyes toward the ceiling. "Ross, our cousin doesn't need a Nurse Goodbody. He needs good care and rest."

"And that's just what he's going to get, sis." Standing at the head of Linc's bed, Ross grinned down at him. "As soon as he moves into the big house with me and Bella."

"Oh no! That's your place. I'm not butting in."

The main ranch house had been built nearly fifty years earlier by Linc's father, Randolf, and Ross's father, Tucker. Back then, the two Ketchum men had been partners, each of them owning half of the T Bar K, a spread that covered several sections in northwestern New Mexico. Initially, both men and their wives had lived together in the monstrous house built of rock and logs. But eventually Randolf had developed heart disease, sold his half to his brother and built a modest house across the ridge from the main estate.

His cousins Seth, Ross and Victoria had always treated Linc as a sibling. All three of them had insisted he always have access to the Ketchum house and the ranch's funds just as if he were their brother. Linc had always been grateful for their generosity, but he'd never taken advantage of it. He was his own man. And he wanted to be able to say he'd earned what he had by hard work, not by handouts.

"Damn it, Linc. The house is yours, too," Ross said now. "It belongs to all of us. Bella and I just happen to be living in it. And you don't have to be told there's plenty of empty rooms in the place. In fact, there's so many Bella doesn't know what to do with them."

Mutiny tightened Linc's jaw as he looked up at his cousin. "You can fill those empty rooms with kids. That would be a damn sight better than hosting a helpless cowboy who can't even button his own jeans."

Ross chuckled. "We're *trying* to fill them with kids, Linc. But that takes time, you know. It will take us a while to fill that many rooms."

"Well, I'm not going to be underfoot," Linc grumbled. "You and Bella are still newlyweds, you need to be alone."

"Tell that to Marina," Victoria wryly interjected.

Marina had been the cook-housekeeper for the Ketchum family since Linc and his cousins had been born. The large Hispanic woman knew more about all of them than they did themselves. She had an extra soft spot for Ross and didn't make any bones about showing it. Nor did she worry about speaking her mind. And no doubt she would demand to help care for Linc.

"That's another thing," Ross quickly put in. "In the big house Marina will be available to the nurse and—"

"No!" Linc interrupted. "Marina already has too much to do. I'll not be piling more problems on her old shoulders."

"Damn it, Linc, you're acting like a child."

Since Linc couldn't use either hand or elbow, it took some doing for him to lever himself off the mattress, but he finally managed to sit up and glare hotly at his cousin. "All right, you cocky bastard. If you think—"

"Stop it! Stop it right now!" Victoria shouted at the two men. "There's no need for all this arguing."

"You're damn right, there's not," Ross said flatly. "Linc is going to do what I say!"

"Like hell!" Linc muttered.

Victoria interceded once again. "That's enough. Nobody is going to make Linc do something he doesn't want to do," she said to Ross and then resting her hands on the footboard of the bed, she leaned toward Linc and smiled encouragingly. "I have the solution, Linc. Your parents' old house is empty.

Grady, the foreman on the fence-building crew moved out a week ago. He bought a place of his own. So we'll have the house clean and ready for you by tomorrow."

Relief washed over Linc's face. "Victoria, you're a real darlin'."

"My husband tells me that very same thing everyday," she teased, then walked to the head of the bed, where she bent down and placed a kiss on Linc's clammy forehead. "Don't worry, cuz, I'm not going to let anyone badger you. Especially my mean ol' brother."

"Aw, Victoria, quit babying the man," Ross complained, but there was a half grin on his face to soften his words. "You'll have him so spoiled by the time he gets well, he'll be worthless to all of us."

This time Linc didn't let Ross's jabs rile him. Now that he knew where he was going to go once he was released from the hospital, there was another pressing problem on his mind.

"Sounds good, Victoria, but what about a nurse? I can't imagine any woman wanting to stay out at the ranch. Especially not round the clock."

Victoria frowned at him. "Why not? The ranch is beautiful. And even though the house isn't anything fancy, it's very nice."

Linc shrugged as memories of his mother pushed at the edges of his thoughts. Darla had hated the ranch. The dust, the livestock, the isolation and the constant work it took from her husband to make the place go. He could still remember her arguing fiercely with his father and constantly throwing in his face threats to leave him and the whole mess behind.

Eventually his mother *had* left the ranch. But not until his father had died from the heart disease that had slowly debilitated him. Linc had been a young teenager when his father had finally passed away and at the time he'd often wondered why Darla bothered to hang around. She'd obviously not given a hoot for her husband. And she had not shown much more concern for Linc. She'd been content to let him run loose on the ranch and more or less take care of himself.

Darla had remarried quickly after his father's death and to his amazement, she'd demanded that Linc move to the east coast with her and her new husband. If the idea hadn't been so ludicrous it would have been laughable. Linc had lived his whole life on the T Bar K. He'd grown up with cousins who were his own age. The place was his home and would always be his home. He wasn't about to move to some city, away from everything he loved. So he'd chosen to stay behind and his mother had walked away without a backward glance.

"Well, yeah," he finally said to Victoria. "But some women—"

"I'm not going to hire just some woman," Victoria assured him. "If she isn't nice and reasonable, dedicated and completely qualified, then she isn't going to step foot on the ranch. Understand?"

Linc wanted to tell her that there wasn't any such woman of that sort who'd be willing to live under the same roof with him, even in a nurse/patient situation. But he kept his mouth shut. He'd already done enough arguing and complaining and Victoria was doing the best she could. At the very least, he was grateful.

"Where are you going to find a woman like that?" Ross questioned his sister. "They don't grow on trees around here, you know."

She made a face at her brother. "I am a doctor, remember? I do have sources. Trust me, I'll find one."

Quickly skirting the bed, Ross looped his arm through Victoria's and tugged her toward the door. "Sounds like a big job to me. You'd better get out of here and get started on it. Linc and I have important things to discuss."

"I hope it's horses," Linc said from his seat on the bed. "Because I'm sure sick of discussing nurses!"

"Oh, all right, I'm out of here," Victoria said with a helpless shake of her head. "But just remember, Linc, you can't get back to work until you heal. And you'll need a nurse to get you there."

"Yeah. Well, I guess a man can stand most anything if he has to," Linc muttered.

* * *

Later that afternoon, Nevada Ortiz was in the middle of trying to immunize a baby boy, who was displaying a whale of a screaming fit, when her boss, Dr. Victoria Hastings called to her.

"Nevada, as soon as you're finished there, I want to see you in my office."

Nevada swiped the baby's thigh with an alcohol square and tried to still his kicking foot.

"What about Mr. Buckhorn?" Nevada called to her. "He's in the waiting room and Joyce says he already went outside twice to smoke a cigarette."

Clearly frustrated, Victoria let out a sigh. "All right. I'll finish up with him and then I'll see you in my office."

"She sounds like she means business," the young woman holding the baby said. "What have you done wrong, Nevada?"

Since Aztec, New Mexico, was a small town, almost everyone was acquainted with each other. And since Nevada had worked as a nurse in Aztec for six of her twenty-five years, she'd met lots of people, including the young mother holding squalling Henry.

Nevada shrugged and smiled. "Not too much today. But little Henry may disagree." She rubbed the spot on the baby's thigh where she'd injected him, and after about two seconds his cries were replaced with a dimpled smile. "Now see there," she told the boy, "that wasn't so bad, was it? And look what you get now."

Reaching into her uniform pocket, she pulled out a red lollipop, removed the cellophane and handed the treat to the baby. Grabbing it, he let out a happy coo and Nevada patted his cheek.

"Be sure that you watch him for any signs of fever or rash," she told the mother. "Since this is a booster, I don't expect him to have any problems, but if he does, go ahead and give us a call."

"I will. Thank you, Nevada."

Once she was sure mother and baby were on their way out of the examining room, Nevada hurried to the front of the building to retrieve Mr. Buckhorn's chart from the hundreds that filled the shelves on a wall behind the receptionist's desk.

Leaning down, she whispered in Joyce's ear, "Has he been outside again? Or just having a cussing fit?"

The receptionist didn't have to be told that Nevada was talking about Mr. Buckhorn. He was the only patient left in the waiting room.

"Neither, thank God," the receptionist answered. "I turned the television on to the Western channel. Sunset Carson is keeping him occupied."

Smiling, Nevada picked up the elderly man's chart and walked to the door of the waiting room. "Mr. Buckhorn, you can come back now," she called to him.

The old Navajo slowly turned his head and leveled

an annoyed look at her. "I've already waited too long, young lady." He jabbed a finger in the direction of the television. "I gotta see what this cowboy is gonna do with this gunslinger."

"He's going to shoot him, that's what," Nevada told him. "And Dr. Hastings is going to shoot you if you don't get back here. She doesn't have time to wait around on old men like you."

Mumbling what sounded like Navajo curse words, the old man slapped a beat-up cowboy hat on his head and slowly rose to his feet. By the time he made it to Nevada, though, he was in a better mood and his wide, wrinkled grin made his dark eyes sparkle playfully.

"I'm not so old, missy. I have a girlfriend. See her every day, too."

"Smells like you have a cigarette every day, too. You know that Doc is gonna be angry with you."

His chuckles were full of mischief. "She'll get over it."

More than thirty minutes later, Nevada was finally able to meet with Victoria. The day had been long and both women were exhausted. Nevada practically fell into the stuffed armchair sitting near the doctor's wide desk.

"What a day!" Nevada exclaimed. "How many patients did we see anyway?"

Victoria tried to smile. "I quit counting after we hit twenty."

Reaching up, Nevada began to pull the pins from the braided black bun at the back of her head. Once the last one was removed, the long silky strands fell to her shoulders, and she gave the heavy mane a shake.

"So, what have I done now?" Nevada asked her boss. "Made a patient angry? I know Mr. Tallman complained about the shot I gave him. But honestly, Victoria, the man is a wimp."

Leaning back in her chair, Victoria chuckled tiredly. "You haven't done a thing wrong, Nevada. And you're right, he is a wimp. But none of that is why I wanted to talk to you this evening."

Nevada looked at her boss with interest. "Oh? What's happened? Are you going to take off work or something?"

Victoria slowly shook her head. "Actually, I probably should take off work. But right now it's just not feasible. Dr. Martinez is out of town on vacation and won't be back for one more week. I have no one to replace me. At least, no one that I would trust with my patients." Folding her hands atop the desk, she leaned up and looked intently at Nevada. "You see, I'm having a problem. I'm hunting a dependable nurse. Someone I can really count on."

Shocked, Nevada stared at the other woman. "Oh.

You mean, uh—you think I can't handle all the work around here? I thought you and I worked well together."

Victoria quickly waved a hand at her. "Nevada, my dear, I couldn't do without you. You're my right arm. And I really don't know how I'm going to get through the next few weeks if you agree to this."

"This?" Nevada asked carefully. "What *is* this?"

Massaging her forehead, Victoria said, "I need you to do me a favor. A big favor."

"Of course. Anything," Nevada quickly agreed.

"Wait a minute," Victoria said as her hand fell away from her face. "You'd better hear me out before you agree. This might be a project you won't want to get yourself into."

Nevada scooted onto the edge of her seat. "You've got me curious now. And you know how much I love challenges."

Chuckling, Victoria said, "Well, I have a feeling this will be one. You know my cousin Linc was burned badly in the barn fire at the ranch."

Nevada nodded soberly. "Yes. How is he doing?"

"Actually, he's going to be released from the hospital tomorrow."

Nevada shot her boss a bright smile. "That's good news. From what you told me, his burns were very serious. He must be doing much better."

"He is. And Ross and I persuaded the doctor that he'd do even better if he was allowed to go home. The doctor agreed. But only if we could find a nurse to stay with him round the clock. I thought of you."

"Me!" Nevada's hand fluttered to her chest. "Victoria! I—I couldn't."

Victoria leveled a wry look at her. "You just told me you would do anything."

"Yes, I did. But I didn't have any idea you'd be asking something like this. I don't even know your cousin! And I'd practically be living with the man!"

"You *would* be living with him," Victoria corrected. "He can't be left alone. He can't use his hands in any way. Not yet. So you can imagine how much care he's going to need."

"Yes, I can imagine." Nevada felt awful for Linc Ketchum. Even though she'd never met the man, she understood the pain and suffering he must be going through. She'd attended to many burn patients over her years of nursing and she understood the care he would need. But she didn't really want to leave her home for two or three weeks. And living with a man? Well, she'd always been adventurous but that was taking it a bit too far.

"But I really don't think I'm the nurse you need."

"You're exactly the nurse Linc needs. These injuries haven't just disabled him physically, they've tugged him down emotionally. Normally, Linc is a gentle, easygoing man. Everyone admires and loves him. But this morning he actually cussed at Ross. He needs to get his mind off the fire and off his confinement. If anyone can do that, you can."

Nevada let out an incredulous laugh. "How? By playing dominos or poker with the man? Victoria, I don't know anything about him. I wouldn't even know how to talk to him."

Smiling, Victoria said, "You? Not know how to talk to a man? Come on, my dear, that sort of thing comes to you naturally."

"That's another thing. I have a life here in town. How could I go out on dates if I'm stuck on the T Bar K? You know that I have boyfriends. They won't understand."

"If that's the case, you don't need them."

A long sigh slipped past Nevada's lips. She'd tried, but she could see there was no talking Victoria out of this. "You really mean this, don't you?"

"Nevada. I can't think of anyone better," she said with a soft voice. "No one else would suit Linc. He's a man who needs gentle care."

Nevada studied Victoria's face and could easily see the signs of worry etching her eyes and mouth. "You love your cousin very much, don't you?"

Victoria nodded. "I always have. Linc is special— to all of us. He's like our brother. And yet he's always wanted to remain independent. I don't know why. But he's a strong, compassionate man and it makes me want to sob when I see him like he is now."

Feeling her eyes grow misty, Nevada walked around the desk and place a hand on Victoria's slender shoulder. "Don't worry. You should know I'll take on the job. I can't say no to you even when I want to."

Victoria looked up at her gratefully. "Don't do this just for me, Nevada. Do it for Linc. Okay?"

Uneasiness rippled through Nevada and made her hesitate. But only for a moment and then she smiled. "All right. I'll do this for Linc."

Chapter Two

He was sitting on the porch of his father's old house when a little white sports car covered with the red dust of T Bar K land pulled to a stop a few feet from the rail fence that enclosed the house and yard, a yard which was little more than a patch of raw mountain land filled with boulders, pine trees and sagebrush.

Rising slowly from his chair, Linc ambled toward the fence as his squinted eyes tried to make out the person behind the dusty windshield. And as he waited for the nurse to climb out of the vehicle he told himself it didn't matter what sort of person this woman was just so long as she stayed out of his hair as much as possible.

The door to the car finally swung open and Linc caught the glimpse of jeans-clad legs and long, raven-black hair being blown by the evening breeze.

He watched her catch her flyaway hair with a brown hand as she turned to greet him.

"Hello," she called cheerfully. "I guess you must be Linc."

Dear God, what had Victoria done to him, he wondered. This woman wasn't a nurse. She couldn't be. She was very young and looked more like a sexy siren than a caregiver. Her petite body had more curves than the mountain road leading up to the house and her face was full of dimples, sparkling brown eyes and lips the color of a ripe cherry. This was not the sort of woman he needed sleeping across the hall from him.

"That would be me," he replied, while wondering how he could tell her to go home and still be polite about it.

She walked up to him and smiled. "I'd offer you my hand. But since you can't take it, I'll just say I'm glad to be here."

Topping her jeans was a red jersey shirt that had slipped down on one shoulder. On her small feet were wedge sandals tall enough to break her ankles. Linc couldn't prevent his gaze from climbing up from her painted toenails to the top of her head and back down again. "Where did Victoria find you?" he asked rudely.

The blunt question lifted Victoria's delicate black brows. "Well, not out of a hole if that's what you're thinking. I'm her nurse. I figured you knew that. Haven't you ever been to Victoria's clinic?"

He shook his head while hating the fact that she was making him feel downright stupid. "I don't ever need to be doctored." He frowned as his gaze focused on his bandaged hands. "At least, not until the fire."

"Well, you must be very lucky," Nevada said while her eyes took in the sight of Victoria's cousin.

He practically glowered at her and lifted the thick white bandages directly in front of her face.

"Lucky? You call this lucky?"

Unaffected by his sarcasm, she nodded. "If you've lived all these years without needing a doctor's care, you're a very fortunate man, Linc Ketchum. And as for those—" she inclined her head toward his burns, "better your hands than your whole body being toasted."

She was right and he knew it, but that didn't make him feel any better. Still, he thanked God that he'd gotten out of the fire before it had consumed him.

"Yeah," he said, then walking around her, he peered into the car's back seat. It was piled with enough luggage to fill two closets. His jaw tightened. "It looks like you've come to stay."

Turning slightly toward him, Nevada frowned. "Of course I've come to stay. You need someone here with you at all times."

He drew in a bracing breath then blew it out. "Well, I don't want to sound rude, but I don't think you're gonna be that person."

She whirled completely around to stare at him. "What?"

He shrugged as a sheepish expression stole over his lean face. Normally he went to great lengths to handle people gently, the same way he handled his horses. But this firebrand standing in front of him was scratching his hackles in the wrong direction.

"I said I don't think you're the right person to stay with me."

Nevada's eyes narrowed as her hands came to rest on either side of her waist. "You don't, huh? Well, just what sort of person would you like to have staying with you?" she asked in a voice that dripped sweetness.

"None! Damn it. I can get along without anybody's help. And I have no idea why Victoria sent you up here! I don't even believe you're a nurse!"

Nevada folded her arms against her breasts. This outburst from her patient wasn't too big a surprise. Victoria had already warned her that since the fire Linc had been on a rampage. And she'd heard a long time ago that the man was a recluse. She'd asked

Victoria about the hearsay and the doctor had confirmed it as true, saying she couldn't remember the last time Linc Ketchum had ever stepped foot off the T Bar K. Poor man, Nevada thought. He really needed her help.

"Why not?" she asked simply.

He stepped closer and it was then that Nevada allowed herself to really look at him. When she'd first driven up, she'd gotten the impression of long legs, muscles and shoulders broad enough to carry her weight twice over. Now she could study his face close up and as far as she was concerned it was a work of pure art.

A Roman nose, square jaw and chin, and darkgreen eyes set beneath a pair of black brows. At the moment he was wearing a cowboy hat the color of creamed coffee, but she could see the hair next to it was slightly darker and curled against his head in a touch-me-please way. Victoria had told her that Linc was thirty-eight and all Nevada could think at the moment was what a hunk of a man Linc Ketchum had grown into in those thirty-eight years.

"Because you don't look like a nurse. Or sound like one, either," he answered.

Nevada couldn't help but laugh. "Really? I guess you must be an expert on nurses?"

He grimaced. "No. But—"

Nevada stepped forward and put her hand on his

shoulder. It was warm, rock-hard and caused her skin to sizzle.

"Listen, Linc. Victoria tried to find a nurse other than me. She couldn't. No one was willing to come all the way out here and stay for two weeks."

"That's not surprising," Linc muttered. "If a woman has to go without electricity for one hour, she thinks she's been traumatized."

"Hmm. Is that so? I had to go without electricity for two days last winter. Ice did something to the lines going to my apartment. But you know, I made it okay. Didn't feel a bit traumatized."

Glowering, he looked away from her. "I guess you're trying to say that I should be grateful that you were willing to take care of me?"

Her hand felt as though it was vibrating on his shoulder and she pulled it away, hoping it would put an end to the odd sensation. "Well, you don't have to go so far as to be grateful. Just civil will be enough for me."

His head twisted back around and Nevada felt something jerk in her chest as his dark-green gaze landed on her face. "You're doing this for Victoria's sake, aren't you?" he asked, then quickly added, "No. Don't answer that. I already know that you are."

"Well, well. You not only think you're an expert on nurses, you also think you're a mind reader. You must have many talents, Mr. Ketchum."

Ignoring her sarcasm, he said, "See, you're not even bothering to deny it."

Nevada smiled at him. "Why should I bother? You seem to know the answer already."

He heaved out a heavy breath. "Well, I guess that part of it doesn't matter. I just don't like feeling beholden to anybody."

Nevada's expression turned serious. "Look, Linc, I'm here because I chose to be here. I'm a nurse and when it all boils down, I can't turn away from someone who needs my help. No matter who they're related to. Now if you don't mind, I need to unload my things from the car."

She stepped around him and jerked the car door open. Linc watched with helpless frustration as she pulled out several pieces of luggage and piled them on the ground. Normally, he would never allow a female to lift anything heavier than a plate of food in his presence. But as it was he was so incapacitated he couldn't even pick up her handbag.

"If you need help with that I can call someone up from the main house," he finally offered.

She glanced his way. "Thank you. But they're not a problem for me to carry."

He watched her shove one of the bags beneath her armpit and pick up two more with her hands. How the hell was he going to deal with this woman for two weeks or more, he wondered. She'd already managed to make him feel like a helpless idiot. Moreover, she was just too damn sexy.

"I—uh—I'd help if I could," he felt compelled to say.

She started moving toward the house and he fell in beside her.

"I know that," she said. "Don't apologize for your condition. You can't help it. Just try to get well as quickly as you can."

The two of them crossed the rough ground of the yard and climbed onto the porch. There Nevada turned to look at the view. The house was facing south and some distance over on the next mountain ridge she could spot the top of the main ranch house. Between here and there was nothing but forested mountains.

"This is beautiful," she said with quiet awe.

Linc looked at her, faintly surprised by the sincerity in her voice. "Yeah, but give yourself a few days and you'll be screaming to see town again."

She flashed him a glance. "How could you predict that? You don't even know me."

"Women can't stand the isolation."

Obviously Linc Ketchum wasn't just down on being incapacitated, he was also down on women for some reason that Nevada would very much like to know.

"Excuse me, but Victoria lived her whole life on this ranch until she went to med school and married Jess."

He waved away her words. "Victoria is different. She's a ranch girl, a cowgirl."

Nevada wanted to ask him what he thought she was, but she didn't bother. Now wasn't the time to try to dig into him. If she was going to be able to make it through the next two or three weeks, she needed to keep peace with the man.

"Well, don't worry about me getting cabin fever. I'm sure you'll keep me entertained," she said, then turning to the door, she opened it and stepped inside.

Linc quickly followed her into the small foyer and then into the long living room until she stopped abruptly and stared all around her.

"Oh! This is lovely. This looks almost like the big ranch house. Only smaller."

The room had off-white walls and a high ceiling crossed with heavy oak beams stained a deep brown. The floor was covered with a shiny brown-and-beige tile and a good portion of the north wall was built of plate glass. The landscape past the window was breathtaking and framed the peaks of the distant San Juan Mountains, which, in spite of it being midsummer, still hung on to their caps of snow.

"You sound surprised," Linc said as he watched her drop her bags and walk slowly around the room. "What were you expecting?"

She shot him a frank glance. "Nothing like this. Victoria told me this was just a small ranch house that they leased to any of the ranch hands who had a family and were in need of housing."

"She told you right."

"Goodness! This is so—beautiful!" Continuing her walk around the room, she inspected the leather furniture, the Western photos and paintings on the walls and the wagon wheel that dropped from the center beam in the ceiling. The wooden wheel was circled with lights that were fashioned in the shape of old-time lanterns.

The fact that she was so taken with the house both surprised and pleased Linc. He hadn't expected such a reaction from her. To look at her, she seemed like the modern-apartment type.

"I'm sure it seems dated and stuffy to you."

"Not at all," she said as she headed toward an opening that looked as though it would lead to the kitchen area.

Linc followed her into the kitchen to a pine table and benches located near another wide window. From here Nevada could look down upon the ranch. From this angle, looking left, she could see a meadow filled with black Angus cattle and the sparkling ribbon that was the Animas River.

"Where do you live?" Linc wanted to know.

She glanced away from the window and over to him. He was standing only a couple of feet away from her and she picked up the faint masculine scent of his body. An inward shiver raced through her as she looked at him, and she hoped the reaction wasn't showing on her face. The last thing she needed was for this man to think she was attracted to him.

Which she wasn't. She couldn't be. He was a patient.

"In Aztec. In an apartment." She grinned wryly. "My kitchen view is of an alleyway. The only good thing about it is that I get to see an assortment of stray cats hunting through the garbage cans."

"Hmmph. I'll bet you're the kind of woman who pours feed out for them."

She laughed guiltily. "Well, I am soft-hearted when it comes to animals," she admitted. "And I'd never let one go hungry for any reason."

"You like animals?" he asked.

Once again he sounded surprised and Nevada wondered where he'd formed his opinions about women.

"Very much. In fact when I first started college I had plans to become a veterinarian. But then a close friend of mine became seriously ill and I decided that maybe I was meant to help people get well."

"Did you help your friend?"

Shaking her head, Nevada turned away from him. He didn't need to see any sort of sadness or woe on her face. Not now. Linc Ketchum needed to see bright skies ahead and she was determined to show them to him. "No. She died. And that only reinforced my resolve to stay in medicine." Turning she smiled at him. "But that's in the past. And right now I think I'd better go carry in the rest of my things and get settled in."

She turned and walked out of the kitchen and Linc found himself wanting to follow her, talk to her, if for no other reason than to hear her voice. Which didn't make one iota of sense to him.

Linc didn't talk to women just for the sake of making conversation. Sure there were women who came to the T Bar K looking to buy a horse or colt or have a mare bred by one of the ranch's champion stallions. And Linc didn't have any problems dealing with them. But as far as his personal life went, he'd always made it a policy to steer clear of women.

It wasn't that he disliked the opposite sex. To Linc, women were pretty much like the horses he tended. Most of them were very beautiful, but they were also high-strung and unpredictable. If he ever let his guard down around one, even the sweet-natured ones, he was taking a big risk of getting hurt, and hurt badly. So he stayed alert and safe around his horses and the women he happened to come in contact with.

The front door opened and closed for a second time and he realized Nevada had already returned to the house. He quickly left the kitchen and walked out to the living room to see her hefting three more bags.

"If you'll show me where I'll be sleeping, I'll get these things out of the way," she told him.

As he walked across the long room to join her, he thought about having her sleep in the small upstairs bedroom. The farther he could put her away from him, the better he'd feel. And the room did have a pretty view and a nice set of oak bedroom furniture. But it would be mean of him to make her climb the stairs with all those things. So he motioned for her to follow him down a long wide hall that was covered with more tile.

Halfway down the corridor, he motioned to their left. "There's two rooms here that are pretty much the same. Take your pick. It doesn't matter to me," he lied.

Her gaze went from one door to the other, then across the hall to where two more doors were located. "Where is your room?" she asked.

Frowning, he asked, "Is that really important?"

She made a face of disbelief. "You *are* my patient. I need to be as close as possible. It will make things easier for me and you both."

"I don't need help getting to bed."

Dropping the bags, she turned a disgusted look on him. "Really? You can unbutton your jeans and shirt? You can pull back the covers?"

Dear Lord, he was going crazy. Of course he couldn't do those things. But how in hell could he let this woman undress him? To have her pretty brown

hands touching him in such a way would be downright decadent.

"Well, I can manage somehow. There's no
need—"

"Look, Linc Ketchum, this is no time to be bashful or modest. I'm a nurse. I know all about men's
anatomies. Helping you out of your jeans won't turn
me three shades of red or make me want to attack you
with lust in my eyes."

She was so cute and sassy and reasonable that it
made him furious. But he tried his best to bite it all
back and behave as the cool cowboy he'd always believed himself to be.

"Miss Ortiz, you've just relieved all my worries,"
he said curtly.

She studied his face, the faint grin on her lips
coming and going along with the dimples in her
cheeks. Linc forced himself to stay put even though
her nearness was affecting him the way the scent of
a wild deer excites a docile horse.

"I'm glad we got all that straight," she said. "It
would be awkward if we rubbed each other the
wrong way right from the start."

As far as Linc was concerned it would be awkward if they rubbed each other any way. But then he
couldn't rub her even if he wanted to. Not with hands
that resembled two white clubs.

Trying not to look petulant, he jerked his head toward the door behind him. "That's my room. So this one—" he motioned to the door behind her shoulder. "Would be the closest to mine."

"Okay."

She turned and opened the door and Linc felt compelled to follow her into the bedroom.

"Oh! This is lovely, too. Goodness, Victoria must have sent an army of maids up here. Everything looks so beautiful and it smells like wood polish."

She walked over and trailed her fingers over the fat carved end post of the bed. Linc was surprised that she was so impressed with the house and its furnishings. He expected that as a nurse she made a very nice salary. Victoria wanted the best in her clinic, and he knew she would be willing to pay far more than hospital wages to this woman. But apparently she wasn't used to expensive surroundings.

"Then I take it that the room is okay with you?" he asked.

She glanced around the room which had a small alcove that held a desk, chair and a graceful floor lamp.

"It's more than okay. It's just great," she murmured as she ran fingers along the silky comforter on the bed. Turning to him, she smiled. "I've never lived anywhere this nice before. I'm not going to know how to feel," she said, then laughing, she bounced on the edge of the mattress. "No broken springs or sags in the middle."

"I'm sure your apartment is very nice," he said as he stood watching her playful antics and wondering how it must feel to be that young and carefree. It had been so long, years and years, since he'd raced over the ranch yard with Ross and Seth and yelled at the top of his lungs with the pure joy of being alive and happy.

Seeing the sober look on his face took away some of the pleasure Nevada was feeling and the smile faded from her face. "It is nice for what I can afford. It takes a lot of money for rent and everything else that goes with making a living. Especially when you're trying to save, too."

Linc suddenly felt a little ashamed of himself. He'd never had to worry about money. His father had left him a fairly large inheritance and since then he'd earned plenty by managing the horse-breeding program for the ranch. In fact, money was something Linc rarely thought about. His home was on the ranch and he didn't want for many material things. But apparently Nevada didn't have it so easy.

"What are you saving for?"

She appeared surprised that he asked the question and frankly, he'd surprised himself. It was none of his business what she did with herself or her money. But something seemed to have happened to his common sense since Nevada Ortiz stepped out of her dusty little car.

She shrugged. "Oh, well, you know, the normal things. Mainly the future. For a family."

His brows slowly lifted as he watched her wavy black hair slide over one pert little breast. "You have someone you're planning to make a family with?"

Laughing softly, she rose from the mattress. "Goodness no! I have plenty of boyfriends, but none of them are husband material."

His frown was tinged with disgust. "If they're not husband material, then what are they?"

"Well, I'm sure you have girlfriends. It's the same thing. They're just companions, guys that I enjoy doing things with."

Linc wanted to kick himself for suddenly feeling so disillusioned. Just what was he expecting from this woman? he asked himself. She was young and beautiful. No doubt she had plenty of men friends she enjoyed herself with. To her they were probably nothing more than toys.

Ignoring the part about the girlfriends, he said, "If that's the case, then what do you call husband material?"

Pursing her lips with displeasure she shook her head. "I'm not really thinking about that now. I'm only twenty-five. I'm not ready to settle down. In fact, I'm not sure that I ever want to get married."

"You just said you wanted a family," he reminded her.

Her expression went stone-sober as she walked past him and picked up one of the cases she'd left in the doorway.

"I do. I just can't figure out how to have one without having a man in the house with me. Unfortunately you need one to produce children." Sighing, she placed the duffel bag upon the bed and began to pull out a stack of blue jeans. "But I keep hoping that someday I'll meet a man who will change my mind about love."

Love. Now that was a word he never spoke, didn't believe in, or want it discussed in his presence. It made him feel very squeamish.

Realizing it was long past time he left the room, Linc turned toward the door only to have her call after him.

"Where are you going?"

Without looking at her, he said, "To call down to the ranch to see if they can round you up a television from the big house. You're going to need something to keep you busy."

Her tinkling laugh filled the bedroom. "I don't need a television. I've got you to keep me busy."

Like hell, Linc thought.

Chapter Three

More than an hour passed before Nevada finished unpacking her things and arranging them just as she wanted in the big bedroom. The dresser and chest were massive, along with the walk-in closet. She could have brought every piece of clothing and toiletries she owned and they wouldn't have filled half the available space.

Nevada couldn't believe the house had been built just for the sole purpose of extra housing for ranch workers. It was too beautiful and, in spite of its old age, had been kept in perfect condition. Someone had taken great pains to copy the big ranch house and rich details could be seen in the dark oak casings around the windows and doors, the expensive tiling on the floor, not to mention the nice furnishings.

The first moment she'd walked into the house, she'd felt some sort of strange connection, a feeling that made her wonder if she was experiencing what it felt like to go home. Which had been an odd reaction for Nevada. Since she'd been a very young child, she hadn't ever felt like she had a home. At least, not like regular folks.

Even though she'd grown up in a house with two parents, it had been far from a normal home. Her mother and father had quarreled incessantly until their arguments had become out-and-out fights that included throwing fists and objects. Nevada had often hidden in the closet praying for the noise to stop and praying, too, that she would someday be able to escape the house that seemed to be filled with nothing but hate.

No. Nevada wasn't exactly sure what a real home would feel like, but she was certain this old house might hold the answers.

Giving one last look over her shoulder, she left the room. Her medical bag was still in the car and she wanted to get Linc's bandages changed before it was time for dinner. Something she was to cook, she supposed, since the closest restaurants or delis were at least twenty miles away. Nevada wasn't exactly brilliant in the kitchen, but if necessary she could put something edible on the table.

Humming to herself, she stepped onto the porch and immediately spotted Linc sitting a few steps away in a wooden rocker. His felt hat was pulled down over his eyes, but the moment he heard her footsteps and the creaking of the screen door closing behind her, he pushed it back on his forehead and cocked an eye at her.

"What are you doing?"

The question seemed comical to her and she laughed softly. "Does it matter?"

He scooted up from his slumped position in the chair. "No. Since you're going to be here for a while, I can't start worrying whether you can take care of yourself or not."

She walked over to him. "What do you mean, take care of myself?"

He shrugged one thick shoulder. "I just meant you surely have enough sense not to do silly things. Like walk out in the woods by yourself."

Nevada frowned. "Why shouldn't I walk in the woods?"

He let out a long sigh. "Bears for one thing. Another, you'd turn around once and be lost. The mountains and the basins begin to all look the same. You'd probably be to the Colorado border before you realized you were going north."

Nevada had to admit she wasn't necessarily good with directions and as for bears, one of those hairy creatures was the last thing she wanted to meet up with.

Smiling at him, she said, "You're probably right about that. I have to take a map with me just to find my way around Santa Fe. But that doesn't mean I can't get out in the woods. You'll be along to help me find the way."

Linc's mouth fell open. "Bullsh—"

He stopped abruptly before he released the last of the curse word and Nevada only smiled wider.

"What's the matter now? You don't like to take walks?" she asked.

Linc rolled his eyes. "I use my legs for a purpose. I walk all over the ranch yard. I don't walk for a woman's entertainment."

"But you're not working down at the ranch yard now," she sweetly pointed out. "And if it's safe to ask, just what do you do to entertain a woman? Can you sing or play the guitar?"

He scowled. "No and no."

"Oh," she said with feigned disappointment. "I thought all cowboys could do those two things."

"Only on television," he grumbled.

"Well, I'm sure you have some talents. And I'm bound to discover what they are before I leave here."

"Don't bet on that."

Laughing softly, Nevada stepped off the porch

and walked to her car. Once she had the medical bag out of the trunk, she carried it to the porch and motioned for Linc to follow her inside.

"What do you have there?" he asked suspiciously without making a move to do her bidding.

"My medical bag. And there's not a thing in here that will hurt you. So get to your feet and come along."

"I don't need any medicine. I've already taken it for today," he said as he managed to rise to his feet without the help of his arms or hands.

The man must have rock-hard abs, Nevada thought, to raise himself up with no help from his upper limbs. But she didn't need to be thinking about Linc Ketchum's abs or the whipcord strength of his body. She was here to nurse, not daydream.

"I'm not going to give you any medicine," she assured him, then shot him a little smile that was a bit wicked. "I have other things I need to do to you."

Eying her through narrowed lashes, Linc stopped in his tracks. "Whoa now," he said firmly. "If you think I'm going to blindly follow your orders, you're crazy, woman."

Nevada lifted her gaze to the ceiling of the porch and hummed a bit of a song about suspicious minds.

Linc cursed under his breath. "I'm not suspicious. I just want to know what's going on. It's my body after all," he practically barked.

Compassion filled Nevada's soft heart and with a smile she walked over to him and put her hand on his shoulder. "I'm sorry, Linc. I was only teasing you a little. It's a proven fact that patients get well much faster if they laugh. You really need to loosen up and let loose with a few chuckles."

"I don't have anything to laugh about," he grumbled.

Nevada tugged on his arm and urged him toward the door. "Of course you do. You can laugh at me. I won't mind at all. Besides, I have a nice surprise for you."

As Linc allowed her to lead him into the house and then the kitchen, he didn't question her further. He was too busy noticing how it felt to have her arm wrapped around his, her hip and thigh softly brushing against him.

He couldn't remember the last time he'd touched a woman. Apparently he'd allowed too much time to pass since he'd gone on the prowl for a little female companionship. Otherwise, he wouldn't be having such a strong reaction to Nevada Ortiz. Sexual starvation could be the only reason he was suddenly noticing the scent of her hair and wondering what she looked like beneath her clothes.

The two of them entered the kitchen and she pointed to the table. "Okay, sit down there while I get everything ready."

Since he was in such a vulnerable condition, it was obvious he was going to have to trust this woman completely. And if Victoria thought so highly of her, she must be a good nurse, Linc told himself. But she didn't look or act like any nurse he'd ever known. And he didn't feel like any normal patient would feel whenever she touched him. But that was something he was going to have to get over. And fast.

With that resolution in his head, he eased down on the long bench and rested his bandaged arms and hands on the table. Like a colorful bird flitting happily from one limb to the next, she moved around the kitchen gathering scissors, towels, tape and a bowl of yellow goop that looked like the sulfur poultices he sometimes used on his horses' cuts and wounds.

"Before I headed out here today," she said as she sat down next to him, "I went by Dr. Olstead's office to pick up my orders for you. He says it's time for you to see that you still have fingers."

Linc's expression was a bit confused. "I've seen my fingers since they were burned. I know that they're still there."

"Yes. But this is going to last for more than just a few minutes," she said, then smiled broadly at his perplexed expression. "Just wait and see."

She picked up a pair of the small scissors that she'd pulled from the medical bag and began to cut through the bandage on his right arm. The white gauze was thickly wrapped and the instrument chewed slowly as Nevada guided it through the material.

While she carefully worked over his arm, Linc studied the shiny crown of her black hair and the dark crescent of long lashes shadowing her cheeks. There wasn't anything about the woman that wasn't fresh and young and lovely. Everything about her glowed like a star plucked from a night sky.

"You like being a nurse?" he asked in hopes that a little conversation would take his mind to more normal things.

"Very much," she answered. "I like helping people."

"Is your mother a nurse?"

His question must have surprised her because she looked up from her task and frowned.

"Heavens no. Mom would run off screaming if she had to change a bandage or a bedpan."

"What does she do?"

Nevada's gaze slipped back to the job of cutting through the bandage and then she shrugged. "She works as a barmaid. In a tavern over in Bloomfield."

"Oh."

He didn't think there had been any note of disgust in his one word, but she must have thought so. She looked up again and this time her lips were set in a grim line.

"Yeah. Oh. Her job is not something I approve of. But she seems to like it. She says the tips are good." With a heavy sigh, she went back to cutting the last of the gauze away from his arm. "Believe me, Linc, my mother wasn't always—well, let's just say in the past years she's allowed her standards to fall."

Linc didn't know why he'd even questioned her about her mother. He'd thought that maybe she'd gotten her personality from the woman. But apparently mother and daughter weren't on the same wavelength.

"Why is that?"

She kept her gaze focused on her job. "She became—well, I guess you could call it disillusioned with a lot of things. She just gave up on ever having any sort of decent life. You know, a husband, a home, a good job."

"Your parents are divorced?"

She nodded. "For a long time now. Dad liked women. I couldn't count all the affairs he had before the two of them finally ended their marriage."

Linc started to ask her if that was why she hadn't yet married. But he stopped himself. He didn't talk about marriage with any woman. Even in a passing way. And he certainly didn't want this glamour girl to think he had any sort of matrimonial thoughts in his mind.

"That's too bad," was all he could say.

"Yes. Very bad," she said in a resigned voice. "Because of my dad, my mother stopped taking care of herself. She began having affairs just to spite him. And after that everything went downhill."

She looked up at him and he could see shame and

sadness in her brown eyes. "I don't really know why I told you all that. It's not something I go around discussing with anyone."

"I never repeat things told to me in confidence," he said, just in case she was worrying he would tell others about her family.

Shaking her head, she said, "I wasn't worried that you would. It's just not something I talk about."

Linc understood what she meant. Darla, his own mother, was never discussed by him or his cousins. Years ago, her name was brought up from time to time, but now there didn't seem any point to it. None of them really knew if the woman was still alive. And apparently she didn't care enough to let them know.

He noticed Nevada was beginning to peel away the layers of gauze away from his arm and he was relieved by the distraction. He didn't want to think about mothers or parents or ruined marriages. All of which were very unpleasant subjects to Linc.

"Good lord, that arm looks like the skin of a baby mouse," Linc exclaimed as she pulled the gauze completely away from his arm and then carefully rested his elbow on a clean towel.

"That's good. It's pink. It means it's alive and getting good blood flow."

It should be getting plenty of blood flow, Linc thought grimly. Each time the woman got near him he could feel his heart thump into overdrive. A silly reaction and one he'd certainly never experienced before.

He glanced down at his arm and tried not to feel deflated. The new skin was so thin it was practically transparent. All the hair was gone and in places he could see blue blood veins running just below the surface.

"I guess it is healing," he had to concede.

"It is and very nicely, too. That's the way we want to keep things going." With her hand on his upper arm, she carefully twisted his arm back and forth so that she could inspect the top and underneath. "Boy, you really did a number on this one. Is the other arm like this one?" she asked.

"Pretty much."

She glanced up at him and he could feel the touch of her brown eyes as it slipped all over his face.

"Victoria tells me that you were a hero. She said if it hadn't been for you several of the horses would have burned to death."

He grimaced. "Victoria is biased. She thinks of herself as my sister. She'd never say anything bad about me."

Nevada shot him a faint smile. "Do you think of yourself as her brother?"

Linc had never had such a question put to him and for a moment it took him aback. All these years he'd thought of himself as the cousin, the one standing just on the outside. And it wasn't because Ross or Seth or Victoria had tried to make him feel that way. In reality it had been quite the opposite. Tucker's children had treated him as though he'd been one of Tucker's offspring, too. But there was no escaping facts. He wasn't one of them. And yet he loved them just as much or more than if they had truly been his siblings.

"Yeah. I guess I do," he murmured.

"I'm glad. Because she thinks you're just about the next best thing to pajamas."

Glancing away from her, he said, "I didn't do anything special. Anyone would have gone in after those horses. I just happened to be the first one at the barn."

That wasn't the way Nevada had heard it. Victoria had told her that several of the ranch hands had been at the barn and they'd tried to hold Linc and keep him from running back into the burning building. They had not been able to stop him, and by the time Linc had emerged from the flames, the entire group had begun to think he was dead.

"Well, I'm sure your horses are happy about it. But I'll bet they miss you."

"Dr. Olstead won't let me go near them. Bacteria, he reasons," Linc muttered. "Hell, they're cleaner than I am. The stalled ones get a bath every day."

Nevada smiled with understanding. "Dr. Olstead is right. You don't want to risk getting any sort of infection. It's not that he thinks the horses are unclean, but there's other things around a barn that might harbor bacteria. Like flies and things like that."

"Yeah. I understand. But that doesn't mean I have to like it."

"No. You don't have to like it," she agreed.

Reaching for the scissors, she began to cut away the bandages on his hands. This task took longer, but Linc didn't mind. In spite of all his protests it was more than nice to have this lovely woman touching him so gently, touching him as though she really cared about his health and well being.

Don't start thinking along those lines, Linc. Just because a woman acts sweet and gentle on the outside doesn't mean she's all goodness on the inside.

His hands had been burned even worse than his arms and Nevada clicked her tongue with misgivings as she unwrapped each finger. "God, this must have been painful. Does any of it still hurt you?" she asked. "If it does, just let me know. I have painkillers in my bag."

"No. None of it hurts. In fact, it mostly doesn't have any feeling at all," he told her. "If I touched your arm, I doubt I'd feel it." At least not in his fingertips, Linc thought. But the rest of his body darn sure would.

She nodded soberly. "The nerve endings in your skin were burned."

"Will it always be that way?"

Her brows pulled together as she gave her head a little shake. "I'm not sure about that, Linc. I think that problem will get better in time, but I can't make you any promises. I'm just an RN not a doctor."

She proceeded to clean his hand and arm and then slather it with the yellow goo. Once she had every spot of his limb covered with the stuff, she began to wind clean gauze around his arm.

"I guess there'll be plenty of scars once the skin heals," he mused aloud. "What about the hair on my forearms? Will it ever come back?"

She looked up at him and gently smiled. "I'm not totally certain about that either. I'd say probably. At least part of it. But who cares whether you have hair on your forearms? You can always wear long sleeves. They look more masculine to me, anyway."

He drew in a deep breath and pushed it out. "You have an answer for everything, don't you?"

She shot him an annoyed look, then laughed softly. "Look, Linc, I'm going to be honest with you. A few scars or a lack of hair is nothing to what you could have had. It's a miracle you're alive. So you'd better be thankful."

He glowered at her. "You think I need your preaching to tell me that?"

"You haven't heard preaching from me—yet," she warned.

"Hmmph," he snorted. "For someone so little you're sure full of sass."

"That's to make up for my size," she reasoned pleasantly.

As far as Linc was concerned, he didn't see a thing wrong with her size. Everything was put together perfectly. Too perfectly for his peace of mind.

"Can I wiggle my fingers?" he asked as he forced himself to focus on anything but her.

She raised up from ministering to his arm. "Sure. Wiggle all you want."

Linc attempted to flex his bare fingers, which still looked like sticks of watermelon to him. "All the time I was in the hospital, I kept thinking how good it would feel to bend my fingers. But it—well," he grimaced as he tried to close them into his fist. "It doesn't feel all that good. They're stiff."

"That will soon change," she promised. "I'm going to bandage each finger lightly so you can move them around and maybe use them just a little. But I mean very little."

He looked at her with surprise. "You mean I don't have to go around with my hands plastered against boards?"

She gave him a happy smile. "Nope. Now, isn't that good news? And aren't you sorry about all this whining and griping?"

The expression that stole over his face was mostly sheepish, but the upward curve of the corner of his lips told her he was definitely pleased.

"Maybe I have been a little cranky," he admitted.

She couldn't help but laugh. "Is that normally your nature?"

He frowned. "Why do you ask that?"

Nevada made a palms up gesture. "Because I don't know you, Linc Ketchum. I don't know if you're usually grouchy or cheerful or sweet or mean or what."

"You're not here to analyze my personality," he reasoned. "And you don't need to know any of those things just to doctor my hands."

Nevada was going to be doing more than doctoring his hands, she wanted to point out, but she didn't say that to him. She could see that it was disturbing to this man to have her here in the house. So far she'd tried to keep everything as light and playful as she could. And she hoped she could keep their time together on that same track. It wouldn't do for both of them to get serious.

"Well, I guess I'll learn for myself," she said as she picked up a roll of gauze and started one end of it around his thumb. "Do you think you can tell me what you like to eat? Or is that a secret, too?"

"You don't need to worry yourself about that either," he told her. "Marina will be bringing up supper from the big house each evening."

This was news to Nevada. Victoria really hadn't had time yesterday to discuss some of the details about her stay here or her duties to Linc. She'd expected to be preparing some sort of meals for him and herself.

"That's nice. But I hope she'll allow me to do breakfast and lunch."

He studied her through drooped lids and for the first time in Nevada's life she felt her whole body react to a man in a purely sexual way. Heat filled her cheeks and she felt as though her whole body was soon going to be glowing like a firefly.

"What does a nurse know about cooking?"

Nevada drew in a bracing breath and told herself not to look at him. She couldn't look at him if she expected to get her senses back under control.

"Probably about as much as a cowboy does," she muttered.

He caught her off guard by releasing a low chuckle. "You might be surprised at what I know how to do in the kitchen."

Nevada couldn't keep her gaze from latching on to him and the minute it did her stomach did a nervous jump. Was he talking about cooking, she wondered, or something altogether different?

"Really. Then maybe you could teach me a few things," she ventured.

The amusement on his face disappeared like a cloud slipping past the sun and his gaze traveled from her face to her bosom and back again. "I'm sure you've already learned everything there is to know."

Chapter Four

Something about Linc's words struck Nevada hard and deep. And for the next few minutes she didn't say anything as she finished bandaging his fingers then went to work on his left arm to repeat the same process.

She really didn't know why his remark had bothered her so. Maybe it was the note of disgust she'd picked up in his voice or maybe it was the lewd way he'd looked at her. Either way, it didn't matter, she told herself. Linc Ketchum wouldn't be the first person to think she was a promiscuous young woman. Some of her so-called friends had also accused her of sleeping with a long list of boyfriends. But in reality nothing could be further from the truth. Nevada was a virgin. And so far she hadn't met one man who would make her want to change that fact.

Even so, she wasn't going to explain any of this to Linc Ketchum. Her sexual habits were none of his business. Pure and simple.

Later that evening, after she'd finished dressing Linc's burns, Nevada went outside to explore the rugged landscape of the yard. She was at the back of the house enjoying the sight of the far-distant San Juans when she heard the sound of an approaching vehicle.

Carefully picking her way through the rocks and clumps of blooming sage, she skirted the end of the building to see Marina climbing out of an old red pickup truck.

"Marina! Hello!" she called to the housekeeper.

The large Mexican lady with a heavy braid pinned to the back of her head, turned in the direction of Nevada's voice and smiled broadly when she spotted her.

Nevada waved and hurried over to the woman. Without uttering a word of welcome, she hugged Marina tightly. Nevada didn't get to see her old friend that often. Yet somehow from the very first time Victoria had introduced Nevada to the housekeeper, Marina had felt like the mother that Nevada had always wanted.

"It's good to see you," she said in a thick voice.

Marina's broad face was wreathed in smiles as she stepped back and patted Nevada's cheek. "Lord, Lord, you don't know how glad I am to see you, *chica*. You look beautiful. Just what Linc needs."

Nevada scowled at the other woman. "Marina! I'm not up here for eye candy. I'm nursing Linc."

"Hmmph. There's different ways of nursing, you know."

Nevada decided it would be better to let Marina's remark drop completely and she sniffed at the delicious smell of food wafting from the open window of Marina's truck.

"Mmm. Something sure smells good."

Marina stepped back to the truck and opened the door. Inside on the bench seat was a cardboard box draped with a white towel. "Nothing special. Just some smothered steak and vegetables. Oh, and a few sourdough biscuits."

Nevada groaned. "Marina, don't you be bringing stuff like that up here every evening. I'll weigh a ton before I leave here," she admonished in a teasing voice.

"You could use a little more weight on those bones," the housekeeper told Nevada. "Besides, I know how much Linc loves to eat. And he needs good nourishment to get well."

Nevada was about to assure Marina that she'd make sure the man ate right, when the sound of the front door opening caught her attention.

Both women turned their heads to see Linc stepping out onto the porch. He eyed the two women for a moment before he walked over and took a seat in one of the lawn chairs.

Her face filled with deep concern, Marina lowered her head toward Nevada and said in a quiet voice, "I'm very worried about Linc, *chica.*"

"You shouldn't be," Nevada stated with confidence. "His arms and hands are coming along very well. It won't be long before he'll be well again and able to work."

Marina shook her head. "That's not what I'm worried about. His body will heal, yes. But his insides, his heart…it's troubled."

Even though the two of them were too far away from Linc for him to catch any of their words, Nevada felt as if he was hearing every syllable that was being uttered about him.

Turning her back to him, Nevada pretended to examine the items in Marina's food box. "Marina, Linc has been through trauma. It's normal for him to be a little down."

The older woman rolled her eyes toward the sky. "Down? *Chica,* he's never acted like this in his life. Linc has always been the quiet, gentle one of the bunch. He's always been kind through and through. But now, he's like a monster!"

Nevada hadn't known Linc before the accident, but she could agree with that last description. The man certainly hadn't come across as kind and gentle since she'd arrived. He clearly didn't trust her abilities as a nurse and he'd practically accused her of being a slut. How much nicer could a man get, she wondered wryly.

Out loud she said, "That's because he probably feels like a monster, Marina. Think about it. He can't do any of the things he loves to do. That would bother you, too. Don't you think?"

Marina's head tilted from one side to the other as she considered Nevada's explanation. "I guess so. But I'm still worried." She lowered her head even closer to Nevada's and whispered. "I haven't told anyone about this, *chica,* but I've been seeing Linc's momma in my dreams. I don't know what she's doing there and it scares me."

A cool shiver raced down Nevada's back. She'd never been a superstitious woman and she had her doubts about anyone *seeing* things that weren't visible to anyone else. But Marina had a bit of a track record for envisioning forthcoming events. The night before the barn fire, she'd warned Ross that something was about to happen. Unfortunately, she had not *seen* enough details to predict exactly what would actually occur. If the housekeeper was now dreaming about Linc's mother, it had to mean something.

"I've known for a long time that Linc's father, Randolf, had passed away. I don't know any of the circumstances around his mother. Is she still living?"

Once again, Marina lifted her brown eyes toward the heavens. "Only God knows that, Nevada."

Nevada looked at her thoughtfully. "You mean, Linc doesn't hear from her? He doesn't know about his own mother?"

Shaking her head, Marina muttered in a disgusted voice, "She left here a long time ago, after Randolf died. Had a new husband on her arm. And she wanted Linc to go with them."

Nevada's gaze drifted thoughtfully to the next ridge of mountain where the tiled top of the big ranch house could be seen above the treetops.

"He didn't go?" she asked.

With another shake of her head, Marina answered, "No. His home, his family had always been here. She couldn't have dragged that boy away from his horses and his cousins to go live somewhere on the east coast. She should have known better. And I expect she did. But she wanted to get away from here—no matter about her son," Marina added with a disapproving sniff. "She was a hard woman to understand. Guess that's 'cause she never did talk much. Linc got that from her. But that's about all he got from that woman."

Nevada was beginning to get the picture and it was one she didn't like. "Well, I wouldn't worry about your dreams, Marina. Sounds like Darla Ketchum is totally out of the picture and has been for some time. I seriously doubt Linc's mood is connected to her in any way."

Marina grimaced. "Darla Ketchum may be out of the picture now, but she could always come back."

Nevada resisted the urge to look over her shoulder to make sure Linc was still in his chair on the porch. "Were you serious when you said no one knew whether she was alive?"

"That's the truth. As far as I know, no one has heard from her in many years." Marina shook her head back and forth. "Linc's a private man, though. If he received any kind of communication from his mother, the rest of us on the ranch might not ever hear about it."

That wasn't surprising news to Nevada. She figured getting anything personal out of him would be worse than trying to give a toddler a dose of medicine.

"Are you two going to yap out there all evening?" Linc suddenly called from the porch. "Or do we get to eat some time before midnight?"

"See," Marina said through tight lips as she looked beyond Nevada's shoulder to the porch. "Listen to him. That's not the Linc I've always known and loved."

Seeing the woman was truly concerned, Nevada patted her shoulder. "Quit worrying, Marina. He'll come out of this, I promise."

The other woman reached into the truck cab to retrieve the box of food. "I hope you're right, *chica*. If anyone can get him back to normal it ought to be you."

Nevada didn't know what normal was for Linc Ketchum, but for everyone's sake she was going to try to find it.

After handing the box to Nevada, Marina climbed into the truck and started the engine.

"You don't want to go say hello to him?" Nevada asked her as the housekeeper ground the gearshift into Reverse.

"No. Tell him I don't like him no more."

"Marina!" Nevada scolded. "You ought—"

"I'm only kidding. But it won't hurt him to think I'm a little put out with him. Maybe it'll get his mind off himself." She grinned then and gunned the truck down the hill.

Nevada waved the housekeeper off and then headed to the house. As she stepped up on the porch, Linc was eyeing her thoughtfully.

"I didn't realize you were chummy with Marina. You know her?"

"Of course. I've treated her in the clinic. And I've also visited the ranch several times. Her husband was a distant cousin to my father. Both of them sorry men," she added matter-of-factly, then inclined her head toward the door. "Let's go in and eat. I'm starving."

He followed her into the house and on to the kitchen. She sat the boxed meal on the table and began to pull out the plastic containers that Marina had sealed it in.

"I'll get plates," he said, turning toward the row of oak cabinets.

Nevada's mouth opened as she looked over her shoulder to voice a protest, but just as quickly she stopped herself. She'd bandaged his hands and fingers thickly enough to provide a cushion. It wouldn't hurt anything to allow him to carry a couple of plates to the table. And would probably do his mental attitude a wealth of good.

"It looks like she's even sent iced tea," Nevada told him. "Is that all right with you?"

"Anything wet will be fine."

He returned to the table carrying two plates, forks and knives and placed one setting at the end of the table and the other across from it. Apparently, Nevada thought, he'd rather have her sitting across from him than right next to him.

Well, that was all right with her. She didn't need to be any closer to the man than she had to be. Something about him made her edgy and flushed, and it didn't have anything to do with his caustic remarks. But she figured it had a whole lot to do with his hard, handsome face and lean, rugged body. One look at him and anyone could see he was a man's man. His body was hewn from years of manual labor, and she realized his physical build was a heck of a lot sexier than some of her male friends who constantly worked out at the gym.

After Nevada poured the tea into glasses and fetched napkins and salt and pepper from the cabinets, the two of them sat down and began to fill their plates.

"Do you think you can manage all right?" Nevada asked. "I can fill your plate for you if you'd like."

His lips a tight line, Linc shook his head. "I'll clean up whatever I spill."

Nevada sighed. "I wasn't worried about that. I don't want you hurting yourself."

"By lifting a spoon with some vegetables in it?" he asked sarcastically.

Exasperated, she waved a dismissive hand at him. "Go ahead. What do I care if your fingers split open? Victoria will probably fire me, is all."

"Worried about your job, are you?"

Normally, Nevada could hold her temper—especially around trying patients. But something about Linc Ketchum really got under her skin and heated her to the boiling point. In spite of his vulnerable condition, she wanted to whack him.

Tossing down her fork, she looked at him. "I think I've had just about enough of you for one evening."

"Think you're about ready to pack up and head back into town?"

As Nevada looked at him she suddenly realized he'd been goading her on purpose, testing her just to see if she was weak-willed enough to bend and run. Well, he was certainly in for a shock if he expected her to quit anything. She wasn't a quitter.

"No. I'd just like to eat my meal without getting indigestion. I'll take my plate to the porch and eat. If you don't mind. Or even if you do."

She started to rise to her feet and was shocked when he reached over and placed his bandaged hand on her arm.

"Sit down."

"I'm not sure I want to."

"Sit down anyway."

Nevada plopped her plate back onto the table, then reached across and plucked the brown cowboy hat from his head.

"Hey! What do you think you're doing?" he practically yelled at her.

She placed the hat on the bench beside her and tried not to stare at the hair she'd exposed. The chocolate-brown strands were thick and curled recklessly around his head in a way-too-sexy way. And suddenly she was wondering how many women had ever run their fingers through those glossy curls. How many had touched his face and kissed his lips? The questions were not something that crossed her mind about other men and the fact that Linc Ketchum had piqued her curiosity was enough to fill her with embarrassed heat.

Looking down at her plate, she said, "We're eating a meal together. The least you can do is respect me enough to take off your hat."

Linc lifted his hand halfway to his rumpled hair before he realized he couldn't do much finger-combing. Dropping his hand back to the table he glanced across the table to her. He felt like a damn idiot for being so nasty with her. But something seemed to be pushing him to say things to her that he'd never say to anyone, much less a beautiful woman like Nevada. He wasn't sure what had come over him, but the moment she'd driven up and stepped from her car, he'd felt like a ruffled rooster.

"Nevada?"

This was the first time he'd said her name and the way she looked up at him told Linc the sound of it surprised her.

"Yes," she replied.

Like a boy who'd been naughty but never wanted to admit it, he fought the itch to squirm in his seat. "I...uh...guess I've pretty much acted like an ass since you've arrived."

Her brown eyes flicked warily back and forth across his face and Linc wondered what it would feel like to have her soft little body draped over his and be able to look deep into those liquid brown pools.

"Oh. I don't know that I'd say that. Maybe a donkey would be more like it," she said in a teasing manner.

The idea that she seemed to take what he dished out and still managed to smile was quite a surprise to Linc. Most women would have already been out the door. Is that what he'd been trying to do? he wondered. Send her away before he had the chance to like her? Really like her?

He sighed. "Earlier you asked me about my personality. I don't know if anyone knows how to describe himself. But I do know that since you arrived you haven't been seeing my normal self. I've behaved badly and I'm sorry about it."

The last thing Nevada had been expecting from him was an apology and for long moments she sat studying his rugged face.

"There's no need for you to apologize, Linc. I understand how it is to be unable to work, to do all the things you like to do."

His expression sober, he worked to maneuver the fork between his bandaged fingers. "Being temporarily incapacitated doesn't give me the right to be rude or forget my manners."

"Sometimes it does," she said softly.

"You're too damn understanding. You know that?"

Smiling, she rose from the bench and eased around the table until she was standing next to his shoulder. "Here," she offered, "let me cut the meat up for you."

He wanted to tell her that he was a big, strong man. He didn't need a flirty little thing like her to feed him. But he couldn't. Not if he wanted to enjoy Marina's smothered steak.

Handing his knife and fork up to her he said, "Go ahead before I have the whole plate in my lap."

She chuckled. "You'll do better soon. The more you try to bend your fingers the more flexible they'll become. And tomorrow evening when we redo the bandages it might be possible that I can make the gauze just a bit thinner. That should help, too."

She leaned across him to reach his plate and Linc was suddenly swamped with the female scent of her skin and hair and the warmth of her body that was so very, very close she was practically touching him.

"I hope so," he said thickly.

Long seconds passed as she cut the steak into bite-size pieces. Linc tried his best to keep his breathing even and his mind on anything but her. But it didn't work and eventually the whole lower half of his body was standing at rigid attention.

"There you go," she said. "Think you can manage the fork?"

Linc released a long breath as she finished the

task and moved away from him. "I can manage," he muttered.

While he'd been in the hospital, he'd been dependent on the nurses to feed him. But Nevada was a hell of a sight different than any of the nurses that had cared for him and there was no way he could endure her feeding him bite after bite until his plate was empty.

"Well, you have to start somewhere," she said as she took her seat across from him. "I guess tonight is as good as any."

Without looking at her, Linc somehow managed to maneuver the fork between his bandaged thumb and forefinger. Once he had it positioned, he discovered it wasn't all that difficult to push it into the piles of food on his plate.

For the next few minutes the two of them concentrated on eating until Nevada finally glanced across the table at him.

"Victoria told me that you normally live in the bunkhouse with the hands that are quartered here on the ranch. But she didn't say why." She looked around the kitchen with its beautiful oak cabinets and up-to-date appliances. "Why don't you live in this house? Or in the big house with Ross and Bella?"

He didn't bother to glance up. "Because I like being around the guys. They're like family, too. Ross and Bella are great. But they're newlyweds. They don't need another person in the house with them."

Nevada studied him thoughtfully. "I'm aware of how big that house is. They'd never know you were around, unless you wanted them to know it."

"I don't belong in that house," he said curtly.

Her brows inched upward, yet Linc didn't see her reaction to his remark. He appeared to be completely obsessed with the food on his plate.

"Why? You're a Ketchum, too."

"Yes. I'm a Ketchum. But I'm not Tucker's son."

"So what? I don't think your cousins want to split hairs over that issue."

He looked up at her, his eyes thoughtful as they roamed her pretty face.

"What would you know about it?"

She shrugged one shoulder as she lifted a piece of steak to her mouth and chewed. After she'd swallowed the bite, she answered, "Maybe I can't speak for the men of the family, but I can speak for Victoria. She considers you the same as her brother. She thinks you're Mr. Wonderful."

A faint grin came and went on his face. "So you told me before. She's misguided, but you're right. None of them have ever shown me any difference because I was Randolf's son. And before your little head starts spinning, I'll tell you that, no, I don't go around with a chip on my shoulder or anything. I live in the bunkhouse because I like it. There isn't any need for me to live in the big house or in this house. Why would one man take up all this space?" he asked as he motioned a hand around his head.

"I see your point," she said, then a curious frown wrinkled her forehead. "Who built this house anyway? And why? It's far too nice to be just a rental."

Releasing a heavy breath, he leaned back in his chair and looked at her. "You are a nosey little thing, aren't you?"

Nevada smiled at him. "Yes. I guess you could say that. I like learning about the people I care for. It makes it nicer. And—" she broke off as she glanced away from him, then began again. "In nursing school we're taught not to get close to or attached to our patients. But in reality that's a bunch of hogwash. A real nurse feels for the person she's caring for. If she didn't—well, she wouldn't be human."

The idea of Nevada Ortiz getting close or attached to Linc made warning bells clang loudly in his head. It was okay for Victoria to love him as a brother and consider him Mr. Wonderful. She was his cousin. But a woman like Nevada was a different matter altogether. She was beautiful and sexy and the kind of female that could easily make a man forget he was supposed to be a loner.

Feeling it was far safer to talk about the house than nurse/patient relationships, he said, "My father built this house about twenty-five years ago."

Her brown eyes widened with total fascination. "Really? That long ago?"

Linc nodded. "You see my Uncle Tucker and he were partners and started building this ranch together in the late fifties and early sixties. The two of them built the big house first. And that's one of the reasons it has so many wings. Both families lived there together. But then my dad developed a bad heart problem and was no longer able to do the physical labor of a rancher. He sold his half of the ranch to Tucker and built this house for himself and my mom."

"I see. Is that what eventually took your father? Heart disease?"

For a second time, Linc nodded and Nevada could see a regretful shadow cross his face.

"Yeah. I was just a teenager. It hit me pretty hard. We were buddies, my dad and I. He was a gifted horseman and taught me everything he knew about the animals."

A smile touched Nevada's lips. "It must have been very nice to have had a father like that."

"Yeah. But I lost him way too early." He awkwardly stabbed his fork into a piece of steak. "My dad was a quiet, gentle man. He never raised his voice or hurt anyone. Now my Uncle Tucker was just the opposite. My cousins would be the first to tell you he was a hellish rounder. Two different men, but they both died of bad hearts. Guess I should make sure I eat right," he said with a bit of dark humor.

Nevada wasn't going to start preaching to him about how he could be genetically prone to heart disease. Now wasn't the time to be a nurse. Tonight she was talking to Linc as a woman and a friend.

She carefully sipped her tea, then dared to ask, "You don't ever communicate with your mother?"

He glanced up at her through narrowed eyes. "Who told you that?"

Her tanned cheeks turned a hot pink. "Marina," she confessed.

Linc snorted. "Marina is just like a tape recorder. She doesn't forget anything and if you push the right buttons, she'll repeat it all."

Nevada put her fork down. "I'm sorry if I shouldn't have brought up the subject of your mother."

"Don't worry about it," he muttered as he turned his attention to the food left on his plate. "There's nothing to tell about her anyway. We don't talk."

"Oh. I'm sorry."

"No need to be sorry." He lifted his eyes to hers. "There wouldn't be much point in trying to communicate with a woman who's only capable of thinking about herself."

Questions pummeled her from every direction. But she managed to stifle them all, except one. "Is that what you think about all women?"

His lips twisted to a mocking slant. "I have more important things to think about than women."

After that sardonic remark, Nevada didn't bother to attempt to make more conversation. She finished her meal then excused herself from the table to gather makings for coffee.

She was waiting for it to drip when she turned around to see that Linc had left the table and slipped out of the kitchen. Which was just as well, Nevada thought. He'd made it clear that he didn't put much stock in a woman's company.

The idea that any man could be so callous and cynical was enough to snap Nevada's back teeth together in an angry grind. But then she quickly scolded herself for allowing his attitude to rile her. She wasn't here to socialize with the man. Or even to like him as a person. Her job was simply to care for his burns and his physical needs. And from now on that was all she intended to do.

Chapter Five

Once the coffee was ready to serve, Nevada poured two cups and carried them out of the kitchen. The living room was empty, so she stepped out on the porch to see if Linc had returned to his willow chair.

Sure enough, she found him there. His boots were crossed at the ankles, his gaze on the moon rising above the eastern mesas.

"I wasn't sure whether you liked coffee or not. But I brought you a cup anyway," she told him. "It's black."

He looked around to where she stood by the screen door and Nevada could see a flicker of surprise cross his face.

"You needn't have bothered," he told her. "I would have gotten it later."

"No bother."

She handed him the cup and made sure he could manage holding it before she turned back toward the door.

"Where are you going?"

The question caught her totally off guard and she paused long enough to glance over her shoulder at him. "Inside. I—have some reading to do."

"Oh."

"If you need anything I'll be in my room," she told him, then went into the house before he could say more.

She had just gotten comfortable with her book when the telephone near the head of her bed rang. Nevada tossed the book to one side and rolled across the mattress to lift the receiver.

"Hello."

"Nevada, it's Victoria. I just wanted to check and see how things have been going. Is Linc there with you?"

Nevada sat up on the side of the bed. "He's outside on the porch. He can't hear what I say."

"Good. Then tell me how things went. Has he been giving you a difficult time?"

Nevada breathed in deeply then slowly released it. Linc Ketchum was like no man she'd ever encountered before. She'd never had a man make her so angry one moment, then filled with empathy the next.

"When you said you wanted a favor from me, you meant a *big* favor," she said wryly.

"Oh dear. He's been that bad?" Victoria asked with concern.

"No. Not exactly. But he is—well, he isn't ordinary, I'll say that much."

Victoria sighed. "You have to understand, Nevada, that Linc isn't your ordinary man. He's not like the other single ranch hands on the T Bar K. Outside of his horses, he doesn't have much of a life. And now the burns have taken that away. Just be as gentle as you can be without losing your mind. I promise, you'll get a big bonus out of this."

Nevada frowned. She hadn't taken this job for money. In fact, she really didn't want extra pay for it. She already owed Victoria so much for giving her such a special job at the clinic.

"I'm not concerned about any of that," she told the doctor.

"Nonsense. You've always dreamed about taking a vacation to Hawaii. When all of this is over with I'm going to make sure you're going."

Under any other circumstances, Nevada would have been shouting for joy at the idea of heading to the tropical island. But something just didn't feel right about using Linc's misfortune for her gain. "We'll talk about that later," Nevada told her.

"Okay. Is there anything you need? Something

you might have forgotten to take with you? A book on patience?" Victoria teased.

Nevada had to laugh. "Oh, he hasn't been all that bad," she tried to assure the other woman. "Just a little bad. And I'm dealing with it."

"That's good. I know you will, Nevada. And I still believe you'll be the best medicine for Linc."

Nevada chuckled with disbelief. "Apparently you don't know your cousin too well. He doesn't like women."

Aghast, Victoria asked, "He told you that?"

"Not in so many words. But it meant the same."

Victoria didn't reply for several long seconds, then she said, "Linc doesn't trust too many women."

Nevada grimaced. "That's obvious. He—uh—he told me a little about his mother. Well, it was very little. But he said she'd only thought about herself and that the two of them didn't communicate. Is that true, Victoria?"

This time an even longer pause passed before Victoria responded. "Linc talked to you about his mother?"

"Yes. Why?"

"Well, frankly, I'm shocked. He doesn't speak about her to anyone. Even in a remote way."

Surprise parted Nevada's lips. "Oh. I didn't realize."

"What did you do to the man anyway?"

"Victoria, what kind of question is that? I didn't do *anything* to the man!"

Victoria laughed softly in her ear. "I meant what did you do to get him talking."

"Irritated him, I think."

"Well, it sounds like you're doing the right thing. Just keep it up. Now, how about you? Are you comfortable enough? Did you find everything in the house you needed?"

"Yes. My room is lovely. Everything is fine." Except that each time I look at your cousin my pulse does silly flip-flops, Nevada silently added.

"Good," Victoria told her. "Then maybe the next couple of weeks or so won't seem like being in prison to you."

Nevada assured the other woman that she didn't feel locked away and then the conversation turned to work at the clinic and for the next few minutes they spoke of other patients and problems.

Eventually, baby Sam began to cry in the background and Victoria ended the conversation to see about her son.

Nevada hung up the telephone and reached for her book while wondering what it would feel like to go home every night to a husband and children.

When she looked at Victoria's life, it all seemed so wonderful. Even though her husband, Jess, was a lawman and often had to work odd hours, he made sure that he and Victoria spent special time together and Victoria did the same for him. Their children were the center of their lives and when they were all together Nevada could see a glow of love encircling the family.

But as far as Nevada was concerned, the Hastings weren't the norm. Most of her young married friends often complained about philandering, selfishness, fights and everything else that happened when a male and female butted heads.

Nevada didn't want that for herself. She'd already seen too much of it as a child. And she realized the chance of finding a special love like Victoria and Jess had was minuscule. She wasn't willing to gamble her heart with those sorts of odds. No matter how lonely she became.

Later, after Nevada had finally managed to read several chapters of her paperback, she got up from the bed and changed into a pair of black pajamas and a white robe trimmed in black.

She was pulling a hairbrush through her long hair when she heard a soft tapping on her bedroom door and went to open it.

Linc was standing on the other side of the threshold. His expression was just a bit disgusted and a little apologetic.

"Were you asleep?" he asked.

Nevada lifted the hairbrush for him to see. "Brushing my hair. But I was thinking about going to bed. Do you need something?"

He grimaced as though her question was inane. "Hell, yes!" he burst out, then with a dismal shake of his head he apologized. "Sorry, Nevada. I'm just feeling too damn helpless, that's all. I need for you to help me get undressed. I managed to slip off my boots. But the shirt and the jeans are another matter. I tried to work the buttons loose, but the bandages are still too thick to catch hold of something so small."

"Oh, Linc," she said contritely, "I'm so sorry! I'd forgotten all about your clothing. And you must be getting tired."

He wasn't exactly tired, Linc thought. In fact, he couldn't remember a time he'd felt so worked up and restless. He felt as if he could jump at least ten barbed-wire fences and never get a scratch. Which was a damn stupid feeling for a man his age.

"Yeah. It's been a long day," he replied as casually as he could.

"Just let me put away my brush, and if you want to go across to your room, I'll be right there."

He nodded, and she whirled back into her room. Linc released a shaky breath as he turned and walked into his own bedroom.

Damn it, he thought, as he switched on a lamp next to the head of the bed. He shouldn't be feeling so nervous about any of this. He'd had women undress him before. And most any man would be envious of his position—a young, beautiful woman taking off his clothes. But he wasn't like most men. And Nevada surely wasn't like most nurses.

When Nevada knocked lightly on the door, he was trying to decide whether it would be best to sit down on the bed or stand. He very nearly jumped at the sound and quickly muttered a curse at himself. She wasn't going to eat him. And he wasn't going to bite her. The two of them weren't like the mares and stallions he bred for the ranch's remuda.

"Come in," he called gruffly.

The room was L-shaped and she stuck her head around the corner and shot him a brief smile. "Ready?" she asked.

"Well, I don't want to sleep in my clothes," he assured her.

Ignoring the sarcastic tone of his remark, Nevada moved into the bedroom and went to stand in front of him. The light by the bed was fashioned from a stack of horseshoes and shaded with a thin sheet of rawhide. The illumination slanting across the two of them was muted but enough for Nevada to see where the buttons on his shirt started and ended.

She reached for the first one and quickly slipped it through the slot. The fabric of his shirt was starched and crisp, a stark contrast to his warm smooth skin. She tried her best to keep her fingers from touching his chest. Not only for his sake, but her own, too. Yet it was virtually impossible to maneuver the buttons without having her fingers touch his skin. Each time she did, her hands received a sizzling jolt and she wondered if he was feeling any of the same sort of reactions she was experiencing.

One, two, three, four. Finally, she reached the eighth button and the two pieces of fabric fell apart. Barely glancing at the skin above his belt, she said, "Now hold your arms out slightly so that I can pull the sleeves down over your bandages. I don't want to disturb the gauze."

He did as she instructed and Nevada carefully pushed the shirt off his shoulders until it draped against his back. By the time she'd moved to the sleeves, she was struggling to keep her breathing at an even keel. The physical reaction she was having to Linc totally shocked her and though she'd assured him that undressing him wouldn't turn her face red, she felt heat seeping into every inch of her body, including her cheeks.

Linc stood stock-still and barely breathing as her hands slowly and carefully worked the sleeves down one arm and then the other. Each time her fingers brushed against his skin, the muscles in his throat clenched to rigid bands. He tried to put his thoughts on other things, but he couldn't think about the weather, his horses or the men down at the bunkhouse when every particle inside him wanted to reach out and touch this woman standing before him.

"Can't you hurry this up," he said with a faint growl. "The roosters are going to be crowing before I ever get to bed."

She looked up at him, her expression turning sardonic. "You'll get there soon enough. Besides, I doubt there's a rooster within miles of here."

He grunted a laugh. "Don't leave your window up tonight. Marina has two roosters and both of them like to crow."

"Don't all men," she muttered under her breath.

"What?"

She drew in a long breath and blew it out. "Nothing. I'll keep the windows shut. By the way, what time do you get up?"

He looked down at her. "Normally I get up at four-thirty. But that's when I'm working. Why does it matter?"

"Do you want to walk around the house in your underwear? Or would you like me to help you get into your jeans first?" she asked dryly.

Oh Lord, he thought desperately. This whole dressing and undressing thing was going to have to go on for several days. Probably until the bandages on his fingers came off completely. And after looking at their fragile appearance tonight, he doubted that would be any time soon.

He didn't answer immediately and she spoke up before he could decide exactly what he wanted to tell her.

"Maybe I should send for some sweat pants or pajamas. You could pull them on yourself and not have to endure me touching you." The shirt finally slipped down his arm and she tossed the garment onto the bed.

Linc's brows shot upward at her testy remark. "Who said I didn't want you touching me?"

"I can tell. It's killing you."

It was killing him all right, but not in the way she was thinking, Linc thought dismally. He had not expected any of this to feel so intimate and personal. He certainly hadn't expected this deep desire to reach out and touch her hair, her skin, her face.

"You're a nurse. This is your job," he pointed out more for himself than her.

"That's right. I've done this very thing many times before," she said matter-of-factly as she reached for the button on the waistband of his jeans. "It's all old hat."

He sucked in such a sharp breath it as if someone had taken a knife to his throat. "I'll bet."

Nevada's lips twisted and she glanced up at him with hard brown eyes. "That's the second time you've implied that I'm promiscuous. What gave you that idea?"

"You. You said you had boyfriends. Or did I misunderstand you?"

With a shake of her head, she focused her gaze on the fly of his jeans. "No. You didn't misunderstand. And aren't you glad I've got experience. Otherwise,

I might just get you all tangled up in this zipper," she added cattily.

Linc started to growl a warning at her, but the loud sound of the zipper peeling open caused his mouth to snap shut. Now wasn't the time to press his luck, he thought. And if she didn't step away from him soon, and leave the room, he was going to do something crazy. Like grab her and kiss her until she couldn't say one more sassy word to him.

She yanked the jeans down over his hips then put her palm in the middle of his chest. "Sit down on the bed and I'll pull them off," she ordered.

He looked down at her soft brown hand pressing against his flesh, then lifted his gaze to hers. Something about the way she was touching him, looking at him, stirred him in ways he'd never experienced before and the feelings shocked and scared him. She was seducing him without even trying and he wanted to yell at her to get out and leave him alone. He didn't want a woman turning his insides out. Especially not a woman who enjoyed playing the field.

He sat down and Nevada grabbed onto the hem of his jeans and tugged the heavy denim down over his feet. Once they were free of his body, she tossed them onto his shirt and stepped back, noticing thankfully that he was wearing a pair of white boxers loose enough to hide the shape of his manhood.

Clearing her throat, she asked as professionally as

she could, "Is there anything else you need? Can you turn the covers back without my help?"

"Yeah," he muttered, "I can manage."

She looked across the room to where the curtains fluttered in the night breeze. "Do you normally sleep with the windows open?"

He glanced over his shoulder to follow her gaze. "Yes. When the nights are cool, we usually keep the bunkhouse open. But that doesn't mean that you have to turn off the air conditioner," he assured her. "I'm sure you're accustomed to artificial heating and cooling. I wouldn't want you to be uncomfortable just for my sake."

If his words had been sincere she would have been drawn to his thoughtfulness. But the sarcasm in his voice told her that he apparently had the idea that she was a spoiled princess who fooled around. The idea was laughable, yet at the moment she couldn't find it in her to be amused.

"I'm not concerned about myself," she said coolly. "If you're not accustomed to sleeping in a draft, you'll wind up with a cold. And that's the last thing your body needs when its trying to repair itself."

Even in the muted light, she could see his gaze flicking up and down her body. The sight caused her to unconsciously tighten the lapels of her robe together.

"I'll be fine," he said curtly.

"Good. I'll say good-night, then."

Turning, she started to leave the room. But before she rounded the corner that would hide her from his view, he called her name.

Pausing, she stifled a sigh and wondered how she'd ever gotten into such an awkward ordeal.

Nevada glanced over her shoulder at him just in time to see him swallow and she was suddenly struck with the fact that he was nervous, that her touch had left him just as unsettled as she was feeling. The idea made her look at him in a totally different way and she felt her heart softening in spite of all the tacky comments he'd said to her.

"Thanks," he said quietly. "I appreciate your help."

Turning slightly back to him, she said, "You sure have a funny way of expressing it."

He grimaced. "Don't expect me to be good at communicating, Nevada. I do most of my talking to horses and they're much smarter than humans. Just a few words to them gets the point across."

Curious now, she walked back to him. "Is that really true? Do horses understand what you're saying?"

A soft glow lit his dark-green eyes. "Hell yes, they understand. In fact, most of the time you don't have to say a word. They just know what you want even before you do."

She smiled wanly. "That sounds very nice. To be understood. But then I guess most animals have that inner instinct. I don't know anything about horses. I've only ridden twice in my life."

"That's a shame."

In the back of her mind, Nevada knew she shouldn't be standing here in Linc's bedroom, talking to him about anything other than his physical condition or needs. But she understood that he needed to talk, he needed to realize that sharing his thoughts with another person could actually be a nice experience.

"While I was growing up several of my friends had horses, but my family couldn't afford to have a horse. I felt left out when they got together and went on rides."

"Your family was poor?"

She nodded. "Not dirt-poor. But we didn't have much for any sort of extras."

His gaze was beginning to wonder over her face and hair and she could feel her stomach doing silly little jumps and twirls. He was an extremely handsome man. Not in a suave or smooth way, but in a very, very masculine way and she could hardly keep her eyes off his broad, thick shoulders or wide expanse of chest sprinkled with curly brown hair.

"How did you manage to go to nursing school?" he asked.

"I worked my way through with different part-time jobs. I worked in a dry cleaners, a café, a pharmacy, an insurance office. The last one paid the best, but I hated it. The day was filled with people demanding money and threatening lawsuits. It wasn't for me. But at least it kept my bills and tuition paid. And I received a couple of scholarships that helped get me through."

"What about your parents? They didn't help with your education?"

Nevada shook her head. "Mom does well to take care of herself. And Dad left a long time ago. He calls and comes around once in a while, but that's about it." Her gaze dropped to her bare toes. "He always figured I'd take care of myself. And I always have."

Linc tried to tell himself that her accomplishments weren't that big a deal. It wasn't uncommon for women to succeed on their own. Yet that was usually after they were grown and standing on secure ground. He figured Nevada had scrapped and scraped from the time she was big enough to work at odd jobs. He admired her greatly for that, even if he didn't like her list of boyfriends.

"Uh—I know I can't do anything with the horses now. But later on you might like to take a ride." He didn't add, *with me*. He told himself he wasn't necessarily making the offer as a way to spend time with her. He wanted to pay her back in some way and a horseback ride was as common as breathing to him.

A slow grin lifted the corners of her lips and Linc

realized he'd like to kiss those corners until her lips parted and her eyelids drifted shut.

"You must already be planning how to pay me back," she said teasingly. "I guess you've already got your worst bronc in mind to put me on."

That brought a smile to his face. "There's not a horse in my remuda that's a bronc. They're not bred to buck. They're bred to work cattle."

He leaned over to the nightstand and opened a door at the bottom. Several books were stacked inside and his bandaged hand shuffled awkwardly through them until he reached the one he was searching for.

"Here," he said, offering the book out to her. "You might like to look through this. If you're not interested, that's all right, too."

Nevada stepped forward and took the book from him. *"The American Quarter Horse,"* she read aloud, then glanced at him. "Is that what you raise here on the ranch?"

He nodded.

Smiling, she clutched the book to her breasts. "Thank you, Linc. I'll take this to bed with me."

As Linc watched her leave his bedroom he couldn't help but wonder what it would be like if she took him to bed. But that wasn't something he could allow his mind to dwell on. Because going to bed with Nevada Ortiz was something that would never, ever happen.

Chapter Six

The next morning when Nevada climbed out of bed, the first thing that caught her attention was the smell of coffee. Which could only mean that Linc was already up and in the kitchen. How he'd managed to make coffee with his bandaged hands, she didn't know, but she was certainly going to find out.

After a quick trip to the bathroom, she tied on her robe and stuck her feet into a pair of satin mules. Once she left the bedroom, she headed straight to the kitchen expecting to find Linc there, but the room was empty.

She poured herself a cup of coffee, which still smelled quite fresh, stirred in a hefty amount of cream, then walked over to the back door to glance onto the patio.

The sight of Linc sitting there in a green motel chair took her by complete surprise. A moment ago, when she'd discovered he wasn't in the kitchen, she'd assumed he'd be on the front porch. He seemed to feel more comfortable outdoors and probably enjoyed drinking his morning coffee in the fresh air. She hadn't expected to find him at the back of the house.

Opening the door, she stepped down onto the patio and carried her coffee over to where he sat with his long legs out in front of him. He hadn't bothered to put on his hat and the faint yellow glow of the rising sun made the brown strands glisten with streaks of gold. The shirt he was wearing wasn't buttoned. Neither were his jeans, but she could see he'd somehow managed to zip them up enough to keep them on his hips.

"Good morning," she greeted him while telling herself not to notice how damn sexy he looked. Those broad thick shoulders and square jaw didn't make up for his moodiness, she told herself. Besides, he'd been a bachelor for years and from all that she could tell, he didn't much like women. It would be foolish of her to fantasize about the man.

"Good morning," he replied.

"Sorry I wasn't up to help you dress," she told him. "Why didn't you wake me?"

Linc glanced over as she took a seat in a nearby

lawn chair. Her white satin robe clung to every curve of her body and her black hair draped her shoulders like wild, tangled vines. The makeup she'd been wearing yesterday had been washed away and now he could see the true smoothness of her rosy-tan cheeks and the long silkiness of her lashes. Her lips reminded him of dark-pink roses, the kind his aunt Amelia used to grow in a sheltered corner of the big house garden.

Nevada Ortiz was a naturally beautiful woman, he thought. Just like the rising of the sun in the azure New Mexican sky.

"It wasn't necessary to wake you," he said after a moment.

"You've been using your hands too much," she scolded. "When I unwrap them this evening, I'd better not find that you've disturbed the skin, or you and I will both be in big-time trouble. I really don't relish being chewed out by two doctors."

"Two doctors?"

"Dr. Olstead and Dr. Hastings," she explained.

"Don't worry," he said with a faint frown. "I haven't put a lot of pressure on my fingers. They feel fine. In fact, I think they're a little more flexible this morning."

Studying him over the rim of her coffee cup, she was surprised to see he appeared relaxed this morning. The grim, tight expression he'd worn most of yesterday was gone and his green eyes were much softer. She was happy to see the change in him, yet at the same time she realized that like this, he was much more dangerous to her well-being.

"Good. I'm glad. You're going to be surprised how quickly you heal. I know it probably seems like you've been bundled up in bandages for a long time now. But later, when you look back on all of this, you'll realize it wasn't all that long. And it certainly beats being turned into a charred piece of toast." She sipped her coffee, then glanced at him from the corner of her eye, "Do you think the fire was an accident?"

He frowned as he continued to watch the glow of morning sunlight breaking over the red mesas. "I really don't know. The barn was built back in the sixties and had been updated through the years. In fact, the electrical wiring was replaced only last year. I can't imagine what might have set off the flames. But I can't imagine anyone deliberately setting the building on fire. Not with helpless mares locked inside their stalls." His jaw turned to granite. "But if it was arson, I'd want to kill the bastard."

The tone of his voice was just menacing enough to have Nevada studying him even closer. Even though he was man who kept to himself, she figured he wouldn't be bashful about going after any one who'd crossed him.

"Well," she said. "I'm sure it was an accident."

She was silent a moment as she remembered the other well-publicized goings on at the T Bar K… "But so many things have happened on the T Bar K this past year it makes a person wonder if something else might be going on."

"Yeah. I thought the same, too."

Nevada thoughtfully turned her attention to her coffee and for the next few minutes the two of them sat in silence as the magpies sang from a nearby pine tree.

The solitude of being in the mountains and alone with Linc was something altogether different for Nevada. Aztec wasn't a busy metropolis by any means, but it was a darn sight more active than this place. At this time of the morning, she was usually already up and dressed and hurrying to work with one hand on the steering wheel while she tried to gulp down a cup of coffee with the other. Patients of all ages from cranky adults to crying babies would be crammed into the waiting room of the clinic and she would have to deal with each one kindly and methodically before Dr. Hastings made her entrance into the examining room.

Every day was a busy day for Nevada. And not too many of her nights were spent alone in front of the television. More often than not, she went out with friends to a movie or dinner, or a nearby concert. In her opinion, life was too fun and too short to spend it alone.

Yet there was something cozy and extremely intimate about sitting here in the morning sun and wearing only a robe and pajamas while a sinfully sexy man lounged mere inches away. And the fact that his jeans and shirt weren't buttoned only added to the pleasant picture around her.

"I'm getting hungry," he said suddenly. "Do you know how to cook breakfast?"

So much for leisurely sipping her coffee, Nevada thought wryly. But then she wasn't here to sit around admiring her patient. This was a job, not a romantic getaway.

"Sure I do. My mother could hardly boil water, but my grandmother is a wonderful cook and she made me work in the kitchen from the time I was a small girl. She said a woman would never be out of a job if she knew how to cook." Nevada tossed him a wry grin. "Thankfully, I'm past being the grill cook at the Wagon Wheel."

Surprise marked his face. "You worked at the Wagon Wheel as a cook?"

Nodding, she carefully rose from the chair while balancing her coffee cup. "For about a year. Remember? I told you I worked in a café."

"Yeah. But I didn't know your job was cook and I didn't know it was at the Wagon Wheel. They always have good food."

She chuckled. "Thanks for the vote of confidence.

In a few minutes you can judge for yourself if I've lost my touch."

Nevada left him on the patio and went to her bedroom to dress. She wasn't about to cook breakfast in her night clothes. That would be behaving too much like a wife. And she certainly didn't want Linc to get the notion that she had that kind of idea about him or any man. Lord, what an embarrassing situation that would be.

Pulling on a pair of blue jeans and a pale-yellow T-shirt that buttoned down the front, she fastened her long hair at the nape of her neck with a brown tortoiseshell barrette. After a quick dab of face powder and lipstick, she hurried out to the kitchen and began to assemble the fixings for breakfast.

She was frying bacon and link sausage when she heard the back door open and close, then Linc's footsteps grow closer and closer before they stopped somewhere behind her.

His nearness caused the nerve endings on Nevada's skin to stand like metal shavings on a magnet and she drew in a deep, bracing breath before she turned to look at him.

"I have things going," she said as she tried to keep her eyes off the strip of bare chest and hard abdomen exposed by the loose tails of his shirt. "How do hot cakes sound? Or would you rather have fried eggs or an omelette?"

This was not the way he'd expected his nurse to be treating him—as though he was royalty and could pick anything from the kitchen that his heart desired. Was she trying to impress him for some reason? he wondered. There wasn't any need for her to lift a hand to prepare meals. Marina would be more than glad to send every meal to them. Especially since she had plenty of leftovers, some of which usually made their way to the bunkhouse. Old Cook wasn't too happy when Marina's treats appeared in his kitchen. He was protective of his position and didn't like it threatened by a woman trying to outshine him. But Nevada was a nurse, she didn't need to stand over a cookstove. Especially for him. And Linc didn't know whether to be pleased by her attitude or wary of her motives.

"Hot cakes sounds good. But—uh—I'd appreciate it if you could button these things up for me."

He gestured down to his shirt. Nevada put down the fork in her hand and stepped toward him. Before she even reached for the two pieces of fabric hanging against his chest, her heart began to beat fast and faint, her breathing slowed to light little sips of air sucked between her parted lips.

"I'm sorry. I should have offered to do this for you sooner," she said in a thick voice.

Linc felt every part of his body going rigid with anticipation as she moved close and took hold of his shirt. This morning she smelled like honeysuckle and morning dew and he wondered if her dark-pink lips would taste just as sweet and moist.

Damn it, he wasn't a man who went around fantasizing about kissing a woman or imagining the shape of her body beneath her clothing, but he seemed to be doing both with Nevada. And he didn't know how he was going to keep his sanity spending this first day with her, much less two weeks.

"That's all right. Maybe I can do it myself pretty soon." Like tomorrow, Linc thought desperately, then sucked in a fiery breath as her small fingers inadvertently brushed against his belly.

Hearing the sharp intake, Nevada dropped her hands and jumped back. "What's wrong? Did I hurt you?" she asked with great concern.

Linc groaned silently. "No. I just had a—sharp pain in one of my hands. It was nothing," he lied. He wasn't about to admit that the touch of her fingers had filled him with more heat than he'd encountered in the burning horse barn.

"Oh. Maybe I should unwrap it and have a look," she suggested as she reached once again for his shirt.

"No, dammit," he said sharply. "It was just a little pain. Nothing to get all shook up about." Only he *was* shook up, Linc thought. He'd been shook up ever since she'd arrived yesterday and the whole idea made him angry at himself and at Victoria for ever sending the woman up here. For two cents he'd call his cousin and tell her to find someone else, that he was going to send Nevada packing. But what would be his excuse? he wondered. That he found her too attractive? That for the first time in his life he'd met a woman he couldn't push out of his mind?

"All right. But please tell me if you have any more of them," she said. "Now if you'll—suck in a bit, I'll button your jeans."

While she worked to fasten the waistband of his jeans, Linc pulled his eyes away from the shiny crown of her head and looked toward the window. This time she couldn't prevent her fingers from touching him and it was all he could do to remain motionless as she searched for the tongue of the zipper nestled just above his crotch.

His heart began to pound like a hammer, forcing hot blood to parts of his body that he wished would remain cold. "If you knew how much I hated this, you'd hurry it up," he finally barked at her. "And I sure as hell don't want burned bacon for breakfast."

Her lips a tight line, she yanked up the zipper and whirled back to the cookstove. "You think I enjoy dressing you?" she muttered as she whipped the browning bacon on to its other side.

"I don't know. Do you?"

Her mouth fell open as she jerked her head around at him. "Keep asking me questions like that and you can cook your own breakfast the best way you can," she said tightly.

For long, tense moments he stared at her. What the hell was he doing, he wondered. He'd been trying his best to get along with the woman. He didn't really want to insult her. And he sure as heck hadn't meant to ask her such a provocative question. But something strange seemed to happen to him whenever she touched him. His normal personality flew out the window and left behind a rutting buck without any manners.

Raking a bandaged hand over his rumpled hair, he said regretfully, "Aw hell, Nevada. Go ahead and say it. I'm a terrible patient."

Ducking her head, she turned back to the frying meat and lifted the browned strips onto a plate lined with paper towel. "Forget it. I understand."

Not liking the idea that he'd hurt her feelings, he moved forward and placed his hands on her shoulders. The bandages on his hands prevented him from feeling the heat of her body, the softness of her skin, but he could imagine the sensation and it was enough to cause his stomach to clench with desire.

"Do you?" he asked softly.

Slowly she turned and lifted her face to his. There was a challenging tilt to her chin, but there were also shadows in her dark eyes, expressions that he couldn't understand but desperately wanted to.

"I think so. You don't like me near you. You don't like me touching you."

Linc tried not to flinch. He had not expected anything so blunt to come out of her mouth. And he'd especially not expected her to read him so closely.

"Look, Nevada, it isn't that I don't like you—"

"Liking me has nothing to do with it," she interrupted. "You don't like how I make you feel. And you're afraid that I'm feeling the same way toward you."

Linc swallowed as his throat tightened and his heart continued to chug like a laboring freight train. "Since you seem to know so much about me, just how do I feel?"

As Nevada's gaze roamed his sober face, she realized she shouldn't have gotten into this conversation. It was going to lead them to things that neither of them needed to hear or feel. But there was no way she could avoid his question now without looking like more of a fool than she already did.

"I think you find me attractive," she said frankly.

Slowly, his dark brows inched upward and she shivered with surprise as his bandaged hands slid up the sides of her neck and gently cupped her face.

"And how do you find me, Nevada Ortiz?"

The question was spoken so softly she could barely hear it. But she did hear and she couldn't ignore it any more than she could dismiss the sudden pounding of her heart.

"You're a very masculine, good-looking man, Linc. I'm sure you've had plenty of women tell you that."

She watched his nostrils flare and for a moment she believed she'd angered him all over again, but then his face softened and his bandaged thumbs began to move back and forth across her cheeks. In the back of her mind, Nevada realized she wanted to feel the touch of his skin upon hers instead of the coarse gauze wrapped around his fingers. She wanted to know what it was like to be in his arms and have his hard lips kissing hers.

"Do you feed the egos of all your male patients like this?"

The corners of her mouth lifted ever so slightly. "I've never had any male patients like you."

A faint grimace twisted his lips. "What does that mean? That you're still trying to flatter me?"

"I never intended to flatter you. I'm only trying to answer your questions."

"Really."

His one word was full of disbelief and while Nevada's mind was screaming at her to step away from him and put a stop to his touch and the senseless conversation between them, she found that her legs refused to obey her commands.

"That's right," she said as she nervously licked her

lips. "I've attended to plenty of male patients over the years. But they were all housed in a hospital room or medical clinic. They were all bedridden or incapacitated in some way. They weren't strong and virile like you."

The more she spoke, the more pink color seeped into her cheeks, and as Linc's gaze roamed her face he realized her blush surprised him. She'd already admitted she'd had plenty of boyfriends. Surely it didn't make her feel self-conscious to talk about the intimate things that went on between a man and a woman.

"That's the way you see me?"

Desire was growing thick in her throat, followed by a choking lump of fear. Just having this man touch her face was making little earthquakes go off inside her. What would happen if he actually put some effort into it, she wondered wildly.

"Stop this, Linc. I can't be your nurse if you're, well, personal like this. It won't work."

"No. It won't work," he murmured lazily. "But I tried to tell you that yesterday. You should have gotten into your car and driven away when I told you to."

His gaze zeroed in on her lips and Nevada felt every bone in her body turning to liquid fire. "So what are you going to do about it?" she muttered inanely.

"What do you think I'm going to do about it?" he asked with a growl.

"Find another nurse to take my place?"

"It's too late for that," he murmured. "And too late for this, too."

Nevada could see his head bending toward hers yet she couldn't believe that he was going to kiss her until she actually felt the touch of his lips.

The contact was like the strike of a match in a pitch-dark room. The space around them seemed to light up and tiny flames sizzled upon her lips as Linc's mouth dominated hers with a bold search that left her breathless and shaking uncontrollably.

Halfway through the kiss, his hands left her face and gathered at the back of her waist. She stumbled slightly as he tugged her forward and into the circle of his arms. The front of her body landed against his and she was instantly consumed with heat and the wild urge to slip her arms around his neck, to hold on and never let go.

She felt the room receding and her senses being sucked into a velvety-soft place when the shrill sound of the telephone jolted the two of them apart.

They stared at each other in shocked silence before Linc finally turned away and clumsily snatched the ringing receiver from the wall near the cabinets.

Nevada sucked in a deep breath and turned back to the skillet on the cookstove. Thank God she'd turned the burner off beneath the sausage or it would have burned to a crisp by now.

As she put a flame beneath the skillet, she realized her hands were trembling and she couldn't seem to suck in enough air to satisfy her lungs. What had the man done to her? She'd been kissed before. Or so she'd thought. Apparently, none of her past suitors had known what they were doing or the chemistry between them had been bad. And that was all it had been between her and Linc, she firmly told herself. Chemistry. Pure and simple. He was a raw male animal and his rough edges excited her sexually. That's all there was to it.

"That was Marina," he said as he hung up the telephone. "She wanted to know if she needed to send breakfast to us."

Nevada wondered how he could sound so normal, so unaffected when her whole body was still vibrating from the kiss they'd shared. But then maybe he hadn't felt any of the things she'd felt, Nevada decided. Maybe the kiss had been just an impulse that he now regretted.

"What did you tell her?" she asked while hating the fact that her own voice was strained.

"Not to bother. That you were cooking up something. I just didn't know what it was yet."

For the next few moments as Nevada broke eggs into another skillet, the innuendo of his remark didn't sink in. When it finally registered that Linc hadn't been referring to breakfast, she turned around to shoot a few choice words at him. But the room was empty.

Nevada was relieved. She didn't need to get into another war of words with the man. And she certainly didn't need to kiss him again. But she very much wanted to. And even worse than that, he probably knew she did.

Chapter Seven

Linc's cousin Ross arrived shortly after they'd finished eating breakfast. The two men sat together on the front porch and drank coffee while Nevada cleaned the kitchen and tried to assure herself that everything was going to be all right.

Throughout the meal, Linc had never mentioned the kiss and neither did she. Maybe it was better that way, she told herself. Maybe if they both behaved as though it had never happened, then they could forget it and move on.

She *had* to move on to the job at hand, Nevada thought. Because Linc was not a man who'd be interested in any sort of relationship with her. From all that she could see, he didn't even much like women. She didn't need to ruin her life by pining over a man who didn't give a flip about her.

Out on the porch, Linc listened to Ross as he talked about his trip to the livestock auction at Farmington yesterday. Normally he was always interested to hear how cattle and horses were selling on the market, but today Ross wasn't holding his attention.

Damn it, he'd been a big, stupid fool to kiss Nevada. Hell, he didn't even know why he had. Except that he'd wanted to kiss her and had ever since she'd stepped out of her car and faced him with her hands on her shapely little hips. Now it was going to be hell to keep his distance from her. But it was something he was going to have to do. Being indisposed with burns was a minor problem compared to the pains Nevada could cause him.

"Linc, are you sure you're feeling all right?"

He looked over to see Ross studying him with a narrow eye.

"Sure. I'm fine. Or I would be if I could take these damn bandages off and get to work," he answered.

Ross's gaze leveled on Linc's bandaged arms and hands. "Yeah. I guess that would be hell going around like that," he said, then grinned mischievously, "but it might not be all bad to have Bella doing everything for me. Like giving me a bath, helping me dress—"

He broke off suddenly and Linc stared purposely out at the mountain range in the far distance.

"Oh. So that's what's bothering you," Ross said with sudden decisiveness. "You don't like having Miss Ortiz getting that personal."

He turned a glare on his cousin. "Would you?"

Ross chuckled. "Is that supposed to be a trick question? Two years ago I would have loved it. Now, well, I'm a one-woman man. You will be, too, Linc. One of these days before you get too old to make love to a woman."

Linc rose from his chair and walked over to one of the posts supporting the roof over the porch. Propping his shoulder against it, he gazed across the mountain top to the big ranch house where his father had once lived with his mother.

"You don't know what you're talking about, Ross. That sort of thing doesn't interest me at all. Never has and never will. You know that."

"No. I don't know anything of the kind. What I do see is a man who's missing a hell of a lot of living. And I've never understood why."

Glancing over his shoulder at Ross, he said, "Is that what you come up here for? To give me some sort of mental therapy? If it was, then you can just get the hell back down the mountain. I don't need it."

"Why no. It sounds like you're in a wonderful frame of mind," Ross said with sarcasm, then shook his head in a helpless fashion. "I thought Nevada would have already brought you out of this funk you're in, but I can see she hasn't made any headway. Poor woman, she'll probably be ripping those bandages off you way ahead of time if you keep this up."

Linc started to bark back at him, then shut his mouth as he realized he'd be adding fodder to Ross's assessment of him. Jerking the brim of his hat down on his forehead, he asked, "Did you get that supplement for the horses yesterday? I don't want any of the gestating mares to go without."

"Yeah. I got it. Twenty sacks. It was all the feed store had."

"Has Skinny been sitting up nights with Miss Lori?"

"Yeah. He's wearing himself out, too."

Skinny was the oldest wrangler on the T Bar K and, except for Marina, had worked for the ranch longer than anyone. Linc realized the man was heading toward his upper seventies and needed his rest. But there wasn't anyone, other than himself, that he would trust with the young mare.

"You think I don't know that?" Linc retorted the question. "But what the hell am I supposed to do about it? There's an eighty-percent chance she'll foal in the dark. Other than a vet, there's no one besides Skinny that I would want around in case something goes wrong. She's young and this is her first foal. He'll know what to watch for."

Sighing heavily, Ross rose to his feet and walked over to where Linc continued to slump against the porch post.

"Look, Linc, I realize you miss the horses—"

"Do you?" Linc interrupted roughly, then murmured in an easier voice, "I doubt you understand how much. They're my life."

Ross didn't say anything for a few moments and then he gently placed his hand on Linc's shoulder.

"Maybe this is a good time to think about that."

Surprised that his cousin would make such a remark, Linc looked around, but by then Ross was already stepping down from the porch and walking to his truck.

"I'll see you tomorrow," he called over his shoulder.

As Ross turned the vehicle around to head back down the mountain, Linc lifted his hand in a farewell gesture, while desperately wishing he was going down to the ranch yard with his cousin. By this time of morning the place would be quiet. But just after daybreak, the barns and corrals were always buzzing with cowboys spreading feed, catching horses from the remuda and saddling up for the day's work.

Batwing chaps and fringed chinks would slap against jeans-covered legs. Spurs would jingle and sweat-stained felt would shade every eye. Flying horse hair and dust would fill the air and mingle with the lingering smells of breakfast from the bunkhouse.

That was the time of day he loved the most, Linc thought. When everything was starting all fresh and new and he would walk from one end of the horse barn to the other, greeting each velvety nose and big trusting eye with a stroke of his hand and a gentle word.

It was a life that he loved with every fiber of his being. And though Ross pretended to understand his feelings about the matter, his cousin didn't really know the depth of Linc's devotion to the ranch or his horses. After all, Ross had Bella. She was the love of his life now. Not the T Bar K.

By the time lunch rolled around Nevada was still full of the breakfast she'd consumed. But she prepared Linc a bowl of vegetable soup and a hefty beef sandwich and called him into the house.

While he ate she made herself busy in another part of the house. But when she heard him making his way outside to the porch again, she emerged from her bedroom and intercepted him at the front door.

"Don't bother going out and sitting down on the porch again," she said. "You've already done that enough for today."

He glared at her. "You might be my nurse, Nevada, but you're not about to tell me where to sit and how often."

Feeling a little testy herself, she punched his chest with her forefinger. "You got the first part right, partner. I'm your nurse and you're to follow my orders.

You're not a sick man, you just can't use your hands. Yet." She drew in a deep breath and stepped back from him. "And if you ever expect to go back to work, you need to get a little exercise."

The corner of his lip curled upward as his gaze swept over her with a pointed look. "I'm sure a girl like you knows just the sort of exercise I need."

A girl like her. Linc Ketchum didn't know anything about the intimate part of her life. It was beyond her where or why he'd gotten the idea that she was a floozy or something worse. As far as she was concerned, having male friends wasn't decaying her morals. But she wasn't about to start defending or explaining herself to this man. Let him think what he wanted. She would be gone from here soon and he could shoot his moody, cutting remarks at someone else.

"As a matter of fact, I do."

His brows formed a dark line as she looped her arm through his and urged him out the door.

"What are you doing now?" he asked.

"We're going for a walk."

"A walk! Like hell. We're not two kids getting off the school bus and you don't have an arm load of books to carry, so you can go for your own walk and leave me alone."

She pursed her lips with disapproval. "So you can sit here and get soft and flabby? I promised Dr. Olstead—"

"Oh, all right, all right," he conceded. "Let's go. But I can tell you right now that it's silly. A man doesn't walk. Not when he can ride a horse or drive a truck."

"Neither of which you can do at the moment," she pointed out sweetly.

"You like reminding me of that, don't you?"

Her expression sobered as she urged him down the steps. "I don't need to remind you of your injuries. You already feel sorry enough for yourself without that."

Stepping onto the ground, Linc halted and stared at her. "Sorry for myself? In my entire life I've never felt sorry for myself."

"Is that so?"

"Yeah. That's so."

"Hmm. A few minutes ago, in the kitchen, I could hear you raising your voice to Ross out here on the porch. Is that the way you normally talk to him?"

Linc's lips compressed in a tight line. "No. But—"

"You're frustrated because you can't go to work with him. Right?"

"That's right," he clipped. And he was also frustrated because each time he looked upon her face he wanted to touch it with his lips, to taste her sweetness over and over. But that wasn't her fault. Neither was it her fault that he had these damned bandages wrapped around his arms and hands. He needed to quit taking his aggravation out on anyone who crossed his path. Especially this woman, who was only here to help him. If his father could see him now, he'd be ashamed of his son's behavior. Linc was even ashamed of it.

"Is it helping matters to be so angry?" she asked.

A sheepish expression crept over his face before he finally shook his head. "Sorry, Nevada. It seems like all I've been doing since you got here is growling and then trying to apologize. I don't really feel sorry for myself. I understand I'll be well in a few days. And I'm damned thankful for that. But—"

Rather than finish his sentence, he curled his bandaged fingers around her arm and urged her forward. As Nevada walked along beside him, she waited for him to continue. When he didn't add anything else to his remarks, she said, "You're thankful. But. But what?"

Heaving out a breath, he lifted his face to the sky. Gray clouds were beginning to drift across the western sky and Linc carefully surveyed them. Normally the afternoon lightning storms didn't begin until July. The sky should remain calm until the two of them returned to the house.

His gaze returned to her face. "You really want to know?"

Nodding, she said, "That's why I asked."

Shrugging, he halted their forward movement. "All right, Nevada, I'm going to be honest with you.

I hate like hell being unable to work and care for myself. But that's not what's really bothering me. You are."

Nevada shouldn't have been surprised by his comment. Not after the episode that had occurred between them in the kitchen this morning. Still, she had not expected him to be so open and direct with her and it shook her more than she cared to admit.

"I'm sorry," she said in a strained whisper. And she meant it. In spite of Linc's gruff rudeness, she liked him. She respected all the things he'd done with his life and the standards he'd set for himself. "I honestly don't want to cause you any more problems than you already have."

For a moment he closed his eyes and Nevada used the time to study the firm line of his lips, to remember and relish those seconds he had kissed her so passionately. She'd never felt anything like it before and though she was smart enough not to repeat the act, she was aching to tilt her face up to his, to invite his lips back down to hers.

"Nevada, I know that I've been behaving like an ass to you. And I wouldn't blame you if you walked off and told Victoria she had a monster for a cousin."

He glanced away from her and for the first time since she'd met Linc Ketchum she believed she was seeing the real man and not the growling bear who'd been doing his best to scare her away. There was regret on his face and something else that looked like raw need.

Carefully, she touched his arm at a spot above the bandaged area. "There's no need for you to be so hard on yourself, Linc. I understand. I really do," she said softly.

He groaned. "You're so young. How could you?"

She swallowed hard as his dark-green eyes met hers. "Because when you kissed me I was afraid."

A mixture of disbelief and regret washed over his face as he reached out and touched her cheek. "Nevada, I never meant to scare you. I can't even remember the last time I kissed a woman. I guess I've forgotten how to treat one."

Shaking her head, she turned her back to him and drew in a deep breath. "You didn't scare me, Linc. Not in the way you're thinking. I was scared because I liked it—a lot."

For long moments the silence was only broken by the breeze whispering through the pines and the chatter of a nearby magpie to its mate. Nevada could only wonder what the man was thinking. Probably that she was truly a promiscuous woman. Well, it didn't matter, she told herself. All that mattered was that he get well and that she leave this ranch with her senses and her heart intact.

"I liked it, too."

The gentle tone of his voice shocked her even

more than his words and she dared to look over her shoulder at him.

"But it isn't going to happen again," she stated with certainty.

"No. I don't have any interest in having a relationship with a woman. And I'm sure you have plans of your own," he said.

Not serious plans, she thought. Not with any certain man. But she didn't explain any of that to him. He didn't care about her plans. He was just trying to get through the next couple of weeks with a nurse in his house.

"Sure," she murmured, then trying not to feel so deflated, she gave him a wry smile. "Ready to walk now? I realize you don't want to, but it will be good for you. And I'd like to see more of the place. Are there any trails around here that we might follow?"

With a faint look of relief on his face, he nodded. "There used to be one that led away from the back of the house. It's rough, but the view is pretty."

"Good," she said cheerfully. "Let's go."

Linc glanced down at her feet. The strapped sandals she'd been wearing earlier had been replaced with a pair of black cowboy boots and he looked at her with faint surprise.

"You're wearing cowboy boots."

She chuckled. "Sure. I may not be a cowgirl, but

I enjoy Western fashion. And this pair is good to walk in. They have treads on the bottom of the soles."

"So they do," he said with a faint smile, then gently urged her in the direction of the trail.

The track Linc recalled had become so overgrown that it took them a few minutes to find it. But finally they discovered a faint rut covered with pine needles and decaying cottonwood leaves. For several yards the track was mostly on level ground and wound gently through a thick stand of trees and scattered boulders. Then the landscape changed abruptly and they began a slippery descent down the side of the mountain.

"Are you sure you want to continue?" Linc asked as she followed closely behind his lead. "This is getting rough and is likely to get worse the farther we go. Looks like the rains have created some treacherous gullies."

Small stones and loose gravel had already caused Nevada to slip more than once, but she wasn't about to turn around and go back. The view around them was becoming more and more spectacular.

"I'm not worried," she assured him, then asked, "How far does this trail go?"

"I haven't been down it in years, but if I remember right the path goes all the way to a meadow. About three-quarters of the way down there's a spot where I always stopped before I ever reached the meadow. I used to go there as a kid to be by myself."

Nevada took her gaze off the trail long enough to allow herself a glimpse of his wide, rugged back and long, strong legs. What had he been like as a young boy, she wondered. Surely his father's death had affected him deeply. But a death in the family was something that couldn't be helped. According to Marina, Darla Ketchum had chosen to leave her son behind. That was a different matter altogether.

"Sounds as though you've never been a social person," she said.

"Not really. I like people. But I like my own company, too."

"I can see that you're nothing like your cousin Ross. I never had the chance to meet his brother Hugh before he was killed. And I've only met Seth a couple of times. Are you like either one of them?"

Linc shook his head. "Maybe a little like Hugh. He was a quiet homebody."

But even in his short life Hugh had had a wife and child, Nevada thought. Except for his cousins, Linc didn't appear to have any immediate family. And as for him bunking with the ranch hands, that wasn't exactly Nevada's idea of having a home.

He glanced over his shoulder at her. "What about you, Nevada? You don't have any siblings either?"

She shook her head. "No. My mother had some sort of medical problem after she gave birth to me. It prevented her from having more children. I would've loved to have had a brother or sister. It's lonely being the only one. But, well, my mother is the sort who didn't need more children. I'm not sure she even needed me," she added glumly.

Linc paused on the steep trail and she stopped as he stood there looking at her. "That's a bad thing to say."

"Not really. I'm only being realistic. You see, as I told you before, my mother had lots of problems with my dad. He wasn't the nicest man in the world." She looked away and found that she was a bit embarrassed to be admitting such things to this man. Talking about her parents with anyone, even people that she'd been acquainted with for a long time, was difficult. "He abused her in more ways than one."

Sadness tinged Linc's eyes. "I'm sorry about that, Nevada."

Shrugging, she glanced his way. "Me too. But that was a long time ago and I try not to let it bother me now. He went his way and my mother's gone hers. At least there's no more fighting and yelling and cheating and threatening. I would never—"

Her expression turned grim as her words trailed away.

"Never what?" Linc prodded, surprised to find himself interested in the facts about her life.

She shrugged again. "Nothing," she said with a wan smile. "Just that I'd never want to live through it again."

Linc nodded marginally and then turned and started walking on down the trail. While he plodded forward, he couldn't help thinking about his own parents and how much a part of Nevada's story matched his own.

He could still hear his mother yelling threats and demands at his father and even now when a woman raised her voice in Linc's presence, it made him cringe with memories. There was no way he would ever want to put himself or a child of his through such misery.

"I understand."

"Do you?" she asked. "I can't imagine. You've been raised in a nice family."

"Even nice families have their problems, Nevada."

Nevada was wondering what he meant by that comment when the forest around them opened up and the trail they were traveling narrowed down to a rocky path on the edge of a steep bluff.

Linc halted his forward motion and turned to her. "This ground is so washed out here that I'm not sure we should go on."

Nevada looked around her. To their left was a small copse of fir trees, fallen tree trunks and moss-covered boulders. To their immediate right, where the bluff fell away, there was nothing but open air, and at least a hundred-foot drop to the next shelf of the mountain. "Is this the place you used to visit?" she asked.

"No. It's still a bit farther on." Moving toward her, he took by the arm. "Come on. I think we should turn around."

"But I want to see. And I won't fall," she assured him. "I'm as sure-footed as a mule."

Wary, Linc shook his head. "That has to be the craziest thing I've ever heard. I'm supposed to be a patient. And you're the nurse. What are we doing out here mountain-climbing?"

She grinned at him. "Are you tired?"

"No. Not in the least. But—"

"I'm the nurse and I'm making sure that you're getting your exercise. And from what I can see you haven't gotten enough yet," she said impishly.

Before Linc realized what he was doing, a chuckle rumbled up from his chest. "Are you always like this?" he asked.

"Like what?"

The corners of his eyes crinkled with amusement. "Are you always so chipper and adventurous. And happy?"

It was such a joy to hear him laugh and see him smile that Nevada felt as though she was standing on bubbly water instead of rocky ground.

"Usually. It's much more fun than being angry and sad." The afternoon had grown hot and Nevada used the back of her forearm to wipe at the perspiration that dotted her forehead. "Have you ever been happy, Linc?"

He laughed again and Nevada realized she could get addicted to the pleasant sound. It was low and as roughly masculine as the tough brown whiskers on his face.

"You mean, you wonder if I've always been a sulky bastard?"

Her smile was shy and totally enchanting to Linc and he suddenly realized it felt good to be walking in the woods with Nevada. He'd not ever done such a thing with a woman and this excursion was turning out to be far more pleasant than he'd ever expected.

"I didn't use those words. You did," she reminded him.

He shrugged and glanced away from her as the reality of his life begin to edge its way back into his thoughts. He wasn't sure he knew what being happy was. But one thing he did understand, he wasn't the badgered, broken man his father had been.

"I'm mostly happy, Nevada. And that's all a man can hope to be."

A brief smile touched her lips. "Well, I guess that's all a woman can hope to be, too." She stepped forward and carefully took hold of his bandaged hand. "You know what, I'd be even happier if you'd lead me on down the mountain. I want to see where you used to sit and dream as a boy."

He could feel something warm tugging at his insides and he realized he was glad that she'd shaken him out of his dark mood, that the two of them had made a sort of peace between them.

"All right. We'll go on down. Just hold onto my hand. I don't want you to fall," he told her.

Nevada shook her head regretfully. "I can't. If I slipped you'd try to grab me and that wouldn't be good for the new skin forming over your fingers. But don't worry about me. Like I said—"

"You're a surefooted as a mule," he interrupted. "And just about as independent." Turning his back to her, he motioned toward the center of his belt. "Hold onto to my belt loops. And don't argue. The next few feet down are a little scary."

Nevada latched her fingers through the loops of his jeans, while thinking nothing could be as frightening as the strange emotions that were beginning to rush over her like a sudden burst of hot sunshine.

Linc Ketchum was her patient. She wasn't supposed to be feeling anything toward the man except concern for his physical well-being. But everything about him mesmerized her and she could only wonder how long it would be before he totally captivated her heart.

Chapter Eight

Linc hadn't been kidding about the trail turning treacherous. The path was nothing more than a narrow, winding ledge. In several places the earth had washed away to leave gaping cracks. If Nevada allowed herself to look she could see the distant, rocky ground below. But she tried not to look at the danger and simply focused on putting one foot safely in front of the other.

More than once during their downward descent, Nevada desperately wanted to grab on to Linc's waist and hold on for dear life. But she figured he would resent that intimate sort of contact. And after the fragile truce they'd made, she didn't want to have him thinking she was deliberately trying to stir the ashes left behind by the hot kiss they'd shared.

Thankfully, the trail suddenly widened and then they were stepping down onto a wide ledge of solid rock. The sound of tinkling water immediately caught Nevada's attention and she looked to her far left to see a small waterfall pouring over a rim of red rock. About ten feet below, the crystal-clear water pooled in a large dished-out spot that was framed with rocks and dead wood.

"Oh! How absolutely beautiful!" Nevada exclaimed. "Where is the water coming from? The snow melt is over for this summer."

He pointed upward to a crease in the mountain. "There's a natural spring up there. As far as I know it's never gone dry."

Totally enchanted, Nevada released her safety hold on his belt loops and walked closer to the waterfall.

"I don't know much about the outdoors, but it must be unusual to find a spring in this arid climate. We're not totally desert here by any means, but we're not living in a tropical zone either."

Linc walked up beside her. "You're right. I think it is an oddity. On all the thousands of acres on this ranch, I've never discovered another one."

She tilted her head to look up at him and there was a sparkle of pleasure in her eyes that made Linc's stomach do a funny little turn.

"This is just wonderful, Linc," Nevada went on. "Thank you for bringing me here." She glanced around for a place to sit down. "Would it be okay if we rested a few minutes before we start back? I'm not as much of a mountain goat as I thought."

"Sure. Just don't get too close to the edge of the bluff. It's a long drop over. I doubt anything could survive it. Not even a mountain goat."

A few feet away, a fallen log rested near the wall of mountain. Linc gestured toward it. "Let's sit here."

She nodded at his suggestion and the two of them found a comfortable seat on the dead pine trunk.

Nevada sighed with pleasure as she stretched her legs out in front of her and wiped once again at the sweat trickling at her temples.

"I never dreamed there would be a place like this around here," she said as she gazed at the splendorous view before them. "You can see the meadow from here. And there's some of your Angus grazing down there. Is there a chance that we'll see any of your horses down there with them?" she asked.

Linc pushed the black hat he was wearing to the back of his head. "No. We do have part of the remuda pastured now, but they're in a different section of the ranch."

"How big is the remuda?" she asked curiously.

"I think we have about two hundred and ten horses now."

"Wow. That's a lot."

"Quite a few," he agreed. "And that doesn't include the broodmares and colts."

"Why so many?" she asked, then shot him an apologetic look. "Sorry, Linc. I'm sure my questions sound naive. I'm not very educated about ranching, but I find it interesting."

His gaze rested on her face and for a second Nevada thought she spotted a bit of surprise on his face. But then he looked away from her and she lost the chance to gauge his expression.

"We have so many horses," he answered, "because the T Bar K does everything just as it was done sixty, sixty-five years ago. You won't find helicopters or four-wheelers taking the place of horses here. Our cowboys do all the cutting and roundups on horseback. It's a tradition that will never change as long as a Ketchum is breathing."

His statement told her a lot about his feelings for the ranch and how much his heritage and place in it meant to him. It was a trait she admired. Most of the men she came in contact with weren't interested in their past or where their roots originated. But then, some of them were like her; their roots were rotten.

"Tell me about this place," she urged. "How did it get started?"

He looked at her once more and this time she could see faint skepticism pulling his brows together.

"You really want to know?" he asked.

"Sure. Why wouldn't I?" she asked with a puzzled frown. "The T Bar K is known far and wide. But I've never actually heard its history."

Maybe she was truly interested, Linc thought. Or maybe she was only pretending to be just to butter him up a bit.

Hell, Linc, why would she want to do that? She doesn't want anything from you. And she sure didn't need to patronize him just to get his attention. All she had to do was button his shirt and he melted like a snowflake on a hot tongue.

"Well, it began with my father, Randolf, and his brother Tucker. They were both born in Texas and raised there. Their father, Nate, was a big cattleman and he owned a ranch near Goliad that had been handed down to him through generations of Ketchums. It was prime land and worth a fortune."

Already enthralled by the story, Nevada said, "Oh. So why did they come up here to New Mexico?"

He shook his head at her with faint amusement. "I thought nurses were supposed to be patient creatures."

"All right. Go on. I won't interrupt with questions," she promised.

"My cousins and I have heard lots of tales from our fathers. But we're not really sure if it was the way things really happened back then. All of us believe they didn't want us to know the entire truth of the matter."

"Hmm. Why do you think that?"

Linc dangled his bandaged hands between his knees as he stared off into the distance. "We're not sure. Except that we believe something scandalous happened. But that would be after Nate got into financial trouble and began to sell off blocks of land. That was during the Depression and the land didn't sell for much. Randolf and Tucker were just young boys then, but they recalled the hard times. Eventually though, Nate pulled things together somehow and after the war started, cattle were in demand again. He began to make piles of money and he bought back the land he'd sold."

"Well, that sounds like everything began to get better," Nevada remarked.

"I guess it got too good," he said with a wry grimace. "You know, the more money a man has, the more troubles he seems to acquire. Anyway—and here's where the story gets sketchy—our grandmother, Sarah, caught Granddad cheating with another woman. And—"

"Cheating! But weren't they old by then?" Nevada interrupted.

"I guess some men never get too old to have a roaming eye. Anyway that was when the trouble started brewing. Eventually Sarah demanded a divorce and her half of the cattle empire."

"Let me guess," Nevada replied, "Nate refused."

Linc nodded. "I think the ranch turned into a hellish place after that. Our grandfather wound up being murdered. He'd been shot and his body thrown into a thick patch of weesatche."

Nevada was shocked. "Oh no. What happened? Do you know?"

Linc shook his head. "Not really. People down there believed Sarah shot him and had her lover hide the body."

By now Nevada was incredulous. "She had a lover too?"

His expression turned to disgust. "Yeah. For spite, I guess. Isn't it nice to hear you come from such a loving family?" he asked sarcastically.

So Linc's parents hadn't been the only ones with marriage problems, Nevada decided. No wonder he had a bad view of relationships between men and women. He must think that all marriages were flawed and painful as those of his grandparents and his own parents had been.

She wanted to tell him that nothing could be further from the truth. There were married people who truly loved each other, who would die for each other. All he had to do was take a look at his cousins. But she didn't say anything. It would be hypocritical of her when she'd made a promise to herself always to be a free and independent woman.

"What happened to Sarah? Was she charged for his death?"

"No. Seems there wasn't enough evidence. So after Nate was buried, Randolf and Tucker decided they didn't want any part of the ranch. They told Sarah to keep it and good riddance."

Nevada shook her head sadly. "They believed she murdered their father."

This time Linc was the one who looked surprised. "Well, don't you?"

"How could I know that without hearing all the facts? It's not good for a person to jump to conclusions too quickly. You might turn out to be wrong."

"I've been wrong before and it didn't kill me. Better to be wrong about a person than dead. If Noah Rider could talk to us, I'm sure he'd agree with that."

Noah Rider was the old foreman who'd been murdered on T Bar K land about two years ago. His body had been discovered in a dry arroyo several miles away from the ranch house. The incident had garnered interest far and wide and Victoria's husband, Jess, had nearly died from a gunshot wound received while investigating the crime. Nevada could remember what a trying time it had been for the whole Ketchum family. But it sounded as though trouble was not something new to this clan.

"So your dad and uncle came up here and started this ranch," Nevada mused aloud. "Where did they get the money to build on?"

Linc shook his head ever so slightly as he peered into the hazy distance. "Well, that's another place where the story gets a little foggy. My dad always told me that he and his brother got their grubstake from their mother. You see, her family had owned lots of oil rights and she'd given her two sons part of the royalties. But Tucker always told a different version. He said that the money they'd used to start the T Bar K had belonged to Nate and when they'd left Texas they'd taken a share of their father's estate."

"How odd that they would tell the story so differently," Nevada commented. "Which one did you believe more? Your father?"

Linc nodded. "Not just because he was my father," he explained. "But Tucker tended to exaggerate the facts at times. And anyway, after all these years it doesn't matter. They made the ranch go and we children are still here keeping their legacy going."

Nevada was fascinated by the story, and as she sat there mulling over everything he'd told her, she realized there were plenty more questions she would have liked to ask about his family. Especially about his mother. What part had she played in all of this? Had she come from Texas, too?

Deciding she didn't want to take the chance on ruining the peace between them, she kept the questions to herself. If Linc ever wanted to talk to her about his mother, he would have to bring up the subject himself.

She looked over to see Linc suddenly squinting up at the sky and she followed his example. Dark-gray clouds were beginning to swirl and mix above them.

"Are those rain clouds?" Nevada asked. "If they are, we're in trouble. It will take us half an hour to get back to the house."

Linc continued to study the skyline. "I think we're in trouble. And I'm not sure if we should try to head back right now. Or wait it out here where we might have shelter."

"Shelter?" Nevada looked around her. Except for one lone juniper jutting out from a crack in the rocks, she didn't see anything that would shield them from lightning and rain. "I don't see any kind of protection around here."

Rising to his feet, Linc pointed toward the waterfall. "That's one of the things that always fascinated me about this place. Have you ever seen one of those old movies where the bandits ride beneath the waterfall and enter a hideout cave?"

Nevada nodded. "Sure. Hasn't everyone? But don't tell me there's a cave behind this waterfall. That's just too much to believe."

He took her by the arm. "Come on. I'll show you."

Nevada pulled back. "Linc! We'll get wet. Your

bandages will get soaked and that would be bad. Let's head to the house."

He started to say something when a loud crack split the air around them and rumbled down the mountainside.

Nevada jumped back to the safety of Linc's side and instinctively clutched his upper arm. "What are we going to do? I don't relish getting fried by lightning."

"Neither do I," he said. "I've already had my share of frying." He looked down at her. "I don't think we have much of a choice. Either way the waterfall or the rain is going to get us wet. At least in the cave we'll be protected from the lightning."

Nevada nodded as another bolt of electricity sizzled through the air and struck a nearby tree. A ball of fire raced up the trunk and Linc quickly tugged on her hand.

"Come on!"

Nevada didn't make any protest as they raced toward the fall of water.

"Duck your head," he warned. "The cave is small."

She did as he instructed and the two of them leaped through the icy flow of water. Once past, Nevada could see they were standing in a natural indentation of the rock. The opening was no more than four feet by six, but it was dry and cozy and would protect them from the violent lightning that was so deadly in this part of the West.

"Not a vacation suite, but at least it's dry," Linc said as the two of them moved toward the back of the enclosure.

"Thank God it's here," Nevada exclaimed. "And I would never have believed it if you hadn't shown me."

"Let's sit down," he suggested. "This might last for a while."

There was just enough room for the two of them to sit side by side with their knees drawn toward them. As Nevada wiped at the water droplets on her hair, she said, "I'm sorry about this, Linc. When I asked you to take a walk, I didn't know it was going to turn into this much of an outing."

"Forget it. And anyway, it's better than being cooped in the house or planted on the porch."

"I know. But it would be awful for you to survive such a horrible fire and then be killed because your nurse had you out in an electrical storm. Lord, I'd never get a job after that."

He looked at her with amusement. "You think Victoria would fire you if that happened?"

"No doubt," Nevada said grimly. "You're her hero."

Linc didn't make any sort of reply to that. Compliments of any sort made him feel awkward and he was already having enough trouble with being jammed in this tiny rock room with Nevada. Their shoulders and arms were squashed together, along with their thighs. The heat from both their bodies was already filling the small space and causing him to sweat beneath his shirt. Or maybe the desire to kiss Nevada again was making him sweat. Either way, he hoped the thunderstorm ended soon.

"It's hard to see through the waterfall. But it looks like it's raining now," Nevada said as she peered intently forward.

A part of Linc's gaze was on the opening in front of them, but the other part was darting to her face, which was only inches away from his. Her rosy-tan skin was as smooth as fine spun silk and along her cheekbone there was a faint bloom of roses. Black hair curled in tiny ringlets against her ear and temple, then fell in shiny waves upon her shoulder.

She was a naturally gorgeous woman and he tried to convince himself that her beauty was the reason he wanted to kiss her, touch her in forbidden places.

Stifling back a groan of desperation, he said, "It's pouring. I can hear it."

Her gaze carefully searched the fall of water a few short feet in front of them, then turned up to his face. "Really?"

He opened his mouth to answer at the same time another crack of lightning hit something outside the cave. Thunder rocked the mountainside like the aftershocks of an explosion. Before Nevada realized what she was doing, she screamed and turned her face into Linc's shoulder.

"Oh God, Linc, we're going to be killed!" she wailed.

Instinctively, Linc's arms curled around her and pressed her head tightly against him. "Sssh. Don't be frightened. It's just noise. The lightning can't get us in here," he said gently.

"Are you sure?" She tilted her head back to peek up at him. "We're sitting on rock! And there's water right in front of us!"

"Yes, but at least we're not targets here like we would be outside. Don't think about the worst happening. Just tell yourself it will all be over in a few minutes."

Before she could make any sort of reply another network of lightning streaked the sky and exploded somewhere outside the cave above their heads.

Nevada buried her face in his shoulder and as Linc gazed down at the top of her head, he realized he didn't know the first thing about calming a frightened woman. The brief times he'd spent in the company of a female hadn't involved situations like this.

But he figured Nevada was no different than a nervous filly that needed a gentle hand on her, so he began to stroke his fingers softly down the black mane of hair resting against her back.

"Don't be scared, little one," he murmured against her temple. "I'm not going to let anything happen to you."

Nevada wasn't usually afraid of electrical storms. The afternoon light shows were a common occurrence in this part of the country. But she'd never been caught out of doors in one before. And certainly not in the mountains where everything was more of a target.

But she trusted Linc to keep them safe and the security of his arms was having a steadying affect on her jumpy nerves. The warmth of his body soothed her while his unique male scent was slowly seducing her senses.

After a few moments she began to forget about the sizzling streaks of lightning and ear-shattering thunder. Being this close to Linc was doing all sorts of things to her body and she realized she desperately wanted to lift her face from his shoulder and turn her lips up to his.

But they'd both vowed to keep their relationship one of patient and nurse. She had to keep her side of the promise, no matter how much she wanted to break it.

Finally, she heard Linc whispering close to her ear, "I think it's letting up now."

Stirring in his arms, she lifted her head and stared toward the front of the cave. From what she could see through the wall of the waterfall, the sky was beginning to lighten. It was time to extract herself from Linc's embrace.

"Uh—it looks like the worst is over. I guess we need to get out of here," she said as she dared to glance up at him.

The moment she lifted her face their eyes collided. Her stomach lurched wildly and her heart began to hammer.

"Yeah—I guess we do," he said in a low voice.

Nevada licked her lips and his gaze settled on them.

"I'm sorry I behaved like such a chicken." But she wasn't sorry that she was here in his arms, her body pressed close to his. It felt like the perfect place for her to be and it was all she could do to keep from sliding her arms around his neck and pressing her cheek against his.

"A person would be crazy not to fear lightning. Don't feel badly because you got a little jumpy." A wry smile twisted his lips as he brought his bandaged hand alongside her face. "Are you okay now? Feel like hiking back home?"

Home. Suddenly that word held a whole new meaning to Nevada. She'd never felt as though she'd had a real home but with Linc she was beginning to imagine what one might be like and the pleasant thought scared her more than she cared to admit.

"Sure. Just let me get on my feet."

"Wait. I'll help you," he said and before she could make a move, he rose to his feet and reached down for her hand.

Nevada shook her head. "Linc, you're forgetting. No pressure on your hands."

"Damn it, for one minute forget about my burns and let me help you," he ordered.

She did as he asked, but she didn't allow him to pull on her weight any more than necessary. Once on her feet, she started to step around him and dash through the waterfall to the outside. But his hand on her waist prevented her from moving.

Darting a glance up at him, she tried not to notice that the two of them were face to face and hip to hip. "Thank you," she said. "For making me not feel so scared."

A faint smile tugged at the corners of his lips. "Thank you for making me come on this walk. It made me realize there's nothing wrong with me that a few days won't cure."

She smiled up at him. "Then I guess we've both made each other feel better."

His hand moved slightly up and down against her rib cage and Nevada was sure the small cave had suddenly lost all its oxygen.

"Uh—we'd better go," she said suddenly.

His hand tightened on her waist and for long moments as Nevada watched his eyes darken and his nostrils flare, she became aware that he wanted to kiss her just as badly as she wanted to kiss him. The realization caused her heart to flutter wildly in her throat and she unconsciously reached out and placed her palms against his chest.

"Nevada—I—"

"What?"

Shaking his head, he removed his hand from her waist and took hold of her arm. "Nothing," he answered grimly. "Let's get out of here before I do something stupid."

He urged her forward and Nevada followed him through the waterfall and back outside onto the ledge of rock. Everything was wet around them, but the sun was beginning to peek through the clouds.

"Look, Linc," Nevada said as she studied the rain-washed sky. "There's a rainbow over our heads. Isn't it beautiful?" She glanced over at him and smiled. "Did you know a rainbow is a promise of good things to come?"

"I always thought it meant that people foolishly chased after things they couldn't have."

"Oh, what a cynic," she said with a playful groan. "Don't you believe in just a little bit of magic?"

Normally Linc would have been quick to spit out the word *no*. But that was before he'd held Nevada in his arms. That was before he'd tasted her lips and felt himself going to a magical place where nothing mattered but making love to her.

Impatient with his soppy thoughts, he nudged her shoulder toward the now-muddy trail. "I believe we'd better get back home before Marina comes up with our supper and has a spell because she can't find us."

The pleasure at spotting the rainbow quickly fell from her face, and she hurried ahead of him to begin the steep climb up the mountain.

Behind her, Linc hated himself for being such a coward. Hated himself for not being able to run after her and admit how much he wanted to make love to her. But the memory of his mother walking away and never looking back was enough to make him keep his place safely behind her.

Chapter Nine

For the next three days Nevada and Linc settled into somewhat of a routine. He'd fixed the problem of showering by having one of the ranch hands come up and help him deal with the task. That usually took away the need for Nevada to help him dress in the mornings. Afterwards she prepared their breakfast and in the evenings, she changed his bandages and urged him to take some sort of exercise.

The walks he took were simple jaunts down the road and back to the house. Nevada never offered to go with him, and he never invited her. Which was probably for the best. Both of them were trying their best to put on an act of indifference, and it was beginning to take its toll.

At night, after the supper that Marina always brought up to them, they would go their separate ways until it was time for bed and then the provocative ordeal of undressing him would have to be gone through all over again.

Nevada's nerves were wearing thin. She'd read more novels than she'd ever read, and the idea of having a television to watch was actually becoming attractive to her.

As for Linc, she wasn't sure how he'd been spending his time. Sometimes she could hear him out on the front porch talking with Ross or some other ranch hand. The last couple of days an old buckaroo named Skinny had come up to visit him.

The first day the older man had arrived, Linc had called Nevada out on the porch to meet him. Which had surprised her somewhat. Several ranch hands had come and gone from the place in the past couple of days and he had not bothered to introduce her to any of them. The fact that he'd wanted her to meet Skinny told her the old man was important to him. And she'd found out that she liked him. He'd had a kind twinkle in his faded blue eyes and it was obvious that he adored Linc.

As for herself, Nevada had almost stopped trying to fool herself. She adored Linc, too. Only she was smart enough to keep her feelings to herself.

The ring of the telephone punctured Nevada's thoughts and she left her seat in the living room to hurry to the kitchen to answer it.

"Nevada, it's Victoria. I'm down here at the big ranch house and I thought I might run up to see you for a few minutes. Are you busy?"

Nevada laughed lightly. "Busy? What would I be doing? It's like a tomb around here."

"Poor thing. I'll bet you're about to go out of your mind."

"Not exactly," Nevada hedged.

"Well, you can tell me all about it in a few minutes. And I've got an appointment card for Linc. Dr. Olstead wants to see him tomorrow at eleven."

"You're just full of news," Nevada remarked, then asked, "Are the babies with you?"

"Brace yourself," Victoria laughed. "I have both of them with me. Better get Linc some earplugs before I get there."

She hung up and Nevada walked through the house in search of her patient.

After a quick peek on the porch and the back patio, she finally found him in his bedroom reading a hardbound book. He was propped against the headboard with a couple of pillows cushioning his back. Heedless of the fancy coverlet, his brown cowboy boots were crossed at the ankles and Nevada could only think it was a good thing he hadn't been walking around in the feed lot.

Since the door was fully open, she knocked lightly on the facing. "Sorry to disturb you, Linc, but that was Victoria who just called. She's coming up to see you—us."

He stood on the floor and with a puzzled frown glanced at his wristwatch. "It's the middle of the afternoon. What's she doing off work?"

"I didn't ask. She probably had Dr. Martinez take her place today. I'll go make coffee before she gets here."

Nevada left him and hurried to the kitchen to put a few refreshments together. The coffeepot was almost full and Marina's famous cowboy cookies were laid out on a tray when Nevada heard Victoria's vehicle arrive in front of the house. As she walked to the front door to greet her boss and friend, she could hear Katrina and little Sam both squealing with loud delight.

Stepping onto the porch, she could see that Linc had already met the little group and had somehow managed to lift Sam up on his back. Katrina was hopping eagerly at his side.

"I wanta ride too, Uncle Linc. Let me ride, too," she pleaded.

"Uncle Linc can't give you a ride now," Victoria told her daughter as the little group headed to the house. "He shouldn't even be carrying Sam. You run on ahead and find Aunt Nevada."

Nevada used that cue to step from the porch and call to the little girl. "Here, Katrina!"

With a loud squeal of excitement, Katrina raced to Nevada and jumped straight into her arms.

Laughing, Nevada lifted the three-and-a-half-year-old high in the air, then set her back on her feet and smacked a big kiss on her cheek.

"Hi, Aunt Nevada! You smell good! And you look pretty, too. Do you think I look pretty? Mommy bought me a new dress." Lifting the pink skirt on both sides, the golden-haired child twirled around on her toes for Nevada.

Her eyes sparkling with love, Nevada kissed the girl's cheek again. "Oh, I wish I had a dress like that. You look like the most beautiful girl in the world."

Beaming, Katrina turned to the other two adults who had reached the porch. "Mommy, Uncle Linc! Nevada says I'm the most beautiful girl in the world."

"Well, you are, aren't you?" Linc asked his niece as he bent down and allowed the dark-headed toddler on his back to step onto the porch. Sam was just over a year old but extremely steady on his feet. Linc had predicted the boy was going to make a championship bronc rider, but Victoria refused to think of her baby doing such a dangerous sport. She was even skittish when Jess rode the tot around on his gentle roping horse.

"Nope," Katrina told him. "I'm just pretty. Nevada is beautiful."

Laughing with embarrassment, Nevada reached out and playfully swatted the girl's bottom. "I think you're making up fairy tales, young lady."

While Katrina giggled and danced, Sam left Linc's side and toddled over to Nevada. Raising his arms up to her, he said, "Nada. Up, Nada!"

Bending down, Nevada lovingly scooped up the boy and cuddled him in her arms. "Come on, Sam, let's go have a cookie. Okay?"

"'Kay!" he shouted with enough enthusiasm to make the adults laugh.

Nevada carried the toddler into the house while Katrina and the other two adults followed. In the kitchen, Victoria settled the children at the table with cookies and milk while Nevada poured fresh coffee for the adults.

"What are you doing off work?" Linc asked his cousin.

Victoria took a seat next to Sam. "I needed a day to get caught up on some personal chores. Dr. Martinez is filling in for me," she answered, then turned a pointed look on Nevada. "He wasn't at all happy when he found out you weren't working at the clinic. He thinks he can't do anything without you."

Nevada frowned. "You're exaggerating even more than your daughter."

"Hmmph. I think he's sweet on you. He's just too shy to say anything to you about it," Victoria remarked.

Across the room, Linc leaned his hip against the cabinet counter and watched Nevada take a seat across from his cousin. He could see a pink tinge of embarrassment on her cheeks and Linc was suddenly struck by the thought that once Nevada left here she would be fair game for any man's attention. The notion irked him, but in the same breath he tried to tell himself that her personal life was none of his business.

"Dr. Martinez is rather old for Nevada, don't you think?" he asked his cousin.

Victoria turned her attention to him. "He's not much older than you, Linc. And he's a good-looking man. If I were Nevada I'd be flattered by his attention."

"Oh, Victoria, don't be silly. I don't need you to round me up a boyfriend. I already have plenty. Besides, if I ever dated the man it would be awkward to work with him later."

"Hmm. That's true," Victoria agreed as she returned her attention to Nevada. "And you're right. You have plenty of guys waiting to date you without me scrounging you up another one. Even if he is a rich, well-to-do doctor."

"Is that what you come up here for?" Linc shot at her. "Just to talk about Nevada's boyfriends?"

Victoria was clearly surprised by Linc's outburst and her mouth fell open as she stared at him. "Is something wrong with that?"

Linc suddenly felt like an idiot and with a deep

frown marring his forehead he marched over to the table and picked up a cookie from the tray.

"No," he answered without bothering to give any explanation for his remark. How could he explain his burst of jealousy, he wondered, when he didn't even understand it himself.

Victoria continued to look at him with a keen eye. "Well, actually, I didn't come up here to discuss anything with Nevada. I came to see you and to check on how you're doing. Nevada tells me you've been in a better mood, but now I'm beginning to wonder if she only told me that to appease me."

Little Sam had eaten most of his cookie and was now placing the last of the crumbs on top of his head, which was making Katrina giggle hysterically and was prompting him to keep repeating the act.

Nevada used the children's antics as a good excuse to leave the table and take the two of them outside.

"I think we'll go pick some wildflowers," she told Victoria. "You go ahead and visit with Linc."

As Nevada hurried the two children out of the kitchen, Linc walked over to the table and sat down across from his cousin.

Victoria heaved out a disgusted sigh. "Well, you managed to run her off without much effort."

Linc lifted his bandaged hands in a gesture of helplessness. "I didn't do any such thing. And why are you suddenly badgering me?"

"Because you make me angry. I want to see my dear cousin Linc and instead you—oh, just forget it. You're just a man."

She reached into the pocket of her shirt, pulled out a small white card and placed it on the table between them.

Ignoring it, Linc asked, "What is that supposed to mean? Are you and Jess having marital problems?"

Tilting her head back, Victoria laughed. "Not in the least. How could you even think such a thing?"

He turned a brooding expression out the window where Nevada was now romping with Sam and Katrina. "It happens," he quipped. "A lot."

"Well, not with us. Never with us. In fact, we're thinking about having another baby," Victoria admitted.

This brought his head around and he stared at her in surprise. "Another baby! But Sam isn't yet two! And you already have two children."

She shrugged as a dreamy expression crossed her face. "So we do. But there's not a limit, is there? We might want four or five or six."

Shaking his head, Linc said, "Kids are nice. But I don't understand your need for more of them. They're lots of work."

Victoria grinned at him. "So are your colts. But you wouldn't understand, Linc. Not until you have a family of your own."

He looked away from her and in spite of himself,

he found his gaze drawn back to the picture Nevada was making as she knelt down to help the children pick wildflowers.

"That won't ever happen," he said lowly.

Silent moments passed before he felt Victoria's hand resting on his arm.

"Why, Linc?" she asked softly. "You know, each month, each year that passes, I keep hoping and praying that someone will come into your life."

Emotions balled in his throat and he did his best to swallow them down before he glanced at her. "You're wasting your prayers on me. You know how I feel about things."

"No. I don't. I know you've never gotten over your mother remarrying and leaving like she did, but—"

"I don't want to talk about her, Victoria. Not now."

Sighing wearily, Victoria pushed the card toward him. "There's your appointment for tomorrow. Dr. Olstead wants to make sure you've been healing all right since you left the hospital."

His arms and hands were healing, he could have told her. But his insides had gone through some sort of trauma that he couldn't shake. Ever since he'd held Nevada in the cave, he'd felt like a different man. When he looked at her now, he didn't only want to make love to her, he also wanted to protect and cherish her. He wanted to see her smile over and over and feel her joy for life flow into him.

Linc had never felt anything like what he was feeling now and he desperately wished Dr. Olstead could heal his state of mind along with his hands.

"All right. Is Nevada going to drive me in or are you going to send up one of the hands to take me?"

His question puckered her dark brows together. "Nevada is going to take you, of course. There's not one man down on the ranch who wants to sit in a doctor's office any more than you do."

"Yeah, guess you're right about that," he said flatly, then inclined his head to the view of the yard. "Sam and Katrina obviously think Nevada is wonderful."

A fond smile crossed Victoria's face. "They call her Aunt Nevada. And she's great with them." Her expression sobered as she added, "It's such a shame that she doesn't want to become a mother. She loves children so much and she'd make such a good parent. But everyone has their own demons to deal with, I suppose."

Struck by Victoria's comments, Linc's gaze traveled back and forth between the sight of Nevada frolicking with his niece and nephew to his cousin's pensive expression.

"What woman wouldn't have demons with a laundry list like Nevada probably has," he remarked. The idea that she'd gone through men the way he did clean shirts left a heavy weight inside him. And he tried to tell himself he was being stupid. He didn't

want to be the next one she put through the wringer
then hung out to dry.

"Oh Linc," Victoria said with a shake of her head,
"you are so—messed up if you think—"

Linc narrowed his eyes on Victoria's lovely face.
"What? What were you about to say?" he demanded.

With another shake of her head, Victoria rose to
her feet and carried her empty cup to the sink.
"Nothing," she told him. "If you want to know anything personal about Nevada, you'll have to ask her
yourself."

And he wasn't about to do that, Linc thought. He
might have slipped that once and kissed her, but since
then he'd kept his distance and he had not allowed
any family or personal talk to come up between them.
The past three days had been lonely and hellish for
him, but he could get through it, he thought, much
better than he could live with a broken heart.

The appointment with Dr. Olstead was at eleven in
the morning. The two of them left the house early
enough to make the drive without having to hurry.

It was the first time Nevada had been back to town
in more than a week and she looked around the place
with renewed interest.

"It's funny how a little time away from a place
makes it all seem new again."

"Guess you've missed it," he said.

Nevada shook her head as she wheeled the car into the parking lot near a block of medical buildings.

"Actually, I'm surprised how little I have missed it. There's been a few times I got to craving the noise of a television. But other than that, I've enjoyed your parents' house."

His parents' house. Funny that Linc had never thought of the place in that way. To him it was his father's house. Darla hadn't seemed a part of it. Not when she'd hated the place so much.

"Well, give me the bunkhouse any day," he said.

Nevada tried not to feel hurt as she looked over at him. "I guess you miss all your buddies." She smiled wryly. "Men get tired of hearing a woman's chatter and I can't talk horse talk with you. I hope Dr. Olstead will give you some good news and you'll be able to go back to work soon."

She picked up her handbag from the console between them and dropped the key inside. Next to her, Linc unbuckled his seat belt then at the last minute before she opened the door, he reached for her hand.

Nevada turned her face around to his. "Yes?"

He grimaced before he cut his eyes away from her. Even so, Nevada could see something was troubling him. His jaw was tight, his lips pressed to a thin line. She hated seeing him like this. Especially when he'd shown her a glimpse of the gentle man he used to be.

"Uh—a minute ago. That bit I said about the

bunkhouse. Don't take that personally. You've done a good job helping me—it's just that I'm more comfortable there with the men."

For some reason his haltingly spoken words saddened her more than anything she could remember and she wound her fingers around his and gently squeezed. "I understand, Linc. Don't try to explain. It'll all be over soon anyway. And I'll be glad for you."

But as for herself, she couldn't imagine what it was going to feel like to go back to her apartment, to live all by herself. There wouldn't be any more breakfasts together. No more sitting on the patio watching the sunrise together. No more helping him into his clothes or sitting close beside him as she tended his bandages. Soon her time with Linc would all be over and she could go back to her happy life and forget about the man with longing written in his eyes and sadness in his voice.

Glancing at her watch, she said, "We'd better go inside. It's almost time for your appointment."

The clinic was full of waiting patients, especially pregnant women and little children. Nevada looked at them and wondered if she would ever be sure enough about someone to start a family with him. As for Linc, he grabbed up a magazine and ignored the whole lot. Including Nevada.

It wasn't long before the nurse stepped out to call Linc's name and usher him back to Dr. Olstead's examining room. Nevada went along with him. Not because he'd asked her to, but because she was his nurse and it would help her care for him better if she heard everything the doctor had to say. She tried to ignore the fact that she wanted to be with him. Just like a wife accompanying her injured or sick husband, she thought with chagrin.

And when Dr. Olstead's nurse began to remove Linc's bandages, Nevada had to fight the urge to push the other woman out of the way and take hold of him herself.

But of course, she had no right or reason to do that so she sat in a plastic chair shoved in one corner of the tiny room while the nurse and the doctor made a thorough examination of Linc's arms and hands.

Thirty minutes later they were back outside the building and as they walked to Nevada's car, one of Linc's rare smiles began to appear on his face.

"Thank God that's over," he said with relief.

"You got a good report."

"Thanks to you," he said.

She scoffed at the compliment. "Anybody can smear medication on a burn. It was nothing."

She walked on ahead of him to the car and for a moment Linc stared thoughtfully after her. He didn't know what had caused the change in her, but something had made her distant, almost indifferent with him. He realized he didn't like it. He wanted her warmth and her smile back. But then he reminded himself that he didn't really deserve Nevada's kindness. Not when he'd been going hot one minute and cold the next; behaving like a jackass who didn't know his head from his tail.

"Is something wrong, Nevada?" he asked as he climbed into the seat next to hers.

Tossing him a glance, she turned the key in the ignition and the engine sprang to life. "Nothing is wrong. Why?"

He shrugged. "I don't know. You just seem a little distant."

Her hand paused on the gearshift. "So? I can't imagine that bothering you."

She put the car into Reverse and gunned it backwards.

"Dr. Olstead said I could go down to the ranch yard and look at the horses," he said.

"If you keep your distance," she reminded him.

"Yeah. Well, it doesn't look like I'm going to make it there anyway. Maybe Skinny will see that all the mares foal as they should and the weanlings are separated from their mothers."

Nevada kept her eyes on the town traffic. "Why aren't you going to make it? Dr. Olstead just gave you a glowing report, not a death sentence."

"I know. But for some reason you're trying to kill

me." He scowled at her. "What's the matter with you, anyway?"

Nevada glanced over at him. What *was* the matter, she asked herself. Was it because she could see her time with him soon ending? That even though he'd only kissed her once since they'd been together, that one kiss had shattered all her preconceived notions about men?

"Nothing, I told you. I'm fine. I guess being in the clinic just made me miss working," she lied.

With Dr. Martinez, he thought, as he stared glumly out the windshield. "Guess you'll be happy to get back to working with Victoria. I'm sure she's a good boss."

"The best."

If you want to know anything personal about Nevada, you should ask her yourself.

As Victoria's words rolled through Linc's mind, he glanced thoughtfully over at Nevada.

"Would you like to go to the Wagon Wheel for lunch?"

She stomped on the brake as the car ahead of them suddenly stopped for a left-hand turn. As they bounced to a halt, Nevada looked over at him.

"You're asking me to go out to lunch with you?"

He surprised her with a low chuckle. "Yes. What's the deal? We eat lunch together everyday anyway."

"True. But this time we'll be in public and you'll be buying." And she couldn't imagine why he might want to linger in town with her. But she wasn't going to question his motives. The man needed an outing in the worst kind of way.

A faint smile touched his rugged face. "I can handle it if you can," he said.

At the next intersection Nevada flipped on the blinker and turned down the street that would take them straight to the diner.

"I think I can survive having lunch with you," she murmured. It was the coming days without him that Nevada was worried about.

Chapter Ten

The Wagon Wheel Café was an eating place that had been in town since the early fifties. Except for a new tile floor and a fresh coat of paint once in a while, it had remained the same simple diner down through the years. The food was good and the eclectic atmosphere was created by the mix of business people dressed in suits and local ranchers in hats and spurs.

Nevada and Linc found a booth in the back of the room and ordered the blue plate special of meat loaf, mashed potatoes, corn and hot rolls. They'd hardly begun to eat when an older man approached their table and greeted Linc.

He turned out to be only one of many to come by their booth and strike up a conversation with Linc. For the most part, Nevada sat quietly eating while Linc answered concerned questions about his health.

She was totally surprised that he seemed to be acquainted with every person in the diner and she said as much to him as they walked out of the building and down the sidewalk to where she'd parked the car.

"You've surprised me, Linc. Here all along I thought you were a stay-at-home kind of guy. Instead, I learn you know half the townspeople."

He shook his head. "I *am* a stay-at-home guy. Each one of those people that came by the table, I met on the ranch," he explained. "You see, anyone who wants to buy a horse from the T Bar K has to go through me. And down through the years we've sold many."

Pausing on the sidewalk she looked at him with interest. "I didn't know you were a trader, too! I've often heard you should never trust a horse trader," she added impishly. "Is that true?"

Chuckling, he took her by the arm and urged her on down the sidewalk. "Depends on what you're trusting him to do."

The meal at the diner and meeting up with old friends appeared to have had a positive effect on Linc. Throughout their drive back to the ranch, he was more talkative and the stilted awkwardness that had been building between them since their time in the cave seemed to ease.

Nevada was relieved with the change between them. It was hard enough for her to hide her burgeoning feelings without having to carefully tiptoe around the man, too.

When they finally reached the main ranch yard, Nevada didn't bother asking him if he wanted to park and take a look at the horses. She simply pulled the car over to an out-of-the-way spot next to a pole corral and killed the motor.

"What are you doing?" he asked with surprise.

"Dr. Olstead said you could look at the horses if you didn't touch anything or get too close. I thought you might like to show me some of your favorites."

Surprise flickered in his eyes and then his whole expression softened. "Only if you're interested. You don't have to give me therapy, you know."

"Maybe I'm the one who needs therapy," she teased, then gently touched his arm. "I'm interested, Linc. Otherwise, I wouldn't have stopped."

Grinning faintly, he tugged his hat down on his forehead and reached for the door handle "Okay. Let's go."

The men who were working around the ranch yard for the afternoon were all surprised to see Linc. As they rushed to greet him, Nevada was careful to remind each of them that because their hands were dirty they couldn't touch their boss and risk giving him an infection.

None of the men seemed to care about that, and they all talked to him at length until Linc finally had to send them on their way.

"You didn't have to do that for my sake," Nevada told him a few minutes later as they walked toward a fenced corral where several mares were chomping at a hay manger filled with dark-green alfalfa. "There's no hurry."

He shrugged. "Don't worry about the men. They all needed to get back to work anyway."

Once they reached the corral, Linc pointed to the mares. There were two blacks, three sorrels and three grays. All of them were in an advanced state of pregnancy.

"These are just a few of our broodmares that will be foaling soon. About a month before time we put them up in this pen so that we can keep a watch on them."

"They're all so beautiful," Nevada said softly as she gazed at the graceful creatures with their long manes and tails. "Is it common for a mare giving birth to have trouble?"

"Not usually. Most have routine births. But sometimes things go wrong. And when they do, you only have a few minutes to try to correct it. Most mares carry their babies for eleven months, so it's a long wait to get one here. And then sometimes they're stillborn. When that happens—well, it really hurts," he murmured.

The emotion in his voice caused her to glance over at him and in that moment as she watched him gazing out at the mares, she realized his rugged body and gruff demeanor was hiding a huge, soft heart. If he were to ever love a woman he would do so with everything inside him, she decided. There wouldn't be any halves with Linc Ketchum.

But Nevada didn't want to think about him loving a woman. Not unless that woman was her. And since that could never happen, she tried not to think about it at all and focus on the horses.

With his arm curled loosely against her back, Linc guided her to the end of a long barn where a railed fence held at least twenty geldings. Three of them were saddled and tethered to a wooden hitching post and Linc explained that the cowboys who'd been riding them had probably come into the bunkhouse for lunch and were planning to go back out on the range again after they ate.

"The rest of this small herd is a portion of our remuda. These are the geldings that the cowboys use every day. They're worked hard, so they require a lot of care. Plenty of feed and hay, morning and night, liniment rubdowns and doctoring. But they're all bred strong. You won't find any fine-boned, timid horses on the T Bar K," he said proudly.

Nevada pointed to a white horse that was splattered with tiny chocolate-brown spots all over his body. "He's gorgeous. If you ever do take me for a ride, Linc, I want to ride him," she told him.

Smiling at her choice, he said, "That's Spotted Bird. He can be a handful at times. But if you pet him and give him a few treats he'll settle right down."

"Sort of like you?" she joked, her brown eyes sparkling.

He chuckled. "Yeah. Sort of like me," he admitted, then taking her by the arm he led her around to the front of the barn. "Let's go in. I want you to see Miss Lori."

She cast him a concerned look. "I'm not sure you should go inside the barn."

Grimacing, he held out his hands and arms. "I know I'm supposed to be careful. But look at this, Nevada. I don't think anything is going to penetrate all these layers of bandages, do you?"

As Nevada studied his injured limbs, she understood that agreeing to let him walk into the barn would be far better medicine than worrying about infection.

"We're going to act like it won't," she said finally. "So let's go. I want to see this Miss Lori that you've been fretting about."

A broad smile slowly parted his lips and, while

watching the transformation come over his face, it suddenly dawned on Nevada that making this man happy had become far too important to her.

Two huge doors were opened at the end of the building and Linc guided her inside where they walked down a wide alleyway filled with the pungent scent of pine-wood shavings. On either side of them were rows of stalls most of which appeared to be empty at the moment.

"At least this barn was saved," she said as she looked all around her. Everything was exceptionally clean. She could smell the disinfectant which had been used to wash down walls and clean water troughs. "Where was the barn that burned?"

"I'll show you when we leave. It was about fifty yards from here. Thank God none of the sparks set any of the other buildings around it on fire."

They reached a fence with a latched gate. Linc opened it and ushered her into an area closed-off from the rest of the structure. A black mare with a star on her forehead was inside the large lot. In one corner Skinny was sitting in an old wooden chair tilted onto its back legs and resting against the fence. The old man was softly playing a harmonica and he finished the little tune before he lowered the instrument to greet the two of them.

"Well, look who's here." A big grin spread over his wrinkled old face as he got up from the chair to join them at the opening of the foaling area. "I thought you weren't supposed to be around the barn."

Linc jerked his head toward Nevada. "She gave me permission."

Skinny's eyes twinkled with appreciation as he looked at Nevada. "You must be even smarter than you are pretty, Miss Nevada. You gonna let him hang around a while?"

Nevada regretfully shook her head. "I'm sorry, Skinny. I can't let him stay but a few minutes. He wanted to show me Miss Lori."

The old wrangler pointed a finger at the black mare. "Well, there she is. She's a beauty, ain't she?"

"Gorgeous," Nevada agreed. "Is it okay if I pet her?"

"Of course," Linc assured her. "Just walk up to her slowly, with your shoulder to her and don't look her straight in the eye until she smells you."

Nevada left the two men and walked over to where the mare was munching on a hay bag filled with alfalfa. Slowly, so as not to startle her, she did as Linc had instructed. After a few moments she was able to reach out and touch the mare's neck with soft, gentle strokes.

Miss Lori turned her head and gazed at Nevada with trusting brown eyes. The exchange with the animal touched her in a way she would never have expected, and she suddenly understood the deep connection Linc felt to his horses. They were truly his family and he felt safe with them because they loved him unconditionally. They would never purposely hurt him.

"She likes you."

Linc's words were murmured gently next to Nevada's ear and she realized she'd been so involved with the mare, she hadn't heard him walk up behind her.

"I'm glad. What would she do if I stroked her on the face? Do horses like that?"

Her question caused his lips to tilt with amusement. "Of course they like it. Don't you?"

She wrinkled her nose at him. "Depends on who's doing the stroking."

A sensual glint sparked his eyes as he reached for her hand and placed it on the mare's nose.

"Picky about that, are you?"

Nevada sucked in an edgy breath as the front of his body brushed against the back of hers. "Much pickier than you think," she muttered.

He didn't say anything to that, and she glanced over her shoulder to see that his expression had sobered. After his playful warmth of this afternoon the sight chilled her.

"I need to talk to Skinny about a few things," he said. "I'll be ready to go in just a minute or two."

Nodding, she turned her gaze back to the mare and told herself to quit acting like a foolish teenage girl. It was crazy for her to allow her feelings to get all tangled up with Linc Ketchum's moods. From the way Dr. Olstead had talked this afternoon, Linc would probably be free of his bandages in another week. After that he would allow him to do light work. At least, he could use his hands enough to see to his own needs. That meant Nevada's job would be finished. And the best thing she could do right now was get ready for the exit.

On the short drive up the mountain to the house, Linc was quiet and Nevada didn't try to engage him in small talk. She wasn't exactly in a talking mood herself. She was feeling a bit defeated and even more angry with herself.

For the past ten of her twenty-five years, she'd pretty much taken care of herself. She had not relied on anyone for financial or emotional support. She had gritted through the poverty and loneliness, and the insecurities of being without a dependable family. She'd finally carved out a niche for herself. She had a good job that she loved. And though she was far from rich, she was secure. She didn't need a man mixed permanently into her life. Not Linc. Not any man.

Later that night, long after they'd eaten dinner and she'd cleared away the dishes, the telephone rang.

Answering it, she found Victoria's husband, Jess, the under-sheriff of San Juan County, on the other end.

"Has Linc already gone to bed?" he asked.

"I don't think so. Let me go find him," she said and put down the phone to hurry through the house.

She found him on the front porch, reading a book beneath the dim glow of a coal-oil lamp. Early in the week, she'd caught him doing the same thing and had asked him why he didn't go inside to read by the light of a proper lamp. He'd told her he felt best when he was outside and that the pioneers who'd settled the nation before them had read just fine by coal-oil lamps.

Nevada hadn't argued with him then and she didn't stop to now as he put down his book and looked up at her.

"You have a telephone call. It's Jess."

Rising from his chair, he blew out the lamp and headed toward the door. "Thanks," he called over his shoulder.

Nevada followed him back into the house but rather than return to the kitchen and intrude on his phone call, she went to her room and began to prepare for bed. She brushed her teeth and cleaned her face and was sitting on the dressing bench brushing her hair when she heard a knock at her door. Turning around, she saw Linc standing in the open doorway. A stricken look was on his face and her heart plummeted.

"What's wrong? What's happened?" she questioned.

He stepped into the room and took a seat on the

foot of her bed, something he'd never done before. He was obviously disturbed.

"Jess called to tell me that he'd just gotten out of a meeting with Sheriff Perez and the fire marshal." His dark gaze caught hers. "The fire at the barn has been ruled to have been arson."

Stunned at the idea that anyone could do such a horrific thing, Nevada could only stare at him. "Arson? I can't believe it. Are they certain?"

He nodded and there was a sick, almost fatalistic look on his face. "Yes. They're sure. The fire marshal says there were two ignition sites, one at each end of the building, and some sort of chemical was used as an accelerator."

"I just can't believe it," Nevada said again in a dazed voice. "Who would do such a thing? You could have been killed! You nearly were!"

Ignoring the implications to his own safety, he said in stunned disbelief, "The horses. How could anyone deliberately set out to kill a barn full of innocent animals? I—"

He stopped and shook his head in dismay. Nevada could see he was clearly shaken by the news Jess had given him.

Feeling the strong urge to console him, Nevada left the dressing table and took a seat next to him on the edge of the mattress.

"I'm so sorry, Linc. So terribly sorry. Your family

has already been through so much with the Rider murder and then Jess nearly being fatally shot. I can't believe that someone else is out to hurt you Ketchums."

"More like out to hurt me. It wasn't unusual for me to stay all night in that barn. Before it was destroyed, that's where I kept most of the pregnant mares and our prize stallion. It was just by the grace of God that there weren't any newborn colts in the barn that night." With a weary groan he lifted one hand and raked it over his face. "Jess is sending out deputies to guard the other buildings in the ranch yard until Ross can come up with some security guards of his own. Hell, what is that going to say to all the people who come here to buy cattle and horses? They'll all be too scared to set a foot on the place!"

Nevada had never seen a raging fire up close, but she could easily imagine the horror of one. The idea that someone had purposely set out to hurt or kill Linc made her shudder.

Reaching over, she placed her hand on his knee. "Linc, try not to think about it," she urged. "Just let Sheriff Perez take care of things. He'll find the person behind all this."

He sucked in a long, shaky breath and then released it in one weary whoosh. "I hope he does. Because if I find him first, I'm going to put these hands around his neck and choke the hell right out of him."

The threat in his voice was cool and deliberate and Nevada had no doubt that he meant what he said.

Suddenly she was very scared for his safety and she clutched his upper arm with both hands.

"Linc, please, don't do anything foolish. You've already been seriously hurt. I—I don't want anything else to happen to you."

Slowly, the dark revenge in his eyes began to fade away and he looked at her with a bit of wonder.

"If I didn't know better," he said softly, "I'd think you really meant that."

Without any warning, Nevada's heart started swelling with emotions and her brown eyes grew misty as she looked up at him. "I do mean it, Linc. I mean it very much."

The room had been quiet before, but now there didn't seem to be any sound at all as the seconds slid by and his gaze slowly searched her face. Finally his attention focused on her lips and caused heat to surge through her body with lightning speed. Desire boiled up inside her and she couldn't stop herself from leaning into him and tilting her face up to his.

"Nevada. Nevada."

Her name was all he said before he bent his head and placed his lips over hers.

He kissed her sweetly, gently, then pulled back to look at her once more.

Nevada could feel the naked longing on her face

and knew that he could see it, too, but her desire for him had grown far too strong to hide.

"Make love to me, Linc."

His bandaged hands rested gently on her shoulders. "You don't know what you're saying."

Her gaze didn't waver on his. "I know exactly what I'm saying."

In the back of Linc's mind, he understood that to reach for Nevada would be as dangerous as reaching for a stick of dynamite. But these past days he'd spent being near her and desperately wanting her had taken a toll on him. He was weak from the constant exertion of trying to resist her.

And why should he keep fighting? he asked himself. The two of them were consenting adults. What happened between them tonight would have no bearing on tomorrow. And maybe, just maybe, having her in his bed would put an end to this maddening ache in his loins.

Without another thought, he pulled her toward him and she fell willingly into his arms.

Over and over Linc kissed her until her arms wound tightly around his neck and she tugged them both down on the mattress.

Lying face to face, he pulled his head back far enough so that his gaze could delve into hers. "I've wanted you from the moment I saw you. But are you sure you want me?" he asked.

With a sensual groan, she lifted a hand to his face and gently stroked his cheek. "I want you, Linc. More than anything," she told him as the truth of those words shattered the resistance she'd desperately been trying to hold on to.

"Little one. My sweet," he murmured.

His soft words of affection caused joy to pour into her heart and she closed her eyes in blissful anticipation as he brought his lips over hers once again.

His searching mouth quickly sent her senses scattering in all directions and before she realized what she was doing, her fingers were loosening the buttons on his shirt, her palms were spreading flat against his hair-roughened chest.

Groaning with pleasure, he deserted her lips to press a moist, tingly trail down the side of her throat.

"Damn it," he murmured with agony. "I can't undress you. My hands can't feel your skin. And I want to feel you, Nevada. So badly."

His urgent words were like an instant aphrodisiac and all she wanted was to please him, to give him anything and everything he wanted. She'd never felt anything close to this before and the reality of what was happening made her whole body hum with love.

And it was love, she told herself. She didn't just want Linc's body. She wanted his heart, his soul to bind with hers. She wanted the two of them to be together like this forever.

"I'll be your hands. Just lean back and let me undress you," she whispered fervently. "Let me make love to you."

He did as she asked, and as Nevada began to remove his boots and then his clothing, she noticed he was watching her through green eyes that were simmering with a fire of their own.

With her gaze fastened firmly on his face, she finally removed his jeans. He was wearing boxer shorts beneath the jeans and she deliberately left them where they were. Even so, she could tell he was already firmly aroused and the sight of his desire left her whole body glowing with heat and her cheeks blooming with color.

"Are you blushing?" he asked teasingly as he watched her fumble with the buttons on her own blouse.

Nevada quickly turned her back to him. "No. It's the dim light in here. In fact, I think we should turn off the lamp."

She started to skirt the bed so that she could reach the small lamp sitting on a table near the headboard. But before she could take more than two steps, Linc caught her by the arm.

"Forget the lamp," he murmured huskily. "I want to see you. I've been wanting to see you for days now."

Nevada had never been naked in front of any man before, and normally the mere thought of being in such a vulnerable position was enough to embarrass her. But Linc's eager request made her feel beautiful and wanted and she wanted to give back to him.

The blue shirt she'd been wearing finally hit the floor and soon her jeans followed. Beneath she was wearing a pale yellow panty and bra set that was made of lace and satin triangles that did little more than cover her nipples and the patch of black hair growing at the apex of her thighs. The soft color glowed like liquid gold against her brown skin and Linc groaned with pleasure as she lay down next to him.

"The rest should be easy enough for you to get off," she whispered against his cheek.

With a low chuckle, he gently rolled her onto her back. "I might just have to chew these things off."

For the next few minutes that was exactly what Nevada thought he was going to do as his mouth explored every crevice, every hill and valley of her body.

Finally, he raised his head and muttered thickly, "Oh honey. Honey. I've got to make you mine. All mine."

Awkwardly, his bandaged fingers pulled at her lingerie, and though she could have helped him remove the pieces of clothing, she understood he needed to do this much of the chore himself.

Once the satin and lace were finally out of the way, he started to position himself over her, but Nevada quickly put a hand against his chest and guided him back to the mattress.

"You can't put pressure on your hands," she gently reminded him. "You'll damage all the healing."

"But—"

He didn't finish the question. He didn't have to as Nevada straddled his waist and flipped her long black hair over her shoulders.

"You little siren," he murmured thickly. "I should have known."

His hands came up to cup her small breasts and though his bandages came between their skins, his touch still excited her beyond anything she could have imagined.

With a groan deep in her throat, she lowered one shoulder so that his mouth could reach her breast. The simple invitation was enough to tell him what she needed and he gladly complied by gently biting down on the chocolate-brown nipple.

"Oooh. Oh Linc. I didn't—know it would be—like this."

Easing back from her slightly, he could see her head was thrown back, her eyes squeezed tightly shut. She was as taut as a violin string just waiting to be plucked and stroked.

"Sure you did, baby. Come here," he crooned. "Come here and let me love you."

With a little help, he pushed his boxer shorts down over his feet and then, placing his hands on both sides of her shapely hips, he guided her up and over his rigid manhood.

The intimate folds of her body were hot and moist and the pleasure of entering her turned Linc's blood to liquid fire. Every nerve, every particle of his body screamed at him to hurry, hurry. But he'd never believed this moment would happen and he wanted it to last. He wanted to watch her face as he slowly filled her body.

Sweat gathered on his face and she began to say his name over and over in a thick, choked voice like a pleading mantra begging him to end her agony.

Finally with a downward tug on her hips, Linc gave one final thrust and her delicious body closed around him like a tight, loving hand.

Nevada bit down hard on her bottom lip, but she couldn't prevent the loud sob from escaping into the quiet bedroom. Yet it wasn't the sound that suddenly paralyzed Linc. It was the thin barrier he'd encountered at the very last moment as he'd joined their bodies.

She was a virgin! A virgin!

"Nevada! What—why didn't you tell me?" he groaned.

He started to push her off him, but she wouldn't budge. Instead, she leaned down and cupped her hands against the sides of his face. "Because it doesn't matter."

Chapter Eleven

"Like hell, I—"

"This is what I want," she interrupted. "And you don't want to stop now, do you?"

He should stop, Linc thought. He should slide away from her this very minute, leave the bedroom and never look back. But his body absolutely refused to listen to any part of that suggestion. Especially when her hips began a slow thrust that turned him inside out.

"You know I don't," he muttered gruffly and then with a groan of surrender, he began to match his movements to hers.

In all of his adult life Linc had never felt such intense pleasure, and though he realized he needed to go slowly to initiate her to their intimate coupling, he couldn't hold back his hunger. Nor could he hide it from her.

Tugging her head down, he feasted on her lips as his hands cupped her rounded bottom and urged her to an even faster pace.

Her breathing became rapid and so did his. Her long hair swung forward and cocooned them inside a curtain of black satin.

Eventually, Nevada's arms got tired and she fell over Linc with an exhausted thump.

"I'm sorry, Linc. My arms—" she said between pants for air.

"Sssh," he whispered as he rolled her onto her back. "Let me finish this."

"Your hands—"

"My hands are the last thing you need to be thinking about," he told her. Then, straddling her body, he lowered himself over her and rested his weight on his elbows. "See how good this is."

Nevada wanted to answer, but she couldn't. His movements were taking her breath away, sending her to a place she'd never been before.

Bright, beautiful stars began to parade behind the back of her closed eyes. Suddenly she felt herself floating upward toward the stars in that velvety sky, until something deep inside her exploded like a meteor shower.

At the same time the thrust of Linc's hips grew frenzied, and with a great groan, he clutched her desperately to him and spilled the warm seeds of his manhood.

It was some time before Nevada was capable of speaking a word. By then Linc had rolled his weight to her side and was studying her with dark, drowsy eyes.

Turning onto her side, she leaned forward and pressed a kiss upon his lips. She had never tasted anything so good in her life, and she wanted to keep on kissing him, but she could see that he wanted to say something so she pulled back and waited.

"Why were you a virgin, Nevada?"

His question seemed ludicrous and she chuckled softly. "I was a virgin because I'd never made love to a man. That's the medical explanation."

"Damn it, I don't want some clinical reason! You—"

She placed a forefinger over his lips. "It's not all that perplexing, Linc. I'd just never met a man I wanted to make love to until you."

He outwardly winced, and she wondered what the reaction meant. Was he already regretting making love to her?

"But you—you let me believe—you talked about your boyfriends and—"

"And you jumped to conclusions. Like a lot of people do where I'm concerned. Just because I have friends that happen to be male, everyone believes I'm a sex siren or something." She rolled her eyes with amusement. "Nothing could be further from the truth."

"Why?"

Her brows lifted in question and he repeated, "Why? Didn't you *feel* anything physical for them?"

She sighed. "Linc, I don't go around experimenting with men. In fact—" Biting down on her lip, she glanced away from him.

"What?" he urged.

"I've been careful to keep my relationships with men only as friendships. That's the way I've always wanted it. And that's the way I always intended it to be. But, you've come along and changed all that."

He couldn't believe any of this. All along, he'd thought Nevada was experienced with men. He'd believed she'd considered them as nothing more than entertainment. At least, that's what he'd wanted to believe. Part of him had desperately been trying to ignore the kind, caring woman who more often than not had put his needs before her own. And now he had to face the fact she'd offered him her innocence and he'd taken it so carelessly.

Linc moved closer, lifted his hand to her brow and gently pushed back her tumbled hair. "You should have told me beforehand, Nevada. I would have—"

"What?" she interrupted. "Not made love to me? Left the room like I had smallpox?"

"I don't know," he admitted truthfully. "But at least I could have been more gentle with you."

Groaning, she scooted forward until the front of her body was pressing into his and her arm was curved around his waist.

"You *were* gentle, Linc. You were perfect. Perfect," she repeated in a whisper as she rubbed her cheek against his chest.

The adoration he heard in her voice pricked him with fear. She wasn't supposed to be all warm and fuzzy and loving toward him. And his heart shouldn't be swelling with the sort of emotions that made him want to hold her close and never let go.

"Honey. You'll know different. When you find a good man."

She pulled her head back and peered dreamily up at him. "I have found a good man."

Linc's heart jerked with a feeling that was both sweet and frightening. "You don't know what you're saying," he said in a husky whisper. "You don't know me, not really."

She smiled at him. A wide show of affection that was full of sensual invitation. "Then maybe you'd better let me learn more."

It was time to stop this thing that was happening between them, Linc told himself. If he didn't stop it both of them were going to suffer. But even the thought of the misery to come was not strong enough to make him move out of her arms.

"Maybe I'd better," he said and with a murmur of pleasure he brought his lips down on hers.

When Nevada woke the next morning, the space next to her was empty and the morning sun was already slanting weakly through the nearby window. She could smell coffee and sausage and the distinct scent of warm flour tortillas filtering through the house, telling her that Linc had been busy in the kitchen.

Linc. She said his name over and over in her mind as she stretched her stiff muscles and climbed out of bed. He was the man she'd thought she would never meet. And though it scared her to think of committing her life to another person, she realized she didn't want to step into the future without him. He made her feel special and loved and she desperately wanted to make him feel the same way.

After tossing on her robe and splashing her face with warm water, she hurried out to the kitchen. She found Linc sitting at the table, his bandaged hands curled around a mug of coffee.

He looked up as she entered the room and smiling she went to him and placed a kiss upon his forehead.

"Good morning," she greeted.

"Good morning."

"I smell food. Have you eaten breakfast yet?" she asked.

Careful to avoid her gaze, he shook his head. "No. I've been waiting on you."

"Linc," she scolded sweetly. "You didn't have to do that. Besides, you should have woken me. I've slept way too late. I hope you haven't needed me for anything."

Oh, he needed her all right, but not as a nurse, Linc thought. But he kept that fact to himself. He could never let her learn exactly what making love to her had done to him. It would give her power over him. And he couldn't allow that. He could never repeat the mistakes of his father.

"I've been fine," he said dully, then ignoring her hand on his shoulder, he rose to his feet. "I've made breakfast tacos. I'll get them."

Nevada trailed after him and painful regret sliced through him as she stared up at him in confusion.

"Linc? Is something wrong?"

"No. Nothing is wrong," he said. "I'm just hungry. Aren't you?"

Her brow remained puckered as she studied his face. "Yes, I am. But—"

She stopped as he turned to pour coffee into a waiting mug. "Here." He handed her the cup. "Get your cream and I'll take the tacos over to the table."

"Linc, aren't you even going to kiss me good

morning?" Surely she deserved that much of a greeting from him, she thought.

He looked away from her. "Don't you think you had enough kissing last night?" he asked sharply.

Stunned by the total change in him, she quietly walked over to the breakfast table and sank onto the end of the bench.

Behind her, Linc gathered up two plates and a basket full of tacos and carried them over to the center of the table. Nevada didn't say anything as he shoved one of the plates and the basket in her direction. She simply picked up one of the tacos and began to eat.

After several minutes of silence had passed, he said in a distant voice, "Look, Nevada, if you got up this morning thinking we were going to start playing house together, then I'm sorry, you got it all wrong."

Funny that he should choose those words, Nevada thought sadly. As a young girl she'd never had the chance to *play* house. She'd had to behave as a grown woman and take care of things that her mother hadn't been capable of dealing with. There had been many times she'd cleaned up after her drunken father and helped him to bed. And back then, she'd vowed to herself that she would never let another man disappoint or hurt her in any way. Too bad she hadn't been able to stick to that vow, she thought.

"I didn't think we'd *play* anything," Nevada said soberly. "And I didn't think I'd wake up this morning to be insulted by you."

A shamed expression suddenly washed over his dark face and he placed his taco on the table, then moved down the bench so that he was sitting only inches from her.

Nevada quivered with hurt and longing as he lifted his hand and touched her cheek.

"I'm sorry, Nevada. I should never have said that. I don't know why I did."

Tears suddenly misted her eyes and she looked down at her lap rather than have him see them. "It's all right, Linc. I understand."

"I doubt it," he said grimly.

Her head jerked up and their gazes locked. "Why do you say that? You think I don't understand that all of this is just as new for you as it is for me?"

He let out a heavy sigh. "Look, Nevada. What happened between us last night was very, very nice. But—"

"But you didn't really mean anything serious by it," she finished for him.

Her voice was thin and flat and the mist in her eyes was growing thicker, but she no longer cared if he knew how much she was beginning to hurt.

He shook his head. "I think you were aware of that from the very beginning."

Yes, maybe she had been, Nevada thought. Maybe in the back of her mind she'd always known that Linc was a free spirit, a loner at heart. Sex with a woman was just that for him and nothing else. Yet the moment he'd kissed her, she'd believed there was something special, something magical flowing from him to her. Apparently she'd been a fool to think he'd felt anything but physical pleasure.

"Linc, it wasn't like I sat for hours and contemplated what was about to happen," she tried to explain. "But even if I had, I wouldn't have changed anything. I would still have wanted you to make love to me."

With a groan of frustration he looked away from her and raked a hand over his dark, tumbled hair. He looked tired, she thought. But more than that he looked anguished, and the idea that she was putting him through such torment was enough to crack her heart right down the middle.

"Nevada, I don't how to explain. Maybe all I should say is that—last night can't happen again. It *won't* happen again. Understand?"

Stiffly, her head jerked back and forth. "No. I don't understand. Why? I thought last night was a beginning for us."

He swallowed hard and then before she could guess his intentions, he rose from the table and crossed over to the kitchen sink where he stood with his back to her and stared out the window.

"There can't be an *us,* Nevada. That's what I'm trying to get across to you."

Nevada left her seat and when she reached his side, she carefully lifted his bandaged hand and cradled it to her face.

"I don't think you really mean that, Linc."

He swallowed hard as he tried to rid himself of the ball of pain burning his throat and creeping into his chest. "I have to mean it," he said flatly. "I've been a bachelor for many years now. That isn't going to change. For you or anyone."

"Why?"

He pulled his hand away from her grasp. "You shouldn't have to ask. You've already told me that you didn't want to get serious about a man. Obviously you have reasons of your own for staying single and I have mine."

She nodded glumly. "That's true. I never wanted this to happen to me. I actually prayed that it wouldn't. Because I know firsthand what it does to a woman to depend solely and completely on a man. My mother adored my father. For a long time she refused to see his shortcomings. And then when his boozing and womanizing became too much to ignore, she still loved him so much she couldn't let him go. It was a horrible situation. Now she drinks to forget it all." Shaking her head, she searched his face. "That's why this scares me, because I've fallen in love with you."

Linc was stunned by her revelation and even though he was telling himself he didn't want or need her love, joy was pouring into his heart. "Nevada, last night wasn't love—"

"Don't, Linc! Just don't ruin everything for me. As far as I'm concerned it was love. And don't try to tell me that all I'm feeling is physical infatuation. I began caring for you the very first day I arrived. I tried to stop my feelings then. But I couldn't. And now I find I don't want to."

He was quaking inside and for once he was glad his hands were hidden behind all the bandages. They were shaking like those of a man who'd drunk too much and slept too little.

"I'm sorry about that, Nevada. If you think I set out to hurt you, you're wrong. Last night just happened and now for both our sakes we've got to put it behind us."

"Why?" she demanded. "I thought what happened between us was wonderful. Wasn't it that way for you?"

He felt sick as he turned away from her and walked over to the windows to stare unseeingly at the distant San Juan Mountains. He couldn't tell her the truth, Linc thought. He couldn't let her know that making love to her had turned him inside out and his world upside down. Linc had always believed sex was just sex, a pleasurable act between a man and a woman. But last night in Nevada's arms he'd experienced something far greater than pleasure. He'd felt linked to her in a deeply spiritual way and that idea was still making him shake with fear.

"Yes, Nevada. It was special," he said in a low, hoarse voice. "But that part of things doesn't matter."

Marching over to him, she forced him to turn and face her. "Doesn't matter?" she asked angrily. "Does *anything* matter to you? Is there anyone on this earth that you care about, other than yourself?"

His expression closed off like a curtain falling over the last scene of a tragic play. "That's a hell of a thing to say."

"That's nothing to what I'd like to say to you," she said tightly.

"What's wrong with you, anyway, Nevada? I understand you were a virgin, but surely you weren't naive enough to think sex equaled a proposal of marriage."

Nevada actually had to clench her fingers to keep from raising her hand and slapping him. "The only thing I was naive about was thinking you had a heart!"

"You've taken my blood pressure enough, you ought to know!" he spat back at her.

The anger and pain boiling up in her head made her lash back at him. "Well you can bet your last dollar that I won't be guilty of checking your blood pressure again. It's obvious you have ice water in your veins!"

He started to make a retort, but Nevada wasn't about to hang around to hear it. She'd already heard far more than she could stand.

"Save it, Linc, I don't want to hear anything else you have to say," she muttered and then hurried out of the kitchen.

By the time she reached the bedroom, her legs were so weak and shaky she could hardly make it to the bed. She sank onto the edge of the mattress and dropped her face into her hands.

This morning when she'd first wakened, she'd felt such a burst of sweet happiness. Making love to Linc had made her whole world bright and beautiful. Too bad her joy couldn't have lasted past breakfast, she thought bitterly.

She was biting back tears, trying to tell herself that he wasn't worth one drop of the salty water running down her cheeks, when she heard him knock on the door.

Deliberately ignoring him, she stared at the wall and desperately tried to swallow away the fiery pain in her throat.

"Nevada. May I come in?"

She didn't answer. She couldn't. It was all she could do to keep the sobs in her chest from bursting past her lips.

Silent moments passed and then she felt his hand upon her back, his fingers threading gently through her tangled hair.

"Nevada, I'm sorry. I'm a bastard. That's all I can say."

Still incapable of looking at him, Nevada shook her head. "No, you could say more if you just would. If it's me—if you've decided you—just don't like me, then tell me. That's all I ask. Tell me the real reason you're trying so hard to push me away."

His hand continued to stroke her back and she could only think of last night and all the ways he'd touched her. Somewhere among all those kisses and touches and whispers, a certainty had filled her heart. Linc was supposed to be her other half. He was the man who was meant to love her, give her children, protect her from the harsh realities of the world.

He sighed. And then in a soft, low voice, he said, "All right. You told me about your family, your parents and all the trouble they'd had. Well, it was pretty much the same way for me. My parents treated their marriage as a prison sentence more than anything else. After what I saw them go through I knew I didn't want any part of it. And I sure didn't want to put a child of mine through it."

Twisting her head around, she stared at him with a wry sort of hope that stabbed Linc right in the chest.

"That's exactly the way I've always seen things.

And that's the main reason I was a virgin. But being here with you, Linc, has changed my way of thinking. I love being close to you, I love living with you. I don't want that to change."

"It has to change," he interrupted flatly. "Because I'm not capable of taking that sort of chance with you or any woman."

A mixture of pain and anger tightened her features. "Why? Because of your mother? Do you think I would be like her?"

Her questions stung him, and he pulled back to stare at her. "What do you know about my mother anyway?"

Nevada could see she was treading on dangerous ground, but she didn't allow that to stop her. Now wasn't the time to tippy-toe around the main issue.

"Only what you've told me," she admitted. "But that's enough to understand that she must have broken your heart when she left here."

"Who told you that?" he muttered.

"Marina. She's been worried about you because she's been having dreams about your mother."

"Bah!" he snorted. "Marina's dreams are just that—dreams. That old housekeeper just likes to gossip and keep things stirred up."

"Linc! The only pot Marina stirs is her cooking pot. So don't belittle her! She loves you."

Dropping his head, Linc pinched the bridge of his

nose. "Yeah. You're right. Hell, she's always been more of a mother to me than my own mother ever was."

"I can't believe your mother didn't love you. Even mine cared about me in her own way. She just had too many problems of her own to be a good mother. Maybe that's the way it was with yours," she reasoned.

Linc lifted his head to look at her and for the first time in his life, he realized he wanted, needed to talk about his mother.

"My mother hated this ranch. She told my father so every day. She wanted him to move to someplace where there was culture and sidewalks, a city where she could buy expensive high heels and get her nails done."

Nevada rolled her eyes. "She could have done that here. If she'd wanted to."

Linc rolled his eyes. "Not in the fashion she wanted. You see, she came from a fairly wealthy family in San Antonio. She was the epitome of a beautiful Texas socialite. Obviously she didn't fit in here and the more my father tried to force her to fit in, the worse things got."

Nevada considered what he was telling her. "She must have known what she was getting into when she married him. This sort of life shouldn't have been that much of a surprise to her," she reasoned. "Maybe your parents had other issues. Things you didn't know about."

Linc's head swung back and forth in disbelief.

"Nothing should have made her walk away from here and never look back."

Nevada's eyes widened. "Marina told me that your mother remarried shortly after Randolf's death and that she tried to get you to go back east with her. You didn't want to go?"

"No. I was a teenager by then. This ranch had been my home for all my life. My cousins were like my own siblings. I didn't want to leave my home or family. From the time I was a little boy, I knew I wanted to do what my father and my uncle did. I wanted to be a cowboy, a rancher with lots of horses that everyone would prize and want to own. If I'd gone away with her to some city, I would have dried up and withered away or turned into a rebellious juvenile delinquent."

Nevada tended to agree. Linc was not the sort of man who'd be content to look up at street lamps rather than a sky full of stars.

"I can understand why you stayed," Nevada said softly. "This is where you felt at home. And that's something I've always wanted. Something I've always dreamed about having. A real home with a family that laughed and loved and stuck together through hard times."

Anguish filled his green eyes. "I'm sorry you've never had that, Nevada. I wish I could be the man to give it all to you. But I don't have it in me and it would be disastrous for both of us if I tried."

Instead of arguing that point, Nevada asked, "How long has it been since you've heard from your mother?"

He let out a sound that was somewhere between a bitter laugh and a snort. "More than twenty years. She was pretty upset that I stayed behind here on the ranch, and for several months I received a few letters and some phone calls from her. But then suddenly they all stopped and that was it. None of us ever heard from Darla Ketchum Carlton again."

"How odd."

"Hell, it was more than odd. It was downright mean," he said, then with a heavy sigh, he got up from his seat beside her and began to walk listlessly around the bedroom. "But then I guess I wasn't a very good son. At least, not to her. I stayed here with Aunt Amelia and Uncle Tucker. They became my parents and she was left out. Maybe I'm the person who's always been wrong here, Nevada. I don't know. That's why—" He paused and looked at her with sad regret. "It's best I always live alone. It's best that I not try to make any woman happy. Especially you."

Chapter Twelve

For the remainder of the day, Nevada couldn't decide what to do. It was apparent that she couldn't sway Linc's way of thinking. At least, she couldn't sway him with talk. Except for when she changed his bandages and choked down the supper Marina brought to them, he avoided her completely. And by that evening, she'd decided that she'd been stupid to believe he cared for her in a special way. Obviously he didn't. And there wasn't any use of her throwing herself at him. She wanted his love, but not that way.

That night when she helped Linc out of his clothes, she kept her touch as impersonal as possible and hurried through the task without ever meeting his gaze. Later, she went to bed feeling like a cold, empty shell and as she lay beneath the light cover all she could think about was Linc lying next to her and how right it had felt to give herself to him.

Nevada tossed and turned for several hours and was finally about to drift off to sleep, when a sound from Linc's room caused her to sit straight up in the bed.

Had he yelled or cried out?

Quickly, she jumped out of bed and ignoring her robe, hurried across the hallway to the open doorway of his bedroom. The faint night lights running along the baseboards in the hallway were enough to allow her to see the outline of his body in bed and fear struck her as she watched him thrash fitfully back and forth upon the mattress.

"Linc." His name whispered from her lips as she hurried to the bedside.

As she leaned over him, she could hear him muttering names and something about stopping the flames.

"Linc, wake up!" She shook his shoulder once, then twice before the thrashing finally stopped and he stared up at her through glazed eyes.

"Nevada? What—are you doing?"

She sat down on the edge of the bed. "You cried out in your sleep. You must have been having a nightmare. Are you okay now?"

He looked around him as though he wasn't quite

sure where they were. "Yeah. I think so." He touched his upper arm to his forehead and it came away wet. "I guess I got hot. I'm sweating."

"You were saying something about flames and names that I suppose belong to some of your horses. Junie and Angel."

He nodded, then allowed his head to fall tiredly back against the pillow. "They're two of my best mares. They were the last ones I pulled from the fire. We'd just made it out of the barn when the roof collapsed."

Nevada's heart ached to comfort him and before she could stop herself she reached out and placed her hand on his damp brow. "Try not to think about it now," she murmured gently. "Can I get you something? Do something for you?"

She could see him closing himself off from her as he turned his eyes away and stared at the wall.

"No. Not unless you can cut these damn bandages off," he said gruffly. "Maybe then you could get back to your own life and I can get back to mine."

Nevada's heart was heavy and numb as she slowly rose from the bedside. "Sorry. I wish I could. I wish you'd never been burned and I had never agreed to help a friend," she said in a stricken voice, then turned and hurried out of the room.

The next morning when she entered the kitchen, she discovered Linc had already eaten breakfast without her and somehow he'd managed to button his jeans. As for his shirt, it was the first time she'd ever seen him in only a T-shirt and he looked almost naked to her, but she didn't make any comment about it. Nor did she scold him for putting enough pressure on his fingers to button his jeans. She knew why he was doing it and she knew right then and there that their days together were over.

After she'd downed a few bites of toast and jelly, she went to her room and called Victoria's office. The moment the other woman heard Nevada's voice, she quickly asked, "What's wrong? Has Linc hurt himself?"

"No. It's nothing like that. I called to see if you were going to be in your office all morning. I'd like to come by and talk to you. It's very important."

"You mean you're going to leave Linc there by himself? You're on the phone with me now, Nevada. Can't we talk like this?"

Even though she was enclosed in her room, she glanced around to make sure Linc wasn't eavesdropping. "I'd rather not. It's too personal."

Victoria let out a long sigh. "Oh dear, this sounds bad."

It *was* bad, Nevada thought, sadly. She'd never felt such anguish in her whole life. "I'll tell you about it when I get there," Nevada told her. "Give me about an hour. If you're in with a patient, I'll wait in your office."

"All right," Victoria agreed, and Nevada quickly said good-bye.

Once she'd hung up the telephone, she quickly packed all her things and left the cases sitting neatly on the bed. She wasn't going to carry them through the house and show Linc her intentions until she'd had a chance to talk with Victoria first. The woman had hired her for this job and she was the person who deserved an explanation.

Minutes later, she told Linc she had to drive into town on business. As she headed her little car down the mountain, she tried not to think that it would be one of the last times she would ever see this wild, beautiful place. Would she ever stop thinking of it as home?

At the clinic she found Victoria engaged with a patient, so she went to the doctor's office to wait. It wasn't long before Victoria hurried into the room. She took hold of Nevada by both shoulders.

"All right. What's happened? You want to quit, don't you? I could hear it in your voice."

Dropping her head, Nevada swung it back and forth. "I'm sorry, Victoria. I realize that doesn't mean much. But there are circumstances that—well, I just can't stay under the same roof with Linc anymore. He doesn't want me there. And I feel very awkward, to say the least."

Her face puckered with confusion, Victoria released her hold on Nevada and crossed the room to the leather chair behind her desk. As she sank into it and crossed her legs, she repeated, "Doesn't want you there? I thought you two were getting along fine."

Nevada could feel a deep blush warming her face. "We were. But things have changed."

Victoria propped her elbows on the desk and studied Nevada with deep concern. "Really? What sort of things? Did Linc get mad about something? Or did you?"

Nevada massaged her aching forehead with shaky fingers. "This is difficult to explain."

"Nevada, I don't have a clue what this is about, but you've been a nurse long enough to know that patients can be difficult. I'm sure Linc's been a bear at times. But if anyone can deal with it, you can."

Nevada let out a long, pent-up breath. "Well, after Jess called and told him about the fire being arson things changed."

"Oh." Victoria leaned wearily back in the leather chair. "That's not surprising. The fire was a very personal thing for him. Those mares are his life and now he learns that someone targeted them and him. I'm sure the news cut his legs out from under him."

Closing her eyes, Nevada said in a low, strained voice, "Yes. He was upset. He came to my bedroom to tell me about it. And—"

She paused not knowing how to go on, then she opened her eyes to see Victoria smiling at her.

"And he kissed you," she said happily.

Groaning now, Nevada shook her head. "Oh Victoria, I wish it had only been a kiss. We—we made love. And now things are just terrible between us. It couldn't be more awful. That's why I'm here—to tell you that I can't stay with Linc any longer. It's just too painful. He doesn't want me there."

Without uttering a word, Victoria rose from the chair and came around the desk to put a comforting arm around Nevada's shoulder.

"Oh honey, no wonder you look so miserable. You must be broken-hearted."

Nevada's eyes grew watery as she looked up at Victoria's concerned face. "I never knew anything could hurt this bad, Victoria. I've fallen in love with Linc. But he doesn't want any sort of relationship with me."

Patting her shoulder, Victoria said, "I'm not surprised. Linc has always wanted to be on his own. But I am very disappointed. You're exactly what he needs in his life. Did he say why he didn't want things to develop between you?"

Wiping her eyes with the back of her hand, Nevada told her, "To put it simply, he doesn't want to go through what his parents went through. Apparently they had a shaky marriage."

"Well, from what Mother told me, Randolf was very possessive and Darla wanted her space. Then there were rumors that Randolf played around and that must have eaten away at her heart."

Nevada's eyes widened at this bit of information. "Does Linc know that?"

Victoria shook her head. "I don't think so. He adored his father. Mother only told me this in total secrecy. And that was long after Randolf had died and Darla had left." Her expression turned earnest. "You won't tell him this, will you, Nevada? I mean, maybe some people would think he ought know the truth of things. But that was so long ago and his mother deserted him. Why pile more heartache on top of that?"

Nevada could see the other woman's reasoning. Yet the idea that Linc didn't know the true facts about his parents' relationship made her chances to have a future with the man practically nil. He was always going to have bitter memories of his mother unless the woman reappeared and explained herself.

"No. I won't tell him. In fact, I won't be telling him anything, except good-bye," she said.

"Oh Nevada," Victoria wailed. "Can't you go back and try to mend fences? At least for another week. By then he ought to be getting his bandages off completely and he'll be able to take care of himself. Right now he needs you."

"Hah!" Nevada said bitterly. "The man doesn't need anyone. Especially me."

"You know that isn't true. He desperately needs your love. He just doesn't know it yet."

Feeling cornered and confused, Nevada jumped to her feet. "I'm going back to the ranch, loading my bags in the car and leaving. You can't change my mind about this, Victoria. I feel badly that I can't finish my end of the bargain. But under circumstances like this I'd hoped you would understand."

Victoria rolled her eyes toward the ceiling. "Oh Nevada, of course I understand. I just wish things could be different. All the way around."

Nevada leaned forward and placed a grateful kiss on Victoria's cheek. "So do I," she whispered tearfully and then turned and hurried out of the office before Victoria could see her break down in sobs.

She drove slowly back to the ranch in hopes the long drive through the countryside would help her pull herself together before she had to face Linc again.

When she arrived, she was thankful not to see him as she hurried to her room to make sure she had everything packed before she carried her bags out to her car.

She was entering the living room, a bag clutched in both hands when Linc stepped out from the kitchen doorway. The moment he spotted her he froze and even from several feet away she could see his eyes narrow.

"What is this?" he asked.

"I think you can figure it out," she said dully. "Your nurse is leaving. You can tear off your bandages—do whatever—I just won't be around to see it."

He crossed the room to where she stood and stared down at her. "What are you doing? You've been here a little more than a week and you're already sick of it?"

His questions caused her to wince. "Don't lay all of that on me, Linc. You know why I'm leaving. And don't act so offended. This is what you want. With me gone, you can breathe a sigh of relief. You won't be tempted to crawl back in bed with me."

His nostrils flared as his gaze searched her face. "Maybe it is for the best," he said flatly. "We sure as hell don't need to keep going on like this."

"I agree," she told him, then with her heart aching, she put on the best professional face she could summon. "Good-bye, Linc. I wish you good luck with your hands and your horses. And I hope whoever tried to hurt you will be caught and punished quickly."

No one could ever hurt him as much as she was doing at this moment, Linc thought. But he understood that her leaving was the best thing, the right thing to do for both of them. He wasn't husband material and Nevada was a woman who deserved a real family. Not a sexual liaison now and then.

Feeling like a wooden statue, he reached out to

take her arms. "I'm sorry about this, Nevada. I never set out to hurt you. I hope you'll find another man— someone you can really love."

She pulled away from him. "Really? You like the idea of another man making love to me the way you made love to me?"

Her questions left him sick inside and for a moment he wanted nothing more than to jerk her into his arms and brand her lips with his. But he couldn't touch her in that way now. If he did, the two of them would only wind up in bed again and if that were to happen he would totally and truly be a lost man.

"Good-bye, Nevada," he said thickly, then turned and walked away before the pain in his heart begged her to stay.

A little more than a week later, Nevada was in the tiny room where all the medicine for the clinic was stored. She was searching through a small refrigerator for a certain antibiotic and not having any luck when Victoria entered the room.

"I'm sorry, Victoria. It's not here. I thought we'd ordered it about a month ago. I'll have Joyce look up all the order sheets. Is there a close substitute we can give the patient?"

"Yes." The doctor reached around Nevada's shoulder and picked up a bottle from the refrigerator shelf. "Give him ten cc's of this and make sure you note it on his chart. I'm going to examining room two and see what I can do for Mrs. Parkins."

"She said she vomited for two hours this morning," Nevada said. "What do you think is wrong with her?"

"Betcha ten dollars she's pregnant," Victoria said with a wink. "And I'd win. I've already read the pregnancy test."

Nevada stared at her in surprise. "Mrs. Parkins! She's forty-two years old!"

Victoria threw a hand over her mouth to stifle a laugh. "Nevada! You're a good nurse. You know that any woman whose equipment is in working order is capable of becoming pregnant, no matter what her age."

"Dear God, she's going to be shocked," Nevada muttered.

"Probably. But she'll be happy even more," Victoria said with a smile. "And speaking of happy, how long is it going to be before I see a smile on your face again? You've been going around here looking like you gave yourself a birthday party and nobody came."

Nevada cast her a wry look. "I'm trying, Victoria. I've been telling myself that Linc Ketchum isn't worth this misery I'm going through. But my heart just doesn't seem to be hearing my words of wisdom."

Victoria sighed with regret. "I know, honey. Before Jess and I got things ironed out, I wasn't fit to be around."

"Yes, but Jess loved you. And both of you did

iron out your differences. There's no hope of that with me and Linc."

"I wouldn't say that, Nevada. Not yet. Ross says Linc hasn't been acting like himself at all. That can only mean that he's fretting over you," Victoria reasoned.

While shoving a needle into the bottle of antibiotic Nevada did her best to ignore Victoria's suggestion. There wasn't any point in giving herself any false hope.

"Victoria, do you think if Linc's mother could be found, he might want to see her?"

"I don't know. I've never thought about it too much. She's been gone for so long—since we were all teenagers. And Linc never mentions her at all."

"Because it hurts him too much," Nevada replied. "And frankly, I don't think he's ever going to be able to love any woman until he resolves this idea that she deserted him because she didn't want him."

Frowning thoughtfully, Victoria said, "You could be right."

"I've been thinking, Victoria. And I've been rolling around the idea of trying to find her. What do you think?"

"I wouldn't know where you might start to track her down. I'll ask Ross and Seth if they have any idea." She shoved the cuff of her white lab coat back to glance at her watch. "Right now I've got to get back to work. Mrs. Parkins has been waiting nearly fifteen minutes!"

* * *

That evening after Nevada got off work, she decided to drive by Neil Rankin's law office. She half expected to find the little log building already closed up for the day, but she found the door still open and Connie still sitting at her desk.

The large Hispanic woman with graying black hair smiled broadly at Nevada. "Well, hello nurse Goodbody," she teased. "What are you up to today?"

"Hi Connie. I need to speak with Neil, if he has a minute to spare," she told the woman.

Connie waved her hand toward the closed door behind her. "Go on in," she told Nevada. "He saw his last client about an hour ago. I think he's just finishing up some paper work before we close up."

"Thanks." Nevada went to the door and rapped on it lightly with her knuckles.

"Come in. I'm fully clothed," Neil called out.

Smiling, Nevada stepped into the lawyer's office. The man was sitting behind a wide oak desk with papers scattered out before him. Wire-rimmed glasses were perched on the end of his nose and his blond hair was rumpled across his forehead. He looked as tired as she felt.

"Hello, Neil. Am I interrupting something important?"

At the sound of her voice, he glanced up. "Nevada!" he exclaimed. "What a great way to end the day!"

Smiling, she waited for him to skirt the desk and walk over to her. As he reached for both her hands, she understood why people came to him whenever they needed help. He was the sort of man who made you feel comfortable and hopeful.

"What a flatterer you are, Neil Rankin. I'm sure you hand a line to every woman who walks through your door."

He chuckled as he took her by the elbow and led her over to one of two armchairs positioned in front of his desk. "Not *every* woman. At least, only the ones who look like you."

Nevada settled herself in the armchair as Neil walked around the desk and took his own seat.

"So I'm hoping you dropped by to say hello to a friend. I'd hate to think you need legal advice."

Nevada shook her head. "Not legal advice. But I do need help. And I didn't know anyone else to turn to."

He studied her with interest. "Well, I'm glad you have that much confidence in me. I don't know if it's really warranted, but shoot your problem at me anyway and I'll try."

Scooting to the edge of the chair she leaned toward his desk. "I want you to help me find someone. A person who used to live here. On the T Bar K, actually."

Instantly, Neil's brows lifted with curiosity. "On the ranch? But surely Victoria could help you with that problem."

"No. She doesn't have a clue about this woman. She's going to talk to her brothers, but I seriously doubt that they know any more than she does."

Neil reached for a pen and scooted a yellow legal pad to the center of his desk. "Does this woman have a name?"

"Darla Ketchum. Darla Ketchum Carlton to be exact."

Neil reared back in his chair. "That's Linc's mother!"

Nevada's head bobbed up and down. "Yes. I want to find her—for him."

A low whistle passed the lawyer's lips. "Boy, maybe you need to think this over, Nevada. Darla Ketchum is a touchy subject. Especially where Linc is concerned."

Nevada grimaced. "You don't have to tell me that. We—uh—we already had a discussion about her and the reasons why she left the ranch."

Neil shrugged. "Well, from what I understand the woman remarried shortly after Randolf died."

"Do you know who the man she married was? Did he live here?"

Neil rubbed his chin thoughtfully. "If I recall right, he wasn't from around here. Because I remember Ross saying something about the man coming up from Texas in a big black limousine. He was just so relieved that Linc wasn't in that car when it left the ranch." He cast her a wry smile. "Funny how those sorts of things stick with kids. And that's what we were at the time, just kids. I might have been sixteen or seventeen and Linc a fraction younger."

How tragic, Nevada thought, for Linc to lose his father and his mother within a short period of time and the loss had occurred when he'd been at such a young, impressionable age. No wonder loneliness had shaped and molded his life.

"Such a long time ago," Nevada said wistfully. "I wonder why he has never been able to ever let go."

"Of his mother's leaving?" Neil asked.

Nevada nodded. "He believes she deliberately deserted him. That she quit communicating with him just to spite him for not leaving the ranch with her."

"Hmm. That's some heavy stuff there, Nevada. I'm not sure we should even try to intervene."

Nevada scooted to the very edge of her seat as her eyes pleaded with the lawyer. "That's the whole problem. No one has been brave enough to confront Linc about this problem. They've allowed him to bottle it all up and try to sweep the whole incident under the rug. The man lost his father and then his mother vanished from his life. Don't you think he deserves to know the truth of the matter? Don't you think it would help him come to terms with issues that he refuses to face?"

Neil held his palms up. "Look, Nevada, I totally

agree with you. But I'd like to know why you've taken on this task? I wasn't aware that you were that closely acquainted with Linc."

Nevada's gaze dropped to her folded hands. "I wasn't acquainted with him until I became his nurse. I guess you weren't aware that I went out to the ranch to care for him after he was released from the hospital."

"I'd heard he was home and doing well. I'd been meaning to drive out for a little visit, but I've been tied up with all sorts of clients. And I had to be out of town all of last week." With a thoughtful look at her, he tapped his pen against the legal pad. "What happened with you and Linc? You got close and he started running backwards?"

Relieved that he understood without her having to explain any embarrassing details, she nodded. "That's it, exactly."

"You must care for him a lot to go to this much trouble to find his mother."

"Very much."

Neil leaned forward and gave her an encouraging smile. "Well, give me what information you have and I'll see what I can do. I'm not a detective, Nevada. So don't expect miracles. But I do have a few friends around the country who work on missing-persons cases."

"I'll be grateful for any sort of help," Nevada told him. "But maybe I should ask how much this sort of thing will cost me. I do have some savings put away. If that's not enough I could take out a loan—"

He lifted a hand to halt her words. "Nevada, that's the last thing you need to be worried about. I don't intend to charge you anything. And as for my contacts, they all enjoy a challenge."

Nevada grimaced. "Yes, but I'm sure they like money, too. They can't make a living giving away their services."

"Believe me, honey, none of them are hurting. They have plenty of rich clients to keep them afloat. You know the sort—spoiled kids who run away from home have to be found."

She breathed a sigh of relief. "All right, if you say so. I won't worry about the money part."

Tossing down his pen, Neil smiled at her with disbelief. "You know, sometimes you women amaze me. I don't understand why you're willing to do so much for us nasty men."

"I care about Linc," she reasoned.

His expression turned to one of wry appreciation. "Yeah. So much so that you're willing to lose all your savings and go in debt for the man."

She drew in a deep breath and blew it out. "I happen to think he's worth it."

Neil chuckled. "You know what, I happen to think he's worth it, too."

Chapter Thirteen

Almost two weeks later, as midnight approached, Miss Lori went into labor. For several nights running Linc had been sitting up with the mare to give Skinny a rest. But tonight Skinny had refused to go to bed. The old wrangler had predicted the full moon would start the mare's birthing engine, and he'd been right.

Easing out of the chair he'd propped against the wall, Linc went over to where Skinny was half sitting, half lying in a bed of straw. He gently shook the old man's shoulder.

"Skinny, wake up. Miss Lori has started."

For a moment the old man looked around in a

dazed stupor until he spotted the mare wringing her tail and bending her nose around to her side.

"Hot damn! Has she laid down yet?"

"Once. Then she bounced back up."

Bones creaked and popped as the old man rose to his feet and rubbed his hands together with excited glee. "It won't be long now! Bet it's going to be a black filly with a star on her forehead."

Linc smiled wryly at the old wrangler. "That's a big stretch. Miss Lori is black with a star on her forehead."

Chuckling, Skinny hopped along on his one good knee until he reached the mare's side. Linc watched as his old friend carefully rubbed his hand over the mare's belly and flank. The man never wanted to miss any of the foals being born. It was a very special time for him, just as it always was for Linc.

A little more than an hour later, the foal was born and as Skinny had predicted it was a black filly with a star on its face. The birth had gone smoothly and the two men had had little more to do than to stand back and watch the miracle in process.

In a matter of minutes after the birth, the mare was on her feet cleaning the little filly of lingering afterbirth. An hour later, the baby was standing up on her long legs, nudging her mother's flank in search of sweet, nourishing milk.

Skinny cackled with pleasure and slapped Linc on

the shoulder. "She's a beauty, Linc. You got a good one on her feet."

"It wasn't just me that got her here, Skinny. You and all the other guys are the reason we have one of the best remudas in six states." He patted Skinny's arm. "Now what do you say me and you go have a cup of coffee?"

The two men slipped into the back of the bunkhouse where the kitchen was located. Linc boiled coffee on the stove and the two men sat at the long table and carefully sipped the steaming brew.

Skinny rattled on about the new filly until he realized that Linc wasn't saying much about anything. The old wrangler set his cup on the wooden table and studied Linc with his faded blue eyes.

"What's the matter with you, boy? Hell, it's been nearly twelve months since we bred Miss Lori. And all that time you've been watching her like a proud papa. I figured you'd be dancing a jig right about now."

Linc rolled his eyes. "Skinny, when have you ever seen me dance? Never. And there isn't anything wrong with me. I'm happy. The filly is great. She's going to be beautiful and smart and tough. What more do you want me to say?"

Skinny shook his head and mumbled into his cup.

"What was that?" Linc asked.

Lifting his head, Skinny scowled at him. "Nothin'. I just thought—well, I thought now that you've got to come back to work, that things would be different.

Like they used to be. I've known you since you were a little tot in diapers. But you aren't that same boy."

Sighing with frustration, Linc left his seat and went over to the cabinets. As he searched around for some leftovers to snack on, he said, "Damn it, Skinny, it wasn't too long ago that these hands of mine were fried. And I was lucky that I hadn't been killed. That does something to a man."

"And whose fault was that?" Skinny shot back at him. "Nobody told you to be a hero and rescue all those mares. The boys in the bunkhouse were coming to help you. If you'd only waited—"

"None of the mares would still be alive," Linc finished sharply. "And the bastard who set the fire is still out there, getting away with near murder. But you expect me to be myself?"

He found half of an apple pie in the refrigerator, whacked out a piece and carried it in his hand over to the table. While he ate, Skinny folded his arms across his chest and looked disgusted.

"If I was you, I don't think I'd be tryin' to blame my behavior on nearly bein' burned to death. Yeah, the thought of that is enough to curl a man's toes, but that ain't your real problem and we both know it."

The pie in Linc's hand stopped midway to his mouth. "What the hell are you talking about now, Skinny? And since when did you become such a psychologist?"

Skinny pushed back his brown felt hat and scrunched up his wrinkled face. "I don't know what that fancy word is and I don't care to know. But a one-eyed man could see you're missin' that pretty little nurse something awful."

Linc started to yell at the old man that he was going senile, but instead, he crammed the remainder of the pie in his mouth and tried to ignore him.

It didn't work. Skinny started again. "She was a nice girl, Linc. Too nice for the likes of you, I guess."

"That's right," Linc said curtly. "She went on to greener pastures."

"Well, I can't blame her. You didn't have much to offer her. Look at yourself. What are you anyway, forty years old now? With her being so young and fresh, she probably thought you were just a few years away from the nursing home."

"I'm thirty-eight, Skinny. And I'm hardly over the hill."

"Well, not like me. Course not. But a young woman like her wants kids of her own. Can't get 'em with a man that goes to sleep every night in a rocking chair."

Linc didn't want to think about Nevada having children or having sex or even touching a man. He didn't want to think of Nevada at all. But for the past two weeks since she'd left, he had not been able to focus his attention on anything. She was always there in his mind, consuming every part of it until he thought he was going crazy.

"All right, old man. I've heard enough of this. You can sit here and keep yapping if you want to. I'm going to bed."

As Linc started to rise from the table, Skinny said, "Where you going to sleep tonight? Going back up to your folks' old house?"

"What if I am?" Linc asked curtly.

"How come?" Skinny asked in a goading voice. "Think that little nurse is going to come back and make you feel better?"

Gritting his teeth, Linc rinsed his cup out and turned it upside down in the sink.

"No. And I don't want her to!"

"You're a damn liar, Linc Ketchum."

No one had ever dared to call him such a thing and it shocked him that Skinny, his best buddy, and a man who had been like an uncle to him all of his life could insult him like this.

Turning slowly away from the sink, Linc walked back over to where Skinny sat with his hat pushed back on his forehead and his chin thrust stubbornly forward.

"Look, Skinny, it's like you said. I don't have anything to offer the woman. And once she found that out—well, I'd be just like my father. Miserable."

Skinny blinked, then swallowed down the last of

his coffee. "No, ain't no way you could be like Randolf. You just ain't made that way."

Funny that Skinny should say such a thing, Linc thought. Everyone had always told him he had mannerisms and a personality just like his father's. "What's that supposed to mean? I can't read your mind."

Skinny wiped a hand across his mouth as though he wished he'd done a bit more thinking before he'd spoken. "Well, it just means that he was different than you. That's all. And it was your mother that carried the misery around. Not your father."

Frowning, Linc sat back down at the table and looked at Skinny. "Don't you think I know that? She was yelling to Dad every day about this dusty, isolated ranch. She wanted away from here and she made him miserable because he wouldn't take her."

Skinny made a tsking noise with his tongue. "Guess I shouldn't have said anything, boy. But seems like you're all messed up about things. And I don't want to see you lose that pretty little nurse. She looked at you like a woman who'd love you 'til the day she died. A man can't find that every day."

Linc didn't have to hear that from Skinny to know it was the truth. He'd been around women all his adult life. He'd shared their company and their beds. But not one of them had touched him the way Nevada had touched him. She'd gilded his heart with sweet honey, she'd lifted away the heavy loneliness inside him and made him wish for little ones sitting around the breakfast table, riding his shoulders and calling him Daddy. Made him dream of nights with Nevada in his arms, making love to him until the end of their days.

"You're right, Skinny," he said finally. "Nevada is one of a kind. But I can't ask her to live here on the ranch with me. She would eventually get sick of the dust, the isolation, the long hours I'd have to give to the horses and not her. She'd want to leave just like my mother and then where would I be?"

"Look, boy, if you think—" He stopped, lifted his hat and scratched the top of his head. "Darla didn't want to leave the ranch because of those things. Oh, she said them enough to your father, I'm sure. But Randolf knew the real reason and he didn't care. As long as he got what he wanted that's all that mattered to him. I guess in that way he was just like Tucker."

Linc was taken completely aback and he stared at Skinny as though the old man had just suffered a stroke. "What's the matter with you, Skinny? Everyone you ask would tell you that Randolf was not like Tucker. Tucker was a tough, indifferent man. Especially to his wife. He was a philanderer, a womanizer and he liked his Kentucky bourbon. Dad was not like that."

"He wasn't? Or was he just careful enough to keep it all hid? He was just as much a Ketchum as

Tucker ever was. They were brothers and they shared the same hot blood. Randolf was more easygoing than Tucker. That much is true. But other than that they were two peas in a pod. If your Daddy hadn't gotten sick with his heart you would have seen for yourself. Before that, you were too young to know what was really going on with your folks."

Stricken by this revelation, Linc reached over and snatched a hold on Skinny's sleeve. "Are you telling me the truth?"

"I've never lied to you before," Skinny said flatly. "Ain't about to start now."

Linc felt sick as all the air drained out of his lungs. "Then why didn't you tell me this before?"

Skinny shook his head. "Wasn't any need to. You always thought highly of your daddy and I didn't want to make you think any less."

"Yes, but you let me go on thinking that my mother—that all their troubles were her fault!"

"Linc, I ain't never been married. But I had a woman once and lost her in an accident. I'm old and maybe you think I don't know about love or any of that stuff. But I do. And I can tell you that there's always two sides to everything."

Linc rose from the table and wiped a weary hand across his face. "She wanted me to go with her. After Dad died, she wanted me to start a new life with her. I didn't want to go. I thought she was demanding. I thought she'd made Dad so miserable it had ruined his heart. But I didn't go. I hurt her for sure. And now—" He shook his head and started toward the door. "I don't want to talk about this anymore, Skinny," he said hoarsely. "I'm going back to the barn."

Hours later, Linc was in the foaling pen, lying on a mound of straw as he watched the new filly toddle after her mother. The baby's black hair was dry now and her legs were straighter. Her little black mane stuck straight up like a punk rocker's hair and each time she walked near Linc she gave him a sassy shake of her head.

If he hadn't felt so rotten, he would have laughed at the filly's antics. But tonight he felt as if his heart had dropped to the bottom of a rocky canyon. He'd thought all along that getting back to work and being able to use his hands would make him a happy man. But it hadn't turned out that way. The job he'd always loved wasn't giving him the same joy he'd felt before the fire and he had to admit to himself, if not to Skinny, that Nevada was the reason.

He would never have believed that he could miss anyone so much. But after she'd packed up and left, the house had felt like a tomb. Only he hadn't been dead; he'd only felt dead.

Long after she was gone, the sound of her laugh and

her sweet voice calling to him had seemed to ricochet off the walls. After the second night, he'd packed up his things and returned to the bunkhouse. At least there Cook had been able to give him a helping hand whenever he needed something. And the conversation of the ranch hands made him feel less lonely.

But nothing felt the same as it had before Nevada came into his life. And now he had to deal with the notion that all the arguments he'd given her for staying apart had been wrong. He'd been wrong. All these years and all the bitterness he'd felt for his mother had painted his image of her as very dark. And he'd transferred that darkness over to Nevada, simply because he'd been afraid of being hurt.

Oh God, how wrong he'd been.

"Linc? You awake?"

At the sound of Skinny's low voice, Linc lifted his head to see the man entering the horse stall. A pen light illuminated his path as he approached the pile of straw where Linc was trying to rest.

"What the hell are you doing out here, Skinny? It's three o'clock in the morning! You should be in bed."

Skinny finally reached Linc's side. There he squatted on his boot heels and dangled his hands between his knees. "I went to bed," he said. "But I couldn't sleep. I felt too ashamed of myself. I—"

"Skinny," Linc interrupted, only to have the old man barge in.

"No, Linc. Let me say my piece. I'm sorry about all that I said back there in the bunkhouse. I shouldn't have. I should have kept my mouth shut. You are just like a son to me. The son I always wanted. I just want you to be happy. And I thought—well—I thought you loved that little gal and that you just needed a nudge her way. I didn't mean to spill all that about your folks."

Pushing himself to a sitting position, Linc reached over and gripped Skinny's forearm. "Don't apologize, Skinny. You did the right thing and I thank you for it. Really thank you for it."

"You mean that?" Skinny asked, his voice full of worried doubt.

Linc chuckled as his heart came to a certain and sudden decision. "You're a bold old codger, you know it? One of these days I'm going to have to name my first son after you. And I don't intend to call him Skinny. So you might as well get ready to cough up your real name and let everybody finally know what it is."

Skinny cackled and patted Linc on the shoulder. "Don't worry, boy. When the time comes, I'll let you know."

The next morning Nevada had just gotten out of the shower when the telephone rang and she moaned with loud frustration. She only had twenty minutes to get her hair dried, her makeup and clothes on and drive to work. She didn't have time for small talk.

Wrapping a towel around her wet hair, she snatched up the receiver. "Hello," she said in a breathless rush.

"Nevada, it's Neil here. Do you have a minute? I wanted to catch you before you left for work."

Nevada's heart began to hammer with anticipation. Two weeks had passed since she'd gone to Neil's office and asked the lawyer for help in finding Darla Ketchum. Since then she hadn't heard any news about the search.

"You've found Linc's mother?" she asked quickly.

"No. Not yet. But we have made a little progress. We found out that her husband is dead and has been for many years. We thought we might be able to locate some of his relatives, but so far we haven't been able to. And as for Darla's relatives, she must have been a black sheep of the family or something. She doesn't appear to be related to anyone that we can find in San Antonio."

Nevada felt deflated, but she told herself that things like this sometimes took months or years. She couldn't expect instant results. And even if Neil managed to find Darla this very day, she didn't know if it would help matters with Linc. She could only hope.

So far, Nevada hadn't heard a word from him. And that really hadn't surprised her. But she'd been hoping and praying he would have a change of heart and realize the two of them were meant to be together.

"Well, at least that's a start," she conceded. "I've been talking to Victoria and Marina and from what they say no one in the family has heard from her. Not since Linc had his last contact with her and that was years ago, shortly after she left the ranch."

Neil said, "Don't worry, Nevada. We'll pick up a trace somewhere, somehow. In the meantime, have you talked with Linc?"

Tears suddenly blurred her eyes and she hated herself for being so emotional and weak. But any thought of Linc crushed her with sadness. "No. As far as I know he hasn't made any effort to contact me." She sighed. "I suppose most people would tell me I'm crazy and that I should give up and forget about the man. But I can't, Neil. Does that make any sense to you?"

"Honey, from what I can see, love doesn't ever make sense. And it's pretty damn hard to find. Hang on 'til you can't hang on any more. That's what I say."

She blinked at the tears spilling over her eyelids. "Thank you, Neil. Let me know if you discover anything at all."

He promised he would, then hung up the phone. Nevada wiped her eyes and hurried to the bathroom to dry her hair.

She'd tossed the towel from her head and was

about to push the button on the blow dryer when she heard the doorbell ring.

The interruption put a weary scowl on her face as she hurried to the front door. Not one of her friends ever stopped by at this hour in the morning. The caller had to be the landlord. He'd been promising to get Nevada new carpet for the past year. Maybe he was finally going to come through, she thought skeptically.

"All right. Just a moment," she called through the door as another ring sounded.

Knowing that the glass storm door was safely latched behind the main wooden door, she didn't take the time to peek out the peephole at the caller. Instead, she swung the panel of wood to one side and then stared with an open mouth.

"Linc!" she finally gasped.

In all of her imaginings, she'd never expected him to show up at her apartment like this with his hat in his hands and a humble look on his face. The sight was enough to make her hands fumble helplessly with the latch on the storm door before she finally managed to open it.

"Hello, Nevada. May I come in?"

Her throat was suddenly so thick she could hardly speak. Sweet, deep emotions began to fill her heart and spill over into the rest of her body like the waterfall where they'd hidden from the storm.

"Of course, Linc."

She pushed the door wider and he stepped past her and into the small apartment.

Nervously, Nevada turned to face him. "I—you'll have to excuse me," she said as she touched a hand to her wet, tangled hair. "I just got out of the shower and I'm still a mess."

He stepped toward her and she noticed his hands wrapped tightly around the brown felt hat. They were free of bandages now and thick scars from the fire were quite evident. Even so, his hands were a beautiful sight to Nevada.

"You look great," he said quietly. "Really great."

Her gaze settled on his rugged face. "So do you," she murmured,

In a nervous gesture, his fingers began to smooth around the brim of his hat. "Uh—I guess you're getting ready to go to work. I wasn't thinking, I'm interrupting."

Nevada's heart suddenly felt so full of anticipation she thought it was going to burst. "Victoria will understand. That's the good thing about having a boss like her."

"She's a pretty good cousin, too," Linc said fondly.

Nevada nodded and then she couldn't stand it any longer. She closed the last few steps between them. "Linc, what are you doing here?"

A groan sounded in his throat as he reached up and raked one hand through his dark hair. "I don't know how to start, or what to say to you. I feel like a damn idiot and I'm sure I look even worse."

"You look tired," she said honestly.

"I've been up all night. Miss Lori finally had her baby last night. A little black filly with a white star."

Nevada had to smile. "That's good. Congratulations."

His expression remained sober. "Miss Lori isn't why I didn't get any sleep though. I haven't been able to sleep much at all since you left," he admitted. "I—"

"Linc," she interrupted, only to have him toss his hat aside and reach for her shoulders.

"Just wait, Nevada. Wait and hear me out. I know you probably want to curse me up one side and down the other. I wouldn't blame you if you hated my guts now. But I'm hoping against hope that you're a forgiving woman."

Hope surged in her heart and that organ began to beat as though it had wings and was soaring higher and higher.

"Why?" she asked simply.

His features twisted with regret. "Because I've been wrong. And stupid. And a few other things that I don't care to repeat."

She looked at him with helpless confusion. "I don't understand, Linc. You said we couldn't be together. You said—"

"I said too many damn things that didn't do anything but hurt both of us," he admitted.

Tentatively, her hands lifted and framed his dear face. "What exactly are you trying to say to me, Linc? I don't understand this change."

With a muffled sound, he tugged her into his arms and buried his face in her damp hair. "I'm trying to say I love you, Nevada."

She shook her head in dazed wonder. "But you were so against that."

"I've learned a lot these past two weeks, Nevada. One is that you can't dictate what your heart feels. It has a mind of its own. I loved you in spite of myself. Living without you has been horrible. And I've come to see that I do want all the things that other men have. A wife and kids, a family that loves me. I was always so afraid of that idea. Afraid that it would turn out like my parents' marriage and then I would be hurt even worse than I was by them. But I've come to realize that I have to move past all that now. I'm different from my dad and you're not Darla. I think we can be happy. What do you think?"

He pulled back his head to look at her and tears of pure joy slipped down Nevada's cheeks as she gazed upon the love in his eyes.

"I *know* we'll be happy, Linc. We both understand how important family is, how necessary it is for children to have two parents who truly love each other. That's why we'll try even harder to do things right."

His eyes glazed over as his arms tightened around her and his head bent down to hers. "Something tells me we won't have to try too hard," he whispered. "I think loving each other is going to come natural."

Nevada couldn't have agreed more and she raised on tiptoe to meet the sweet promise of his kiss. And for long moments their lips searched, their hands clung with need.

Linc was the one who finally lifted his head and presented her with a dazzling smile that took Nevada's breath away. "Go dry your hair and get dressed. We have things to do today. Do you think Victoria will give you the day off?"

"I don't know," she said with a happy laugh. "If my usual replacement will come in, then she will."

"I'll call her right now," Linc said as his gaze darted around the room in search of a phone. "You go get ready. We've got a date with the county clerk to get our marriage license."

He pushed her out of his embrace and turned her toward the door leading out of the small living area, but she quickly whirled back to him.

"Marriage license! Linc! You can't be in that big a hurry. I want us to be married in church with all the beautiful trimmings! You will give me that much, won't you?" she pleaded.

His expression softened and for the first time in his life he knew what it was like to spoil and love and protect a woman. His woman.

"Of course I will, honey. I want us to have a nice wedding, too. Just so you don't make me wait too long. We can still get the license today. It'll keep."

She started to stand on her tiptoes to kiss him again. But at that moment another thought struck her and she looked at him worriedly.

"Linc, uh—maybe before we make any plans I need to confess something to you."

Amusement crinkled his green eyes. "What is it? That you have a passion for stabbing people with needles? I already knew that," he teased.

"No, Linc. I'm serious. I've done something that you should know about." She paused long enough to draw in a bracing breath. "It's about your mother."

A frown puckered his brows and Nevada could only wonder if she'd ruined everything.

"My mother? I don't understand."

"After I left the ranch I was pretty upset. I decided there wouldn't be much chance for us unless something changed your mind. I was hoping to find your mother so that the two of you might work out your differences. I asked Neil Rankin to help me search for her." She reached for his hand and pressed it lovingly between hers. "No matter what you think, Linc, I can't believe that she simply turned her back on you."

He didn't say anything, and Nevada's heart sank as he lowered his head and shook it back and forth.

"Are you angry with me?" she asked after several minutes passed.

Lifting his head, he looked at her with moist eyes. "I'm not angry, darling. I'm floored that you would go to such lengths for me. And I don't think I deserve a woman like you. But I'm going to try like hell to be deserving. Just give me a chance."

She let out a relieved breath. "I was afraid. You've been so bitter about her. And—"

Linc lifted a forefinger to her lips. "There's something I need to tell you, honey. I had an enlightening conversation with Skinny. And it seems that things were not what I thought they were between my parents. Apparently my father wasn't faithful and my mother was very unhappy about it. That's why she wanted to leave the ranch. She wanted the two of us to start over somewhere else." His mouth twisted with regret. "I guess my dad couldn't give up his vices."

"And your mother loved him too much to leave," she added. "Oh, Linc, I'm so sorry. But maybe now if we can find her things could be different for the two of you."

He smiled gently down at her. "My hands are still scarred, but not my heart, my darling. If we're able to track down Mom's whereabouts, I'll be glad. But right now I've found the woman I'm going to love for the rest of my life."

Her eyes were bright with happy tears as she lifted his hand to her lips. "Can we live in your parents' house, Linc? And turn it into a real home?"

"It's waiting for us and all the children we're going to have. And maybe someday, if we do find Mom, we'll be able to present her with grandchildren."

Suddenly, dressing and work and marriage license were put on the back burner as Linc's hands pushed the blue terry robe Nevada was wearing down off her naked body.

"Oh—by the way," he murmured against the curve of her shoulder. "I think I'd better warn you that I've promised Skinny to name our first boy after him."

She giggled. "Skinny?"

"Yeah. But he'll tell us his real name when the times comes."

And that time would come soon, Nevada thought happily. Very soon.

* * * * *

Coming in October to

SPECIAL EDITION™

the fourth book in the new continuity

MOST LIKELY TO…

Eleven Students. One reunion. And a secret
that will change everyone's lives.

THE PREGNANCY PROJECT

(SE #1711)

by reader favorite

Victoria Pade

He was her last chance to have a baby—but his
bedside manner left a lot to be desired. Could
the patient's gentle nature prove to be the best
medicine for the physician's scarred heart?

Don't miss this compelling story—only from
Silhouette Books.

Available at your favorite retail outlet.

Where love comes alive™

SPECIAL EDITION™

Don't miss the latest book from

Sharon De Vita

coming in October 2005!

ABOUT THE BOY

Silhouette Special Edition #1715

When widow Katie Murphy moved back
to Cooper's Cove to run the newspaper,
she sought a role model for her sun, Rusty.
Police chief Lucas Porter proved to be the
perfect mentor—but relations between
Katie and Lucas weren't smooth. Could the
redheaded reporter overcome Lucas's
distrust of the media...and earn
a press pass to his heart?

Available at your favorite retail outlet.

Where love comes alive™

Handwritten: *Oct*

COMING NEXT MONTH

#1711 THE PREGNANCY PROJECT—Victoria Pade
Most Likely To...
Desperate to conceive a child, Ella Gardner's only hope was Jacob Weber, M.D., a fellow Saunders U. alum renowned for his promising fertility treatments and difficult demeanor. But when single Ella saw the surly doctor's softer side, she faced a decision—should she put the pregnancy project on the back burner as her feelings for Jacob heated up?

#1712 ADDING TO THE FAMILY—Gina Wilkins
Family Found
Miranda Martin enjoyed the footloose single life in Little Rock. Her crush on CPA Mark Wallace was just a passing flirtation since she couldn't imagine getting serious with a busy single dad. But when she unexpectedly became the guardian of her five-year-old twin nephews, she needed parenting pointers—*pronto*. And it was Mark to the rescue....

#1713 SHE'S HAVING A BABY—Marie Ferrarella
The Cameo
When her best friend gave her a special cameo and told her to put it on to find true love, MacKenzie Ryan humored her. She had no use for love charms—after all, a recent romance had left her heartbroken...and pregnant! Her skepticism held sway until she crossed paths with her new neighbor, widower Quade Preston....

#1714 ONCE AND AGAIN—Brenda Harlen
Attorney Jessica Harding was about to make partner at a New York law firm. She'd long ago put her hometown and painful memories of first love Nick Armstrong behind her. But when her best friend's child was injured in an accident, Jessica rushed back to Pinehurst...and rediscovered Nick. Was the sharp lawyer now on track for a different sort of partnership?

#1715 ABOUT THE BOY—Sharon De Vita
When widow Katie Murphy moved back to Cooper's Cove to run the newspaper, she sought a role model for her son, Rusty. Police chief Lucas Porter proved to be the perfect mentor—but relations between Katie and Lucas weren't smooth. Could the redheaded reporter overcome Lucas's distrust of the media...and earn a press pass to his heart?

#1716 BLINDSIDED—Leslie LaFoy
After inheriting her brother's failing hockey franchise, recently divorced Catherine Talbott took a shot at turning the team—and her life—around. Her first goal: hire Logan Dupree to coach. His heart hadn't been in hockey since an accident had blinded him in one eye, ending his playing career—but his heart *did* go out to perky, petite Catherine....

Praise for
WITH THE OLD BREED

"In all the literature on the Second World War, there is not a more honest, realistic or moving memoir than Eugene Sledge's. This is the real deal, the real war: unvarnished, brutal, without a shred of sentimentality or false patriotism, a profound primer on what it actually was like to be in that war. It is a classic that will outlive all the armchair generals' safe accounts of—not the 'good war'—but the worst war ever."
—Ken Burns, creator of *The War*

"Of all the books about the ground war in the Pacific, [*With the Old Breed*] is the closest to a masterpiece."
—*The New York Review of Books*

"There are some brilliant memoirs of the savage battle for Okinawa, but E. B. Sledge's is by far the most haunting."
—*The Wall Street Journal*

"The best World War II memoir of an enlisted man."
—*Navy Times*

Awarded number one Best War Story Ever Told by *Men's Journal* magazine

WITH THE
OLD BREED

At Peleliu and Okinawa

E. B. SLEDGE

BALLANTINE BOOKS • NEW YORK

2007 Presidio Press Mass Market Edition

Published in the United States by Presidio Press, an imprint of The Random House Publishing Group, a division of Random House, Inc., New York.

PRESIDIO PRESS and colophon are registered trademarks of Random House, Inc.

Originally published in hardcover in the United States by Presidio Press, an imprint of The Random House Publishing Group, a division of Random House, Inc., in 1981.

The epigraph from Kipling is from "Preface" in *Departmental Ditties and Ballads and Barrack Room Ballads,* Macmillan and Co., 1915.

ISBN 978-0-89141-919-8

Cover design: Carl D. Galian
Cover photograph: © National Archives

Printed in the United States of America

www.presidiopress.com

OPM 29 28 27 26 25 24 23 22

In memory of Capt. Andrew A. Haldane,
beloved company commander of K/3/5,
and to the Old Breed

*The deaths ye died I have watched beside
and the lives ye led were mine.*

——RUDYARD KIPLING

Rifles were high and holy things to them, and they knew five-inch broadside guns. They talked patronizingly of the war, and were concerned about rations. They were the Leathernecks, the old Timers. . . . They were the old breed of American regular, regarding the service as home and war as an occupation; and they transmitted their temper and character and viewpoint to the high-hearted volunteer mass which filled the ranks of the Marine Brigade. . . .

—"The Leathernecks" in *Fix Bayonets* by John W. Thomason, Jr.

Contents

Foreword by Brig. Gen. Walter S. McIlhenny   xi
Preface   xiii
Acknowledgments   xv
Introduction by Victor Davis Hanson   xvii

PART I PELELIU: A NEGLECTED BATTLE

Foreword by Lt. Col. John A. Crown   3
  1. Making of a Marine   5
  2. Preparation for Combat   17
  3. On to Peleliu   49
  4. Assault into Hell   63
  5. Another Amphibious Assault   114
  6. Brave Men Lost   139

PART II OKINAWA: THE FINAL TRIUMPH

Foreword by Capt. Thomas J. Stanley   175
  7. Rest and Rehabilitation   177
  8. Prelude to Invasion   192
  9. Stay of Execution   205
10. Into the Abyss   226
11. Of Shock and Shells   243
12. Of Mud and Maggots   259
13. Breakthrough   283
14. Beyond Shuri   306
15. End of the Agony   330

Appendix: A Roll of Honor   345
Bibliography   347
Index   349

FOREWORD

It was my privilege to assume command of the 3d Battalion, 5th Marines, 1st Marine Division (Reinforced) on 10 April 1944 during the final phase of the New Britain campaign. New Britain was its second combat operation.

Although we didn't know it at the time, two more campaigns lay before the battalion, Peleliu and Okinawa. Each of them would be of greater intensity and extract a greater cost than did the first two. And when the division departed New Britain for a "rest camp" on Pavuvu in the Russell Islands, we began comprehensive training for what was to become Operation Stalemate on Peleliu Island in the Palau Islands. That operation was to receive little publicity or recognition, but it was certainly to be one of the bloodiest and hardest fought in the Pacific war.

Among the replacements who joined us during this period was a young Marine known as "Sledgehammer," more properly listed as Pfc. E. B. Sledge. He was assigned to Company K, under the command of Capt. Andrew Haldane, one of the finest company commanders in the entire Corps.

Sledgehammer has a Ph.D. now and is a professor of biology at the University of Montevallo, Montevallo, Alabama. But he has never forgotten his experiences with Company K during the fights for Peleliu and Okinawa.

Although I commanded the 3d Battalion during its training period for Peleliu, it was my fate—through the vicissitudes of seniority, or the lack thereof—to be transferred to the regimental staff before we sailed for Peleliu. That was a source of deep regret on my part.

It's customary for historical accounts to be written about

military campaigns. It's not unusual for officers to write their personal narratives of such operations. But it's all too rare for an ordinary Marine infantryman to set down in print his own impressions of war. This is the man who actually closes with the enemy, who endures a plethora of privations along with pain and all too often death, who is the lowest common denominator when battle is joined.

Sledgehammer Sledge was such a Marine. In this book we see the war as he himself saw it. Anyone who has served in the ranks will find many situations analogous to his own experiences recounted accurately in the recital of fears, frustrations, and small triumphs. It's fascinating and instructive reading.

—Brig. Gen. Walter S. McIlhenny,
U.S. Marine Corps Reserve (Ret.),
Avery Island, Louisiana

PREFACE

This book is an account of my World War II experiences in training and in combat with Company K, 3d Battalion, 5th Marine Regiment, 1st Marine Division during the Peleliu and Okinawa campaigns. It is not a history, and it is not my story alone. I have attempted, rather, to be the spokesman for my comrades, who were swept with me into the abyss of war. I hope they will approve my efforts.

I began writing this account immediately after Peleliu while we were in rest camp on Pavuvu Island. I outlined the entire story with detailed notes as soon as I returned to civilian life, and I have written down certain episodes during the years since then. Mentally, I have gone over and over the details of these events, but I haven't been able to draw them all together and write them down until now.

I have done extensive research with published and unpublished histories and documents pertaining to my division's role in the Peleliu and Okinawa campaigns. I have been amazed at the vast difference in the perception of events recounted in these narratives as contrasted to my experience on the front line.

My Pacific war experiences have haunted me, and it has been a burden to retain this story. But time heals, and the nightmares no longer wake me in a cold sweat with pounding heart and racing pulse. Now I can write this story, painful though it is to do so. In writing it I'm fulfilling an obligation I have long felt to my comrades in the 1st Marine Division, all of whom suffered so much for our country. None came out unscathed. Many gave their lives, many their health, and some their sanity. All who survived will long remember the horror they would rather forget. But they suffered and they did their duty so a sheltered homeland can enjoy the peace that was purchased at such a high cost. We owe those Marines a profound debt of gratitude.

E.B.S.

ACKNOWLEDGMENTS

Although this is a personal account, which was originally written for my family, there have been numerous people who have helped shape it into book form for the general reader.

First I want to thank Jeanne, my wonderful wife. She typed the Peleliu portion of the manuscript from stacks of my handwritten pages, and was the first to suggest that this narrative might be of interest to others than our family. She has encouraged and aided me with ideas, advice, editing, and typing. That the lengthy original manuscript was completed after years of spare-time writing and research during graduate school and child rearing is due as much to her assistance as to my efforts.

Deepest appreciation is extended to my editor, Lt. Col. Robert W. Smith, USMC (Ret.). During his last year as editor of the *Marine Corps Gazette,* he became interested in seeing this complete account in book form during our work on extracts, which appeared as a three-part article, "Peleliu: A Neglected Battle." His interest has been my good fortune. In addition to his vast editing skill, Bob has been an inexhaustible source of good ideas and advice. On more than one occasion he has bolstered my sagging morale when I've become weary with what is not a happy subject. His objectivity has guided me through the forest when I couldn't see the trees, and when it was painful to both of us to omit parts of the original. I am grateful for his sensitivity and impeccable professionalism.

I want to thank my publisher, Col. Robert V. Kane, USA (Ret.), and Adele Horwitz, Editor in Chief of Presidio Press, who saw in my verbose original manuscript a story that should be told.

This book could not have been written without the benefit of Marine Corps historical material. My requests for help were rapidly and efficiently granted in every instance. For this I want to thank Brig. Gen. Edwin H. Simmons, USMC (Ret.), Director of Marine Corps History and Museums Benis Frank; Ralph Donnelly; and Henry I. Shaw.

For their help and encouragement I express my gratitude to Brig. Gen. Walter McIlhenny, USMC (Ret.); Lt. Col. John A. Crown, USMC (Ret.); Brig. Gen. Austin Shofner, USMC (Ret.); Capt. John A. Moran, USMC (Ret.); and Maj. Allan Bevilacqua, USMC (Ret.).

M. Sgt. Robert F. Fleischauer, USMC (Ret.), is due recognition and thanks for his fine work on the maps and sketches.

I thank Mrs. Hilda Van Landingham for typing the first draft of the Okinawa portion. Mary Francis Tipton, Reference Librarian at the University of Montevallo, merits my deepest appreciation for her help. Dr. Lucille Griffith, Professor Emeritus of History, University of Montevallo, was one of the first people to suggest this account be published. Her faith in it is redeemed, and I thank her.

My heartiest thanks to my old K/3/5 buddies who have assisted so much in verifying company casualty figures, countless other details, and photograph identification: Ted (Tex) Barrow, Henry A. Boyes, Valton Burgin, Jessie Crumbacker, Art Dimick, John Hedge, T. L. Hudson, William Leyden, Sterling Mace, Tom Matheny, Jim McEney, Vincent Santos, George Sarrett, Thomas (Stumpy) Stanley. If I have omitted any names, I apologize. Any errors in the manuscript are solely mine.

I appreciate the cooperation and understanding of my sons John and Henry and their patience with a father who was often preoccupied with past events.

A grant from the University of Montevallo Faculty Research Committee aided in the preparation of the manuscript.

E.B.S.

INTRODUCTION
By Victor Davis Hanson

Until the millennium arrives and countries cease trying to enslave others, it will be necessary to accept one's responsibilities and to be willing to make sacrifices for one's country—as my comrades did. As the troops used to say, "If the country is good enough to live in, it's good enough to fight for." With privilege goes responsibility.

So E. B. Sledge ends his memoir of the horrors of the Marines' fighting in late 1944 and spring 1945 against the imperial Japanese on Peleliu and Okinawa. We should recall these concluding thoughts about patriotic duty because *With the Old Breed* has now achieved the status of a military classic—in part on the perception of Sledge's blanket condemnation of the brutality and senselessness of war itself.

Although there are horrors aplenty in the graphic accounts of the 1st Marine Division's ordeal in these two invasions, his message is still not so darkly condemnatory. The real power of Sledge's memoir is not just found in his melancholy. Even in his frequent despair over the depravity seen everywhere around him, there is an overriding sense of tragedy: until the nature of man himself changes, reluctant men such as E. B. Sledge will be asked to do things that civilization should not otherwise ask of its own—but must if it is to survive barbarity.

Who, in fact, was Eugene Bondurant Sledge—a previously unknown retired professor who late in life published his first book, originally intended only as a private memoir for his family? Yet within two decades of publication that draft became acknowledged as the finest literary account to emerge about the Pacific war.

Despite the still growing acclaim given *With the Old Breed*—first published more than twenty years earlier by the

Presidio Press of Novato, California—the death of Sledge at seventy-seven, in March 2001, garnered little national attention. After his retirement, Sledge had remained a mostly private person who rarely entered the public arena.

Even with his perfect Marine name, E. B. Sledge might have seemed an unlikely combat veteran. Born the son of a prominent local physician in Mobile, Alabama, the articulate, slight, and shy Sledge spent only a year at Marion Military Institute, and then enrolled at the Georgia Institute of Technology—before choosing instead to leave the officers' training program to enlist in late 1943 in the U.S. Marine Corps as a private. This early intimate experience with officer training, together with the subsequent decision to prefer service with the enlisted corps, colors much of the narrative of *With the Old Breed*. Sledge repeatedly takes stock of officers, and both the worst and best men in the Corps prove to be its second lieutenants and captains.

After the defeat of Japan, Sledge served in the American occupying force in China; his account of that tour was published posthumously as *China Marine*. Sledge later remarked he found the return to civilian life difficult after Peleliu and Okinawa, as did many veterans of island fighting in the Pacific who could not "comprehend people who griped because America wasn't perfect, or their coffee wasn't hot enough, or they had to stand in line and wait for a train or bus." Yet Sledge adjusted well enough to graduate in 1949 with his B.S. degree. By 1960 he had completed his Ph.D. in zoology and settled on an academic career; at thirty-nine he joined the University of Montevallo, where he taught microbiology and ornithology until his retirement.

His scholarly expertise and precision of thought and language, gained from nearly thirty years as a teacher and scientist, perhaps explain much of the force of *With the Old Breed*. The narrative is peppered with wide-ranging empirical observations of his new surroundings—and philosophical shrugs about the incongruity of it all: "There the Okinawans had tilled their soil with ancient and crude farming methods; but the war had come, bringing with it the latest and most refined technology for killing. It seemed so insane, and I realized that the war was like some sort of disease afflicting man."

The look back at the savagery of Peleliu and Okinawa—based on old battle notes he had once kept on slips of paper in his copy of the New Testament—is presented with the care of a clinician. Sledge's language is modest; there is no bombast. The resulting autopsy of battle is eerie, almost dreamlike. Dispassionate understatement accentuates rather than sanitizes the barbarity. Sledge describes a dead Japanese medical corpsman torn apart by American shelling thusly: "The corpsman was on his back, his abdominal cavity laid bare. I stared in horror, shocked at the glistening viscera bespecked with fine coral dust. This can't have been a human being, I agonized. It looked more like the guts of one of the many rabbits or squirrels I had cleaned on hunting trips as a boy. I felt sick as I stared at the corpses."

We readers are dumbfounded by the first few pages—how can such a decent man have endured such an inferno, emerged apparently whole, and now decades later brought us back to these awful islands to write so logically about such abject horrors? On the eve of the invasion of Peleliu, the ever curious Sledge matter-of-factly asks an intelligent-looking but doomed Marine what he plans to do after the war, and then he describes the reply, " 'I want to be a brain surgeon. The human brain is an incredible thing; it fascinates me,' he replied. But he didn't survive Peleliu to realize his ambition."

The Pacific ground theater of World War II from Guadalcanal to Okinawa that nearly consumed Sledge, as it did thousands of American youths, was no dream, but a nightmare unlike any other fighting in the nation's wartime history. It was an existential struggle of annihilation. And the killing was fueled by political, cultural—and racial—odium in which no quarter was asked or given: "A brutish, primitive hatred," Sledge reminds us decades later, "as characteristic of the horror of war in the Pacific as the palm trees and the islands."

The sheer distances across the seas, the formidable size of the imperial Japanese fleet, and the priority of the United States in defeating Nazi Germany first, all meant that the odds were often with the enemy. In particular theaters the Japanese had advantages over the Americans in numbers, choice of terrain, and even supply. We now might underestimate the wartime technology of imperial Japan, forgetting that it was often as good as, or even superior to, American munitions. On both islands Sledge writes in detail of the singular Japanese mortars and artillery that wheeled out, fired, and then withdrew in safety behind heavy steel doors. Especially feared was "a 320-mm-spigot-mortar unit equipped to fire a 675-pound shell. Americans first encountered this awesome weapon on Iwo Jima."

As Sledge relates, the heat, rugged coral peaks, and incessant warm rain of the exotic Pacific islands, so unlike the European theater, were as foreign to Americans as the debilitating tropical diseases. Land crabs and ubiquitous jungle rot ate away leather, canvas—and flesh. "It was gruesome," Sledge the biologist writes of Peleliu, "to see the stages of decay proceed from just killed to bloated to maggot-infested rotting to partially exposed bones—like some biological clock marking the inexorable passage of time." He adds of the stench, "At every breath one inhaled hot, humid air heavy with countless repulsive odors."

The awfulness was not just that the fanatical nature of the Japanese resistance meant that America's Depression-era draftees were usually forced to kill rather than wound or capture their enemy. Rather, there grew a certain dread or even bewilderment among young draftees about the nature of an ideology that could fuel such elemental hatred of the Americans. On news of the Japanese surrender after Hiroshima and Nagasaki, the veteran Sledge remained puzzled: "We thought the Japanese would never surrender. Many refused to believe it. Sitting in stunned silence, we remembered our dead. So many dead. So many maimed. So many bright futures consigned to the ashes of the past."

E. B. Sledge's story begins with his training as a Marine in Company K, 3d Battalion, 5th Marine Regiment, 1st Marine Division. The memoir centers on two nightmarish island battles that ultimately ruined the division. The first was at Peleliu (Operation Stalemate II, September 15–November 25,

1944), where in 10 weeks of horrific fighting some 8,769 Americans were killed, wounded, or missing. About 11,000 Japanese perished—nearly the entire enemy garrison on the island. Controversy raged—and still does about the wisdom of storming many of the Pacific islands—whether Gen. Douglas MacArthur really needed the capture of the Japanese garrison on Peleliu to ensure a safe right flank on his way to the Philippines.

Yet such arguments over strategic necessity count little for Sledge. His concern is instead with the survival of his 235 comrades in Company K, which suffered 150 killed, wounded, or missing. And so there is little acrimony over the retrospective folly of taking on Peleliu. Sledge's resignation might be best summed up as something like, "The enemy held the island; we took it; they lost, and we moved on."

Operation Iceberg (April 1, 1945–July 2, 1945) the next year to capture Okinawa was far worse. Indeed it was the most nightmarish American experience of the entire Pacific war—over 50,000 American casualties, including some 12,500 soldiers and sailors killed, and the greatest number of combat fatigue cases ever recorded of a single American battle.

My namesake Victor Hanson, of the 6th Marine Division, 29th Regiment, was killed near the Shuri Line, in the last assault on the heights, a few hours before its capture on May 19, 1945. His letters, and those of his commanding officer notifying our family of his death, make poignant reading—including the account of his final moments on Sugar Loaf Hill. Indeed, the very name Okinawa has haunted the Hanson family, as it had Sledge's and thousands of other American households, for a half century hence. For decades in the United States no one really knew—or wished not to know—what really went on at Okinawa.

In fact, neither of Sledge's two battles, despite their ferocity and the brutal eventual American victories—being in obscure, distant places and in the so-called second theater—garnered the public attention of Normandy Beach or the Battle of the Bulge. In the case of Okinawa, the savagery was overshadowed, first, by the near simultaneous death of

Franklin Roosevelt on April 12, and the May 8 German sur-render in Europe; and then later by the dropping of the atomic bombs on Hiroshima and Nagasaki (August 6 and 9), just over five weeks after the island was declared finally secured on July 2.

Sandwiched in between these momentous events, tens of thousands of Americans in obscurity slowly ground their way down the island. They accepted that they might have to kill everyone in most of the last crack Japanese units, led by the most accomplished officers in the Japanese military, the bril-liant but infamous generals Mitsuru Ushijima and Isamu Cho and the gifted tactician Col. Hiromichi Yahara.

When the battle was over, the U.S. Navy had suffered its worst single-battle losses in its history. The newly formed 6th Marine Division and Sledge's veteran 1st Marine Division were wrecked, with almost half their original strength either killed or wounded. The commander of all U.S. ground forces on Okinawa, Gen. Simon Bolivar Buckner, Jr., became the highest-ranking soldier to die in combat in World War II. The destructive potential of thousands of kamikaze suicide bombers, together with the faulty prebattle intelligence that had sorely underestimated the size, armament, and ferocity of the island resistance, created a dread about the upcoming November 1 scheduled assault on the Japanese mainland (Operation Olympic).

Controversy still rages over the morality of dropping the two atomic bombs that ended the war before the American in-vasions of Kyushu and Honshu. But we forget that President Truman's decision was largely predicated on avoiding the nightmare that Marines like E. B. Sledge had just endured on Peleliu and Okinawa. If today Americans in the leisure of a long peace wonder whether our grandfathers were too hasty in their decision to resort to atomic weapons, they forget that many veterans of the Pacific wondered why they had to suffer through an Okinawa when the successful test at Alamogordo, New Mexico, on July 16 came just a few days after the island was declared secure. Surely the carnage on Okinawa could have been delayed till late summer to let such envisioned weapons convince the Japanese of the futility of prolonging the war.

There are fine memoirs of Okinawa and narrative accounts of the battle's role in the American victory over Japan, most notably William Manchester's beautifully written *Goodbye, Darkness,* and George Feifer's comprehensive *Tennozan: The Battle of Okinawa and the Atomic Bomb.* But E. B. Sledge's harrowing story remains unmatched, told in a prose that is dignified, without obscenities or even much slang—all the more memorable since the author was not a formal stylist nor given to easy revelations of his own strong passions. John Keegan, Paul Fussel, and Studs Turkel have all praised Sledge's honesty, especially his explicit acknowledgment that he experienced the same hatred, but fought daily against the barbarity that drove others to nearly match the atrocities of their Japanese enemies.

Unlike the case of many postwar memoirs, the accuracy of Sledge's facts has never been called into question. He does not magnify his own achievements or those of his own Company K. Sledge sometimes uses a few footnotes of explication at the bottom of the page. Often they are heartbreaking asterisks that apprise the reader that the wonderful officer Sledge has just described in the text was later shot or blown up on Peleliu or Okinawa. He reminds his readers that his Marines, being as human as any other soldiers, were capable of great cruelty—"a passionate hatred for the Japanese burned through all Marines I knew." But that being said, Sledge's own moral censure reveals a certain American exceptionalism that such barbarism should and usually was to be condemned as deviance rather than accepted as the norm—quite different from the Japanese:

> *In disbelief I stared at the face as I realize that the Japanese had cut off the dead Marine's penis and stuffed it into his mouth. My emotions solidified into rage and a hatred for the Japanese beyond anything I ever had experienced. From that moment on I never felt the least pity or compassion for them no matter what the circumstances. My comrades would field strip their*

*packs and pockets for souvenirs and take gold teeth, but
I never saw a Marine commit the kind of barbaric
mutilation the Japanese committed if they had access
to our dead.*

What I find most haunting about *With the Old Breed* is
Sledge's empathy with those whom he might not have been
expected to share a natural affinity, among them even at times
the enemy—whom he often wishes not to kill gratuitously
and whose corpses he refuses to desecrate. His is a very mannered Southern world where the martial chivalry of an Alabama, Louisiana, or Texas soldier shine through; implicit is
a pride in the stereotyped manhood or the Old South, but also
love for his Yankee comrades who he knows fight as well as
his kinsmen. Sledge admits fear, occasionally acknowledg-
ing that his courage was the only result of desperation or ra-
tional calculation. He only incidentally notes his skill as a
Marine. Yet through his own matter-of-fact descriptions the
reader easily surmises why his comrades nicknamed a man of
135 pounds "Sledgehammer."

Sledge's heroes amid the desolation of the charred
islands—Sergeants Baily and Haney, Lieutenant "Hillbilly"
Jones, and the beloved Captain Haldane—are singled out for
their reticence, reflection, and humanity. Of Jones, Sledge
writes, "He had that rare ability to be friendly yet familiar
with enlisted men. He possessed a unique combination of
those qualities of bravery, leadership, ability, integrity, dignity, straightforwardness, and compassion. The only other officer I knew who was his equal in all these qualities was
Captain Haldane."

While the reader is astonished at the élan and skill of
Sledge's young compatriots, Sledge nevertheless describes
them as apprentices in the shadows of the real "old-time"
Marines—a near mythical generation that came of age between the wars and was made of even sterner stuff, fighting
and winning the initial battles of the Pacific at Guadalcanal
and Cape Gloucester on New Britain against the supposedly
invincible and ascendant Japanese of 1942 and 1943. Of
Gunnery Sgt. Elmo Haney, who scrubbed his genitals with a

bristle brush and cleaned his M1 and bayonet three times daily, Sledge concludes, "Despite his personal idiosyncrasies, Haney inspired us youngsters in Company K. He provided us with a direct link to the 'Old Corps'. To us he *was* the old breed. We admired him—and we loved him."

Indeed, in Sledge's Pacific, there are Homeric heroes of all sorts of an age now long gone by. Bob Hope at the height of his Hollywood career turns up as the devoted patriot at out-of-the-way Pavuvu, flying in at some danger to entertain the troops. And the future Illinois senator Paul Douglas—noted author and University of Chicago economics professor—appears in the worst of combat at Peleliu as a gray-haired, bespectacled fifty-three-year-old Marine enlistee, handing out ammo to the young Sledge. Douglas later becomes severely wounded at Okinawa and receives the Silver Star and Purple Heart. Again, if modern readers are amazed at the courageous breed of young Marines who surround Sledge, he advises us that we are even more removed than we think from these earlier Americans, since the real "old breed" antedated and was even superior to his own.

Sledge shares a hatred for the brutality of the Japanese, but it never blinds him to their shared horrible fate of being joined together in death at awful places such as Peleliu and Okinawa. So he is furious when he sees a fellow Marine yanking the gold teeth out of a mortally wounded, but very much alive, Japanese soldier on Okinawa: "It was uncivilized, as is all war, and was carried out with the particular savagery that characterized the struggle between the Marines and the Japanese. It wasn't simply souvenir hunting or looting the enemy dead; it was more like Indian warriors taking scalps. Such was the incredible cruelty that decent men could commit when reduced to a brutish existence in their fight for survival amid the violent death, terror, tension, fatigue, and filth that was the infantryman's war."

Indeed at the heart of Sledge's genius of recollection is precisely his gift to step aside to condemn the insanity of war, to deplore its bloodletting, without denying that there is often a reason for it, and a deep love that results for those who share its burdens.

War is brutish, inglorious, and a terrible waster. Combat leaves an inedible mark on those who are forced to endure it. The only redeeming factors were my comrades' incredible bravery and their devotion to each other. Marine Corps training taught us to kill efficiently and to try to survive. But it also taught us loyalty to each other—and love. That esprit de corps sustained us.

There is a renewed timeliness to Sledge's memoir. *With the Old Breed* has never been more relevant than after September 11—war being the domain of an unchanging human nature and thus subject to predictable lessons that transcend time and space. It is not just that American Marines of the new millennium also face a novel strain of suicide bombers, or fanatic enemies emboldened by a frightening anti-Western creed, or once again the similar terror of Sledge's mines, mortars, and hand-to-hand battle in places like Iraqi's Haditha or Ramadi.

Rather, Sledge reminds us of the lethality of what we might call the normal American adolescent in uniform, a grim determinism that we also recognized in the Hindu Kush and Kirkuk. Raised amid bounty and freedom, the American soldier seems a poor candidate to learn *ex nihilo* the craft of killing. How can a suburban teenager suddenly be asked to face and defeat the likes of zealots, whether on Okinawa's Shuri Line or at Fallujah in the Sunni Triangle? "Would I do my duty or be a coward?" Sledge wonders on his initial voyage to the Pacific. "Could I kill?"

But read *With the Old Breed* to be reminded how a certain American reluctance to kill and the accompanying unease with militarism have the odd effect of magnifying courage, as free men prove capable of almost any sacrifice to preserve their liberty.

Or as E. B. Sledge once more reminds us thirty-six years after surviving Okinawa:

In writing I am fulfilling an obligation I have long felt to my comrades in the 1st Marine Division, all of whom suffered so much for our country. None came out unscathed. Many gave their lives, many their health, and some their sanity. All who survived will long remember the horror they would rather forget. But they suffered and they did their duty so a sheltered homeland can enjoy the peace that was purchased at such high cost. We owe those Marines a profound debt of gratitude.

We owe the same to the late E. B. Sledge. He reminds us in a "sheltered homeland" that America is never immune from the "insanity" of war. So he brings alive again the names, faces, and thoughts of those who left us at Okinawa and Peleliu, but who passed on what we must in turn bequeath to others to follow.

PART I

Peleliu:
A Neglected Battle

FOREWORD TO PART I

The 1st Marine Division's assault on the Central Pacific island of Peleliu thirty-seven years ago was, in the overall perspective of World War II, a relatively minor engagement. After a war is over, it's deceptively easy to determine which battles were essential and which could have gone unfought. Thus, in hindsight, Peleliu's contribution to total victory was dubious. Moreover, World War II itself has faded into the mists with the more immediate combat in Korea and Vietnam.

To the men of the 1st Marine Division who made the assault on Peleliu (the youngest of whom are in their fifties today), there was nothing minor about it. For those who were there, it was a bloody, wearying, painful, and interminable engagement. For a single-division operation, the losses were extraordinarily heavy.

Eugene B. Sledge served in Company K, 3d Battalion, 5th Marines throughout the battle. I had the privilege of commanding Company I of the same battalion in the same period. His account awoke vivid memories which had lain dormant for years.

Don't read this personal narrative seeking the significance of the battle or of grand strategy. Rather read it for what it is, intense combat as seen by an individual Marine rifleman. For those who have experienced battle elsewhere, the similarities will be obvious.

John A. Crown
Lieutenant Colonel
U.S. Marine Corps
Atlanta, Georgia

CHAPTER ONE

Making of a Marine

I enlisted in the Marine Corps on 3 December 1942 at Marion, Alabama. At the time I was a freshman at Marion Military Institute. My parents and brother Edward had urged me to stay in college as long as possible in order to qualify for a commission in some technical branch of the U.S. Army. But, prompted by a deep feeling of uneasiness that the war might end before I could get overseas into combat, I wanted to enlist in the Marine Corps as soon as possible. Ed, a Citadel graduate and a second lieutenant in the army, suggested life would be more beautiful for me as an officer. Mother and Father were mildly distraught at the thought of me in the Marines as an enlisted man—that is, "cannon fodder." So when a Marine recruiting team came to Marion Institute, I compromised and signed up for one of the Corps' new officer training programs. It was called V-12.

The recruiting sergeant wore dress blue trousers, a khaki shirt, necktie, and white barracks hat. His shoes had a shine the likes of which I'd never seen. He asked me lots of questions and filled out numerous official papers. When he asked, "Any scars, birthmarks, or other unusual features?" I described an inch-long scar on my right knee. I asked why such a question. He replied, "So they can identify you on some Pacific beach after the Japs blast off your dog tags." This was my introduction to the stark realism that characterized the Marine Corps I later came to know.

The college year ended the last week of May 1943. I had the month of June at home in Mobile before I had to report 1 July for duty at Georgia Tech in Atlanta.

I enjoyed the train trip from Mobile to Atlanta because the

train had a steam engine. The smoke smelled good, and the whistle added a plaintive note reminiscent of an unhurried life. The porters were impressed and most solicitous when I told them, with no little pride, that I was on my way to becoming a Marine. My official Marine Corps meal ticket got me a large, delicious shrimp salad in the dining car and the admiring glances of the steward in attendance.

On my arrival in Atlanta, a taxi deposited me at Georgia Tech, where the 180-man Marine detachment lived in Harrison Dormitory. Recruits were scheduled to attend classes year round (in my case, about two years), graduate, and then go to the Marine base at Quantico, Virginia, for officers' training.

A Marine regular, Capt. Donald Payzant, was in charge. He had served with the 1st Marine Division on Guadalcanal. Seeming to glory in his duty and his job as our commander, he loved the Corps and was salty and full of swagger. Looking back, I realize now that he had survived the meat grinder of combat and was simply glad to be in one piece with the good fortune of being stationed at a peaceful college campus.

Life at Georgia Tech was easy and comfortable. In short, we didn't know there was a war going on. Most of the college courses were dull and uninspiring. Many of the professors openly resented our presence. It was all but impossible to concentrate on academics. Most of us felt we had joined the Marines to fight, but here we were college boys again. The situation was more than many of us could stand. At the end of the first semester, ninety of us—half of the detachment—flunked out of school so we could go into the Corps as enlisted men.

When the navy officer in charge of academic affairs called me in to question me about my poor academic performance, I told him I hadn't joined the Marine Corps to sit out the war in college. He was sympathetic to the point of being fatherly and said he would feel the same way if he were in my place.

Captain Payzant gave the ninety of us a pep talk in front of the dormitory the morning we were to board the train for boot camp at the Marine Corps Recruit Depot, San Diego, California. He told us we were the best men and the best Marines in the detachment. He said he admired our spirit for wanting to get into the war. I think he was sincere.

After the pep talk, buses took us to the railway station. We sang and cheered the whole way. We were on our way to war at last. If we had only known what lay ahead of us!

Approximately two and a half years later, I came back through the Atlanta railway station on my way home. Shortly after I stepped off the car for a stroll, a young army infantryman walked up to me and shook hands. He said he had noticed my 1st Marine Division patch and the campaign ribbons on my chest and wondered if I had fought at Peleliu. When I said I had, he told me he just wanted to express his undying admiration for men of the 1st Marine Division.

He had fought with the 81st Infantry Division (Wildcats), which had come in to help us at Peleliu.* He was a machine gunner, had been hit by Japanese fire on Bloody Nose Ridge, and was abandoned by his army comrades. He knew he would either die of his wounds or be cut up by the Japanese when darkness fell. Risking their lives, some Marines had moved in and carried him to safety. The soldier said he was so impressed by the bravery, efficiency, and esprit of the Marines he saw on Peleliu that he swore to thank every veteran of the 1st Marine Division he ever ran across.

The "Dago people"—as those of us bound for San Diego were called—boarded a troop train in a big railroad terminal in Atlanta. Everyone was in high spirits, as though we were headed for a picnic instead of boot camp—and a war. The trip across the country took several days and was uneventful but interesting. Most of us had never been west, and we enjoyed the scenery. The monotony of the trip was broken with card games, playing jokes on each other, and waving, yelling, and

*Together with the 1st Marine Division, the U.S. Army's 81st Infantry Division comprised the III Amphibious Corps commanded by Maj. Gen. Roy S. Geiger, USMC. For the Palau operation, the 1st Marine Division assaulted Peleliu on 15 September 1944 while the 81st Division took Angaur Island and provided a regiment as corps reserve. The 81st Division relieved the 1st Marine Division on Peleliu on 20 October and secured the island on 27 November.

whistling at any and all women visible. We ate some meals in dining cars on the train; but at certain places the train pulled onto a siding, and we ate in the restaurant in the railroad terminal.

Nearly all of the rail traffic we passed was military. We saw long trains composed almost entirely of flatcars loaded with tanks, halftracks, artillery pieces, trucks, and other military equipment. Many troop trains passed us going both ways. Most of them carried army troops. This rail traffic impressed on us the enormousness of the nation's war effort.

We arrived in San Diego early one morning. Collecting our gear, we fell into ranks outside our cars as a first sergeant came along and told the NCOs on our train which buses to get us aboard. This first sergeant looked old to us teenagers. Like ourselves, he was dressed in a green wool Marine uniform, but he had campaign ribbons on his chest. He also wore the green French *fourragère* on his left shoulder. (Later, as a member of the 5th Marine Regiment, I would wear the braided cord around my left arm with pride.) But this man sported, in addition, two single loops outside his arm. That meant he had served with a regiment (either the 5th or 6th Marines) that had received the award from France for distinguished combat service in World War I.

The sergeant made a few brief remarks to us about the tough training we faced. He seemed friendly and compassionate, almost fatherly. His manner threw us into a false sense of well-being and left us totally unprepared for the shock that awaited us when we got off those buses.

"Fall out, and board your assigned buses!" ordered the first sergeant.

"All right, you people. Get aboard them buses!" the NCOs yelled. They seemed to have become more authoritarian as we approached San Diego.

After a ride of only a few miles, the buses rolled to a stop in the big Marine Corps Recruit Depot—boot camp. As I looked anxiously out the window, I saw many platoons of recruits marching along the streets. Each drill instructor (DI) bellowed his highly individual cadence. The recruits looked as rigid as sardines in a can. I grew nervous at seeing how serious—or rather, scared—they seemed.

"All right, you people, off them damned buses!"

We scrambled out, lined up with men from the other buses, and were counted off into groups of about sixty. Several trucks rolled by carrying work parties of men still in boot camp or who had finished recently. All looked at us with knowing grins and jeered, "You'll be sorreee." This was the standard, unofficial greeting extended to all recruits.

Shortly after we debused, a corporal walked over to my group. He yelled, "Patoon, teehut. Right hace, forwart huah. Double time, huah."

He ran us up and down the streets for what seemed hours and finally to a double line of huts that would house us for a time. We were breathless. He didn't even seem to be breathing hard.

"Patoon halt, right hace!" He put his hands on his hips and looked us over contemptuously. "You people are stupid," he bellowed. From then on he tried to prove it every moment of every day. "My name is Corporal Doherty. I'm your drill instructor. This is Platoon 984. If any of you idiots think you don't need to follow my orders, just step right out here and I'll beat your ass right now. Your soul may belong to Jesus, but your ass belongs to the Marines. You people are *recruits*. You're *not* Marines. You may not have what it takes to be Marines."

No one dared move, hardly even to breathe. We were all humbled, because there was no doubt the DI meant exactly what he said.

Corporal Doherty wasn't a large man by any standard. He stood about five feet ten inches, probably weighed around 160 pounds, and was muscular with a protruding chest and flat stomach. He had thin lips, a ruddy complexion, and was probably as Irish as his name. From his accent I judged him to be a New Englander, maybe from Boston. His eyes were the coldest, meanest green I ever saw. He glared at us like a wolf whose first and foremost desire was to tear us limb from limb. He gave me the impression that the only reason he didn't do so was that the Marine Corps wanted to use us for cannon fodder to absorb Japanese bullets and shrapnel so genuine Marines could be spared to capture Japanese positions.

That Corporal Doherty was tough and hard as nails none of us ever doubted. Most Marines recall how loudly their DIs yelled at them, but Doherty didn't yell very loudly. Instead he shouted in an icy, menacing manner that sent cold chills through us. We believed that if he didn't scare us to death, the Japs couldn't kill us. He was always immaculate, and his uniform fitted him as if the finest tailor had made it for him. His posture was erect, and his bearing reflected military precision.

The public pictures a DI wearing sergeant stripes. Doherty commanded our respect and put such fear into us that he couldn't have been more effective if he had had the six stripes of a first sergeant instead of the two of a corporal. One fact emerged immediately with stark clarity: this man would be the master of our fates in the weeks to come.

Doherty rarely drilled us on the main parade ground, but marched or double-timed us to an area near the beach of San Diego Bay. There the deep, soft sand made walking exhausting, just what he wanted. For hours on end, for days on end, we drilled back and forth across the soft sand. My legs ached terribly for the first few days, as did those of everyone else in the platoon. I found that when I concentrated on a fold of the collar or cap of the man in front of me or tried to count the ships in the bay, my muscles didn't ache as badly. To drop out of ranks because of tired legs was unthinkable. The standard remedy for such shirking was to "double-time in place to get the legs in shape"—before being humiliated and berated in front of the whole platoon by the DI. I preferred the pain to the remedy.

Before heading back to the hut area at the end of each drill session, Doherty would halt us, ask a man for his rifle, and tell us he would demonstrate the proper technique for holding the rifle while creeping and crawling. First, though, he would place the butt of the rifle on the sand, release the weapon, and let it drop, saying that anyone who did that would have a miserable day of it. With so many men in the platoon, it was uncanny how often he asked to use my rifle in this demonstration. Then, after demonstrating how to cradle the rifle, he ordered us to creep and crawl. Naturally, the men in front kicked sand onto the rifle of the one behind him. With this and several other techniques, the DI made it necessary for us to clean our rifles several times each day. But we learned quickly and well an old Marine Corps truism, "The rifle is a Marine's best friend." We always treated it as just that.

During the first few days, Doherty once asked one of the recruits a question about his rifle. In answering, the hapless recruit referred to his rifle as "my gun." The DI muttered some instructions to him, and the recruit blushed. He began trotting up and down in front of the huts holding his rifle in one hand and his penis in the other, chanting, "This is my rifle," as he held up his M1, "and this is my gun," as he moved his other arm. "This is for Japs," he again held aloft his M1; "and this is for fun," he held up his other arm. Needless to say, none of us ever again used the word "gun" unless referring to a shotgun, mortar, artillery piece, or naval gun.

A typical day in boot camp began with reveille at 0400 hours. We tumbled out of our sacks in the chilly dark and hurried through shaves, dressing, and chow. The grueling day ended with taps at 2200. At any time between taps and reveille, however, the DI might break us out for rifle inspection, close-order drill, or for a run around the parade ground or over the sand by the bay. This seemingly cruel and senseless harassment stood me in good stead later when I found that war allowed sleep to no man, particularly the infantryman. Combat guaranteed sleep of the permanent type only.

We moved to two or three different hut areas during the first few weeks, each time on a moment's notice. The order was "Platoon 984, fall out on the double with rifles, full individual equipment, and seabags with all gear properly stowed, and prepare to move out in ten minutes." A mad scramble would follow as men gathered up and packed their equipment. Each man had one or two close buddies who pitched in to help each other don packs and hoist heavy seabags onto sagging shoulders. Several men from each hut would stay behind to clean up the huts and surrounding area as the other men of the platoon struggled under their heavy loads to the new hut area.

Upon arrival at the new area, the platoon halted, received hut assignments, fell out, and stowed gear. Just as we got into the huts we would get orders to fall in for drill with rifles, cartridge belts, and bayonets. The sense of urgency and hurry never abated. Our DI was ingenious in finding ways to harass us.

One of the hut areas we were in was across a high fence from an aircraft factory where big B-24 Liberator bombers were made. There was an airstrip, too, and the big four-engine planes came and went low over the tops of the huts. Once one belly-landed, going through the fence near our huts. No one was hurt, but several of us ran down to see the crash. When we got back to our area, Corporal Doherty delivered one of his finest orations on the subject of recruits never leaving their assigned area without the permission of their DI. We were all impressed, particularly with the tremendous number of push-ups and other exercises we performed instead of going to noon chow.

During close-order drill, the short men had the toughest time staying in step. Every platoon had its "feather merchants"—short men struggling along with giant strides at the tail end of the formation. At five feet nine inches, I was about two-thirds of the way back from the front guide of Platoon 984. One day while returning from the bayonet course, I got out of step and couldn't pick up the cadence. Corporal Doherty marched along beside me. In his icy tone, he said, "Boy, if you don't get in step and stay in step, I'm gonna kick you so hard in the behind that they're gonna have to take both of us to sick bay. It'll take a major operation to get my foot outa your ass." With those inspiring words ringing in my ears, I picked up the cadence and never ever lost it again.

The weather became quite chilly, particularly at night. I had to cover up with blankets and overcoat. Many of us slept in dungaree trousers and sweat shirts in addition to our Skivvies. When reveille sounded well before daylight, we only had to pull on our boondockers [field shoes] before falling in for roll call.

Each morning after roll call, we ran in the foggy darkness to a large asphalt parade ground for rifle calisthenics. Atop a wooden platform, a muscular physical training instructor led several platoons in a long series of tiring exercises. A public-address system played a scratchy recording of "Three O'-Clock in the Morning." We were supposed to keep time with the music. The monotony was broken only by frequent whispered curses and insults directed at our enthusiastic instructor, and by the too frequent appearance of various DIs who stalked the extended ranks making sure all hands exercised vigorously. Not only did the exercises harden our bodies, but our hearing became superkeen from listening for the DIs as we skipped a beat or two for a moment of rest in the inky darkness.

At the time, we didn't realize or appreciate the fact that the discipline we were learning in responding to orders under stress often would mean the difference later in combat—between success or failure, even living or dying. The ear training also proved to be an unscheduled dividend when Japanese infiltrators slipped around at night.

Shortly we received word that we were going to move out to the rifle range. We greeted the announcement enthusiastically. Rumor had it that we would receive the traditional broad-brimmed campaign hats. But the supply ran out when our turn came. We felt envious and cheated every time we saw those salty-looking "Smokey Bear" hats on the range.

Early on the first morning at the rifle range, we began what was probably the most thorough and the most effective rifle marksmanship training given to any troops of any nation during World War II. We were divided into two-man teams the first week for dry firing, or "snapping-in." We concentrated on proper sight setting, trigger squeeze, calling of shots, use of the leather sling as a shooting aid, and other fundamentals.

It soon became obvious why we all received thick pads to be sewn onto the elbows and right shoulders of our dungaree jackets: during this snapping-in, each man and his buddy practiced together, one in the proper position (standing, kneeling, sitting, or prone) and squeezing the trigger, and the other pushing back the rifle bolt lever with the heel of his hand, padded by an empty cloth bandolier wrapped around the palm. This procedure cocked the rifle and simulated recoil.

The DIs and rifle coaches checked every man continuously. Everything had to be just so. Our arms became sore from being contorted into various positions and having the leather sling straining our joints and biting into our muscles. Most of us had problems perfecting the sitting position (which I never saw used in combat). But the coach helped everyone the way he did me—simply by plopping his weight on my shoulders until I was able to "assume the correct position." Those familiar with firearms quickly forgot what they knew and learned the Marine Corps' way.

Second only to accuracy was safety. Its principles were pounded into us mercilessly. "*Keep* the piece pointed toward the target. *Never* point a rifle at anything you don't intend to shoot. *Check* your rifle *each* time you pick it up to be sure it isn't loaded. Many *accidents* have occurred with 'unloaded' rifles."

We went onto the firing line and received live ammunition the next week. At first, the sound of rifles firing was disconcerting. But not for long. Our snapping-in had been so thorough, we went through our paces automatically. We fired at round black bull's-eye targets from 100, 300, and 500 yards. Other platoons worked the "butts."* When the range officer ordered, "Ready on the right, ready on the left, all ready on the firing line, commence firing," I felt as though the rifle was part of me and vice versa. My concentration was complete.

Discipline was ever present, but the harassment that had been our daily diet gave way to deadly serious, businesslike instruction in marksmanship. Punishment for infractions of the rules came swiftly and severely, however. One man next to me turned around slightly to speak to a buddy after "cease firing" was given; the action caused his rifle muzzle to angle

---

*"Butts" refers to the impact area on a rifle range. It consists of the targets mounted on a vertical track system above a sheltered dugout, usually made of concrete, in which other shooters operate, mark, and score the targets for those on the firing line.

away from the targets. The sharp-eyed captain in charge of the range rushed up from behind and booted the man in the rear so hard that he fell flat on his face. The captain then jerked him up off the deck and bawled him out loudly and thoroughly. We got his message.

Platoon 984 took its turn in the butts. As we sat safely in the dugouts and waited for each series of firing to be completed, I had somber thoughts about the crack and snap of bullets passing overhead.

Qualification day dawned clearly and brightly. We were apprehensive, having been told that anyone who didn't shoot high enough to qualify as "marksman" wouldn't go overseas. When the final scores were totaled, I was disappointed. I fell short of "expert rifleman" by only two points. However, I proudly wore the Maltese Cross–shaped sharpshooter's badge. And I didn't neglect to point out to my Yankee buddies that most of the high shooters in our platoon were Southern boys.

Feeling like old salts, we returned to the recruit depot for the final phases of recruit training. The DIs didn't treat us as veterans, though; harassment picked up quickly to its previous intensity.

By the end of eight grueling weeks, it had become apparent that Corporal Doherty and the other DIs had done their jobs well. We were hard physically, had developed endurance, and had learned our lessons. Perhaps more important, we were tough mentally. One of our assistant drill instructors even allowed himself to mumble that we might become Marines after all.

Finally, late in the afternoon of 24 December 1943, we fell in without rifles and cartridge belts. Dressed in service greens, each man received three bronze Marine Corps globe-and-anchor emblems, which we put into our pockets. We marched to an amphitheater where we sat with several other platoons.

This was our graduation from boot camp. A short, affable-looking major standing on the stage said, "Men, you have successfully completed your recruit training and are now United States Marines. Put on your Marine Corps emblems and wear them with pride. You have a great and proud tradition to uphold. You are members of the world's finest fighting outfit, so be worthy of it." We took out our emblems and put one on each lapel of our green wool coats and one on the left side of the overseas caps. The major told several dirty jokes. Everyone laughed and whistled. Then he said, "Good luck, men." That was the first time we had been addressed as men during our entire time in boot camp.

Before dawn the next day, Platoon 984 assembled in front of the huts for the last time. We shouldered our seabags, slung our rifles, and struggled down to a warehouse where a line of trucks was parked. Corporal Doherty told us that each man was to report to the designated truck as his name and destination was called out. The few men selected to train as specialists (radar technicians, aircraft mechanics, etc.) were to turn in their rifles, bayonets, and cartridge belts.

As the men moved out of ranks, there were quiet remarks of, "So long, see you, take it easy." We knew that many friendships were ending right there. Doherty called out, "Eugene B. Sledge, 534559, full individual equipment and M1 rifle, infantry, Camp Elliott."

Most of us were designated for infantry, and we went to Camp Elliott or to Camp Pendleton.* As we helped each other aboard the trucks, it never occurred to us why so many were being assigned to infantry. We were destined to take the places of the ever mounting numbers of casualties in the rifle or line companies in the Pacific. We were fated to fight the war first hand. We were cannon fodder.

After all assignments had been made, the trucks rolled out, and I looked at Doherty watching us leave. I disliked him, but I respected him. He had made us Marines, and I wondered what he thought as we rolled by.

---

*Camp Elliott was a small installation located on the northern outskirts of San Diego. It has been used rarely since World War II. Thirty-five miles north of San Diego lies Camp Joseph H. Pendleton. Home today of the 1st Marine Division, it is the Marine Corps' major west coast amphibious base.

CHAPTER TWO

Preparation for Combat

INFANTRY TRAINING

Most of the buildings at Camp Elliott were neat wooden barracks painted cream with dark roofs. The typical two-story barracks was shaped like an H, with the squad bays in the upright parts of the letter. The many-windowed squad bays held about twenty-five double-decker metal bunks. The room was big, roomy, and well lighted. The ensuing two months were the only period during my entire service in World War II that I lived in a barracks. The remaining time I slept under canvas or the open sky.

No one yelled at us or screamed orders to hurry up. The NCOs seemed relaxed to the point of being lethargic. We had the free run of the camp except for certain restricted areas. Taps and lights-out were at 2200. We were like birds out of a cage after the confinement and harassment of boot camp. With several boys who bunked near me, I sampled the draft beer at the slop chute (enlisted men's club), bought candy and ice cream at the PX (post exchange), and explored the area. Our newly found freedom was heady stuff.

We spent the first few days at Camp Elliott at lectures and demonstrations dealing with the various weapons in a Marine infantry regiment. We received an introduction to the 37mm antitank gun, 81mm mortar, 60mm mortar, .50 caliber machine gun, .30 caliber heavy and light machine guns, and the Browning Automatic Rifle (BAR). We also ran through combat tactics for the rifle squad. Most of our conversation around the barracks concerned the various weapons and whether or not it would be "good duty" to be on a 37mm gun crew, light machine gun or 81mm mortar. There was always one man, frequently—in fact, usually—a New Englander who knew it all and claimed to have the latest hot dope on everything.

"I talked to a guy over at the PX who had been through 81mm mortar school, and he said them damn mortars are so heavy he wished to hell he had gotten into 37mm guns so he could ride in a jeep while it pulled the gun."

"I talked to a guy over at Camp Pendleton, and he said a mortar shell blew up over there just as it was fired and killed the instructor and all the crew. I'm getting into light machine guns; they say that's a good deal."

"Like hell. My uncle was in France in World War I, and he said the average life of a machine gunner was about two minutes. I'm gonna be a rifleman, so I won't have to tote all that weight around."

So it went. None of us had the slightest idea what he was talking about.

One day we fell in and were told to separate into groups according to which weapon we wanted to train with. If our first choice was filled, we made a second selection. The mere fact that we had a choice amazed me. Apparently the idea was that a man would be more effective on a weapon he had picked rather than one to which he had been assigned. I chose 60mm mortars.

The first morning, those in 60mm mortars marched behind a warehouse where several light tanks were parked. Our mortar instructor, a sergeant, told us to sit down and listen to what he had to say. He was a clean-cut, handsome blond man wearing neat khakis faded to just that right shade that indicated a "salty" uniform. His bearing oozed calm self-confidence. There was no arrogance or bluster about him, yet he was obviously a man who knew himself and his job and would put up with no nonsense from anybody. He had an intangible air of subdued, quiet detachment, a quality possessed by so many of the combat veterans of the Pacific campaigns whom I met at that time. Sometimes his mind seemed a million miles away, as though lost in some sort of melancholy reverie. It was a genuine attribute, unrehearsed and spontaneous. In short, it couldn't be imitated consciously. I noted this carefully in my early days in the Marine Corps but never understood it until I observed the same thing in my buddies after Peleliu.

One man raised his hand, and the sergeant said, "OK, what's your question?"

The man began with, "Sir." The sergeant laughed and said, "Address me as sergeant, not sir."

"Yes, sir."

"Look, you guys are U.S. Marines now. You are not in boot camp anymore. Just relax, work hard, and do your job right, and you won't have any trouble. You'll have a better chance of getting through the war." He won our respect and admiration instantly.

"My job is to train you people to be 60mm mortarmen. The 60mm mortar is an effective and important infantry weapon. You can break up enemy attacks on your company's front with this weapon, and you can soften enemy defenses with it. You will be firing over the heads of your own buddies at the enemy a short distance away, so you've got to know exactly what you're doing. Otherwise there'll be short rounds and you'll kill and wound your own men. I was a 60mm mortarman on Guadalcanal and saw how effective this weapon was against the Japs there. Any questions?"

On the chilly January morning of our first lesson in mortars, we sat on the deck under a bright sky and listened attentively to our instructor.

"The 60mm mortar is a smoothbore, muzzle-loaded, high-angle-fire weapon. The assembled gun weighs approximately forty-five pounds and consists of the tube—or barrel—bipod, and base plate. Two or sometimes three 60mm mortars are in each rifle company. Mortars have a high angle of fire and are particularly effective against enemy troops taking cover in defilades or behind ridges where they are protected from our artillery. The Japs have mortars and know how to use 'em, too. They will be particularly anxious to knock out our mortars and machine guns because of the damage these weapons can inflict on their troops."

The sergeant then went over the nomenclature of the gun.

He demonstrated the movements of gun drill, during which the bipod was unstrapped and unfolded from carrying position, the base plate set firmly on the deck, the bipod leg spikes pressed into the deck, and the sight snapped into place on the gun. We were divided into five-man squads and practiced these evolutions until each man could perform them smoothly. During subsequent lessons he instructed us in the intricacies of the sight with its cross-level and longitudinal-level bubbles and on how to lay the gun and sight it on an aiming stake lined up with a target. We spent hours learning how to take a compass reading on a target area, then place a stake in front of the gun to correspond to that reading.

Each squad competed fiercely to be the fastest and most precise in gun drill. When my turn came to act as number one gunner, I would race to the position, unsling the mortar from my right shoulder, set it up, sight in on the base stake, remove my hands from it and yell, "Ready." The sergeant would check his stopwatch and give the time. Many shouts of encouragement came from a gunner's squad urging each man on. Each of us rotated as number one gunner, as number two gunner (who dropped the shells into the tube at number one's command), and as ammo carriers.

We were drilled thoroughly but were quite nervous about handling live ammunition for the first time. We fired at empty oil drums set on a dry hillside. There were no mishaps. When I saw the first shell burst with a dull *bang* about two hundred yards out on the range, I suddenly realized what a deadly weapon we were dealing with. A cloud of black smoke appeared at the point of impact. Flying steel fragments kicked up little puffs of dust all around an area about nine by eighteen yards. When three shells were fired from one weapon, the bursts covered an area about thirty-five by thirty-five yards with flying fragments.

"Boy, I'd pity any Jap that had all that shrapnel flying around him," murmured one of my more thoughtful buddies.

"Yeah, it'll tear their asses up all right. But don't forget they're gonna be throwing stuff at you just as fast as they can," said the mortar sergeant.

This, I realized, was the difference between war and hunting. When I survived the former, I gave up the latter.

We also received training in hand-to-hand combat. This consisted mostly of judo and knife fighting. To impress us with the effectiveness of his subject, the judo instructor methodically slammed each of us to the ground as we tried to rush him.

"What good is this kind of fighting gonna do us if the Japs can pick us off with machine guns and artillery at five hundred yards?" someone asked.

"When dark comes in the Pacific," the instructor replied, "the Japs always send men into our positions to try to infiltrate the lines or just to see how many American throats they can slit. They are tough and they like close-in fighting. You can handle them, but you've got to know how." Needless to say, we paid close attention from then on.

"Don't hesitate to fight the Japs dirty. Most Americans, from the time they are kids, are taught not to hit below the belt. It's not sportsmanlike. Well, nobody has taught the Japs that, and war ain't sport. Kick him in the balls before he kicks you in yours," growled our instructor.

We were introduced to the Marine's foxhole companion, the Ka-Bar knife. This deadly piece of cutlery was manufactured by the company bearing its name. The knife was a foot long with a seven-inch-long by one-and-a-half-inch-wide blade. The five-inch handle was made of leather washers packed together and had "USMC" stamped on the blade side of the upper hand guard. Light for its size, the knife was beautifully balanced.

"Everybody has heard a lot about all those kinds of fancy fighting knives that are, or should be, carried by infantry troops: throwing knives, stilettos, daggers, and all that stuff. Most of it is nothing but bull. Sure, you'll probably open more cans of C rations than Japs with this knife, but if a Jap ever jumps in your hole, you're better off with a Ka-Bar than any other knife. It's the very best and it's rugged, too. If you guys were gonna fight Germans, I'd guess you'd never need a fighting knife, but with the Japs it's different. I guarantee that you or the man in the next foxhole will use a Ka-Bar on a Jap infiltrator before the war is over." He was right.*

All of our instructors at Camp Elliott did a professional job. They presented us with the material and made it clear that our chances of surviving the war depended to a great extent on how well we learned. As teachers they had no problem with student motivation.

But I don't recall that anyone really comprehended what was happening outside our own training routine. Maybe it was the naive optimism of youth, but the awesome reality that we were training to be cannon fodder in a global war that had already snuffed out millions of lives never seemed to occur to us. The fact that our lives might end violently or that we might be crippled while we were still boys didn't seem to register. The only thing that we seemed to be truly concerned about was that we might be too afraid to do our jobs under fire. An apprehension nagged at each of us that he might appear to be "yellow" if he were afraid.

One afternoon two veterans of the Bougainville campaign dropped into my barracks to chat with some of us. They had been members of the Marine raider battalion that had fought so well along with the 3d Marine Division on Bougainville. They were the first veterans we had met other than our instructors. We swamped them with questions.

"Were you scared?" asked one of my buddies.

"Scared! Are you kiddin'? I was so goddamn scared the first time I heard slugs coming at me I could hardly hold on to my rifle," came the reply.

The other veteran said, "Listen, mate, everybody gets scared, and anybody says he don't is a damn liar." We felt better.

The mortar school continued during my entire stay at Camp Elliott. Swimming tests were the last phase of special training we received before embarking for the Pacific. Mercifully, in January 1944 we couldn't foresee the events of au-

---

*The U.S. Marine Corps still uses Ka-Bar's fine fighting knife. The manufacturer's name now has become to Marines a noun (*kabar*) meaning their fighting knife.

tumn. We trained with enthusiasm and the faith that the battles we were destined to fight would be necessary to win the war.

Earlier, on 20-23 November 1943, the 2d Marine Division carried out its memorable assault on the coral atoll of Tarawa in the Gilbert Islands. Many military historians and others consider the battle for Tarawa as the first modern head-on amphibious assault.

A coral reef extended out about five hundred yards and surrounded the atoll. Tarawa was subject to unpredictable dodging tides that sometimes lowered water levels and caused Higgins boats (LCVP: Landing Craft, Vehicle and Personnel) to strand on the reef.

Plans called for the use of amphibian tractors (LVTs: Landing Vehicles, Tracked; now called assault amphibians) to carry the troops across the reef. But only enough amtracs existed to take in the first three waves. After the first three assault waves got ashore in amtracs, the supporting waves had to wade across the reef through murderous Japanese fire, because their Higgins boats hung up at the reef's edge.

The 2d Division suffered terrible losses—3,381 dead and wounded. Its Marines killed all but seventeen of the 4,836 Japanese defenders of the tiny atoll.

There was loud and severe criticism of the Marine Corps by the American public and some military leaders because of the number of casualties. Tarawa became a household word in the United States. It took its rightful place with Valley Forge, the Alamo, Belleau Wood, and Guadalcanal as a symbol of American courage and sacrifice.

The young Marines at Camp Elliott didn't have the remotest idea that in about nine months they would participate as part of the 1st Marine Division in the assault on Peleliu. That battle would prove to be so vicious and costly that the division's losses would just about double those of the 2d Marine Division at Tarawa. To add tragedy to its horror, hindsight would show that the seizure of Peleliu was of questionable necessity. As more than one Marine historian has said, it's unfortunate to the memory of the men who fought and died on

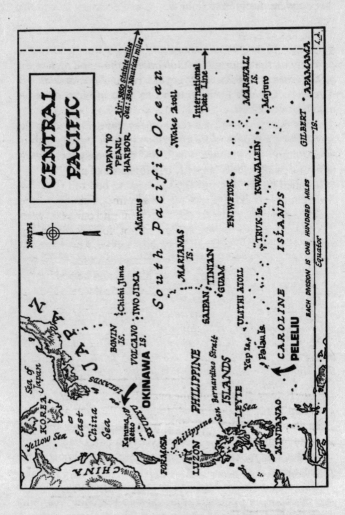

Peleliu that it remains one of the lesser known and poorly understood battles of World War II.

OVERSEAS AT LAST

Early on the morning of 28 February 1944, the men of the 46th Replacement Battalion got off trucks at dockside in San Diego Harbor and lined up to board a troopship that would take us to the Pacific. The *President Polk* had been a luxury liner of the President Line during peacetime. Painted battleship gray, the ship now looked gloomy and ominous with its antiaircraft guns and life rafts. I had the uneasy feeling that this was going to be a one-way trip for some of us.

Loaded down with full transport pack, bed roll (mattress with canvas cover), M1 carbine, and helmet, I struggled up a steep gangplank. Once on deck we went into our troop compartment one deck below. A blast of hot, foul air hit me as I entered the hatch and started down the ladder. About halfway down, the man in front of me slipped and clattered to the bottom. We were all concerned about his fall and helped him up and into his gear again. Later such an incident would elicit almost nothing but a casual glance and a quick helping hand.

We stood crowded in the compartment and waited for what seemed like hours for an officer to check the muster roll and assign each of us to a sack or rack (bunk). Each sack consisted of canvas laced onto a pipe frame hinged to metal uprights, head and foot, extending from deck to the overhead. Chains held each rack onto the ones above and below.

When I crawled onto mine, I realized the rack above was only about two feet away. With mattress unrolled and gear laid out, a man barely had room to stretch out. I had to climb up about four racks to get to mine, which was almost at the highest level.

Dim electric bulbs overhead gave us barely enough light to see. As soon as I could, I went topside searching for relief from the foul, crowded compartment. The deck was jammed, too, but the air was fresh.

Many of us were too excited to sleep, so we explored the

ship for hours, talked to the crewmen, or watched the completion of loading. Finally, around midnight, 1 went below and climbed into my rack. Several hours later I awoke to the vibration of the ship's engine. I pulled on my boondockers and dungaree pants and jacket and raced topside, filled with apprehension and excitement. It was about 0500. The deck was crowded with other Marines subdued by the realization that each turn of the ship's screws would take us farther from home and closer to the unknown.

Harsh questions raced through my mind. Would I ever see my family again? Would I do my duty or be a coward? Could I kill? Fantasy captivated me in the brief period. Maybe I'd be put into a rear-echelon outfit and never see a Japanese. Maybe I'd be an infantryman and disgrace my outfit by running away from the enemy. Or, maybe I'd kill dozens of Japanese and win a Navy Cross or Silver Star and be a national hero.

The tension finally broke as we watched the sailors rushing about casting off hawsers and lines, preparing the ship for the open sea.

The *President Polk* moved on a zigzag course toward a destination unknown to those of us sweltering in her bowels. Our daily routine was dull, even for those like myself who rather enjoyed being aboard a ship. We rolled out of our racks each morning about sunrise. Brushing my teeth and shaving with nonlathering shaving cream was my morning toilet. Each day an officer or NCO led us through an exercise period of calisthenics. And we could always count on a rifle inspection. Other than that, we had practically no duties.

Every few days we had abandon-ship drills, which helped offset the boredom. And the ship's crew conducted gun drills frequently. The first time they held target practice with live ammunition was exciting to watch. Yellow balloons were released from the bridge. As they were caught by the wind, the gunners opened fire upon order from the fire control officer. The rapid-fire 20mm and 40mm antiaircraft guns seemed to do an effective job. But to some of us Marines, the 3-inch and 5-inch cannons didn't accomplish much other than hurt our ears. Considering the number of balloons that escaped, we felt the gun crews should have practiced more. This was probably because none of us had ever had any experience with antiaircraft guns and didn't realize what a difficult type of gunnery was involved.

Beyond some letter writing and a lot of conversation— so-called bull sessions—we spent much of our time waiting in chow lines strung along gangways and passages leading to the ship's galley. Chow was an unforgettable experience. After the inevitable wait in line, I entered the hatch leading to the galley and was met with a blast of hot air laden with a new set of odors differing only slightly from the typical troop compartment aroma. To the same basic ingredients (paint, grease, tobacco, and sweat) were added the smells of rancid cooking and something of a bakery. It was enough to turn a civilian's stomach inside out, but we rapidly and necessarily adjusted.

We moved along the cafeteria-style line and indicated to sweating navy messmen what foods we wanted served onto shining compartmentalized steel trays. The messmen wore Skivvy shirts and were tattooed profusely on their arms. They all mopped the sweat from their faces constantly. Amid the roar of ventilators, we ate standing at long folding tables. Everything was hot to the touch but quite clean. A sailor told me that the tables had been used as operating tables for Marine casualties that the ship took on during one of the earlier Pacific campaigns. That gave me a strange feeling in the pit of my stomach every time I went to chow on the *President Polk.*

The heat was intense—at least 100 degrees—but I gulped down a cup of hot "joe" (black coffee), the stuff that replaced bread as the staff of life for Marines and sailors. I grimaced as the dehydrated potatoes battered my taste buds with an unsavory aftertaste characteristic of all World War II–vintage dehydrated foods. The bread was a shock—heavy, and with a flavor that was a combination of bitterness, sweetness, and uncooked flour. No wonder hot joe had replaced it as the staff of life!

After chow in the steaming galley, we went topside to cool

off. Everyone was soaked with sweat. It would have been a relief to eat on deck, but we were forbidden to take chow out of the galley.

One day, as we moved along some nameless companionway in a chow line, I passed a porthole that gave me a view into the officers' mess. There I saw Navy and Marine officers clad neatly in starched khakis sitting at tables in a well-ventilated room. White-coated waiters served them pie and ice cream. As we inched along the hot companionway to our steaming joe and dehydrated fare, I wondered if my haste to leave the V-12 college life hadn't been a mistake. After all, it would have been nice to have been declared a gentleman by Congress and to have lived like a human being aboard ship. To my immense satisfaction, however, I discovered later that such niceties and privileges of rank were few on the front lines.

During the morning of 17 March we looked out across the bow and saw a line of white breakers on the horizon. The Great Barrier Reef extends for thousands of miles, and we were to pass through it to New Caledonia. As we neared the reef, we saw several hulks of wooden ships stranded high and dry, apparently blown there years ago by some storm.

As we closed on the harbor of Noumea, we saw a small motor launch head our way. The *Polk* signaled with flags and blinker lights to this pilot boat, which soon pulled alongside. The pilot climbed a ladder and boarded the ship. All sorts of nautical protocol and mutual greetings between him and the ship's officers ensued as he went to the bridge to guide us in. This man was a middle-aged, pleasant-looking civilian dressed in a neat white Panama suit, straw hat, and black tie. Surrounded by sailors in blue denim and ship's officers in khaki, he looked like a fictional character out of some long-forgotten era.

The blue water of the Pacific turned to green as we passed into the channel leading into the harbor of Noumea. There was a pretty white lighthouse near the harbor. White houses with tile roofs nestled around it and up the base of slopes of high mountains. The scene reminded me of a photo of some picturesque little Mediterranean seaport.

The *President Polk* moved slowly through the harbor as the speaker system ordered a special sea detail to stand by. We tied up to a dock with long warehouses where United States military personnel were moving crates and equipment. Most of the shipping I saw was U.S. Navy, but there also were some American and foreign merchant freighters along with a few quaint-looking civilian fishing boats.

The first Pacific native I saw wasn't dressed in a hula skirt or waving a spear but nonchalantly driving a freight-moving tractor on the dock. He was a short muscular man—black as ink—clad only in a loin cloth with a bone in his nose and a bushy head of kinky hair like a Fuzzy Wuzzy out of a Kipling story. The incredible thing about this hair was its color, beautiful amber. A sailor explained that the natives were fond of bleaching their hair with blueing they got from Americans in exchange for seashells. Bone in the nose notwithstanding, the man was an admirable tractor driver.

NEW CALEDONIA

After weeks at sea, cramped into a troopship, we were relieved to move onto land again. We piled into Marine Corps trucks and drove through the main section of Noumea. I was delighted to see the old French architecture, which reminded me of the older sections of Mobile and New Orleans.

The trucks sped along a winding road with mountains on each side. We saw small farms and a large nickel mine in the valley. Some of the land was cleared, but thick jungle covered much of the low areas. Although the weather was pleasant and cool, the palms and other growth attested to the tropical climate. After several miles we turned into Camp Saint Louis, where we would undergo further training before being sent "up north" to the combat zone as replacements.

Camp Saint Louis was a tent camp comprised of rows of tents and dirt streets. We were assigned to tents, stowed our gear, and fell in for chow. The galley rested on a hill just past the camp's brig. In full view were two wire cages about the size of phone booths. We were told that those who caused trouble were locked in there, and a high-pressure fire hose was turned on them periodically. The strictness of discipline at Camp Saint Louis caused me to assume the explanation of the cages was true. In any event, I resolved to stay out of trouble.

Our training consisted of lectures and field exercises. Combat veteran officers and NCOs lectured on Japanese weapons, tactics, and combat methods. Most of the training was thorough and emphasized individual attention. We worked in groups of ten or twelve.

I usually was placed in a squad instructed by a big red-headed corporal who had been in a Marine raider battalion during the fighting in the Solomon Islands. Big Red was good-natured but tough as nails. He worked us hard. One day he took us to a small rifle range and taught us how to fire a Japanese pistol, rifle, and heavy and light machine guns. After firing a few rounds from each, Red put about five of us into a pit about five feet deep with a one-foot embankment in front and the steep slope of a ridge behind as a backstop.

"One important thing you must learn fast to survive is exactly what enemy fire sounds like coming at you and what kind of weapon it is. Now when I blow this whistle, get down and stay down until you hear the whistle again. If you get up before the signal, you'll get your head blowed off, and the folks back home will get your insurance."

Red blew the whistle and we got down. He announced each type of Japanese weapon and fired several rounds from it over our hole into the bank. Then he and his assistants fired them all together for about fifteen seconds. It seemed a lot longer. The bullets popped and snapped as they went over. Several machine-gun tracers didn't embed in the bank but bounced off and rolled—white-hot, sizzling, and sputtering—into the hole. We cringed and shifted about, but no one got burned.

 This was one of the most valuable training exercises we underwent. There were instances later on Peleliu and Okinawa which it prepared me to come through unscathed.

A salty sergeant conducted bayonet training. He had been

written about in a national magazine because he was so outstanding. On the cinder-covered street of an old raider camp, I witnessed some amazing feats by him. He instructed us in how to defend ourselves barehanded against an opponent's bayonet thrust.

"Here's how it's done," he said.

He picked me out of the squad and told me to charge him and thrust the point of my bayonet at his chest when I thought I could stick him. I got a mental image of myself behind bars at Mare Island Naval Prison for bayoneting an instructor, so I veered off just before making my thrust.

"What the hell's the matter with you? Don't you know how to use a bayonet?"

"But, Sarge, if I stick you, they'll put me in Mare Island."

"There's less chance of you bayoneting me than of me whipping your ass for not following my orders."

"OK," I thought to myself, "if that's the way you feel about it, we have witnesses."

So I headed for him on the double and thrust at his chest. He sidestepped neatly, grabbed my rifle behind the front sight, and jerked it in the direction I was running. I held on to the rifle and tumbled onto the cinders. The squad roared with laughter. Someone yelled, "Did you bayonet him, Sledgehammer?" I got up looking sheepish.

"Knock it off, wise guy," said the instructor. "You step up here, and let's see what you can do, big mouth."

My buddy lifted his rifle confidently, charged, and ended up on the cinders, too. The instructor made each man charge him in turn. He threw them all.

He then took up a Japanese Arisaka rifle with fixed bayonet and showed us how the Japanese soldiers used the hooked hand guard to lock on to the U.S. blade. Then, with a slight twist of his wrist, he could wrench the M1 rifle out of the opponent's hands and disarm him. He coached us carefully to hold the M1 on its side with the left side of the blade toward the deck instead of the cutting edge, as we had been taught in the States. This way, as we parried a Japanese's blade, he couldn't lock ours.

We went on long hikes and forced marches through the

jungles, swamps, and over endless steep hills. We made countless practice landings from Higgins boats on small islets off the coast. Each morning after chow we marched out of camp equipped with rifles, cartridge belts, two canteens of water, combat pack, helmet, and K rations. Our usual pace was a rapid route step for fifty minutes with a ten-minute rest. But the officers and NCOs always hurried us and frequently deleted the ten-minute rest.

When trucks drove along the road, we moved onto the sides, as columns of infantry have done since early times. The trucks frequently carried army troops, and we barked and yapped like dogs and kidded them about being dogfaces. During one of these encounters, a soldier hanging out of a truck just ahead of me shouted, "Hey, soldier. You look tired and hot, soldier. Why don't you make the army issue you a truck like me?"

I grinned and yelled, "Go to hell."

His buddy grabbed him by the shoulder and yelled, "Stop calling that guy soldier. He's a Marine. Can't you see his emblem? He's not in the army. Don't insult him."

"Thanks," I yelled. That was my first encounter with men who had no esprit. We might grumble to each other about our officers or the chow or the Marine Corps in general, but it was rather like grumbling about one's own family—always with another member. If an outsider tried to get into the discussion, a fight resulted.

One night during exercises in defense against enemy infiltration, some of the boys located the bivouac of Big Red and the other instructors who were supposed to be the infiltrators and stole their boondockers. When the time came for their offense to commence, they threw a few concussion grenades around and yelled like Japanese but didn't slip out and capture any of us. When the officers realized what had happened, they reamed out the instructors for being too sure of themselves. The instructors had a big fire built in a ravine. We sat around it, drank coffee, ate K rations, and sang some songs. It didn't seem like such a bad war so far.

All of our training was in rifle tactics. We spent no time on heavy weapons (mortars and machine guns), because when we went "up north" our unit commander would assign us where needed. That might not be in our specialties. As a result of the field exercises and obstacle course work, we reached a high level of physical fitness and endurance.

During the last week of May we learned that the 46th Replacement Battalion would go north in a few days. We packed our gear and boarded the USS *General Howze* on 28 May 1944. This ship was quite different from the *President Polk*. It was much newer and apparently had been constructed as a troopship. It was freshly painted throughout and spic and span. With only about a dozen other men, I was assigned to a small, well-ventilated compartment on the main deck, a far cry from the cavernous, stinking hole I bunked in on the *Polk*. The *General Howze* had a library from which troop passengers could get books and magazines. We also received our first atabrine tablets. These small, bitter, bright yellow pills prevented malaria. We took one a day.

On 2 June the *General Howze* approached the Russell Islands and moved into an inlet bordered by large groves of coconut palms. The symmetrical groves and clear water were beautiful. From the ship we could see coral-covered roadways and groups of pyramidal tents among the coconut palms. This was Pavuvu, home of the 1st Marine Division.

We learned we would debark the next morning, so we spent our time hanging over the rail, talking to a few Marines on the pier. Their friendliness and unassuming manner struck me. Although clad neatly in khakis or dungarees, they appeared hollow-eyed and tired. They made no attempt to impress us green replacements, yet they were members of an elite division known to nearly everybody back home because of its conquest of Guadalcanal and more recent campaign at Cape Gloucester on New Britain. They had left Gloucester about 1 May. Thus, they had been on Pavuvu about a month.

Many of us slept little during the night. We checked and rechecked our gear, making sure everything was squared away. The weather was hot, much more so than at New Caledonia. I went out on deck and slept in the open air. With a mandolin and an old violin, two of our Marines struck up some of the finest mountain music I'd ever heard. They played and sang folk songs and ballads most of the night. We thought it was mighty wonderful music.

WITH THE OLD BREED

About 0900 the morning of 3 June 1944, carrying the usual mountain of gear, I trudged down the gangplank of the *General Howze*. As we moved to waiting trucks, we passed a line of veterans waiting to go aboard for the voyage home. They carried only packs and personal gear, no weapons. Some said they were glad to see us, because we were their replacements. They looked tanned and tired but relieved to be headed home. For them the war was over. For us, it was just beginning.

In a large parking area paved with crushed coral, a lieutenant called out our names and counted us off into groups. To my group of a hundred or more he said, "Third Battalion, Fifth Marines."

If I had had an option—and there was none, of course—as to which of the five Marine divisions I served with, it would have been the 1st Marine Division. Ultimately, the Marine Corps had six divisions that fought with distinction in the Pacific. But the 1st Marine Division was, in many ways, unique. It had participated in the opening American offensive against the Japanese at Guadalcanal and already had fought a second major battle at Cape Gloucester, north of the Solomon Islands. Now its troops were resting, preparing for a third campaign in the Palau Islands.

Of regiments, I would have chosen the 5th Marines. I knew about its impressive history as a part of the 1st Marine Division, but I also knew that its record went back to France in World War I. Other Marines I knew in other divisions were proud of their units and of being Marines, as well they should have been. But the 5th Marines and the 1st Marine Division carried not only the traditions of the Corps but had traditions and a heritage of their own, a link through time with the "Old Corps."

The fact that I was assigned to the very regiment and division I would have chosen was a matter of pure chance. I felt as though I had rolled the dice and won.*

The trucks drove along winding coral roads by the bay and through coconut groves. We stopped and unloaded our gear near a sign that said "3rd Bn., 5th Marines." An NCO assigned me to Company K. Soon a lieutenant came along and took aside the fifteen or so men who had received crew-served weapons training (mortars and machine guns) in the States. He asked each of us which weapon he wanted to be assigned to in the company. I asked for 60mm mortars and tried to look too small to carry a seventy-pound flamethrower. He assigned me to mortars, and I moved my gear into a tent that housed the second squad of the 60mm mortar section.

For the next several weeks I spent most of my time during the day on work parties building up the camp. The top sergeant of Company K, 1st Sergeant Malone, would come down the company street shouting, "All new men outside for a work party, on the double." Most of the time the company's veterans weren't included. Pavuvu was supposed to be a rest camp for them after the long, wet, debilitating jungle campaign on Cape Gloucester. When Malone needed a large work party he would call out, "I need every available man." So we referred to him as "Available" Malone.

None of us, old hands or replacements, could fathom why

---

*The history of the 5th Marines continued after World War II. The regiment fought in the Korean War and again in Vietnam. Thus it is the only Marine regiment to have fought in all of the nation's major wars in this century.

No Marine division fought in World War I. [The 5th and 6th Marine Regiments fought in France as part of the 2d Division (Regular) American Expeditionary Force (AEF), a mixed unit of Marine and Army brigades.] But the 1st Marine Division was the only Marine division to fight in Korea. Along with the 3d Marine Division, it also fought in Vietnam. It is, therefore, the sole Marine division to have fought in all of our major wars during the past sixty years.

Today the 5th Marines still forms a part of the 1st Marine Division. Stationed on the west coast, the division can deploy units for duty in the western Pacific.

the division command chose Pavuvu. Only after the war did I find out that the leaders were trying to avoid the kind of situation the 3d Marine Division endured when it went into camp on Guadalcanal after its campaign on Bougainville. Facilities on Guadalcanal, by then a large rear-area base, were reasonably good, but the high command ordered the 3d Division to furnish about a thousand men each day for working parties all over the island. Not only did the Bougainville veterans get little or no rest, but when replacements came, the division had difficulty carrying out its training schedule in preparation for the next campaign, Guam.

If Pavuvu seemed something less than a tropical paradise to us replacements fresh from the States and New Caledonia, it was a bitter shock to the Gloucester veterans.* When ships entered Macquitti Bay, as the *General Howze* had, Pavuvu looked picturesque. But once ashore, one found the extensive coconut groves choked with rotting coconuts. The apparently solid ground was soft and turned quickly to mud when subjected to foot or vehicular traffic.

Pavuvu was the classical embodiment of the Marine term "boondocks." It was impossible to explain after the war what life on Pavuvu was like. Most of the griping about being "rock happy" and bored in the Pacific came from men stationed at the big rear-echelon bases like Hawaii or New Caledonia. Among their main complaints were that the ice cream wasn't good, the beer not cold enough, or the USO shows too infrequent. But on Pavuvu, simply living was difficult.

For example, most of the work parties I went on in June and July were pick-and-shovel details to improve drainage or pave walkways with crushed coral, just to get us out of the water. Regulations called for wooden decks in all tents, but I never saw one on Pavuvu.

Of all the work parties, the one we hated most was collect-

---

*After Guadalcanal, the 1st Marine Division went to Melbourne, Australia, for rest and refitting for the New Britain campaign. When Cape Gloucester ended, the men assumed they were headed back to Australia. Instead they were dumped on a deserted island in the Russell Islands group, sixty miles from Guadalcanal.

ing rotten coconuts. We loaded them onto trucks to be dumped into a swamp. If we were lucky, the coconut sprout served as a handle. But more often, the thing fell apart, spilling stinking coconut milk over us.

We made sardonic, absurd jokes about the vital, essential, classified work we were doing for the war effort and about the profundity and wisdom of the orders we received. In short, we were becoming "Asiatic," a Marine Corps term denoting a singular type of eccentric behavior characteristic of men who had served too long in the Far East. I had done a good deal of complaining about Pavuvu's chow and general conditions during my first week there; one of the veterans in our company, who later became a close friend, told me in a restrained but matter-of-fact way that, until I had been in combat, there was really nothing to complain about. Things could be a good deal worse, he said, and advised me to shut up and quit whining. He shamed me thoroughly. But for the first weeks on Pavuvu, the stench of rotting coconuts permeated the air. We could even taste it in the drinking water. I'm still repulsed even today by the smell of fresh coconut.

The most loathsome vermin on Pavuvu were the land crabs. Their blue-black bodies were about the size of the palm of a man's hand, and bristles and spines covered their legs. These ugly creatures hid by day and roamed at night. Before putting on his boondockers each morning, every man in the 1st Marine Division shook his shoes to roust the land crabs. Many mornings I had one in each shoe and sometimes two. Periodically we reached the point of rage over these filthy things and chased them out from under boxes, seabags, and cots. We killed them with sticks, bayonets, and entrenching tools. After the action was over, we had to shovel them up and bury them, or a nauseating stench developed rapidly in the hot, humid air.

Each battalion had its own galley, but chow on Pavuvu consisted mainly of heated C rations: dehydrated eggs, dehydrated potatoes, and that detestable canned meat called Spam. The synthetic lemonade, so-called battery acid, that remained after chow was poured on the concrete slab deck of the galley to clean and bleach it. It did a nice job. As if hot C rations didn't get tedious week in and week out, we experienced a period of about four days when we were served oatmeal morning, noon, and night. Scuttlebutt was that the ship carrying our supplies had been sunk. Whatever the cause, our only relief from monotonous chow was tidbits in packages from home. The bread made by our bakers was so heavy that when you held a slice by one side, the rest of the slice broke away of its own weight. The flour was so massively infested with weevils that each slice of bread had more of the little beetles than there are seeds in a slice of rye bread. We became so inured to this sort of thing, however, that we ate the bread anyway; the wits said, "It's a good deal. Them beetles give you more meat in your diet."

We had no bathing facilities at first. Shaving each morning with a helmet full of water was simple enough, but a bath was another matter. Each afternoon when the inevitable tropical downpour commenced, we stripped and dashed into the company street, soap in hand. The trick was to lather, scrub, and rinse before the rain stopped. The weather was so capricious that the duration of a shower was impossible to estimate. Each downpour ended as abruptly as it had begun and never failed to leave at least one or more fully lathered, cursing Marines with no rinse water.

Morning sick call was another bizarre sight during the early days on Pavuvu. The Gloucester veterans were in poor physical condition after the wettest campaign in World War II, during which men endured soakings for weeks on end. When I first joined the company, I was appalled at their condition: most were thin, some emaciated, with jungle rot in their armpits and on their ankles and wrists. At sick call they paired off with a bottle of gentian violet and cotton swabs, stood naked in the grove, and painted each other's sores. So many of them needed attention that they had to treat each other under a doctor's supervision. Some had to cut their boondockers into sandals, because their feet were so infected with rot they could hardly walk. Needless to say, Pavuvu's hot, humid climate prolonged the healing process.

"I think the Marine Corps has forgotten where Pavuvu is," one man said.

"I think God has forgotten where Pavuvu is," came a reply.

"God couldn't forget because he made everything."

"Then I bet he wishes he could forget he made Pavuvu."

This exchange indicates the feeling of remoteness and desolation we felt on Pavuvu. On the big island bases, men had the feeling of activity around their units and contact through air and sea traffic with other bases and with the States. On Pavuvu we felt as though we were a million miles from not only home but from anything else that bespoke of civilization.

I believe we took in stride all of Pavuvu's discomforts and frustrations for two reasons. First, the division was an elite combat unit. Discipline was stern. Our esprit de corps ran high. Each man knew what to do and what was expected of him. All did their duty well, even while grumbling.

NCOs answered our complaining with, "Beat your gums. It's healthy." Or, "Whatta ya griping for? You volunteered for the Marine Corps, didn't ya? You're just gettin' what ya asked for."

No matter how irritating or uncomfortable things were on Pavuvu, things could always be worse. After all, there were no Japanese, no bursting shells, no snapping and whining bullets. And we slept on cots. Second, makeup of the division was young: about 80 percent were between the ages of eighteen and twenty-five; about half were under twenty-one when they came overseas. Well-disciplined young men can put up with a lot even though they don't like it; and we were a bunch of high-spirited boys proud of our unit.

But we had another motivating factor, as well: a passionate hatred for the Japanese burned through all Marines I knew. The fate of the Goettge patrol was the sort of thing that spawned such hatred.* One day as we piled stinking coconuts, a veteran Marine walked past and exchanged greetings with a couple of our "old men." One of our group asked us if we knew who he was.

---

*During the first week of the Guadalcanal campaign, the Marines captured a Japanese soldier who claimed some of his starving comrades west of the Matanikau River would surrender if the Marines would "liberate" them. With twenty-five picked men (scouts, intelligence specialists, a surgeon, and a linguist) from the division's headquarters and the 5th Marines, Col. Frank Goettge—the division's intelligence officer—went on a mission more humanitarian than military. The Japanese ambushed the patrol as it debarked from landing craft in the darkness. Only three Marines escaped.

"No, I never saw him," someone said.

"He's one of the three guys who escaped when the Goettge patrol got wiped out on Guadalcanal. He was lucky as hell."

"Why did the Japs ambush that patrol?" I asked naively.

A veteran looked at me with unbelief and said slowly and emphatically, "Because they're the meanest sonsabitches that ever lived."

The Goettge patrol incident plus such Japanese tactics as playing dead and then throwing a grenade—or playing wounded, calling for a corpsman, and then knifing the medic when he came—plus the sneak attack on Pearl Harbor, caused Marines to hate the Japanese intensely and to be reluctant to take prisoners.

The attitudes held toward the Japanese by noncombatants or even sailors or airmen often did not reflect the deep personal resentment felt by Marine infantrymen. Official histories and memoirs of Marine infantrymen written after the war rarely reflect that hatred. But at the time of battle, Marines felt it deeply, bitterly, and as certainly as danger itself. To deny this hatred or make light of it would be as much a lie as to deny or make light of the esprit de corps or the intense patriotism felt by the Marines with whom I served in the Pacific.

My experiences on Peleliu and Okinawa made me believe that the Japanese held mutual feelings for us. They were a fanatical enemy; that is to say, they believed in their cause with an intensity little understood by many postwar Americans—and possibly many Japanese, as well.

This collective attitude, Marine and Japanese, resulted in savage, ferocious fighting with no holds barred. This was not the dispassionate killing seen on other fronts or in other wars. This was a brutish, primitive hatred, as characteristic of the horror of war in the Pacific as the palm trees and the islands. To comprehend what the troops endured then and there, one must take into full account this aspect of the nature of the Marines' war.

Probably the biggest boost to our morale about this time on Pavuvu was the announcement that Bob Hope would come over from Banika and put on a show for us. Most of the men in the division crowded a big open area and cheered as a Piper Cub circled over us. The pilot switched off the engine briefly, while Jerry Colonna poked his head out of the plane and gave his famous yell, "Ye ow ow ow ow ow." We went wild with applause.

Bob Hope, Colonna, Frances Langford, and Patti Thomas put on a show on a little stage by the pier. Bob asked Jerry how he liked the trip over from Banika, and Jerry answered that it was "tough sledding." When asked why, he replied, "No snow." We thought it was the funniest thing we had ever heard. Patti gave several boys from the audience dancing lessons amid much grinning, cheering, and applause. Bob told many jokes and really boosted our spirits. It was the finest entertainment I ever saw overseas.*

Bob Hope's show remained the main topic of conversation as we got down to training in earnest for the coming campaign. Pavuvu was so small that most of our field exercises were of company size rather than battalion or regimental. Even so, we frequently got in the way of other units involved in their training exercises. It was funny to see a company move forward in combat formation through the groves and become intermingled with the rigid ranks of another company standing weapons inspection, the officers shouting orders to straighten things out.

We held numerous landing exercises—several times a week, it seemed—on the beaches and inlets around the island away from camp. We usually practiced from amtracs. The newest model had a tailgate that dropped as soon as the tractor was on the beach, allowing us to run out and deploy.

"Get off the beach fast. Get off the damned beach as fast as

*I renewed my acquaintance with Bob Hope last spring when he played in a charity golf tournament in Birmingham, Alabama. Earlier I had sent him copies of the *Marine Corps Gazette* (November and December 1979 and January 1980) that had serialized portions of my Peleliu story. He was enthusiastic about the account and remembered well the young Marines of the 1st Marine Division on Pavuvu. Despite a clamoring public on a hectic day in Birmingham, this most gracious man took the time to reminisce with me about the old breed.

you can and move inland. The Nips are going to plaster it with everything they've got, so your chances are better the sooner you move inland," shouted our officers and NCOs. We heard this over and over day after day. During each landing exercise, we would scramble out of our tractors, move inland about twenty-five yards, and then await orders to deploy and push forward.

The first wave of tractors landed rifle squads. The second wave landed more riflemen, machine gunners, bazooka gunners, flamethrowers, and 60mm mortar squads. Our second wave typically trailed about twenty-five yards behind the first as the machines churned through the water toward the beach. As soon as the first wave unloaded, its amtracs backed off, turned around, and headed past us out to sea to pick up supporting waves of infantry from Higgins boats circling offshore. It all worked nicely on Pavuvu. But there were no Japanese there.

In addition to landing exercises and field problems before Peleliu, we received refresher instructions and practice firing all small arms assigned to the company: M1 rifle, BAR, carbine, .45 caliber pistol, and Thompson submachine gun. We also learned how to operate a flamethrower.

During instruction with the flamethrower, we used a palm stump for a target. When my turn came, I shouldered the heavy tanks, held the nozzle in both hands, pointed at the stump about twenty-five yards away, and pressed the trigger. With a whoosh, a stream of red flame squirted out, and the nozzle bucked. The napalm hit the stump with a loud splattering noise. I felt the heat on my face. A cloud of black smoke rushed upward. The thought of turning loose hellfire from a hose nozzle as easily as I'd water a lawn back home sobered me. To shoot the enemy with bullets or kill him with shrapnel was one of the grim necessities of war, but to fry him to death was too gruesome to contemplate. I was to learn soon, however, that the Japanese couldn't be routed from their island defenses without it.

About this time I began to feel a deeper appreciation for the influence of the old breed on us newer Marines. Gunnery Sergeant Haney* provided a vivid example of their impact.

I had seen Haney around the company area but first noticed him in the shower one day because of the way he bathed. About a dozen naked, soapy replacements, including myself, stared in wide-eyed amazement and shuddered as Haney held his genitals in his left hand while scrubbing them with a GI brush the way one buffs a shoe. When you consider that the GI brush had stiff, tough, split-fiber bristles embedded in a stout wooden handle and was designed to scrub heavy canvas 782 (web) gear, dungarees, and even floors, Haney's method of bathing becomes truly impressive.

I first saw him exert his authority one day on a pistol range where he was in charge of safety. A new second lieutenant, a replacement like myself, was firing from the position I was to assume. As he fired his last round, another new officer behind me called to him. The lieutenant turned to answer with his pistol in his hand. Haney was sitting next to me on a coconut-log bench and hadn't uttered a word except for the usual firing range commands. When the lieutenant turned the pistol's muzzle away from the target, Haney reacted like a cat leaping on its prey. He scooped up a large handful of coral gravel and flung it squarely into the lieutenant's face. He shook his fist at the bewildered officer and gave him the worst bawling out I ever heard. Everyone along the firing line froze, officers as well as enlisted men. The offending officer, with his gold bars shining brightly on his collar, cleared his weapon, holstered

---

*Gunnery Sgt. Elmo M. Haney served with Company K, 3d Battalion, 5th Marines in France during World War I. Between the two world wars, he taught school in Arkansas for about four years, then rejoined the Marine Corps where he was assigned to his old unit. He fought on Guadalcanal and at Cape Gloucester with Company K. In the latter action he won a Silver Star for heroism when he "took care of some Japs by himself with a few hand grenades," as one Marine described the scene.

Haney was more than fifty years old when the 1st Marine Division assaulted Peleliu. Although a gunnery sergeant by rank, he held no official position in Company K's chain of command. In the field he seemed to be everywhere at once, correcting mistakes and helping out. He withdrew himself from the front lines on the second day of Peleliu, admitting sadly that he could no longer take the heat and the battle.

it, and took off rubbing his eyes and blushing visibly. Haney returned to his seat as though nothing had happened. Along the firing line, we thawed. Thereafter we were much more conscious of safety regulations.

Haney was about my size, at 135 pounds, with sandy crew-cut hair and a deep tan. He was lean, hard, and muscular. Although not broad-shouldered or well-proportioned, his torso reminded me of some anatomy sketch by Michelangelo: every muscle stood out in stark definition. He was slightly barrel-chested with muscles heaped up on the back of his shoulders so that he almost had a hump. Neither his arms nor his legs were large, but the muscles in them reminded me of steel bands. His face was small-featured with squinting eyes and looked as though it was covered with deeply tanned, wrinkled leather.

Haney was the only man I ever knew in the outfit who didn't seem to have a buddy. He wasn't a loner in the sense that he was sullen or unfriendly. He simply lived in a world all his own. I often felt that he didn't even see his surroundings; all he seemed to be aware of was his rifle, his bayonet, and his leggings. He was absolutely obsessed with wanting to bayonet the enemy.

We all cleaned our weapons daily, but Haney cleaned his M1 before muster, at noon chow, and after dismissal in the afternoon. It was a ritual. He would sit by himself, light a cigarette, fieldstrip his rifle, and meticulously clean every inch of it. Then he cleaned his bayonet. All the while he talked to himself quietly, grinned frequently, and puffed his cigarette down to a stump. When his rifle was cleaned he reassembled it, fixed his bayonet, and went through a few minutes of thrust, parry, and butt-stroke movements at thin air. Then Haney would light up another cigarette and sit quietly, talking to himself and grinning while awaiting orders. He carried out these proceedings as though totally unaware of the presence of the other 235 men of the company. He was like Robinson Crusoe on an island by himself.

To say that he was "Asiatic" would be to miss the point entirely. Haney transcended that condition. The company had many rugged individualists, characters, old salts, and men who were "Asiatic," but Haney was in a category by himself. I felt that he was not a man born of woman, but that God had issued him to the Marine Corps.

Despite his personal idiosyncracies, Haney inspired us youngsters in Company K. He provided us with a direct link to the "Old Corps." To us he *was* the old breed. We admired him—and we loved him.

Then there was Company K's commanding officer, Capt. "Ack Ack" Haldane.* Late one afternoon as we left the rifle range, a heavy rain set in. As we plodded along Pavuvu's muddy roads, slipping and sliding under the downpour, we began to feel that whoever was leading the column had taken a wrong turn and that we were lost. At dusk in the heavy rain, every road looked alike: a flooded trail cut deeply with ruts, bordered by towering palms, winding aimlessly through the gloom. As I struggled along feeling chilled and forlorn and trying to keep my balance in the mud, a big man came striding from the rear of the column. He walked with the ease of a pedestrian on a city sidewalk. As he pulled abreast of me, the man looked at me and said, "Lovely weather, isn't it, son?"

I grinned at Haldane and said, "Not exactly, sir." He recog-

---

*Capt. Andrew Allison Haldane, USMCR, was born 22 August 1917 in Lawrence, Massachusetts. He graduated from Bowdoin College, Brunswick, Maine, in 1941.

Captain Haldane served with the 1st Marine Division on Guadalcanal and was commanding officer of Company K at Cape Gloucester, where he won the Silver Star. During a five-day battle, he and his Marines repulsed five Japanese bayonet charges within one hour in the predawn darkness. He led Company K through most of the fight for Peleliu. On 12 October 1944, three days before the Marines came off the lines, he died in action. The Marines of Company K, and the rest of the division who knew him, suffered no greater loss during the entire war.

Bowdoin College annually honors the memory of Captain Haldane by presenting the Haldane Cup to the graduating senior who has displayed outstanding qualities of leadership and character. The cup was a gift from officers who had served with Captain Haldane in the Pacific. Among them was the late senator from Illinois, Paul Douglas, himself a member of the 5th Marines on Peleliu and Okinawa.

nized me as a replacement and asked how I liked the company. I told him I thought it was a fine outfit.

"You're a Southerner, aren't you?" he asked. I told him I was from Alabama. He wanted to know all about my family, home, and education. As we talked the gloom seemed to disappear, and I felt warm inside. Finally he told me it wouldn't rain forever, and we could get dry soon. He moved along the column talking to other men as he had to me. His sincere interest in each of us as a human being helped to dispel the feeling that we were just animals training to fight.

Acclaimed by superiors and subordinates alike for his leadership abilities, Captain Haldane was the finest and most popular officer I ever knew. All of the Marines in Company K shared my feelings. Called the "skipper," he had a strong face full of character, a large, prominent jaw, and the kindest eyes I ever saw. No matter how often he shaved or how hard he tried, he always had a five o'clock shadow. He was so large that the combat pack on his back reminded me of the bulge of his wallet, while mine covered me from neck to waist.

Although he insisted on strict discipline, the captain was a quiet man who gave orders without shouting. He had a rare combination of intelligence, courage, self-confidence, and compassion that commanded our respect and admiration. We were thankful that Ack Ack was our skipper, felt more secure in it, and felt sorry for other companies not so fortunate. While some officers on Pavuvu thought it necessary to strut or order us around to impress us with their status, Haldane quietly told us what to do. We loved him for it and did the best job we knew how.

Our level of training rose in August and so did the intensity of "chicken" discipline. We suffered through an increasing number of weapons and equipment inspections, work parties, and petty cleanup details around the camp. The step-up in harassment, coupled with the constant discomforts and harsh living conditions of Pavuvu, drove us all into a state of intense exasperation and disgust with our existence before we embarked for Peleliu.

"I used to think the lieutenant was a pretty good joe, but damned if I ain't about decided he ain't nothin' but a hoss's ass," grumbled one Marine.

"You said that right, ole buddy," came back another.

"Hell, he ain't the only one that's gone crazy over insisting that everything be just so, and then bawlin' us out if it ain't. The gunny's mean as hell, and nothin' suits him anymore," responded yet another man.

"Don't let it get you down, boys. It's just part of the USMC plan for keeping the troops in fighting shape," calmly remarked a philosophical old salt of prewar service.

"What the hell you talking about?" snapped an irritated listener.

"Well, it's this way," answered the philosopher. "If they get us mad enough, they figure we'll take it out on the Nips when we hit this beach coming up. I saw it happen before Guadalcanal and Gloucester. They don't pull this kind of stuff on rear-echelon boys. They want us to be mean, mad, and malicious. That's straight dope, I'm telling you. I've seen it happen every time before we go on a campaign."

"Sounds logical. You may be right. But what's malicious?" someone said.

"Forget it, you nitwit," the philosopher growled.

"Right or not, I'm sure tired of Pavuvu," I said.

"That's the plan, Sledgehammer. Get you fed up with Pavuvu, or wherever the hell you happen to be, and you'll be hot to go anywhere else even if the Nips are there waiting for you," the philosopher said.

We fell silent, thinking about that and finally concluded he was right. Many of the more thoughtful men I knew shared his view.

I griped as loudly as anyone about our living conditions and discipline. In retrospect, however, I doubt seriously whether I could have coped with the psychological and physical shock and stress encountered on Peleliu and Okinawa had it been otherwise. The Japanese fought to win. It was a savage, brutal, inhumane, exhausting, and dirty business. Our commanders knew that if we were to win and survive, we must be trained realistically for it whether we liked it or not.*

---

*In the postwar years, the Marine Corps came in for a great deal of undeserved criticism, in my opinion, from well-meaning persons who did not comprehend the magnitude of stress and horror that combat can be. The technology that developed the rifled barrel, the machine gun, and high-explosive shells has turned war into prolonged, subhuman slaughter. Men must be trained realistically if they are to survive it without breaking mentally and physically.

CHAPTER THREE

On to Peleliu

In late August we completed our training. About the 26th, Company K boarded LST (landing ship, tank) 661* for a voyage that would end three weeks later on the beach at Peleliu.

Each rifle company assigned to the assault waves against Peleliu made the trip in an LST carrying the amtracs that would take the men ashore. Our LST lacked sufficient troop compartment space to accommodate all of the men of the company, so the platoon leaders drew straws for the available space. The mortar section got lucky. We were assigned to a troop compartment in the forecastle with an entrance on the main deck. Some of the other platoons had to make themselves as comfortable as possible on the main deck under and around landing boats and gear secured there.

Once loaded, we weighed anchor and headed straight for Guadalcanal, where the division held maneuvers in the Tassafaronga area. This area bore little resemblance to the beaches we would have to hit on Peleliu, but we spent several days in large- and small-unit amphibious landing exercises.

Some of our Guadalcanal veterans wanted to visit the island's cemetery to pay their respects to buddies killed during the division's first campaign. The veterans I knew were not allowed to make the trip to the cemetery, and there was a great

*LSTs were a class of shallow-draft amphibious ships developed just before World War II. An LST could drive its front end directly onto a beach and then unload its cargo of vehicles through the large clamshell doors that formed the ship's bow when closed. Or as in the case at Peleliu, LSTs could debark troop-carrying assault amphibians (amtracs) at sea. Advanced models of the LST serve the American fleet today.

deal of understandable bitterness and resentment on their part because of this.

Between training exercises, some of us explored the beach area and looked over the stranded wrecks of Japanese landing barges, the troopship *Yamazuki Maru,* and a two-man submarine. One of the Guadalcanal veterans told us what a helpless feeling it had been to sit back in the hills and watch Japanese reinforcements come ashore unopposed during the dark days of the campaign when the Japanese navy was so powerful in the Solomon Islands. Evidence of earlier fighting remained in the goodly number of shattered trees and several human skeletons we found in the jungle growth.

We also had our lighter moments. When the amtracs returned us to the LST each afternoon, we hurried to our quarters, stowed our gear, stripped, and went below to the tank deck. After all the amtracs were aboard, the ship's CO (commanding officer) obligingly left the bow doors open and the ramp down so we could swim in the blue waters of Sealark Channel (called more appropriately Iron Bottom Bay because of all the ships that had been sunk there during the Guadalcanal campaign). We dove, swam, and splashed in the beautiful water like a bunch of little boys, and for a few fleeting hours forgot why we were there.

The thirty LSTs carrying the 1st Marine Division's assault companies finally weighed anchor early on the morning of 4 September to make the approximately 2,100-mile voyage to Peleliu. The trip proved to be uneventful. The sea was smooth, and we ran into rain squalls only once or twice.

After chow each morning, several of us went aft to the ship's fantail to watch Gunnery Sergeant Haney's show. Dressed in khaki shorts, boondockers, and leggings, Haney went through his ritual of bayonet drill and rifle cleaning. He kept the scabbard on his bayonet and used a canvas-covered stanchion running down from the ship's superstructure as his target. It was a poor substitute for a moving parry stick, but Haney didn't let that stop him. For about an hour he went through his routine, complete with monologue, while dozens of Company K men lounged around on coils of rope and other gear, smoking and talking. Sometimes a spirited game of pinochle went on almost under his feet. He was as oblivious of the players as they were of him. Occasionally a sailor would come by and stare in disbelief at Haney. Several asked me if he were Asiatic. Not being able to overcome the temptation to kid them a bit, I told them no, he was just typical of our outfit. Then they would stare at me as they had at Haney.

I always had the feeling that sailors looked on Marine infantrymen as though we were a bit crazy, wild, or reckless. Maybe we were. But maybe we had to develop a don't-give-a-damn attitude to keep our sanity in the face of what we were about to endure.

In the ranks, we knew little about the nature of the island that was our objective. During a training lecture on Pavuvu we learned that Peleliu must be taken to secure Gen. Douglas MacArthur's right flank for his invasion of the Philippines, and that it had a good airfield that could support MacArthur. I don't recall when we heard the name of the island, although we viewed relief maps and models during lectures. (It had a nice sounding name, Pel' e loo.) Although our letters from Pavuvu were carefully censored, our officers apparently feared taking a chance on some character writing in code to someone back home that we were to hit an island named Peleliu. As a buddy said to me later, however, no one back home would have known where to look for it on a map anyway.

The Palaus, the westernmost part of the Caroline Islands chain, consist of several large islands and more than a hundred smaller ones. Except for Angaur in the south and a couple of small atolls in the north, the whole group lies within an encircling coral reef. About five hundred miles to the west lie the southern Philippines. To the south at about the same distance is New Guinea.

Peleliu, just inside the Palau reef, is shaped like a lobster's claw, extending two arms of land. The southern arm reaches northeastward from flat ground to form a jumble of coral islets and tidal flats overgrown thickly with mangroves. The longer northern arm is dominated by the parallel coral ridges of Umurbrogol Mountain.

North to south, the island is about six miles long, with a width of approximately two miles. On the wide, largely flat southern section, the Japanese had constructed an airfield shaped roughly like the numeral 4. The ridges and most of the island outside the airfield were thickly wooded; there were only occasional patches of wild palms and open grass areas. The thick scrub so completely masked the true nature of the terrain that aerial photographs and pre–D day photos taken by United States submarines gave intelligence officers no hint of its ruggedness.

The treacherous reef along the landing beaches and the heavily defended coral ridges inland made the invasion of Peleliu a combination of the problems of Tarawa and of Saipan. The reef, over six hundred yards long, was the most formidable natural obstacle. Because of it, troops and equipment making the assault had to be transported in amtracs; Higgins boats could not negotiate across the rough coral and the varying depths of water.

Before leaving Pavuvu, we had been told that the 1st Marine Division would be reinforced to about 28,000 men for the assault on Peleliu. As every man in the ranks knew, however, a lot of those people included in the term *reinforced* were neither trained nor equipped as combat troops. They were specialists attached to the division to implement the landing and supply by working on ships and later on the beaches. They would not be doing the fighting.

Upon sailing for Peleliu, the 1st Marine Division numbered 16,459 officers and men. (A rear echelon of 1,771 remained on Pavuvu.) Only about 9,000 were infantrymen in the three infantry regiments. Intelligence sources estimated that we would face more than 10,000 Japanese defenders on Peleliu. The big topic of conversation among us troops had to do with those comparative strengths.

"Hey, you guys, the lieutenant just told me that the 1st Division is gonna be the biggest Marine division to ever make a landing. He says we got reinforcements we never had before."

A veteran looked up from cleaning his .45 automatic and said, "Boy, has that shavetail lieutenant been smoke-stacking you!"

"Why?"

"Use your head, buddy. Sure we got the 1st Marines, the 5th Marines, and the 7th Marines; them's infantry. The 11th Marines is our division artillery. Where the hell's all them people who is supposed to 'reinforce' the division? Have you seen 'em? Who the hell are they, and where the hell are they?"

"I don't know, I'm just telling you what the lieutenant said."

"Well, I'll tell you who them 'reinforcements' is. They's all what they call specialists, and they ain't line company Marines. Remember this, buster. When the stuff hits the fan, and you and me are trying to live through that shootin' and the shellin', them damned specialists'll be settin' on they cans back at division CP [command post] on the beach, writin' home about how war is hell. And who is gonna have all the casualties and lose all the men fightin' the Nips? The 1st Marines, the 5th Marines, and the 7th Marines'll all catch hell, and the 11th Marines'll lose some men too. Wake up, boy, them shavetail lieutenants is as useless as tits on a boar hog. The NCOs run things when the shootin' starts."*

D MINUS 1

After evening chow on 14 September 1944, a buddy and I leaned against the rail of LST 661 and talked about what we would do after the war. I tried to appear unconcerned about

---

*During World War II, amphibious planners considered the safe ratio of attackers to defenders in an amphibious assault to be three to one. To the leaders at Peleliu, the total Marine force of 30,000 provided a safe margin over the Japanese. Although at least one regimental commander—the redoubtable Col. Lewis B. ("Chesty") Puller—pointed out the disparity in actual combat forces, the division's commander, Maj. Gen. William H. Rupertus, and his staff believed his fears were groundless.

the next day, and he did too. We may have fooled each other and ourselves a little, but not much. As the sun disappeared below the horizon and its glare no longer reflected off a glassy sea, I thought of how beautiful the sunsets always were in the Pacific. They were even more beautiful than over Mobile Bay. Suddenly a thought hit me like a thunderbolt. Would I live to see the sunset tomorrow? My knees nearly buckled as panic swept over me. I squeezed the railing and tried to appear interested in our conversation.

The ships in the convoy turned into dark hulks gliding along as the squawk box interrupted our conversation, "Now hear this. Now hear this." Talking quietly in pairs and small groups, the men around us seemed to pay more than the usual attention to the command. "All troops lay below to quarters. All troops lay below to quarters."

My buddy and I went to our forecastle compartment. One of our NCOs sent a work party to another compartment to draw rations and ammunition. After it returned, our lieutenant came in, gave us "at ease," and said he had some things to say. His brow was knit, his face drawn, and he looked worried.

"Men, as you probably know, tomorrow is D day. General Rupertus says the fighting will be extremely tough but short. It will be over in four days, maybe three. A fight like Tarawa. It's going to be rough but fast. Then we can return to a rest area.

"Remember what you've been taught. Keep your heads down going in on the amtrac. A lot of unnecessary casualties at Saipan were the result of men looking over the side to see what was happening. As soon as the amtrac stops on the beach, get out on the double, and get off the beach fast. Keep out of the way of amtracs on their way back out to pick up more troops from the supporting waves. Our tanks will be coming in behind us, too. The drivers have their hands full and can't dodge around the infantry, so you keep out of their way. Get off the beach fast! The Japs will plaster it with everything they've got, and if we get pinned down on the beach, artillery and mortars will ruin us.

"Have your weapons ready because the Japs always try to stop us at the beach line. They may meet us at the beach with bayonets as soon as our naval gunfire barrage lifts and moves inland. So come out of the amtracs ready for anything. Have a round in the chamber of your small arms and lock your pieces [snap on the safety]. Have the canister containers of your high-explosive mortar rounds untaped and stowed in your ammo bags ready for immediate use as soon as we are called on to deliver fire on the company front. Fill your canteens, draw rations and salt tablets, and clean your weapons. Reveille will be before daylight, and H hour will be at 0830.

Hit the sack early. You will need the rest. Good luck and carry on."

He left the compartment and the NCOs issued us ammo, K rations, and salt tablets.

"Well," said one man, "that scuttlebutt we heard during maneuvers on Guadalcanal about how this blitz gonna be rough but fast must be true if the division CG says so."

"San Antone," muttered a Texan. "Imagine, only four, maybe three days for a battle star. Hell, I can put up with anything for no longer than that."

He reflected the feelings of most of us, and we were encouraged by the commanding general's announcement confirming the oft-repeated "rough but fast" rumors we had been hearing.* We kept trying to convince ourselves that the CG knew what he was talking about. We all dreaded a long, protracted campaign that would drag on beyond endurance like Guadalcanal and Cape Gloucester. Our morale was excellent, and we were trained for anything no matter how rough. But we prayed that we could get it over with in a hurry.

We sat on our sacks, cleaned our weapons, packed our combat packs, and squared away our gear. Throughout history, combat troops of various armies have carried packs weighing many pounds into action; but we traveled light, carrying only absolute necessities—the way fast-moving Confederate infantry did during the Civil War.

My combat pack contained a folded poncho, one pair of socks, a couple of boxes of K rations, salt tablets, extra carbine ammo (twenty rounds), two hand grenades, a fountain pen, a small bottle of ink, writing paper in a waterproof wrapper, a toothbrush, a small tube of toothpaste, some photos of my folks along with some letters (in a waterproof wrapper), and a dungaree cap.

---

*In a sealed letter opened D day minus 1 by civilian news correspondents assigned to cover the battle, Maj. Gen. William H. Rupertus predicted that Peleliu would fall in four days after a short, tough fight. His forecast colored the tactical thinking ashore for much of the next month. Because of his optimism, many of the thirty-six newsmen never went ashore; of those who did, only six stayed through the critical early stages of the battle. Thus, the medium's eyes saw little of what actually happened.

My other equipment and clothing were a steel helmet covered with camouflaged-cloth covering, heavy green dungaree jacket with a Marine emblem and *USMC* dyed above it on the left breast pocket, trousers of the same material, an old toothbrush for cleaning my carbine, thin cotton socks, ankle-high boondockers, and light tan canvas leggings (into which I tucked my trouser legs). Because of the heat, I wore no Skivvy drawers or shirt. Like many men, I fastened a bronze Marine emblem to one collar for good luck.

Attached to my web pistol belt, I carried a pouch containing a combat dressing, two canteens, a pouch with two fifteen-round carbine magazines—clips, we called them, and a fine brass compass in a waterproof case. My kabar hung in its leather sheath on my right side. Hooked over the belt by its spoon (handle), I carried a grenade. I also had a heavy-bladed knife similar to a meat cleaver that my dad had sent me; I used this to chop through the wire braces wrapped around the stout crates of 60mm mortar shells.

On the stock of my carbine I fastened an ammo pouch with two extra clips. I carried no bayonet, because the model carbine I had lacked a bayonet lug. Onto the outside of my pack, I hooked my entrenching tool in its canvas cover. (The tool proved useless on Peleliu, because of the hard coral.)

All officers and men dressed much the same. The main differences among us were in the type of web belt worn and the individual weapon carried.

We tried to appear unconcerned and talked about anything but the war. Some wrote last latters.

"What are you going to do after the war, Sledgehammer?" asked a buddy sitting across from me. He was an extremely intelligent and intellectually active young man.

"I don't know, Oswalt. What are you planning to do?"

"I want to be a brain surgeon. The human brain is an incredible thing; it fascinates me," he replied.

But he didn't survive Peleliu to realize his ambition.

Slowly the conversations trailed off, and the men hit the sack. It was hard to sleep that night. I thought of home, my parents, my friends—and whether I would do my duty, be wounded and disabled, or be killed. I concluded that it was impossible for me to be killed, because God loved me. Then I told myself that God loved us all and that many would die or be ruined physically or mentally or both by the next morning and in the days following. My heart pounded, and I broke out in a cold sweat. Finally, I called myself a damned coward and eventually fell asleep saying the Lord's Prayer to myself.

D DAY, 15 SEPTEMBER 1944

I seemed to have slept only a short time when an NCO came into the compartment saying, "OK, you guys, hit the deck." I felt the ship had slowed and almost stopped. If only I could hold back the hands of the clock, I thought. It was pitch dark with no lights topside. We tumbled out, dressed and shaved, and got ready for chow—steak and eggs, a 1st Marine Division tradition honoring a culinary combination learned from the Australians. Neither the steak nor the eggs was very palatable, though; my stomach was tied in knots.

Back in my compartment, a peculiar problem had developed. Haney, who had been one of the first to return from chow about forty-five minutes earlier, had ensconced himself on the seat of one of the two toilets in the small head on our side of the compartment. There he sat, dungaree trousers down to his knees, his beloved leggings laced neatly over his boondockers, grinning and talking calmly to himself while smoking a cigarette. Nervous Marines lined up using the other toilet one after another. Some men had been to the head on the other side of the compartment while others, in desperation, dashed off to the heads in other troop compartments. The facilities in our compartment normally were adequate, but D day morning found us all nervous, tense, and afraid. The veterans already knew what I was to find out: during periods of intense fighting, a man might not have the opportunity to eat or sleep, much less move his bowels. All the men grumbled and scowled at Haney, but because he was a gunnery sergeant, no one dared suggest he hurry. With his characteristic detachment, Haney ignored us, remained unhurried, and left when he pleased.

The first light of dawn was just appearing as I left my gear on my bunk, all squared away and ready to put on, and went out onto the main deck. All the men were talking quietly, smoking, and looking toward the island. I found Snafu* and stayed close by him; he was the gunner on our mortar, so we stuck together. He was also a Gloucester veteran, and I felt more secure around veterans. They knew what to expect.

He pulled out a pack of cigarettes and drawled, "Have a smoke, Sledgehammer."

"No thanks, Snafu. I've told you a million times I don't smoke."

"I'll bet you two bits, Sledgehammer, that before this day is over you'll be smokin' the hell outa every cigarette you can get your hands on."

I just gave him a sickly grin, and we looked toward the island. The sun was just coming up, and there wasn't a cloud in the sky. The sea was calm. A gentle breeze blew.

A ship's bell rang, and over the squawk box came, "Get your gear on and stand by." Snafu and I hurried to our bunks, nodding and speaking to other grim-faced buddies who were rushing to get their gear. In the crowded compartment we helped each other with packs, straightened shoulder straps, and buckled on cartridge belts. Generals and admirals might worry about maps and tons of supplies, but my main concern at the moment was how my pack straps felt and whether my boondockers were comfortable.

The next bell rang. Snafu picked up the forty-five pounds of mortar and slung the carrying strap over his shoulder. I slung my carbine over one shoulder and the heavy ammo bag over the other. We filed down a ladder to the tank deck where an NCO directed us to climb aboard an amtrac. My knees got weak when I saw that it wasn't the newer model with the tail-gate ramp for troop exit in which we had practiced. This meant that once the amtrac was on the beach, we'd have to jump over the high sides, exposed much more to enemy fire. I was too scared and excited to say much, but some of the guys grumbled about it.

*Cpl. Merriell A. ("Snafu") Shelton came from Louisiana.

The ship's bow doors opened and the ramp went down. All the tractors' engines roared and spewed out fumes. Exhaust fans whirred above us. Glaring daylight streamed into the tank deck through the opened bow of the ship as the first amtrac started out and clattered down the sloping ramp.

Our machine started with a jerk, and we held on to the sides and to each other. The amtrac's treads ground and scraped against the iron ridges on the ramp, then it floated freely and settled onto the water like a big duck. Around us roared the voices of the ships' guns engaged in the preassault bombardment of Peleliu's beaches and defensive positions.

The Marine Corps had trained us new men until we were welded with the veterans into a thoroughly disciplined combat division. Now the force of events unleashed on that two-mile by six-mile piece of unfriendly coral rock would carry us forward unrelentingly, each to his individual fate.

Everything my life had been before and has been after pales in the light of that awesome moment when my amtrac started in amid a thunderous bombardment toward the flaming, smoke-shrouded beach for the assault on Peleliu.

Since the end of World War II, historians and military analysts have argued inconclusively about the necessity of the Palau Islands campaign. Many believed after the battle—and still believe today—that the United States didn't need to fight it as a prerequisite to General MacArthur's return to the Philippines.

Adm. William F. ("Bull") Halsey suggested calling off the Palau operation after high-level planners learned that Japanese air power in the Philippines wasn't as strong as intelligence originally had presumed it to be. But MacArthur believed the operation should proceed, and Adm. Chester W. Nimitz said it was too late to cancel the operation, because the convoy was already under way.

Because of important events in Europe at the time and the lack of immediate, apparent benefits from the seizure of Peleliu, the battle remains one of the lesser known or understood of the Pacific war. Nonetheless, for many it ranks as the roughest fight the Marines had in World War II.

Maj. Gen. (later Lt. Gen.) Roy S. Geiger, the rugged commander of the III Amphibious Corps, said repeatedly that Peleliu was the toughest battle of the entire Pacific war. A former commandant of the Marine Corps, Gen. Clifton B. Cates, said Peleliu was one of the most vicious and stubbornly contested battles of the war, and that nowhere was the fighting efficiency of the U.S. Marine demonstrated more convincingly.

Peleliu also was important to the remainder of the Marines' war in the Pacific because of the changes in Japanese tactics encountered there. The Japanese abandoned their conventional all-out effort at defending the beach in favor of a complex defense based upon mutually supporting, fortified positions in caves and pillboxes extending deeply into the interior of the island, particularly in the ridges of Umurbrogol Mountain.

In earlier battles, the Japanese had exhausted their forces in banzai charges against the Marines once the latter had firmly established a beachhead. The Marines slaughtered the wildly charging Japanese by the thousands. Not a single banzai charge had been successful for the Japanese in previous campaigns.

But on Peleliu the Japanese commander, Col. Kunio Nakagawa, let the Marines come to him and the approximately 10,000 troops of his proud 14th Infantry Division. From mutually supporting positions, the Japanese covered nearly every yard of Peleliu from the beach inland to the center of Nakagawa's command post, deep beneath the coral rock in the center of the ridge system. Some positions were large enough to hold only one man. Some caves held hundreds. Thus the Marines encountered no one main defense line. The Japanese had constructed the perfect defense-in-depth with the whole island as a front line. They fought until the last position was knocked out.

Aided by the incredibly rugged terrain, the new Japanese tactics proved so successful that the 1st Marine Division suffered more than twice as many casualties on Peleliu as the 2d Marine Division had on Tarawa. Proportionately, United States casualties on Peleliu closely approximated those suf-

fered later on Iwo Jima where the Japanese again employed an intricate defense-in-depth, conserved forces, and fought a battle of attrition. On an even greater scale, the skillful, tenacious defense of the southern portion of Okinawa used the same sophisticated, in-depth defensive system first tested on Peleliu.

CHAPTER FOUR

Assault into Hell

H hour, 0800. Long jets of red flame mixed with thick black smoke rushed out of the muzzles of the huge battleships' 16-inch guns with a noise like a thunderclap. The giant shells tore through the air toward the island, roaring like locomotives.

"Boy, it must cost a fortune to fire them 16-inch babies," said a buddy near me.

"Screw the expense," growled another.

Only less impressive were the cruisers firing 8-inch salvos and the host of smaller ships firing rapid fire. The usually clean salty air was strong with the odors of explosives and diesel fuel. While the assault waves formed up and my amphibious tractor lay still in the water with engines idling, the tempo of the bombardment increased to such intensity that I couldn't distinguish the reports of the various types of weapons through the thunderous noise. We had to shout at each other to be heard. The big ships increased their fire and moved off to the flanks of the amtrac formations when we started in so as not to fire over us at the risk of short rounds.

We waited a seeming eternity for the signal to start toward the beach. The suspense was almost more than I could bear. Waiting is a major part of war, but I never experienced any more supremely agonizing suspense than the excruciating torture of those moments before we received the signal to begin the assault on Peleliu. I broke out in a cold sweat as the tension mounted with the intensity of the bombardment. My stomach was tied in knots. I had a lump in my throat and swallowed only with great difficulty. My knees nearly buckled, so I clung weakly to the side of the tractor. I felt nauseated and feared that my bladder would surely empty itself and reveal me to be the coward I was. But the men around me looked just about the way I felt. Finally, with a sense of fatalistic relief mixed with a flash of anger at the navy officer who was our wave commander, I saw him wave his flag toward the beach. Our driver revved the engine. The treads churned up the water, and we started in—the second wave ashore.

We moved ahead, watching the frightful spectacle. Huge geysers of water rose around the amtracs ahead of us as they approached the reef. The beach was now marked along its length by a continuous sheet of flame backed by a thick wall of smoke. It seemed as though a huge volcano had erupted from the sea, and rather than heading for an island, we were being drawn into the vortex of a flaming abyss. For many it was to be oblivion.

The lieutenant braced himself and pulled out a half-pint whiskey bottle.

"This is it, boys," he yelled.

Just like they do in the movies! It seemed unreal.

He held the bottle out to me, but I refused. Just sniffing the cork under those conditions might have made me pass out. He took a long pull on the bottle, and a couple of the men did the same. Suddenly a large shell exploded with a terrific concussion, and a huge geyser rose up just to our right front. It barely missed us. The engine stalled. The front of the tractor lurched to the left and bumped hard against the rear of another amtrac that was either stalled or hit. I never knew which.

We sat stalled, floating in the water for some terrifying moments. We were sitting ducks for the enemy gunners. I looked forward through the hatch behind the driver. He was wrestling frantically with the control levers. Japanese shells were screaming into the area and exploding all around us. Sgt. Johnny Marmet leaned toward the driver and yelled something. Whatever it was, it seemed to calm the driver, because he got the engine started. We moved forward again amid the geysers of exploding shells.

Our bombardment began to lift off the beach and move inland. Our dive bombers also moved inland with their strafing and bombing. The Japanese increased the volume of their fire against the waves of amtracs. Above the din I could hear the ominous sound of shell fragments humming and growling through the air.

"Stand by," someone yelled.

I picked up my mortar ammo bag and slung it over my left shoulder, buckled my helmet chin strap, adjusted my carbine sling over my right shoulder, and tried to keep my balance. My heart pounded. Our amtrac came out of the water and moved a few yards up the gently sloping sand.

"Hit the beach!" yelled an NCO moments before the machine lurched to a stop.

The men piled over the sides as fast as they could. I followed Snafu, climbed up, and planted both feet firmly on the left side so as to leap as far away from it as possible. At that instant a burst of machine-gun fire with white-hot tracers snapped through the air at eye level, almost grazing my face. I pulled my head back like a turtle, lost my balance, and fell awkwardly forward down onto the sand in a tangle of ammo bag, pack, helmet, carbine, gas mask, cartridge belt, and flopping canteens. "Get off the beach! Get off the beach!" raced through my mind.

Once I felt land under my feet, I wasn't as scared as I had been coming across the reef. My legs dug up the sand as I tried to rise. A firm hand gripped my shoulder. "Oh god, I thought, it's a Nip who's come out of a pillbox!" I couldn't reach my kabar—fortunately, because as I got my face out of the sand and looked up, there was the worried face of a Marine bending over me. He thought the machine-gun burst had hit me, and he had crawled over to help. When he saw I was unhurt, he spun around and started crawling rapidly off the beach. I scuttled after him.

Shells crashed all around. Fragments tore and whirred, slapping on the sand and splashing into the water a few yards behind us. The Japanese were recovering from the shock of our prelanding bombardment. Their machine gun and rifle fire got thicker, snapping viciously overhead in increasing volume.

Our amtrac spun around and headed back out as I reached

the edge of the beach and flattened on the deck. The world was a nightmare of flashes, violent explosions, and snapping bullets. Most of what I saw blurred. My mind was benumbed by the shock of it.

I glanced back across the beach and saw a DUKW (rubber-tired amphibious truck) roll up on the sand at a point near where we had just landed. The instant the DUKW stopped, it was engulfed in thick, dirty black smoke as a shell scored a direct hit on it. Bits of debris flew into the air. I watched with that odd, detached fascination peculiar to men under fire, as a flat metal panel about two feet square spun high into the air then splashed into shallow water like a big pancake. I didn't see any men get out of the DUKW.

Up and down the beach and out on the reef, a number of amtracs and DUKWs were burning. Japanese machine-gun bursts made long splashes on the water as though flaying it with some giant whip. The geysers belched up relentlessly where the mortar and artillery shells hit. I caught a fleeting glimpse of a group of Marines leaving a smoking amtrac on the reef. Some fell as bullets and fragments splashed among them. Their buddies tried to help them as they struggled in the knee-deep water.

I shuddered and choked. A wild desperate feeling of anger, frustration, and pity gripped me. It was an emotion that always would torture my mind when I saw men trapped and was unable to do anything but watch as they were hit. My own plight forgotten momentarily, I felt sickened to the depths of my soul. I asked God, "Why, why, why?" I turned my face away and wished that I were imagining it all. I had tasted the bitterest essence of war, the sight of helpless comrades being slaughtered, and it filled me with disgust.

I got up. Crouching low, I raced up the sloping beach into a defilade. Reaching the inland edge of the sand just beyond the high-water mark, I glanced down and saw the nose of a huge black and yellow bomb protruding from the sand. A metal plate attached to the top served as a pressure trigger. My foot had missed it by only inches.

I hit the deck again just inside the defilade. On the sand immediately in front of me was a dead snake about eighteen inches long. It was colorful, somewhat like American species I had kept as pets when a boy. It was the only snake I saw on Peleliu.

Momentarily I was out of the heavy fire hitting on the beach. A strong smell of chemicals and exploding shells filled the air. Patches of coral and sand around me were yellowed from the powder from shell blasts. A large white post about four feet high stood at the edge of the defilade. Japanese writing was painted on the side facing the beach. To me, it appeared as though a chicken with muddy feet had walked up and down the post. I felt a sense of pride that this was enemy territory and that we were capturing it for our country to help win the war.

One of our NCOs signaled us to move to our right, out of the shallow defilade. I was glad, because the Japanese probably would pour mortar fire into it to prevent it being used for shelter. At the moment, however, the gunners seemed to be concentrating on the beach and the incoming waves of Marines.

I ran over to where one of our veterans stood looking to our front and flopped down at his feet. "You'd better get down," I yelled as bullets snapped and cracked all around.

"Them slugs are high, they're hittin' in the leaves, Sledgehammer," he said nonchalantly without looking at me.

"Leaves, hell! Where are the trees?" I yelled back at him.

Startled, he looked right and left. Down the beach, barely visible, was a shattered palm. Nothing near us stood over knee high. He hit the deck.

"I must be crackin' up, Sledgehammer. Them slugs sound just like they did in the jungle at Gloucester, and I figured they were hittin' leaves," he said with chagrin.

"Somebody gimme a cigarette," I yelled to my squad mates nearby.

Snafu was jubilant. "I toldja you'd start smokin', didn't I, Sledgehammer?"

A buddy handed me a smoke, and with trembling hands we got it lit. They really kidded me about going back on all my previous refusals to smoke.

I kept looking to our right, expecting to see men from the

3d Battalion, 7th Marines (3/7), which was supposed to be there. But I saw only the familiar faces of Marines from my own company as we moved off the beach. Marines began to come in behind us in increasing numbers, but none were visible on our right flank.

Unfamiliar officers and NCOs yelled and shouted orders, "K Company, first platoon, move over here," or "K Company, mortar section, over here." Considerable confusion prevailed for about fifteen minutes as our officers and the leaders from our namesake company in the 7th Marines straightened out the two units.

From left to right along the 2,200-yard beach front, the 1st Marines, the 5th Marines, and the 7th Marines landed abreast. The 1st Marines landed one battalion on each of the two northern White beaches. In the division's center, the 5th Marines landed its 1st Battalion (1/5) over Orange Beach One and its 3d Battalion (3/5) over Orange Beach Two. Forming the right flank of the division, the 7th Marines was to land one battalion (3/7) in the assault over Orange Beach Three, the southernmost of five designated beaches.

In the confusion of the landing's first few minutes, K/3/5 actually got in ahead of the assault companies of 3/7 and slightly farther to the right than intended. As luck would have it, the two companies got mixed together as the right flank of the division. For about fifteen minutes we were the exposed right flank of the entire beachhead.

We started to move inland. We had gone only a few yards when an enemy machine gun opened up from a scrub thicket to our right. Japanese 81mm and 90mm mortars then opened up on us. Everyone hit the deck; I dove into a shallow crater. The company was completely pinned down. All movement ceased. The shells fell faster, until I couldn't make out individual explosions, just continuous, crashing rumbles with an occasional ripping sound of shrapnel tearing low through the air overhead amid the roar. The air was murky with smoke and dust. Every muscle in my body was as tight as a piano wire. I shuddered and shook as though I were having a mild convulsion. Sweat flowed profusely. I prayed, clenched my teeth, squeezed my carbine stock, and cursed the Japanese. Our lieutenant, a Cape Gloucester veteran who was nearby, seemed to be in about the same shape. From the meager protection of my shallow crater I pitied him, or anyone, out on that flat coral.

The heavy mortar barrage went on without slackening. I thought it would never stop. I was terrified by the big shells arching down all around us. One was bound to fall directly into my hole, I thought.

If any orders were passed along, or if anyone yelled for a corpsman, I never heard it in all the noise. It was as though I was out there on the battlefield all by myself, utterly forlorn and helpless in a tempest of violent explosions. All any man could do was sweat it out and pray for survival. It would have been sure suicide to stand up in that firestorm.

Under my first barrage since the fast-moving events of hitting the beach, I learned a new sensation: utter and absolute helplessness. The shelling lifted in about half an hour, although it seemed to me to have crashed on for hours. Time had no meaning to me. (This was particularly true when under a heavy shelling. I never could judge how long it lasted.) Orders then came to move out and I got up, covered by a layer of coral dust. I felt like jelly and couldn't believe any of us had survived that barrage.

The walking wounded began coming past us on their way to the beach where they would board amtracs to be taken out to one of the ships. An NCO who was a particular friend of mine hurried by, holding a bloody battle dressing over his upper left arm.

"Hit bad?" I yelled.

His face lit up in a broad grin, and he said jauntily, "Don't feel sorry for me, Sledgehammer. I got the million-dollar wound. It's all over for me."

We waved as he hurried on out of the war.

We had to be alert constantly as we moved through the thick sniper-infested scrub. We received orders to halt in an open area as I came upon the first enemy dead I had ever seen, a dead Japanese medical corpsman and two riflemen. The medic apparently had been trying to administer aid when he was killed by one of our shells. His medical chest lay open beside him, and the various bandages and medicines were arranged neatly in compartments. The corpsman was on his back, his abdominal cavity laid bare. I stared in horror, shocked at the glistening viscera bespecked with fine coral dust. This can't have been a human being, I agonized. It looked more like the guts of one of the many rabbits or squirrels I had cleaned on hunting trips as a boy. I felt sick as I stared at the corpses.

A sweating, dusty Company K veteran came up, looked first at the dead, and then at me. He slung his M1 rifle over his shoulder and leaned over the bodies. With the thumb and forefinger of one hand, he deftly plucked a pair of horn-rimmed glasses from the face of the corpsman. This was done as casually as a guest plucking an hors d'oeuvre from a tray at a cocktail party.

"Sledgehammer," he said reproachfully, "don't stand there with your mouth open when there's all these good souvenirs laying around." He held the glasses for me to see and added, "Look how thick that glass is. These sonsabitches must be half blind, but it don't seem to mess up their marksmanship any."

He then removed a Nambu pistol, slipped the belt off the corpse, and took the leather holster. He pulled off the steel helmet, reached inside, and took out a neatly folded Japanese flag covered with writing. The veteran pitched the helmet on the coral where it clanked and rattled, rolled the corpse over, and started pawing through the combat pack.

The veteran's buddy came up and started stripping the other Japanese corpses. His take was a flag and other items. He then removed the bolts from the Japanese rifles and broke the stocks against the coral to render them useless to infiltrators. The first veteran said, "See you, Sledgehammer. Don't take any wooden nickels." He and his buddy moved on.

I hadn't budged an inch or said a word, just stood glued to the spot almost in a trance. The corpses were sprawled where the veterans had dragged them around to get into their packs and pockets. Would I become this casual and calloused about enemy dead? I wondered. Would the war dehumanize me so that I, too, could "field strip" enemy dead with such nonchalance? The time soon came when it didn't bother me a bit.

Within a few yards of this scene, one of our hospital corpsmen worked in a small, shallow defile treating Marine wounded. I went over and sat on the hot coral by him. The corpsman was on his knees bending over a young Marine who had just died on a stretcher. A blood-soaked battle dressing was on the side of the dead man's neck. His fine, handsome, boyish face was ashen. "What a pitiful waste," I thought. "He can't be a day over seventeen years old." I thanked God his mother couldn't see him. The corpsman held the dead Marine's chin tenderly between the thumb and fingers of his left hand and made the sign of the cross with his right hand. Tears streamed down his dusty, tanned, grief-contorted face while he sobbed quietly.

The wounded who had received morphine sat or lay around like zombies and patiently awaited the "doc's" attention. Shells roared overhead in both directions, an occasional one falling nearby, and machine guns rattled incessantly like chattering demons.

We moved inland. The scrub may have slowed the company, but it concealed us from the heavy enemy shelling that was holding up other companies facing the open airfield. I could hear the deep rumble of the shelling and dreaded that we might move into it.

That our battalion executive officer had been killed a few moments after hitting the beach and that the amtrac carrying most of our battalion's field telephone equipment and operators had been destroyed on the reef made control difficult. The companies of 3/5 lost contact with each other and with 3/7 on our right flank.*

*Historical accounts of battles often leave a reader with the impression that the individual participants had a panoramic view of events. Such is not the case, however. Even the historians have never been able to piece together completely what happened to 3/5 on D day at Peleliu.

As I passed the different units and exchanged greetings with friends, I was astonished at their faces. When I tried to smile at a comment a buddy made, my face felt as tight as a drumhead. My facial muscles were so tensed from the strain that I actually felt it was impossible to smile. With a shock I realized that the faces of my squad mates and everyone around me looked masklike and unfamiliar.

As we pushed eastward, we halted briefly along a North-South trail. Word was passed that we had to move forward faster to a trail where we would come up abreast of 3/7.

We continued through the thick scrub and heavy sniper fire until we came out into a clearing overlooking the ocean. Company K had reached the eastern shore. We had reached our objective. To our front was a shallow bay with barbed-wire entanglements, iron tetrahedrons, and other obstacles against landing craft. I was glad we hadn't tried to invade this coast.

About a dozen Company K riflemen commenced firing at Japanese soldiers wading along the reef several hundred yards away at the mouth of the bay. Other Marines joined us. The enemy were moving out from a narrow extension of the mangrove swamp on the left toward the southeastern promontory on our right. About a dozen enemy soldiers were alternately swimming and running along the reef. Some of the time only their heads were above the water as my buddies sent rifle fire into their midst. Most of the running enemy went down with a splash.

We were elated over reaching the eastern shore, and at being able to fire on the enemy in the open. A few Japanese escaped and scrambled among the rocks on the promontory.

"OK, you guys, line 'em up and squeeze 'em off," said a sergeant. "You don't kill 'em with the noise. It's the slugs that do it. You guys couldn't hit a bull in the ass with a bass fiddle," he roared.

Several more Japanese ran out from the cover of the mangroves. A burst of rifle fire sent every one of them splashing. "That's better," growled the sergeant.

The mortarmen put down our loads and stood by to set up the guns. We didn't fire at the enemy with our carbines. Rifles were more effective than carbines at that range. So we just watched.

Firing increased from our rear. We had no contact with Marine units on our right or left. But the veterans weren't concerned with anything but the enemy on the reef.

"Stand by to move out!" came the order.

"What the hell," grumbled a veteran as we headed back into the scrub. "We fight like hell and reach our objective, and they order us to fall back." Others joined in the grumbling.

"Aw, knock it off. We gotta gain contact with the 7th Marines," an NCO said.

We headed back into the thick scrub. For some time I completely lost my bearings and had no idea where we were going.

Unknown to the Marines, there were two parallel North–South trails about two hundred yards apart winding through the thick scrub. Poor maps, poor visibility, and numerous snipers made it difficult to distinguish the two trails.

When 3/5, with Company K on its right flank, reached the first (westernmost) trail, it was then actually abreast of 3/7. However, due to poor visibility, contact couldn't be made between the two battalions. It was thought 3/5 was too far to the rear. So, 3/5 was ordered to move forward to come abreast of 3/7. By the time this error was realized, 3/5 had pushed 300–400 yards ahead of the 7th Marine's flank. For the second time on D day, K/3/5 was the forwardmost exposed right flank element of the division. The entire 3d Battalion, 5th Marines formed a deep salient reaching into enemy territory to the east coast. To make matters worse, the battalion's three companies had lost contact with each other. These isolated units were in critical danger of being cut off and surrounded by the Japanese.

The weather was getting increasingly hot, and I was soaked with sweat. I began eating salt tablets and taking frequent drinks of tepid water from my canteens. We were warned to save our water as long as possible, because no one knew when we would get any more.

A sweating runner with a worried face came up from the rear. "Hey, you guys, where's K Company's CO?" he asked. We told him where we thought Ack Ack could be located.

"What's the hot dope?" someone asked, with that same anxious question always put to runners.

"Battalion CP says we just gotta establish contact with the 7th Marines, 'cause if the Nips counterattack they'll come right through the gap," he said as he hurried on.

"Jesus!" said a man near me.

We moved forward and came up with the rest of the company in a clearing. The platoons formed up and took casualty reports. Japanese mortar and artillery fire increased. The shelling became heavy, indicating the probability of a counterattack. Most of their fire whistled over us and fell to our rear. This seemed strange although fortunate to me at the time. The order came for us to move out a short distance to the edge of the scrub. At approximately 1650 I looked out across the open airfield toward the southern extremities of the coral ridges—collectively called Bloody Nose Ridge—and saw vehicles of some sort moving amid swirling clouds of dust.

"Hey," I said to a veteran next to me, "what are those amtracs doing all the way across the airfield toward the Jap lines?"

"Them ain't amtracs; they're Nip tanks!" he said.

Shell bursts appeared among the enemy tanks. Some of our Sherman tanks had arrived at the edge of the airfield on our left and opened fire. Because of the clouds of dust and the shellfire, I couldn't see much and didn't see any enemy infantry, but the firing on our left was heavy.

Word came for us to deploy on the double. The riflemen formed a line at the edge of the scrub along a trail and lay prone, trying to take what cover they could. From the beginning to the end on Peleliu, it was all but impossible to dig into the hard coral rock, so the men piled rocks around themselves or got behind logs and debris.

Snafu and I set up our 60mm mortar a few yards behind them, across the trail in a shallow crater. Everyone got edgy as the order came, "Stand by to repel counterattack. Counter-attack hitting I Company's front."

I didn't know where Company I was, but I thought it was on our left—somewhere. Although I had great confidence in our officers and NCOs, it seemed to me that we were alone and confused in the middle of a rumbling chaos with snipers everywhere and with no contact with any other units. I thought all of us would be lost.

"They needta get some more damned troops up here," growled Snafu, his standard remark in a tight spot.

Snafu set up the gun, and I removed an HE (high explosive) shell from a canister in my ammo bag. At last we could return fire!

Snafu yelled, "Fire!"

Just then a Marine tank to our rear mistook us for enemy troops. As soon as my hand went up to drop the round down the tube, a machine gun cut loose. It sounded like one of ours—and from the rear of all places! As I peeped over the edge of the crater through the dust and smoke and saw a Sherman tank in a clearing behind us, the tank fired its 75mm gun off to our right rear. The shell exploded nearby, around a bend in the same trail we were on. I then heard the report of a Japanese field gun located there as it returned fire on the tank. Again I tried to fire, but the machine gun opened up as before.

"Sledgehammer, don't let him hit that shell. We'll all be blown to hell," said a worried ammo carrier crouched in the crater near me.

"Don't worry, that's my hand he just about hit," I snapped.

Our tank and the Japanese field gun kept up their duel.

"By god, when that tank knocks out that Nip gun he'll swing his 75 over thisaway, and it'll be our ass. He thinks we're Nips," said a veteran in the crater.

"Oh, Jesus!" someone moaned.

A surge of panic rose within me. In a brief moment our tank had reduced me from a well-trained, determined assistant mortar gunner to a quivering mass of terror. It was not just that I was being fired at by a machine gun that unnerved me so terribly, but that it was one of ours. To be killed by the enemy was bad enough; that was a real possibility I had prepared myself for. But to be killed by mistake by my own comrades was something I found hard to accept. It was just too much.

An authoritative voice across the trail yelled, "Secure the mortar."

A volunteer crawled off to the left, and soon the tank ceased firing on us. We learned later that our tankers were firing on us because we had moved too far ahead. They thought we were enemy support for the field gun. This also explained why the enemy shelling was passing over and exploding behind us. Tragically, the marine who saved us by identifying us to the tanker was shot off the tank and killed by a sniper.

The heavy firing on our left had about subsided, so the Japanese counterattack had been broken. Regrettably, I hadn't helped at all, because we were pinned down by one of our own tanks.

Some of us went along the trail and looked at the Japanese field gun. It was a well-made, formidable-looking piece of artillery, but I was surprised that the wheels were the heavy wooden kind typical of field guns of the nineteenth century. The Japanese gun crew was sprawled around the piece.

"Them's the biggest Nips I ever saw," one veteran said.

"Look at them sonsabitches; they's all over six foot tall," said another.

"That must be some of that 'Flower of the Kwantung Army' we've been hearing about," put in a corporal.

The Japanese counterattack was no wild, suicidal *banzai* charge such as Marine experience in the past would have led us to expect. Numerous times during D day I heard the dogmatic claim by experienced veterans that the enemy would *banzai.*

"They'll pull a *banzai,* and we'll tear their ass up. Then we can get the hell offa this hot rock, and maybe the CG will send the division back to Melbourne."

Rather than a *banzai,* the Japanese counterthrust turned out to be a well-coordinated tank-infantry attack. Approximately one company of Japanese infantry, together with about thirteen tanks, had moved carefully across the airfield until annihilated by the Marines on our left. This was our first warning that the Japanese might fight differently on Peleliu than they had elsewhere.

Just before dusk, a Japanese mortar concentration hit 3/5's command post. Our CO, Lt. Col. Austin C. Shofner,* was hit while trying to establish contact among the companies of our battalion. He was evacuated and put aboard a hospital ship.

Companies I, K, and L couldn't regain contact before nightfall. Each dug in in a circular defense for the night. The situation was precarious. We were isolated, nearly out of water in the terrible heat, and ammunition was low. Lt. Col. Lewis Walt, accompanied by only a runner, came out into that pitch-dark, enemy-infested scrub, located all the companies, and directed us into the division's line on the airfield. He should have won a Medal of Honor for that feat!†

Rumor had it, as we dug in, that the division had suffered heavy casualties in the landing and subsequent fighting. The veterans I knew said it had been about the worst day of fighting they had ever seen.‡

It was an immense relief to me when we got our gun pit completed and had registered in our gun by firing two or three rounds of HE into an area out in front of Company K. My thirst was almost unbearable, my stomach was tied in knots, and sweat soaked me. Dissolving some K ration dextrose

---

*Shofner had assumed command of 3/5 before the Peleliu campaign. Not only was he highly respected, but his men considered him someone special. As a captain, he had survived the fighting on Corregidor, been captured by the Japanese, escaped, and had returned to combat. He came back to the division later, and commanded the 1st Battalion, 1st Marines on Okinawa. He retired from the Corps as a brigadier general.

†Walt was the executive officer of the 5th Marines when the battle for Peleliu began. He remained with 3/5 for a few days as its commanding officer until a replacement was named. A combat Marine in the truest sense, Walt had served with the 1st Marine Division on Guadalcanal and at Cape Gloucester. He had won the Navy Cross for heroism. He went on to serve in the Korean War and later in Vietnam where, as a lieutenant general, he commanded the III Marine Amphibious Corps for nearly two years. He retired as a general after serving as assistant commandant of the Marine Corps.

‡Casualty figures for the 1st Marine Division on D day reflected the severity of the fighting and the ferocity of the Japanese defense. The division staff had predicted D day losses of 500 casualties, but the total figure was 1,111 killed and wounded, not including heat prostration cases.

tablets in my mouth helped, and I took the last sip of my dwindling water supply. We had no idea when relief would get through with additional water. Artillery shells shrieked and whistled back and forth overhead with increasing frequency, and small-arms fire rattled everywhere.

In the eerie green light of star shells swinging pendulum-like on their parachutes so that shadows danced and swayed around crazily, I started taking off my right shoe.

"Sledgehammer, what the hell are you doin'?" Snafu asked in an exasperated tone.

"Taking off my boondockers; my feet hurt," I replied.

"Have you gone Asiatic?" he asked excitedly. "What the hell are you gonna do in your stockin' feet if the Nips come bustin' outa that jungle, or across this field? We may have to get outa this hole and haul tail if we're ordered to. They're probably gonna pull a *banzai* before daybreak, and how do you reckon you'll move around on this coral in your stockin's?"

I said that I just wasn't thinking. He reamed me out good and told me we would be lucky to get our shoes off before the island was secured. I thanked God my foxhole buddy was a combat veteran.

Snafu then nonchalantly drew his kabar and stuck it in the coral gravel near his right hand. My stomach tightened and gooseflesh chilled my back and shoulders at the sight of the long blade in the greenish light and the realization of why he placed it within such easy reach. He then checked his .45 automatic pistol. I followed his example with my kabar as I crouched on the other side of the mortar, checked my carbine, and looked over the mortar shells (HE and flares) stacked up within reach. We settled down for the long night.

"Is that theirs or ours, Snafu?" I asked each time a shell went over.

There was nothing subtle or intimate about the approach and explosion of an artillery shell. When I heard the whistle of an approaching one in the distance, every muscle in my body contracted. I braced myself in a puny effort to keep from being swept away. I felt utterly helpless.

As the fiendish whistle grew louder, my teeth ground

against each other, my heart pounded, my mouth dried, my eyes narrowed, sweat poured over me, my breath came in short irregular gasps, and I was afraid to swallow lest I choke. I always prayed, sometimes out loud.

Under certain conditions of range and terrain, I could hear the shell approaching from a considerable distance, thus prolonging the suspense into seemingly unending torture. At the instant the voice of the shell grew the loudest, it terminated in a flash and a deafening explosion similar to the crash of a loud clap of thunder. The ground shook and the concussion hurt my ears. Shell fragments tore the air apart as they rushed out, whirring and ripping. Rocks and dirt clattered onto the deck as smoke of the exploded shell dissipated.

To be under a barrage of prolonged shelling simply magnified all the terrible physical and emotional effects of one shell. To me, artillery was an invention of hell. The onrushing whistle and scream of the big steel package of destruction was the pinnacle of violent fury and the embodiment of pent-up evil. It was the essence of violence and of man's inhumanity to man. I developed a passionate hatred for shells. To be killed by a bullet seemed so clean and surgical. But shells would not only tear and rip the body, they tortured one's mind almost beyond the brink of sanity. After each shell I was wrung out, limp and exhausted.

During prolonged shelling, I often had to restrain myself and fight back a wild, inexorable urge to scream, to sob, and to cry. As Peleliu dragged on, I feared that if I ever lost control of myself under shell fire my mind would be shattered. I hated shells as much for their damage to the mind as to the body. To be under heavy shell fire was to me by far the most terrifying of combat experiences. Each time it left me feeling more forlorn and helpless, more fatalistic, and with less confidence that I could escape the dreadful law of averages that inexorably reduced our numbers. Fear is many-faceted and has many subtle nuances, but the terror and desperation endured under heavy shelling are by far the most unbearable.

The night wore on endlessly, and I was hardly able to catch even so much as a catnap. Toward the predawn hours, numerous enemy artillery pieces concentrated their fire on the area

D-DAY

⊔⊔⊔⊔⊔⊔   FRONT LINES

—————   REGIMENTAL BOUNDARIES

◀━━━   MAIN COUNTERATTACK

◁━   SECONDARY COUNTERATTACKS
       OR STRONG PRESSURE

1000   500   0   1000 YDS

of scrub jungle from which Lt. Col. Lewis Walt had brought us. The shells screeched and whined over us and crashed beyond in the scrub.

"Whoo, boy, listen to them Nip gunners plaster that area," said a buddy in the next hole.

"Yeah," Snafu said, "they must think we're still out there and I betcha they'll counterattack right across through that place, too."

"Thank God we are here and not out there," our buddy said.

The barrage increased in tempo as the Japanese gave the vacant scrub jungle a real pounding. When the barrage finally subsided, I heard someone say with a chuckle, "Aw, don't knock it off now, you bastards. Fire all your goddamn shells out there in the wrong place."

"Don't worry, knucklehead, they'll have plenty left to fire in the right place, which is going to be where they see us when daylight comes," another voice said.

Supplies had been slow in keeping up with the needs of the 5th Marines' infantry companies on D day. The Japanese kept heavy artillery, mortar, and machine-gun fire on the entire regimental beach throughout the day; enemy artillery and mortar observers called down their fire on amphibian vehicles as soon as they reached the beach. This made it difficult to get the critical supplies ashore and the wounded evacuated. All of Peleliu was a front line on D day. No one but the dead was out of reach of enemy fire. The shore party people* did their best, but they couldn't make up for the heavy losses of amtracs needed to bring the supplies to us.

We weren't aware of the problems on the beach, being too occupied with our own. We griped, cursed, and prayed that water would get to us. I had used mine more sparingly than some men had, but I finally emptied both of my canteens by the time we finished the gun pit. Dissolving dextrose tablets in my mouth helped a little, but my thirst grew worse through

*The shore party battalion consisted of Marines assigned the mission of unloading and handling supplies and of directing logistics traffic on the beach during an amphibious assault.

the night. For the first time in my life, I appreciated fully the motion picture cliche of a man on a desert crying, "Water, water."

Artillery shells still passed back and forth overhead just before dawn, but there wasn't much small-arms fire in our area. Abruptly, there swept over us some of the most intense Japanese machine-gun fire I ever saw concentrated in such a small area. Tracers streaked and bullets cracked not more than a foot over the top of our gun pit. We lay flat on our backs and waited as the burst ended.

The gun cut loose again, joined by a second and possibly a third. Streams of bluish white tracers (American tracers were red) poured thickly overhead, apparently coming from somewhere near the airfield. The cross fire kept up for at least a quarter of an hour. They really poured it on.

Shortly before the machine guns opened fire, we had received word to move out at daylight with the entire 5th Marine regiment in an attack across the airfield. I prayed the machine-gun fire would subside before we had to move out. We were pinned down tightly. To raise anything above the edge of the gun pit would have resulted in its being cut off as though by a giant scythe. After about fifteen minutes, firing ceased abruptly. We sighed in relief.

D PLUS 1

Dawn finally came, and with it the temperature rose rapidly.

"Where the hell is our water?" growled men around me. We had suffered many cases of heat prostration the day before and needed water or we'd all pass out during the attack, I thought.

"Stand by to move out!" came the order. We squared away all of our personal gear. Snafu secured the gun, took it down by folding the bipod and strapping it, while I packed my remaining shells in my ammo bag.

"I've got to get some water or I'm gonna crack up," I said.

At that moment, a buddy nearby yelled and beckoned to us, "Come on, we've found a well."

I snatched up my carbine and took off, empty canteens bouncing on my cartridge belt. About twenty-five yards away, a group of Company K men gathered at a hole about fifteen feet in diameter and ten feet deep. I peered over the edge. At the bottom and to one side was a small pool of milky-looking water. Japanese shells were beginning to fall on the airfield, but I was too thirsty to care. One of the men was already in the hole filling canteens and passing them up. The buddy who had called me was drinking from a helmet with its liner removed. He gulped down the milky stuff and said, "It isn't beer, but it's wet." Helmets and canteens were passed up to those of us waiting.

"Don't bunch up, you guys. We'll draw Jap fire sure as hell," shouted one man.

The first man who drank the water looked at me and said, "I feel sick."

A company corpsman came up yelling, "Don't drink that water, you guys. It may be poisoned." I had just lifted a full helmet to my lips when the man next to me fell, holding his sides and retching violently. I threw down my water, milky with coral dust, and started assisting the corpsman with the man who was ill. He went to the rear, where he recovered. Whether it was poison or pollution we never knew.

"Get your gear on and stand by," someone yelled.

Frustrated and angry, I headed back to the gun pit. A detail came up about that time with water cans, ammo, and rations. A friend and I helped each other pour water out of a five-gallon can into our canteen cups. Our hands shook, we were so eager to quench our thirst. I was amazed that the water looked brown in my aluminum canteen cup. No matter, I took a big gulp—and almost spit it out despite my terrible thirst. It was awful. Full of rust and oil, it stunk. I looked into the cup in disbelief as a blue film of oil floated lazily on the surface of the smelly brown liquid. Cramps gripped the pit of my stomach.

My friend looked up from his cup and groaned, "Sledgehammer, are you thinking what I'm thinking?"

"I sure am, that oil drum steam-cleaning detail on

Pavuvu," I said wearily. (We had been together on a detail assigned to clean out the drums.)

"I'm a sonofabitch," he growled. "I'll never goof off on another work party as long as I live."

I told him I didn't think it was our fault. We weren't the only ones assigned to the detail, and it was obvious to us from the start (if not to some supply officer) that the method we had been ordered to use didn't really clean the drums. But that knowledge was slight consolation out there on the Peleliu airfield in the increasing heat. As awful as the stuff was, we had to drink it or suffer heat exhaustion. After I drained my cup, a residue of rust resembling coffee grounds remained, and my stomach ached.

We picked up our gear and prepared to move out in preparation for the attack across the airfield. Because 3/5's line during the night faced south and was back-to-back with that of 2/5, we had to move to the right and prepare to attack northward across the airfield with the other battalions of the regiment. The Japanese shelling of our lines began at daylight, so we had to move out fast and in dispersed formation. We finally got into position for the attack and were told to hit the deck until ordered to move again. This suited me fine, because the Japanese shelling was getting worse. Our artillery, ships, and planes were laying down a terrific amount of fire in front on the airfield and ridges beyond in preparation for our attack. Our preattack barrage lasted about half an hour. I knew we would move out when it ended.

As I lay on the blistering hot coral and looked across the open airfield, heat waves shimmered and danced, distorting the view of Bloody Nose Ridge. A hot wind blew in our faces.

An NCO hurried by, crouching low and yelling, "Keep moving out there, you guys. There's less chance you'll be hit if you go across fast and don't stop."

"Let's go," shouted an officer who waved toward the airfield. We moved at a walk, then a trot, in widely dispersed waves. Four infantry battalions—from left to right 2/1, 1/5, 2/5, and 3/5 (this put us on the edge of the airfield)—moved across the open, fire-swept airfield. My only concern then was my duty and survival, not panoramic combat scenes. But I often wondered later what that attack looked like to aerial observers and to those not immersed in the firestorms. All I was aware of were the small area immediately around me and the deafening noise.

Bloody Nose Ridge dominated the entire airfield. The Japanese had concentrated their heavy weapons on high ground; these were directed from observation posts at elevations as high as three hundred feet, from which they could look down on us as we advanced. I could see men moving ahead of my squad, but I didn't know whether our battalion, 3/5, was moving across behind 2/5 and then wheeling to the right. There were also men about twenty yards to our rear.

We moved rapidly in the open, amid craters and coral rubble, through ever-increasing enemy fire. I saw men to my right and left running bent as low as possible. The shells screeched and whistled, exploding all around us. In many respects it was more terrifying than the landing, because there were no vehicles to carry us along, not even the thin steel sides of an amtrac for protection. We were exposed, running on our own power through a veritable shower of deadly metal and the constant crash of explosions.

For me the attack resembled World War I movies I had seen of suicidal Allied infantry attacks through shell fire on the Western Front. I clenched my teeth, squeezed my carbine stock, and recited over and over to myself, "The Lord is my shepherd; I shall not want. Yea, though I walk through the valley of the shadow of death, I will fear no evil, for Thou art with me; Thy rod and Thy staff comfort me. . . ."

The sun bore down unmercifully, and the heat was exhausting. Smoke and dust from the barrage limited my vision. The ground seemed to sway back and forth under the concussions. I felt as though I were floating along in the vortex of some unreal thunderstorm. Japanese bullets snapped and cracked, and tracers went by me on both sides at waist height. This deadly small-arms fire seemed almost insignificant amid the erupting shells. Explosions and the hum and the growl of shell fragments shredded the air. Chunks of blasted coral stung my face and hands while steel fragments spattered down on the hard rock like hail on a city street. Everywhere shells flashed like giant firecrackers.

Through the haze I saw Marines stumble and pitch forward as they got hit. I then looked neither right nor left but just straight to my front. The farther we went, the worse it got. The noise and concussion pressed in on my ears like a vise. I gritted my teeth and braced myself in anticipation of the shock of being struck down at any moment. It seemed impossible that any of us could make it across. We passed several craters that offered shelter, but I remembered the order to keep moving. Because of the superb discipline and excellent esprit of the Marines, it had never occurred to us that the attack might fail.

About halfway across, I stumbled and fell forward. At that instant a large shell exploded to my left with a flash and a roar. A fragment ricocheted off the deck and growled over my head as I went down. On my right, Snafu let out a grunt and fell as the fragment struck him. As he went down, he grabbed his left side. I crawled quickly to him. Fortunately the fragment had spent much of its force, and luckily hit against Snafu's heavy web pistol belt. The threads on the broad belt were frayed in about an inch-square area.

I knelt beside him, and we checked his side. He had only a bruise to show for his incredible luck. On the deck I saw the chunk of steel that had hit him. It was about an inch square and a half inch thick. I picked up the fragment and showed it to him. Snafu motioned toward his pack. Terrified though I was amid the hellish chaos, I calmly juggled the fragment around in my hands—it was still hot—and dropped it into his pack. He yelled something that sounded dimly like, "Let's go." I reached for the carrying strap of the mortar, but he pushed my hand away and lifted the gun to his shoulder. We got up and moved on as fast as we could. Finally we got across and caught up with other members of our company who lay panting and sweating amid low bushes on the northeastern side of the airfield.

How far we had come in the open I never knew, but it must have been several hundred yards. Everyone was visibly shaken by the thunderous barrage we had just come through. When I looked into the eyes of those fine Guadalcanal and

Cape Gloucester veterans, some of America's best, I no longer felt ashamed of my trembling hands and almost laughed at myself with relief.

To be shelled by massed artillery and mortars is absolutely terrifying, but to be shelled in the open is terror compounded beyond the belief of anyone who hasn't experienced it. The attack across Peleliu's airfield was the worst combat experience I had during the entire war. It surpassed, by the intensity of the blast and shock of the bursting shells, all the subsequent horrifying ordeals on Peleliu and Okinawa.

The heat was incredibly intense. The temperature that day reached 105 degrees in the shade (we were *not* in the shade) and would soar to 115 degrees on subsequent days. Corpsmen tagged numerous Marines with heat prostration as being too weak to continue. We evacuated them. My boondockers were so full of sweat that my feet felt squishy when I walked. Lying on my back, I held up first one foot and then the other. Water literally poured out of each shoe.

"Hey, Sledgehammer," chuckled a man sprawled next to me, "you been walking on water."

"Maybe that's why he didn't get hit coming across that airfield," laughed another.

I tried to grin and was glad the inevitable wisecracks had started up again.

Because of the shape of the airfield, 3/5 was pinched out of the line by 2/5 on our left and 3/7 on our right after our crossing. We swung eastward and Company K tied in with 3/7, which was attacking in the swampy areas on the eastern side of the airfield.

As we picked up our gear, a veteran remarked to me with a jerk of his head toward the airfield where the shelling continued, "That was rough duty; hate to have to do that every day."

We moved through the swamps amid sniper fire and dug in for the night with our backs to the sea. I positioned my mortar in a meager gun pit on a slight rise of ground about fifteen feet from a sheer rock bluff that dropped about ten feet to the ocean. The jungle growth was extremely thick, but we had a clear hole in the jungle canopy above the gun pit through which we could fire the mortar without having shells hit the foliage and explode.

Most of the men in the company were out of sight through the thick mangroves. Still short of water, everyone was weakened by the heat and the exertions of the day. I had used my water as sparingly as possible and had to eat twelve salt tablets that day. (We kept close count of these tablets. They caused retching if we took more than necessary.)

The enemy infiltration that followed was a nightmare. Illumination fired above the airfield the previous night (D day) had discouraged infiltration in my sector, but others had experienced plenty of the hellish sort of thing we now faced and would suffer every night for the remainder of our time on Peleliu. The Japanese were noted for their infiltration tactics. On Peleliu they refined them and practiced them at a level of intensity not seen in the past.

After we had dug in late that afternoon we followed a procedure used nearly every night. Using directions from our observer, we registered in the mortar by firing a couple of HE shells into a defilade or some similar avenue of approach in front of the company not covered by our machine-gun or rifle fire where the enemy might advance. We then set up alternate aiming stakes to mark other terrain features on which we could fire. Everyone lighted up a smoke, and the password for the night was whispered along the line, passed from foxhole to foxhole. The password always contained the letter *L,* which the Japanese had difficulty pronouncing the way an American would.

Word came along as to the disposition of the platoons of the company and of the units on our flanks. We checked our weapons and placed equipment for quick access in the coming night. As darkness fell, the order was passed, "The smoking lamp is out." All talking ceased. One man in each foxhole settled down as comfortably as he could to sleep on the jagged rock while his buddy strained eyes and ears to detect any movement or sound in the darkness.

An occasional Japanese mortar shell came into the area, but things were pretty quiet for a couple of hours. We threw up a few HE shells as harassing fire to discourage movement in front of the company. I could hear the sea lapping gently against the base of the rocks behind us.

The Japanese soon began trying to infiltrate all over the company front and along the shore to our rear. We heard sporadic bursts of small-arms fire and the bang of grenades. Our fire discipline had to be strict in such situations so as not to mistakenly shoot a fellow Marine. The loose accusation was often made during the war that Americans were "trigger happy" at night and shot at anything that moved. This accusation was often correct when referring to rear-area or inexperienced troops; but in the rifle companies, it was also accepted as gospel that anybody who moved out of his hole at night without first informing the men around him, and who didn't reply immediately with the password upon being challenged, could expect to get shot.

Suddenly movement in the dried vegetation toward the front of the gun pit got my attention. I turned cautiously around and waited, holding Snafu's cocked .45 automatic pistol at the ready. The rustling movements drew closer. My heart pounded. It was definitely not one of Peleliu's numerous land crabs that scuttled over the ground all night, every night. Someone was slowly crawling toward the gun pit. Then silence. More noise, then silence. Rustling noises, then silence—the typical pattern.

It must be a Japanese trying to slip in as close as possible, stopping frequently to prevent detection, I thought. He probably had seen the muzzle flash when I fired the mortar. He would throw a grenade at any moment or jump me with his bayonet. I couldn't see a thing in the pale light and inky blackness of the shadows.

Crouching low so as to see better any silhouette against the sky above me, I flipped off the thumb safety on the big pistol. A helmeted figure loomed up against the night sky in front of the gun pit. I couldn't tell from the silhouette whether the helmet was U.S. or Japanese. Aiming the automatic at the center of the head, I pressed the grip safety as I also squeezed the trigger slightly to take up the slack. The thought raced through my mind that he was too close to use his grenade so

he would probably use a bayonet or knife on me. My hand
was steady even though I was scared. It was he or I.

"What's the password?" I said in a low voice.

No answer.

"Password!" I demanded as my finger tightened on the
trigger. The big pistol would fire and buck with recoil in a
moment, but to hurry and jerk the trigger would mean a miss
for sure. Then he'd be on me.

"Sle-Sledgehammer!" stammered the figure.

I eased up on the trigger.

"It's de l'Eau, Jay de l'Eau. You got any water?"

"Jay, why didn't you give the password? I nearly shot you!"
I gasped.

He saw the pistol and moaned, "Oh, Jesus," as he realized

what had nearly happened. "I thought you knew it was me," he said weakly.

Jay was one of my closest friends. He was a Gloucester veteran and knew better than to prowl around the way he had just done. If my finger had applied the last bit of pressure to that trigger, Jay would have died instantly. It would have been his own fault, but that wouldn't have mattered to me. My life would have been ruined if I had killed him, even under those circumstances.

My right hand trembled violently as I lowered the big automatic. I had to flip on the thumb safety with my left hand; my right thumb was too weak. I felt nauseated and weak and wanted to cry. Jay crept over and sat on the edge of the gun pit.

"I'm sorry, Sledgehammer. I thought you knew it was me," he said.

After handing him a canteen, I shuddered violently and thanked God that Jay was still alive. "Just how in the hell could I tell it was you in the dark with Nips all over the place?" I snarled. Then I reamed out one of the best friends I ever had.

HEADING NORTH

"Get your gear on and stand by to move out."

We shouldered our loads and began moving slowly out of the thick swamp. As I passed a shallow foxhole where Robert B. Oswalt had been dug in, I asked a man nearby if the word were true about Oswalt being killed. Sadly, he said yes. Oswalt had been fatally wounded in the head. A bright young mind that aspired to delve into the mysteries of the human brain to alleviate human suffering had itself been destroyed by a tiny chunk of metal. What a waste, I thought. War is such self-defeating, organized madness the way it destroys a nation's best.

I wondered also about the hopes and aspirations of a dead Japanese we had just dragged out of the water. But those of us caught up in the maelstrom of combat had little compassion for the enemy. As a wise, salty NCO had put it one day on

Pavuvu when asked by a replacement if he ever felt sorry for the Japanese when they got hit, "Hell no! It's them or us!"

We moved out, keeping our five-pace interval, through the thick swamp toward the sound of heavy firing. The heat was almost unbearable, and we were halted frequently to prevent heat prostration in the 115-degree temperature.

We came to the eastern edge of the airfield and halted in the shade of a scrub thicket. Throwing down our gear, we fell on the deck, sweating, panting, exhausted. I had no more than reached for a canteen when a rifle bullet snapped overhead.

"He's close. Get down," said an officer. The rifle cracked again. "Sounds like he's right through there a little way," the officer said.

"I'll get him," said Howard Nease.

"OK, go ahead, but watch yourself."

Nease, a Gloucester veteran, grabbed his rifle and took off into the scrub with the nonchalance of a hunter going after a rabbit in a bush. He angled to one side so as to steal up on the sniper from the rear. We waited a few anxious moments, then heard two M1 shots.

"Ole Howard got him," confidently remarked one of the men.

Soon Howard reappeared wearing a triumphant grin and carrying a Japanese rifle and some personal effects. Everyone congratulated him on his skill, and he reacted with his usual modesty.

"Rack 'em up, boys," he laughed.

We moved out in a few minutes through some knee-high bushes onto the open area at the edge of the airfield. The heat was terrific. When we halted again, we lay under the meager shade of the bushes. I held up each foot and let the sweat pour out of my boondockers. A man on the crew of the other weapon in our mortar section passed out. He was a Gloucester veteran, but Peleliu's heat proved too much for him. We evacuated him, but unlike some heat prostration cases, he never returned to the company.

Some men pulled the rear border of their camouflaged helmet cover out from between the steel and the liner so the cloth hung down over the backs of the necks. This gave them some protection against the blistering sun, but they looked like the French foreign legion in a desert.

After a brief rest, we continued in dispersed order. We could see Bloody Nose Ridge to our left front. Northward from that particular area, 2d Battalion, 1st Marines (2/1) was fighting desperately against Japanese hidden in well-protected caves. We were moving up to relieve 1st Battalion, 5th Marines (1/5) and would tie in with the 1st Marines. Then we were to attack northward along the eastern side of the ridges.

On this particular day, 17 September, the relief was slow and difficult. As 3/5 moved in and the men of 1/5 moved out, the Japanese in the ridges on our left front poured on the artillery and mortar fire. I pitied those tired men in 1/5 as they tried to extricate themselves without casualties. Their battalion, as with the others in the 5th Marines, had had a rough time crossing the airfield through the heavy fire the previous day. But once they got across they met heavy resistance from pillboxes on the eastern side. We had been more fortunate: after getting across the airfield, 3/5 moved into the swamp, which wasn't defended as heavily.

With the relief of 1/5 finally completed, we tied in with the 1st Marines on our left and 2/5 on our right. Our battalion was to attack during the afternoon through the low ground along the eastern side of Bloody Nose, while 2/5 was to clean out the jungle between our right flank and the eastern shore.

As soon as we moved forward, we came under heavy flanking fire from Bloody Nose Ridge on our left. Snafu delivered his latest communiqué on the tactical situation to me as we hugged the deck for protection: "They need to git some more damn troops up here," he growled.

Our artillery was called in, but our mortars could fire only to the front of the company and not on the left flank area, because that was in the area of the 1st Marines. The Japanese observers on the ridge had a clear, unobstructed view of us. Their artillery shells whined and shrieked, accompanied by the deadly whispering of the mortar shells. Enemy fire grew more intense, until we were pinned down. We were getting the first bitter taste of Bloody Nose Ridge, and we had increasing compassion for the 1st Marines on our left who were battering squarely into it.

The Japanese ceased firing when our movement stopped. Yet as surely as three men grouped together, or anyone started moving, enemy mortars opened up on us. If a general movement occurred, their artillery joined in. The Japanese began to demonstrate the excellent fire discipline that was to characterize their use of all weapons on Peleliu. They fired only when they could expect to inflict maximum casualties and stopped firing as soon as the opportunity passed. Thus our observers and planes had difficulty finding their well-camouflaged positions in the ridges.

When the enemy ceased firing artillery and mortars from caves, they shut protective steel doors and waited while our artillery, naval guns, and 81mm mortars blasted away at the rock. If we moved ahead under our protective fire support, the Japanese pinned us down and inflicted serious losses on us, because it was almost impossible to dig a protective foxhole in the rock. No individual events of the attack stuck in my mind, just the severe fire from our left and the feeling that any time the Japanese decided to do so, they could have blown us sky high.

Our attack was called off late in the afternoon, and we were ordered to set up our mortar for the night. An NCO came by and told me to go with him and about four others from other platoons to unload an amtrac bringing up supplies for Company K. We arrived at the designated place, dispersed a little so as not to draw fire, and waited for the amtrac. In a few minutes it came clanking up in a swirl of white dust.

"You guys from K Company, 5th Marines?" asked the driver.

"Yeah, you got chow and ammo for us?" asked our NCO.

"Yeah, sure have. Got a unit of fire,* water, and rations.

---

*Determined from experience, a unit of fire was the amount of ammunition that would last, on average, for one day of heavy fighting. A unit of fire for the M1 rifle was 100 rounds; for the carbine, 45 rounds; for the .45 caliber pistol, 14 rounds; for the light machine gun, 1,500 rounds; and for the 60mm mortar, 100 rounds.

Better get it unloaded as soon as you can, or we'll draw fire," the driver said as his machine lurched to a halt and he climbed down.

The tractor was an older model such as I had landed from on D day. It didn't have a drop tailgate; so we climbed aboard and hefted the heavy ammo boxes over the side and down onto the deck.

"Let's go, boys," our NCO said as he and a couple of us climbed onto the tractor.

I saw him gaze in amazement down into the cargo area of the tractor. At the bottom, wedged under a pile of ammo boxes, we saw one of those infernal fifty-five-gallon oil drums of water. Filled, they weighed several hundred pounds. Our NCO rested his arms on the side of the tractor and remarked in an exasperated tone, "It took a bloody genius of a supply officer to do that. How in the hell are we supposed to get that drum outa there?"

"I don't know," said the driver. "I just bring it up."

We cursed and began unloading the ammo as fast as possible. We had expected the water to be in several five-gallon cans, each of which weighed a little more than forty pounds. We worked as rapidly as possible, but then we heard that inevitable and deadly *whisshh-shh-shh*. Three big mortar shells exploded, one after the other, not far from us.

"Uh oh, the stuff's hit the fan now," groaned one of my buddies.

"Bear a hand, you guys. On the double," said our NCO.

"Look, you guys, I'm gonna hafta get this tractor the hell outa here. If it gets knocked out and it's my fault, the lieutenant'll have my can in a crack," groaned the driver.

We had no gripe with the driver, and we didn't blame him. The amtrac drivers on Peleliu were praised by everyone for doing such a fine job. Their bravery and sense of responsibility were above question. We worked like beavers as our NCO said to him, "I'm sorry, ole buddy, but if we don't get these supplies unloaded, it's *our* ass!"

More mortar shells fell out to one side, and the fragments swished through the air. It was apparent that the Japanese mortar crew was trying to bracket us, but was afraid to fire too much for fear of being seen by our observers. We sweated and panted to get the ammo unloaded. We unloaded the water drum with a rope sling.

"You fellows need any help?" asked a Marine who appeared from the rear.

We hadn't noticed him before he spoke. He wore green dungarees, leggings, and a cloth-covered helmet like ourselves and carried a .45 caliber automatic pistol like any mortar gunner, machine gunner, or one of our officers. Of course, he wore no rank insignia, being in combat. What astonished us was that he looked to be more than fifty years old and wore glasses—a rarity (for example, only two men in Company K wore them). When he took off his helmet to mop his brow, we saw his gray hair. (Most men forward of division and regimental CPs were in their late teens or early twenties. Many officers were in their mid-twenties.)

When asked who he was and what unit he was in, he replied, "Capt. Paul Douglas. I was division adjutant until that barrage hit the 5th Marines' CP yesterday, then I was assigned as R-1 [personnel officer] in the 5th Regiment. I am very proud to be with the 5th Marines," he said.

"Gosh, Cap'n! You don't have to be up here at all, do you?" asked one of our detail in disbelief as he passed ammo boxes to the fatherly officer.

"No," Douglas said, "but I always want to know how you boys up here are making out and want to help if I can. What company are you fellows from?"

"From K Company, sir," I answered.

His face lit up, and he said, "Ah, you're in Andy Haldane's company."

We asked Douglas if he knew Ack Ack. He said, yes, that they were old friends. As we finished unloading, we all agreed that there wasn't a finer company commander than Captain Haldane.

A couple more mortar shells crashed nearby. Our luck would run out soon. Japanese gunners usually got right on target. So we yelled, "Shove off," to the driver. He waved and clanked away in his unloaded amtrac. Captain Douglas helped us stack some of the ammo and told us we had better disperse.

I heard a buddy ask, "What's that crazy old gray-headed guy doing up here if he could be back at regiment?"

Our NCO growled, "Shut up! Knock it off, you eightball! He's trying to help knuckleheads like you, and he's a damned good man."*

Each man in our detail took up a load of supplies, bade Captain Douglas "so long," and started back to the company lines. Other men went back to bring up the rest of the supplies before dark. We ate chow and finished preparations for the night. That was the first night on Peleliu that I was able to make up a cup of hot bouillon from the dehydrated tablets in my K rations and a canteen cup of heated, polluted, oily water. Hot as the weather was, it was the most nourishing and refreshing food I had eaten in three days. The next day we got fresh water. It was a great relief after that polluted stuff.

Dug in next to our gun pit were 1st Lt. Edward A. ("Hillbilly") Jones, Company K's machine-gun platoon leader, and a salty sergeant, John A. Teskevich. Things were quiet in our area except for our artillery's harassing fire pouring over; so after dark obscured us from Japanese observers, the two of them slipped over and sat at the edge of our gun pit. We shared rations and talked. The conversation turned out to be one of the most memorable of my life.†

Hillbilly was second only to Ack Ack in popularity among the enlisted men in Company K. He was a clean-cut, handsome, light-complexioned man—not large, but well built.

---

*Paul Douglas became a legend in the 1st Marine Division. This remarkable man was fifty-three years old, had been an economics professor at the University of Chicago, and had enlisted in the Marine Corps as a private. In the Peleliu battle he was slightly wounded carrying flamethrower ammunition up to the lines. At Okinawa he was wounded seriously by a bullet in the arm while carrying wounded for 3/5. Even after months of therapy, he didn't regain complete use of the limb.

Years after the war, I had the great pleasure of meeting and visiting with Senator Paul Douglas. I told him about the remark referring to him as the "crazy old gray-headed guy." He laughed heartily and expressed great pride in having served with the 1st Marine Division.

†Both Hillbilly and Teskevich were later killed.

Hillbilly told me he had been an enlisted man for several prewar years, had gone to the Pacific with the company, and had been commissioned following Guadalcanal. He didn't say why he was made an officer, but the word among the men was that he had been outstanding on Guadalcanal.

It was a widespread joke among men in the ranks during the war that an officer was made an officer and a gentleman by an act of Congress when he was commissioned. An act of Congress may have made Hillbilly an officer, but he was born a gentleman. No matter how filthy and dirty everyone was on the battlefield, Hillbilly's face always had a clean, fresh appearance. He was physically tough and hard and obviously morally strong. He sweated as much as any man but somehow seemed to stand above our foul and repulsive living conditions in the field. Hillbilly had a quiet and pleasant voice even in command. His accent was soft, more that of the deep South, which was familiar to me, than that of the hill country.

Between this man and all the Marines I knew there existed a deep mutual respect and warm friendliness. He had that rare ability to be friendly yet not familiar with enlisted men. He possessed a unique combination of those qualities of bravery, leadership, ability, integrity, dignity, straightforwardness, and compassion. The only other officer I ever knew who was his equal in all these qualities was Captain Haldane.

That night Hillbilly talked about his boyhood and his home in West Virginia. He asked me about mine. He also talked about his prewar years in the Marine Corps. Later I remembered little of what he said, but the quiet way he talked calmed me. He was optimistic about the battle in progress and seemed to understand and appreciate all my fears and apprehensions. I confided in him that many times I had been so terrified that I felt ashamed, and that some men didn't seem to be so afraid. He scoffed at my mention of being ashamed, and said that my fear had been no greater than anyone else's but that I was just honest enough to admit its magnitude. He told me that he was afraid, too, and that the first battle was the hardest because a man didn't know what to expect. Fear dwelled in everyone, Hillbilly said. Courage meant overcoming fear and doing one's duty in the presence of danger, not being unafraid.

The conversation with Hillbilly reassured me. When the sergeant came over and joined in after getting coffee, I felt almost lighthearted. As conversation trailed off, we sipped our joe in silence.

Suddenly, I heard a loud voice say clearly and distinctly, "You will survive the war!"

I looked first at Hillbilly and then at the sergeant. Each returned my glance with a quizzical expression on his face in the gathering darkness. Obviously they hadn't said anything.

"Did y'all hear that?" I asked.

"Hear what?" they both inquired.

"Someone said something," I said.

"I didn't hear anything. How about you?" said Hillbilly, turning to the sergeant.

"No, just that machine gun off to the left."

Shortly the word was passed to get settled for the night. Hillbilly and the sergeant crawled back to their hole as Snafu returned to the gun pit. Like most persons, I had always been skeptical about people seeing visions and hearing voices. So I didn't mention my experience to anyone. But I believed God spoke to me that night on that Peleliu battlefield, and I resolved to make my life amount to something after the war.

That night—the third since landing—as I settled back in the gun pit, I realized I needed a bath. In short, I stunk! My mouth felt, as the saying went, like I had gremlins walking around in it with muddy boots on. Short as it was, my hair was matted with dust and rifle oil. My scalp itched, and my stubble beard was becoming an increasing source of irritation in the heat. Drinking water was far too precious in those early days to use in brushing one's teeth or in shaving, even if the opportunity had arisen.

The personal bodily filth imposed upon the combat infantryman by living conditions on the battlefield was difficult for me to tolerate. It bothered almost everyone I knew. Even the hardiest Marine typically kept his rifle and his person clean. His language and his mind might need a good bit of cleaning up but not his weapon, his uniform, or his person.

We had this philosophy drilled into us in boot camp, and many times at Camp Elliott I had to pass personal inspection, to the point of clean fingernails, before being passed as fit to go on liberty. To be anything less than neat and sharp was considered a negative reflection on the Marine Corps and wasn't tolerated.

It was tradition and folklore of the 1st Marine Division that the troops routinely referred to themselves when in the field as "the raggedy-ass Marines." The emphasis during maneuvers and field problems was on combat readiness. Once back in camp, however, no matter where in the boondocks it was situated, the troops cleaned up before anything else.

In combat, cleanliness for the infantryman was all but impossible. Our filth added to our general misery. Fear and filth went hand in hand. It has always puzzled me that this important factor in our daily lives has received so little attention from historians and often is omitted from otherwise excellent personal memoirs by infantrymen. It is, of course, a vile subject, but it was as important to us then as being wet or dry, hot or cold, in the shade or exposed to the blistering sun, hungry, tired, or sick.

Early the next morning, 18 September, our artillery and 81mm mortars shelled Japanese positions to our front as we prepared to continue the previous day's attack northward on the eastern side of Bloody Nose Ridge. A typical pattern of attack in our company, or any other rifle company, went something like this. Our two mortars would fire on certain targets or areas known or thought to harbor the enemy. Our light-machine-gun squads fired on areas in front of the rifle platoons they were attached to support. Then two of the three rifle platoons moved out in dispersed order. The remaining platoon was held in company reserve.

Just before the riflemen moved out, we ceased fire with the mortars. The machine guns stopped also unless they were situated where they could fire over the heads of the advancing riflemen. The latter moved out at a walk to conserve energy. If they received enemy fire, they moved from place to place in short rushes. Thus they advanced until they reached the objective. The mortars stood by to fire if the riflemen ran into strong opposition, and the machine-gun squads moved forward to add their fire support.

The riflemen were the spearhead of any attack. Consequently they caught more hell than anybody else. The machine gunners had a tough job, because the Japanese concentrated on trying to knock them out. The flamethrower gunner had it rough and so did the rocket launcher gunners and the demolitions men. The 60mm mortarmen caught it from Japanese counterbattery fire of mortars and artillery, snipers (who were numerous), and bypassed Japanese machine guns (which were common). The tankers caught hell from mortar and artillery fire and mines. But it was always the riflemen who had the worst job. The rest of us only supported them.

Marine Corps tactics called for bypassing single snipers or machine guns in order to keep forward momentum. Bypassed Japanese were knocked out by a platoon or company of infantry in reserve. Thus mortars fired furiously on the enemy to the front while a small battle raged behind between bypassed, entrenched Japanese and Marines in reserve. These Japanese frequently fired from the rear, pinning down the advance and causing casualties. Troops had to be well disciplined to function this way, and leadership had to be the best to coordinate things under such chaotic conditions. Marine tactics resembled those developed by the Germans under Gen. Erich Ludendorff which proved so successful against the Allies in the spring of 1918.

If the riflemen hit heavy opposition, our 81mm mortars, artillery, tanks, ships, and planes were called on for support. These tactics worked well on Peleliu until the Marines hit the mutually supporting complex of caves and pillboxes in the maze of coral ridges. As heavy casualties mounted, the reserve rifle platoon, mortarmen, company officers, and anybody else available acted as stretcher bearers to get the wounded out from under fire as fast as possible. Every man in Company K, no matter what his rank or job, did duty as a ri-

fleman and stretcher bearer on numerous occasions on
Peleliu and later on Okinawa.

Shelling from the ridge positions on our left slowed us
down. Our planes made air strikes and our ships and artillery
attacked the ridges, but Japanese shells kept coming in. The
company had an increasing number of casualties. We moved
our mortar several times to avoid the shelling, but the Japanese artillery and mortar fire got so heavy and caused such
losses to the battalion that our attack was finally called off
about noon.

On our right 2/5 made better progress. That battalion
moved forward through thick jungle shielded from enemy
observers, then turned east and moved out onto the smaller
prong of Peleliu's "lobster claw." We moved behind 2/5 eastward across the causeway road to exploit their gain. Again
shielded by thick woods, we moved away from Bloody Nose.

We pitied the 1st Marines attacking the ridges. They were
suffering heavy casualties.

"The word is the 1st Marines catchin' hell," said Snafu.

"Poor guys, I pity 'em," another man said.

"Yeah, me too, but I hope like hell they take that damn
ridge, and we don't have to go up there," said another.

"That shelling coming from up there was hell, and you
couldn't even locate the guns with field glasses," added
someone else.

From what we had seen thrown at us from the left flank
during the past two days, and what I saw of the ridges then, I
felt sure that sooner or later every battalion of every regiment
in the division would get thrown against Bloody Nose. I was
right.

The 1st Marines' predicament at the time was worse than
ours in 3/5. They were attacking the end of the ridge itself,
and not only received heavy shelling from enemy caves there
but deadly accurate small-arms fire as well. Being tied in
with the 1st Marines at the time, we got "the word" straight
from the troops themselves and not from some overly optimistic officer in a CP putting pins on a map.

The word passed along the line to us told that when the
men of 2/1 moved up toward the Japanese positions follow-

ing preassault artillery fire, the enemy fired on them from
mutually supporting positions, pinning them down and inflicting heavy losses. If they managed to get onto the slopes,
the Japanese opened fire point-blank from caves as soon as
our artillery lifted. The enemy then moved back into their
caves. If Marines got close enough to an enemy position to attack it with flamethrowers and demolition charges, Japanese
in mutually supporting positions raked them with cross fire.
Each slight gain by the 1st Marines on the ridges came at almost prohibitive cost in casualties. From what little we could
see of the terrain and from the great deal we heard firsthand
of the desperate struggle on our left, some of us suspected
that Bloody Nose was going to drag on and on in a long battle
with many casualties.

The troops got paid to do the fighting (I made sixty dollars
a month), and the high command the thinking; but the big
brass were predicting optimistically that the Japanese defenses in the ridges would be "breached any day" and Peleliu
would be secured in a few days.*

As 3/5 moved eastward on 18 September, a buddy commented sadly, "You know, Sledgehammer, a guy from the 1st
Marines told me they got them poor boys makin' frontal attacks with fixed bayonets on that damn ridge, and they can't
even see the Nips that are shootin' at 'em. That poor kid was
really depressed; don't see no way he can come out alive.
There just ain't no sense in that. They can't get nowhere like
that. It's slaughter."

"Yeah, some goddamn glory-happy officer wants another
medal, I guess, and the guys get shot up for it. The officer gets
the medal and goes back to the States, and he's a big hero.
Hero, my ass; gettin' troops slaughtered ain't being no hero,"
said a veteran bitterly.

And bitterness it was. Even the most optimistic man I knew

---

*For nearly a week of bitter combat, Maj. Gen. William H. Rupertus insisted
that the 1st Marine Division could handle the job on Peleliu alone. Only after
the 1st Marine Regiment was ground down to a nub—suffering 56 percent
casualties—did Maj. Gen. Roy Geiger, commander of the III Marine Amphibious Corps, overrule Rupertus and order in the U.S. Army's 321st Infantry Regiment to help the Marines.

believed our battalion must take its turn against those incredible ridges—and dreaded it.

DEATH PATROL

As we moved toward the smaller "lobster claw," Snafu
chanted, "Oh, them mortar shells are bustin' up that ole gang
of mine," to the tune of "Those Wedding Bells Are Breaking
Up That Old Gang of Mine." We halted frequently to rest
briefly and to keep down the number of cases of heat prostration.

Although not heavy, my pack felt like a steaming-hot wet
compress on my shoulders and upper back. We were sopping
wet with sweat, and at night or during a halt in the shade our
dungarees dried out a bit. When they did, heavy white lines of
fine, powdery salt formed, as though drawn by chalk, along
the shoulders, waist, and so on. Later, as the campaign
dragged on and our dungarees caked with coral dust, they felt
like canvas instead of soft cotton.

I carried a little Gideon's New Testament in my breast
pocket, and it stayed soaked with sweat during the early days.
The Japanese carried their personal photos and other papers
in waterproof green rubber pocket-sized folding bags. I "lib-
erated" one such bag from a corpse and used it as a covering
for my New Testament. The little Bible went all the way
through Okinawa's rains and mud with me, snug in its captured cover.

During one halt along a sandy road in the woods, we heard
the words "hot chow" passed.

"The hell you say," someone said in disbelief.

"Straight dope; pork chops."

We couldn't believe it, but it was true. We filed past a cylin-
drical metal container, and each of us received a hot, delicious pork chop. The chow had been sent ashore for
Company K by the crew of LST 661. I vowed if the chance
ever came I would express my thanks to those sailors for that
chow.*

---

*I fulfilled that vow in July 1945 after the battle for Okinawa ended.

As we sat along the road eating pork chops with our fingers, a friend sitting on his helmet next to me began to examine a Japanese pistol he had captured. Suddenly the pistol fired. He toppled over on his back but sprang up immediately, holding his hand to his forehead. Several men hit the deck, and we all ducked at the sound of the shot. I had seen what happened but ducked instinctively with an already well-developed conditioned reflex. I stood up and looked at the man's face. The bullet merely had creased his forehead. He was lucky. When the other men realized he wasn't hurt, they really began to kid him unmercifully. Typical comments went something like:

"Hey, ole buddy, I always knew you had a hard head, but I didn't know slugs would bounce off of it."

"You don't need a helmet except to sit on when we take ten."

"You're too young to handle dangerous weapons."

"Some people will do anything to get a Purple Heart."

"Is this the sort of thing you used to do to attract your mother's attention?"

He rubbed his forehead, embarrassed, and mumbled, "Aw, knock it off."

We moved along a causeway and finally halted on the edge of a swamp where the company deployed and dug in for the night. Things were fairly quiet. The next morning the company swung south, pushing through the heavy growth behind a mortar and artillery barrage. We killed a few Japanese throughout the area. Late in the day Company K deployed again for the night.

The following day, Company K received a mission to push a strong combat patrol to the east coast of the island. Our orders were to move through the thick growth onto the peninsula that formed the smaller "claw" and set up a defensive position at the northern tip of the land mass on the edge of a mangrove swamp. Our orders didn't specify the number of days we were to remain there.

First Lt. Hillbilly Jones commanded the patrol consisting of about forty Marines plus a war dog, a Doberman pinscher. Sgt. Henry ("Hank") Boyes was the senior NCO. As with all combat patrols, we were heavily armed with rifles and BARs.

We also had a couple of machine-gun squads and the mortar squad with us. Never missing an opportunity to get into the action with his cold steel, Sgt. Haney volunteered to go along.

"G-2 [division intelligence] reports there are a couple thousand Japs somewhere on the other side of that swamp, and if they try to move across it to get back to the defensive positions in Bloody Nose, we're to hold them up until artillery, air strikes, and reinforcements can join us," a veteran NCO said in a terse voice. Our mission was to make contact with the enemy, test his strength, or occupy and hold a strategic position against enemy attack. I wasn't enthusiastic about it.

We picked up extra rations and ammunition as we filed through the company lines exchanging parting remarks with friends. Heading into the thick scrub brush, I felt pretty lonesome, like a little boy going to spend his first night away from home. I realized that Company K had become my home. No matter how bad a situation was in the company, it was still home to me. It was not just a lettered company in a numbered battalion in a numbered regiment in a numbered division. It meant far more than that. It was home; it was "my" company. I belonged in it and nowhere else.

Most Marines I knew felt the same way about "their" companies in whatever battalion, regiment, or Marine division they happened to be. This was the result of, or maybe a cause for, our strong esprit de corps. The Marine Corps wisely acknowledged this unit attachment. Men who recovered from wounds and returned to duty nearly always came home to their old company. This was not misplaced sentimentality but a strong contributor to high morale. A man felt that he belonged to his unit and had a niche among buddies whom he knew and with whom he shared a mutual respect welded in combat. This sense of family was particularly important in the infantry, where survival and combat efficiency often hinged on how well men could depend on one another.*

*During and after the war, army men told me that if a soldier got wounded and later returned to infantry duty, there was little chance it would be to his old company. They all agreed that was regrettable. They didn't like the practice, because a recuperated veteran became just another replacement in a strange outfit.

We moved through the thick growth quietly in extended formation, with scouts out looking out for snipers. Things in our area were quiet, but the battle rumbled on Bloody Nose. Thick jungle growth clogged the swamp, which also contained numerous shallow tidal inlets and pools choked with mangroves and bordered by more mangroves and low pandanus trees. If a plant were designed especially to trip a man carrying a heavy load, it would be a mangrove with its tangle of roots.

I walked under a low tree that had a pair of man-o-war birds nesting in its top. They showed no fear as they cocked their heads and looked down from their bulky stick nest. The male saw little of interest about me and began inflating his large red throat pouch to impress his mate. He slowly extended his huge seven-foot wingspan and clicked his long hooked beak. As a boy, I had seen similar man-o-war birds sailing high over Gulf Shores near Mobile, but never had I seen them this close. Several large white birds similar to egrets also perched nearby, but I couldn't identify them.

My brief escape from reality ended abruptly when a buddy scolded in a low voice, "Sledgehammer, what the hell you staring at them birds for? You gonna get separated from the patrol," as he motioned vigorously for me to hurry. He thought I'd lost my senses, and he was right. That was neither the time nor the place for something as utterly peaceful and ethereal as bird watching. But I had had a few delightful and refreshing moments of fantasy and escape from the horror of human activities on Peleliu.

We moved on and finally halted near an abandoned Japanese machine-gun bunker built of coconut logs and coral rock. This bunker served as our patrol's CP. We deployed around it and dug in. The area was just a few feet above the water level, and the coral was fairly loose. We dug the mortar gun pit within a few feet of the swamp water, about thirty feet from the bunker. Visibility through the swamp was limited to a few feet by the dense tangle of mangrove roots on three sides of the patrol's defense perimeter. We didn't register in the gun, because we had to maintain absolute quiet at all times. If we made noise, we would lose the element of surprise should the

Japanese try to come across the area. We simply aimed the mortar in the direction we would be most likely to fire. We ate our rations, checked our weapons, and prepared for a long night.

We received the password as darkness settled on us, and a drizzling rain began. We felt isolated listening to moisture dripping from the trees and splashing softly into the swamp. It was the darkest night I ever saw. The overcast sky was as black as the dripping mangroves that walled us in. I had the sensation of being in a great black hole and reached out to touch the sides of the gun pit to orient myself. Slowly the reality of it all formed in my mind: we were expendable!

It was difficult to accept. We come from a nation and a culture that values life and the individual. To find oneself in a situation where your life seems of little value is the ultimate in loneliness. It is a humbling experience. Most of the combat veterans had already grappled with this realization on Guadalcanal or Gloucester, but it struck me out in that swamp.

George Sarrett, a Gloucester veteran, was in the gun pit with me, and we tried to cheer each other up. In low tones he talked of his boyhood in Texas and about Gloucester.

Word came that Haney was crawling along checking positions.

"What's the password?" whispered Haney as he crawled up to us. George and I both whispered the password. "Good," said Haney. "You guys be on the alert, you hear?"

"OK, Haney," we said. He crawled over to the CP where I assumed he settled down.

"I guess he'll be still for a while now," I said.

"Hope the hell you're right," answered George.

Well, I wasn't, because in less than an hour Haney made the rounds again.

"What's the password?" he whispered as he poked his head up to the edge of our hole.

We told him. "Good," he said. "You guys check your weapons. Got a round in the chamber?" he asked each of us.

We answered yes. "OK, stand by with that mortar. If the Nips come through this swamp at high port with fixed bayonets, you'll need to fire HE and flares as fast as you can." He crawled off.

"Wish that Asiatic old boy would settle down. He makes me nervous. He acts like we are a bunch of green boots," my companion growled. George was a cool-headed, self-possessed veteran, and he spoke my sentiments. Haney was making me jittery, too.

Weary hours dragged on. We strained our eyes and ears in the dripping blackness for indications of enemy movement. We heard the usual jungle sounds caused by animals. A splash, as something fell into the water, made my heart pound and caused every muscle to tighten. Haney's inspection tours got worse. He obviously was getting more nervous with each hour.

"I wish to hell Hillbilly would grab him by the stackin' swivel and anchor him in the CP," George mumbled.

The luminous dial of my wristwatch showed the time was after midnight. In the CP a low voice sounded, "Oh, ah, oh" and trailed off, only to repeat the sound louder.

"What's that?" I asked George anxiously.

"Sounds like some guy havin' a nightmare," he replied nervously. "They sure as hell better shut him up before every Nip in this damned swamp knows our position." We heard someone moving and thrashing around in the CP.

"Knock it off," several men whispered near us.

"Quiet that man down!" Hillbilly ordered in a stern low voice.

"Help! help! Oh God, help me!" shouted the wild voice. The poor Marine had cracked up completely. The stress of combat had finally shattered his mind. They were trying to calm him down, but he kept thrashing around. In a firm voice filled with compassion, Hillbilly was trying to reassure the man that he was going to be all right. The effort failed. Our comrade's tragically tortured mind had slipped over the brink. He screamed more loudly. Someone pinioned the man's arms to his sides, and he screamed to the Doberman pinscher, "Help me, dog; the Japs have got me! The Japs have got me and they're gonna throw me in the ocean." I heard the sickening crunch of a fist against a jaw as someone tried to knock the man unconscious. It didn't faze him. He fought like a wildcat, yelling and screaming at the top of his voice.

Our corpsman then gave him an injection of morphine in the hope of sedating him. It had no effect. More morphine; it had no effect either. Veterans though they were, the men were all getting jittery over the noise they believed would announce our exact location to any enemy in the vicinity.

"Hit him with the flat of that entrenching shovel!" a voice commanded in the CP. A horrid *thud* announced that the command was obeyed. The poor man finally became silent.

"Christ a'mighty, what a pity," said a Marine in a neighboring foxhole.

"You said that right, but if the goddamn Nips don't know we're here, after all that yellin', they'll never know," his buddy said.

A tense silence settled over the patrol. The horror of the whole affair stimulated Haney to check our positions frequently. He acted like some hyperactive demon and cautioned us endlessly to be on the alert.

When welcome dawn finally came after a seemingly endless blackness, we all had frayed nerves. I walked the few paces over to the CP to find out what I could. The man was dead. Covered with his poncho, his body lay next to the bunker. The agony and distress etched on the strong faces of Hillbilly, Hank, and the others in the CP revealed the personal horror of the night. Several of these men had received or would receive decorations for bravery in combat, but I never saw such agonized expressions on their faces as that morning in the swamp. They had done what any of us would have had to do under similar circumstances. Cruel chance had thrust the deed upon them.

Hillbilly looked at the radioman and said, "I'm taking this patrol in. Get battalion for me."

The radioman tuned his big pack-sized radio and got the battalion CP. Hillbilly told the battalion CO, Major Gustafson, that he wanted to bring in the patrol. We could hear the major tell Hillbilly he thought we should stay put for a couple of days until G-2 could determine the disposition of the Japanese. Hillbilly, a first lieutenant, calmly disagreed, saying we hadn't fired a shot, but because of circumstances we all had a pretty bad case of nerves. He felt strongly that we should come in. I saw several old salts raise their eyebrows and smile as Hillbilly stated his opinion. To our relief, Gus agreed with him; I have always thought it was probably because of his respect for Hillbilly's judgment.

"I'll send a relief column with a tank so you won't have any trouble coming in," said the major's voice. We all felt comforted. The word went rapidly through the patrol that we were going in. Everyone breathed easier. In about an hour we heard a tank coming. As it forced its way through the thick growth, we saw familiar faces of Company K men with it. We placed the body on the tank, and we returned to the company's lines. I never heard an official word about the death thereafter.

RELIEF FOR THE 1ST MARINES

Over the next few days, the 5th Marines patrolled most of the southern "claw." We had set up defensive positions to prevent any possible counterlanding by the Japanese along the exposed southern beaches.

On about 25 September (D + 10) the battered 1st Marine Regiment was relieved by the U.S. Army's 321st Infantry Regiment of the 81st Infantry Division. The 1st Marines moved into our area where they were to await a ship to return them to Pavuvu. We picked up our gear and moved out from the relative quiet of the beach to board trucks that would speed our regiment to a position straddling the west road. From there we would attack northward along the western side of the ridges.

As we walked along one side of a narrow road, the 1st Marines filed along the other side to take over our area. I saw some familiar faces as the three decimated battalions trudged past us, but I was shocked at the absence of so many others whom I knew in that regiment. During the frequent halts typical to the movement of one unit into the position of another, we exchanged greetings with buddies and asked about the fate of mutual friends. We in the 5th Marines had many a dead or wounded friend to report about from our ranks, but the men in the 1st Marines had so many it was appalling.

"How many men left in your company?" I asked an old Camp Elliott buddy in the 1st Marines.

He looked at me wearily with bloodshot eyes and choked as he said, "Twenty is all that's left in the whole company, Sledgehammer. They nearly wiped us out. I'm the only one left out of the old bunch in my company that was with us in mortar school at Elliott."

I could only shake my head and bite my lip to keep from getting choked up. "See you on Pavuvu," I said.

"Good luck," he said in a dull resigned tone that sounded as though he thought I might not make it.

What once had been companies in the 1st Marines looked like platoons; platoons looked like squads. I saw few officers. I couldn't help wondering if the same fate awaited the 5th Marines on those dreadful ridges. Twenty bloody, grueling, terrible days and nights later, on 15 October (D + 30) my regiment would be relieved. Its ranks would be just about as decimated as those we were filing past.

We boarded trucks that carried us southward along the east road then some distance northward along the west road. As we bumped and jolted past the airfield, we were amazed at all the work the Seabees (naval construction battalions) had accomplished on the field. Heavy construction equipment was everywhere, and we saw hundreds of service troops living in tents and going about their duties as though they were in Hawaii or Australia. Several groups of men, Army and Marine service troops, watched our dusty truck convoy go by. They wore neat caps and dungarees, were clean-shaven, and seemed relaxed. They eyed us curiously, as though we were wild animals in a circus parade. I looked at my buddies in the truck and saw why. The contrast between us and the onlookers was striking. We were armed, helmeted, unshaven, filthy, tired, and haggard. The sight of clean comfortable noncombatants was depressing, and we tried to keep up our morale by discussing the show of U.S. material power and technology we saw.

We got off the trucks somewhere up the west road parallel

to the section of the ridges on our right that was in American hands. We heard firing on the closest ridge. The troops I saw along the road as we unloaded were army infantrymen from the 321st Infantry Regiment, veterans of Angaur.

As I exchanged a few remarks with some of these men, I felt a deep comradeship and respect for them. Reporters and historians like to write about interservice rivalry among military men; it certainly exists, but I found that frontline combatants in all branches of the services showed a sincere mutual respect when they faced the same danger and misery. Combat soldiers and sailors might call us "gyrenes," and we called them "dogfaces" and "swabbies," but we respected each other completely.

After the relief of 1st Marines, a new phase of the fight for Peleliu began. No longer would the Marines suffer prohibitive casualties in fruitless frontal assaults from the south against the ridges. Rather they would sweep up the western coast around the enemy's last-ditch defenses in search of a better route into the final pocket of resistance.

Although the bitter battle for Peleliu would drag on for another two months, the 1st Marine Division seized all of the terrain of strategic value in the first week of bitter fighting. In a series of exhausting assaults, the division had taken the vital airfield, the commanding terrain above it, and all of the island south and east of Umurbrogol Mountain. Yet the cost had been high: 3,946 casualties. The division had lost one regiment as an effective fighting unit, and had severely depleted the strength of its other two.

CHAPTER FIVE

Another Amphibious Assault

The 5th Marines now had the mission to secure the northern part of the island—that is, the upper part of the larger "lobster claw." Following that chore the regiment was to move south again on the eastern side of the Umurbrogol ridges to complete the isolation and encirclement. Most of us in the ranks never saw a map of Peleliu except during training on Pavuvu, and had never heard the ridge system referred to by its correct name, Umurbrogol Mountain. We usually referred to the whole ridge system as "Bloody Nose," "Bloody Nose Ridge," or simply "the ridges."

As we moved through the army lines, Japanese machine guns were raking the crest of the ridge on our right. The slugs and bluish white tracers pinned down the American troops on the ridge but passed high above us on the road. The terrain was flat and sparsely wooded. Tanks supported us, and we were fired on by small arms, artillery, and mortars from the high coral ridges to our right and from Ngesebus Island a few hundred yards north of Peleliu.

Our battalion turned right at the junction of West Road and East Road, headed south along the latter, and stopped at dusk. As usual, there wasn't much digging in as such, mostly finding some crater or depression and piling rocks around it for what protection we could get.

I was ordered to carry a five-gallon can of water over to the company CP. When I got there, Ack Ack was studying a map by the light of a tiny flashlight that his runner shielded with another folded map. The company's radioman was sitting with him, quietly tuning his radio and calling an artillery battery of the 11th Marines.

Putting the water can down, I sat on it and watched my skipper with admiration. Never before had I regretted so profoundly my lack of artistic talent and inability to draw the scene before me. The tiny flashlight faintly illuminated Captain Haldane's face as he studied the map. His big jaw, covered with a charcoal stubble of beard, jutted out. His heavy brow wrinkled with concentration just below the rim of his helmet.

The radioman handed the phone to Ack Ack. He requested a certain number of rounds of 75mm HE to be fired out to Company K's front. A Marine on the other end of the radio questioned the need for the request.

Haldane answered pleasantly and firmly, "Maybe so, but I want my boys to feel secure." Shortly the 75s came whining overhead and started bursting in the dark thick growth across the road.

Next day I told several men what Ack Ack had said. "That's the skipper for you, always thinking of the troops' feelings," was the way one man summed it up.

Several hours passed. It was my turn to be on watch in our hole. Snafu slept fitfully and ground his teeth audibly, which he usually did during sleep in combat. The white coral road shone brightly in the pale moonlight as I strained my eyes looking across into the wall of dark growth on the other side.

Suddenly two figures sprang up from a shallow ditch directly across the road from me. With arms waving wildly, yelling and babbling hoarsely in Japanese, they came. My heart skipped a beat, then began pounding like a drum as I flipped off the safety of my carbine. One enemy soldier angled to my right, raced down the road a short distance, crossed over, and disappeared into a foxhole in the line of the company on our right flank. I focused on the other. Swinging a bayonet over his head, he headed at me.

I dared not fire at him yet, because directly between us was a foxhole with two Marines in it. If I fired just as the Marine on watch rose up to meet the Japanese intruder, my bullet would surely hit a comrade in the back. The thought flashed through my mind, "Why doesn't Sam or Bill fire at him?"

With a wild yell the Japanese jumped into the hole with the

two Marines. A frantic, desperate, hand-to-hand struggle ensued, accompanied by the most gruesome combination of curses, wild babbling, animalistic guttural noises, and grunts. Sounds of men hitting each other and thrashing around came from the foxhole.

I saw a figure pop out of the hole and run a few steps toward the CP. In the pale moonlight, I then saw a Marine nearest the running man jump up. Holding his rifle by the muzzle and swinging it like a baseball bat, he blasted the infiltrator with a smashing blow.

From our right, where the Japanese had gone into the company on our flank, came hideous, agonized, and prolonged screams that defied description. Those wild, primitive, brutish yellings unnerved me more than what was happening within my own field of vision.

Finally a rifle shot rang out from the foxhole in front of me, and I heard Sam say, "I got him."

The figure that had been clubbed by the rifle lay groaning on the deck about twenty feet to the left of my hole. The yelling over to our right ceased abruptly. By this time, of course, everyone was on the alert.

"How many Nips were there?" asked a sergeant near me.

"I saw two," I answered.

"There must'a been more," someone else put in.

"No," I insisted, "only two came across the road here. One of them ran to the right where all that yelling was, and the other jumped into the hole where Sam shot him."

"Well, then, if there were just those two Nips, what's all that groanin' over here then?" he asked, indicating the man felled by the rifle butt.

"I don't know, but I didn't see but two Nips, and I'm sure of it," I said adamantly—with an insistence that has given me peace of mind ever since.

A man in a nearby hole said, "I'll check it out." Everyone sat still as he crawled to the groaning man in the shadows. A .45 pistol shot rang out. The moaning stopped, and the Marine returned to his hole.

A few hours later as objects around me became faintly visible with the dawn, I noticed that the still form lying to my left didn't appear Japanese. It was either an enemy in Marine dungarees and leggings, or it was a Marine. I went over to find out which.

Before I got to the prone body, its identity was obvious to me. "My God!" I said in horror.

Several men looked at me and asked what was the matter.

"It's Bill," I said.

An officer and an NCO came over from the CP.

"Did he get shot by one of those Japs?" asked the sergeant.

I didn't answer, just looked at him with a blank stare and felt sick. I looked at the man who had crawled past me to check on the groaning man in the dark. He had shot Bill through the temple, mistakenly assuming him to be a Japanese. Bill hadn't told any of us he was leaving his foxhole.

As the realization of his fatal mistake hit him, the man's face turned ashen, his jaw trembled, and he looked as though he were going to cry. Man that he was, though, he went straight over and reported to the CP. Ack Ack sent for and questioned several men who were dug in nearby, including myself, to ascertain exactly what had happened.

Ack Ack was seated off to himself. "At ease, Sledge," he said. "Do you know what happened last night?"

I told him I had a pretty good idea.

"Tell me exactly what you saw."

I told him, making clear I had seen two, and only two, Japanese and had said so at the time. I also told him where I saw those enemy soldiers go.

"Do you know who killed Bill?" the captain asked.

"Yes," I said.

Then he told me it had been a tragic mistake that anyone could have made under the circumstances and never to discuss it or mention the man's name. He dismissed me.

As far as the men were concerned, the villain in the tragedy was Sam. At the time of the incident Sam was supposed to be on watch while Bill was taking his turn at getting much-needed sleep. It was routine that at a preagreed time, the man on watch woke his buddy and, after reporting anything he had seen or heard, took his turn at sleep.

This standard procedure in combat on the front line was

based on a fundamental creed of faith and trust. You could depend on your buddy; he could depend on you. It extended beyond your foxhole, too. We felt secure, knowing that one man in each hole was on watch through the night.

Sam had betrayed that basic trust and had committed an unforgivable breach of faith. He went to sleep on watch while on the line. As a result his buddy died and another man would bear the heavy burden of knowing that, accident though it was, he had pulled the trigger.

Sam admitted that he might have dozed off. The men were extremely hard on him for what had happened. He was visibly remorseful, but it made no difference to the others who openly blamed him. He whined and said he was too tired to stay awake on watch, but he only got sworn at by men who were equally tired yet reliable.

We all liked Bill a great deal. He was a nice young guy, probably in his teens. On the neatly typewritten muster roll for the 3d Battalion, 5th Marines on 25 September 1944, one reads these stark words: "_____, William S., killed in action against the enemy (wound, gunshot, head)—remains interred in grave #3/M." So simply stated. Such an economy of words. But to someone who was there, they convey a tragic story. What a waste.

The Japanese who had come across the road in front of me were probably members of what the enemy called a "close-quarter combat unit." The enemy soldier shot by Sam was not dressed or equipped like their typical infantryman. Rather he wore only tropical khaki shorts, short-sleeved shirt, and *tabi* footwear (split-toed, rubber-soled canvas shoes). He carried only his bayonet. Why he entered our line where he did may have been pure accident, or he may have had an eye on our mortar. His comrade angled off toward the right near a machine gun on our flank. Mortars and machine guns were favorite targets for infiltrators on the front lines. To the rear, they went after heavy mortars, communications, and artillery.

Before Company K moved out, I went down the road to the next company to see what had happened during the night. I learned that those blood-chilling screams had come from the

Japanese I had seen run to the right. He had jumped into a foxhole where he met an alert Marine. In the ensuing struggle each had lost his weapon. The desperate Marine had jammed his forefinger into his enemy's eye socket and killed him. Such was the physical horror and brutish reality of war for us.

NGESEBUS ISLAND

Early the next morning our battalion made a successful assault on a small hill on the narrow neck of northern Peleliu. Because of its isolated position, it lacked the mutual support from surrounding caves that made most of the ridges on the island impregnable.

At this time the rest of the regiment was getting a lot of enemy fire from Ngesebus Island. The word was that several days earlier the Japanese had slipped reinforcements by barge down to Peleliu from the larger islands to the north; some of the barges had been shot up and sunk by the navy, but several hundred enemy troops got ashore. It was a real blow to our morale to hear this.*

"Sounds just like Guadalcanal," said a veteran. "About the time we think we got the bastards boxed in, the damn Nips bring in reinforcements, and it'll go on and on."

"Yeah," said another, "and once them slant-eyed bastards get in these caves around here, it'll be hell to pay."

On 27 September army troops took over our positions. We moved northward.

"Our battalion is ordered to hit the beach on Ngesebus Island tomorrow," an officer told us.†

I shuddered as I recalled the beachhead we had made on 15 September. The battalion moved into an area near the northern peninsula and dug in for the night in a quiet area. It was

---

*On the night of 22–23 September about six hundred Japanese of the 2d Battalion, 15th Regiment came down from Babelthuap and got ashore on Peleliu as reinforcements.

†Ngesebus had to be captured to silence the enemy fire coming into the 5th Marines' flank and to prevent its use as a landing place for Japanese reinforcements from the north. There was also an airfield on Ngesebus—a fighter strip—that was supposed to be useful for American planes.

sandy, open, and had some shattered, drooping palms. We didn't know what to expect on Ngesebus. I prayed the landing wouldn't be a repeat of the holocaust of D day.

Early in the morning of 28 September (D + 3) we squared away our gear and stood by to board the amtracs that would take us across the 500–700 yards of shallow reef to Ngesebus.

"We'll probably get another battle star for this beachhead," said a man enthusiastically.

"No we won't," answered another. "It's still just part of the Peleliu operation."

"The hell you say; it's still another beachhead," the first man responded.

"I don't make the regulation, ole buddy, but you check with the gunny, and I'll betcha I'm right." Several mumbled comments came out about how stingy the high command was in authorizing battle stars, which were little enough compensation for combat duty.

We boarded the tractors and tried to suppress our fear. Ships were firing on Ngesebus, and we saw Marine F4U Corsair fighter planes approaching from the Peleliu airfield to the south. "We gonna have lots of support for this one," an NCO said.

Our amtracs moved to the water's edge and waited for H hour as the thunderous prelanding naval gunfire bombardment covered the little island in smoke, flame, and dust. The Corsairs from Marine Fighter Squadron (VMF) 114 peeled off and began bombing and strafing the beach. The engines of the beautiful blue gull-winged planes roared, whined, and strained as they dove and pulled out. They plastered the beach with machine guns, bombs, and rockets. The effect was awesome as dirt, sand, and debris spewed into the air.*

Our Marine pilots outdid themselves, and we cheered, yelled, waved, and raised our clenched fists to indicate our approval. Never during the war did I see fighter pilots take

---

*Ngesebus was one of the first American amphibious assaults where air support for the landing force came exclusively from Marine aircraft. In earlier landings, air support came from navy and sometimes army planes.

such risks by not pulling out of their dives until the very last instant. We were certain, more than once, that a pilot was pulling out too late and would crash. But, expert flyers that they were, they gave that beach a brutal pounding without mishap to plane or pilot. We talked about their spectacular flying even after the war ended.

Out to sea on our left, with a cruiser, destroyers, and other ships firing support, was a huge battleship. Someone said it was the USS *Mississippi,* but I never knew for sure. She ranked with the Corsairs in the mass of destruction she hurled at Ngesebus. The huge shells rumbled like freight cars—as the men always used to describe the sound of projectiles from full-sized battleships' 16-inch guns.

At H hour our tractor driver revved up his engine. We moved into the water and started the assault. My heart pounded in my throat. Would my luck hold out? "The Lord is my shepherd," I prayed quietly and squeezed my carbine stock.

To our relief we received no fire as we approached the island. When my amtrac lurched to a stop well up on the beach, the tailgate went down with a bump, and we scrambled out. With its usual din and thunder the bombardment moved inland ahead of us. Some Company K Marines on the beach were already firing into pillboxes and bunkers and dropping in grenades. With several other men, I headed inland a short distance. But as we got to the edge of the airstrip, we had to dive for cover. A Nambu (Japanese light machine gun) had cut loose on us.

A buddy and I huddled behind a coral rock as the machine-gun slugs zipped viciously overhead. He was on my right. Because the rock was small, we pressed shoulder to shoulder, hugging it for protection. Suddenly there was a sickening crack like someone snapping a large stick.

My friend screamed, "Oh God, I'm hit!" and lurched over onto his right side. He grabbed his left elbow with his right hand, groaning and grimacing with pain as he thrashed around kicking up dust.

A bypassed sniper had seen us behind the rock and shot him. The bullet hit him in the left arm, which was pressed tightly against my right arm as we sought cover from the machine gun out front. The Nambu was firing a bit high, but there was no doubt the sniper had his sights right on us. We were between a rock and a hard place. I dragged him around the rock out of sight of the sniper as the Nambu bullets whizzed overhead.

I yelled, "Corpsman!" and Ken (Doc) Caswell,* the mortar section corpsman, crawled over, opening his pouch to get at his first aid supplies as he came. Another man also came over to see if he could help. While I cut away the bloody dungaree sleeve from the injured arm with my kabar, Doc began to tend the wound. As he knelt over his patient, the other Marine placed his kabar under the injured man's pack strap and gave a violent upward jerk to cut away the shoulder pack. The razor-sharp blade sliced through the thick web pack strap as though it were a piece of string. But before the Marine could arrest its upward motion, the knife cut Doc in the face to the bone.

Doc recoiled in pain from the impact of the knife thrust. Blood flowed down his face from the nasty gash to the left of his nose. He regained his balance immediately and returned to his work on the smashed arm as though nothing had happened. The clumsy Marine cursed himself for his blunder as I asked Doc what I could do to help him. Despite considerable pain, Doc kept at his work. In a quiet, calm voice he told me to get a battle dressing out of his pouch and press it firmly against his face to stop the bleeding while he finished work on the wounded arm. Such was the selfless dedication of the navy hospital corpsmen who served in Marine infantry units. It was little wonder that we held them in such high esteem. (Doc later got his face tended and was back with the mortar section in a matter of a few hours.)

While I did as Doc directed, I yelled at two Marines coming our way and pointed toward the sniper. They took off quickly toward the beach and hailed a tank. By the time a stretcher team came up and took my wounded friend, the two

---

*Habitually and affectionately, Marines call all U.S. Navy corpsmen who serve with them "Doc."

men trotted by, waved, and one said, "We got the bastard; he ain't gonna shoot nobody else."

The Nambu had ceased firing, and an NCO signaled us forward. Before moving out, I looked toward the beach and saw the walking wounded wading back toward Peleliu.

After we moved farther inland, we received orders to set up the mortars on the inland side of a Japanese pillbox and prepare to fire on the enemy to our company's front. We asked Company K's gunnery sergeant, Gy. Sgt. W. R. Saunders, if he knew of any enemy troops in the bunker. It appeared undamaged. He said some of the men had thrown grenades through the ventilators, and he was sure there were no live enemy inside.

Snafu and I began to set up our mortar about five feet from the bunker. Number One mortar was about five yards to our left. Cpl. R. V. Burgin was getting the sound-powered phone hooked up to receive fire orders from Sgt. Johnny Marmet, who was observing.

I heard something behind me in the pillbox. Japanese were talking in low, excited voices. Metal rattled against an iron grating. I grabbed my carbine and yelled, "Burgin, there're Nips in that pillbox."

All the men readied their weapons as Burgin came over to have a look, kidding me with, "Shucks, Sledgehammer, you're crackin' up." He looked into the ventilator port directly behind me. It was rather small, approximately six inches by eight inches, and covered with iron bars about a half inch apart. What he saw brought forth a stream of curses in his best Texas style against all Nippon. He stuck his carbine muzzle through the bars, fired two quick shots, and yelled, "I got 'em right in the face."

The Japanese inside the pillbox began jabbering loudly. Burgin was gritting his teeth and calling the enemy SOBs while he fired more shots through the opening.

Every man in the mortar section was ready for trouble as soon as Burgin fired the first shot. It came in the form of a grenade tossed out of the end entrance to my left. It looked as big as a football to me. I yelled "Grenade!" and dove behind the sand breastwork protecting the entrance at the end of the pillbox. The sand bank was about four feet high and L-shaped to protect the entrance from fire from the front and flanks. The grenade exploded, but no one was hit.

The Japanese tossed out several more grenades without causing us injury, because we were hugging the deck. Most of the men crawled around to the front of the pillbox and crouched close to it between the firing ports, so the enemy inside couldn't fire at them. John Redifer and Vincent Santos jumped on top. Things got quiet.

I was nearest the door, and Burgin yelled to me, "Look in and see what's in there, Sledgehammer."

Being trained to take orders without question, I raised my head above the sand bank and peered into the door of the bunker. It nearly cost me my life. Not more than six feet from me crouched a Japanese machine gunner. His eyes were black dots in a tan, impassive face topped with the familiar mushroom helmet. The muzzle of his light machine gun stared at me like a gigantic third eye.

Fortunately for me, I reacted first. Not having time to get my carbine into firing position, I jerked my head down so fast my helmet almost flew off. A split second later he fired a burst of six or eight rounds. The bullets tore a furrow through the bank just above my head and showered sand on me. My ears rang from the muzzle blast and my heart seemed to be in my throat choking me. I knew damned well I had to be dead! He just couldn't have missed me at that range.

A million thoughts raced through my terrified mind: of how my folks had nearly lost their youngest, of what a stupid thing I had done to look directly into a pillbox full of Japanese without even having my carbine at the ready, and of just how much I hated the enemy anyway. Many a Marine veteran had already lost his life on Peleliu for making less of a mistake than I had just made.

Burgin yelled and asked if I were all right. A hoarse squawk was all the answer I could muster, but his voice brought me to my senses. I crawled around to the front, then up on top of the bunker before the enemy machine gunner could have another try at me.

Redifer yelled, "They've got an automatic weapon in

there." Snafu disagreed, and a spirited argument ensued. Redifer pointed out that there surely was an automatic weapon in there and that I should know, because it came close to blowing off my head. But Snafu was adamant. Like much of what I experienced in combat, this exchange was unreal. Here we were: twelve Marines with a bull by the tail in the form of a well-built concrete pillbox containing an unknown number of Japanese with no friendly troops near us and Snafu and Redifer—veterans—in a violent argument.

Burgin shouted, "Knock it off," and they shut up.

Redifer and I lay prone on top of the bunker, just above the door. We knew we had to get the Japanese while they were bottled up, or they would come out at us with knives and bayonets, a thought none of us relished. Redifer and I were close enough to the door to place grenades down the opening and move back before they exploded. But the Japanese invariably tossed them back at us before the explosion. I had an irrepressible urge to do just that. Brief as our face-to-face meeting had been, I had quickly developed a feeling of strong personal hate for that machine gunner who had nearly blasted my head off my shoulders. My terror subsided into a cold, homicidal rage and a vengeful desire to get even.

Redifer and I gingerly peeped down over the door. The machine gunner wasn't visible, but we looked at three long Arisaka rifle barrels with bayonets fixed. Those bayonets seemed ten feet long to me. Their owners were jabbering excitedly, apparently planning to rush out. Redifer acted quickly. He held his carbine by the barrel and used the butt to knock down the rifles. The Japanese jerked their weapons back into the bunker with much chattering.

Behind us, Santos yelled that he had located a ventilator pipe without a cover. He began dropping grenades into it. Each one exploded in the pillbox beneath us with a muffled *bam*. When he had used all of his, Redifer and I handed him our grenades while we kept watch at the door.

After Santos had dropped in several, we stood up and began to discuss with Burgin and the others the possibility that anyone could still be alive inside. (We didn't know at the time that the inside was subdivided by concrete baffles for extra protection.) We got our answer when two grenades were tossed out. Luckily for the men with Burgin, the grenades were thrown out the back. Santos and I shouted a warning and hit the deck on the sand on top of the pillbox, but Redifer merely raised his arm over his face. He took several fragments in the forearm but wasn't wounded seriously.

Burgin yelled, "Let's get the hell outa here and get a tank to help us knock this damn thing out." He ordered us to pull back to some craters about forty yards from the pillbox. We sent a runner to the beach to bring up a flamethrower and an amtrac armed with a 75mm gun.

As we jumped into the crater, three Japanese soldiers ran out of the pillbox door past the sand bank and headed for a thicket. Each carried his bayoneted rifle in his right hand and held up his pants with his left hand. This action so amazed me that I stared in disbelief and didn't fire my carbine. I wasn't afraid, as I had been under shell fire, just filled with wild excitement. My buddies were more effective than I and cut down the enemy with a hail of bullets. They congratulated each other while I chided myself for being more curious about strange Japanese customs than with being combat effective.

The amtrac rattling toward us by this time was certainly a welcome sight. As it pulled into position, several more Japanese raced from the pillbox in a tight group. Some held their bayoneted rifles in both hands, but some of them carried their rifles in one hand and held up their pants with the other. I had overcome my initial surprise and joined the others and the amtrac machine gun in firing away at them. They tumbled onto the hot coral in a forlorn tangle of bare legs, falling rifles, and rolling helmets. We felt no pity for them but exulted over their fate. We had been shot at and shelled too much and had lost too many friends to have compassion for the enemy when we had him cornered.

The amtrac took up a position on a line even with us. Its commander, a sergeant, consulted Burgin. Then the turret gunner fired three armor-piercing 75mm shells at the side of the pillbox. Each time our ears rang with the familiar *wham bam* as the report of the gun was followed quickly by the explosion of the shell on a target at close range. The third shell tore a hole entirely through the pillbox. Fragments kicked up dust around our abandoned packs and mortars on the other side. On the side nearest us, the hole was about four feet in diameter. Burgin yelled to the tankers to cease firing lest our equipment be damaged.

Someone remarked that if fragments hadn't killed those inside, the concussion surely had. But even before the dust settled, I saw a Japanese soldier appear at the blasted opening. He was grim determination personified as he drew back his arm to throw a grenade at us.

My carbine was already up. When he appeared, I lined up my sights on his chest and began squeezing off shots. As the first bullet hit him, his face contorted in agony. His knees buckled. The grenade slipped from his grasp. All the men near me, including the amtrac machine gunner, had seen him and began firing. The soldier collapsed in the fusillade, and the grenade went off at his feet.

Even in the midst of these fast-moving events, I looked down at my carbine with sober reflection. I had just killed a man at close range. That I had seen clearly the pain on his face when my bullets hit him came as a jolt. It suddenly made the war a very personal affair. The expression on that man's face filled me with shame and then disgust for the war and all the misery it was causing.

My combat experience thus far made me realize that such sentiments for an enemy soldier were the maudlin meditations of a fool. Look at me, a member of the 5th Marine Regiment—one of the oldest, finest, and toughest regiments in the Marine Corps—feeling ashamed because I had shot a damned foe before he could throw a grenade at me! I felt like a fool and was thankful my buddies couldn't read my thoughts.

Burgin's order to us to continue firing into the opening interrupted my musings. We kept up a steady fire into the pillbox to keep the Japanese pinned down while the flame-thrower came up, carried by Corporal Womack from Mississippi. He was a brave, good-natured guy and popular with the troops, but he was one of the fiercest-looking Marines I ever

saw. He was big and husky with a fiery red beard well pow-
dered with white coral dust. He reminded me of some wild
Viking. I was glad we were on the same side.

Stooped under the heavy tanks on his back, Womack approached the pillbox with his assistant just out of the line of
our fire. When they got about fifteen yards from the target, we
ceased firing. The assistant reached up and turned a valve on
the flamethrower. Womack then aimed the nozzle at the opening made by the 75mm gun. He pressed the trigger. With a
whoooooooosh the flame leaped at the opening. Some muffled screams, then all quiet.

Even the stoic Japanese couldn't suppress the agony of
death by fire and suffocation. But they were no more likely to
surrender to us than we would have been to them had we ever
been confronted with the possibility of surrender. In fighting
the Japanese, surrender was not one of our options.

Amid our shouts of appreciation, Womack and his buddy
started back to battalion headquarters to await the summons
to break another deadlock somewhere on the battlefield—or
lose their lives trying. The job of flamethrower gunner was
probably the least desirable of any open to a Marine infantryman. Carrying tanks with about seventy pounds of flamma-
ble jellied gasoline through enemy fire over rugged terrain in
hot weather to squirt flames into the mouth of a cave or pillbox was an assignment that few survived but all carried out
with magnificent courage.

We left the craters and approached the pillbox cautiously.
Burgin ordered some of the men to cover it while the rest of
us looked over the fallen Japanese to be sure none was still
alive; wounded Japanese invariably exploded grenades when
approached, if possible, killing their enemies along with
themselves. All of them were dead. The pillbox was out of action thanks to the flamethrower and the amtrac. There were
seven enemy dead inside and ten outside. Our packs and mortars were only slightly damaged by the fire from the amtrac's
75mm gun.

Of the twelve Marine mortarmen, our only casualties were
Redifer and Leslie Porter, who had taken some grenade fragments. They weren't hurt seriously. Our luck in the whole af-

fair had been incredible. If the enemy had surprised us and rushed us, we might have been in a bad fix.

During this lull the men stripped the packs and pockets of the enemy dead for souvenirs. This was a gruesome business, but Marines executed it in a most methodical manner. Helmet headbands were checked for flags, packs and pockets were emptied, and gold teeth were extracted. Sabers, pistols, and *hari-kari* knives were highly prized and carefully cared for until they could be sent to the folks back home or sold to some pilot or sailor for a fat price. Rifles and other larger weapons usually were rendered useless and thrown aside. They were too heavy to carry in addition to our own equipment. They would be picked up later as fine souvenirs by the rear-echelon troops. The men in the rifle companies had a lot of fun joking about the hair-raising stories these people, who had never seen a live Japanese or been shot at, would probably tell after the war.

The men gloated over, compared, and often swapped their prizes. It was a brutal, ghastly ritual the likes of which have occurred since ancient times on battlefields where the antagonists have possessed a profound mutual hatred. It was uncivilized, as is all war, and was carried out with that particular savagery that characterized the struggle between the Marines and the Japanese. It wasn't simply souvenir hunting or looting the enemy dead; it was more like Indian warriors taking scalps.

While I was removing a bayonet and scabbard from a dead Japanese, I noticed a Marine near me. He wasn't in our mortar section but had happened by and wanted to get in on the spoils. He came up to me dragging what I assumed to be a corpse. But the Japanese wasn't dead. He had been wounded severely in the back and couldn't move his arms; otherwise he would have resisted to his last breath.

The Japanese's mouth glowed with huge gold-crowned teeth, and his captor wanted them. He put the point of his kabar on the base of a tooth and hit the handle with the palm of his hand. Because the Japanese was kicking his feet and thrashing about, the knife point glanced off the tooth and sank deeply into the victim's mouth. The Marine cursed him

① TOP VIEW

DOOR — DOOR

SAND BANK — SAND BANK

FRONT

PILL BOX CONCRETE COVERED WITH SAND

② FRONT VIEW

VENT PIPES

4 FEET

FIRING PORTS

③ REAR VIEW

④

and with a slash cut his cheeks open to each ear. He put his foot on the sufferer's lower jaw and tried again. Blood poured out of the soldier's mouth. He made a gurgling noise and thrashed wildly. I shouted, "Put the man out of his misery." All I got for an answer was a cussing out. Another Marine ran up, put a bullet in the enemy soldier's brain, and ended his agony. The scavenger grumbled and continued extracting his prizes undisturbed.

Such was the incredible cruelty that decent men could commit when reduced to a brutish existence in their fight for survival amid the violent death, terror, tension, fatigue, and filth that was the infantryman's war. Our code of conduct toward the enemy differed drastically from that prevailing back at the division CP.

The struggle for survival went on day after weary day, night after terrifying night. One remembers vividly the landings and the beachheads and the details of the first two or three days and nights of a campaign; after that, time lost all meaning. A lull of hours or days seemed but a fleeting instant of heaven-sent tranquillity. Lying in a foxhole sweating out an enemy artillery or mortar barrage or waiting to dash across open ground under machine-gun or artillery fire defied any concept of time.

To the noncombatants and those on the periphery of action, the war meant only boredom or occasional excitement; but to those who entered the meat grinder itself, the war was a netherworld of horror from which escape seemed less and less likely as casualties mounted and the fighting dragged on and on. Time had no meaning; life had no meaning. The fierce struggle for survival in the abyss of Peleliu eroded the veneer of civilization and made savages of us all. We existed in an environment totally incomprehensible to men behind the lines—service troops and civilians.

A trip inside the pillbox by Redifer and Burgin solved the mystery of how some of the occupants had survived the grenades and shell bursts. (Burgin shot a soldier inside who was feigning death.) Concrete walls partitioned the bunker into compartments connected by small openings. Three or four enemy soldiers occupied each compartment, which had its own firing ports to the outside. Each would have had to be put out of action individually had we not had the help of Womack and his flamethrower.

When our gunny came by and saw the results of our encounter with the pillbox he had thought was empty, he looked sheepish. He gazed in amazement at the enemy dead scattered around. We really razzed him about it—or rather, we gave him the nearest thing approaching the razz that we Marine privates dared hand out to the austere personage of Gy. Sergeant Saunders. I have thought often that Burgin should have been decorated for the fine leadership he exhibited in coordinating and directing the knockout of the pillbox. I'm sure men have been decorated for less.

We set up our two mortars in a large crater near the now knocked-out pillbox and registered in the guns for the night. The ammo carriers dug into the softer coral around the edge of the crater. An amtrac brought up rations and a unit of fire for the company. The wind began to blow briskly, and it got cloudy and heavily overcast. As darkness settled, heavy clouds scudded across the sky. The scene reminded me of hurricane weather on the Gulf Coast back home.

Not far behind us, the heat of the fire burning in the pillbox exploded Japanese grenades and small-arms ammunition. All night occasional shifts of wind blew the nauseating smell of burning flesh our way. The rain fell in torrents, and the wind blew hard. Ships fired star shells to illuminate the battlefield for our battalion. But as soon as the parachute of a star shell opened, the wind swept it swiftly along like some invisible hand snatching away a candle. In the few hundred yards they still held at the northern end of the island, the enemy was fairly quiet.

The next morning, again with the help of tanks and amtracs, our battalion took most of the remainder of Ngesebus. Our casualties were remarkably low for the number of Japanese we killed.* In midafternoon we learned that an army

---

*Official accounts vary somewhat as to the actual casualty figures for Ngesebus. However, the Marines suffered about 15 killed and 33 wounded, while the Japanese lost 470 killed and captured. Company K suffered the largest portion

unit would relieve us shortly and complete the job on the northern end of Ngesebus.

Our mortar section halted to await orders and dispersed among some open bushes. In our midst was the wreckage of a Japanese heavy machine gun and the remains of the squad that had been wiped out by Company K. The squad members had been killed in the exact positions to be occupied by such a squad "according to the book."

At first glance the dead gunner appeared about to fire his deadly weapon. He still sat bolt upright in the proper firing position behind the breech of his machine gun. Even in death his eyes stared widely along the gun sights. Despite the vacant look of his dilated pupils, I couldn't believe he was dead. Cold chills ran along my spine. Gooseflesh tickled my back. It seemed as though he was looking through me into all eternity, that at any instant he would raise his hands—which rested in a relaxed manner on his thighs—grip the handles on the breech, and press the thumb trigger. The bright shiny brass slugs in the strip clip appeared as ready as the gunner, anxious to speed out, to kill, and to maim more of the "American devils." But he would rot, and they would corrode. Neither he nor his ammo could do any more for the emperor.

The crown of the gunner's skull had been blasted off, probably by one of our automatic weapons. His riddled steel helmet lay on the deck like a punctured tin can. The assistant gunner lay beside the gun. Apparently, he had just opened a small green wooden chest filled with strip clips of machine-gun cartridges when he was killed. Several other Japanese soldiers, ammo carriers, lay strung out at intervals behind the gun.

A Company K rifleman who had been in the fight that knocked out the machine-gun crew sat on his helmet nearby and told us the story. The action had taken place the day before while the mortar section was fighting at the pillbox. The rifleman said, "The thing that I just couldn't believe was the way those Nip ammo carriers could chop chop around here

---

of the casualties in 3/5 by losing 8 killed and 24 wounded. This undoubtedly resulted from the presence of a ridge and caves on Ngesebus in our sector.

on the double with those heavy boxes of ammo on their backs."

Each ammo box had two leather straps, and each ammo carrier had a heavy box on his back with the straps around his shoulders. I lifted one of the ammo chests. It weighed more than our mortar. What the Japanese lacked in height, they certainly compensated for in muscle.

"I'd sure hate to hafta lug that thing around, wouldn't you?" asked the Marine. "When they got hit," he continued, "they fell to the deck like a brick because of all that weight."

As we talked, I noticed a fellow mortarman sitting next to me. He held a handful of coral pebbles in his left hand. With his right hand he idly tossed them into the open skull of the Japanese machine gunner. Each time his pitch was true I heard a little splash of rainwater in the ghastly receptacle. My buddy tossed the coral chunks as casually as a boy casting pebbles into a puddle on some muddy road back home; there was nothing malicious in his action. The war had so brutalized us that it was beyond belief.

I noticed gold teeth glistening brightly between the lips of several of the dead Japanese lying around us. Harvesting gold teeth was one facet of stripping enemy dead that I hadn't practiced so far. But stopping beside a corpse with a particularly tempting number of shining crowns, I took out my kabar and bent over to make the extractions.

A hand grasped me by the shoulder, and I straightened up to see who it was. "What are you gonna do, Sledgehammer?" asked Doc Caswell. His expression was a mix of sadness and reproach as he looked intently at me.

"Just thought I'd collect some gold teeth," I replied.

"Don't do it."

"Why not, Doc?"

"You don't want to do that sort of thing. What would your folks think if they knew?"

"Well, my dad's a doctor, and I bet he'd think it was kinda interesting," I replied, bending down to resume my task.

"No! The germs, Sledgehammer! You might get germs from them."

I stopped and looked inquiringly at Doc and said, "Germs? Gosh, I never thought of that."

"Yeah, you got to be careful about germs around all these dead Nips, you know," he said vehemently.

"Well, then, I guess I'd better just cut off the insignia on his collar and leave his nasty teeth alone. You think that's safe, Doc?"

"I guess so," he replied with an approving nod.

Reflecting on the episode after the war, I realized that Doc Caswell didn't really have germs in mind. He was a good friend and a fine, genuine person whose sensitivity hadn't been crushed out by the war. He was merely trying to help me retain some of mine and not become completely callous and harsh.

There was little firing going on now because 3/5 was preparing to pull back as it was relieved by an army battalion. Our tanks, two of which had been parked near us, started toward the beach. As they rattled and clanked away, I hoped they weren't leaving prematurely.

Suddenly we were jolted by the terrific blast of a Japanese 75mm artillery piece slightly to our right. We flung ourselves flat on the deck. The shriek and explosion of the shell followed instantly. Fragments tore through the air. The gun fired again rapidly.

"Jesus, what's that?" gasped a man near me.

"It's a Nip 75, and God is he close," another said.

Each time the gun fired I felt the shock and pressure waves from the muzzle blast. I was terror stricken. We began to hear shouts of "Corpsman" on our right.

"For chrissake, get them tanks back up here," someone yelled. I looked toward the tanks just in time to see several wheel around and come speeding back to help the pinned-down infantrymen.

"Mortar section, stand by," someone yelled. We might be called to fire on the enemy gun, but as yet we didn't know its location.

The tanks went into action and almost immediately knocked out the weapon. Calls came from our right for corpsmen and stretcher bearers. Several of our ammo carriers went with the corpsmen to act as stretcher bearers. Word filtered along to us that quite a number of casualties had been caused by the terrible point-blank fire of the enemy cannon. Most of those hit were members of the company that was tied in with us on our right.

Our ammo carriers and corpsmen returned shortly with a distressing account of the men next to us caught directly in front of the Japanese gun when it opened fire from a camouflaged position. When I saw one of our men's face, I knew how bad it had been. He appeared absolutely stricken with horror. I often had seen him laugh and curse the Japanese when we were under heavy shelling or scrambling out of the way of machine-gun or sniper fire. Never during the entire Peleliu campaign, or later during the bloody fighting on Okinawa, did I see such an expression on his face.

He grimaced as he described how he and the man with him put one of the casualties, someone we all knew, on a stretcher. "We knew he was hit bad, and he had passed out. I tried to lift the poor guy under his shoulders, and he [pointing to the other mortarman] lifted his knees. Just as we almost got him on the stretcher, the poor guy's body came apart. God! It was awful!"

He and the man with him looked away as everyone groaned and slowly shook their heads. We had been terrified by the enemy gun firing point-blank like that. It was an awful experience. It had been bad enough on us, but it was unbearable for those unfortunates who were in the direct line of fire.

Our company had been off to one side and had suffered no casualties during the ordeal, but it was one of the more shocking experiences I endured during the war. As I have said earlier, to be shelled was terrifying, and to be shelled in the open on your feet was horrible; but to be shelled point-blank was so shocking that it almost drove the most resilient and toughest among us to panic. Words can't convey the awesome sensation of actually feeling the muzzle blasts that accompanied the shrieks and concussions of those artillery shells fired from a gun so close by. We felt profound pity for our fellow Marines who had caught its full destructive force.

During mid-afternoon as we waited for the army infantry,

we sat numbly looking at nothing with the "bulkhead stare." The shock, horror, fear, and fatigue of fifteen days of combat were wearing us down physically and emotionally. I could see it in the dirty, bearded faces of my remaining comrades: they had a hollow-eyed vacant look peculiar to men under extreme stress for days and nights on end.

"Short but rough. Three days, maybe four," the division CG had said before Peleliu. Now we had been at it fifteen terrible days with no end in sight.

I felt myself choking up. I slowly turned my back to the men facing me, as I sat on my helmet, and put my face in my hands to try to shut out reality. I began sobbing. The harder I tried to stop the worse it got. My body shuddered and shook. Tears flowed out of my scratchy eyes. I was sickened and re-volted to see healthy young men get hurt and killed day after day. I felt I couldn't take any more. I was so terribly tired and so emotionally wrung out from being afraid for days on end that I seemed to have no reserve strength left.

The dead were safe. Those who had gotten a million-dollar wound were lucky. None of us left had any idea that we were just midway through what was to be a monthlong ordeal for the 5th Marines and the 7th Marines.

I felt a hand on my shoulder and looked up at the tired, bloodshot eyes of Duke, our lieutenant. "What's the matter, Sledgehammer?" he asked in a sympathetic voice. After I told him how I felt, he said, "I know what you mean. I feel the same way. But take it easy. We've got to keep going. It'll be over soon, and we'll be back on Pavuvu." His understanding gave me the strength I needed, enough strength to endure fif-teen more terrible days and nights.

When long files of soldiers accompanied by amtracs loaded with barbed wire and other supplies came by, we re-ceived orders to move out. We were glad to see those army men. As we shouldered our weapons and loads, a buddy said to me, "Sure wish we could dig in behind barbed wire at night. Makes a fella' feel more secure." I agreed as we walked wearily toward the beach.

After crossing back to northern Peleliu on 29 September, 3/5 bivouacked east of Umurbrogol Mountain in the Ngardololok area. We were familiar with this area from the first week of the campaign. It was fairly quiet and had been the bivouac area of the shattered 1st Marines for about a week after they came off the line and awaited ships to take them to Pavuvu.

We were able to rest, but we were uneasy. As usual we asked about the fate of friends in other units, more often than not with depressing results. Rumor had the 5th Marines slated to join the 7th Marines already fighting on those dreaded coral ridges that had been the near destruction of the 1st Marines. The men tried not to think about it as they sat around in the muggy shade, brewed hot coffee in their canteen cups, and swapped souvenirs and small talk. From the north came the constant rattle of machine guns and the rumble of shells.

CHAPTER SIX

Brave Men Lost

"OK, you people, stand by to draw rations and ammo. The battalion is going to reinforce the 7th Marines in the ridges."

We received the unwelcome but inevitable news with fatalistic resignation as we squared away our weapons and gear. Our information had the casualty figure of the 7th Marines rapidly approaching that of the 1st Marines. And our own regimental strength wasn't much better than that of the 7th. All of Peleliu except the central ridges was now in our hands. The enemy held out in the Umurbrogol Pocket, an area about 400 yards by 1,200 yards in the ruggedest, worst part of the ridges.*

The terrain was so unbelievably rugged, jumbled, and confusing, that I rarely knew where we were located. Only the officers had maps, so locations meant nothing in my mind. One ridge looked about like another, was about as rugged, and was defended as heavily as any other. We were usually told the name of this or that coral height or ridge when we attacked. To me it meant only that we were attacking the same objective where other Marine battalions had been shot up previously.

We were resigned to the dismal conclusion that our battalion wasn't going to leave the island until all the Japanese

---

*My memory of the remaining events of horror and death and violence amid the Peleliu ridges is as clear and distinct as a long nightmare where specific events are recalled vividly the next day. I remember clearly the details of certain episodes that occurred before or after certain others and can verify these with my notes and the historical references. But time and duration have absolutely no meaning in relation to those events from one date to the next. I was well aware of this sensation then.

were killed, or we had all been hit. We merely existed from hour to hour, from day to day. Numbed by fear and fatigue, our minds thought only of personal survival. The only glimmer of hope was a million-dollar wound or for the battle to end soon. As it dragged on and on and casualties mounted, a sense of despair pervaded us. It seemed that the only escape was to be killed or wounded. The will for self-preservation weakened. Many men I knew became intensely fatalistic. Somehow, though, one never could quite visualize his own death. It was always the next man. But getting wounded did seem inevitable. In a rifle company it just seemed to be a matter of time. One couldn't hope to continue to escape the law of averages forever.

On 3 October our battalion made an attack on the Five Sisters, a rugged coral hill mass with five sheer-walled peaks. Before the attack the 11th Marines covered the area with artillery fire. We fired a heavy mortar barrage on the company front, and the machine guns laid down covering fire.

As we ceased firing briefly, we watched the riflemen of 3/5 move forward onto the slopes before Japanese fire stopped them. We fired the mortars rapidly to give our men cover as they pulled back. The same fruitless attack was repeated the next day with the same dismal results.* Each time we got orders to secure the guns after the riflemen stopped advancing, the mortar section stood by to go up as stretcher bearers. (We always left a couple of men on each gun in case mortar fire was needed.) We usually threw phosphorous and smoke grenades as a screen, and the riflemen covered us, but enemy snipers fired as rapidly as possible at stretcher bearers. The Japanese were merciless in this, as in everything else in combat.

Because of the rugged, rock-strewn terrain and intense heat on Peleliu, four men were needed to carry one casualty on a stretcher. Everyone in the company took his turn as a stretcher bearer nearly every day. All hands agreed it was backbreaking, perilous work.

My heart pounded from fear and fatigue each time we

*K/3/5 lost eight killed and twenty-two wounded at the Five Sisters.

lifted a wounded man onto a stretcher, raised it, then stumbled and struggled across the rough ground and up and down steep inclines while enemy bullets snapped through the air and ricochets whined and pinged off the rocks. The snipers hit a stretcher bearer on more than one occasion. But luckily, we always managed to drag everybody behind rocks until help came. Frequently enemy mortars added their shells in an effort to stop us.

Each time I panted and struggled with a stretcher under fire, I marveled at the attitude of the casualty. When conscious, the wounded Marine seemed at ease and supremely confident we would get him out alive. With bullets and shells coming in thick and fast, I sometimes doubted any of us could make it. Even discounting the effects of shock and the morphine administered by the corpsmen, the attitude of the wounded Marine seemed serene. When we reached a place out of the line of fire, the man usually would encourage us to put him down so we could rest. If he wasn't wounded severely, we stopped and all had a smoke. We would cheer him up by asking him to think of us when he got on board the hospital ship.

Invariably the not-so-seriously hurt were in high spirits and relieved. They were on their way out of hell, and they expressed pity for those of us left behind. With the more seriously wounded and the dying, we carried the stretcher as fast as possible to an amtrac or ambulance jeep, which then rushed them to the battalion aid station. After getting them into a vehicle, we would throw ourselves down and pant for breath.

When acting as a stretcher bearer—struggling, running, crawling over terrain so rugged that sometimes the carriers on one end held the stretcher handles above their heads while those on the other end held their handles almost on the rocks to keep the stretcher level—I was terrified that the helpless casualty might fall off onto the hard, sharp coral. I never saw this happen, but we all dreaded it.

The apparent calmness of our wounded under fire stemmed in part from the confidence we shared in each other. None of us could bear the thought of leaving wounded behind. We never did, because the Japanese certainly would have tortured them to death.

During the period between attacks by our battalion on the Five Sisters, our front line was formed on fairly level ground. The mortars were dug in some yards behind the line. The entire company was out in the open, and we knew the Japanese were watching us at all times from their lairs in the Five Sisters. We came under sniper and mortar fire only when the Japanese were sure of inflicting maximum casualties. Their fire discipline was superb. When they shot, someone usually got hit.

When night came it was like another world. Then the enemy came out of their caves, infiltrating or creeping up on our lines to raid all night, every night. Raids by individual enemy soldiers or small groups began as soon as darkness fell. Typically, one or more raiders slipped up close to Marine positions by moving during dark periods between mortar flares or star shells. They wore *tabi,* and their ability to creep in silently over rough rocks strewn with pulverized vegetation was incredible. They knew the terrain perfectly. Suddenly they rushed in jabbering or babbling incoherent sounds, sometimes throwing a grenade, but always swinging a saber, bayonet, or knife.

Their skill and daring were amazing, matched only by the coolheaded, disciplined manner in which Marines met their attacks. Strict fire discipline on our part was required to avoid shooting friends if the enemy got into a position before he was shot. All we could do was listen in the dark to the desperate animalistic sounds and the thrashing around when a hand-to-hand fight occurred.

No one was allowed out of his position after dark. Each Marine maintained a keen watch while his buddy tried to sleep. Mutual trust was essential. Frequently our men were killed or wounded in these nightly fights, but we invariably killed the foe.

One night so many Japanese crept around in front of the company and slipped in among the rocks and ground litter between some of the forward positions that much of the following morning was occupied with trying to kill them all. This was difficult, because in any direction one fired one might hit a Marine. The excellent discipline and control exhibited by the Marines finally got all the Japanese without any Company K casualties.

The only "injury" that occurred was to my friend Jay's dungaree trousers. Jay walked past my foxhole with a deliberate, stiff-kneed gait and wearing a wry expression on his face.

"What happened to you?" I asked.

"Aw hell, I'll tell you later." He grinned sheepishly.

"Go on, tell him, Jay," another man near him yelled teasingly.

Several men laughed. Jay grinned and told them to shut up. He waddled on back to battalion like a tiny child who had soiled his pants, which was just what he had done. We all had severe cases of diarrhea by this time, and it had gotten the best of Jay. Considering what had happened, the incident really wasn't funny, but it was understandable.

At daylight Jay had slung his carbine over his shoulder and walked a short distance from his foxhole to relieve himself. As he stepped over a log, his foot came down squarely on the back of a Japanese lying in hiding. Jay reacted instantaneously and so did the enemy soldier. Jay brought his carbine to bear on the Japanese's chest as the latter sprang to his feet. Jay pulled the trigger. "Click." The firing pin was broken, and the carbine didn't fire. As the enemy soldier pulled the pin from a hand grenade, Jay threw the carbine at him. It was more an act of desperation than anything else.

As Jay spun around and ran back toward us yelling, "shoot him," the Japanese threw his grenade, striking my friend in the middle of the back. It fell to the deck and lay there, a dud. The Japanese then drew his bayonet. Waving it like a sword, he took off after Jay at a dead run.

Jay had spotted a BARman and fled in his direction, yelling for him to shoot the enemy. The BARman stood up but didn't fire. The Japanese came on. Jay was running and yelling as hard as he could. After agonizing moments, the BARman took deliberate aim at the enemy soldier's belt buckle and fired most of a twenty-round magazine into him. The soldier collapsed in a heap. The blast of automatic rifle fire had cut his body nearly in two.

Terrified and winded, Jay had had a close call. When he asked the BARman why in the hell he had waited so long to fire, that character grinned. I heard him reply something to the effect that he thought he'd just let the Japanese get a little closer to see if he could cut him into two pieces with his BAR.

Jay obviously didn't appreciate his close call being used as the subject of an experiment. As all the men laughed, Jay received permission to go back to battalion headquarters to draw a clean pair of trousers. The men kidded him a great deal about the episode, and he took it all with his usual good nature.

During the entire period among the Umurbrogol ridges, a nuisance Marine infantrymen had to contend with was the rear-echelon souvenir hunters. These characters came up to the rifle companies during lulls in the fighting and poked around for any Japanese equipment they could carry off. They were easy to spot because of the striking difference between their appearance and that of the infantry.

During the latter phase of the campaign the typical infantryman wore a worried, haggard expression on his filthy, unshaven face. His bloodshot eyes were hollow and vacant from too much horror and too little sleep. His camouflaged helmet cover (if it hadn't been torn off against the rocks) was gray with coral dust and had a tear or two in it. His cotton dungaree jacket (originally green) was discolored with coral dust, filthy, greasy with rifle oil, and as stiff as canvas from being soaked alternately with rain and sweat and then drying. His elbows might be out, and his knees frequently were, from much "hitting the deck" on the coral rock. His boondockers were coated with gray coral dust, and his heels were worn off completely by the sharp coral.

The infantryman's calloused hands were nearly blackened by weeks of accumulation of rifle oil, mosquito repellant (an oily liquid called Skat), dirt, dust, and general filth. Overall he was stooped and bent by general fatigue and excessive

physical exertion. If approached closely enough for conver-
sation, he smelled bad.

The front-line infantry bitterly resented the souvenir hunters.
One major in the 7th Marines made it a practice of putting
them into the line if they came into his area. His infantrymen
saw to it that the "visitors" stayed put until released to return
to their respective units in the rear areas.

During a lull in our attacks on the Five Sisters, I was on an
ammo-carrying detail and talking with a rifleman friend after
handing him some bandoliers. It was quiet, and we were sitting on the sides of his shallow foxhole as his buddy was
bringing up K rations. (By quiet I mean we weren't being
fired on. But there was always the sound of firing somewhere
on the island.) Two neat, clean, fresh-looking souvenir
hunters wearing green cloth fatigue caps instead of helmets
and carrying no weapons walked past us headed in the direction of the Five Sisters, several hundred yards away. When
they got a few paces in front of us, one of them stopped and
turned around, just as I was on the verge of calling to them to
be careful where they went.

The man called back to us asking, "Hey, you guys, where's
the front line?"

"You just passed through it," I answered serenely. The second souvenir hunter spun around. They looked at each other
and then at us in astonishment. Then, grabbing the bills of
their caps, they took off on the double back past us toward the
rear. They kicked up dust and never looked back.

"Hell, Sledgehammer, you should'a let 'em go on so they'd
get a good scare," chided my friend. I told him we couldn't
just let them walk up on a sniper. "Serve them rear-echelon
bastards right. And they call them guys Marines," he grumbled. (In fairness, I must add that some of the rear-area service troops volunteered and served as stretcher bearers.)

In our myopic view we respected and admired only those
who got shot at, and to hell with everyone else. This was un-
fair to noncombatants who performed essential tasks, but we
were so brutalized by war that we were incapable of making
fair evaluations.

A LEADER DIES

By 5 October (D + 20) the 7th Marines had lost about as many men as the 1st Marines had lost earlier in the battle. The regiment was now finished as an assault force on the regimental level. The 5th Marines, the last of the 1st Marine Division's infantry regiments, began to relieve the 7th Marines that day. Some of the men of the battered regiment would be killed or wounded in subsequent actions in the draws and valleys among the ridges of Peleliu, but the 7th Marines were through as a fighting force for the campaign.

On 7 October 3/5 made an assault up a large draw called Horseshoe Valley, known commonly as "the Horseshoe." There were numerous enemy heavy guns in caves and emplacements in the ridges bordering the Horseshoe to the west, north, and east. Our battalion was supposed to knock out as many of them as possible. We were supported by six army tanks, because the Marine 1st Tank Battalion had been relieved on 1 October to be sent back to Pavuvu. Somebody erroneously assumed there would be no further need for tanks on Peleliu.

My guess is that the 1st Tank Battalion was relieved not because the men were "badly depleted and debilitated"—the official reason given—but because the machines were. Machines wore out or needed overhauling and maintenance, but men were expected to keep going. Tanks, amtracs, trucks, aircraft, and ships were considered valuable and difficult to replace way out in the Pacific. They were maintained carefully and not exposed needlessly to wear or destruction. Men, infantrymen in particular, were simply expected to keep going beyond the limits of human endurance until they got killed or wounded or dropped from exhaustion.

Our attack on the Horseshoe was preceded by terrific artillery fire from our big guns. The shells swished and whined toward the ridges for two and a half hours. The mortars added their bit, too. The attack was surprisingly successful. The Horseshoe wasn't secured, but many Japanese were killed. We also knocked out many caves containing heavy guns, but only after several of the tanks took hits from them.

In the estimation of the Marines, the army tankers did a good job. Here the tanks operated with our riflemen attached. It was a case of mutual support. The tanks pulled up to the caves and fired into them point-blank with their 75mm cannon—*wham bam*. Their machine guns never seemed to stop. A tank unattended by riflemen was doomed to certain destruction from enemy suicide crews carrying mines. And the riflemen got a lot of protection from the tanks.

About the only instance I know of where tanks tried to operate without riflemen in the Pacific was a case of army tanks on Okinawa. Predictably, the Japanese knocked out most of those tanks. Marine tanks always operated with riflemen, like a dog with his fleas. But with tanks and riflemen, it was mutually beneficial.

After the attack of 7 October on the Horseshoe, 3/5 pulled back some distance from the ridges. Shortly thereafter we again went up toward the northern part of the island.

Between 8 and 11 October we emplaced our 60mm mortars between the West Road and the narrow beach. We were only a few yards from the water. Thus set up, we fired over the West Road, our front line beyond, and onto the ridges. We had an observer somewhere across the road who sent us orders by the sound-powered phone.

We kept up a brisk rate of fire because Japanese had infiltrated into positions on the ridge next to the road and were sniping at vehicles and troops with deadly effect. Our mortar fire helped pin them down and clean them out. We had good gun emplacements among some rocks and were screened by a narrow strip of thick foliage between us and the road and, therefore, from the enemy in the ridge beyond.

I was extremely confused as to where we had left our company. An NCO told me our mortars were detached temporarily from Company K and were supporting another unit hard-pressed by snipers. The enemy were firing from positions that were almost impossible to locate and they shot any and everybody they could—even casualties being evacuated by amtracs. More than one desperate amtrac driver, as he raced down the West Road toward the Regimental Aid Station, arrived only to find his helpless cargo slaughtered where they lay.

While we were in this position we were particularly vulnerable to infiltrators who might slip in along the beach as well as from the water to our rear. We kept watch in all directions at night; in this place, there were no friendly troops to our rear, just the water's edge about ten feet away and then the ocean-covered reef. The water was only about knee deep for quite a distance out. The Japanese would wade out, slip along the reef, and come in behind us.

One night while I was firing flare shells, James T. (Jim) Burke, a Marine we called the Fatalist, was manning Number One gun. Between firing missions, I could see him sitting on his helmet next to his gun, keeping watch to our left and rear.

"Hey, Sledgehammer, let me see your carbine a minute," he whispered nonchalantly in his usual laconic manner. He had a .45 pistol which was of little use at much distance. I handed him my carbine. I didn't know what he saw, so I followed his gaze as he pointed my carbine toward the sea. In the pale light a shadowy figure was moving slowly and silently along the reef parallel to the shoreline in the shallow water. The man couldn't have been more than thirty yards away or we couldn't have seen him in the dim moonlight. There was no doubt that he was a Japanese trying to get farther along to where he could slip ashore and creep up on our mortars.

No challenge or demand for password was even considered in a situation like that. No Marine would be creeping along the reef at night. The Fatalist rested his elbows on his knees and took careful aim as the figure moved slowly through the glassy-smooth water. Two quick shots; the figure disappeared.

The Fatalist flipped the safety back on, handed me my carbine, and said, "Thanks, Sledgehammer." He appeared as unconcerned as ever.

During the morning of 12 October, an NCO brought word that we were to take up our guns. The mortar section was to rejoin Company K. We gathered our gear and mortar. Snafu, George Sarrett, and I got into a jeep parked along a sheltered part of the road. We had to hang on because the driver took off with a lurch in a cloud of dust and drove like hell down the West Road bordered by the sniper-infested ridge. It was my first—and only—jeep ride during my entire enlistment. It was an eventful day because of that.

Shortly the driver stopped and let us off in a supply area where we waited for an NCO who was to guide us up into the ridges. Directly the rest of the Company K mortarmen arrived with directions to reach the company. We hoisted our mortar and other weapons and gear and headed across the road. We picked our way around the end of the ridge, then headed up a narrow valley filled with skeletons of shattered trees jutting up here and there on the slopes amid crazy-angled coral masses.

Johnny Marmet came striding down the incline of the valley to meet us as we started up. Even before I could see his face clearly, I knew from the way he was walking that something was dreadfully amiss. He lurched up to us, nervously clutching the web strap of the submachine gun slung over his shoulder. I had never seen Johnny nervous before, even under the thickest fire, which he seemed to regard as a nuisance that interfered with his carrying out his job.

His tired face was contorted with emotion, his brow was knitted tightly, and his bloodshot eyes appeared moist. It was obvious he had something fearful to tell us. We shuffled to a halt.

My first thought was that the Japanese had slipped in thousands of troops from the northern Palaus and that we would never get off the island. No, maybe the enemy had bombed some American city or chased off the navy as they had done at Guadalcanal. My imagination went wild, but none of us was prepared for what we were about to hear.

"Howdy, Johnny," someone said as he came up to us.

"All right, you guys, let's get squared away here," he said looking in every direction but at us. (This was strange, because Johnny wasn't the least reluctant to make eye contact with death, destiny, or the general himself.) "OK, you guys, OK, you guys," he repeated, obviously flustered. A couple of men exchanged quizzical glances. "The skipper is dead. Ack

Ack has been killed," Johnny finally blurted out, then looked quickly away from us.

I was stunned and sickened. Throwing my ammo bag down, I turned away from the others, sat on my helmet, and sobbed quietly.

"Those goddamn slant-eyed sonsabitches," someone behind me groaned.

Never in my wildest imagination had I contemplated Captain Haldane's death. We had a steady stream of killed and wounded leaving us, but somehow I assumed Ack Ack was immortal. Our company commander represented stability and direction in a world of violence, death, and destruction. Now his life had been snuffed out. We felt forlorn and lost. It was the worst grief I endured during the entire war. The intervening years have not lessened it any.

Capt. Andy Haldane wasn't an idol. He was human. But he commanded our individual destinies under the most trying conditions with the utmost compassion. We knew he could never be replaced. He was the finest Marine officer I ever knew. The loss of many close friends grieved me deeply on Peleliu and Okinawa. But to all of us the loss of our company commander at Peleliu was like losing a parent we depended upon for security—not our physical security, because we knew that was a commodity beyond our reach in combat, but our mental security.

Some of the men threw their gear violently to the deck. Everybody was cursing and rubbing his eyes.

Finally Johnny pulled himself together and said, "OK, you guys, let's move out." We picked up mortars and ammo bags. Feeling as though our crazy world had fallen apart completely, we trudged slowly and silently in single file up the rubble-strewn valley to rejoin Company K.*

---

*At the time of Captain Haldane's death, the bulk of Company K was operating with its parent battalion (3/5) on Hill 140 within the Umurbrogol Pocket. In an attempt to orient himself to the strange terrain his company was occupying, Haldane raised his head and looked over a ridge. A sniper's bullet killed him instantly. First Lt. Thomas J. ("Stumpy") Stanley succeeded him as commander of K/3/5. Stanley led Company K through the remainder of the Peleliu campaign and on to Okinawa the following spring.

So ended the outstanding combat career of a fine officer who had distinguished himself at Guadalcanal, Cape Gloucester, and Peleliu. We had lost our leader and our friend. Our lives would never be the same. But we turned back to the ugly business at hand.

THE STENCH OF BATTLE

Johnny led us on up through a jumble of rocks on Hill 140. Company K's line was emplaced along a rock rim, and we set up the mortars in a shallow depression about twenty yards behind it. The riflemen and machine gunners in front of us were in among rocks along the rim of Hill 140 facing east toward Walt Ridge and the northern end of the infamous Horseshoe. We had previously attacked that valley from its southern end. From the rim of Hill 140 the rock contours dropped away in a sheer cliff to a canyon below. No one could raise his head above the rim rock without immediately drawing heavy rifle and machine-gun fire.

The fighting around the pocket was as deadly as ever, but of a different type from the early days of the campaign. The Japanese fired few artillery or mortar barrages, just a few rounds at a time when assured of inflicting maximum casualties. That they usually did, and then secured the guns to escape detection. Sometimes there was an eerie quiet. We knew they were everywhere in the caves and pillboxes. But there was no firing in our area, only the sound of firing elsewhere. The silence added an element of unreality to the valleys.

If we moved past a certain point, the Japanese opened up suddenly with rifle, machine-gun, mortar, and artillery fire. It was like a sudden storm breaking. More often than not we had to pull back, and not a man in the company had seen a live enemy anywhere.

They couldn't hope to drive us off by then or to be reinforced themselves. From that point onward, they killed solely for the sake of killing, without hope and without higher purpose. We were fighting in Peleliu's ridges and valleys, in terrain the likes of which most Americans could not even visualize, against an enemy unlike anything most Americans could imagine.

The sun bore down on us like a giant heat lamp. Once I saw a misplaced phosphorous grenade explode on the coral from the sun's intense heat. We always shaded our stacked mortar shells with a piece of ammo box to prevent this.

Occasional rains that fell on the hot coral merely evaporated like steam off hot pavement. The air hung heavy and muggy. Everywhere we went on the ridges the hot humid air reeked with the stench of death. A strong wind was no relief; it simply brought the horrid odor from an adjacent area. Japanese corpses lay where they fell among the rocks and on the slopes. It was impossible to cover them. Usually there was no soil that could be spaded over them, just the hard, jagged coral. The enemy dead simply rotted where they had fallen. They lay all over the place in grotesque positions with puffy faces and grinning buck-toothed expressions.

It is difficult to convey to anyone who has not experienced it the ghastly horror of having your sense of smell saturated constantly with the putrid odor of rotting human flesh day after day, night after night. This was something the men of an infantry battalion got a horrifying dose of during a long, protracted battle such as Peleliu. In the tropics the dead became bloated and gave off a terrific stench within a few hours after death.

Whenever possible we removed Marine dead to the rear of the company's position. There they were usually laid on stretchers and covered with ponchos which stretched over the head of the corpse down to the ankles. I rarely saw a dead Marine left uncovered with his face exposed to sun, rain, and flies. Somehow it seemed indecent not to cover our dead. Often, though, the dead might lie on the stretchers for some time and decompose badly before the busy graves registration crews could take them for burial in the division cemetery near the airfield.

During the fighting around the Umurbrogol Pocket, there was a constant movement of one weary, depleted Marine company being relieved by another slightly less weary, depleted company. We seemed to rotate from one particularly dangerous part of the line to one slightly less so and back again continuously.

There were certain areas we moved into and out of several times as the campaign dragged along its weary, bloody course. In many such areas I became quite familiar with the sight of some particular enemy corpse, as if it were a landmark. It was gruesome to see the stages of decay proceed from just killed, to bloated, to maggot-infested rotting, to partially exposed bones—like some biological clock marking the inexorable passage of time. On each occasion my company passed such a landmark we were fewer in number.

Each time we moved into a different position I could determine the areas occupied by each rifle company as we went into that sector of the line. Behind each company position lay a pile of ammo and supplies and the inevitable rows of dead under their ponchos. We could determine how bad that sector of the line was by the number of dead. To see them so always filled me with anger at the war and the realization of the senseless waste. It depressed me far more than my own fear.

Added to the awful stench of the dead of both sides was the repulsive odor of human excrement everywhere. It was all but impossible to practice simple, elemental field sanitation on most areas of Peleliu because of the rocky surface. Field sanitation during maneuvers and combat was the responsibility of each man. In short, under normal conditions, he covered his own waste with a scoop of soil. At night when he didn't dare venture out of his foxhole, he simply used an empty grenade canister or ration can, threw it out of his hole, and scooped dirt over it next day if he wasn't under heavy enemy fire.

But on Peleliu, except along the beach areas and in the swamps, digging into the coral rock was nearly impossible. Consequently, thousands of men—most of them around the Umurbrogol Pocket in the ridges, many suffering with severe diarrhea, fighting for weeks on an island two miles by six miles—couldn't practice basic field sanitation. This fundamental neglect caused an already putrid tropical atmosphere to become inconceivably vile.

Added to this was the odor of thousands of rotting, discarded Japanese and American rations. At every breath one inhaled hot, humid air heavy with countless repulsive odors. I felt as though my lungs would never be cleansed of all those foul vapors. It may not have been that way down on the airfield and in other areas where the service troops were encamped, but around the infantry in the Umurbrogol Pocket, the stench varied only from foul to unbearable.

In this garbage-filled environment the flies, always numerous in the tropics anyway, underwent a population explosion. This species was not the unimposing common housefly (the presence of one of which in a restaurant is enough to cause most Americans today to declare the place unfit to serve food to the public). Peleliu's most common fly was the huge blowfly or bluebottle fly. This creature has a plump, metallic, greenish-blue body, and its wings often make a humming sound during flight.

The then new insecticide DDT was sprayed over the combat areas on Peleliu for the first time anywhere. It supposedly reduced the adult fly population while Marines were still fighting on the ridges, but I never noticed that the flies became fewer in number.

With human corpses, human excrement, and rotting rations scattered across Peleliu's ridges, those nasty insects were so large, so glutted, and so lazy that some could scarcely fly. They could not be waved away or frightened off a can of rations or a chocolate bar. Frequently they tumbled off the side of my canteen cup into my coffee. We actually had to shake the food to dislodge the flies, and even then they sometimes refused to move. I usually had to balance my can of stew on my knee, spooning it up with my right hand while I picked the sluggish creatures off the stew with my left. They refused to move or to be intimidated. It was revolting, to say the least, to watch big fat blowflies leave a corpse and swarm into our C rations.

Even though none of us had much appetite, we still had to eat. A way to solve the fly problem was to eat after sunset or before sunrise when the insects were inactive. Chow had to be unheated then, because no sterno tablets or other form of light could be used after dark. It was sure to draw enemy sniper fire.

Each morning just before sunrise, when things were fairly quiet, I could hear a steady humming sound like bees in a hive as the flies became active with the onset of daylight. They rose up off the corpses, refuse, rocks, brush, and wherever else they had settled for the night like a swarm of bees. Their numbers were incredible.

Large land crabs crawled all over the ridges at night, attracted by corpses. Their rustling through dry debris often was indistinguishable from prowling enemy soldiers. We responded by tossing a grenade at the sound.

In addition to rotting corpses and organic waste, the litter of smashed and worn out equipment of every type became more abundant as the battle dragged on and the size of the Umurbrogol Pocket shrank slowly. The ridges and ravines were littered with the flotsam of fierce combat. Debris of battle was everywhere and became more noticeable as the weeks dragged on.

I still see clearly the landscape around one particular position we occupied for several days. It was a scene of destruction and desolation that no fiction could invent. The area was along the southwestern border of the pocket where ferocious fighting had gone on since the second day of battle (16 September). The 1st Marines, the 7th Marines, and now the 5th Marines, all in their turn, had fought against this same section of ridges. Our exhausted battalion, 3/5, moved into the line to relieve another slightly more exhausted battalion. It was the same old weary shuffling of one tired, depleted outfit into the line to relieve another whose sweating men trudged out of their positions, hollow-eyed, stooped, grimy, bearded zombies.

The Company K riflemen and machine gunners climbed up the steep ridge and into the crevices and holes of the company we relieved. Orders were given that no one must look over the crest of the ridge, because enemy rifle and machine-gun fire would kill instantly anyone who did.

As usual the troops pulling out gave our men "the dope" on

the local conditions: what type fire to expect, particular danger spots and possible infiltration routes at night.

My mortar went into a gun pit occupied by one of the 60mm mortars of the company we were relieving. The gun pit was among coral rocks about twenty yards from the foot of the ridge. An extremely youthful Marine was just buckling the leather strap around the bipod and tube of his 60mm mortar as I walked up near the position and put down my heavy ammo bag. I sat on my helmet and started talking to him as the rest of our squad moved into their positions. As the young man looked up, I was struck by the agonized expression on his face. He didn't seem happy, the way he should have, about being relieved.

"You guys watch out for the Japs at night. Two of the bastards got into this gun pit last night and cut up our gunner and assistant gunner," he said.

He told me in a strained voice that the crew was so occupied firing the mortar during the previous night that two Japanese who slipped through the line on the ridge managed to creep up close to the pit without detection. They jumped in and cut up the two men working the mortar before nearby mortar ammo carriers killed them. The wounded Marines had been evacuated, but one of them had died, and the other was in poor condition. The bodies of the Japanese had been thrown into some nearby bushes.

The man telling me of the tragedy and another crouching beside the gun pit had been ammo carriers but had now assumed new duties as gunner and assistant. I noticed that as the new gunner folded and strapped his gun to leave, he seemed reluctant to touch the bottom or sides of the emplacement. When he left and we came closer to the gun pit to set up our mortar, I saw why. The white coral sides and bottom were spattered and smeared with the dark red blood of his two comrades.

After we got our gun emplaced, I collected up some large scraps of cardboard from ration and ammo boxes and used them to cover the bottom of the pit as well as I could. Fat, lazy blowflies were reluctant to leave the blood-smeared rock.

I had long since become used to the sight of blood, but the

idea of sitting in that bloodstained gun pit was a bit too much for me. It seemed almost like leaving our dead unburied to sit on the blood of a fellow Marine spilled out on the coral. I noticed that my buddy looked approvingly at my efforts as he came back from getting orders for our gun. Although we never discussed the subject, he apparently felt as I did. As I looked at the stains on the coral, I recalled some of the eloquent phrases of politicians and newsmen about how "gallant" it is for a man to "shed his blood for his country," and "to give his life's blood as a sacrifice," and so on. The words seemed so ridiculous. Only the flies benefited.

The wind blew hard. A drizzling rain fell out of a leaden sky that seemed to hang just above the ridge crest. Shattered trees and jagged rocks along the crest looked like stubble on a dirty chin. Most green trees and bushes had long since been shattered and pulverized by shell fire. Only the grotesque stumps and branches remained. A film of fine coral dust covered everything. It had been dust before the rain, but afterward it was a grimy coating of thin plaster.

The overwhelming grayness of everything in sight caused sky, ridge, rocks, stumps, men, and equipment to blend into a grimy oneness. Weird, jagged contours of Peleliu's ridges and canyons gave the area an unearthly alien appearance. The shattered vegetation and the dirty-white splotches peppering the rocks where countless bullets and shell fragments had struck off the weathered gray surfaces contributed to the unreality of the harsh landscape.

Rain added the final touch. On a battlefield rain made the living more miserable and forlorn and the dead more pathetic. To my left lay a couple of bloated Japanese corpses teaming with maggots and inactive flies who seemed to object to the rain as much as I did. Each dead man still wore the two leather cartridge boxes, one on either side of his belt buckle, neat wrap leggings, *tabi* shoes, helmets, and packs. Beside each corpse lay a shattered and rusting Arisaka rifle, smashed against a rock by some Marine to be certain it wasn't used again.

Cans of C rations and K ration boxes, opened and unopened, lay around our gun pit along with discarded grenade and mortar shell canisters. Scattered about the area were discarded U.S. helmets, packs, ponchos, dungaree jackets, web cartridge belts, leggings, boondockers, ammo boxes of every type, and crates. The discarded articles of clothing and the inevitable bottle of blood plasma bore mute testimony that a Marine had been hit there.

Many tree stumps had a machine-gun ammo belt draped over them. Some of these belts were partially filled with live cartridges. Amid all this evidence of violent combat, past and continuing, I was interested in the fact that spent, or partially so, machine-gun ammo belts so often seemed to be draped across a shattered stump or bush rather than lying on the ground. In combat, I often experienced fascination over such trivia, particularly when exhausted physically and strained emotionally. Many combat veterans told me they also were affected the same way.

All around us lay the destruction and waste of violent combat. Later, on the muddy clay fields and ridges of Okinawa, I would witness similar scenes on an even vaster scale. There the battlefield would bear some resemblance to others described in World War II. During the muddy stalemate before Shuri, the area would resemble descriptions I had read of the ghastly corpse-strewn morass of Flanders during World War I.

Those, though, were typical modern battlefields. They were nothing like the crazy-contoured coral ridges and rubble-filled canyons of the Umurbrogol Pocket on Peleliu. Particularly at night by the light of flares or on a cloudy day, it was like no other battlefield described on earth. It was an alien, unearthly, surrealistic nightmare like the surface of another planet.

I have already mentioned several times the exhaustion of the Marines as the campaign wore on. Our extreme fatigue was no secret to the Japanese either. As early as 6 October, nine days before we were relieved, a captured document reported that we appeared worn out and were fighting less aggressively.

The grinding stress of prolonged heavy combat, the loss of sleep because of nightly infiltration and raids, the vigorous physical demands forced on us by the rugged terrain, and the unrelenting, suffocating heat were enough to make us drop in our tracks. How we kept going and continued fighting I'll never know. I was so indescribably weary physically and emotionally that I became fatalistic, praying only for my fate to be painless. The million-dollar wound seemed more of a blessing with every weary hour that dragged by. It seemed the only escape other than death or maiming.

In addition to the terror and hardships of combat, each day brought some new dimension of dread for me: I witnessed some new, ghastly, macabre facet in the kaleidoscope of the unreal, as though designed by some fiendish ghoul to cause even the most hardened and calloused observer among us to recoil in horror and disbelief.

Late one afternoon a buddy and I returned to the gun pit in the fading light. We passed a shallow defilade we hadn't noticed previously. In it were three Marine dead. They were lying on stretchers where they had died before their comrades had been forced to withdraw sometime earlier. (I usually avoided confronting such pitiful remains. I never could bear the sight of American dead neglected on the battlefield. In contrast, the sight of Japanese corpses bothered me little aside from the stench and the flies they nourished.)

As we moved past the defilade, my buddy groaned, "Jesus!" I took a quick glance into the depression and recoiled in revulsion and pity at what I saw. The bodies were badly decomposed and nearly blackened by exposure. This was to be expected of the dead in the tropics, but these Marines had been mutilated hideously by the enemy. One man had been decapitated. His head lay on his chest; his hands had been severed from his wrists and also lay on his chest near his chin. In disbelief I stared at the face as I realized that the Japanese had cut off the dead Marine's penis and stuffed it into his mouth. The corpse next to him had been treated similarly. The third had been butchered, chopped up like a carcass torn by some predatory animal.

My emotions solidified into rage and a hatred for the Japanese beyond anything I ever had experienced. From that moment on I never felt the least pity or compassion for them no matter what the circumstances. My comrades would field-strip their packs and pockets for souvenirs and take gold teeth, but I never saw a Marine commit the kind of barbaric mutilation the Japanese committed if they had access to our dead.

When we got back to the gun pit, my buddy said, "Sledge-hammer, did you see what the Nips did to them bodies? Did you see what them poor guys had in their mouths?" I nodded as he continued, "Christ, I hate them slant-eyed bastards!"

"Me too. They're mean as hell," was all I could say.

Victory at High Cost

Twelve October continued to be an eventful day for us on Hill 140. Following Captain Haldane's death in the morning, we set up our mortars below and behind a 75mm pack how-itzer tied down within Company K's lines. We were to fire our usual support for the company, but we also were to provide covering fire for the artillery piece.

Johnny Marmet was observing for us through a crack in the coral rock up near the howitzer when he suddenly called down to us that he saw some Japanese officers just outside the mouth of a cave. Apparently confident they were sheltered from American fire, they were just sitting down to eat at a table on a ledge beneath a thatched canopy.

Johnny called the range to us and the order to fire five rounds. Snafu sighted in on the proper aiming stake, repeated Johnny's range, and yelled, "Fire one." I grabbed a shell, re-peated the range and charge, pulled off the proper number of powder increments from between the tail fins, put my right thumb over the safety pin, pulled the safety wire, and dropped the shell into the muzzle. Snafu realigned the sight after the recoil, grabbed the bipod feet, and yelled, "Fire two." I prepared the second shell and dropped it into the tube. It went smoothly and we got all the rounds off in short order. We listened tensely for them to explode on target. My heart pounded away the seconds. It was a rare occasion to get Japanese officers bunched up and rarer indeed on Peleliu for them to expose themselves.

After seemingly endless seconds of suspense we heard the dull boom as each shell exploded over the ridge and across the valley. Something was wrong though. I heard one less explosion than the number of shells we had fired. We looked anxiously up at Johnny who had his eyes glued to the target. Suddenly he spun around, snapped his finger, and stamped his foot. Scowling down at us he yelled, "Right on target, zeroed in! But the first damned round was a *dud*! What the hell happened?" We groaned and cursed with frustration. The first shell had gone right through the thatched roof and the Japanese officers dove for the cave. But the shell didn't explode. Our remaining shells were right on target, too, smashing up and blowing apart the thatched canopy and the table. But the enemy officers were safe inside the cave. Our pinpoint accuracy had been remarkable for a 60mm mortar that normally functioned to neutralize an area with fragments from its bursting shells. Our golden opportunity had vanished because of a dud shell. We set about trying to figure out what had gone wrong.

Everybody in the mortar section was cursing and groaning. Suddenly Snafu accused me of forgetting to pull the safety wire to arm that first shell. I was confident that I had pulled the pin. Some defense worker in an ammunition plant back in the States had made a mistake in the manufacture of the shell, I contended. Snafu wouldn't accept that, and we got into a hot argument. I was angry and frustrated enough myself. We had missed our one chance in a million to avenge the death of our CO. But Snafu was in a rage. It was a matter of pride with him, because he was the gunner and, therefore, in command of our mortar crew.

Snafu was a good Marine and an expert mortarman. His performance of his duties bore absolutely no resemblance to his nickname, "Situation Normal All Fouled Up." He felt it was a reflection on him that a chance to clobber several Japanese officers had failed because his assistant gunner hadn't pulled the safety wire on a shell. He was proud of a newspaper clipping from his hometown paper in Louisiana describing the effective fire his "mortar gun" had poured on the Japs during the bloody fighting for Hill 660 on Cape

Gloucester. Snafu was a unique character known and respected by everybody. The guys loved to kid him about his intrepid "mortar gun" on Hill 660, and he thrived on it. But this foul-up and escape of those enemy officers because of a dud shell was another matter.

As we argued, I knew that unless I could prove the dud wasn't my fault, I'd never hear the end of it from Snafu and the other Company K survivors of Peleliu. Fortunately, luck was on my side. We had fired only a couple of shells to register the gun before Johnny called on us to fire on the Japanese. Consequently I had an accurate count of the number of rounds we had fired from this position. While Snafu ranted and raved I crawled around on all fours a few feet in front of the gun. With incredible good luck I found what I was seeking amid the coral gravel and pulverized plant material. I retrieved the safety wire from each shell we had fired.

I held them out to Snafu and said, "OK, count them and then tell me I didn't pull the wires on all those rounds."

He counted them. We knew that no other 60mm mortar had occupied this newly captured position, so all the wires were ours. I was angry the shell had been a dud and the Japanese had escaped, but I was delighted that it wasn't due to my carelessness. I heard no more about the dud. We all wanted to forget it.

Word also came that day that the high command had declared the "assault phase" of the Palau Islands operation at an end. Many profane and irreverent remarks were made by my buddies to the effect that our leaders were as crazy as hell if they thought that held true on Peleliu. "Somebody from the division CP needs to come up here and tell them damned Nips the 'assault phase' is over," grumbled one man.

After dark the Japanese reinfiltrated some of the positions they had been driven out of around Hill 140. It was the usual hellish night in the ridges, exhausted Marines trying to fight off incredibly aggressive Japanese slipping all around. It was mortar flares, HE shells, grenades, and small-arms fire. I was so tired I held one eye open with the fingers of one hand to stay awake while clutching a grenade or other weapon with the other hand.

The next day, 13 October, 3/5 was ordered to renew the offensive and to straighten our lines, forming a salient on Hill 140. Our battalion was the only unit of the 5th Marines still on the lines and ordered to attack. Snipers raised hell all over the place. It seemed to me the fighting would never end, as we fired covering fire for our weary riflemen. Our artillery fired heavy support. The next morning, 14 October, Corsairs made a napalm strike against the Japanese on our right. Company I made a probing attack after a mortar barrage was halted by heavy sniper fire. Companies K and L improved their positions and put out more sandbags and concertina wire.

The battalion's efforts at attacking seemed like the gasping of a tired steam engine struggling to pull its string of cars up a steep grade. We were barely making it. Rumors flew that army troops would relieve us the next day, but my cynicism kept me from believing them.

We found some Japanese rifles and ammunition in our area. Hidden under pieces of corrugated iron, I discovered two boxes containing about a dozen Japanese grenades. I suggested to an NCO that we take them in case we needed them during the coming night, but he said we could get them later if necessary. We got busy on firing missions with our mortar, and the first time I glanced back toward the boxes, the souvenir hunters had moved in and were emptying them. Another mortarman and I yelled at the scavenging pests. They left, but all the Japanese grenades were gone.

A wave of hope and excitement spread through the ranks that evening when we got solid information that we would be relieved by the army the next morning. I got less sleep that night than ever. With the end in sight, I didn't want to get my throat slit at the last moment before escaping from the meat grinder.

During the morning of 15 October soldiers of the 2d Battalion, 321st Infantry Regiment, 81st Infantry Division (Wildcats) began moving single file into our area. I couldn't believe it! We were being relieved at last!

As the soldiers filed by us into position, a grizzled buddy squatting on his battered helmet eyed them critically and remarked, "Sledgehammer, I don't know about them dogfaces.

Major McIlhenny and his company commanders: 3d Bn, 5th Marines, 1st Marine Division, Pavuvu, June 1944. (L to R: Capt. Bishop, Capt. Neville, Capt. McAuliffe, McIlhenny, Capt. Haldane, Capt. Crown).

To Gene Sledge
Here's Pavuvu
Bob Hope

Pavuvu. Bob Hope and 1st Marine Division officers during his show before Peleliu.

Capt. Andrew A. Haldane. Photo by Lt. Col. John A. Crown.

D day, Peleliu. Smoke from naval and aerial bombardment hiding the beach. USMC photo.

Platoon Sgt. John Marmet, returning from Peleliu. Private photo.

D day, Peleliu. The inferno on the beach before we started in. National Archives photo.

An amphibious tractor burns on the beach as Marines take shelter under a DUKW. D day, Peleliu. Private photo (Pfc. John J. Smith).

Orange Beach 3 on D day, Peleliu, to the right of where K/3/5 had landed earlier. USMC photo.

Caliber .30 aircooled machine gun in action. Peleliu. USMC photo.

D day afternoon
after Marines
smashed Japanese
tank attack. Peleliu.
USMC photo.

Japanese soldier
killed alongside his
field piece. Note Jap
grenade in center
foreground. Peleliu.
USMC photo.

77mm howitzer of
the 11th Marines
fires close support
for frontline troops.
Peleliu. USMC
photo.

Men of the 5th Marines attack across the open fireswept airfield on 16 September. Peleliu. USMC photo.

The wounded could not survive long without water in the 115° F heat. Peleliu. USMC photo.

Dead Marines lying on the north end of Airfield D-4. Peleliu. USMC photo.

81mm mortar in action. Peleliu. USMC photo.

Typical 60mm mortar section emplacement in a bomb crater blasted out of solid coral. Peleliu. USMC photo.

Assault on Ngesebus. View from amphibious amtrac while crossing in third wave from Peleliu. USMC photo.

Ngesebus: Assault troops (K/3/5) move inland. USMC photo.

Flamethrower gunner with supporting rifle fire team burns out enemy emplacement. Peleliu. USMC photo.

Corsair drops napalm on Five Sisters. Peleliu. USMC photo.

View showing the removal of a wounded Marine. Peleliu. USMC photo.

Wounded Marines being removed from the shell-blasted terrain. Peleliu. USMC photo.

Death Valley, looking north. Five Sisters on the right. Peleliu. USMC photo.

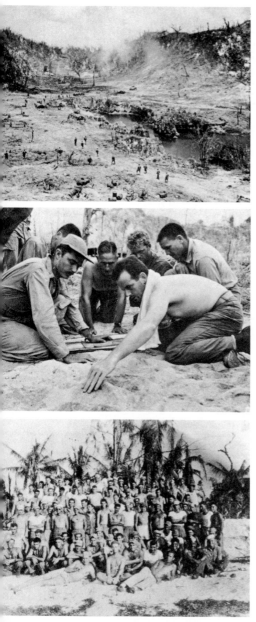

Tank infantry attack in the Horseshoe. Looking north: Five Brothers (left), Walt Ridge (right), Hill 140 (center background). USMC photo.

Col. Harold "Bucky" Harris, 5th Marines, discusses air support with some of his officers: (L to R, Lt. Col. J. R. Bailey, Harris, Maj. John "Gus" Gustafson, Lt. Col. Lewis Walt, Maj. Gordon Gayle). Peleliu. USMC photo.

K/3/5 survivors before boarding ship for Pavuvu.

A dreaded Japanese 150mm gun in its protected cave emplacement. Okinawa. USMC photo.

USS Idaho firing support for troops ashore. Okinawa. USMC photo.

1st Lt. Thomas "Stumpy" Stanley, CO of K/3/5, calling for artillery support.

Carrying the wounded. Okinawa. USMC photo.

Gunnery Sgt. Henry A. Boyes, after the 2 May 1945 attack. Pencil indicates where an enemy bullet went through his cap. Okinawa.

Marines wait to attack as a barrage of white phosphorous shells explodes on enemy positions. USMC photo.

Marines throwing smoke grenades to screen stretcher bearers. Okinawa. USMC photo.

The survivor grieves. Okinawa. USMC photo.

Passing through a small village. Note split-toe tabi on dead Japanese soldier. April 1945, Okinawa. USMC photo.

Shell-blasted Wana Ridge. Okinawa. USMC photo.

Flamethrower tank cleaning out enemy. Okinawa. USMC photo.

Pfc. Paul Isen of the 5th Marines dashing across through Japanese machine-gun fire as he crosses "death valley." Okinawa. USMC photo.

Wana Ridge. Marine on left has Thompson submachine gun; his buddy has a BAR. Okinawa. USMC photo.

Collecting supplies air-dropped on Shuri Ridge after mud halted land movement to the front. USMC photo.

Rubble of the walls of Shuri Castle. Okinawa. USMC photo.

At battle's end, three weary K Company mortarmen: L to R, John Redifer, Vincent Santos, Gene Farrar. Photo by Gene Farrar.

Author at the end of the campaign. Tent camp on Okinawa. Unknown photographer.

Eugene B. Sledge after return from Peking in 1946.

Look how many of 'em wearin' glasses, and they look old enough to be my daddy. Besides, them pockets on their dungaree pants sure do look baggy."

"They look fine to me. They're our replacements," I answered.

"I guess you're right. Thank God they're here," he said reflectively.

His observations were correct though, because most of our fellow Marines hadn't reached the age of twenty-one yet, and army dungarees did have large side pockets.

"We sure are glad to see you guys," I said to one of the soldiers.

He just grinned and said, "Thanks." I knew he wasn't happy to be there.*

The relief, which had gone smoothly, was completed by 1100, and we were on our way to the northern defense zone of Peleliu. Our battalion deployed along the East Road facing seaward, where we were to stop any counterlanding the Japanese might try.

My mortar was emplaced near the road so we could fire on the strip of mangrove swamp between the narrow beach and the sea as well as up the road toward the Umurbrogol Pocket if necessary. There was a sloping ridge to our rear along which the rest of the company dug in defensively. We stayed there from the time we came off the line until the last week of the month.

The area was quiet. We relaxed as much as we could with the nagging fear that we might get thrown into the line again if an emergency developed.

We learned that our battalion would leave Peleliu as soon as a ship was available to transport us back to Pavuvu. By day we rested and swapped souvenirs, but we had to be on the alert at night for possible Japanese movement. To the south we could hear the constant rattle of machine guns and the

*By 15 October, the Marines had compressed the Umurbrogol Pocket to an area of about 400 to 500 yards. Yet the soldiers of the 81st Infantry Division faced six more weeks of fighting before the process of constant pressure and attrition wiped out the final vestiges of Japanese opposition.

thud of mortars and artillery as the 81st Infantry Division kept up the pressure around the Umurbrogol Pocket.

One day a buddy told me he had a unique souvenir to show me. We sat on a rock as he carefully removed a package from his combat pack. He unwrapped layers of waxed paper that had originally covered rations and proudly held out his prize for me to see.

"Have you gone Asiatic?" I gasped. "You know you can't keep that thing. Some officer'll put you on report sure as hell," I remonstrated as I stared in horror at the shriveled human hand he had unwrapped.

"Aw, Sledgehammer, nobody'll say anything. I've got to dry it in the sun a little more so it won't stink," he said as he carefully laid it out on the rock in the hot sun. He explained that he thought a dried Japanese hand would be a more interesting souvenir than gold teeth. So when he found a corpse that was drying in the sun and not rotting, he simply took out his kabar and severed the hand from the corpse, and here it was, and what did I think?

"I think you're nuts," I said. "You know the CO will raise hell if he sees that."

"Hell no, Sledgehammer, nobody says anything about the guys collecting gold teeth, do they?" he argued.

"Maybe so," I said, "but it's just the idea of a human hand. Bury it."

He looked grimly at me, which was totally out of character for his amiable good nature. "How many Marines you reckon that hand pulled the trigger on?" he asked in an icy voice.

I stared at the blackened, shriveled hand and wondered about what he said. I thought how I valued my own hands and what a miracle to do good or evil the human hand is. Although I didn't collect gold teeth, I had gotten used to the idea, but somehow a hand seemed to be going too far. The war had gotten to my friend; he had lost (briefly, I hoped) all his sensitivity. He was a twentieth-century savage now, mild mannered though he still was. I shuddered to think that I might do the same thing if the war went on and on.

Several of our Marines came over to see what my buddy

had. "You dumb jerk, throw that thing away before it begins to stink," growled an NCO.

"Hell yes," added another man, "I don't want you going aboard ship with me if you got that thing. It gives me the creeps," he said as he looked disgustedly at the souvenir.

After several other men chimed in with their disapproval, my friend reluctantly flung his unique souvenir among the rocks.

We had good rations and began to eat heartily and enjoy being out of the line as we relaxed more each day. Good water came up by jeep with the rations, and I never brushed my teeth so many times a day. It was a luxury. Rumors began to spread that we would soon board ship and leave Peleliu.

Toward the end of October, we moved to another part of the island. Our spirits soared. We bivouacked in a sandy, flat area near the beach. Jeeps brought in our jungle hammocks and our knapsacks.* We received orders to shave and to put on the clean dungarees we all carried in our knapsacks.

Some men complained that it would be easier to clean up aboard ship. But one NCO laughed and said that if our scroungy, stinking bunch of Marines climbed a cargo net aboard ship, the sailors would jump over the other side as soon as they saw us.

My hair, though it had been short on D day, had grown into a thick matted mass plastered together with rifle oil and coral dust. Long ago I had thrown away my pocket comb, because most of the teeth had broken out when I tried to comb my hair. I managed now to clean up my head with soap and water, and it took both edges of two razor blades and a complete tube of shaving soap to shave off the itching, greasy tangle of coral-encrusted beard. I felt like a man freed of a hair shirt.

My dungaree jacket wasn't torn, and I felt I must keep it as a souvenir of good luck. I rinsed it in the ocean, dried it in the sun, and put it into my pack.†

---

*A knapsack was the lower half of the two-part World War II Marine combat pack. The upper part was called the haversack. The latter half was the part a Marine normally carried with him into a fight.

†I later wore this same lucky jacket through the long, muddy Okinawa campaign. Faded now, it hangs peacefully in my closet, one of my most prized possessions.

My filthy dungaree trousers were ragged and torn in the knees so I threw them into a campfire along with my stinking socks. The jagged coral had worn away the tough, inch-thick cord soles of my new boondockers of 15 September to the thin innersoles. I had to keep these until we returned to Pavuvu, because my replacement shoes were back there in my seabag.

That afternoon, 29 October, we learned that we would board ship the next day. With a feeling of intense relief, I climbed into my hammock at dusk and zipped up the mosquito netting along the side. I was delighted at how comfortable it was to lie on something other than hard, rocky ground. I lay back, sighed, and thought of the good sleep I should get until my turn for sentry duty came around. I could look inland and see the ragged crest of those terrible ridges against the skyline. Thank goodness that section was in U.S. hands, I thought.

Suddenly, *zip, zip, zip, zip,* a burst of Japanese machine-gun fire (blue-white tracers) slashed through the air *under* my hammock! The bullets kicked up sand on the other side of a crater beneath me. I jerked open the hammock zipper. Carbine in hand, I tumbled out into the crater. After all I had been through, I wasn't taking any chances on getting my rear end shot off in a hammock.

Judging from the sound made by the bullets, the machine gun was a long way off. The gunner was probably firing a burst toward the army lines over on some ridge between him and me. But a man could get killed just as dead by a stray bullet as an aimed one. So after my brief moments of comfort in the hammock, I slept the rest of the night in the crater.

Next morning, 30 October, we squared away our packs, picked up our gear, and moved out to board ship. Even though we were leaving bloody Peleliu at last, my mind was distracted by an oppressive feeling that Bloody Nose Ridge was pulling us back like some giant, inexorable magnet. It had soaked up the blood of our division like a great sponge. I believed that it would get us yet. Even if we boarded ship, we would get jerked off and thrown into the line to help stop a counterattack or some threat to the airfield. I suppose I had become completely fatalistic; our casualties had been so heavy that it was impossible for me to believe we were actually leaving Peleliu. The sea was quite rough, and I looked back at the island with great relief as we put out for the ship.

We pulled alongside a big merchant troopship, the *Sea Runner*, and prepared to climb a cargo net to get aboard. We had done this sort of thing countless times in our training but never when we were so terribly exhausted. We had a hard time even getting started up the net because we kept bobbing up and down in the heavy sea. Several men stopped to rest on the way, but no one fell. As I struggled upward with my load of equipment, I felt like a weary insect climbing a vine. But at last I was crawling up out of the abyss of Peleliu!

We were assigned to quarters in troop compartments belowdecks. I stowed my gear on my rack and went topside. The salt air was delicious to breathe. What a luxury to inhale long deep breaths of fresh clean air, air that wasn't heavy with the fetid stench of death.

The cost in casualties for a tiny island was terrible. The fine 1st Marine Division was shattered. It suffered a total loss of 6,526 men (1,252 dead and 5,274 wounded). The casualties in the division's infantry regiments were: 1st Marines, 1,749; 5th Marines, 1,378; 7th Marines, 1,497. These were severe losses considering that each infantry regiment started with about 3,000 men. The army's 81st Infantry Division would lose another 3,278 men (542 dead and 2,736 wounded) before it secured the island.

Most of the enemy garrison on Peleliu died. Only a few were captured. Estimates as to the exact losses by the Japanese vary somewhat, but conservatively, 10,900 Japanese soldiers died and 302 became prisoners. Of the prisoners only 7 were soldiers and 12 sailors. The remainder were laborers of other oriental extractions.

Company K, 3d Battalion, 5th Marines went into Peleliu with approximately 235 men, the normal size of a World War II Marine rifle company. It left with only 85 unhurt. It suffered 64 percent casualties. Of its original seven officers, two remained for the return to Pavuvu.

For its actions on Peleliu and Ngesebus, the 1st Marine Division received the Presidential Unit Citation.

Even at a distance Peleliu was ugly with the jagged ridges and shattered trees. Haney came up alongside me and leaned on the rail. He looked gloomily at the island and puffed a cigarette.

"Well, Haney, what did you think of Peleliu?" I asked. I really was curious what a veteran with a combat record that included some of the big battles of the Western Front during World War I thought of the first battle in which I had participated. I had nothing in my experience to make a comparison with Peleliu.

Instead of the usual old salt comment—something like, "You think that was bad, you oughta been in the old Corps,"—Haney answered with an unexpected, "Boy, that was terrible! I ain't never seen nothin' like it. I'm ready to go back to the States. I've had enough after that."

A common perception has it that the "worst battle" to any man is the one he had been in himself. In view of Haney's comments, I concluded that Peleliu must have been as bad as I thought it was even though it was my first battle. Haney's long Marine Corps career as a combat infantryman certainly qualified him as a good judge of how bad a battle had been. His simple words were enough to convince me about the severity of the fight we had just been through.

None of us would ever be the same after what we had endured. To some degree that is true, of course, of all human experience. But something in me died at Peleliu. Perhaps it was a childish innocence that accepted as faith the claim that man is basically good. Possibly I lost faith that politicians in high places who do not have to endure war's savagery will ever stop blundering and sending others to endure it.

But I also learned important things on Peleliu. A man's ability to depend on his comrades and immediate leadership is absolutely necessary. I'm convinced that our discipline, esprit de corps, and tough training were the ingredients that equipped me to survive the ordeal physically and mentally—given a lot of good luck, of course. I learned realism, too. To defeat an enemy as tough and dedicated as the Japanese, we had to be just as tough. We had to be just as dedicated to America as they were to their emperor. I think this was the essence of Marine Corps doctrine in World War II, and that history vindicates this doctrine.

To this private first class, Peleliu was also a vindication of Marine Corps training, particularly of boot camp. I speak only from a personal viewpoint and make no generalizations, but for me, in the final analysis, Peleliu was:

- thirty days of severe, unrelenting inhuman emotional and physical stress;
- proof that I could trust and depend completely on the Marine on each side of me and on our leadership;
- proof that I could use my weapons and equipment efficiently under severe stress; and
- proof that the critical factor in combat stress is duration of the combat rather than the severity.

Boot camp taught me that I was expected to excel, or try to, even under stress. My drill instructor was a small man. He didn't have a big mouth. He was neither cruel nor sadistic. He wasn't a bully. But he was a strict disciplinarian, a total realist about our future, and an absolute perfectionist dedicated to excellence. To him more than to my disciplined home life, a year of college ROTC before boot camp, and months of infantry training afterward I attribute my ability to have withstood the stress of Peleliu.

The Japanese were as dedicated to military excellence as U.S. Marines. Consequently, on Peleliu the opposing forces were like two scorpions in a bottle. One was annihilated, the other nearly so. Only Americans who excelled could have defeated them.

Okinawa would be the longest and largest battle of the Pacific war. There my division would suffer about as many casualties as it did on Peleliu. Again the enemy garrison would fight to the death. On Okinawa I would be shelled and shot at more, see more enemy soldiers, and fire at more of them with my mortar and with small arms than on Peleliu. But there was a ferocious, vicious nature to the fighting on Peleliu that made it unique for me. Many of my veteran comrades agreed.

Perhaps we can say of Peleliu as the Englishman, Robert Graves, said of World War I, that it:

> . . . gave us infantrymen so convenient a measuring-stick for discomfort, grief, pain, fear, and horror, that nothing since has greatly daunted us. But it also brought new meanings of courage, patience, loyalty, and greatness of spirit; incommunicable, we found to later times.*

As I crawled out of the abyss of combat and over the rail of the *Sea Runner,* I realized that compassion for the sufferings of others is a burden to those who have it. As Wilfred Owen's poem "Insensibility" puts it so well, those who feel most for others suffer most in war.

*Graves, Robert, "Introduction" in *Old Soldiers Never Die* by Frank Richards, Berkley Publishing Corp., N.Y. 1966.

PART II

Okinawa: The Final Triumph

FOREWORD TO PART II

Peleliu took its toll. As the executive officer and then commander of Company K, 3d Battalion, 5th Marines, I saw in the eyes of each survivor the price he paid for thirty days of unrelenting close combat on that hunk of blasted coral.

For those weary men returning to Pavuvu in November 1944, the war was far from over. Pavuvu was a better place the second time around than when we had left it. But it wasn't a rest haven. The survivors of Peleliu weren't allowed such a luxury. There was little time for licking wounds. We had to absorb a lot of new men as replacements for those lost on Peleliu and for the rotation home of the Guadalcanal veterans who by then had fought three campaigns.

Peleliu was something special for the Marines of K/3/5—for all of the 1st Marine Division. It has remained so down through the years. Yet Okinawa had its own character, more forbidding in many ways than its predecessor. There the 1st Marine Division fought a different war under a new set of rules where tactics and movement were used in a fashion previously unknown to the island-fighting Marines.

Okinawa is a large island, more than sixty miles long and from two to eighteen miles wide. It introduced the Marines to "land" warfare for the first time. Even in 1945 it had a city, towns and villages, several large airfields, an intricate road network, and a good-sized civilian population. Most important, the Japanese defended it with more than 100,000 of their best troops. Okinawa was Japanese territory. They knew it was our final stepping-stone to the home islands of Japan.

The Marines had learned a lot on the way to Okinawa. We had improved our force structure, tactics, and techniques for combat along the way. The Japanese had learned, too. On Okinawa we faced a set of defenses and defensive tactics made sophisticated by the Japanese through application of lessons learned from all of their previous losses. They also fought with an intensity born of a certain knowledge that if they failed, nothing remained to prevent our direct assault into their homeland.

Irrespective of the new elements, the battle for Okinawa was fought and ultimately decided the way all battles have been fought and won or lost. The men on both sides, facing each other day after day across the sights of a rifle, determined the outcome. Pfc. Eugene B. Sledge was one of those men. In this book he gives us a unique experience of seeing and feeling war at its most important level, that of the enlisted fighting man. His words ring true, clean of analysis and reaction to past events. They simply reflect what happened to him and, therefore, to all of the Marines who fought there. I know, because I fought with them.

For the men of the "old breed" who struggled, bled, died, and eventually won on Peleliu and Okinawa, Sledgehammer is their most eloquent spokesman. I'm proud to have served with them—and with him.

Capt. Thomas J. Stanley
U.S. Marine Corps Reserve (Ret.)
Houston, Texas

CHAPTER SEVEN

Rest and Rehabilitation

Early next morning the *Sea Runner,* in convoy with other ships including those carrying the survivors of the 7th Marines, put out for Pavuvu. I was glad to be aboard ship again, even a troopship. I drank gallons of ice cold water from the electrically cooled "scuttlebutts."*

Most of my old friends in rifle companies had been wounded or killed. It was terribly depressing, and the full realization of our losses bore down heavily on me as we made inquiries. The survivors on board gave us all the details regarding our friends who hadn't made it through Peleliu. We thanked them and moved on. After a few of the visits and bad news about lost friends, I began to feel that I hadn't been just lucky but was a survivor of a major tragedy.

One day after noon chow a friend and I were sitting on our racks discussing things in general. The conversation drifted off, and we fell silent. Suddenly he looked at me with an intense, pained expression on his face and said, "Sledgehammer, why the hell did we have to take Peleliu?" I must have looked at him blankly, because he began to argue that our losses on Peleliu had been useless and hadn't helped the war effort at all, and that the island could have been bypassed. "Hell, the army landed troops on Morotai [Netherlands East Indies] with light opposition the same day we landed on Peleliu, and we caught hell, and the damn place still ain't secured. And while we were still on Peleliu, MacArthur hit

*This is a naval slang word referring either to water coolers aboard ship or to rumors. Perhaps the double meaning derived from a habit of sailors and Marines of swapping rumors when gathered around a water cooler for a drink.

Leyte [in the Philippines, 20 October] and walked ashore standing up. I just don't see where we did any good," he continued.

I replied gloomily, "I don't know." He just stared at the bulkhead and sadly shook his head. He was the same friend who had been with me the time we saw the three terribly mutilated Marine dead. I could imagine what he was thinking.

Despite these momentary lapses, the veterans of Peleliu knew they had accomplished something special. That these Marines had been able to survive the intense physical exertion of weeks of combat on Peleliu in that incredibly muggy heat gave ample evidence of their physical toughness. That we had survived emotionally—at least for the moment—was, and is, ample evidence to me that our training and discipline were the best. They prepared us for the worst, which is what we experienced on Peleliu.

On 7 November 1944, (three days after my twenty-first birthday) the *Sea Runner* entered Macquitti Bay. After passing familiar islets, she dropped anchor off Pavuvu's steel pier. I was surprised at how good Pavuvu looked after the desolation of Peleliu.

We picked up our gear and debarked shortly. On the beach we walked over to one of several tables set up nearby. There I saw—of all things—an American Red Cross girl. She was serving grapefruit juice in small paper cups. Some of my buddies looked at the Red Cross woman sullenly, sat on their helmets, and waited for orders. But together with several other men, I went over to the table where the young lady handed me a cup of juice, smiled, and said she hoped I liked it. I looked at her with confusion as I took the cup and thanked her. My mind was so benumbed by the shock and violence of Peleliu that the presence of an American girl on Pavuvu seemed totally out of context. I was bewildered. "What the hell is she doing here?" I thought. "She's got no more business here than some damn politician." As we filed past to board trucks, I resented her deeply.

Next to a table counting off the men to board the trucks stood a brand-spanking-new boot second lieutenant. He was so obviously fresh from the States and officers' candidate school that his khakis were new, and he wasn't even suntanned. As I moved slowly by the table he said, "OK, sonny, move out." Since my enlistment in the Marine Corps, I had been called about everything imaginable—printable and unprintable. But fresh off of Peleliu I was unprepared for "sonny." I turned to the officer and stared at him blankly. He returned my gaze and seemed to realize his mistake. He looked hurriedly away. My buddies' eyes still carried that vacant, hollow look typical of men recently out of the shock of battle. Maybe that's what the young lieutenant saw in mine, and it made him uncomfortable.

The trucks sped past neat tent areas, much improved since we had last seen Pavuvu. We arrived at our familiar camp area to find numerous self-conscious replacements sitting and standing in and around the tents. We were the "old men" now. They appeared so relaxed and innocent of what lay ahead of us that I felt sorry for them. We took off our packs and settled into our tents. In the best way we could, we tried to unwind and relax.

Shortly after we arrived back at Pavuvu and on an occasion when all the replacements were out of the company area on work parties, 1st Sgt. David P. Bailey yelled "K Company, fall in." As the survivors of Peleliu straggled out of their tents into the company street, I thought about how few remained out of the 235 men we started with.

Dressed in clean khakis and with his bald head shining, Bailey walked up to us and said, "At ease, men." He was a real old-time salty Marine and a stern disciplinarian, but a mild-mannered man whom we highly respected. Bailey had something to say, and it wasn't merely a pep talk. Unfortunately, I don't remember his exact words, so I won't attempt to quote him, but he told us we should be proud. He said we had fought well in as tough a battle as the Marine Corps had ever been in, and we had upheld the honor of the Corps. He finished by saying, "You people have proved you are good Marines." Then he dismissed us.

We returned silently and thoughtfully to our tents. I heard no cynical comments about Bailey's brief remarks. Words of praise were rare from the heart of such a stern old salt who expected every man to do his best and tolerated nothing less. His straightforward, sincere praise and statement of respect and admiration for what our outfit had done made me feel like I had won a medal. His talk was not the loud harangue of a politician or the cliché-studded speech of some rear-echelon officer or journalist. It was a quiet statement of praise from one who had endured the trials of Peleliu with us. As far as being a competent judge of us, there was nobody better qualified than an old combat Marine and a senior NCO like Bailey, who had observed us and endured the fight himself. His words meant a lot to me, and they apparently did to my comrades, too.

One of our first activities after getting settled in our Pavuvu tents was to renew our old feud with the rats and land crabs. Our seabags, cots, and other gear had been stacked around the center tent pole while we were gone. The land crabs had moved in and made themselves at home. When several of my tent mates and I started unstacking the items around the tent pole, the crabs swarmed out. The men started yelling, cursing the crabs and smashing them with bayonets and entrenching tools. Some character sprayed cigarette lighter fluid on a crab as it ran into the company street and then threw a match at it. The flaming crab moved a couple of feet before being killed by the flames.

"Hey, you guys, did you see that? That crab looked just like a burning Jap tank."

"Good oh," yelled another man as Marines rushed around trying to find more cans of lighter fluid to spray on the hated land crabs. Men started taking orders for cans of lighter fluid and raced off to the 5th Marines PX tent to buy up all they could find. We killed over a hundred crabs from my tent alone.

One evening after chow as I sprawled on my cot wishing I were back home, I noticed one of Company K's two surviving officers carrying some books and papers down the company street in the twilight. He passed my tent and went to the fifty-five-gallon oil drum that served as a trash can. The lieutenant tossed some maps and papers into the can. He held up a thick book and with obvious anger slammed it into the trash can. He then turned and walked slowly back up the street.

Curious, I went out to have a look. The maps were combat maps of Peleliu. I dropped them back into the trash (and have since regretted I didn't salvage them for future historical reference). Then I found the book. It was a large hardback volume of about a thousand pages, bound in dark blue, obviously not a GI field manual or book of regulations.

Always seeking good reading material, I looked at the spine of the book and read its title, *Men At War* by Ernest Hemingway. This is interesting history, I thought, and was puzzled as to why the lieutenant had thrown it so violently into the trash. I opened the cover. In the twilight I saw written in a bold strong hand, *A. A. Haldane.* A lump rose in my throat as I asked myself why I'd want to read about war when Peleliu had cost us our company commander and so many good friends. I, too, slammed the book down into the trash can in a gesture of grief and disgust over the waste of war I had already experienced firsthand.

After we had been back on Pavuvu about a week, I had one of the most heartwarming and rewarding experiences of my entire enlistment in the Marine Corps. It was after taps, all the flambeaus were out, and all of my tent mates were in their sacks with mosquito nets in place. We were all very tired, still trying to unwind from the tension and ordeal of Peleliu.

All was quiet except for someone who had begun snoring softly when one of the men, a Gloucester veteran who had been wounded on Peleliu, said in steady measured tones, "You know something, Sledgehammer?"

"What?" I answered.

"I kinda had my doubts about you," he continued, "and how you'd act when we got into combat, and the stuff hit the fan. I mean, your ole man bein' a doctor and you havin' been to college and bein' sort of a rich kid compared to some guys. But I kept my eye on you on Peleliu, and by God you did OK; you did OK."

"Thanks, ole buddy," I replied, nearly bursting with pride. Many men were decorated with medals they richly earned for their brave actions in combat, medals to wear on their blouses

for everyone to see. I was never awarded an individual decoration, but the simple, sincere personal remarks of approval
by my veteran comrade that night after Peleliu were like a
medal to me. I have carried them in my heart with great pride
and satisfaction ever since.

As Christmas approached, rumor had it we were going to
have a feast of real turkey. There were several days out of the
year when the Marine Corps tried to give us good chow:
10 November (the Marine Corps' birthday), Thanksgiving,
Christmas, and New Year's. The rest of the time in the Pacific
war, chow was canned or dehydrated. Refrigeration facilities
for large quantities of food were not available, at least not to a
unit as mobile and as lacking in all luxuries as a combat division in the Fleet Marine Force. But the scuttlebutt was that
there were frozen turkeys for us in the big refrigerators on
Banika.

We had special Christmas Eve church services in the palm-
thatched regimental chapel that had been constructed skillfully by Russell Island natives. That was followed by a
special Christmas program at the regimental theater where
we sat on coconut logs and sang carols. I enjoyed it a great
deal but felt pretty homesick. Then we had our roast turkey,
and it was excellent.

New Year's celebration was even more memorable for me.
On New Year's Eve after chow, I heard some yelling and other
commotion over at the battalion mess hall. The messmen had
just about finished squaring away the galley for the night
when a sentry shouted, "Corporal of the guard, fire at post
number three!"

I saw cooks and messmen in the mess hall who were cleaning up by lamplight all rush outside to a fire burning in a
grove of trees near the galley. I thought one of the gasoline
heaters that boiled water in tubs where we cleaned our mess
kits had caught fire. By the light of the flames I could see men
running around the galley yelling, and I could hear the mess
sergeant cursing and shouting orders. I also saw two figures
slide through the shadows toward our company street, but
paid them little heed. In a few minutes the fire was put out,

just a can of gasoline some distance from the mess hall that had somehow caught fire, somebody said.

A friend of mine appeared at my tent and said in a low voice, "Hey, you guys, Howard says come on down to his tent; plenty of turkey for everybody!"

We followed him on the double. As I entered the tent, there sat Howard Nease on his cot, a flambeau flickering beside him, and a towel on his lap under a huge, plump roast turkey.

"Happy New Year, you guys," Howard said with his characteristically broad grin.

We filed past him as he deftly sliced off huge slabs of turkey with his razor-sharp kabar, and placed them into our opened hands. Others came in, and we broke out our two cans of warm beer that each had been issued. Someone produced a can of jungle juice that had been "working." A guitar, a fiddle, and a mandolin struck up the "Spanish Fandango" as Howard sliced turkey until the carcass was cleaned. Then he directed the music, using his kabar as a baton. Howard told us the burning can of gasoline had been merely a diversion to distract the mess sergeant while he and a couple of other daredevils entered the galley and made a moonlight requisition of two turkeys.

We, the survivors of that recent bloodbath on Peleliu, forgot our troubles and howled with laughter at the story. Enjoying the comradeship forged by combat, we had the finest New Year's Eve party I've ever attended. The 11th Marines fired an artillery salute at midnight—as a peaceful gesture.

It was typical of Howard that he pulled off his turkey requisition so neatly and just as typical that he shared it with as many of his buddies as he could. He was one of those wonderfully buoyant souls, always friendly and joking, coolheaded in combat, and though much admired, very modest. When Howard was killed by a Japanese machine gun in the early days of the Okinawa battle (his third campaign), every man who knew him was deeply saddened. By his example, he taught me more than anyone else the value of cheerfulness in the face of adversity.

One of my most treasured memories is the mental picture of Howard Nease sitting on his bunk carving a huge turkey on his lap with his kabar by the light of a flambeau in his tent under Pavuvu's palms on New Year's Eve 1944, grinning and saying, "Happy New Year, Sledgehammer." I profited greatly from knowing him.

Our new division commander, Maj. Gen. Pedro del Valle, former commander of the 11th Marines, ordered regular close-order drills, parades, and reviews. This was better than work parties moving rotting coconuts and added a "spit and polish" to our routine that helped morale. A regular beer ration of two cans a man each week also helped. During close-order drill we dressed in clean khakis, which each man pressed under his mattress pad on his canvas bunk. As we marched back and forth on the neat coral-covered parade ground, I thought about home or some book I was reading and wasn't at all bored.

One day we had a 5th Regiment parade. Decorations and medals were awarded to those cited for outstanding service on Peleliu. Many of our wounded had returned from the hospitals by then. When the Purple Heart medal was awarded to those who had been wounded, there weren't many of us who didn't qualify for it.

During those parades we took great pride in seeing our regimental flag carried with us. Like all the regimental flags, it had a large Marine Corps emblem on it with "United States Marine Corps" emblazoned across the top. Below the emblem was "Fifth Marine Regiment."

But the thing that made our flag unique was the number of battle streamers attached at the top of the staff. These streamers (ribbons about a foot long with the names of battles printed on them) represented battles the 5th Marines had fought in and decorations the regiment had won, all the way back to Belleau Wood (World War I) and the Banana Wars (in South America). We had just added Peleliu to the World War II collection. Those streamers represented more battles than any other Marine regiment had fought in. One buddy said our flag had so many battle streamers, decorations, and ribbons that it looked like a mop—an unsophisticated yet straight-from-the-shoulder summation of a proud tradition!

After we had been back on Pavuvu several weeks, I was told one day to dress in clean khakis and to report to the company headquarters tent promptly at 0100. There was some vague reference to an interview that might lead to officers' candidate school back in the States.

"Hey, Sledgehammer, you'll have it made, being an officer and all that, wheeling and dealing Stateside," a buddy said as I got ready for the interview.

"If you're lucky maybe you can land a desk job," another said.

Some of my buddies were obviously envious as I left and walked nervously down the street. The thoughts in my head were that I didn't want or intend to leave Company K (unless as a casualty or rotated home for good) and why on earth had I been chosen for an interview regarding OCS.

When I arrived at the company headquarters, I was sent to a tent a short distance away, near the battalion headquarters. I reported to the tent and was greeted cordially by a first lieutenant. He was an extremely handsome man and, I gathered from his composure and modest self-confidence, a combat veteran.

He asked me in detail about my background and education. He was sincere and friendly. I felt he was trying carefully to determine whether the men he interviewed were suitable to be Marine officers. He and I hit it off well, and I was perfectly honest with him. He asked me why I had not succeeded in the V-12 officers' candidate program, and I told him how I felt about joining the Marine Corps and being sent to college.

"How do you feel about it now that you've been in combat?" he asked.

I told him it would be nice to be back in college. I said I had seen enough on Peleliu to satisfy my curiosity and ardor for fighting. "In fact," I said, "I'm ready to go home."

He laughed good-naturedly and knowingly. He asked me how I liked the Marine Corps and my unit. I told him I was proud to be a member. He asked me how I liked being a 60mm mortar crewman, and I said it was my first choice. Then he got very serious and asked, "How would you feel about sending men into a situation where you knew they would be killed?"

Without hesitation 1 answered, "I couldn't do it, sir."

The lieutenant looked at me long and hard in a friendly, analytical way. He asked me a few more questions, then said, "Would you like to be an officer?"

"Yes, sir, if it meant I could go back to the States," I said. He laughed and with a few more friendly remarks told me that was all.

My buddies asked me for all the details of the interview. When I told them all about it one said, "Sledgehammer, damn if you ain't got to be as Asiatic as Haney. Why the hell didn't you snow that lieutenant so you could go into OCS?"

I replied that the lieutenant was experienced and too wise to fall for a snow job. That was true, of course, but I really had no desire to leave Company K. It was home to me, and I had a strong feeling of belonging to the company no matter how miserable or dangerous conditions might be. Besides, I had found my niche as a mortarman. The weapon and its deployment interested me greatly, and if I had to fight again, I was confident of doing the Japanese far more damage as a mortarman than as a second lieutenant. I had no desire to be an officer or command anybody; I just wanted to be the best mortar crewman I could—and to survive the war.

There was nothing heroic or unique in my attitude. Other men felt the same way. Actually, in combat our officers caught just as much hell as the enlisted men. They also were burdened with responsibility. As one buddy (a private) said, "When the stuff hits the fan, all I have to do is what I'm told, and I can look out for just me and my buddy. Them officers all the time got to be checkin' maps and squarin' people away."

We began to assimilate the new replacements into the company, and we added a third mortar to my section. The battalion ordnance section checked all weapons, and we got new issues for those worn out in the fight for Peleliu.

There were some drafted Marines among the new replacements and also a sprinkling of NCOs who had been in navy yards and other stateside duty stations. The presence of the NCOs caused some bitterness among a few of the Gloucester and Peleliu veterans who were by then senior in their squads because of the heavy casualties on Peleliu. The latter wouldn't get promoted with new NCOs entering the company to take our leadership positions. From what I saw, however, the new NCOs were mostly men with numerous years of service, although not combat veterans. They did a good job of assuming their authority while respecting us combat veterans for our experience.

The drafted Marines took a good bit of kidding about being "handcuffed volunteers" from those of us who had enlisted into the Marine Corps. Some of the drafted men insisted vehemently that they were volunteers who had enlisted like most of us. But they were careful to conceal their records and identification, because "SS" (for Selective Service) appeared after the serial number if a man had been drafted.

The draftees sometimes had their laugh on us, though. If we griped and complained, they grinned and said, "What you guys bitchin' about? You asked for it, didn't you?" We just grumbled at them; no one got angry about it. For the most part, the replacements were good men, and the company retained its fighting spirit.

Our training picked up in intensity, and rumors began to fly regarding the next "blitz" (a term commonly used for a campaign). We heard that the 1st Marine Division was to be put into an army to invade the China coast or Formosa (Taiwan). Many of my buddies feared that we would lose our identity as Marines and that the Marine Corps would finally be absorbed into the U.S. Army (a fate that has caused anxiety to U.S. Marines of many generations, as history well documents). Our training emphasized street fighting and cooperation with tanks in open country. But we still didn't know the name of our objective. After we were shown maps (without names) of a long, narrow island, we still didn't know.

One day Tom F. Martin, a friend of mine in Company L, who also had been in the V-12 program and was a Peleliu veteran, came excitedly to my tent and showed me a *National Geographic* map of the Northern Pacific. On it we saw the same oddly shaped island. Located 325 miles south of the southern tip of the Japanese home island of Kyushu, it was called Okinawa Shima. Its closeness to Japan assured us of one thing beyond any doubt: Whatever else happened, the battle for Okinawa was bound to be bitter and bloody. The Japanese never had sold any island cheaply, and the pattern of the war until then had shown that the battles became more vicious the closer we got to Japan.

We made practice landings, fired various small arms, and underwent intensive mortar training. With a third weapon added to our mortar section, I felt as though we were Company K's artillery battery.

At this time hepatitis broke out among the troops. We called it yellow jaundice, and I got a bad case. We could look at a man and tell whether he had the malady by the yellowing of the whites of his eyes. Even our deeply tanned skins took on a sallow appearance. I felt terrible, was tired, and the smell of food nauseated me. Pavuvu's muggy heat didn't help any either. I went to sick call one morning, as other Marines were doing in increasing numbers. The medical officer gave me a "light duty slip," a piece of paper officially relieving me from the intense exertion of routine training but still making me subject to minor work parties such as picking up trash, straightening tent ropes, and the like. It was the only time during my entire service in the Marine Corps that I got out of regular duties because of illness.

Had we been civilians, I'm confident those of us with hepatitis would have been hospitalized. Instead, we received APC pills from a corpsman.* This medication was the standard remedy for everything except bayonet, gunshot, or shrapnel wounds. After several days I was pronounced recovered enough for resumption of regular duties and surrendered my cherished light duty slip to an officer in sick bay.

Training intensified. During January 1945 the company boarded an LCI† and, in convoy with other such vessels, went

---

*A nonprescription, all-purpose painkiller containing aspirin and caffeine, among other ingredients.

†Landing craft, infantry: a sort of miniature LST that carried about a company of infantry plus a few vehicles.

to Guadalcanal for maneuvers. After a division-sized field problem, we returned to Pavuvu on 25 January.

Then we listened daily with sympathetic interest to the news reports of the terrible fighting encountered by the 3d, 4th, and 5th Marine divisions during the battle for Iwo Jima that began on 19 February.

"It sounds just like a larger version of Peleliu," a buddy of mine said one day.

He didn't realize how correct he was. The new pattern of defense-in-depth and no *banzai* charges that the Japanese had tried on the 1st Marine Division at Peleliu was repeated on Iwo Jima. When that island was declared secured on 16 March, the cost to the three Marine divisions that fought there sounded like our Peleliu casualties magnified three times.

During our training we were told that we would have to climb over a seawall or cliff (exact height unknown) to move inland during the coming battle. Several times we practiced scaling a sheer coral cliff (about forty feet high) across the bay from the division's camp on Pavuvu. We had no more than two ropes to get the entire company up and over the cliff. Supposedly we would be furnished rope ladders before D day, but I never saw any.

While we stood at the foot of the cliff during those exercises, waiting our turn and watching other men struggle up the ropes to the top of the cliff with all their combat gear, I heard some choice comments from my buddies regarding the proceedings. The company officers (all new except First Lieutenant Stanley, the CO) were rushing around with great enthusiasm urging the troops up the cliff like it was some sort of college football training routine.

"What a fouled-up bunch of boot lieutenants if I ever saw any. Just what the hell do they think them goddamn Nips are gonna be doin' while we climb up that cliff one at a time?" grumbled a veteran machine gunner.

"Seems pretty stupid to me. If that beach is anything like Peleliu, we'll get picked off before anybody gets up any cliff," I said.

"You said that right, Sledgehammer, and them Nips ain't

gonna be sittin' around on their cans; they're gonna bracket that beach with mortars and artillery, and machine guns are gonna sweep the top of that cliff," he said with melancholy resignation.

Our new mortar section leader was a New Englander out of an Ivy League college. Mac was blond, not large, but was well built, energetic, and talkative, with a broad New England accent. He was a conscientious officer, but he irritated the veterans by talking frequently and at great length about what he was going to do to the Japanese when we went into action again. We sometimes heard such big talk from enlisted replacements who were trying to impress someone (mostly themselves) with how brave they would be under fire, but Mac was about the only officer I ever heard indulge in it.

Whenever he got started with, "The first time one of our guys gets hit, its gonna make me so mad that I'm gonna take my kabar between my teeth and my .45 in my hand and charge the Japs," all the veterans would sit back and smirk. We threw knowing glances at each other and rolled our eyes like disgusted schoolboys listening to a coach brag that he could lick the opposing team single-handed.

I felt embarrassed for Mac, because it was so obvious he conceived combat as a mixture of football and a boy scout campout. He wouldn't listen to the few words of caution from some of us who suggested he had a shock coming. I agreed with a buddy from Texas who said, "I hope to God that big-mouth Yankee lieutenant has to eat every one of them words of his when the stuff hits the fan." The Texan's wish came true on Okinawa, and it was one of the funniest things I ever saw under fire.

Before the next campaign, we had to take the usual inoculations plus some additional ones. Our arms were sore, and many men became feverish. The troops hated getting injections, and the large number (someone said it was seven) before Okinawa made us crotchety. The plague shot burned like fire and was the worst.

Most of our corpsmen did a good job of making the shots as painless as possible, and this helped. But we had one arrogant corpsman who was unfeeling about other people's pain.

He wasn't popular, to say the least. (I hasten to add that he was the one—and only—U.S. Navy hospital corpsman I knew in the Marine Corps who didn't conduct himself in an exemplary manner. All other corpsmen I saw were probably more highly respected by Marines—as a group, and as individuals—than any other group of people we were involved with.)

Directly in front of me as we lined up for shots was a buddy who was a Peleliu veteran. In front of him were several new replacements. The more new men "Doc Arrogant" stuck with the needle, the worse he became. He was just plain mean by the time he got to my buddy. "Doc Arrogant" was in a hurry and didn't look up to recognize my buddy as the latter stepped up to the table. It nearly cost Doc dearly. He held the needle like a dart, plunged it into my friend's arm, depressed the plunger, and said, "Move out!"

My friend didn't flinch from the painful shot. He turned slowly, shook his fist in the corpsman's face, and said, "You sonofabitch, if you want to do some bayonet practice, I'll meet you out on the bayonet course with fixed bayonets and no scabbards on the blades, and then see what you can do."

"Doc Arrogant" looked shocked. He was speechless when he realized that the arm he had punctured so roughly wasn't attached to a meek replacement but to a seasoned veteran.

Then my friend said, "If you ever give me another shot like that, I'll grab you by the stacking swivel and beat you down to parade rest. I'll whip your ass so bad you won't even be able to make this next blitz, because they'll hafta award you a Purple Heart when I finish with you, wise guy."

"Doc Arrogant" changed instantly into "Doc Meek." When I stepped up for my shot, he administered it with a gentleness that would have done credit to Florence Nightingale.

We started packing up our gear. Soon we got word that we would have more maneuvers on Guadalcanal, then shove off for our next fight—Okinawa.

Chapter Eight

Prelude to Invasion

From the standpoint of personal satisfaction I've always been glad that as long as we had to pull maneuvers somewhere in preparation for Peleliu and Okinawa, this training took place on Guadalcanal. The name of that island was embroidered in white letters down the red number *One* on our division patch of which we were all very proud. Guadalcanal had great symbolic significance. I was glad I got to see some of the areas fought over by the 1st Marine Division during the campaign and got some firsthand accounts on the spot of what had taken place from veterans who had participated in making that history.

During one period of maneuvers on Guadalcanal, we stayed ashore for two or three weeks and bivouacked in an area that had been the camp of the 3d Marine Division before its troops went into the hell of Iwo Jima. We strung our jungle hammocks and made ourselves as comfortable as possible. Each day for several days we went out into the hills, jungles, and *kunai* grass fields for training. And we enjoyed a cool shower each afternoon after coming in from the field.

Guadalcanal was a big base by early 1945 and had many service troops and rear-echelon units on it. Across the road from us was a battalion of "Seabees" (naval construction battalion). Late one afternoon three or four of us went over and eased quietly into the end of their chow line. Their cooks recognized us as Marines but didn't say anything. We loaded up on real ice cream, fresh pork chops, fresh salad, and good bread (all unheard-of delicacies on Pavuvu) and sat at a clean table in a spacious mess hall. It sure beat C rations in a bivouac area. As intruders, we expected to be thrown out any minute. No one seemed to notice us, though.

Next afternoon we returned along with other Marines who had the same idea and enjoyed another excellent supper. Next day we tried it again, easing quietly and slowly along to the chow line, trying not to attract attention. To my amazement a large neatly painted white sign with blue letters and blue border had been placed above the entrance to the chow line since the previous evening. I don't remember the exact wording, but it went something close to this, "Marines welcomed in this chow line after all CB personnel have been through."

We were as embarrassed as we were delighted. Those Seabees had been fully aware of us all along and knew exactly how many Marines were slipping into their chow line. But they were willing and glad to share their extra chow with us as long as it lasted. The sign was necessary, because the Seabees knew we would spread the word and more hungry Marines would swarm over their chow line each day like ants.

We were elated and went through the chow line grinning and thanking the messmen. They were the friendliest bunch I ever saw and made us feel like adopted orphans. The sign may have been made earlier for 3d Division Marines who liked the Seabees' food as much as we, or it may have been put up for our benefit. In any event we appreciated the good food and good treatment. It strengthened our respect for the Seabees.

The 3d Battalion, 5th Marines had been in the assault waves at Peleliu; therefore, in the Okinawa campaign we were assigned as regimental reserve. For the voyage to the island, consequently, we would be loaded aboard the attack transport ship USS *McCracken* instead of LSTs. Such APA transports sent troops ashore in LCVPs (small, open landing craft known as Higgins boats) rather than amphibious tractors.

One afternoon following landing exercises and field problems, our company returned to the beach to await the return of the Higgins boats that would pick us up and return us to the ship. Late afternoon sunlight danced on the beautiful blue waves, and a large fleet of ships stood offshore in Sealark

Channel. Dozens of Higgins boats and other amphibious craft plied from the ships to shore, loading Marines and ferrying them out to the ships. It looked like some sort of boating festival except that all the craft were military.

One by one the Higgins boats picked up men (about twenty-five at a time) from our beach area. We waited as the sun sank low in the west. The ships formed up in convoy and moved past us, parallel to the beach. We had no rations or extra water, were tired from daylong maneuvers, and had no desire to spend the night on a mosquito-infested beach.

Finally, as the last ship showed us its stern, a Higgins boat came plowing through the spray toward us. We were the only troops left on the beach. The coxswain revved his engine, ran the bow of the shallow-draft boat up on the beach, and dropped the bow ramp with a bang. We clambered aboard and someone yelled the customary, "Shove off, coxswain, you're loaded." We held on to the bulwarks of the boat as he raised the ramp, reversed engines, turned, and headed out at full throttle toward the disappearing ship.

The sea was rough. As usual Snafu started getting seasick, so he lay down on his side on the deck of the boat. We were crowded: two machine-gun squads and two 60mm mortar squads packed the Higgins boat, along with all our combat gear, small arms, mortars, and machine guns.

A Higgins boat, like any powerful motor-driven boat under full throttle, normally settled down at the stern end with bow elevated and moved easily over the water. But our boat was so loaded with men and equipment that, even though we crowded as far back in the stern as possible, the squared-off bow ramp wasn't elevated sufficiently to skip over the waves. It drove straight against some large waves, and water poured in through an open view port. Usually, this three-foot by two-foot panel rode well above water level. The coxswain yelled instructions to close the folding steel shutters on the panel, which we did as quickly as possible. But water still sprayed over the bow ramp and in through the cracks around the panel.

In the gathering twilight we could see the stern of a transport far ahead of us. It was the last ship in the convoy that had passed from view around the end of Guadalcanal. Our coxswain made as much speed as possible to catch the transport, and we shipped more and more water. If we didn't catch up with that transport before dark we didn't know when we would get back to our ship.

Water began filling the bilges below the floor decking, so the coxswain started the pumps to keep us afloat. We stood by to bail with our helmets, but by the time the water rose above the flooring where we could get at it, the boat would probably sink because of its heavy load. The situation was grim, and I dreaded the thought of trying to swim the couple of miles through rough water to the beach. What irony, I thought, if some of us should die after surviving Peleliu by drowning on maneuvers in Iron Bottom Bay.

Slowly we gained on the transport and finally drew alongside. Towering above us, the ship was packed with Marines. We shouted up to them for help. A navy officer leaned over the rail and asked us which ship we were from. We told him we had missed the *McCracken* and requested to come aboard or we might sink. He gave orders to our coxswain to pull in close under a pair of davits. He did so, and two cables with hooks were lowered to us. Just as the hooks were fastened to rings in the floor, our Higgins boat seemed to start sinking. Only the cables held it up. A cargo net was lowered to us, and we scrambled up and aboard the ship. We were all mighty relieved to be out of that small boat.

Several hours after dark, the ship arrived at the fleet anchorage. A signalman on the bridge went to work with his blinker light sending code to other ships. The *McCracken* was located, and we were soon back aboard.

"Where the hell you guys been so long?" asked a man in my troop compartment as we fell into our racks.

"We went to 'Frisco for a beer," someone answered.

"Wise guy," he replied.

After maneuvers were completed, our convoy sailed from the Russell Islands on 15 March 1945. We were bound for Ulithi Atoll where the convoy would join the gathering invasion fleet. We anchored off Ulithi on 21 March and remained there until 27 March.*

We lined the rails of our transport and looked out over the vast fleet in amazement. We saw ships of every description: huge new battleships, cruisers, sleek destroyers, and a host of fast escort craft. Aircraft carriers were there in greater numbers than any of us had ever seen before. Every conceivable type of amphibious vessel was arrayed. It was the biggest invasion fleet ever assembled in the Pacific, and we were awed by the sight of it.

Because of tides and winds, the ships swung about on their anchor chains, and each day the fleet looked new and different. When I came topside each morning, I felt disoriented. It was a strange sensation, as though I were in a different frame of reference and had to learn my surroundings anew.

The first afternoon at Ulithi a fellow mortarman said, "Break out the field glasses, and let's see how many kinds of ships we can identify." We passed the mortar section's field glasses around and whiled away many hours studying the different ships.

Suddenly someone gasped, "Look over there at that hospital ship off our port bow! Look at them nurses! Gimme them field glasses!"

Lining the rail of the hospital ship were about a dozen American nurses looking out over the fleet. A scuffle erupted among us over who would use the field glasses first, but we all finally had a look at the girls. We whistled and waved, but we were too far away to be heard.

Aside from the huge new battleships and carriers, we talked most about a terribly scorched and battered aircraft carrier anchored near us. A navy officer told us she was the *Franklin*.† We could see charred and twisted aircraft on her

---

*Ulithi Atoll lies about 260 miles northeast of Peleliu on the western edge of the Caroline Islands. It was captured by an element of the 81st Infantry Division as a part of the Palau Islands operation. Ulithi consists of about thirty islets surrounding an enormous lagoon some nineteen miles long and five to ten miles wide. It became the major U.S. fleet anchorage in the Central Pacific.
†During carrier raids on Japan (18–21 March), Japanese suicide planes had crashed into the American carriers *Wasp, Yorktown,* and *Franklin.* The *Franklin*

flight deck, where they had been waiting loaded with bombs and rockets to take off when the ship was hit. It must have been a flaming inferno of bursting bombs and rockets and burning aviation gasoline. We looked silently at the battered, listing hulk until one man said, "Ain't she a mess! Boy, them poor swabbies musta' caught hell." Those of us who had lived through the blast and fire of Peleliu's artillery barrages could appreciate well the bravery of the sailors on the *Franklin*.

While we were anchored at Ulithi, we went ashore on the tiny islet of Mog Mog for recreation and physical conditioning. After some calisthenics, and to the delight of all hands, our officers broke out warm beer and Cokes. We had one of the most enjoyable baseball games I ever played. Everybody was laughing and running like a bunch of little boys. It was good to get off the cramped transport, stretch our legs, and relieve the monotony. We hated to board the Higgins boats at sunset to return to the ship and our cramped quarters.

At Ulithi we received briefings on the coming battle for Okinawa. This time there was no promise of a short operation. "This is expected to be the costliest amphibious campaign of the war," a lieutenant said. "We will be hitting an island about 350 miles from the Japs' home islands, so you can expect them to fight with more determination than ever. We can expect 80 to 85 percent casualties on the beach."

A buddy next to me leaned over and whispered, "How's that for boosting the troops' morale?" I only groaned.

The lieutenant continued, "We may have trouble getting over that cliff or seawall in our sector. Also, according to G-2 there is a large Jap gun, maybe 150mm, emplaced just on the right flank of our battalion sector. We hope naval gunfire can knock it out. Be on the alert for a Jap paratrooper attack in our rear, particularly at night. It's pretty certain the Nips will pull off a massive counterattack, probably supported by tanks,

---

was the most heavily damaged of the three; her loss was 724 killed and 265 wounded. That the ship was saved at all and later towed some 12,000 miles to New York for repairs was a tribute to the bravery and the skill of her crew.

sometime during our first night ashore or just before dawn. They'll *banzai* and try to push us off the beachhead."*

On 27 March the loudspeaker came on with, "Now hear this, now hear this. Special sea detail stand by." Sailors assigned to the detail moved to their stations where they weighed anchor.

"Well, Sledgehammer, they're raising the hook, so it won't be long before we're in it again ole buddy," a friend said.

"Yeah," I said, "and I'm not in any hurry, either."

"You can say that again." He sighed.

The huge convoy got under way like clockwork. Just watching that host of different vessels kept my mind off what was ahead. As we proceeded I was conscious of how cool the weather had become. We had our wool-lined field jackets with us, and it was comfortable on deck, particularly at night. To those of us who had lived and fought in the sweltering tropics for months, cooler weather was very significant.

Most of our voyage from Ulithi was uneventful. Each night during the northward trip I had noticed the beautiful Southern Cross constellation slipping lower and lower on the starlit horizon. Finally it disappeared. It was the only thing about the South and Central Pacific I would miss. The Southern Cross formed a part of our 1st Marine Division shoulder patch and was, therefore, especially symbolic.

We had intense pride in the identification with our units and drew considerable strength from the symbolism attached to them. As we drew closer to Okinawa, the knowledge that I was a member of Company K, 3d Battalion, 5th Marine Regiment, 1st Marine Division helped me prepare myself for what I knew was coming.†

---

*By this time in the Pacific war, official unit designations recognized the prevailing system of task organization for combat where supporting elements reinforced the infantry. Such units became regimental combat teams (RCT) and battalion landing teams (BLT); hence official designations were 5th RCT or 3d BLT. But the rank and file infantryman never forgot who he was. Throughout the war I never heard a Marine infantryman refer to his unit by other than its base name. We were always "K/3/5," "3d Battalion, 5th," or "5th Marines."

†Our planners still hadn't realized that this costly large-scale suicide charge tactic had been abandoned for good. The Japanese had shifted to the defense-in-depth tactic as the best means of defeating us. This tactical shift had pro-

Map of Okinawa showing IE SHIMA, MOTOBU PENINSULA, ISHIKAWA ISTHMUS, YONTAN AIRFIELD, HAGUSHI, LANDING BEACHES, KADENA AIRFIELD, EASTERN ISLANDS, KERAMA RETTO, NAHA, SHURI, NAKAGUSUKU WAN (BUCKNER BAY), OROKU PENINSULA, YONABARU, ITOMAN, MINATOGA. Scale in NAUTICAL MILES.

Okinawa is a large island, some sixty miles long and from two to eighteen miles wide. Like most islands in the Pacific, it is surrounded by a coral reef. But on the west coast that reef lies close to shore, particularly along the invasion beaches at Hagushi.

Through the center of the island runs a ridge rising some 1,500 feet in the wild, mountainous north. South of the Ishikawa Isthmus, the land levels out considerably but is cut by several prominent streams. In 1945, as it remains today, the southern portion of the island contained the bulk of the civilian population.

longed our fight on Peleliu and had been repeated with the same murderous results against the Marines on Iwo Jima.

Of primary importance to the defense of the island were three east–west ridge systems crossing the southern part of the island. To the north and just below the invasion beaches lay the ridges of Kakazu and Nishibaru. In the middle, running west from Shuri Castle, was the most formidable of the ridges, cut by sheer cliffs and deep draws. Above the extreme southern tip of the island lay Kunishi, Yuza-Dake, and Yaeju-Dake. Together these ridges formed a series of natural defensive barriers to the American forces advancing from the north.

Into these natural barriers, Lt. Gen. Mitsuru Ushijima threw the bulk of his 110,000-man Thirty-second Japanese Army. Natural and man-made barriers were transformed into a network of mutually supporting positions linked by a system of protected tunnels. Each of the ridge lines was held in great strength until it became untenable; then the enemy withdrew to the next defense line. Thus the Japanese drew on their experiences at Peleliu, Saipan, and Iwo Jima to construct a highly sophisticated and powerful defense-in-depth. There they waited and fought to exhaust the will and the resources of the American Tenth Army.

Tension mounted on the eve of D day. We received final orders to move in off the beach as fast as possible. We were also reminded that although we were in regimental reserve, we would probably "get the hell kicked out of us" coming on the beach. We were advised to hit the sack early; we would need all the rest we could get.*

A predawn reveille ushered in Easter Sunday—April Fool's Day—1945. The ship seethed with activity. We had chow of steak and eggs, the usual feast before the slaughter. I returned to our troop compartment and squared away my ammunition, combat pack, and mortar ammunition bag. The ship's crew manned battle stations and stood by to repel

---

*Three/Five was scheduled to land after the 1st and 2d battalions of the 5th Marines on the extreme right of the regimental beach. It would form the right flank of the III Marine Amphibious Corps and link with the U.S. Army's XXIV Corps landing to the south.

kamikaze attacks.* Dawn was breaking, and the preassault bombardment of the beaches had begun. Above it I could hear the drone of enemy aircraft inbound to the attack.

I went into the head to relieve my distressed colon, cramped by fear and apprehension. On the big transport ships the toilet facilities consisted of a row of permanent wooden seats situated over a metal trough through which ran a constant flow of seawater. There were about twenty seats—no limited facilities here with Haney to delay us as at Peleliu.

Most of the men in my troop compartment had already been to the head and by then had donned their gear and moved out on deck, so I was about the last one in the head. I settled comfortably on a seat. Next to me I noticed a cagelike chute of iron mesh coming through the overhead [ceiling] near one of the 40mm antiaircraft gun tubs. It extended down, through the deck, and into the compartment below.

Startled out of my wits by an incredibly loud sound of clattering, clanking, scraping, and rasping metal, I sprang up with a reflex born of fear and tried to bolt out of the head into the troop compartment. I knew a kamikaze had crashed into our ship right above me. My trousers around my ankles hobbled me, and I nearly fell. As I reached to pull them up, the loud clanking and clattering—like a thousand cymbals falling down stone steps—continued. I looked over at the iron mesh chute and saw dozens of empty brass 40mm shell cases cascading down from the guns above. They clattered and clanked through the chute to some collecting bin below decks. My fright subsided into chagrin.

I got on my gear and joined the other men on deck to await orders. We milled around, each man sticking close to his buddy. Higgins boats would take us to rendezvous areas and transfer us to amtracs that previously had delivered the assault waves of infantry across the reef to the beach.

The bombardment of the beach by our warships had grown

*Manned suicide planes that dived into American ships. Faith in the kamikaze's ("divine wind") ability to cut off the American fleet's support of the landing force ashore was an important element in the Japanese defensive scheme.

in intensity, and our planes had joined in with strafing, rockets, and bombing. Japanese planes flew over the fleet at some distance from us. Many of our ships were firing at them.

An order came for all troops to go below (this was to prevent casualties from strafing enemy planes). Loaded with our battle gear, we squeezed our way back through the doorlike hatches into our compartment. Packed like sardines in the aisles between the racks, we waited in the compartment for orders to move back on deck. Sailors on deck dogged our hatches [sealed the doors by turning U-shaped handles positioned all around them]. Like men locked in a closet, we waited and listened to the firing outside. The compartment wasn't large, and the air soon became foul. It was difficult to breathe. Although the weather was cool, we began to sweat.

"Hey, you guys, the blowers [electric ventilating fans] are off. By God, we'll smother in this damn place!" yelled one man. I was next to the hatch, and several of us started yelling at the sailors outside, telling them we needed air. They yelled back from the other side of the steel door that it couldn't be helped, because the electricity was needed to operate the gun mounts. "Then, by God, let us out on deck!"

"Sorry, we've got orders to keep this hatch dogged down."

We all started cursing the sailors, but they were following orders, and I'm sure they didn't want to keep us locked in that stuffy compartment. "Let's get the hell outa here," a buddy said. We all agreed it would be better to get strafed on deck than to suffocate in the compartment. Grasping the levers and moving them to the unlock position, we tried to open the hatch. As fast as we turned each lever, the sailors outside turned it back and kept it dogged down. Other desperate Marines joined us in trying to unclamp the hatch. There were only two sailors outside, so with our combined efforts, we finally got all the clamps open, shoved open the hatch, and burst out into the cool, fresh air.

About that time other Company K men poured out of a hatch on the other side of the compartment. One of the sailors got pushed over and rolled across the deck. In an instant we were all outside breathing in the fresh air.

"All right, you men, return to your quarters. No troops topside. That's an order!" came a voice from a platform slightly aft and above us. We looked up and saw a navy officer, an ensign, standing against the rail glaring at us. He wore khakis, an officer's cap, and insignia bars on his collar, in stark contrast to us dressed in green dungarees, tan canvas leggings, and camouflaged helmet covers, and loaded with battle equipment, weapons, and gear. He wore a web pistol belt with a .45 automatic in the holster.

None of our officers was in the area, so the navy ensign had it all to himself. He swaggered back and forth, ordering us into the foul air of the troop compartment. If he had been a Marine officer, we would have obeyed his order with mutterings and mumblings, but he was so unimposing that we just milled around. Finally, he began threatening us all with courts-martial if we didn't obey him.

A friend of mine spoke up, "Sir, we're goin' to hit that beach in a little while and a lot of us might not be alive an hour from now. We'd rather take a chance on gettin' hit by a Jap plane out here than go back in there and smother to death."

The officer spun around and headed for the bridge—to get help, we assumed. Shortly some of our own officers came up and told us to stand by to go down the nets to the waiting boats. As far as I know, our breakout of the troop compartment for fresh air was never mentioned.

We picked up our gear and moved to assigned areas along the bulwarks of the ship. The weather was mostly clear and incredibly cool (about 75 degrees) after the heat of the South Pacific. The bombardment rumbled and thundered toward the island. Everything from battleships down to rocket and mortar boats were plastering the beaches along with our dive bombers. Japanese planes, their engines droning and whining, came in over the huge convoy, and many ships' antiaircraft fire began bursting in the air. I saw two enemy planes get hit some distance from our ship.

We were all tense, particularly with the intelligence estimate that we could expect 80–85 percent casualties on the beach. Although I was filled with dread about the landing, I wasn't nearly so apprehensive as I had been at Peleliu. Perhaps it was because I was already a combat veteran. I had survived the Peleliu landing and knew what to expect from the Japanese, as well as from myself. Climbing down the cargo net to the Higgins boat, I was still afraid; but it was different from Peleliu.

In addition to the invaluable experience of being a combat veteran, the immensity of our fleet gave me courage. Combat vessels and armed transports ranged as far as we could see. I have no idea how many of our planes were in the air, but it must have been hundreds.

We climbed down the net and settled into the Higgins boat. Someone said, "Shove off, coxswain, you're loaded," as the last Marine climbed into our boat. The coxswain gunned the engine and pulled away from the ship. Other boats loaded with Marines from 3/5 were pulling out all along the side of the ship. I sure hated to leave it. Amphibious craft of every description floated on the water around us. The complexity of the huge invasion was evident everywhere we looked.

Our boat ran some distance from our ship, then began circling slowly in company with other boats loaded with men from our battalion. The bombardment of the Hagushi beaches roared on with awesome intensity. Sitting low in the water, we really couldn't see what was going on except in our immediate vicinity. We waited nervously for H hour, which was scheduled for 0830.

Some of the ships began releasing thick white smoke as a screen for the convoy's activity. The smoke drifted lazily and mingled in with that of the exploding shells. We continued to circle on the beautiful blue water made choppy by the other boats in our group.

"It's 0830 now," someone said.

"The first wave's goin' in now. Stand by for a ram," Snafu said.

The man next to me sighed. "Yeah, the stuff's gonna hit the fan now."

CHAPTER NINE

Stay of Execution

"The landing is unopposed!"

We looked with amazement at the Marine on the amtrac with which our Higgins boat had just hooked up.

"The hell you say," one of my buddies shot back.

"It's straight dope. I ain't seen no casualties. Most of the Nips musta hauled ass. I just saw a couple of mortar shells fallin' in the water; that's all. The guys went in standin' up. It beats anything I ever saw."

Images of the maelstrom at Peleliu had been flashing through my mind, but on Okinawa there was practically no opposition to the landing. When we overcame our astonishment, everybody started laughing and joking. The release of tension was unforgettable. We sat on the edge of the amtrac's troop compartment singing and commenting on the vast fleet surrounding us. No need to crouch low to avoid the deadly shrapnel and bullets. It was—and still is—the most pleasant surprise of the war.

It suddenly dawned on me, though, that it wasn't at all like the Japanese to let us walk ashore unopposed on an island only 350 miles from their homeland. They were obviously pulling some trick, and I began to wonder what they were up to.

"Hey, Sledgehammer, what's the matter? Why don't you sing like everybody else?"

I grinned and took up a chorus of the "Little Brown Jug."

"That's more like it!"

As our wave moved closer to the island, we got a good view of the hundreds of landing boats and amtracs approaching the beach. Directly ahead of us, we could see the men of our regiment moving about in dispersed combat formations like tiny toy soldiers on the rising landscape. They appeared unhurried and nonchalant, as if on maneuvers. There were no enemy shells bursting among them. The island sloped up gently from the beach, and the many small garden and farm plots of the Okinawans gave it the appearance of a patchwork quilt. It was beautiful, except where the ground cover and vegetation had been blasted by shells. I was overcome with the contrast to D day on Peleliu.

When our wave was about fifty yards from the beach, I saw two enemy mortar shells explode a considerable distance to our left. They spewed up small geysers of water but caused no damage to the amtracs in that area. That was the only enemy fire I saw during the landing on Okinawa. It made the April Fool's Day aspect even more sinister, because all those thousands of first-rate Japanese troops on that island had to be somewhere spoiling for a fight.

We continued to look at the panorama around our amtrac with no thought of immediate danger as we came up out of the water. The tailgate banged down. We calmly picked up our gear and walked onto the beach.

A short distance down the beach on our right, the mouth of Bishi Gawa emptied into the sea. This small river formed the boundary between the army divisions of the XXIV Corps, to the south, and the III Amphibious Corps, to the north of the river. On our side of the mouth of the river, on a promontory jutting out into the sea, I saw the remains of the emplacement containing the big Japanese gun that had concerned us in our briefings. The seawall in our area had been blasted down into a terracelike rise a few feet high over which we moved with ease.

We advanced inland, and I neither heard nor saw any Japanese fire directed against us. As we moved across the small fields and gardens onto higher elevations, I could see troops of the 6th Marine Division heading toward the big Yontan Airfield on our left. Jubilation over the lack of opposition to the landing prevailed, particularly among the Peleliu veterans. Our new replacements began making remarks about amphibious landings being easy.

SOUTHERN
OKINAWA

1   0   1   2   3

Scale in Miles

*   *   *

Lt. Gen. Simon Bolivar Buckner, Jr., USA, commanded the Tenth Army in the assault against Okinawa. Left (north) of the American landing was the III Marine Amphibious Corps led by Maj. Gen. Roy S. Geiger, which consisted of the 1st and 6th Marine divisions with the latter on the left. To the right (south) landed the army's XXIV Corps commanded by Maj. Gen. John R. Hodge and made up of the 7th and 96th Infantry divisions with the latter on the far right. Backing up the XXIV Corps was the 77th Infantry Division with the 27th Infantry Division afloat in reserve. Across the island stood the 2d Marine Division, which had conducted an elaborate, full-scale feint at the southeastern beaches. Altogether, Lt. Gen. Buckner had 541,866 men at his disposal.

Of the 50,000 troops ashore on D day, the four assault divisions lost only 28 killed, 104 wounded, and 27 missing.

The plan of attack called for the four divisions to cross the island, cutting it in two. The Marines would then turn left and move north to secure the upper two-thirds of the island while the army forces wheeled right into line and proceeded south.

By late afternoon on D day we were ordered to dig in for the night. My squad set up in a small field of recently harvested grain. The clay/loam soil was just right for digging in, so we made a good gun pit. Our company's other two mortars were positioned nearby. We registered in on likely target areas to our front with a couple of rounds of HE, then squared away our ammo for the night. Everybody was expecting a big counterattack with tanks because of the open nature of the countryside.

Once set up, several of us went over to the edge of the field and cautiously explored a neat, clean Okinawan farmhouse. It was a likely hiding place for snipers, but we found it empty.

As we were leaving the house to return to our positions, Jim Dandridge, one of our replacements, stepped on what appeared to be a wooden cover over an underground rainwater cistern at the corner of the house. Jim was a big man, and the wooden planks were rotten. He fell through, sinking in above his waist. The hole wasn't a cistern but a cesspool for the sewage from the house. Jim scrambled out bellowing like a mad bull and smelling worse. We all knew it might be weeks before we could get a change of dungarees, so it was no laughing matter to Jim. But we started kidding him unmercifully about his odd taste in swimming holes. Jim was good-natured, but he quickly had enough and chased a couple of the men back across the field to our positions. They laughed but kept out of his reach.

No sooner had we gotten back to our foxholes than we heard the unmistakable drone of a Japanese aircraft engine. We looked up and saw a Zero coming directly over us. The fighter was high, and the pilot apparently had bigger game than us in mind. He headed out over the beach toward our fleet offshore. Several ships began firing furiously as he circled lazily and then dove. The plane's engine began to whine with increasing intensity as the kamikaze pilot headed straight down toward a transport. We saw the smoke where he hit the ship, but it was so far away we couldn't determine what damage had been done. The troops had debarked earlier, but the ship's crew probably had a rough time of it. It was the first kamikaze I had seen crash into a ship, but it wasn't the last.

In the gathering dusk we turned our attention to our immediate surroundings and squared away for the night. We each had been issued a small bottle containing a few ounces of brandy to ward off the chill of D day night. Knowing my limited taste, appreciation, and capacity for booze, my buddies began trying to talk me out of my brandy ration. But I was cold after sundown, and thought the brandy might warm me up a bit. I tried a sip, concluding immediately that Indians must have had brandy in mind when they supposedly spoke of "firewater." I traded my brandy for a can of peaches, then broke out my wool-lined field jacket and put it on. It felt good.

We waited in the clear, chilly night for the expected Japanese attack. But all was quiet, with no artillery fire nearby and rarely any rifle or machine-gun fire—stark contrast to the rumbling, crashing chaos of D day night on Peleliu.

When Snafu woke me about midnight for my turn on

watch, he handed me our "Tommy" (submachine) gun. (I don't remember how, where, or when we got the Tommy gun, but Snafu and I took turns carrying it and the mortar throughout Peleliu and Okinawa. A pistol was fine but limited at close range, so we valued our Tommy greatly.)

After a few minutes on watch, I noticed what appeared to be a man crouching near me at the edge of a line of shadows cast by some trees. I strained my eyes, averted my vision, and looked in all directions, but I couldn't be sure the dark object was a man. The harder I looked the more convinced I was. I thought I could make out a Japanese fatigue cap. It wasn't a Marine, because none of our people was placed where the figure was. It was probably an enemy infiltrator waiting for his comrades to get in place before acting.

I couldn't be sure in the pale light. Should I fire or take a chance? My teeth began to chatter from the chill and the jitters.

I raised the Tommy slowly, set it on full automatic, flipped off the safety, and took careful aim at the lower part of the figure (I mustn't fire over his head when the Tommy recoiled). I squeezed the trigger for a short burst of several rounds. Flame spurted out of the muzzle, and the rapid explosions of the cartridges shattered the calm. I peered confidently over my sights, expecting to see a Japanese knocked over by the impact of the big .45 caliber slugs. Nothing happened. The enemy didn't move.

Everyone around us began whispering, "What's the dope? What did you see?"

I answered that I thought I had seen a Japanese crouching near the shadows.

There were enemy in the area, for just then we heard shouts in Japanese, a high-pitched yell: "Nippon banzai," then incoherent babbling followed by a burst of firing from one of our machine guns. Quiet fell.

When dawn broke, the first dim light revealed my infiltrator to be a low stack of straw. My buddies kidded me for hours about a Peleliu veteran firing at a straw Japanese.

RACE ACROSS THE ISLAND

On 2 April (D + 1) the 1st Marine Division continued its attack across the island. We moved out with our planes overhead but without artillery fire, because no organized body of Japanese had been located ahead of us. Everyone was asking the same question: "Where the hell are the Nips?" Some scattered small groups were encountered and put up a fight, but the main Japanese army had vanished.

During the morning I saw a couple of dead enemy soldiers who apparently had been acting as observers in a large leafless tree when some of the prelanding bombardment killed them. One still hung over a limb. His intestines were strung out among the branches like garland decorations on a Christmas tree. The other man lay beneath the tree. He had lost a leg, which rested on the other side of the tree with the leggings and trouser leg still wrapped neatly around it. In addition to their ghoulish condition, I noted that both soldiers wore high-top leather hobnail shoes. That was the first time I had seen that type of Japanese footwear. All the enemy I had seen on Peleliu had worn the rubber-soled canvas split-toed *tabi*.

We encountered some Okinawans—mostly old men, women, and children. The Japanese had conscripted all the young men as laborers and a few as troops, so we saw few of them. We sent the civilians to the rear where they were put into internment camps so they couldn't aid the enemy.

These people were the first civilians I had seen in a combat area. They were pathetic. The most pitiful things about the Okinawan civilians were that they were totally bewildered by the shock of our invasion, and they were scared to death of us. Countless times they passed us on the way to the rear with fear, dismay, and confusion on their faces.

The children were nearly all cute and bright-faced. They had round faces and dark eyes. The little boys usually had close-cropped hair, and the little girls had their shiny jet-black locks bobbed in the Japanese children's style of the period. The children won our hearts. Nearly all of us gave them all the candy and rations we could spare. They were quicker to lose their fear of us than the older people, and we had some good laughs with them.

One of the funnier episodes I witnessed involved two Okinawan women and their small children. We had been ordered to halt and "take ten" (a ten-minute rest) before resuming our rapid advance across the island. My squad stopped near a typical Okinawan well constructed of stone and forming a basin about two feet deep and about four feet by six feet on the sides. Water bubbled out of a rocky hillside. We watched two women and their children getting a drink. They seemed a bit nervous and afraid of us, of course. But life had its demands with children about, so one woman sat on a rock, nonchalantly opened her kimono top, and began breast-feeding her small baby.

While the baby nursed, and we watched, the second child (about four years old) played with his mother's sandals. The little fellow quickly tired of this and kept pestering his mother for attention. The second woman had her hands full with a small child of her own, so she wasn't any help. The mother spoke sharply to her bored child, but he started climbing all over the baby and interfering with the nursing. As we looked on with keen interest, the exasperated mother removed her breast from the mouth of the nursing baby and pointed it at the face of the fractious brother. She squeezed her breast just as you would milk a cow and squirted a jet of milk into the child's face. The startled boy began bawling at the top of his lungs while rubbing the milk out of his eyes.

We all roared with laughter, rolling around on the deck and holding our sides. The women looked up, not realizing why we were laughing, but began to grin because the tension was broken. The little recipient of the milk in the eyes stopped crying and started grinning, too.

"Get your gear on; we're moving out," came the word down the column. As we shouldered our weapons and ammo and moved out amid continued laughter, the story traveled along to the amusement of all. We passed the two smiling mothers and the grinning toddler, his cute face still wet with his mother's milk.

Moving rapidly toward the eastern shore, we crossed terrain often extremely rugged with high, steep ridges and deep gullies. In one area a series of these ridges lay across our line of advance. As we labored up one side and down the other of each ridge, we were tired but glad the Japanese had abandoned the area. It was ideal for defense.

During another halt, we spent our entire break rescuing an Okinawan horse. The animal had become trapped in a narrow flooded drainage ditch about four feet deep. He couldn't climb out or move forward or backward. When we first approached the animal, he plunged up and down in the water rolling his eyes in terror. We calmed him, slipped a couple of empty cartridge belts beneath his belly, and heaved him up out of the ditch.

We had plenty of help, because Texans and horse lovers gravitated to the scene from all over our battalion, which ranged in columns along the valley and surrounding ridges. The city men looked on and gave useless advice. When we got the little horse out of the ditch, he stood on wobbly legs as the water dripped off him, shook himself, and headed for a patch of grass.

No sooner had we washed the mud off the cartridge belts than the word came to move out. We didn't get any rest during that break, and we were tired, but we had the satisfaction of knowing that little horse wouldn't starve to death bogged down in the ditch.

The clear cool weather compensated for our rapid advance over the broken terrain. Those of us with experience in the tropics felt as though we had been delivered from a steam room. The hills and ridges on Okinawa were mostly clay, but it was dry, and we didn't slip or slide with our heavy loads. Pine trees grew everywhere. I had forgotten what a delicious odor the needles gave off. We also saw Easter lilies blooming.

Completing the initial assignment of the 1st Marine Division to cut the island in two, we reached the east coast in an area of marshes and what appeared to be large freshwater reservoirs. Offshore was a bay called Chimu Wan.

We arrived on the afternoon of 4 April, some eight to thirteen days ahead of schedule. Our rapid movement had been possible, of course, only because of the widely scattered opposition. These first four days had been too easy for us. We were confused as to what the Japanese were doing. We knew they weren't about to give up the island without a fierce, drawn-out fight.

And we didn't have to wait long to find out where the enemy was. Later that day rumors began that the army divisions were meeting increasingly stiff opposition as they tried to move south. We knew that sooner or later we'd be down there with them in the thick of it.

We also learned that our namesake company in the 7th Marines had been ambushed to the north of us near the village of Hizaonna and had suffered losses of three killed and twenty-seven wounded. Thus, despite the relative ease with which our division had moved across the center of the island, the Japanese were still there and still hurting the Marines.

The 1st Marine Division spent the remainder of April mopping up the central portion of Okinawa. Elements of the division, including the 3d Battalion, 5th Marines, conducted a shore-to-shore amphibious operation toward the end of the month to secure the Eastern Islands which lay on the outer edge of Chimu Wan Bay. The purpose was to deny them to the Japanese as an operating base in the rear of the American forces, much the same reason 3/5 had assaulted Ngesebus during the fight for Peleliu.

The 6th Marine Division moved north during April and captured the entire upper part of the island. The task wasn't easy. It involved a rough, costly seven-day mountain campaign against strongly fortified Japanese positions in the heights of Motobu Peninsula.

Meanwhile three army divisions were coming up short against fierce Japanese resistance in the Kakazu–Nishibaru ridgeline, the first of three main enemy defense lines in the southern portion of the island. Stretched from left to right across Okinawa, the 7th, 96th, and 27th Infantry divisions were getting more than they could handle and were making little progress in their attacks.

PATROLS

Hardly had we arrived on the shore of Chimu Wan Bay than we received orders to move out. We headed inland and north into an area of small valleys and steep ridges, where we settled into a comfortable bivouac area and erected our two-man pup tents. It was more like maneuvers than combat; we didn't even dig foxholes. We could see Yontan Airfield in the distance to the west. Rain fell for the first time since we had landed five days earlier.

The next day our company began patrolling through the general area around our bivouac site. We didn't need the mortars because of the scattered nature of the enemy opposition. Stowing them out of the weather in our tents, those of us in the mortar section served as riflemen on the patrols.

Mac, our new mortar section leader, led the first patrol I made. Our mission was to check out our assigned area for signs of enemy activity. Burgin was our patrol sergeant. I felt a lot more comfortable with him than with Mac.

On a clear, chilly morning, with the temperature at about 60 degrees, we moved out through open country on a good, rock-surfaced road. The scenery was picturesque and beautiful. I saw little sign of war. We had strict orders not to fire our weapons unless we saw a Japanese soldier or Okinawans we were certain were hostile. No shooting at chickens and no target practice.

"Mac, where we headed?" someone had asked before we left.

"Hizaonna," the lieutenant answered without batting an eye.

"Jesus Christ! That's where K Company, 7th got ambushed the other night," one of the new replacements said.

"Do you mean us few guys are supposed to patrol that place?"

"Yeah, that's right, Hood," Burgin answered. (We had nick-named a big square-jawed man from Chicago "Hoodlum" because of the notorious gangs of John Dillinger and others in that city during the days of Prohibition.)

My reaction on hearing our destination had been to thrust

my Tommy gun toward another new man who wasn't assigned to the patrol and say, "Take this; don't you wanta go in
my place?"

"Hell, no!" he replied.

So, off we went, with Mac striding along like he was still in
OCS back in Quantico, Virginia. The veterans among us
looked worried. The new men, like Mac, seemed unconcerned. Because of the strange absence of anything but scattered opposition, some of the new men were beginning to
think war wasn't as bad as they had been told it was. Some of
them actually chided us about giving them an exaggerated account of the horrors and hardships of Peleliu. Okinawa in
April was so easy for the 1st Marine Division that the new
men were lulled into a false sense of well-being. We warned
them, "When the stuff hits the fan, it's hell," but they grew
more and more sure that we veterans were "snowing" them.

Mac didn't help matters either by his loud pronouncements
of how he would take his kabar in his teeth and his .45 in hand
and charge the Japanese as soon as one of our guys got hit.
The April stay of execution tended to lull even the veterans
into a state of wishful thinking and false security, although
we knew better.

Soon, however, our idyllic stroll on that perfect April
morning was broken by an element of the horrid reality of the
war that I knew lurked in wait for us somewhere on that beautiful island. Beside a little stream below the road, like a
hideous trademark of battle, lay a Japanese corpse in full
combat gear.

From our view above, the corpse looked like a gingerbread
man in a helmet with his legs still in the flexed position of
running. He didn't appear to have been dead many days then,
but we passed that same stream many times throughout April
and watched the putrid remains decompose gradually into the
soil of Okinawa. I was thankful the windswept road with the
sweet, fresh smell of pine needles filling our nostrils was too
high for us to sense his presence in any way but visually.

As we patrolled in the vicinity of Hizaonna, we moved
through some of the area where Company K, 7th Marines had
been ambushed a few nights before. The grim evidence of a

hard fight lay everywhere. We found numerous dead Japanese where they had fallen. Bloody battle dressings, discarded articles of bloody clothing, and bloodstains on the ground indicated where Marines had been hit. Empty cartridge cases were piled where various Marine weapons had been.

I remember vividly an Okinawan footpath across a low hillock where the Marine column apparently had been attacked from both sides. On the path were empty machine-gun ammo boxes, ammo clips for M1 rifles, and carbine shell cases; discarded dungaree jackets, leggings, and battle dressings; and several large bloodstains, by then dark spots on the soil. Scattered a short distance on both sides of the path were about a score of enemy dead.

The scene was like reading a paragraph from a page of a history book. The Marines had suffered losses, but they had inflicted worse on the attacking Japanese. We saw no Marine dead; all had been removed when the relief troops had come in and aided K/3/7 to withdraw from the ambush.

As I looked at the flotsam of battle scattered along that little path, I was struck with the utter incongruity of it all. There the Okinawans had tilled their soil with ancient and crude farming methods; but the war had come, bringing with it the latest and most refined technology for killing. It seemed so insane, and I realized that the war was like some sort of disease afflicting man. From my experience at Peleliu I had unconsciously come to associate combat with stifling hot, fire-swept beaches, steaming mangrove-choked swamps, and harsh, jagged coral ridges. But there on Okinawa the disease was disrupting a place as pretty as a pastoral painting. I understood then what my grandmother had really meant when she told me as a boy that a blight descended on the land when the South was invaded during the Civil War.

While a buddy and I were looking over the area, Burgin told us to check out a section of sunken roadway nearby. The sunken portion was about thirty yards long and about ten feet deep; the banks were steep and sloping. Heavy bushes grew along their edges at ground level so all we could see was the sky overhead and the sloping road in front and behind us.

When we were about halfway along the sunken road, carbine shots rang out from where we had left Burgin and Mac.

"Ambush!" snarled my buddy, a veteran with combat experience stretching back to Cape Gloucester.

We went into a low crouch instinctively, and I put my finger on the safety catch of the Tommy. Hurrying over to the bank toward the sound of the shots, we scrambled up and peered cautiously through the bushes. We both knew we wouldn't have a chance if we got pinned down in that ditchlike road where we could be shot from above. My heart pounded, and I felt awfully lonely as I looked out. There, where we had left him, stood Mac in the farmyard, calmly pointing his carbine straight down toward the ground by his feet at some object we couldn't see. My comrade and I looked at each other in amazement. "What the hell?" my buddy whispered. We climbed out of the sunken road and went toward Mac as he fired his carbine at the ground again. Other members of the patrol were converging cautiously on the area. They looked apprehensive, thinking we were being ambushed.

Burgin stood a short distance behind Mac, shaking his head slowly in disgust. As we came up, I asked Mac what he had fired at. He pointed to the ground and showed us his target: the lower jaw of some long-dead animal. Mac said he just wanted to see if he could shoot any of the teeth loose from the jawbone.

We stared at him in disbelief. There we were, a patrol of about a dozen Marines, miles from our outfit, with orders not to fire unless at the enemy, in an area with dead Japanese scattered all over the place, and our lieutenant was plinking away with his carbine like a kid with a BB gun. If Mac had been a private, the whole patrol would probably have stuck his head in a nearby well. But our discipline was strict, and we just gritted our teeth.

Burgin made some tactful remark to remind Mac he was the officer in charge of a patrol and that the enemy might jump us at any time. Thereupon Mac began spouting off, quoting some training manual about the proper way for troops to conduct themselves on patrol.

Mac wasn't stupid or incompetent. He just didn't seem to

realize there was a deadly war going on and that we weren't involved in some sort of college game. Strange as it seemed, he wasn't mature yet. He had enough ability to complete Marine Corps OCS—no simple task—but occasionally he could do some of the strangest things, things only a teenage boy would be expected to do.

Once on another patrol, I saw him taking great pains and effort to position himself and his carbine near a Japanese corpse. After getting just the right angle, Mac took careful aim and squeezed off a couple of rounds. The dead Japanese lay on his back with his trousers pulled down to his knees. Mac was trying very carefully to blast off the head of the corpse's penis. He succeeded. As he exulted over his aim, I turned away in disgust.

Mac was a decent, clean-cut man but one of those who apparently felt no restraints under the brutalizing influence of war—although he had hardly been in combat at that time. He had one ghoulish, obscene tendency that revolted even the most hardened and callous men I knew. When most men felt the urge to urinate, they simply went over to a bush or stopped wherever they happened to be and relieved themselves without ritual or fanfare. Not Mac. If he could, that "gentleman by the act of Congress" would locate a Japanese corpse, stand over it, and urinate in its mouth. It was the most repulsive thing I ever saw an American do in the war. I was ashamed that he was a Marine officer.

During the early part of that beautiful April in our happy little valley—while we veterans talked endlessly in disbelief about the lack of fighting—a few of us had a close view of a Japanese Zero fighter plane. One clear morning after a leisurely breakfast of K rations, several of us sauntered up a ridge bordering our valley to watch an air raid on Yontan Airfield. None of us was scheduled for patrols that day, and none of us was armed. We had violated a fundamental principle of infantrymen: "Carry your weapon on your person at all times."

As we watched the raid, we heard an airplane engine to our right. We turned, looked down a big valley below our ridge, and saw a plane approaching. It was a Zero flying up the valley toward us, parallel to and level with the crest of our ridge. It was moving so slowly it seemed unreal. Unarmed, we gawked like spectators at a passing parade as the plane came across our front. It couldn't have been more than thirty or forty yards away. We could see every detail of the plane and of the pilot seated in the cockpit inside the canopy. He turned his head and looked keenly at our little group watching him. He wore a leather flight helmet, goggles pushed up on his forehead, a jacket, and a scarf around his neck.

The instant the Zero pilot saw us, his face broke into the most fiendish grin I ever saw. He looked like the classic cartoon Japanese portrayed in American newspapers of the war years, with buck teeth, slanted eyes, and a round face. He grinned like a cat, for we were to be his mice. We were a fighter pilot's strafing dream, enemy infantry in the open with no antiaircraft guns and no planes to protect us.

One of my buddies muttered in surprise as the plane went on by to our left, "Did you see that bastard grin at us—that slant-eyed sonofabitch. Where the hell's my rifle?"

It happened so fast, and we were all so astonished at the sight of a plane cruising by at eye level, we almost forgot the war. The Japanese pilot hadn't. He banked, climbed to gain altitude, and headed around another ridge out of sight. It was obvious he was coming back to rake us over. It would be difficult to avoid getting hit. No savior was in sight for us.

As we started to spin around and rush back down the ridge seeking safety, we again heard a plane. This time it wasn't the throb of a cruising engine, but the roar of a plane at full throttle. The Zero streaked past us, going down the valley in the opposite direction from which he had first appeared. He was still flying at eye level and he was in a big hurry, as if the devil were after him. His devil was our savior, a beautiful blue Marine Corsair. That incredible Corsair pilot bore in right behind the Japanese as they roared out of sight over the ridge tops. The planes were moving too fast to see either pilot's face, but I'm confident the emperor's pilot had lost his grin when he saw that Corsair.

On our patrols during April, we investigated many Okinawan villages and farms. We learned a lot about the people's customs and ways of life. Particularly appealing to me were the little Okinawan horses, really shaggy oversized ponies.

The Okinawans used a type of halter on those horses that I had never seen before. It consisted of two pieces of wood held in place by ropes. The wooden pieces on either side of the horse's head were shaped like the letter F. They were carved out of fine-grained brown wood and were about as big around as a man's thumb. A short piece of rope or cord held the pieces together across the front, and a rope across the top of the animal's head held the pieces in place on each side of the head just above the opening of the mouth. Two short ropes at the back of the wooden pieces merged into a single rope. When pull was exerted on this single rope, the wooden pieces clamped with gentle pressure against the sides of the animal's face above the mouth, and the animal stopped moving. This apparatus combined the qualities of a halter and a bridle without the need for a bit in the horse's mouth.

I was so intrigued by the Okinawan halter that I took one off a horse we kept with us for several days and replaced it with a rope halter. My intention was to send the wooden halter home—I remember that a bright piece of red cord held the front ends together—so I put it into my pack. After 1 May, however, it seemed increasingly doubtful that I would ever get home myself, and my equipment seemed to get heavier as the mud got deeper. Regretfully, I threw away the halter.

We grew quite attached to the horse our squad had adopted, and he didn't seem to mind when we slung a couple of bags of mortar ammo across his back.

When the time came at the end of April for us to leave our little horse, I removed the rope halter and gave him a lump of ration sugar. I stroked his soft muzzle as he switched flies with his tail. He turned, ambled across a grassy green meadow, and began grazing. He looked up and back at me once. My eyes grew moist. However reluctant I was to leave him, it was for the best. He would be peaceful and safe on the slopes of that green, sunlit hill. Being civilized men, we were duty-bound to return soon to the chaotic netherworld of shells and bullets and suffering and death.

Ugly rumors began to increase about the difficulties the

army troops were having down on southern Okinawa. From high ground on clear nights I could see lights flickering and glowing on the southern skyline. A distant rumble was barely audible sometimes. No one said much about it. I tried unsuccessfully to convince myself it was thunderstorms, but I knew better. It was the flash and the growl of guns.

A HAPPY LANDING

On 13 April (12 April back in the States) we learned of the death of President Franklin D. Roosevelt. Not the least bit interested in politics while we were fighting for our lives, we were saddened nonetheless by the loss of our president. We were also curious and a bit apprehensive about how FDR's successor, Harry S. Truman, would handle the war. We surely didn't want someone in the White House who would prolong it one day longer than necessary.

Not long after hearing of Roosevelt's death, we were told to prepare to move out. Apprehension grew in the ranks. We thought the order meant the inevitable move into the inferno down south. On the contrary, it was to be a shore-to-shore amphibious operation against one of the Eastern Islands. We learned that Company K was to land on Takabanare Island, and that there might not be any Japanese there. We were highly skeptical. But so far Okinawa had been a strange "battle" for us; anything could happen.

Our battalion boarded trucks and headed for the east coast. We went aboard amtracs and set out into Chimu Wan to make the short voyage to Takabanare. The other companies of our battalion went after other islands of the group.

We landed with no opposition on a narrow, clean, sandy beach with a large rock mass high on our left. The rock hill looked foreboding. It was a vantage point from which flanking fire could have raked the beach. But all went well, and we pushed rapidly over the entire island without seeing a single enemy soldier.

After we moved across the island and found nothing but a few civilians, we recrossed the island to the beach where we set up defensive positions. My squad was situated partway up the slope of the steep rocky hill overlooking the beach. Our mortar was well emplaced among some rocks, so that we could fire on the beach or its approaches in the bay. A small destroyer escort was anchored offshore at the base of the hill. It had been standing by during our landing and remained with us during the several days we stayed on Takabanare. We felt important, as though we had our own private navy.

The weather was pleasant, so sleeping in the open was comfortable. We had few duties other than standing by to prevent a possible enemy move to occupy the island. I wrote letters, read, and explored the area around our positions. Some of the Marines swam the short distance to the ship and went aboard, where the navy people welcomed them and treated them to hot chow and all the hot coffee they wanted. I was content to laze in the sun and the cool air and eat K rations.

We left Takabanare after several days and returned to our bivouac on Okinawa. There we resumed patrolling in the central area of the island. As April wore on, rumors and bad news increased about the situation the army was facing down south. Scuttlebutt ran rampant about our future employment down there. Our fear increased daily, and we finally got the word that we'd be moving south on 1 May to replace the 27th Infantry Division on the right flank of the Tenth Army.

About mid-April the 11th Marines, the 1st Marine Division's artillery regiment, had moved south to add the weight of its firepower to the army's offensive. On 19 April the 27th Infantry Division launched a disastrous tank-infantry attack against Kakazu Ridge. Thirty army tanks became separated from their infantry support. The Japanese knocked out twenty-two of them in the ensuing fight. The 1st Marine Division's tank battalion offered the closest replacements for the tanks lost by the army.

Lt. Gen. Simon B. Buckner, Tenth Army commander, ordered Maj. Gen. Roy S. Geiger, III Amphibious Corps commander, to send the 1st Tank Battalion south to join the 27th Infantry Division. Geiger objected to the piecemeal employment of his Marines, so Buckner changed his orders and sent the entire 1st Marine Division south to relieve the 27th In-

fantry Division on the extreme right of the line just north of Machinato Airfield.

During the last days of April, some of our officers and NCOs made a trip down south to examine the positions on the line that we were to move into. They briefed us thoroughly on what they saw, and it didn't sound promising.

"The stuff has hit the fan down there, boys. The Nips are pouring on the artillery and mortars and everything they've got," said a veteran sergeant. "Boys, they're firing knee mortars as thick and fast as we fire M1s."

We were given instructions, issued ammo and rations, and told to square away our gear. We rolled up our shelter halves (I wished I could crawl into mine and hibernate) and packed our gear to be left behind with the battalion quartermaster.

The first of May dawned cloudy and chilly. A few of us mortarmen built a small fire next to a niche in the side of the ridge to warm ourselves. The dismal weather and our impending move south made us gloomy. We stood around the fire eating our last chow before heading south. The fire crackled cheerily, and the coffee smelled good. I was nervous and hated to leave our little valley. We tossed our last ration cartons and wrappers onto the fire—the area must be left cleaner than when we arrived—and a few of the men drifted away to pick up their gear.

"Grenade!" yelled Mac as we heard the pop of a grenade primer cap.

I saw him toss a fragmentation grenade over the fire into the niche. The grenade exploded with a weak bang. Fragments zipped out past my legs, scattering sparks and sticks from the fire. We all looked astonished, Mac not the least so. No one was hit. I narrowly missed the million-dollar wound (it would have been a blessing in view of what lay ahead of us). The men who had just moved away from the fire undoubtedly would have been hit if they hadn't moved, because they had been standing directly in front of the niche.

All eyes turned on our intrepid lieutenant. He blushed and mumbled awkwardly about making a mistake. Before we moved to board the trucks, Mac had thought it would be funny to play a practical joke on us. So he staged the well-known trick of pouring out the explosive charge from a fragmentation grenade, screwing the detonation mechanism back on the empty "pineapple," and pitching it into the middle of a group of people. When the primer cap went "pop," the perpetrator of the joke could watch with sadistic delight as everyone scrambled for cover expecting the fuse to burn down and the grenade to explode.

By his own admission, however, Mac had been careless. Most of the explosive charge remained in the grenade; he had poured out only part of it. Consequently, the grenade exploded with considerable force and threw out its fragments. Luckily, Mac threw the grenade into the niche in the ridge. If he had thrown it into the open, most of the Company K mortar section would have been put out of action by its own lieutenant before we ever got down south. Fortunately for Mac, the company commander didn't see his foolish joke. We regretted he hadn't.

What a way to start our next fight!

CHAPTER TEN

Into the Abyss

We boarded trucks and headed south over dusty roads. In this central portion of Okinawa we first passed many bivouacs of service troops and vast ammunition and supply dumps, all covered with camouflage netting. Next we came to several artillery positions. From the piles of empty brass shell cases, we knew they had fired a lot. And from the numerous shell craters gouged into the fields of grass, we could tell that the Japanese had thrown in plenty of counterbattery fire.

At some unmarked spot, we stopped and got off the trucks. I was filled with dread. We took up a single file on the right side of a narrow coral road and began walking south. Ahead we could hear the crash and thunder of enemy mortar and artillery shells, the rattle of machine guns, and the popping of rifles. Our own artillery shells whistled southbound.

"Keep your five-pace interval," came an order.

We did not talk. Each man was alone with his thoughts.

Shortly a column of men approached us on the other side of the road. They were the army infantry from 106th Regiment, 27th Infantry Division that we were relieving. Their tragic expressions revealed where they had been. They were dead beat, dirty and grisly, hollow-eyed and tight-faced. I hadn't seen such faces since Peleliu.

As they filed past us, one tall, lanky fellow caught my eye and said in a weary voice, "It's hell up there, Marine."

Nervous about what was ahead and a bit irritated that he might think I was a boot, I said with some impatience, "Yeah, I know. I was at Peleliu."

He looked at me blankly and moved on.

We approached a low, gently sloping ridge where Company K would go into the line. The noise grew louder.

"Keep your five-pace interval; don't bunch up," yelled one of our officers.

The mortar section was ordered off the road to the left in dispersed order. I could see shells bursting between us and the ridge. When we left the road, we severed our umbilical connection with the peaceful valley up north and plunged once more into the abyss.

As we raced across an open field, Japanese shells of all types whizzed, screamed, and roared around us with increasing frequency. The crash and thunder of explosions was a nightmare. Rocks and dirt clattered down after each erupting shell blew open a crater.

We ran and dodged as fast as we could to a place on a low gentle slope of the ridge and flung ourselves panting onto the dirt. Marines were running and crawling into position as soldiers streamed past us, trying desperately to get out alive. The yells for corpsmen and stretcher bearers began to be heard. Even though I was occupied with my own safety, I couldn't help but feel sorry for the battle-weary troops being relieved and trying not to get killed during those few critical minutes as they scrambled back out of their positions under fire.

Japanese rifle and machine-gun fire increased into a constant rattle. Bullets snapped and popped overhead. The shelling grew heavier. The enemy gunners were trying to catch men in the open to inflict maximum casualties on our troops running into and out of position—their usual practice when one of our units was relieving another on the line.

It was an appalling chaos. I was terribly afraid. Fear was obvious on the faces of my comrades, too, as we raced to the low slope and began to dig in rapidly. It was such a jolt to leave the quiet, beautiful countryside that morning and plunge into a thunderous, deadly storm of steel that afternoon. Going onto the beach to assault Peleliu and attacking across the airfield there, we had braced ourselves for the blows that fell. But the shock and shells of 1 May at Okinawa, after the reprieve of a pleasant April, caught us off balance.

Fear has many facets, and I do not minimize my fear and

terror during that day. But it was different. I was a combat
veteran of Peleliu. With terror's first constriction over, I knew
what to expect. I felt dreadful fear but not near-panic. Experience had taught me what to expect from the enemy guns.
More important, I knew I could control my fear. The terrible
dread that I might panic was gone. I knew that all anyone
could do under shell fire was to hug the deck and pray—and
curse the Japanese.

There was the brassy, metallic twang of the small 50mm
knee mortar shells as little puffs of dirty smoke appeared
thickly around us. The 81mm and 90mm mortar shells
crashed and banged all along the ridge. The *whiz-bang* of the
high-velocity 47mm gun's shells (also an antitank gun),
which was on us with its explosion almost as soon as we
heard it whizz into the area, gave me the feeling the Japanese
were firing them at us like rifles. The slower screaming, whining sound of the 75mm artillery shells seemed the most abundant. Then there was the roar and rumble of the huge enemy
150mm howitzer shell, and the *kaboom* of its explosion. It
was what the men called the big stuff. I didn't recall having
recognized any of it in my confusion and fear at Peleliu. The
bursting radius of these big shells was of awesome propor-
tions. Added to all this noise was the swishing and fluttering
overhead of our own supporting artillery fire. Our shells
could be heard bursting out across the ridge over enemy positions. The noise of small-arms fire from both sides resulted in
a chaotic bedlam of racket and confusion.

We were just below the crest of a low sloping section of the
ridge. It was about ten feet high and on the left of our company's zone. Snafu and I began to dig the gun pit, and the
ammo carriers dug in with two-man foxholes. Digging in
Okinawa's claylike soil was easy, a luxury after the coral rock
of Peleliu.

No sooner had we begun to dig in than terrible news arrived about mounting casualties in the company. The biggest
blow was the word that Privates Nease and Westbrook had
been killed. Both of these men were liked and admired by us
all. Westbrook was a new man, a friendly curly-headed blond
and one of the youngest married men in the outfit. I believe he

wasn't yet twenty. Howard Nease was young in years but an old salt with a combat record that started at Cape Gloucester.

Many men were superstitious about one's chances of surviving a third campaign. By that time one's luck was wearing thin, some thought. I heard this idea voiced by Guadalcanal veterans who also had survived Gloucester and then struggled against the odds on Peleliu.

"Howard's luck just run out, that's all. Ain't no damn way a guy can go on forever without gittin' hit," gloomily remarked a Gloucester veteran who had joined Company K with Nease two campaigns before Okinawa.

We took the news of those deaths hard. Added to the stress of the day, it put us into an angry frame of mind as we dug in. Against whom should we pour out our anger while we were unable to fire at the enemy?

Most of us had finished digging in when we suddenly noticed that our pugnacious lieutenant, Mac, was still digging feverishly. He was excavating a deep one-man foxhole and throwing out a continuous shower of dirt with his entrenching shovel. While shells were still coming in, the fire had slackened a bit in our area. But Mac continued to burrow underground.

I don't know who started it, but I think it was Snafu who reminded Mac of his oft-repeated promise to charge the enemy line as soon as any of our guys got hit. Once the kidding began, several of us veterans chimed in and vigorously encouraged Mac to keep his promise.

"Now that Nease and Westbrook been killed, ain't it about time you took your kabar and .45 and charged them Nips, Mac?" Snafu asked.

Mac never stopped digging; he simply answered that he had to dig in. I told him I would lend him my kabar, but another man said with mock seriousness, "Naw, Sledgehammer, he might not be able to return it to you."

"Boy, when Mac gets over to them Nips, he's gonna clean house, and this blitz gonna be a pushover," someone else said.

But Mac only grunted and showed no inclination to charge the enemy—or to stop digging. He burrowed like a badger. Our jibes didn't seem to faze him. We kept our comments respectful because of his rank, but we gave it to him good for all the bravado and nonsense he had been mouthing off with ever since he joined the company.

"Mac, if you dig that hole much deeper they'll get you for desertion," someone said.

"Yeah, my mom use'ta tell me back home if I dug a hole deep enough I'd come through to China. Maybe if you keep digging you'll get through to the States, and we can all crawl in there and go home, Mac," came one comment accompanied by a grin.

Mac could hear us but was totally oblivious to our comments. It's hard to believe that we actually talked that way to a Marine officer, but it happened, and it was hilarious. He deserved every bit of it.

When he finally got his foxhole deep enough, he began laying wooden boards from ammo boxes over all of the top except for one small opening through which he could squirm. Then he threw about six inches of soil on top of the boards. We sat in our holes, watching him and the shelling to our right rear. When he had completed the cover over his hole, which actually made it a small dugout with limited visibility, Mac got in and proudly surveyed his work. He had been too occupied to pay much heed to us, but now he explained carefully to us how the boards with soil on top would protect him from shell fragments.

George Sarrett, who wasn't interested in the lecture, inched up the little slope several feet and peeped over the crest to see if there were any enemy troops moving around out front. He didn't look long, because a Japanese on the next ridge saw him and fired a burst from a machine gun that narrowly missed him. As the slugs came snapping over, George jerked his head down, lost his balance, slid back down the slope, and landed on top of Mac's dugout, causing the roof to cave in. The startled lieutenant jumped up, pushing boards and soil aside like a turtle rearing up out of a pile of debris.

"You ruined my foxhole!" Mac complained.

George apologized, and I had to bite my lip to keep from laughing. The other men smirked and grinned. We never heard any more from Mac about charging the Japanese line with his kabar and .45 caliber pistol. That enemy shelling had one beneficial result: it dissolved his bravado.

We got our positions squared away for the night and ate some K rations, as well as one could with a stomach tied in knots. More details reached us about the loss of Nease, Westbrook, and others killed and wounded. We regretted any American casualties, but when they were close friends it was terribly depressing. They were just the first of what was to grow into a long tragic list before we would come out of combat fifty hellish days later.*

Before dark we learned there would be a big attack the next morning all along the U.S. line. With the heavy Japanese fire poured onto us as we moved into that line, we dreaded the prospect of making a push. An NCO told us that our objective was to reach the Asato Gawa, a stream about 1,500 yards south of us that stretched inland and eastward to an area near the village of Dakeshi.

Rain ushered in a gloomy dawn. We were apprehensive but hopeful. There was some small-arms fire along the line, and a few shells passed back and forth during early morning. The rain slackened temporarily and we ate some K rations. On the folding pocket-sized tripod issued to us, I heated up a canteen cup of coffee with a sterno tablet. I had to hover over it to keep the rain from drowning it out.

As the seconds ticked slowly toward 0900, our artillery and ships' guns increased their rate of fire. The rain poured down, and the Japanese took up the challenge from our artillery. They started throwing more shells our way, many of which passed over us and exploded far to our rear where our own artillery was emplaced.

Finally we received orders to open fire with our mortars. Our shells exploded along a defilade to our front. Our machine guns opened up in earnest. Our artillery, ships' guns,

---

*The 27th Infantry Division had been in action since 15 April. It had suffered heavily in the attacks of 19 April in capturing Kakazu Ridge, Machinato Airfield, and the surrounding area. After the 1st Marine Division relieved it, the 27th Infantry Division went north for patrolling and guard duty.

and 81mm mortars increased the tempo to an awesome rate as the time for the attack approached. The shells whistled, whined, and rumbled overhead, ours bursting out in front of the ridge and the enemy's exploding in our area and to the rear. The noise increased all along the line. Rain fell in torrents, and the soil became muddy and slippery wherever we hurried around the gun pit to break out and stack our ammo.

I looked at my watch. It was 0900. I gulped and prayed for my buddies in the rifle platoons.

"Mortars cease firing and stand by."

We were ready to fire or to take up the mortars at a moment's notice and move forward. Some of our riflemen moved past the crest of the ridge to attack. Noise that had been loud now grew into deafening bedlam. The riflemen hardly got out of their foxholes when a storm of enemy fire from our front and left flank forced them back. The same thing was happening to the battalions on our right and left.

The sound of the many machine guns became one incredible rattle against a thundering and booming of artillery. Rifles popped everywhere along the line, while Japanese slugs snapped over the low ridge behind which we lay. We fired some white phosphorous shells to screen our withdrawing troops. Just as we heard "Cease firing," a Marine came running through the mud on the slope to our right, yelling, "The guys pulling back need a stretcher team from mortars!"

Three other mortarmen and I took off on the double after the messenger. With bullets snapping and popping overhead, we ran along for about forty yards, keeping just below the crest of the ridge. We came to a road cut through the ridge about eight feet below the crest; an officer told us to stand behind him until we were ordered to go out and bring in the casualty. This was the exact spot where Nease and Westbrook had been machine-gunned the day before. Japanese bullets were zipping and swishing through the cut like hail pouring through an open window.

A couple of Company K rifle squads were running back toward us from the abortive attack. They rushed along the road in small groups and turned right and left as soon as they got through the cut to get out of the line of fire. Incredibly, none got hit by the thick fire coming through the cut. I knew most of them well, although some of the new men not as well as the veterans. They all wore wild-eyed, shocked expressions that showed only too vividly they were men who had barely escaped chance's strange arithmetic. They clung to their Mls, BARs, and Tommy guns and slumped to the mud to pant for breath before moving behind the ridge toward their former foxholes. The torrential rain made it all seem so much more unbelievable and terrible.

I hoped fervently that we wouldn't have to step out into that road to pick up a casualty. I felt ashamed for thinking this, because I knew full well that if I were lying out there wounded, my fellow Marines wouldn't leave me. But I didn't see how anyone could go out and get back now that the volume of fire was so intense; since most of our attacking troops had fallen back, the Japanese could concentrate their fire on the stretcher teams as I had seen them do at Peleliu. They showed medical personnel no mercy.

Our company gunnery sergeant, Hank Boyes, was the last man through the cut. He made a quick check of the men and announced—to my immense relief—that everyone had made it back; casualties had been brought back farther down the line where the machine-gun fire hadn't been as heavy.

Boyes was amazing. He had dashed out to the men pinned down in front of the ridge, where he threw smoke grenades to shield them from the Japanese fire. He returned with a hole shot through his dungaree cap (he wasn't wearing his helmet) and another through his pants leg. He had been hit in the leg with fragments from a Japanese knee mortar shell but refused to turn in.*

---

*Gy. Sgt. Henry A. Boyes was a former dairy farmer from Trinidad, California. He fought with K/3/5 at Cape Gloucester and landed on Peleliu as a squad leader. He won a Silver Star there and became a platoon sergeant after the assault on Ngesebus. Wounded during the fighting around the Five Sisters, he was evacuated, but returned in time for the landing on Okinawa. Wounded early in May he refused evacuation and became first sergeant of Company K. After the company commander, 1st Lt. Stumpy Stanley, was evacuated in late May with malaria, Boyes shared the primary leadership role with 1st Lt. George Loveday. A powerfully built man, Hank Boyes was

The officer told us we wouldn't be needed as stretcher bearers and to return to our posts. As we took off on the double to the gun pits, the shells kept up their heavy traffic back and forth, but the bullets began to slacken off somewhat with all our men by then under cover of the ridge. I jumped into the gun pit, and my temporary replacement hurried back to his hole.*

We crouched in our foxholes in the pouring rain, cursing the Japanese, the shells, and the weather. The enemy gunners poured fire into our company area to discourage another attack. Word came down the line that all attacking Marine units had suffered considerable casualties, so we would remain inactive until the next day. That suited us fine. The Japanese shelling continued viciously for some time. We all felt depressed about the failure of the attack and we still didn't know how many friends we had lost, an uncertainty that always bore down on every man after an attack or fire fight.

From the gun pit, which contained several inches of water, we looked out on a gloomy scene. The rain had settled into a steady pelting that promised much misery. Across the muddy fields we saw our soaked comrades crouching forlornly in their muddy holes and ducking, as we did, each time a shell roared over.

This was my first taste of mud in combat, and it was more detestable than I had ever imagined. Mud in camp on Pavuvu was a nuisance. Mud on maneuvers was an inconvenience. But mud on the battlefield was misery beyond description. I had seen photographs of World War I troops in the mud—the men grinning, of course, if the picture was posed. If not posed, the faces always wore a peculiarly forlorn, disgusted expression, an expression I now understood. The air was

---

stern but compassionate. No matter how low morale got, he was always there inspiring like some inexhaustible dynamo. Today he and his family run a successful logging and cattle business in Australia.

*At some time during the attack, Burgin ran out and exposed himself to heavy machine-gun fire from a weapon that no one could locate. He called back a fire mission to the mortars after he spotted the machine gun. Our mortar fire hit on target and knocked out the gun. Burgin won a Bronze Star for his actions.

chilly and clammy, but I thanked God we weren't experiencing this misery in Europe where the foxholes were biting cold as well as wet.

The shelling finally subsided, and things got fairly quiet in our area. We squatted thankfully in our holes and grumbled about the rain. The humid air hung heavily with the chemical odor of exploded shells.

Shortly, to our left rear, we saw a Marine stretcher team bringing a casualty back through the rain. Instead of turning left behind the ridge we were on, or right behind the one farther across the field, the team headed straight back between the two low ridges. This was a mistake, because we knew the Japanese could still fire on that area.

As the stretcher team approached the cover of some trees, Japanese riflemen to our left front opened up on them. We saw bullets kicking up mud and splashing in the puddles of water around the team. The four stretcher bearers hurried across the slippery field. But they couldn't go faster than a rapid walk, or the casualty might fall off the stretcher.

We requested permission to fire 60mm phosphorous shells as a smoke screen (we were too far away to throw smoke grenades to cover the stretcher team). Permission was denied. We weren't allowed to fire across our company front because of the possibility of hitting unseen friendly troops. Thus we watched helplessly as the four stretcher bearers struggled across the muddy field with bullets falling all around them. It was one of those terribly pathetic, heartrending sights that seemed to rule in combat: men struggling to save a wounded comrade, the enemy firing at them as fast as they could, and the rest of us utterly powerless to give any aid. To witness such a scene was worse than personal danger. It was absolute agony.

To lighten their loads, the four carriers had put all of their personal equipment aside except for a rifle or carbine over their shoulders. Each held a handle of the stretcher in one hand and stretched out the other arm for balance. Their shoulders were stooped with the weight of the stretcher. Four helmeted heads hung low like four beasts of burden being flogged. Soaked with rain and spattered with mud, the dark green dungarees hung forlornly on the men. The casualty lay inert on the narrow canvas stretcher, his life in the hands of the struggling four.

To our dismay, the two carriers in the rear got hit by a burst of fire. Each loosened his grip on the stretcher. Their knees buckled, and they fell over backwards onto the muddy ground. The stretcher pitched onto the deck. A gasp went up from the men around me, but it turned almost immediately into roars of relief. The two Marines at the other end of the stretcher threw it down, spun around, and grabbed the stretcher casualty between them. Then each supported a wounded carrier with his other arm. As we cheered, all five assisted one another and limped and hobbled into the cover of the bushes, bullets still kicking up mud all around them. I felt relief and elation over their escape, matched only by a deepened hatred for the Japanese.

Before nightfall we received information that Company K would push again the next day. As the rain slowly diminished and then ceased, we made our grim preparations.

While receiving extra ammo, rations, and water, I saw our company officers and NCOs gathering nearby. They stood or squatted around the CO, talking quietly. Our company commander was obviously in charge, giving orders and answering questions. The senior NCOs and the veteran officers stood by with serious, sometimes worried expressions as they listened. Those of us in the ranks watched their familiar faces carefully for signs of what was in store for us.

The faces of the replacement lieutenants reflected a different mood. They showed enthusiastic, animated expressions with eyebrows raised in eager anticipation of seeing the thing through like a successful field problem at OCS in Quantico. They were very conscientious and determined to do their best or die in the effort. To me, those young officers appeared almost tragic in their naive innocence and ignorance of what lay ahead for us all.

The new officers bore a heavy burden. Not only were they going into combat with all its terrors and unknowns for the first time—conditions even the best of training couldn't possibly duplicate—but they were untried officers. Combat was the acid test. Faced with heavy responsibilities and placed in a position of leadership amid hardened, seasoned Marine combat veterans in a proud, elite division like the First was a difficult situation and a terrific challenge for any young lieutenant. No one I knew in the ranks envied them in the least.

During the course of the long fighting on Okinawa, unlike at Peleliu, we got numerous replacement lieutenants. They were wounded or killed with such regularity that we rarely knew anything about them other than a code name and saw them on their feet only once or twice. We expected heavy losses of enlisted men in combat, but our officers got hit so soon and so often that it seemed to me the position of second lieutenant in a rifle company had been made obsolete by modern warfare.

After the CO dismissed his junior officers, they returned to their respective platoons and briefed the troops about the impending push. Mac was crisp and efficient in his orders to Burgin and the rest of the mortar section NCOs. In turn they told us what to prepare for. (It was good to see Mac divested of his cockiness.) We would get maximum support from heavy artillery and other weapons; casualties would be given swift aid. So we prepared our equipment and waited nervously.

A friend came over from one of the rifle platoons that was to be in the next day's assault. We sat near the gun pit on our helmets in the mud and had a long talk. I lit my pipe and he a cigarette. Things were quiet in the area, so we were undisturbed for some time. He poured out his heart. He had come to me because of our friendship and because I was a veteran. He told me he was terribly afraid about the impending attack. I said everybody was. But I knew he would be in a more vulnerable position than some of us, because his platoon was in the assault. I did my best to cheer him up.

He was so appalled and depressed by the fighting of the previous day that he had concluded he couldn't possibly survive the next day. He confided his innermost thoughts and secrets about his parents and a girl back home whom he was going to marry after the war. The poor guy wasn't just afraid of death or injury—the idea that he might never return to those he loved so much had him in a state of near desperation.

I remembered how Lt. Hillbilly Jones had comforted and helped me through the first shock of Peleliu, and I tried to do the same for my friend. Finally he seemed somewhat relieved, or resigned to his fate, whatever it might be. We got up and shook hands. He thanked me for our friendship, then walked slowly back to his foxhole.

There was nothing unique in the conversation. Thousands like it occurred every day among infantrymen scheduled to enter the chaos and inferno of an attack. But it illustrates the value of camaraderie among men facing constant hardship and frequent danger. Friendship was the only comfort a man had.

It seems strange how men occupied themselves after all weapons and gear had been squared away for an impending attack. We had learned in boot camp that no pack straps should be left with loose ends dangling (any such loose straps on a Marine's pack were called "Irish pennants"—why Irish I never knew—and resulted in disciplinary action or a blast from the drill instructor). So, from pure habit I suppose, we carefully rolled up the loose straps and shaped up our packs. There was always a bit of cleaning and touching up to be done on one's weapon with the toothbrush most of us carried for that purpose. A man could always straighten up his lacings on his leggings, too. With such trivia, doomed men busily occupied themselves, as though when they got up and moved forward out of their foxholes it would be to an inspection rather than to oblivion.

We were partially successful with our attack on 3 May. The knockout of the Japanese heavy machine gun by our mortars the previous day helped our company's advance to the next low ridgeline. But we couldn't hold the hills. Heavy enemy machine-gun and mortar fire drove us back about a hundred yards. Thus we gained about three hundred yards for the entire day.

We moved into a quiet area back of the front lines well before dark. Word came that because of heavy casualties over the past two days' fighting, Company K would go into battalion reserve for a while. We dug in around the battalion aid station for its defense.

Our casualties were still coming back from the afternoon's action as we moved into position. Much to my joy I saw the friend with whom I'd had the conversation the night before. He wore a triumphant look of satisfaction, shook hands with me heartily, and grinned as a stretcher team carried him by with a bloody bandage on his foot. God or chance—depending on one's faith—had spared his life and lifted his burden of further fear and terror in combat by awarding him a million-dollar wound. He had done his duty, and the war was over for him. He was in pain, but he was lucky. Many others hadn't been as lucky the last couple of days.

COUNTERATTACK

We settled into our holes for the night, feeling more at ease off the line and in a quiet area. My foxhole partner had the first watch, so I dropped off to sleep, confident that we would have a fairly quiet night. I hadn't slept long before he woke me with, "Sledgehammer, wake up. The Nips are up to something." Startled, I awoke and instinctively unholstered my .45 automatic.

I heard a stern order from an NCO, "Stand by for a ram, you guys. One hundred percent alert!"

I heard heavy artillery and small-arms firing up on the line. It seemed to come mostly from the area beyond our division's left flank where army troops were located. The firing directly forward had increased, too. Our artillery shells swished overhead in incredible numbers. It wasn't just the usual harassing fire against the Japanese; there was too much of it for that.

"What's the dope?" I asked nervously.

"Beats me," said my buddy, "but something sure the hell's going on up on the line. Nips probably pulling a counterattack."

From the increasing fire, enemy as well as friendly, it was obvious something big was happening. As we waited in our holes hoping to get word about what was going on, heavy machine-gun and mortar fire broke out abruptly some distance to our right, to the rear of where the 1st Marines' line reached the sea. From our little mound we saw streams of American machine-gun tracers darting straight out to sea under the eerie light of 60mm mortar flares. That could only mean one thing. The enemy was staging an amphibious attack, trying to come ashore behind the right flank of the 1st Marines, which was the right-hand regiment on the 1st Marine Division's line.

"The Nips must be pullin' a counterlanding, and the 1st Marines' givin' 'em hell," someone said tensely.

Could our comrades in the 1st Marine Regiment stop that attack? That was the question on everyone's mind. But one man said confidently in a low voice, "The 1st Marines'll tear their ass up, betcha." We hoped he was right. With no more than we knew, it was clear that if the Japanese got ashore on our right flank and counterattacked heavily on our left and front, our entire division might be isolated. We sat and listened apprehensively in the darkness.

As if things didn't seem grim enough, the next order came along. "Stand by for possible Jap paratroop attack! All hands turn to. Keep your eyes open."

My blood felt like icewater throughout my body, and I shuddered. We weren't afraid of Japanese paratroopers as such. They couldn't be any tougher to deal with than veteran Japanese infantry. But the fear of being cut off from other U.S. troops by having the enemy land behind us filled us with dread. Most nights on Peleliu we had to keep a sharp lookout to front, rear, right, and left. But that night on Okinawa we had to scan even the dark sky for signs of parachutes.

We lived constantly with the fear of death or maiming from wounds. But the possibility of being surrounded by the enemy and wounded beyond the point of being able to defend myself chilled my soul. They were notorious for their brutality.

A couple of Japanese planes flew over during the night (we recognized the sound of the engines), and I experienced a dread I had never known before. But they passed on without dropping parachutists. They were bombers or fighters on their way to attack our ships lying offshore.

The Japanese and American artillery fire to our left front rumbled and roared on and on with frightening intensity, drowning out the rattle of machine guns and rifles. To our right, elements of the 1st Marine Regiment kept up their small-arms and mortar fire out to sea for quite some time. We heard scattered rifle fire far to our rear. This was disturbing, but some optimist said it was probably nothing more than trigger-happy, rear-echelon guys firing at shadows. Rumors passed that some enemy soldiers had broken through the army's line on our left. It was a long night made worse by the uncertainty and confusion around us. I suffered extremely mixed emotions: glad on the one hand to be out of the fighting, but anxious for those Americans catching the fury of the enemy's attack.

At first light we heard Japanese planes attacking our ships and saw the fleet throwing up antiaircraft fire. Despite the aerial attack, the ships' big guns began heavy firing against the Japanese on land. Toward our right and rear, the firing of our infantry units slackened. We learned that radio messages indicated the 1st Marines had slaughtered hundreds of Japanese in the water when they tried a landing behind our division's flank. The sound of scattered firing told us some enemy had slipped ashore, but the major threat was over.

Our artillery increased its support fire to our front, and we were told that our division would attack during the day. We would remain in position, however—an order we found most agreeable.

Word came that the army troops on our left had held off the main Japanese attack, but things were still grim in that area. Some enemy had gotten through, and others were still attacking. While 3/5 remained in reserve, the 1st Marine Division began its attack to our front, and we heard that the opposition was ferocious. We received orders to be on the lookout for any enemy that might have slipped around the division's flank during the night. There were none.

There was a massive enemy air attack against our fleet at this time. We saw a kamikaze fly through a thick curtain of flak and crash-dive into a cruiser. A huge white smoke ring rose thousands of feet into the air. We heard shortly that it was the cruiser USS *Birmingham* that had suffered considerable damage and loss of life among her crew.

The Japanese counterattack of 3–4 May was a major effort aimed at confusing the American battle plan by isolating and destroying the 1st Marine Division. The Japanese made a night amphibious landing of several hundred men on the east coast behind the 7th Infantry Division. Coordinated with that landing was another on the west coast behind the 1st Marine Division. The Japanese plan called for the two elements to move inland, join up, and create confusion to the rear while the main counterattack hit the American center.

The Japanese 24th Infantry Division concentrated its frontal attack on the boundary between the American army's 7th and 77th Infantry divisions. The enemy planned to send a separate brigade through the gap in the American lines created by the 24th Division's attack, swing it to the left behind the 1st Marine Division, and hit the Marines as the Japanese 62d Infantry Division attacked the 1st Marine Division's front.

If the plan succeeded, the enemy would isolate and destroy the 1st Marine Division. It failed when the two American army divisions stopped the frontal assault, except for a few minor penetrations, with more than 6,000 Japanese dead counted. At the same time, the 1st Marines (on the right of the 1st Marine Division) discovered the enemy landing on the west coast. They killed over 300 enemy in the water and on the beach.

CHAPTER ELEVEN

Of Shock and Shells

Heavy rains began on 6 May and lasted through 8 May, a preview of the nightmare of mud we would endure from the end of the second week of May until the end of the month. Our division had reached the banks of the Asato Gawa at a cost of 1,409 casualties (killed and wounded). I knew losses had been heavy during the first week of May because of the large number of casualties I saw in just the small area we were operating in.

On 8 May Nazi Germany surrendered unconditionally. We were told this momentous news, but considering our own peril and misery, no one cared much. "So what" was typical of the remarks I heard around me. We were resigned only to the fact that the Japanese would fight to total extinction on Okinawa, as they had elsewhere, and that Japan would have to be invaded with the same gruesome prospects. Nazi Germany might as well have been on the moon.

The main thing that impressed us about V-E Day was a terrific, thundering artillery and naval gunfire barrage that went swishing, roaring, and rumbling toward the Japanese. I thought it was in preparation for the next day's attack. Years later I read that the barrage had been fired on enemy targets at noon for its destructive effect on them but also as a salute to V-E Day.

The 6th Marine Division moved into the line on our right, and our division shifted toward the left somewhat. This put us in the center of the American front. As we crouched in our muddy foxholes in the cold rain, the arrival of the 6th Marine Division plus the massive artillery barrage did more for our morale than news about Europe.

The 5th Marines approached the village of Dakeshi and ran into a strong enemy defensive system in an area known as the Awacha Pocket. Talk was that we were approaching the main Japanese defense line, the Shuri Line. But Awacha and Dakeshi confronted us before we reached the main ridges of the Shuri Line.

When our battalion dug in in front of Awacha, our mortars were emplaced on the slope of a little rise about seventy-five yards behind the front line. The torrents of rain were causing us other problems besides chilly misery. Our tanks couldn't move up to support us. Amtracs had to bring a lot of supplies, because the jeeps and trailers bogged down in the soft soil.

Ammunition, boxes of rations, and five-gallon cans of water were brought up as close to us as possible. But because of the mud along a shallow draw that ran to the rear of the mortar section, all the supplies were piled about fifty yards away in a supply dump on the other side of the draw. Working parties went off to carry the supplies from the dump across the draw to the rifle platoons and the mortar section.

Carrying ammo and rations was something the veterans had done plenty of times before. With the others I had struggled up and down Peleliu's unbelievably rugged rocky terrain in the suffocating heat, carrying ammo, rations, and water. Like carrying stretcher cases, it was exhausting work. But this was my first duty on a working party in deep mud, and it surpassed the drudgery of any working party I had ever experienced.

All ammunition was heavy, of course, but some was easier to handle than others. We praised the manufacturers of hand-grenade and belted machine-gun ammunition boxes. The former were wooden with a nice rope handle on each side; the latter were metal and had a collapsible handle on top. But we cursed the dolts who made the wooden cases our .30 caliber rifle ammo came in. Each box contained 1,000 rounds of ammunition. It was heavy and had only a small notch cut into either end. This allowed only a fingertip grip by the two men usually needed to handle a single crate.

We spent a great deal of time in combat carrying this heavy ammunition on our shoulders to places where it was needed—spots often totally inaccessible to all types of vehicles—and breaking it out of the packages and crates. On Okinawa this was often done under enemy fire, in driving rain, and through knee-deep mud for hours on end. Such activity drove the infantryman, weary from the mental and physical stress of combat, almost to the brink of physical collapse.

A great number of books and films about the war ignored this grueling facet of the infantryman's war. They gave the impression that ammunition was always "up there" when needed. Maybe my outfit just happened to get a particularly bad dose of carrying ammo into position on Peleliu because of the heat and rugged terrain and on Okinawa because of the deep mud. But the work was something none of us would forget. It was exhausting, demoralizing, and seemingly unending.

In this first position before Awacha, those of us detailed to the working parties had made a couple of trips across the shallow draw when a Nambu light machine gun opened up from a position to our left. I was about midway across the draw, in no particular hurry, when the Japanese gunner fired his first bursts down the draw. I took off at a run, slipping and sliding on the mud, to the protected area where the supply dump was placed. Slugs snapped viciously around me. The men with me also were lucky as we dove for the protection of a knoll beside the supplies. The enemy machine gunner was well concealed up the draw to our left and had a clear field of fire anytime anyone crossed where we were. We were bound to lose men to that Nambu if we kept moving back and forth. Yet we had to get the ammo distributed for the coming attack.

We looked across the draw toward the mortar section and saw Redifer throw out a phosphorous grenade to give us smoke-screen protection when we came back across. He threw several more grenades, which went off with a muffled *bump* and a flash. Thick clouds of white smoke billowed forth and hung almost immobile in the heavy, misty air. I grabbed a metal box of 60mm mortar ammo in each hand. Each of the other men also picked up a load. We prepared to cross. The Nambu kept firing down the smoke-covered draw. I was reluctant to go, as were the others, but we could see Redifer standing out in the draw, throwing more phosphorous grenades to hide us. I felt like a coward. My buddies must have felt the same way as we glanced anxiously at each other. Someone said resignedly, "Let's go, on the double, and keep your five-pace interval."

We dashed into the smoky, murky air. I lowered my head and gritted my teeth as the machine-gun slugs snapped and zipped around us. I expected to get hit. So did the others. I wasn't being brave, but Redifer was, and I would rather take my chances than be yellow in the face of his risks to screen us. If he got hit while I was cringing in safety, I knew it would haunt me the rest of my life—that is, if I lived much longer, which seemed more unlikely every day.

The smoke hid us from the gunner, but he kept firing inter-mittent bursts down the draw to prevent our crossing. Slugs popped and snapped, but we made it across. We rushed be-hind the knoll and flung the heavy ammo boxes down on the mud. We thanked Redifer, but he seemed more concerned with solving the problem at hand than talking.

"Boy, that Nip's got the best-trained trigger finger I ever heard. Listen to them short bursts he gets off," a buddy said. We panted and listened to the machine gun half in terror and half in admiration of the Japanese gunner's skill. He contin-ued to fire across the rear of our position. Each burst was two or three rounds and spaced: *tat, tat . . . tat, tat, tat . . . tat, tat.*

Just then we heard the engine of a tank some distance across the draw. Without a word, Redifer sped across the draw toward the sound. He got across safely. We could see him dimly through the drifting smoke as he contacted the tankers. Shortly we saw him backing toward us slowly, giving the tankers hand signals as he directed the big Sherman across the draw. The Nambu kept firing blindly through the smoke as we watched Redifer anxiously. He seemed unhur-ried and reached us safely with the tank.

The tankers had agreed to act as a shield for us in our haz-ardous crossing. With several of us crouching in the welcome protection it afforded us, the tank moved back and forth across the draw, always between us and the enemy machine gun. We loaded up on ammo and moved slowly across the machine-gun-swept draw, hugging the side of the tank like chicks beside a mother hen. We kept this up until all the ammo was brought safely across.

The troops often expressed the opinion that whether an enlisted man was or wasn't recommended for a decoration for outstanding conduct in combat depended primarily on who saw him perform the deed. This certainly was true in the case of Redifer and what he had done to get the ammunition across the draw. I had seen other men awarded decorations for less, but Redifer was not so fortunate as to receive the official praise he deserved. Just the opposite happened.

As we finished the chore of moving the ammo across the draw, a certain first lieutenant, who by some unlucky chance had been assigned to Company K after Peleliu, came up. We called him simply "Shadow." A tall, skinny man, he was the sloppiest Marine—officer or enlisted—I ever saw.

His dungarees hung on him like old, discarded clothes on a scarecrow; his web pistol belt was wrapped around his waist like a loose sash on a dressing gown; his map case flopped around; and every pack strap dangled more "Irish pennants" than any new recruit had in boot camp. Shadow never wore canvas leggings when I saw him. His trouser legs were rolled up unevenly above his skinny ankles. He didn't fit his camouflaged cloth helmet cover tightly over his helmet like most Marines. It sagged to one side like some big stocking cap. For some reason, he frequently carried his helmet upside down in his left hand clutched against his side like a football. On his head he wore a green cloth fatigue cap like the rest of us wore under our helmets. But his cap was torn across the top so that his dark hair protruded like straw through a scarecrow's hat.

Shadow's disposition was worse than his appearance. Moody, ill-tempered, and highly excitable, he cursed the veteran enlisted men worse than most DIs did recruits in boot camp. When he was displeased with a Marine about something, he didn't reprimand the man the way our other officers did. He threw a tantrum. He would grab his cap by the bill, fling it onto the muddy deck, stamp his feet, and curse everyone in sight. The veteran sergeant who accompanied Shadow would stand silently by during these temper displays, torn between a compulsion to reprimand us, if it seemed his duty to do so, and embarrassment and disapproval over his officer's childish behavior.

In all fairness, I don't know how competent an officer Shadow was considered to be by his superiors. Needless to say, he wasn't highly regarded in the ranks, simply on the basis of his lack of self-control. But he was brave. I'll give him that.

Shadow "pitched a fit" in reaction to what Redifer had done in facilitating our ammo transportation across the draw. It was just the first of many such performances I was to witness, and they never ceased to amaze as well as disgust me.

He went to Redifer and unleashed such a verbal assault against him that anyone who didn't know better would have assumed that Redifer was a coward who had deserted his post in the face of the enemy instead of having just performed a brave act. Shadow yelled, gesticulated, and cursed Redifer for "exposing himself unnecessarily to enemy fire" when he was throwing the smoke grenades into the draw and when he went to contact the tank.

Redifer took it quietly, but he was obviously dismayed. We looked on in disbelief, having expected Shadow to praise the man for showing bravery and initiative under fire. But here was this ranting, raving officer actually cursing and berating a man for doing something any other officer would have considered a meritorious act. It was so incredibly illogical that we couldn't believe it.

Finally, having vented his rage on a Marine who rightfully deserved praise, Shadow strode off grumbling and cursing the individual and collective stupidity of enlisted men. Redifer didn't say anything. He just looked off into the distance. We growled mightily, though.

As midday approached on 9 May, everyone was tense about the coming attack. Ammunition had been issued, men had squared away their gear and had done their last-minute duties: adjusting cartridge belts, pack straps, leggings, and leather rifle slings—all those forlorn little gestures of no value that released tension in the face of impending terror. We had previously registered our mortars on selected targets and had stacked HE and phosphorous shells off the mud on pieces of boxes for quick access.

The ground having dried sufficiently for our tanks to maneuver, several stood by with engines idling, hatches open, and the tankers waiting—waiting like everyone else. War is mostly waiting. The men around me sat silently with drawn faces. Some replacements had come into the company to make up for our earlier losses. These new men looked more confused than afraid.

The big guns had fired periodically during the morning, but then had died away. There wasn't much noise as we waited for the preattack bombardment to begin.

Then the preassault bombardment commenced. The big shells swished overhead as each battery of our artillery and each ship's guns began to shell the Japanese Awacha defenses ahead of us. At first we could identify each type of shell— 75mm, 105mm, and 155mm artillery, along with the 5-inch ship's guns—as it added to the storm of steel.

We saw our planes overhead, Corsairs and dive bombers. Air strikes began as the planes dove, firing rockets, dropping bombs, and strafing to our front. The firing thundered and rumbled until finally even the experienced ears of the veterans could distinguish nothing, only that we were glad that all that stuff was ours.

Enemy artillery and mortar shells began coming in as the Japanese tried to disrupt the attack. The replacements looked utterly bewildered amid the bedlam. I remembered my first day in combat and sympathized with them. The sheer massiveness of the preattack bombardment was an awesome and frightening thing to witness as a veteran, let alone as a new replacement.

Soon the order came, "Mortar section, stand by." We took directions from Burgin, who was up on the observation post to spot targets and direct our fire. Although our 60mm shells were small compared to the huge shells rushing overhead, we could fire close-in to the company front where bigger mortars and the artillery couldn't shoot without endangering our own people. This closeness made it doubly critical that we fire skillfully and avoid short rounds.

We had fired only a few rounds when Snafu began cursing the mud. With each round, the recoil pushed the mortar's base plate against the soft soil in the gun pit, and he had trouble re-sighting the leveling bubbles to retain proper alignment of the gun on the aiming stake.

After we completed the first fire mission, we quickly moved the gun a little to one side of the pit onto a harder sur-face and resighted it. At Peleliu we often had to hold the base plate as well as the bipod feet onto the coral rock to prevent the recoil from making the base plate bounce aside, knocking the mortar's alignment out too far. On Okinawa's wet clay soil, just the opposite happened. The recoil drove the base plate into the ground with each round we fired. This problem got worse as the rains increased during May, and the ground became softer and softer.

The order came to secure the guns and to stand by. The air strike ended, and the artillery and ships' guns slacked off. The tanks and our riflemen moved out as tank-infantry teams, and we waited tensely. Things went well for a couple of hundred yards during this attack made by 3/5 and 3/7 before heavy fire from Japanese on the left flank stopped the attack. Our OP (observation post) ordered us to fire smoke because heavy enemy fire was coming from our left. We fired phosphorous rapidly to screen the men from the enemy observers.

Our position got a heavy dose of Japanese 90mm mortar counterbattery fire. We had a difficult time keeping up our firing with those big 90mm shells crashing around us. Shell fragments whined through the air, and the big shells slung mud around. But we had to keep up our fire. The riflemen were catching hell from the flank and had to be supported. Our artillery began firing again at the enemy positions to our left to aid the harassed riflemen.

We always knew when we were inflicting losses on the Japanese with our 60mm mortars by the amount of counter-battery mortar and artillery fire they threw back at us. If we weren't doing them any damage, they usually ignored us un-less they thought they could inflict a lot of casualties. If the

Japanese counterbattery fire was a real indicator of our effectiveness in causing them casualties, we were satisfyingly effective during the Okinawa campaign.

During the attack of 9 May against Awacha, Company K suffered heavy losses. It was the same tragic sight of bloody, dazed, and wounded men benumbed with shock, being carried or walking to the aid station in the rear. There also were the dead, and the usual anxious inquiries about friends. We were all glad when the word came that 3/5 would move into reserve for the 7th Marines—for a couple of days, it turned out. The 7th Marines were fighting to our right against Dakeshi Ridge.

In the path of the 1st Marine Division, from north to south, lay Awacha, Dakeshi Ridge, Dakeshi Village, Wana Ridge, Wana Village, and Wana Draw. South of the latter lay the defenses and the heights of Shuri itself. All these ridges and villages were defended heavily by well-prepared, mutually supporting fortifications built into a skillful system of defense-in-depth. Similarly powerful defensive positions faced the 6th Marine Division on the right and the army infantry divisions on the left. The Japanese ferociously defended every yard of ground and conserved their strength to inflict maximum losses on the American forces. The tactics turned Okinawa into a bloodbath.

The battle against Awacha raged on to our left. We dug in for the night in the wet ground. Our mortars weren't set up. We were to act as riflemen and to keep watch across an open, sloping valley. Above us the other two mortar squads dug in in two parallel lines about twenty feet apart and perpendicular to the line of the crest of the embankment above us. Water and rations were issued and mail brought to us.

Mail usually was a big morale booster, but not for me that time. There was a chilly drizzling rain off and on. We were weary and my spirits weren't the best. I sat on my helmet in the mud and read a letter from my parents. It brought news that Deacon, my beloved spaniel, had been hit by an automobile, had dragged himself home, and had died in my father's arms. He had been my constant companion during the several years before I had left home for college. There, with the sound of heavy firing up ahead and the sufferings and deaths of thousands of men going on nearby, big tears rolled down my cheeks, because Deacon was dead.

During the remainder of the night, the sound of firing toward Dakeshi Ridge indicated that the 7th Marines were having a lot of trouble trying to push the Japanese off the ridge. Just before dawn we could hear heavy firing off to our left front where 1/5 and 2/5 were fighting around the Awacha Pocket.

"Stand by, you guys, and be prepared to move out," came the order from an NCO on the embankment above us.

"What's the hot dope?" a mortarman asked.

"Don't know, except the Nips are counterattacking on the 5th Marines' front and the battalion [3/5] is on standby to go up and help stop 'em."

We greeted the news with an understandable lack of enthusiasm. We were still tired and tense from the punishment the battalion took at Awacha the day before. What's more, we didn't relish moving anywhere in the darkness. But we squared away our gear, chewing gum nervously or gnawing on ration biscuits. The sound of firing rose and fell to our left front as we waited and wondered.

Finally, during the misty gray light of early morning, the order came, "OK, you guys, let's go." We picked up our loads and moved toward the front lines.

Other than occasional shells whining over in both directions, things were rather calm. Our column moved along a ridge just below the crest to the emplacements of the Marines who had been under attack. We found them assessing the damage they had done to the Japanese and caring for their own wounded. Some of the men told us the enemy had come into bayonet range before being repulsed. "But we tore their ass up, by God," one man said to me as he pointed out at about forty Japanese corpses sprawled beyond the Marine foxholes.

In the pale dawn, the air was misty and still smoky from phosphorous shells the enemy had fired to hide their approach. There was a big discussion in the ranks. Comments passed along to us from the Marines in place had it that somebody had seen a woman advancing with the attacking Japanese and that she was probably among the dead out there. We couldn't see her from our positions.

Then word came, "About face; we're moving back." In short, our help wasn't needed, so we were to be deployed somewhere else. Back through the rain and the mud we went.

All movements during most of May and early June were physically exhausting and utterly exasperating because of the mud. Typically, we moved in single file, five paces apart, slipping and sliding up and down muddy slopes and through boggy fields. When the column slowed or stopped, we tended to bunch up, and the NCOs and officers ordered sternly, "Keep your five-pace interval; don't bunch up." The everpresent danger of shells even far behind the lines made it necessary that we stay strung out. However, sometimes it was so dark that in order not to get separated and lost, each man was ordered to hold on to the cartridge belt of the man in front of him. This made the going difficult over rough and muddy terrain. Often if a man lost his footing and fell, several others went down with him, sprawling over each other in the mud. There were muffled curses and exasperated groans as they wearily disentangled themselves and regained their footing, groping about in the inky darkness to reform the column.

As soon as we stopped, the order came, "Move out." So the column always moved forward but like an accordion or an inchworm: compressed, then strung out, stopping and starting. If a man put down his load for a brief respite, he was sure to hear, "Pick up your gear; we're moving out!" So the load had to be hoisted onto shoulders again. But if you didn't put it down, chances were you missed an opportunity to rest for a few seconds, or even up to an hour, while the column halted up ahead for reasons usually unknown. To sit down on a rock or on a helmet when drunk with fatigue was like pressing a button to signal some NCO to shout, "On your feet; pick up your gear; we're moving out again." So the big decision in every man's mind at each pause in the column's forward progress was whether to drop his load and hope for a lengthy pause or to stand there and support all the weight rather than putting it down and having to pick it up again right away.

The column wound around and up and down the contours of terrain, which in May and early June was covered nearly always with slippery mud varying in depth from a few inches to knee deep. The rain was frequent and chilly. It varied from drizzles to wind-driven, slashing deluges that flooded our muddy footprints almost as soon as we made them. The helmet, of course, kept one's head dry, but a poncho was the only body protection we had. It was floppy and restricted movement greatly. We had no raincoats. So, rather than struggle over slippery terrain with our loads, encumbered further by a loose-fitting poncho, we just got soaking wet and shivered in misery.

We tried to wisecrack and joke from time to time, but that always faded away as we grew more weary or closer to the front lines. That kind of movement over normal terrain or on roads would try any man's patience, but in Okinawa's mud it drove us to a state of frustration and exasperation bordering on rage. It can be appreciated only by someone who has experienced it.

Most men finally came to the state where they just stood stoically immobile with a resigned expression when halted and waited to move out. The cursing and outbursts of rage didn't seem to help, although no one was above it when goaded to the point of desperation and fatigue with halting and moving, slipping and sliding, and falling in the mud. Mud didn't just interfere with vehicles. It exhausted the man on foot who was expected to keep on where wheels or treaded vehicles couldn't move.

At some point during our moves, our mortar section completely wiped out an enemy force that had held an elongated ridge for three days against repeated Marine infantry attacks supported by heavy artillery fire. Burgin was observing. He reasoned that there must have been a narrow gully running along the ridge that sheltered the Japanese from the artillery fire. He registered our three mortars so that one fired from right to left, another from left to right, and the third along the crest of the ridge. Thus the Japanese in the gully couldn't escape.

Lieutenant Mac ordered Burgin not to carry out the fire mission. He said we couldn't spare the ammo. Burgin, a three-campaign veteran and a skillful observer, called the company CP and asked if they could get us the ammo. The CP told him yes.

Over the sound-powered phone, Burgin said, "On my command, fire."

Mac was with us at the gun pits and ordered us not to fire. He told Burgin the same over the phone.

Burgin told him to go to hell and yelled, "Mortar section, fire on my command; commence firing!"

We fired as Mac ranted and raved.

When we finished firing, the company moved against the ridge. Not a shot was fired at our men. Burgin checked the target area and saw more than fifty freshly killed Japanese soldiers in a narrow ravine, all dead from wounds obviously caused by our mortar fire. The artillery shells had exploded in front of or to the rear of the Japanese who were protected from them. Our 60mm mortar shells fell right into the ravine, however, because of their steeper trajectory.

We had scored a significant success with the teamwork of our mortar section. The event illustrated the value of experience in a veteran like Burgin compared with the poor judgment of a "green" lieutenant.

The short period of rest in May helped us physically and mentally. Such periodic rests off the lines, lasting from a day to several days, enabled us to keep going. The rations were better. We could shave and clean up a bit using our helmets for a basin. Although we had to dig in because of long-range artillery or air raids, two men could make a simple shelter with their ponchos over their hole and be relatively (but not completely) dry on rainy nights. We could relax a little.

I'm convinced we would have collapsed from the strain and exertion without such respites. But I found it more difficult to go back each time we squared away our gear to move forward into the zone of terror. My buddies' joking ceased as we trudged grim-faced back into that chasm where time had no meaning and one's chances of emerging unhurt dwindled with each encounter. With each step toward the distant rattle and rumble of that hellish region where fear and horror tortured us like a cat tormenting a mouse, I experienced greater and greater dread. And it wasn't just dread of death or pain, because most men felt somehow they wouldn't be killed. But each time we went up, I felt the sickening dread of fear itself and the revulsion at the ghastly scenes of pain and suffering among comrades that a survivor must witness.

Some of my close friends told me they felt the same way. Significantly, those who felt it most acutely were the more battle-wise veterans for whom Okinawa was their third campaign. The bravest wearied of the suffering and waste, even though they showed little fear for their own personal safety. They simply had seen too much horror.

The increasing dread of going back into action obsessed me. It became the subject of the most tortuous and persistent of all the ghastly war nightmares that have haunted me for many, many years. The dream is always the same, going back up to the lines during the bloody, muddy month of May on Okinawa. It remains blurred and vague, but occasionally still comes, even after the nightmares about the shock and violence of Peleliu have faded and been lifted from me like a curse.

The 7th Marines secured Dakeshi Ridge on 13 May after a bitter fight. Some of the Peleliu veterans in that regiment noted that the vicious battle resembled the fighting on Bloody Nose Ridge. We could see the ridge clearly. It certainly looked like Bloody Nose. The crest was rugged and jagged on the skyline and had an ugly thin line of blackened, shattered trees and stumps.

Our company moved into a smashed, ruined village that an officer told me was Dakeshi. Some of us moved up to a stout stone wall where we were ordered to hold our fire while we watched a strange scene about one hundred yards to our front. We had to stand there inactive and watch as about forty or fifty Japanese soldiers retreated through the ruins and rubble. They had been flushed by men of the 7th Marines. But we were in support of the 7th Marines, some elements of which were forward of us on the right and left, out of our field of vision. We couldn't risk firing for fear of hitting those Marines. We could only watch the enemy trotting along holding their rifles. They wore no packs, only crossed shoulder straps supporting their cartridge belts.

As they moved through the rubble with helmets bobbing up and down, a man next to me fingered the safety catch on his M1 rifle and said in disgust, "Look at them bastards out there in the open, and we can't even fire at 'em."

"Don't worry, the 7th Marines will catch them in a cross fire farther on," an NCO said.

"That's the word," said an officer confidently.

Just then a swishing, rushing sound of shells passing low overhead made us all duck reflexively, even though we recognized the sound as our own artillery. Large, black, sausage-shaped clouds of thick smoke erupted in the air over the Japanese as each of those deadly 155mm bursts exploded with a flash and a *karump*. The artillerymen were zeroed in on target. The Japanese broke into a dead run, looking very bowlegged to me (as they always did when running). Even as they ran away under that deadly hail of steel, showing us their backs, I felt there was an air of confident arrogance about them. They didn't move like men in panic. We knew they simply had been ordered to fall back to other strongly prepared defensive positions to prolong the campaign. Otherwise they would have stayed put or attacked us, and in either case fought to the death.

More of our 155s swished over, erupting above the Japanese. We stood in silence and watched as the artillery fire took its toll of them. It was a grim sight, still vivid in my mind. The survivors moved out of sight through drifting smoke as we heard the rattle of Marine machine guns on our right and left front.

We received orders to move out along a little road bordered by stone walls. We passed through the ruins of what had been a quaint village. What had been picturesque little homes with straw-thatched or tiled roofs were piles of smoldering rubble.

After bitter fighting, the Awacha defenses and then those around Dakeshi fell to our division. Yet, between us and Shuri, there remained another system of heavy Japanese defenses: Wana. The costly battle against them would become known as the battle for Wana Draw.

CHAPTER TWELVE

Of Mud and Maggots

The boundary between the III Amphibious Corps (Marines) and the XXIV Corps (Army) ran through the middle of the main Japanese defensive position on the heights of Shuri. As the Marines moved southward, the 1st Marine Division remained on the left in the III Amphibious Corps' zone of action with the 6th Marine Division on the right. Within the 1st Marine Division's zone of action, the 7th Marines occupied the left flank and the 5th Marines the right. The 1st Marines was in reserve.

Beyond Awacha-Dakeshi, the Marines next faced Wana Ridge. On the other side of Wana Ridge lay Wana Draw, through which meandered the Asato Gawa. Forming the southern high ground above Wana Draw was yet another ridge, this one extending eastward from the city of Naha and rising to the Shuri Heights. This second ridge formed a part of the main Japanese defensive positions, the Shuri Line.

Wana Draw aimed like an arrow from the northwest directly into the heart of the Japanese defenses at Shuri. Within this natural avenue of approach, the Japanese took advantage of every difficult feature of terrain; it couldn't have provided a better opportunity for their defense if they had designed it. The longest and bloodiest ordeal of the battle for Okinawa now faced the men of the 1st Marine Division.

For the attack against Wana on 15 May 1945, the 5th Marines sent 2/5 forward with 3/5 in close support. The 1st Battalion came behind in reserve.

Before 2/5's attack began, we moved into a position behind that battalion. We watched tanks firing 75s and M7s firing

105s thoroughly shell the draw. The tanks received such heavy Japanese fire in return that the riflemen of 2/5 assigned to attack with the tanks had to seek any protection they could in ditches and holes while they covered the tanks from a distance; no man on his feet could have survived the hail of shells the enemy fired at the tanks. And the tanks couldn't move safely beyond the cover the riflemen provided because of Japanese suicide tank-destroyer teams. Finally, we saw the tanks pull back after suffering some hits. Our artillery and naval gunfire threw a terrific barrage at the Japanese positions around the draw. Shortly after that the tanks withdrew. Then an air strike was made against the draw. The bombardment of the draw seemed very heavy to us, but it wasn't anything compared to what was to become necessary before the draw was taken.

We moved from one position to another behind 2/5 until I was so confused I had no idea where we were. Late in the afternoon, we halted temporarily along a muddy trail running along the treeless slope of a muddy ridge. Marines of 2/5 moved past us going the other direction. Japanese shells whistled across the ridge and burst to the rear. Our artillery roared and swished overhead, the explosions booming and thundering out in the draw across the ridge.

Nearby our regimental Protestant chaplain had set up a little altar made out of a box from which he was administering Holy Communion to a small group of dirty Marines. I glanced at the face of a Marine opposite me as the file halted. He was filthy like all of us, but even through a thickly mud-caked dark beard I could see he had fine features. His eyes were bloodshot and weary. He slowly lowered his light machine gun from his shoulder, set the handle on his toe to keep it off the mud, and steadied the barrel with his hand. He watched the chaplain with an expression of skepticism that seemed to ask, "What's the use of all that? Is it gonna keep them guys from gettin' hit?" That face was so weary but so expressive that I knew he, like all of us, couldn't help but have doubts about his God in the presence of constant shock and suffering. Why did it go on and on? The machine gunner's buddy held the gun's tripod on his shoulder, glanced briefly at the muddy little communion service, and then stared blankly off toward a clump of pines to our rear—as though he hoped to see home back there somewhere.

"Move out," came along their file.

The machine gunner hoisted the heavy weapon onto his shoulder as they went slipping and sliding around a bend in the trail into the gathering dusk.

We were told to spread out, take cover, and await further orders. Some of us found holes. Others scooped out what they could. Soon several Japanese shells exploded not far from me. I heard a shout for a corpsman and then, "Hey, you guys, Doc Caswell got hit!"

I forgot about the shells and felt sick. I ran in the direction of the shout to look for Kent Caswell, praying with every step that he wasn't hurt badly. Several other Marines were already with Doc, and a fellow corpsman was bandaging his neck. Doc Caswell lay back in the foxhole and looked up at me as I bent over him and asked him how he was doing (no doubt a stupid question, but my throat was constricted with grief). He opened his lips to speak, and blood trickled out from between them. I was heartbroken, because I didn't see how he could possibly survive. I feared that vital blood vessels in his neck had been severed by the shell fragments.

"Don't talk Doc, they'll get you outa here, and you'll be OK," I managed to stammer.

"OK you guys, let's get him outa here," the corpsman said as he finished his aid.

As I said so long to Doc and got up to leave, I noticed a cloverleaf of 60mm mortar shells lying on the side of the fox-hole. A shell fragment had sliced a gash through the thick black metal endplate. I shuddered as I wondered whether it had passed first through Doc's neck.*

Our massive artillery, mortar, naval gunfire, and aerial bombardment continued against Wana Draw on our front and Wana Ridge on our left. The Japanese continued to shell

---

*Some time later we learned that Doc had survived the trip to the aid station with the stretcher team and that he would live. He returned to his native Texas where he remains one of my most faithful friends from our days in K/3/5.

everything and everybody in the area, meeting each tank–infantry attack with a storm of fire. A total of thirty tanks, including four flamethrowers, blasted and burned Wana Draw. Our artillery, heavy mortars, ships' guns, and planes then plastered the enemy positions all over again until the noise and shock made me wonder what it was like to be in a quiet place. We had been under and around plenty of "heavy stuff" at Peleliu, but not on nearly so massive a scale or for such unending periods of time as at Wana. The thunderous American barrages went on and on for hours and then days. In return, the Japanese threw plenty of shells our way. I had a continuous headache I'll never forget. Those thunderous, prolonged barrages imposed on me a sense of stupefaction and dullness far beyond anything I ever had experienced before.

It didn't seem possible for any human being to be under such thunderous chaos for days and nights on end and be unaffected by it—even when most of it was our own supporting weapons, and we were in a good foxhole. How did the Japanese stand up under it? They simply remained deep in their caves until it stopped and then swarmed up to repulse each attack, just as they had done at Peleliu. So our heavy guns and air strikes had to knock down, cave in, or otherwise destroy the enemy's well-constructed defensive positions.

At some time during the fight for Wana Draw, we crossed what I supposed was the draw itself, somewhere near its mouth. To get to that point, we fought for days. I had lost count of how many. Marines of 2/5 had just gone across under fire, while we waited in an open field to move across. We eased up to the edge of the draw to cross in dispersed order. An NCO ordered three men and me to cross at a particular point and to stay close behind the 2/5 troops directly across the draw from us. The other side looked mighty far away. Japanese machine guns were firing down the draw from our left, and our artillery was swishing overhead.

"Haul ass, and don't stop for anything till you get across," said our NCO. (We could see other Marines of our battalion starting across on our right.) He told me to leave my mortar ammo bag and that someone else would bring it. I had the Thompson (submachine gun) slung over my shoulder.

We left the field and slid down a ten-foot embankment to the sloping floor of the draw. My feet hit the deck running. The man ahead of me was a Company K veteran whom I knew well, but the other two were replacements. One I knew by name, but the other not at all. I ran as fast as I could, and was glad I was carrying only my Tommy, pistol, and combat pack.

The valley sloped downward toward a little stream and then upward to the ridge beyond. The Japanese machine guns rattled away. Bullets zipped and snapped around my head, the tracers like long white streaks. I looked neither right nor left, but with my heart in my throat raced out, splashed across the little stream, and dashed up the slope to the shelter of a spur of ridge projecting out into the draw to our left. We must have run about three hundred yards or more to get across.

Once behind the spur I was out of the line of machine-gun fire, so I slowed to a trot. The veteran ahead of me and a little to my right slowed up, too. We glanced back to see where the two new men were. Neither one of them had made more than a few strides out into the draw from the other side. One was sprawled in a heap, obviously killed instantly. The other was wounded and crawling back. Some Marines ran out, crouching low, to drag him to safety.

"Jesus, that was close, Sledgehammer," said the man with me.

"Yeah," I gasped. That was all I could say.

We went up the slope and contacted a couple of riflemen from 2/5.

"We got a kid right over there just got hit. Can you guys get him out?" one of them said. "There's some corpsmen set up in a ravine along the ridge there." He pointed out the location of the casualty and then the dressing station.

We hailed two Company K men coming along the ridge, and they said they would help. One ran back along the ridge to get a stretcher. We other three moved up the ridge and into some brush where we found the wounded Marine. He lay on his back still clutching his rifle. As we came up he said, "Boy, am I glad to see you guys."

"You hit bad?" I asked as I knelt beside him.

"Look out, you guys! Nips right over there in the bushes."

I unslung my Tommy and, watching where he indicated the Japanese were, I talked to him. My two buddies knelt beside us with their weapons ready, watching for enemy soldiers through the brush while we waited for the stretcher.

"Where you hit?" I asked the wounded Marine.

"Right here," he said, pointing to the lower right portion of his abdomen.

He was talkative and seemed in no pain—obviously still shocked and dazed from his wound. I knew he would hurt badly soon, because he was hit in a painful area. I saw a smear of blood around a tear in his dungaree trousers, so I unhooked his cartridge belt and then his belt and his trousers to see how serious the wound was. It wasn't the round, neat hole of a bullet, but the gash characteristic of a shell fragment. About two inches long, it oozed a small amount of blood.

"What hit you?" I asked.

"Our company sixty mortars," answered the wounded Marine.

I felt a sharp twinge of conscience and thought some 60mm mortarman in the poor guy's own company fouled up and dropped some short rounds.

Almost as though he had read my thoughts, he continued, "It was my own damn fault I got hit, though. We were ordered to halt back there a way and wait while the mortars shelled this area. But I saw a damn Nip and figured if I got a little closer I could get a clear shot at the sonofabitch. When I got here the mortars came in, and I got hit. Guess I'm lucky it wasn't worse. I guess the Nip slipped away."

"You better take it easy now," I said as the stretcher came up.

We got the young Marine on the stretcher, put his rifle and helmet alongside him, and moved back down the ridge a little way to a corpsman. Several corpsmen were at work in a deep ravine cut into the ridge by erosion. It had sheer walls and a level floor and was perfectly protected. About a dozen wounded, stretcher cases and walking wounded were there already.

As we set our casualty onto the floor of the ravine, he said,

"Thanks a lot you guys; good luck." We wished him luck and a quick trip to the States.

Before we left, I paused and watched the corpsmen a moment. It was admirable how efficiently they handled the wounded, with more coming in continuously as stretcher teams left for evacuation centers with those already given field first aid.

We split up, moved apart a little, and sought shelter along the slope to await orders. I found a commodius two-man standing foxhole commanding a perfect wide view of the draw for a long distance right and left. It obviously had been used as a defensive position against any movement in the draw and probably had sheltered a couple of Japanese riflemen or perhaps a light machine gunner. The hole was well dug in dry clay soil; the ridge sloped up steeply behind it. But the hole and its surroundings were devoid of any enemy equipment or trash of any kind. There wasn't so much as an empty cartridge case or ammo carton to be seen. But there were enemy tracks in the soft soil thrown out of the hole, tracks of *tabi* sneakers and hobnail-sole field shoes.

The Japanese had become so security-conscious they not only removed their dead when possible but sometimes even picked up their expended "brass" just as we did on a rifle range. Sometimes all we found were bloodstains on the ground where one had been killed or wounded. They removed everything they could when possible to conceal their casualties. But when they removed even empty cartridge cases, and we found only tracks, we got an eerie feeling—as though we were fighting a phantom enemy.

During their battle on the Motobu Peninsula in April, Marines of the 6th Division had seen evidence of increased security consciousness on the part of the Japanese. But we had seen nothing like it on Peleliu, and Guadalcanal veterans had told me nearly every Japanese they "field stripped" had a diary on him. The same was said about Gloucester.

After sitting out another thunderous barrage of friendly artillery fire, the three of us shouldered our weapons and moved along the ridge to rejoin Company K. Once together, our company formed into extended file and headed westward toward the regimental right flank. (I lost track of the date, as we moved about for several days.) The shell-blasted terrain was treeless and increasingly low and flat. We dug in, were shelled off and on, and were thoroughly bewildered as to where we were, other than we were said to be still somewhere in Wana Draw. Shuri loomed to our left front.

About that time Burgin was wounded. He was hit in the back of the neck by a shell fragment. Fortunately, he wasn't killed. Burgin was a Texan and as fine a sergeant as I ever saw. He was a Gloucester veteran whose luck had run out. We would miss him from the mortar section, and were delighted when he returned later after eighteen days of convalescence.

The weather turned cloudy on 21 May, and the rains began. By midnight the drizzle became a deluge. It was the beginning of a ten-day period of torrential rains. The weather was chilly, and mud, mud, mud was everywhere. We slipped and slid along the trails with every step we took.

While the 1st Marine Division was fighting the costly, heartbreaking battle against the Wana positions, the 6th Marine Division (on the right and slightly forward) had been fighting a terrible battle for Sugar Loaf Hill. Sugar Loaf and the surrounding pieces of prominent terrain—the Horse Shoe and Half Moon—were located on the main ridge running from Naha to Shuri. Like Wana, they were key Japanese defensive positions in the complex that guarded the Shuri Heights.

During the morning of 23 May, the boundary between the 1st Marine Division and the 6th Marine Division shifted to the right (west) so the latter could rearrange its lines. The 3d Battalion, 5th Marines went into line on the right to take over the extended front.

I remember the move vividly, because we entered the worst area I ever saw on a battlefield. And we stayed there more than a week. I shudder at the memory of it.

We shouldered our weapons and gear, and the column telescoped its way circuitously through muddy draws, slipping and sliding along the slopes of barren hills to avoid observation and consequent shelling by the enemy. It rained off and on. The mud got worse the farther we went. As we approached our destination, the Japanese dead, scattered about in most areas since 1 May, became more numerous.

When we had dug in near enemy dead and conditions permitted, we always shoveled soil over them in a vain effort to cut down the stench and to control the swarming flies. But the desperate fighting for ten days against and around Sugar Loaf Hill and the continued, prolonged Japanese artillery and mortar fire had made it impossible for the Marine units there to bury the enemy dead.

We soon saw that it also had been impossible to remove many Marine dead. They lay where they had fallen—an uncommon sight even to the veterans in our ranks. It was a strong Marine tradition to move our dead, sometimes even at considerable risk, to an area where they could be covered with a poncho and later collected by the graves registration people. But efforts to remove many Marines killed in the area we entered had been in vain, even after Sugar Loaf Hill had been captured following days of terrible fighting.

The rains had begun 21 May, almost as soon as Sugar Loaf Hill had been secured by men of the 6th Marine Division. Because of the deep mud, the able-bodied could scarcely rescue and evacuate their wounded and bring up vital ammo and rations. Regrettably, the dead had to wait. It couldn't have been otherwise.

We slogged along through a muddy draw around the base of a knoll. On our left we saw six Marine corpses. They were lying facedown against a gentle muddy slope where they apparently had hugged the deck to escape Japanese shells. They were "bunched up"—in a row, side by side, scarcely a foot apart. They were so close together that they probably had all been killed by the same shell. Their browning faces lay against the mud in an even row. One could imagine the words of fear or reassurance that had been passed among them as they lay under the terror of the shelling. Each clutched a rusting rifle, and every sign indicated that those tragic figures were new replacements, fresh to the shock of combat.

The first man's left hand was extended forward, palm down. His fingers clutched the mud in a death grip. A beautiful, shiny gold watch was held in place around the decaying wrist by an elaborate gold metal stretch band. (Most of the men I knew—and myself—wore plain, simple luminous-dial, waterproof, shockproof wristwatches with a plain green cloth wristband.) How strange, I thought, for a Marine to wear a flashy, conspicuous watch while on the front lines, stranger still that some Japanese hadn't slipped out during a dark night and taken it.

As we filed past the dead Marines, each of my buddies turned his head and gazed at the horrible spectacle with an expression that revealed how much the scene inwardly sickened us all.

I had heard and read that combat troops in many wars became hardened and insensitive to the sight of their own dead. I didn't find that to be the case at all with my comrades. The sight of dead Japanese didn't bother us in the least, but the sight of Marine dead brought forth regret, never indifference.

HALF MOON HILL

While the artillery swished and whined overhead in both directions, we moved to our new positions in the westernmost extension of Wana Draw. By twos and threes, the Company K men forming the front line eased onto a barren, muddy, shell-torn ridge named Half Moon Hill and into the foxholes of the company we were relieving. Our mortar section went into place behind a low rise of ground below the ridge and about a hundred yards back of the front lines. The terrain between us and Half Moon was nearly flat. The little elevation behind which we emplaced our guns was so low that when we stood up beside the gun pit, we could see clearly up to the company's forward lines on the ridge.

Readily visible beyond that, to the left front, were the still higher, smoke-shrouded Shuri Heights, the heart of the Japanese defensive system. That ominous and formidable terrain feature was constantly under bombardment of varying intensity from our artillery, heavy mortars, and gunfire support ships. No matter, though. It didn't seem to deter the enemy observers from directing their artillery and heavy mortars in shelling our whole area frequently, every day and every night.

We faced south on Half Moon. A narrow-gauge railroad track lay a short distance to our right and ran south through a flat area between Half Moon and a ridge to our right known as the Horse Shoe. Beyond that it swung westward toward Naha. An officer told us that the ridge to our right (west) and slightly to our rear across the railroad was Sugar Loaf Hill.

Company K was on the right flank of 3/5 and moved up onto the western part of the base of Half Moon. The Japanese still occupied caves in both of the southward-pointing tips of the crescent. The right-flank foxhole of our company was dug on the crest at the western edge of the end of the base of Half Moon. Below it to the right the ridge dropped away to low flat ground.

Our company CP was situated in the sunken railroad bed to the right of our mortar section's position. A nice tarpaulin was stretched over the CP from one side of the railroad embankment to the other. This kept the post snug and dry while torrents of chilly rain kept shivering riflemen, machine gunners, and mortarmen soaked, cold, and miserable day and night in open foxholes. The rain greeted us as we moved into our assigned area.

The almost continuous downpour that started on 21 May turned Wana Draw into a sea of mud and water that resembled a lake. Tanks bogged down and even amtracs could not negotiate the morass. Living conditions on the front lines were pitiful. Supply and evacuation problems were severe. Food, water, and ammunition were scarce. Foxholes had to be bailed out constantly. The men's clothing, shoes, feet, and bodies remained constantly wet. Sleep was nearly impossible. The mental and physical strain took a mounting toll on the Marines.

Making an almost impossible situation worse were the deteriorating bodies of Marines and Japanese that lay just outside the foxholes where they had fallen during the five days of ferocious fighting that preceded Company K's arrival on Half Moon. Each day's fighting saw the number of corpses increase. Flies multiplied, and amoebic dysentery broke out. The men of Company K, together with the rest of the 1st Marine Division, would live and fight in that hell for ten days.

We dispersed our guns and dug gun pits as best we could in the mud. Snafu and I took compass readings and set aiming stakes based on the readings from our observer. As soon as we fired a couple of rounds of HE to register in my gun, it was obvious we had a bad problem with the base plate of our mortar being driven farther into the soft soil with the recoil of each shell. We reasoned the rain would soon stop, however, or if it didn't, a couple of pieces of ammo box under the base plate would hold it firm. What a mistake!

After digging in the gun, registering in on the aiming stakes, and preparing ammo for future use, I had my first opportunity to look around our position. It was the most ghastly corner of hell I had ever witnessed. As far as I could see, an area that previously had been a low grassy valley with a picturesque stream meandering through it was a muddy, repulsive, open sore on the land. The place was choked with the putrefaction of death, decay, and destruction. In a shallow defilade to our right, between my gun pit and the railroad, lay about twenty dead Marines, each on a stretcher and covered to his ankles with a poncho—a commonplace, albeit tragic, scene to every veteran. Those bodies had been placed there to await transport to the rear for burial. At least those dead were covered from the torrents of rain that had made them miserable in life and from the swarms of flies that sought to hasten their decay. But as I looked about, I saw that other Marine dead couldn't be tended properly. The whole area was pocked with shell craters and churned up by explosions. Every crater was half full of water, and many of them held a Marine corpse. The bodies lay pathetically just as they had been killed, half submerged in muck and water, rusting weapons still in hand. Swarms of big flies hovered about them.

"Why ain't them poor guys been covered with ponchos?" mumbled my foxhole buddy as he glanced grimly about with a distraught expression on his grizzled face. His answer came the moment he spoke. Japanese 75mm shells came whining and whistling into the area. We cowered in our hole as they crashed and thundered around us. The enemy gunners on the commanding Shuri Heights were registering their artillery and mortars on our positions. We realized quickly that anytime any of us moved out of our holes, the shelling began immediately. We had a terrible time getting our wounded evacuated through the shell fire and mud without the casualty and stretcher bearers getting hit. Thus it was perfectly clear why the Marine dead were left where they had fallen.

Everywhere lay Japanese corpses killed in the heavy fighting. Infantry equipment of every type, U.S. and Japanese, was scattered about. Helmets, rifles, BARs, packs, cartridge belts, canteens, shoes, ammo boxes, shell cases, machine-gun ammo belts, all were strewn around us up to and all over Half Moon.

The mud was knee deep in some places, probably deeper in others if one dared venture there. For several feet around every corpse, maggots crawled about in the muck and then were washed away by the runoff of the rain. There wasn't a tree or bush left. All was open country. Shells had torn up the turf so completely that ground cover was nonexistent. The rain poured down on us as evening approached. The scene was nothing but mud; shell fire; flooded craters with their silent, pathetic, rotting occupants; knocked-out tanks and amtracs; and discarded equipment—utter desolation.

The stench of death was overpowering. The only way I could bear the monstrous horror of it all was to look upward away from the earthly reality surrounding us, watch the leaden gray clouds go scudding over, and repeat over and over to myself that the situation was unreal—just a nightmare—that I would soon awake and find myself somewhere else. But the ever-present smell of death saturated my nostrils. It was there with every breath I took.

I existed from moment to moment, sometimes thinking death would have been preferable. We were in the depths of the abyss, the ultimate horror of war. During the fighting around the Umurbrogol Pocket on Peleliu, I had been depressed by the wastage of human lives. But in the mud and driving rain before Shuri, we were surrounded by maggots and decay. Men struggled and fought and bled in an environment so degrading I believed we had been flung into hell's own cesspool.

Not long after 3/5 took over Half Moon, several of us were on a work party, struggling through knee-deep mud to bring ammo from the rear up to the mortar positions. We passed near the company CP in the railroad bed.

"Hey, you guys, looka there; Stumpy's in bad shape!" said a Marine in an excited low voice. We all stopped and looked toward the CP. There was our CO, Stumpy Stanley, just outside the edge of the tarpaulin, trying to stand by himself. But he had to be supported by a man on each side. He looked haggard and weary and was shaking violently with malarial chills. He could barely hold up his head. The men supporting him seemed to be arguing with him. He was objecting as best he could. But it was a feeble effort, because he was so sick.

"Po' Stumpy got that goddamn bug so bad he can't hardly

stand up. But looka there; he's all man, by God. He don't wanna be 'vacuated," said Snafu gravely.

"He's a damn good Joe," someone else said.

We thought highly of Stumpy and respected him greatly. He was a good skipper, and we had confidence in him. But malaria made him too ill to stay on his feet. The chilly rain, the emotional stress, and the physical exertion and strain of those days were enough to make a well man collapse. Obviously those who had malarial infections couldn't possibly keep going. So, for the second time in May, we lost our commanding officer. Stumpy was the last of our Peleliu officers, and his evacuation ended an era for me. He was the last tie to Capt. Andy Haldane. For me, Company K was never the same after that day.

As we feared, Shadow became the CO. It's best that I don't record what we said about that.

At daybreak the morning after we took over the line on Half Moon, George Sarrett and I went up onto the ridge to our observation post. Half Moon was shaped like a crescent, with the arms pointing southward. Our battalion line stretched along the crest of the ridge as it formed the base of the crescent. The arms extended outward beyond our front lines, and Japanese occupied caves in the reverse slopes of those arms, particularly the one on the left (east). They made our line a hot spot.

To our front, the ridge sloped down sharply from the crest, then more gently all the way to a big road embankment approximately three hundred yards out and running parallel to our lines. A large culvert opened toward us through the embankment. The area to our front was well drained and as bare as the back of one's hand. It wasn't heavily cratered. Two shallow ditches about fifty yards apart ran across the area between the southern tips of the Half Moon. These ditches were closer to the road embankment than to our lines. The sloping area leading to the culvert resembled an amphitheater bordered by the base of the crescent (where we were) to the north, the arms of the crescent extending southward, and the high road embankment running east and west at the southern end. Our visibility within the amphitheater was perfect (except for the reverse slopes of the arms of the crescent).

Marines of 2/4 had warned us as they departed that the Japanese came out of the caves in the reverse slopes of the crescent's arms at night and generally raised hell. To combat that, our ships kept star shells aloft, and our 60mm mortars kept flares burning in the wet sky above the ridge all night every night we were there.

As the dawn light grew brighter, we could see the lay of the land through the drizzle and thin fog. So we registered the mortar section's three guns with an aiming stake on one of each of three important terrain features. We had one gun register in on the reverse slope of the left-hand extension of the Half Moon. A second mortar we registered on the reverse slope of the road embankment. We registered the third gun to cover the area around the mouth of the culvert.

No sooner had we registered the guns than we got a reaction. Big 90mm Japanese mortar shells began crashing along the crest of the ridge. They came so thick and so fast we knew an entire enemy mortar section was firing on us, not an isolated gun. They were zeroed in on the ridge and traversed along the crest from my left to the far right end of the company's line. It was an awful pounding. Each big shell fluttered and swished down and went off with a flash and an ear-splitting crash. Shrapnel growled through the air, and several men were wounded badly. Each shell threw stinking mud around when it exploded. The wounded were moved down behind the ridge with great difficulty because of the slippery, muddy slopes. A corpsman gave them aid, and they were carried to the rear—shocked, torn, and bleeding.

An uneasy quiet then settled along the line. Suddenly, someone yelled, "There goes one." A single Japanese soldier dashed out of the blackness of the culvert. He carried his bayoneted rifle and wore a full pack. He ran into the open, turned, and headed for shelter behind the tip of the southern end of the crescent arm on our left front. It looked as though he had about a thirty-yard dash to make. Several of our riflemen and BARmen opened up, and the soldier was bowled over by their bullets before he reached the shelter of the ridge. Our men cheered and yelled when he went down.

As the day wore on, more Japanese ran out of the culvert in ones and twos and dashed for the shelter of the same ridge extension. It was obvious they wanted to concentrate on the reverse slope there from where they could launch counterattacks, raids, and infiltration attempts on our front line. Obviously, it was to our best interest to stop them as quickly as possible. Any enemy soldier who made it in behind that slope might become one's unwelcome foxhole companion some night.

When the Japanese ran out of the culvert, our men fired on them and nearly always knocked them down. The riflemen, BARmen, and machine gunners looked on it as fine target practice, because we received no return small-arms fire, and the Japanese mortars were quiet.

I kept busy with the field glasses, observing, adjusting range, and calling fire orders onto the slope and the road embankment. I had the Tommy with me, but it wasn't as steady and accurate at the two- to three-hundred-yard range as an M1 Garand rifle. We had an M1 and an ammo belt in our OP, though, and I wanted to throw down that phone and the field glasses and grab up that M1 every time an enemy popped into view. As long as our mortar section was firing a mission, I had no choice but to continue observing.

The Japanese kept up their efforts to move behind the slope. Some made it, because our men missed them. Our 60mm mortar shells crashed away steadily on the target areas. We could see Japanese emerge from the culvert and be killed by our shells.

The longer this action continued without our receiving any return fire, the more relaxed my buddies became. The situation began to take on certain aspects of a rifle range, or more likely, an old-fashioned turkey shoot. My buddies started making bets about who had hit which Japanese. Lively arguments developed, but with rifles, BARs, and several machine guns firing simultaneously, no one could tell for sure who hit which enemy soldier.

The men yelled and joked more and more in one of their

few releases from weeks of tension under the pounding of heavy weapons. So they began to get careless and to miss some of the Japanese scurrying for the slope. Shadow saw this. He ran up and down our firing line cursing and yelling at everybody. Then the men settled down and took more careful aim. Finally the enemy stopped coming, and I received orders to call "cease firing" to our mortars. We sat and waited.

During the lull, I moved over into the machine-gun emplacement next to our mortar OP to visit with the gunner. It contained a Browning .30 caliber water-cooled heavy machine gun manned by a gunner who had joined Company K as a replacement after Peleliu. On Pavuvu, he and I had become good friends. We called him "Kathy" after a chorus girl he knew in California. He was married and very much in love with his wife, so he bore a heavy burden of guilt because he had had an affair with Kathy on his way overseas and couldn't get her out of his mind.

As we sat alone in the machine-gun pit, he asked me whether I wanted to see a picture of Kathy. I said yes. He carefully and secretively picked up his rain-soaked combat pack and took out a waterproof plastic map holder. Folding back the canvas cover, he said, "Here she is."

My eyes nearly popped out of my head. The eight-by-ten-inch photo was a full-length portrait of one of the most beautiful girls I ever saw. She was dressed, or undressed, in a scanty costume that exposed a good portion of her impressive physical endowments.

I gasped audibly, and "Kathy" said, "Isn't she a beauty?"

"She really is!" I told him, and added, "You've got a problem on your hands with a girl like that chorus girl and a wife you love." I kidded him about the possible danger of getting the letters to his wife and his girl crossed up and in the wrong envelopes. He just laughed and shook his head as he looked at the photo of the beautiful girl.

The scene was so unreal I could barely believe it: two tired, frightened young men sitting in a hole beside a machine gun in the rain on a ridge, surrounded with mud—nothing but stinking mud, with so much decaying human flesh buried or half buried in it that there were big patches of wriggling fat maggots marking the spots where Japanese corpses lay—looking at the picture of a beautiful seminude girl. She was a pearl in a mudhole.

Viewing that picture made me realize with a shock that I had gradually come to doubt that there really was a place in the world where there were no explosions and people weren't bleeding, suffering, dying, or rotting in the mud. I felt a sense of desperation that my mind was being affected by what we were experiencing. Men cracked up frequently in such places as that. I had seen it happen many times by then. In World War I they had called it shell shock or, more technically, *neuresthenia*. In World War II the term used was combat fatigue.

Strange that such a picture provoked such thoughts, but I vividly recall grimly making a pledge to myself. The Japanese might kill or wound me, but they wouldn't make me crack up. A peaceful civilian back home who sat around worrying about losing his mind probably didn't have much to occupy him, but in our situation there was plenty of reason for the strongest-willed individuals to crack up.

My secret resolve helped me through the long days and nights we remained in the worst of the abyss. But there were times at night during that period when I felt I was slipping. More than once my imagination ran wild during the brief periods of darkness when the flares and star shells burned out.

"There comes another one," somebody yelled. "Kathy" quickly stowed his picture in his pack, spun around, gripped the machine-gun handle in his left hand, poised his trigger finger, and grabbed the aiming knob with his right hand. His assistant gunner appeared from out of nowhere and jumped to his post to feed the ammo belt into the gun. I started back to the OP hole but saw that George had phone in hand, and the mortars were still "secured." So I grabbed up an M1 rifle "Kathy" had in the machine-gun emplacement.

I saw enemy soldiers rushing out of the culvert. Our line started firing as I counted the tenth Japanese to emerge. Those incredibly brave soldiers formed a skirmish line abreast, with a few yards between each other, and started trotting silently toward us across open ground about three hundred yards away. Their effort was admirable but so hopeless. They had no supporting fire of any kind to pin us down or even to make us cautious. They looked as though they were on maneuvers. They had no chance of getting close to us.

I stood up beside the machine gun, took aim, and started squeezing off shots. The Japanese held their rifles at port arms and didn't even fire at us. Everybody along our line was yelling and firing. The enemy soldiers wore full battle gear with packs, which meant they had rations and extra ammo, so this might be the beginning of a counterattack of some size.

Within seconds, eight of the ten enemy soldiers pitched forward, spun around, or slumped to the deck, dead where they fell. The remaining two must have realized the futility of it all, because they turned around and started back toward the culvert. Most of us slackened our fire and just watched. Several men kept firing at the two retreating enemy soldiers but missed, and it looked as though they might get away. Finally one Japanese fell forward near one of the shallow ditches. The surviving soldier kept going.

Just as "Kathy" got his machine-gun sights zeroed in on him, the order "cease firing" came along the line. But the machine gun was making so much noise we didn't hear the order. "Kathy" had his ammo belts loaded so that about every fifth cartridge was a tracer. He squeezed off a long burst of about eight shots. The bullets struck the fleeing Japanese soldier in the middle of his pack and tore into him between his shoulders.

I was standing directly behind "Kathy," looking along his machine-gun barrel. The tracers must have struck the man's vertebrae or other bones and been deflected, because I clearly saw one tracer flash up into the air out of the soldier's right shoulder and another tracer come out of the top of his left shoulder. The Japanese dropped his rifle as the slugs knocked him face down into the mud. He didn't move.

"I got him; I got the bastard," "Kathy" yelled, jumping around slapping me on the back, and shaking hands with his assistant gunner. He had reason to be proud. He had made a good shot.

The enemy soldier who fell near the ditch began crawling

and flopped into it. Some of the men started firing at him again. The bullets kicked up mud all around the soldier as he slithered desperately along in the shallow ditch which didn't quite hide him. Machine-gun tracers ricocheted off the ground like vicious red arrows as the Japanese struggled along the shallow ditch.

Then, on one of the rare occasions I ever saw compassion expressed for the Japanese by a Marine who had to fight them, one of our men yelled, "Knock it off, you guys. The poor bastard's already hit and ain't got a snowball's chance in hell."

Someone else yelled angrily, "You stupid jerk; he's a goddamn Nip, ain't he? You gone Asiatic or something?"

The firing continued, and bullets hit the mark. The wounded Japanese subsided into the muddy little ditch. He and his comrades had done their best. "They died gloriously on the field of honor for the emperor," is what their families would be told. In reality, their lives were wasted on a muddy, stinking slope for no good reason.

Our men were in high spirits over the affair, especially after being pounded for so long. But Shadow was yelling, "Cease firing, you dumb bastards." He came slipping and sliding along the line, cursing and stopping at intervals to pour out storms of invective on some smiling, muddy Marine. He carried his helmet in his left hand and periodically took off his cap and flung it down into the mud until it was caked. Each man looked glum and sat or stood motionless until Shadow had finished insulting him and moved on.

As Shadow passed the machine-gun pit, he stopped and screamed at "Kathy," who was still jumping around in jubilation over his kill. "Knock it off, you goddamn fool!" Then he glared at me and said, "You're supposed to be observing for the mortars; put that goddamn rifle down, you bastard."

I wasn't impetuous, but, had I thought I could get away with it, I would certainly have clubbed him over the head with that M1 rifle.

I didn't, but Shadow's asinine conduct and comment did make me rash enough to say, "The guns are secured, sir. We were all sent out here to kill Nips, weren't we? So what difference does it make what weapon we use when we get the chance?"

His menacing expression turned into surprise and then doubt. With a quizzical look on his face, he cocked his head to one side as he pondered my remark, while I stood silently with the realization that I should have kept my mouth shut. The fine sergeant accompanying Shadow half glared and half smiled at me. Suddenly, without another glance, Shadow strode off along the ridge crest, cursing and yelling at the Marines in each foxhole as he passed them. I resolved to keep my mouth shut in the future.

As daylight waned, I looked out to our front through the drizzling rain falling through the still, foul air. A wisp of smoke rose straight up from the pack of the Japanese soldier "Kathy" had shot. The tracers had set something on fire. The thin finger of smoke rose high and then spread out abruptly to form a disc that appeared to rest on the column. So delicate and unreal, the smoke stood in the stagnant, fetid air like a marker over the corpse. Everything out there was motionless, only death and desolation among the enemy bodies.

George and I got orders to return to our mortar gun pits. Someone else would man the OP for the night. Getting back to the mortar emplacements from the company's front line was a major effort and an extremely dangerous one. From the moment we stepped to the rear of the crest of the ridge to descend the muddy slope, it was like trying to walk down a greased slide.

A large and unknown number of Japanese all over the ridge had been killed during the early counterattacks. They had been covered with soil as soon as possible. And Japanese were still being killed out front. Infiltrators also were being killed all along the ridge at night. Our men could only spade mud over them.

The situation was bad enough, but when enemy artillery shells exploded in the area, the eruptions of soil and mud uncovered previously buried Japanese dead and scattered chunks of corpses. Like the area around our gun pits, the ridge was a stinking compost pile.

If a Marine slipped and slid down the back slope of the

muddy ridge, he was apt to reach the bottom vomiting. I saw more than one man lose his footing and slip and slide all the way to the bottom only to stand up horror-stricken as he watched in disbelief while fat maggots tumbled out of his muddy dungaree pockets, cartridge belt, legging lacings, and the like. Then he and a buddy would shake or scrape them away with a piece of ammo box or a knife blade.

We didn't talk about such things. They were too horrible and obscene even for hardened veterans. The conditions taxed the toughest I knew almost to the point of screaming. Nor do authors normally write about such vileness; unless they have seen it with their own eyes, it is too preposterous to think that men could actually live and fight for days and nights on end under such terrible conditions and not be driven insane. But I saw much of it there on Okinawa and to me the war was insanity.

CHAPTER THIRTEEN

Breakthrough

The rains became so heavy that at times we could barely see our buddies in the neighboring foxhole. We had to bail out our gun pit and foxholes during and after each downpour or they filled with water.

Snafu and I dug a deep foxhole close to the gun pit and placed pieces of wooden ammo crates across braces set on the muddy clay at the bottom. At one end of this foxhole, beyond the extension of the boards, we dug a sump. As the surface water poured into our foxhole and down under the boards, we bailed out the sump with a C ration can for a day or two. But the soil became so saturated by continued downpours that water poured in through the four sides of the foxhole as though it were a colander. We then had to use a discarded helmet to bail out the sump, because the ration can couldn't take out water fast enough to keep up with that pouring in.

The board "floor" kept us out of the water and mud, provided we worked diligently enough at the bailing detail. Necessity being the mother of invention, we had "reinvented" the equivalent of duckboards commonly used in flooded World War I trenches. The duckboards pictured and described in 1914–18 in Flanders were, of course, often prefabricated in long sections and then placed in the trenches by infantrymen. But the small board floor we placed in our foxhole served the same function.

Continued firing finally caused my mortar's base plate to drive the pieces of wood supporting it deep into the mud in the bottom of the gun pit. We couldn't sight the gun properly. We tugged and pulled the gun up out of the mud, then it was a choice of emplacing it either on some firmer base in the gun pit or on the surface outside. The latter prospect would have meant sure death from the enemy shelling, so we had to come up with something better in a hurry.

Somebody got the bright idea of building a "footing" on which to rest the base plate. So in the bottom of the gun pit, we dug out a deep square hole larger than the base plate and lined it with boards. We next placed several helmets full of coral gravel we found in the side of the railroad bed into the footing. We set the mortar's base plate on the firm coral footing, resighted the gun, and had no more trouble with recoil driving the base plate into the mud. I suppose the other two squads in our mortar section fixed their guns' base plates in the same manner.

The Japanese infantry kept up their activity to our front and tried to infiltrate our lines every night, sometimes with success. Snafu made good about then on the threat he had made to the CP on Peleliu about any enemy headed toward the Company K CP. On Peleliu one night after we came off the lines Snafu shot two Japanese with his Thompson. He had killed one and fatally wounded the other. A sergeant made Snafu bury the dead soldier. Snafu objected strenuously because he said, and rightly so, if he hadn't shot the Japanese they would have kept on going right into the company CP. Sarge said maybe so, but the corpse had to be buried, and since Snafu had shot it, he must bury it. Snafu promised he would never shoot another enemy soldier headed for the CP.

One day as dawn broke with a thin fog and a pelting rain, Snafu woke me out of the nearest thing to sleep that could be attained in that miserable place with, "Halt who goes there? What's the password?"

Jolted out of my fatigue stupor, I saw Snafu's face silhouetted against the gray sky. Rain poured off his helmet, and drops of moisture on the end of each whisker of the thick stubbly beard on his jutting square jaw caught the dim light like glass beads. I snatched the Tommy up off my lap as he raised his .45 pistol and aimed it toward two dim figures striding along about twenty yards away. Visibility was so poor in the dim light, mist, and rain that I could tell little about the shadowy figures other than they wore U.S. helmets. At the sound of Snafu's challenge, the two men speeded up instead of halting and identifying themselves.

"Halt or I'll fire!" he yelled.

The two took off for the railroad bed as fast as they could on the slippery ground. Snafu fired several shots with his .45 but missed. Shortly we heard a couple of American grenades explode in the railroad bed. Then a buddy yelled that the Japanese had been killed by his grenades. Daylight came rapidly, so we went over to the railroad embankment to ask what had happened.

When Snafu and I got to the foxhole by the railroad embankment, we found two Marine snipers grinning and laughing. The grenade explosions had scared awake the Marines in the dryness under the tarpaulin in the company CP and had chased them out into the rain. They were drifting back to the shelter as we arrived. We waved, but got only glares in return.

We took a look at the dead enemy before returning to our foxhole. They had been wearing Marine helmets but otherwise were dressed in Japanese uniforms. A grenade had exploded in the face of one. There was no face and little head remaining. The other wasn't as badly mangled.

Snafu and I returned to our hole and got settled just in time to see Hank come stalking along from the CP. He was stopping at every foxhole along the way to find out who had been so negligent as to let the Japanese soldiers get past them and almost to the CP. Hank arrived at our foxhole and asked us why we hadn't seen the two soldiers pass if one of us was on watch as we were supposed to be.

Snafu spoke up immediately and said, "Hell, I saw 'em go right by here, but I reckoned they was headed for the company CP." (He didn't mention his challenging the Japanese or firing at them.)

Hank looked astonished and said, "What do you mean, Snafu?"

Snafu swelled with indignation and answered, "You remember when they made me bury that Nip I shot on Peleliu when them two was headed for the CP?"

"Yeah, so what?" answered Hank in a low, menacing voice.

"Well, I told them then if they made me bury 'im, then by God, next time I seen a Nip headin' for the CP I wasn't gonna' stop 'im!"

I groaned in a low voice, "Oooh, shut up, Snafu."

One didn't talk like that to a senior NCO and get away with it. Hank was a very formidable person and merited the tremendous respect we felt for him, but woe be unto the Marine who didn't do a task properly and incurred his wrath. Hank treated us with respect and compassion—if we followed orders and did our best. I had no desire to see what he would do to someone who didn't, but I thought I was about to. So I turned my head and half closed my eyes, as did all the awestruck men in the foxholes within earshot who had been watching Snafu and Hank.

Nothing happened. I glanced at Snafu and Hank as they stood there glaring at each other, a bantam rooster glaring up at a mighty eagle.

Finally Hank said, "You'd better not let that happen again!" He turned and stalked back to the CP.

Snafu mumbled and grumbled. The rest of us sighed with relief. I fully expected Hank at least to order Snafu to bury the two Japanese down there on the railroad, and then Snafu, as my corporal, would order me onto the burial detail as had happened on Peleliu. But he didn't, and someone else spaded mud over the two corpses.

Much later, when Hank was leaving Company K for home after an outstanding record in three campaigns, I asked him what he had thought about that incident. He just looked at me and grinned, but wouldn't say anything about it. His grin revealed, however, that he respected Snafu and knew he wasn't lax in any way, and probably that he himself had been ordered by some officer to look into the affair.

Because of the surroundings, our casualties during the stalemate on Half Moon were some of the most pathetic I ever had seen. Certainly a beautiful landscape didn't make a wound less painful or a death less tragic. But our situation before Shuri was the most awful place conceivable for a man to be hurt or to die.

Most of the wounds resulted from enemy shell fragments, but it seemed to me we had more than the usual number of cases of blast concussion from exploding shells. That was understandable because of the frequent heavy shellings we were subjected to. All the casualties were muddy and soaking wet like the rest of us. That seemed to accentuate the bloody battle dressings on their wounds and their dull expressions of shock and pain, which made the horror and hopelessness of it all more vivid as we struggled through the chilly driving rain and deep mud to evacuate them.

Some of the concussion cases could walk and were helped and led (some seemed to have no sure sense of direction) to the rear like men walking in their sleep. Some wore wild-eyed expressions of shock and fear. Others whom I knew well, though could barely recognize, wore expressions of idiots or simpletons knocked too witless to be afraid anymore. The blast of a shell had literally jolted them into a different state of awareness from the rest of us. Some of those who didn't return probably never recovered but were doomed to remain in mental limbo and spend their futures in a veteran's hospital as "living dead."

The combat fatigue cases were distressing. They ranged in their reactions from a state of dull detachment seemingly unaware of their surroundings, to quiet sobbing, or all the way to wild screaming and shouting. Stress was the essential factor we had to cope with in combat, under small-arms fire, and in warding off infiltrators and raiders during sleepless, rainy nights for prolonged periods; but being shelled so frequently during the prolonged Shuri stalemate seemed to increase the strain beyond that which many otherwise stable and hardened Marines could endure without mental or physical collapse. From my experience, of all the hardships and hazards the troops had to suffer, prolonged shell fire was more apt to break a man psychologically than anything else.

In addition to the wounded, quite a number of men were evacuated and described in the muster rolls simply as "sick." Some of them suffered attacks of malaria. Others had fever, respiratory problems, or were just exhausted and seemed to have succumbed to the rigors of exposure and the chilly rains. There were numerous cases of pneumonia. Many men weren't evacuated, although they suffered serious ailments resulting from the cold rains and being soaking wet for more than a week.

Most of us had serious trouble with our feet. An infantry-man with sore feet was in miserable shape under the best of living conditions. During a period of about fourteen or fifteen days, as near as I can calculate the time (from 21 May to 5 June), my feet and those of my buddies were soaking wet, and our boondockers were caked with sticky mud. Being up on the line and frequently shelled prevented a man from taking off his boondockers to put on a pair of dry socks. And even if he had dry socks, there was no way to clean and dry the leather boondockers. Most of us removed our mud-caked canvas leggings and tucked our trouser cuffs into our sock tops, but it didn't help our feet much. Consequently most men's feet were in bad condition.

My feet were sore, and it hurt to walk or run. The insides of my boondockers gave me the sensation of being slimy when I wiggled my toes to try to warm my feet with increased circulation. The repulsive sensation of slippery, slimy feet grew worse each day. My sore feet slid back and forth inside my soaked boondockers when I walked or ran. Fortunately they never became infected, a miracle in itself.

Sore feet caused by prolonged exposure to mud and water was called immersion foot, I learned later. In World War I they called the same condition trench foot. To me it was an unforgettable sensation of extreme personal filth and painful discomfort. It was the kind of experience that would make a man sincerely grateful for the rest of his life for clean, dry socks. As simple a condition as dry socks seemed a luxury.

The almost constant rain also caused the skin on my fingers to develop a strange shrunken and wrinkled appearance. My nails softened. Sores developed on the knuckles and backs of both hands. These grew a little larger each day and hurt whenever I moved my fingers. I was always knocking the scabs off against ammo boxes and the like. Similar sores had tormented combat troops in the South Pacific campaigns and were called jungle rot or jungle sores.*

Our own mail came up to us in canvas bags, usually with the ammo and rations. It was of tremendous value in boosting sagging morale. On several occasions I actually had to bend over my letters and read as rapidly as possible to shield them from the torrents of rain before the ink was smeared across the soggy paper and the writing became illegible.

Most of us received letters from family and civilian friends. But occasionally we received letters from old Company K buddies who had returned to the States. Their early letters expressed relief over being back with family or with "wine, women, and song." But later the letters often became disturbingly bitter and filled with disillusionment. Some expressed a desire to return if they could get back into the old battalion. Considering the dangers and hardships those men had been through before they were sent home, and considering our situation in front of Shuri, the attitudes of our buddies who had returned Stateside puzzled us.

They expressed themselves in various ways, but the gist of their disillusionment was a feeling of alienation from everyone but their old comrades. Although there was gasoline and meat rationing back in the States, life was safe and easy. Plenty of people were ready to buy a Marine combat veteran wearing campaign ribbons and battle stars a drink or a beer anytime. But all the good life and luxury didn't seem to take the place of old friendships forged in combat.

There was talk of war profiteers and able-bodied men who got easy duty at the expense of others. Some letters said simply that folks back in the States "just don't understand what the hell it's all about, because they have had it so easy." I heard more than one buddy express the opinion, as we sat in the mud, that civilians would "understand" if the Japanese or

---

*After the campaign on Okinawa ended, a battalion surgeon told me the sores on my hands were probably caused by malnutrition, the filth we lived in, or both. The festering sores that developed on my hands in late May didn't heal until nearly five months after we came out of combat.

the Germans bombed an American city. Some men thought that would have been a good idea *if* no American civilians got killed, just scared. But nobody wanted it to be *his* hometown.

It was hard to believe that some of our old friends who had wanted so much to return home actually were writing us that they thought of volunteering again for overseas duty. (Some actually did.) They had had enough of war, but they had greater difficulty adjusting to civilians or to comfortable Stateside military posts. We were unable to understand their attitudes until we ourselves returned home and tried to comprehend people who griped because America wasn't perfect, or their coffee wasn't hot enough, or they had to stand in line and wait for a train or bus.

Our buddies who had gone back had been greeted enthusiastically—as those of us who survived were received later on. But the folks back home didn't, and in retrospect couldn't have been expected to, understand what we had experienced, what in our minds seemed to set us apart forever from anyone who hadn't been in combat. We didn't want to indulge in self-pity. We just wished that people back home could understand how lucky they were and stop complaining about trivial inconveniences.

Siegfried Sassoon, an English combat infantry officer and poet in World War I, experienced the same feeling when he returned home. He summed it up in the following verse:

> *You smug-faced crowds with kindling eye*
> *Who cheer when soldier lads march by,*
> *Sneak home and pray you'll never know*
> *The hell where youth and laughter go.* *

The poet might just as well have been referring to Peleliu or to the mudfields in front of Shuri as to France in World War I.

Some of the younger replacements who came to us then had trouble adjusting, and not just to the shelling. That was enough to shake up the strongest veteran, but they were ut-

*Sassoon, Siegfried, "Suicide in Trenches" in *Collected Poems,* Viking Press, N.Y. 1949.

terly dismayed by our horrible surroundings. Numerous Marine replacements for combat units on Okinawa never had their names added to their units' muster rolls, because they got hit before notice of their transfer from their replacement draft to the combat unit ever reached Headquarters, U.S. Marine Corps. So they were listed on the casualty rolls as members of various replacement drafts.

It was also common throughout the campaign for replacements to get hit before we even knew their names. They came up confused, frightened, and hopeful, got wounded or killed, and went right back to the rear on the route by which they had come, shocked, bleeding, or stiff. They were forlorn figures coming up to the meat grinder and going right back out of it like homeless waifs, unknown and faceless to us, like unread books on a shelf. They never "belonged" to the company or made any friends before they got hit.

Of course, those replacements who got hit right away with the "million-dollar wound" were actually fortunate.*

Our food usually consisted of a cold can of C rations and, rarely, a canteen cup of hot coffee. When we could brew it up, it was a treat. It was difficult to warm anything with our little heat tablets because of the almost constant rain. Sometimes I had to hunch over and shield a can of C-ration stew from the rain, because the can would fill up with rainwater as fast as I spooned the cold stew into my mouth.

We ate only because hunger forced us to do so. No other stimulus could have forced me to eat when my nostrils were so saturated with the odor of decay that I frequently felt sick. I ate little during that period, but drank hot coffee or bouillon at every opportunity.

The constant rain caused our weapons to rust. Most of us lined the holsters for our .45 automatic pistols with the green plastic covers we were issued. These came in long sleevelike pieces and could be placed over carbines, rifles, and Tommy

---

*K/3/5 landed at full strength of 235 officers and men on 1 April 1945. The company joined 250 replacements during the campaign for a total of 485 serving. Of the fifty men left at the end of the campaign, only twenty-six had made the landing.

guns. We kept a plastic hood draped over our mortar when it wasn't in use. This plastic cover was issued to be placed over ourselves while crouching down to avoid being sprayed with mustard gas, should that weapon have been used by the Japanese. We kept our weapons heavily oiled and actually had little trouble with them considering the battlefield conditions.

Field sanitation was nonexistent because of the shelling and the mud. Each man simply used a grenade canister or ammo carton and threw his own waste out into the already foul mud around his foxhole.

By day the battlefield was a horrible scene, but by night it became the most terrible of nightmares. Star shells and flares illuminated the area throughout the nights but were interspersed with moments of chilling, frightening blackness.

Sleep was almost impossible in the mud and cold rain, but sometimes I wrapped my wet poncho around me and dozed off for brief periods while my foxhole mate was on watch and bailing out the hole. One usually had to attempt sleep while sitting or crouching in the foxhole.

As usual, we rarely ventured out of our foxholes at night unless to care for wounded or to get ammunition. When a flare or star shell lighted the area, everyone froze just as he was, then moved during the brief periods of darkness. When the area lighted up with that eerie greenish light, the big raindrops sparkled like silver shafts as they slanted downward. During a strong wind they looked as though they were being driven along almost horizontal to the deck. The light reflected off the dirty water in the craters and off the helmets and weapons of the living and the dead.

I catalogued in my mind the position of every feature on the surrounding terrain. There was no vegetation, so my list consisted of mounds and dips in the terrain, foxholes of my comrades, craters, corpses, and knocked-out tanks and amtracs. We had to know where everyone, living and dead, was located. If one of us fired at an enemy infiltrating or on a raid, he needed to know where his comrades were so as not to hit them. The position and posture of every corpse was important, because infiltrating Japanese also would freeze when illuminating shells lit up. So they might go unnoticed among the dead.

The longer we stayed in the area, the more unending the nights seemed to become. I reached the state where I would awake abruptly from my semisleep, and if the area was lit up, note with confidence my buddy scanning the terrain for any hostile sign. I would glance about, particularly behind us, for trouble. Finally, before we left the area, I frequently jerked myself up into a state in which I was semiawake during periods between star shells.

I imagined Marine dead had risen up and were moving silently about the area. I suppose these were nightmares, and I must have been more asleep than awake, or just dumbfounded by fatigue. Possibly they were hallucinations, but they were strange and horrible. The pattern was always the same. The dead got up slowly out of their waterlogged craters or off the mud and, with stooped shoulders and dragging feet, wandered around aimlessly, their lips moving as though trying to tell me something. I struggled to hear what they were saying. They seemed agonized by pain and despair. I felt they were asking me for help. The most horrible thing was that I felt unable to aid them.

At that point I invariably became wide awake and felt sick and half-crazed by the horror of my dream. I would gaze out intently to see if the silent figures were still there, but saw nothing. When a flare lit up, all was stillness and desolation, each corpse in its usual place.

Among the craters off the ridge to the west was a scattering of Marine corpses. Just beyond the right edge of the end foxhole, the ridge fell away steeply to the flat, muddy ground.*

---

*The flat, muddy, cratered landscape to the west of Half Moon Hill was a noman's-land to the railroad and beyond to the Horse Shoe and Sugar Loaf Hill, where the left flank of the 6th Marine Division was located. At no time did I see any Americans in that low, flooded ground astride the railroad. Thus a gap of considerable size existed between the 1st and 6th Marine Divisions.

An officer told me that machine guns and strongpoints to the right rear covered the area. He said the low flat terrain was so vulnerable to Japanese fire from the heights of Shuri that extending the lines to meet on that flooded ground would have sentenced the men involved to sure death. At night star shells illuminated the area so that the enemy couldn't infiltrate across it.

Next to the base of the ridge, almost directly below me, was a partially flooded crater about three feet in diameter and probably three feet deep. In this crater was the body of a Marine whose grisly visage has remained disturbingly clear in my memory. If I close my eyes, he is as vivid as though I had seen him only yesterday.

The pathetic figure sat with his back toward the enemy and leaned against the south edge of the crater. His head was cocked, and his helmet rested against the side of the crater so that his face, or what remained of it, looked straight up at me. His knees were flexed and spread apart. Across his thighs, still clutched in his skeletal hands, was his rusting BAR. Canvas leggings were laced neatly along the sides of his calves and over his boondockers. His ankles were covered with muddy water, but the toes of his boondockers were visible above the surface. His dungarees, helmet, cover, and 782 gear appeared new. They were neither mud-spattered nor faded.

I was confident that he had been a new replacement. Every aspect of that big man looked much like a Marine "taking ten" on maneuvers before the order to move out again. He apparently had been killed early in the attacks against the Half Moon, before the rains began. Beneath his helmet brim I could see the visor of a green cotton fatigue cap. Under that cap were the most ghastly skeletal remains I had ever seen— and I had already seen too many.

Every time I looked over the edge of that foxhole down into that crater, that half-gone face leered up at me with a sardonic grin. It was as though he was mocking our pitiful efforts to hang on to life in the face of the constant violent death that had cut him down. Or maybe he was mocking the folly of the war itself: "I am the harvest of man's stupidity. I am the fruit of the holocaust. I prayed like you to survive, but look at me now. It is over for us who are dead, but you must struggle, and will carry the memories all your life. People back home will wonder why you can't forget."

During the day I sometimes watched big raindrops splashing into the crater around that corpse and remembered how as a child I had been fascinated by raindrops splashing around a

large green frog as he sat in a ditch near home. My grandmother had told me that elves made little splashes like that,
and they were called water babies. So I sat in my foxhole
and watched the water babies splashing around the green-
dungaree-clad corpse. What an unlikely combination. The
war had turned the water babies into little ghouls that danced
around the dead instead of little elves dancing around a
peaceful bullfrog. A man had little to occupy his mind at
Shuri—just sit in muddy misery and fear, tremble through
the shellings, and let his imagination go where it would.

One of the very few humorous incidents I saw during those
terrible days before Shuri occurred toward the end of the awful stalemate. Two Marines from the other mortar squad were
dug in to the left of my gun pit. One morning at the first pale
light of dawn I heard a commotion in their foxhole. I could
hear a poncho being flung aside as someone began thrashing
around. There were grunts and swearing. I strained my eyes
through the steaming rain and brought the Tommy gun up to
my shoulder. From all indications, one or more Japanese had
slipped up on the weary occupants of the foxhole, and they
were locked in a life-and-death struggle. But I could do nothing but wait and alert other men around us.

The commotion grew louder, and I could barely make out
two dark figures struggling in the foxhole. I was utterly helpless to aid a buddy in distress, because I couldn't identify who
was Marine and who was Japanese. None of us dared leave
his own foxhole and approach the two. The enemy soldier
must have already knifed one of the Marines and was grap-
pling with the other, I thought.

The dark figures rose up. Standing toe to toe, they leaned
into each other and exchanged blows with their fists. Everyone's eyes were fixed on the struggling figures but could see
little in the semidarkness and pouring rain. The mumblings
and swearing became louder and understandable, and we
heard, "You dumb jerk; gimme that range card. It's mine." I
recognized the voice of a man who had come into Company
K before Okinawa.

"No it's not; it's mine. You betta gimme it. I don't take no crap from nobody." The latter was the familiar voice of Santos, a Peleliu veteran. We all started in surprise.

"Hey, you guys, what the hell's goin' on over there?" growled an NCO.

The two struggling figures recognized his voice and immediately stopped hitting each other.

"You two eightballs," the NCO said as he went over to them. "It woulda served ya right if we hada shot you both. We figured a Nip had got in your foxhole."

Each of the two battlers protested that the other was the cause of all the trouble. The light was good by then, and some of us went over to their foxhole to investigate.

"What's all the row about?" I asked.

"This, by God; nothin' but this!" snarled the NCO as he glared at the two sheepish occupants of the foxhole and handed me a range card.

I was puzzled why two Marines would squabble over a range card.* But when I looked at the card, I saw it was special and unique. Impressed on it in lipstick was the ruby red imprint of a woman's lips. The men had found the unique card in a canister while breaking out ammo for the guns the previous afternoon and had argued all night about who would keep it. Toward dawn they came to blows over it.

The NCO continued to chew them out, as I handed the card back to him and returned to my foxhole. We all got a good laugh out of the episode. I often wondered what that woman back in that ammunition factory in the States would have thought about the results of her efforts to add a little morale booster for us in a canister of mortar ammo.

During the last few days of May we received several small but vicious counterattacks from the Japanese soldiers who had been occupying the caves in the reverse slope of Half Moon's left-hand arm. One morning we got a message that a

---

*A five-by-seven-inch range card came in each canister of 60mm mortar ammunition. It contained printed columns of numbers denoting range, sight setting, and number of powder increments to be attached to each mortar shell for a given range. Thus the cards were as common as ammo canisters.

large number of enemy was massing behind the crescent. I was ordered to leave the OP and return to the gun pit in preparation for a big fire mission. I moved down the ridge and across the reeking, shell-pocked wasteland to the gun pits without mishap. Once there, we squared away the three 60mm mortars to fire on the reverse slope of the left crescent arm.

The firing pattern of the mortars was arranged to box in the Japanese and prevent their escape while our three guns shelled the area heavily in an attempt to wipe them out. Consequently, we had to fire rapid-fire, searching and traversing the target area. The ammo carriers were kept busy breaking out more HE shells, but I was so busy on my mortar I didn't have time to notice them. The tube (barrel) became intensely hot. We wrapped a dungaree jacket around the lower half of it, and one of the ammo carriers poured helmets full of water taken from a shell crater over the cloth to cool the steaming barrel, while we continued rapid-fire.*

We fired I don't know how many hundreds of shells before the order came to cease firing. My ears rang. I was exhausted, and had a roaring headache. Beside each of the three gun pits was a huge stack of empty HE canisters and ammo crates from the large number of shells we had fired. We were anxious to know the results of our firing. But our observers couldn't see the target area, because it was on the reverse slope of the ridge.

A few days later when our regiment went forward in the attack, we didn't move through the target area, so we still didn't

---

*I've read accounts of "mortars glowing red" when firing rapidly for long periods. They sound dramatic and impressive. But from my experience I'm skeptical that a mortar can be fired safely and accurately when its barrel is glowing red. My experience was that if a barrel got very hot from rapid fire—so hot that the surrounding air had insufficient cooling effect—it was dangerous to drop a round down the tube. The one time I did, the heat ignited the increments, then the propellant cartridge ignited before the shell slid all the way down the barrel. Consequently, the shell wobbled out of the barrel and fell short after having slid down only about half its length.

Thus, to avoid short rounds, we either had to wait for the air to cool our barrel, fire at a slower rate, or, as in this fire mission, which was an emergency, cool the barrel with water.

see the effects of the fire mission. But one Company K NCO who did see the area told us that he had counted more than two hundred enemy dead who apparently had been trapped and killed by our fire. I assume he was right, because after our barrage, the Japanese ceased activity along the ridge.

SHURI

The rain began to slacken, and rumors spread that we would attack soon. We also heard that the main enemy force had withdrawn from the Shuri line. But the Japanese had left a strong rear guard to fight to the death. So we could expect no signs of weakness. The Japanese had been spotted retreating from Shuri under cover of the bad weather. Our naval guns, artillery, heavy mortars, and even a few airplanes had thrown a terrific bombardment into them. But withdrawal or not, Shuri wasn't going to fall easily. We anticipated a hard fight once the weather cleared.

On a quiet day or two before the 5th Marines moved out for the big push against Shuri, several Marines from the graves registration section came into our area to collect the dead. Those dead already on stretchers presented no problem, but the corpses rotting in shell craters and in the mud were another matter.

We sat on our helmets and gloomily watched the graves registration people trying to do their macabre duty. They each were equipped with large rubber gloves and a long pole with a stiff flap attached to the end (like some huge spatula). They would lay a poncho next to a corpse, then place the poles under the body, and roll it over onto the poncho. It sometimes took several tries, and we winced when a corpse fell apart. The limbs or head had to be shoved onto the poncho like bits of garbage. We felt sympathy for the graves registration men. With the corpses being moved, the stench of rotting flesh became worse (if possible) than ever before.

Apparently the enemy had withdrawn guns and troops from Shuri to the extent that their shelling of our area had all but stopped. A miserable drizzling rain commenced again. Almost out on my feet with fatigue, I decided to take advantage of the quiet. I unfolded an unused stretcher, set it on some boards, lay down on my back, and covered my head and body with my poncho. It was the first time in two months— since leaving my canvas rack aboard ship on 1 April (D day)—that I had been able to lie down on anything but hard ground or mud. The canvas stretcher felt like a deluxe bed, and my poncho shielded all but my mud-caked boondockers and ankles from the rain. For the first time in about ten days I fell into a deep sleep.

How long I slept I don't know, but after a while I became aware of being lifted upward. At first I thought I was dreaming, but then I awoke fully and realized someone had picked up the stretcher. Throwing the poncho away from me, I sprang off the stretcher, spun around, and saw two clean, neatly shaven Marines looking at me in utter astonishment.

Several of my grimy buddies squatting on their muddy helmets nearby began to laugh. The two strangers were graves registration men. They had picked up the stretcher thinking I was just another poncho-covered corpse. It never occurred to them that, instead, I was just a weary Marine trying to catch a nap on a comfortable stretcher who had covered himself to keep off the rain. They grinned when they realized what had happened. I accused my buddies of telling the two men to pick up my stretcher, but they only laughed and asked why my nap had ended so abruptly. I was left with an eerie feeling from the incident, but my buddies enjoyed the joke thoroughly.

Dawn broke clearly without rain on 28 May, and we prepared to attack later in the morning. About 1015 we attacked southward against long-range mortar and machine-gun fire. We were elated that the opposition was so light and that the sun was shining. We actually advanced several hundred yards that day, quite an accomplishment in that sector.

Moving through the mud was still difficult, but we were all glad to get out of the stinking, half-flooded garbage pit around the Half Moon. That night we learned that we would continue the attack the next day by moving directly against the Shuri Ridge.

About midmorning on 29 May, 3/5 attacked the Shuri with

Company L in the lead and Companies K and I following closely. Earlier in the morning Company A, 1st Battalion, 5th Marines had attacked eastward into the rains of Shuri Castle and had raised the Confederate flag. When we learned that the flag of the Confederacy had been hoisted over the very heart and soul of Japanese resistance, all of us Southerners cheered loudly. The Yankees among us grumbled, and the Westerners didn't know what to do. Later we learned that the Stars and Stripes that had flown over Guadalcanal were raised over Shuri Castle, a fitting tribute to the men of the 1st Marine Division who had the honor of being first into the Japanese citadel.*

We all were filled with a sense of accomplishment that night as we dug in somewhere around Shuri Castle. We in the ranks were well aware of its strategic importance to the progress of the campaign.

Although the whole place was in ruins, we could still see that the area around Shuri Castle had been impressive and picturesque before its destruction by the incessant U.S. bombardment. Shuri Castle itself was a mess, and I couldn't tell much about its former appearance. It had been an ancient stone building surrounded by a moat and what appeared to have been terraces and gardens. As we picked our way through the rubble, I looked at the terraced stonework and shattered blackened tree stumps. I thought it must have been a pretty place once.

We dug in that night with the knowledge that even though we were at last in Shuri Castle, there were strongly entrenched Japanese still north of us in Wana Draw, east of us, and south of us. The lines were terribly confused to many of us in the ranks, and we assumed that the enemy could come at

*For the assault against Shuri Castle, 1/5 and 3/5 actually attacked eastward, turning approximately ninety degrees to the left of the southward-facing front. The 5th Marines thus crossed over into the zone of the 77th Infantry Division to reach Shuri Castle. The 77th Infantry Division was located north of Shuri, and a large number of Japanese were still entrenched between the army division and the 5th Marines as the latter moved eastward behind the Japanese who were blocking the 77th Division's advance.

us from almost any direction. But they remained quiet during the night, except for the usual raiders.

We attacked again the next day, and got shelled badly. I was totally confused as to where we were for several days and can't clarify it now in my mind even after careful study of the notes and references at my disposal.

At dusk on one of those last few days of May, we moved onto a muddy, slippery ridge and were told to dig in along the crest. One of the three 60mm mortar squads was to set up its gun down behind the ridge, but my squad and the remaining squad were ordered to dig in along the ridge crest and to function as riflemen during the night. The weather turned bad again, and it started raining.

Mac, our mortar section leader, was nowhere to be seen. But Duke, who had been our section leader on Peleliu and who was by then leading the battalion's 81mm mortar platoon, came up to take charge. He ordered an NCO to have us dig two-man foxholes five yards apart along the crest of the ridge. My buddy went off down the ridge to draw ammo and chow while I prepared to dig.

The ridge was about a hundred feet high, quite steep, and we were on a narrow crest. Several discarded Japanese packs, helmets, and other gear lay scattered along the crest. From the looks of the muddy soil, the place had been shelled heavily for a long time. The ridge was a putrid place. Our artillery must have killed Japanese there earlier, because the air was foul with the odor of rotting flesh. It was just like being back at Half Moon Hill. Off toward our front, to the south, I had only a dim view through the gathering gloom and curtain of rain of the muddy valley below.

The men digging in on both sides of me cursed the stench and the mud. I began moving the heavy, sticky clay mud with my entrenching shovel to shape out the extent of the foxhole before digging deeper. Each shovelful had to be knocked off the spade, because it stuck like glue. I was thoroughly exhausted and thought my strength wouldn't last from one sticky shovelful to the next.

Kneeling on the mud, I had dug the hole no more than six or eight inches deep when the odor of rotting flesh got worse.

There was nothing to do but continue to dig, so I closed my mouth and inhaled with short shallow breaths. Another spadeful of soil out of the hole released a mass of wriggling maggots that came welling up as though those beneath were pushing them out. I cursed, and told the NCO as he came by what a mess I was digging into.

"You heard him, he said put the holes five yards apart."

In disgust, I drove the spade into the soil, scooped out the insects, and threw them down the front of the ridge. The next stroke of the spade unearthed buttons and scraps of cloth from a Japanese army jacket buried in the mud—and another mass of maggots. I kept on doggedly. With the next thrust, metal hit the breastbone of a rotting Japanese corpse. I gazed down in horror and disbelief as the metal scraped a clean track through the mud along the dirty whitish bone and cartilage with ribs attached. The shovel skidded into the rotting abdomen with a squishing sound. The odor nearly overwhelmed me as I rocked back on my heels.

I began choking and gagging as I yelled in desperation, "I can't dig in here! There's a dead Nip here!"

The NCO came over, looked down at my problem and at me, and growled, "You heard him; he said put the holes five yards apart."

"How the hell can I dig a foxhole through a dead Nip?" I protested.

Just then Duke came along the ridge and said, "What's the matter, Sledgehammer?"

I pointed to the partially exhumed corpse. Duke immediately told the NCO to have me dig in a little to the side away from the rotting remains. I thanked Duke and glared at the NCO. How I managed not to vomit during that vile experience I don't know. Perhaps my senses and nerves had been so dulled by constant foulness for so long that nothing could evoke any other response but to cry out and move back.

I soon had a proper foxhole dug to one side of the site of my first attempt. (A few spades full of mud thrown back into that excavation did little to reduce the horrid odor.) My buddy returned, and we began to square away our gear for the coming light. There was some small-arms fire to our left, but all was quiet around us. Duke was down at the foot of the ridge behind us with a map in his hand. He called us to come down for a critique and a briefing on the next day's attack.

Glad to leave the stinking foxhole, I got up and carefully started down the slippery ridge. My buddy rose, took one step down the ridge, slipped, and fell. He slid on his belly all the way to the bottom, like a turtle sliding off a log. I reached the bottom to see him stand erect with his arms partially extended and look down at his chest and belt with a mixed expression of horror, revulsion, and disbelief. He was, of course, muddy from the slide. But that was the least of it. White, fat maggots tumbled and rolled off his cartridge belt, pockets, and folds of his dungaree jacket and trousers. I picked up a stick and handed him another. Together we scraped the vile insect larvae off his reeking dungarees.

That Marine was a Gloucester veteran with whom I had often shared a hole on Peleliu and Okinawa. He was as tough and as hard as any man I ever knew. But that slide was almost too much for him. I thought he was going to scream or crack up. Having to wallow in war's putrefaction was almost more than the toughest of us could bear. He shook himself like a wet dog, however, cursed, and threw down the stick when we got him scraped free of maggots.

Duke's group of eight to ten Marines showed their sympathy for my buddy and their appreciation of the vileness of his accident. Muddy, bearded, and red-eyed with fatigue, Duke called our attention to the map, and that helped us focus on other subjects. He showed us where we were and told us some of the plans for the next day's attack, which was supposed to break completely through the Shuri line.

I was so revolted and sickened by what had just happened and so weary that I didn't remember much of what he told us. It is a pity in retrospect, because that briefing was the only time in my combat experience that an officer ever showed a group of privates a map of the battlefield and explained recent events and future attack plans. Usually an NCO simply relayed the word to us. We then followed orders as they were given, rarely knowing what was going on.

We never knew why Duke held the little critique that night, whether he was ordered to do so or not. I suspect he did it on his own. He realized we wanted to know and understand our role in the overall plan.

It was a historic time, and we were participating in events of key importance to the American effort on Okinawa. All eyes were on Shuri. My buddies and I were key participants at a critical juncture in one of the epic land battles of World War II, and we were having our tiny role in that battle explained. Duke asked if there were any questions. A few were asked, which he answered clearly. I maintained my condition of near stupefaction through it all. Then we slowly climbed back up the filthy ridge after he dismissed us.

That night the rain came down in torrents. It was without exaggeration the most terrific deluge I've ever seen. The wind blew fiercely, slashing the rain horizontally across the crest of the ridge and stinging our faces and hands. The star shells burst but gave little illumination because they were snatched away immediately by the unseen hand of the gale. Visibility was limited to about six feet. We couldn't see our buddies in their foxholes on either side of us. What a terrible night to grapple with Japanese infiltrators or a counterattack, I thought to myself all night long.

Considerable machine-gun fire, bursts of rifle fire, and grenade explosions erupted throughout the night a short way down the line to our left. But all was mercifully quiet, albeit tense, in our immediate area. Next morning I realized why we weren't molested by the enemy as the men to our left had been. For a considerable distance to our right and left, the ridge fell away almost perpendicularly to the valley below. The Japanese simply couldn't crawl up the slick surface.

In the latter days of May while the Japanese held on to the center of their line around Shuri, the U.S. Army divisions to the east and the 6th Marine Division to the west (around Naha) finally made progress to the south. Their combined movements threatened to envelop the main Japanese defense forces in the center. Thus the enemy had to withdraw. By dawn on 30 May, most of the Japanese Thirty-second Army had departed the Shuri line, leaving only rear guards to cover their retreat.

In the sixty-one days of fighting on Okinawa after D day, an estimated 62,548 Japanese soldiers had lost their lives and 465 had been captured. American dead numbered 5,309; 23,909 had been wounded; and 346 were missing in action. It wasn't over yet.

CHAPTER FOURTEEN

Beyond Shuri

We pushed past Shuri over some muddy hills in the army's zone of action and came across a group of about twenty Japanese prisoners. Each man was stripped except for a G-string. They stood barefooted in the mud alongside a trail winding along the slope of a barren hill. Several dirty and battle-weary army infantrymen guarded them. The captured enemy had been ordered by an interpreter (army lieutenant) to stand off the trail so Company K's column could pass.

We slipped and slid wearily toward the sound of firing up ahead. A grizzled rifleman in front of me and I had been cursing the mud and exchanging remarks about how glad we were to be past Shuri. Suddenly a Japanese prisoner stepped in front of my friend, blocking his way.

"Get outa the way, you crazy bastard," growled the Marine.

The soldier folded his arms calmly, raised his chin, and displayed a picture of arrogance. My buddy and I heated up fast. He pushed the Japanese backward and sent him sprawling into the mud. The enemy soldier sprang up quickly and assumed his former position.

"What's that crazy bastard doin'?" I yelled as I dropped my mortar ammo bag and reached for my .45 pistol.

My buddy unslung his rifle, grasped it by the stock with his left hand and by the pistol grip with his right hand. He planted his muddy feet firmly on the trail, flexed his knees, and growled, "Git outa my way, you bastard."

Other Marines behind us had halted when we did. Seeing what was happening, they started cursing the Japanese.

"What's the hold up? Move out," someone behind us yelled.

The army first lieutenant (he was actually wearing his silver bars on his collars), clean-shaven and spotless except for muddy combat boots, came along the column to ascertain the problem. Seeing my buddy's stance and realizing he might soon have one less prisoner, he said, "You can't mistreat these men. They are prisoners of war. According to the Geneva Code, POWs must be treated humanely." He looked desperate; the whole column of muddy, raggedy-ass Marines glared at and cursed the prisoners strung out alongside us on the trail.

"Screw the Geneva Code. If that slant-eyed sonofabitch don't move outa my way, I'll give him a vertical butt stroke in his big mouth and knock out every one of them goddamn buck teeth." My buddy slowly moved his rifle back and forth, and the enemy soldier's arrogant expression began to fade. The army lieutenant knew he had a bad problem on his hands, and he obviously didn't know how to solve it. (It was commonly said that Marines rarely took prisoners.) A couple of GI riflemen of the prisoner-guard detail stood by relaxed and grinned their endorsement of our sentiments. They obviously had been in the "meat grinder" long enough to have no more love for the Japanese than we did. The lieutenant obviously wasn't one of their officers but from some rear-echelon outfit.

Just then, one of our officers hurried up from the rear of the column. The army lieutenant was mighty relieved to see him and explained the situation. Our officers went over and quietly told my buddy to get back into ranks. He then told the army language officer that if he didn't get his prisoners out of the way, he (our officer) couldn't guarantee that some of them wouldn't get hurt. The army officer spoke kindly in Japanese to the POWs, and they all stepped farther back away from the trail, giving us plenty of room. The language officer acted and sounded more like an elementary school teacher giving little children directions than an officer giving orders to a bunch of tough Japanese soldiers.

During the whole episode, most of the Japanese never appeared afraid, merely chagrined or ashamed because they had acted disgracefully by surrendering. Perhaps the one who acted so arrogantly thought that one last act of defiance would soothe his conscience somewhat. Most Americans at the time couldn't comprehend the Japanese determination to win or fight to the death. To the Japanese, surrender was the ultimate disgrace.

We didn't feel that POWs should be mistreated or handled roughly, but neither did we feel that one should be allowed to block our path and get away with the act. My view that some language officers were often overly solicitous about the comfort of prisoners and unduly courteous to them was shared by other infantrymen in the "meat grinder." We were too familiar with the sight of helpless wounded Americans lying flat on their backs on stretchers getting shot by Japanese snipers while we struggled to evacuate them.

After the breakthrough, we moved rapidly through areas where the opposition was light or absent. Our supply lines, communications, and casualty evacuation had a difficult time keeping up with us because the mud was still such a serious problem. Although the rain fell less frequently, it hadn't ceased.

As our column moved along the base of a road embankment on one occasion, a Marine walking along the road above us carrying a field telephone and a small roll of wire shouted down and asked for the identity of our unit. His buddy followed him along the road at a little distance carrying a roll of wire. These men were clean-shaven and neat. They looked suspiciously like rear-echelon people to us.

"Hey, what outfit you guys in?" shouted the first man up on the road.

"K/3/5," I yelled.

His buddy behind him asked him, "What outfit did he say?"

"K/3/5, whatever the hell that means."

The effect on us was instant and dramatic. Men who had paid little attention to what seemed a routine inquiry looked angrily up at the man. I flushed with anger. My unit and I had been insulted. The mortarman next to me threw down his ammo bag and started up the embankment. "I'll show you what the hell it means, you rear-echelon sonofabitch! I'm gonna whip your ass."

I wasn't given to brawling. The Japanese provided me with all the excitement and fighting I wanted. But I lost my head completely. I threw down my ammo bag and started up the embankment. Other mortarmen started up, too.

"What's the dope?" I heard a man back along the column shout.

"That rear-echelon bastard up there cussed K Company," someone answered.

Immediately other Company K men started up the bank. The two men up on the road looked utterly bewildered as they saw bearded, muddy Marine infantrymen cursing, grounding their weapons, dropping their loads, and surging angrily up the embankment. One of our officers and a couple of NCOs saw what had happened and rushed up ahead of us.

The officer turned and yelled, "You people get back in ranks on the double! Move! Move!"

We stopped, each of us knowing that to disobey orders invited severe disciplinary action. The two men on the road had become frightened, and we saw them hustling along the road to the rear. They looked back anxiously several times to see whether they were being followed. We must have been an angry, menacing-looking bunch from their viewpoint. I suspect those two Marines knew the real meaning and essence of esprit de corps after that experience.

We picked up our weapons and gear and moved out again below the road only to halt shortly. The officers consulted their maps, held a critique, and decided that place was as good as any for the company to leave the muddy low ground, go up the bank, and take advantage of the coral-surfaced road (probably the east–west Naha–Yonabaru highway, a segment of which our regiment captured about then). We moved up onto the road, took off our gear, and settled onto the side of a large ridge with a wide grass- and tree-covered crest. Okinawan burial vaults and emplacements lay all along the slope of the ridge, but the Japanese hadn't left many men to defend it. However, they gave a good account of themselves before being wiped out.

Toward dusk, I was examining a Japanese 75mm dual-purpose gun which they had abandoned in perfect condition.

Several of us had a lot of fun turning its cranks and wheels, which we didn't understand but which moved the big barrel up and down, right and left. Our play was interrupted by the shriek of several enemy artillery shells that exploded up on the ridge crest near a group of Company K men.

"Corpsman!"

We raced up onto the ridge, hoping no more shells came in but wondering who was hit and knowing we might be needed to help with the casualties. We could see the smoke from the shells and the Marines scurrying around to aid the casualties and to disperse.

In the gathering twilight, I ran up to a little knot of Marines bending over a casualty. To my dismay, the wounded Marine was good-natured, cigar-chewing Joe Lambert, a demolitions expert I had known so long. I knelt beside him and was distressed to see that he had multiple wounds from shell fragments in his body.

The men had eased a poncho under Lambert and were preparing to carry him down the ridge for evacuation. I wished him luck, made the usual jokes about not being too romantic with the nurses on the hospital ship, and asked him to drink a beer and think of me when he got Stateside—the usual comments one made to a badly wounded friend who had little chance.

Lambert looked up at me in the gathering darkness. With the stump of an unlighted cigar clenched in his teeth, he said with irony in his voice, "Sledgehammer, ain't this a helluva' thing—a man been in the company as long as me, and hafta get carried out on a poncho?"

I made some feeble attempts to comfort him. I knew he was going to die, and I wanted to cry.

"Wish I could light that cigar for you, Cobber, but the smokin' lamp is out."

"That's OK, Sledgehammer."

"One of those good-lookin' nurses'll light it for you," I said as they picked up the poncho and started off down the slope of the ridge with him.

I stood up and looked at a nearby group of beautiful pines silhouetted against the darkening sky. The wind blew their fresh scent into my face, and I thought how much like Southern pine it smelled. But poor, brave Lambert would never get back home again. I was thankful that when his luck finally ran out and he was fatally wounded, it happened on a high, clear, grassy ridge crest near a clump of fragrant pines and not back in the stinking muck of the quagmire around Shuri.

Corporal Lambert was a great favorite in Company K. Any of us who had fought on Peleliu's Bloody Nose Ridge had seen him numerous times standing above some Japanese cave, swinging a satchel charge of explosives on a rope until he got it just right, then releasing the rope and yelling, "Fire in the hole"—just before the muffled explosion. He would grin, then climb down and rejoin us wringing wet with sweat from his face to his boondockers. He would relight his cigar (which served in turn as a lighter for his satchel-charge fuses) and discuss the damage done to the cave. He was big, round-faced, and jovial. Rumor said that he had been scheduled to return to the States after Peleliu but refused because he wanted to remain with Company K. Not long after he was carried out, we learned that Lambert had died. It's one of the war's many personal tragedies that he was killed after having served so long and so bravely.

Next day we moved out into a wide valley below the ridge. We saw Japanese equipment and dead on several roads destroyed by the big U.S. bombardment the last week of May when the enemy had evacuated Shuri. We also encountered numerous Japanese supply dumps. Most of the food and rations didn't suit our tastes. The Japanese iron rations, which I had seen first in gauze sacs on Peleliu, tasted like dog biscuits. But I found several cans of preserved Japanese deep-sea scallops which were delicious. Several cans of these stored in my pack were a welcome change from C and K rations.

We made one rapid advance across a wide grassy valley only to be halted by snipers in some rocks on the crest of the opposite ridge. We set up the guns, registered in on the areas where snipers were, and began firing. Stretcher teams came and went up and down the slope of the open ridge. Four of us were ordered off for a stretcher team to pick up a corpsman who had been hit by sniper fire.

We went up the gently sloping, grass-covered ridge and came to the "doc." Another stretcher team passed us carrying the Marine whom the doc had been tending when he himself was wounded. The Marine had been shot by a sniper, and the corpsman had come to administer medical aid. While he was working over the wounded Marine, a Japanese shot him in the thigh. Although wounded painfully, he continued to work on his patient. Then the sniper had shot Doc in the other thigh. As we arrived, he cautioned us to be careful or we would get hit, too.

We quickly got him on a stretcher and took off as fast as possible. Doc was a fairly tall, well-built man, larger than any of us. We carried him a long distance: down the ridge and across the wide valley to a steep-sided ditch spanned by a footbridge. An ambulance jeep was waiting on the other side of the footbridge. We were all nearly exhausted from the exertions and lack of sleep of the past two weeks, and it was quite a struggle. Twice wounded though he was, he kept insisting we stop and rest for a while. But we four felt obligated to get him to the jeep and evacuated as soon as possible.

Finally, we agreed to stop for a breather. Setting the stretcher down, we fell out flat on the grass, panting for breath. Doc talked to us calmly, admonishing us to take it easy and not to overexert ourselves. I felt ashamed. That unselfish, dedicated corpsman was more concerned because we were so tired from carrying him out than he was with his own wounds.

We picked up the stretcher and got to the ditch. There on the bank I saw a bush with several small red tomatoes. I managed to grab three or four tomatoes and put them on the stretcher as we got Doc across the narrow footbridge. I told him to eat them, that they'd make him feel better. He thanked me, but said we should eat them, because he would get good chow in the hospital.

Who should walk around the jeep just as we were loading our corpsman but Doc Arrogant, notorious for painful shots

on Pavuvu. "I'll take those," he said, reaching for the tomatoes.

"The hell you say!" I exclaimed, snatching them out of his
hand.

One of my buddies went up to him and said, "You bastard,
you'd take candy from a baby, wouldn't ya?"

Arrogant looked surly, turned around, and went back
around the jeep. Our Doc handed me the tomatoes and insisted we eat them. We said we would and wished him luck as
the jeep bumped off to the rear.

We recrossed the footbridge and fell exhausted onto the
grass. We had a smoke, divided up the juicy little tomatoes,
cussed Doc Arrogant, and voiced our admiration for all other
corpsmen.

On 4 June we moved rapidly southward through open
country in a torrential rain. Although the opposition was sporadic, we still had to check out all houses, huts, and former
Japanese emplacements. While searching a small hut, I came
across an old Okinawan woman seated on the floor just inside
the doorway. Taking no chances, I held my Thompson ready
and motioned to her to get up and come out. She remained on
the floor but bowed her old gray head and held her gnarled
hands toward me, palms down, to show the tattoos on the
backs of her hands indicating she was Okinawan.

"No Nippon," she said slowly, shaking her head as she
looked up at me with a weary expression that bespoke of
much physical pain. She then opened her ragged blue kimono
and pointed to a wound in the lower left side of her abdomen.
It was an old wound, probably caused by shell or bomb fragments. It was an awful sight. A large area around the scabbed-
over gash was discolored and terribly infected with gangrene.
I gasped in dismay. I guessed that such a severe infection in
the abdominal region was surely fatal.

The old woman closed her kimono. She reached up gently,
took the muzzle of my Tommy, and slowly moved it so as to
direct it between her eyes. She then released the weapon's
barrel and motioned vigorously for me to pull the trigger. Oh
no, I thought, this old soul is in such agony she actually wants
me to put her out of her misery. I lifted my Tommy, slung it

over my shoulder, shook my head, and said "no" to her. Then I stepped back and yelled for a corpsman.

"What's up, Sledgehammer?"

"There's an old gook woman in there that's been hit in the side real bad."

"I'll see what I can do for her," he said as we met about fifty yards from the hut.

At that moment, a shot rang out from the hut. I spun around. The corpsman and I went down into a crouching position.

"That was an M1," I said.

"Sure was. What the hell?" he said.

Just then a Marine emerged nonchalantly from the hut, checking the safety on his rifle. I knew the man well. He was attached at that time to company headquarters. I called to him by name and said, "Was there a Nip in that hut? I just checked it out."

"No," he said as we approached him, "just an old gook woman who wanted me to put her out of her misery; so I obliged her!"

The doc and I stared at each other, and then at the Marine. That quiet, neat, mild-mannered young man just wasn't the type to kill a civilian in cold blood.

When I saw the crumpled form under the faded blue kimono in the hut door, I blew up. "You dumb bastard! She tried to get me to shoot her, and I called Doc to come help her."

The executioner looked at me with a puzzled expression.

"You sonofabitch," I yelled. "If you want to shoot at somebody so damn bad, why don't you trade places with a BAR-man or a machine gunner and get outa that damn CP and shoot at Nips? They shoot back!"

He stammered apologies, and Doc cursed him.

I said, "We're supposed to kill Nips, not *old women*!"

The executioner's face flushed. An NCO came up and asked what happened. Doc and I told him. The NCO glared and said, "You dirty bastard."

Somebody yelled, "Let's go Sledgehammer, we're movin' out."

"You guys shove off, I'll take care of this," said the NCO to Doc and me. We ran off to catch up with the mortar section while the NCO continued to chew out the executioner. I never knew whether or not he was disciplined for his cold-blooded act.

On the right of the 1st Marine Division, the 7th Marines extended its lines to the west coast and sealed off the Oroku Peninsula. Then the 6th Marine Division came in and fought a ten-day battle of attrition to annihilate the Japanese defenders there. The division killed nearly 5,000 Japanese, taking only 200 prisoners, at a loss of 1,608 Marines killed and wounded.

On 4 June, the 1st Marines relieved the 5th Marines as the assault regiment for the 1st Marine Division's drive to the south. The 5th Marines went into reserve for III Marine Amphibious Force, a stance that still involved much danger for its weary Marines because of a mission to aggressively patrol and mop up behind the forward elements.

We dug in as a secondary line along a low ridge with some ruins of Okinawan houses behind us and a broad open valley stretching south to our front as far as we could see. The rain ended the night of 5–6 June. I'll never forget the sensation of profound physical relief when I removed my soaked, muddy boondockers for the first time in approximately two weeks. As I pulled off my slimy, stinking socks, bits and shreds of dead flesh sloughed off the soles of my feet. A buddy, Myron Tesreau, commented on the overpowering odor, only to discover that his feet were just as bad. My socks, a pair of khaki-colored, woolen army socks (thicker and heavier than our white Marine Corps issue) were so slimy and putrid I couldn't bear to wash them in my helmet. I had traded a candy bar to a soldier for them back in April. They were my prized possession because of their comfort when wet. With regret, I threw my prize socks aside and spaded dirt over them as though covering up a foul corpse.

It was great to wash my feet, holding them up on an ammo box to let the sun shine on them while I wiggled my toes.

Everybody got his feet clean and dry as soon as possible. Mine were extremely sore and red over the entire soles, almost to the point of bleeding. All of the normal friction ridges of the skin had sloughed off, and the soles were furrowed with deep, reddish grooves. But after drying them in the sun and putting on dry socks and boondockers, they soon felt better. Months passed, however, before the soles appeared normal again.

We had our mortars set up in pits at the base of the low ridge along which the Company K line was dug in. George Sarrett and I had a regular two-man foxhole on the ridge next to a road cut that came through at right angles to the ridge. During the nights we were there, we mortarmen took turns on the guns and fired flares periodically over our company area.

Between patrols and nightly vigils we began to get rested and dried out. We had air drops of supplies, food, water, and ammo. During the day we could build campfires and heat rations, which all enjoyed. We had ten-in-one rations there, always a welcome change from C and K rations. The method of air drop used to supply water had not been perfected then. The water was contained in long plastic bags, four of which were stored in a metal cylinder attached to the parachute. Quite often the impact of the cylinder hitting the deck caused one or more of the bags to break, and some or all of the water in it was lost.

We always had a lot of fun when supplies were air-dropped to us, even though it was hard work running through the mud collecting up the ammo, rations, and other supplies attached to the brightly colored chutes. Most of the time Marine torpedo bombers made the drops while flying low over us. Their accuracy was remarkable. During the periods when deep mud covered much of the battlefield we always welcomed a clear day, not only because we hated the rain, but because it meant our planes could be up and supply us with air drops. Otherwise supplies had to be manhandled miles through the mud.

While we were in reserve, another mortarman and I were sent on a routine mission to carry a message to the west coast regarding supplies. It was the kind of ordinary thing every infantryman was called on to do many times. Typically, it was good duty, because we were temporarily out from under the eagle eye of the company gunny sergeant, could move at our own pace, and do a little sightseeing along the way through areas already fought over and secured. It wasn't considered hazardous.

Our instructions were straightforward. Our company gunny, Hank Boyes, told us to keep on the main east–west road all the way to the beach and back. He told us who to contact and what to ask for. Then he warned us against screwing around souvenir hunting and cautioned us about the possibility of bypassed enemy.

We started off in high spirits for what we thought would be an interesting jaunt into the area south of the Oroku Peninsula. We had gotten cleaned up by then. Our dungarees had been washed, and our leggings and boondockers were dry and scraped clean of mud. We carried the usual two canteens of water. We also had ration chocolate bars because we would be gone several hours and could eat those on the move. My buddy was armed with a carbine. I carried the Tommy and my .45 pistol. The weather had dried out, and it was an ideal day for a little harmless diversion from the patrols we had been making.

After we moved out of our battalion area and onto the road, we saw almost no one. As we walked along the silent road, the only sounds in our immediate surroundings were our own voices, the crunching of our boondockers on the road, the muffled sloshing of the water in our canteens, and the occasional thump of our weapons' stocks against our canteens or kabar scabbards. We moved in that silent world that characterized the backwash of battle.

The area was replete with the flotsam of war. The storm front had passed, but its wreckage was left behind. Our experienced eyes read the silent signs and reconstructed the drama and pathos of various life-and-death struggles that had occurred. We encountered numerous enemy corpses, which we always passed on the windward side. We saw no Marine dead. But a bloody dungaree jacket here, a torn boondocker there, a helmet with the camouflage cloth cover and steel beneath ripped by bullets, discarded plasma bottles, and bloody battle dressings gave mute testimony of the fate of their former owners.

We passed through an embankment for a railroad track and entered the outskirts of a town. All buildings were badly damaged, but some were still standing. We stopped briefly to explore a quaint little store. Displayed in its window were various cosmetics. In the street in front of the store lay a corpse clad in a blue kimono. Someone had placed a broken door over the pathetic body. We speculated he had been the proprietor of the little shop. We passed a burned-out bus station with the ticket booth still standing in front. To our right and distant the battle rumbled and rattled as the 6th Marine Division fought the enemy on the Oroku Peninsula.

Without incident we continued through the ruins toward the beach when an amtrac came rattling toward us. The driver was the first living soul we had seen. We hailed him, and it turned out he was expecting us at the beach but had started along the road hoping to locate us. After receiving the information about our unit, he spun his amtrac around and headed back toward the beach. With our mission completed, my buddy and I started back along the road through the ruins.

We passed the little cosmetic shop and the dead Okinawan covered by the door and approached the bus station on our left. A gentle breeze was blowing. Only the clanking of a piece of loose tin on the ruined bus station roof broke the silence. If I blotted out the distant rumble of battle, our surroundings reminded me of walking past some deserted farm building on a peaceful spring afternoon back home. It seemed like an interesting place to take ten, explore the bus station, and eat our ration bars. We had saved time by meeting the amtrac, so we could stop for a while.

The harsh snapping and cracking of a long burst of Japanese machine-gun bullets zipping chest high in front of us sent my buddy and me scrambling for cover. We dove behind the concrete ticket booth and lay on the rubble-strewn concrete, breathing hard.

"God, that was close, Sledgehammer!"

"Too damned close!"

The enemy gunner had been zeroed in perfectly on his elevation, but he had led us too much. The bullets ricocheted and whined around inside the burned-out bus station. We heard the tinkle of glass as the slugs broke windows among the burned-out buses.

"Where the hell is that bastard?" asked my buddy.

"I don't know, but he's probably a couple of hundred yards away from the sound of the gun."

We lay motionless for a moment, the silence interrupted only by the peaceful, lazy clanking of the tin in the breeze. Cautiously I peered out from behind the base of the ticket booth. Another burst of slugs narrowly missed my head and went clattering through the building after striking the concrete alongside us.

"That bastard's zeroed in on us for sure," groaned my buddy.

The ticket booth in front of the building was surrounded by an open expanse of concrete in all directions. The gunner had us pinned down tightly. My buddy peeped around his side of the narrow booth and got the same reception as I had. The enemy machine gunner then fired a burst across the top of the concrete portion of the booth, shattering what was left of the windows in the upper part of the booth. We were sure that the Nambu gunner was up on the south side of the railroad embankment.

"Maybe we can get back among them buses and out of sight and then slip out of the rear of the building," my buddy said. He moved slightly to one side to look behind us, but another burst of fire proved his plan faulty.

"I guess we'll hafta wait it out till dark and then slip out of here," I said.

"Guess you're right. We sure as hell ain't gonna get outa here during the daylight without gettin' hit. He's got us pinned down tight. Sledgehammer, after all the crap we've been through, damned if we ain't between a rock and the hard place. Goddamit to hell!"

The minutes grew into lonely hours as time dragged by. We kept a sharp lookout in all directions in case other Japanese might slip in behind us while we were occupied by the machine gun.

Toward late afternoon we heard a burst of M1 rifle fire over in the direction where the enemy gunner was located. After a few minutes we peeped out. To our delight we saw a group of four or five Company K Marines striding along the road from the direction of the road cut.

"Look out for that Nambu!" we yelled, pointing back toward where the fire had been coming from.

A grinning Marine held up the machine gun and yelled, "Rack 'em up. You guys OK? The gunny figured you'd run into trouble when you didn't come back and sent us out to look for you."

By mid-June familiar faces were scarce in Company K and in all the infantry units of the 1st Marine Division. On 1 June the company lost thirty-six men to enemy action. Ten days later, twenty-two men left with immersion foot and other severe illnesses. Despite midmonth replacements, Company K moved toward its final major fight with about one hundred men and two or three officers—only half of whom had landed at Hagushi two and a half months earlier.

CARNAGE ON KUNISHI RIDGE

Toward the middle of June we began to hear disturbing rumors about a place south of us called Kunishi Ridge. Rumors circulated that our division's other infantry regiments, the 7th Marines and later the 1st Marines, were involved in bitter fighting there and would need our help. Our hopes began to fade that the 5th Marines wouldn't be committed to the front lines again.

We continued our patrols. I enjoyed my canned Japanese scallops and hoped there was no such place as Kunishi Ridge. But, the inevitable day came with the order, "Square away your gear; we're movin' out again."

The weather turned dry and warm as we moved south. The farther we proceeded, the louder the sound of firing became: the bumping of artillery, the thudding of mortars, the inces-

sant rattle of machine guns, the popping of rifles. It was a familiar combination of noise that engendered the old feelings
of dread about one's own chances as well as the horrible images of the wounded, the shocked, and the dead—the inevitable harvest.

*Following the retreat from Shuri, the Japanese defenders
of Okinawa withdrew into their final defensive lines along a
string of ridges near the southern end of the island. The western anchor was Kunishi Ridge. In the middle was Yuza-Dake.
Farther east was Yaeju-Dake.**

*Kunishi Ridge was about 1,500 yards long, a sheer coral
escarpment. The Japanese dug into caves and emplacements
on its forward and reverse slopes. The northern frontal approaches to Kunishi lay wide open: flat grasslands and rice
paddies across which the Japanese had perfect fields of fire.*

*On 12 June the 7th Marines made a predawn attack and
captured a portion of Kunishi. The Marines were on the
ridge, but the enemy was in it. For four days, the Marines of
the 7th Regiment were isolated atop the ridge. Air drops and
tanks supplied them, and tanks removed their dead and
wounded.*

*On 14 June the 1st Marines attacked portions of Kunishi
and suffered heavy losses for their efforts. On the same day,
the 1st Battalion—led by Lt. Col. Austin Shofner (former CO
of 3/5 on Peleliu)—attacked and captured Yuza-Dake but suffered terrible casualties from the Japanese defenders there
and from intense fire sent over from Yaeju-Dake.*

Into the hellish confusion we went on 14 June with the
words still ringing in our ears, "The 5th Marines may not be
committed again." We plodded along the sides of a dusty
road, next to tanks and amtracs moving forward and a steady
stream of ambulance jeeps returning loaded with the youthful human wreckage of the battle for Kunishi Ridge.

That afternoon our company deployed along a row of trees
and bushes on the south side of the road. We saw and heard

*Dake means "hill" in Japanese.

heavy firing on Kunishi Ridge across the open ground ahead. My mortar section dug in near the road with our guns adjusted to fire flares over a picturesque bridge that remained intact over a high stream bank.

A couple of us went to look at the bridge before dark. We walked down to the stream on a trail leading from the road. The water was crystal clear and made a peaceful gurgling sound over a clean pebbly bottom. Ferns grew from the overhanging mossy banks and between rocks on both sides. I had the urge to look for salamanders and crayfish. It was a beautiful place, cool and peaceful, so out of context with the screaming hell close above it.

The next morning we relieved 1/1 on Yuza-Dake. As we moved up along a road, we passed a small tree with all the limbs blasted off. So many communication wires hung from it at all angles that it looked like a big inverted mop. A ricocheting bullet whined between me and the man in front of me. It raised a little dust cloud as it smashed into a pile of dry brush by the roadside. Back into the meat grinder again, I thought, as we moved up toward the sound of heavy firing.

Yuza-Dake looked terrible to me. It resembled one of the hellish coral ridges on Peleliu. We could see Kunishi Ridge on our right and the Yaeju-Dake escarpment on our left. Army tanks were moving against the latter while machine guns and 75mm cannons hammered away.

For the first time in combat I heard the wailing of sirens. We were told that the army had put sirens on their tanks for the psychological effect it might have on the Japanese. To me the sirens just made the whole bloody struggle more bizarre and unnerving. The Japanese rarely surrendered in the face of flamethrowers, artillery, bombs, or anything else, so I didn't understand how harmless sirens would bother them. We got mighty tired of hearing them wailing against the constant rattle of small arms and the crash of shell fire.

While we were on Yuza-Dake under sporadic enemy fire, 2/5 joined the 7th Marines in the bitter fighting to capture the rest of Kunishi Ridge. The Japanese emplacements and caves received terrific bombardment by mortars, artillery, heavy naval gunfire, and air strikes consisting of twenty-five to thirty planes. It reminded me more and more of Bloody Nose Ridge on Peleliu.

The 2d Battalion, 5th Marines gained some ground on Kunishi but needed help. Company K was attached to 2/5 and arrived just in time to help that battalion fight off a company-sized night counterattack on 17 June. Later that night we heard that our company would attack the next morning to seize the remainder of Kunishi Ridge in the 5th Marines' zone of action. Once again we would enter the abyss of close combat.

We learned that we would move out well before daylight and deploy for the attack, because we had to move across a wide-open area to get to the ridge. An officer came along giving us what sounded like a pep talk about how the 5th Marines could finish the job on Kunishi Ridge. (We all knew that the 1st Marines and the 7th Marines had already been terribly shot up taking most of the ridge.)

Moving in the darkness was something the old salts of Gloucester and Peleliu didn't like at all. We were stubborn in our belief that nobody but the Japanese, or damned fools, moved around at night. The new replacements who had come into the company a few days before seemed so pitifully confused they didn't know the difference. But moving up under cover of darkness was the only sane way to approach Kunishi Ridge. The 1st Marines and the 7th Marines had already found it necessary to move that way to get across the open ground without being slaughtered.

We moved slowly and cautiously across dry rice paddies and cane fields. Up ahead we saw shells exploding on and around the ridge as our artillery swished overhead. We heard the familiar popping of rifles, rattle of machine guns, and banging of grenades. Enemy shells also exploded on the ridge. We all knew that this was probably the last big fight before the Japanese were wiped out and the campaign ended. While I plodded along through the darkness, my heart pounding, my throat dry and almost too tight to swallow, near-panic seized me. Having made it that far in the war, I knew my luck would run out. I began to sweat and pray that when I got hit it wouldn't result in death or maiming. I wanted to turn and run away.

We came closer to the ridge silhouetted against the skyline. Its crest looked so much like Bloody Nose that my knees nearly buckled. I felt as though I were on Peleliu and had it all to go through over again.

The riflemen moved up onto the ridge. We mortarmen were positioned to watch out for Japanese infiltrating from the left rear. We didn't set up our weapons: the fighting was so close-in with the enemy on the reverse slope and in the ridge that we couldn't fire high explosives.

Our 105mm artillery was firing over Kunishi Ridge while we moved into position in the dark. To our dismay, a shell exploded short in our company's line. The company CP alerted the artillery observers that we had received short rounds. Another 105 went off with a terrible flash and explosion.

"Corpsman!" someone yelled.

"Goddamit, we're getting casualties from short rounds!" an officer yelled into his walkie-talkie.

"What's the word on those short rounds?" the company executive officer asked.

"Says they'll check it out."

Our artillery was firing across the ridge into and around the town of Kunishi to prevent the enemy from moving more troops onto the ridge. But each time they shot, it seemed that one gun fired its shells in a traversing pattern right along the ridge in Company K's lines. It was enough to drive anyone into a state of desperation.

The Japanese were throwing grenades all along the line, and there was some rifle and machine-gun fire. On the right we began to hear American grenades exploding well within our lines.

"Hey, you guys; Nips musta gotten hold of a box of our grenades. Listen to that, wouldja?"

"Yeah, them bastards'll use anything they can get their hands on."

During the next flurry of grenades, we heard no more U.S. models explode within our area. Then the word came along in the dark to be sure all the new replacements knew exactly how to use grenades properly. One of our new men had been discovered removing each grenade canister from a box of grenades, pulling the sealing tape from the canister, and then throwing the unopened canister at the enemy. The Japanese opened each canister, took out the grenade, pulled the pin, and threw the deadly "pineapple" back at us. The veterans around me were amazed to find out what had happened. The incident, however, was just one of many examples of the poor state of combat readiness of the latest group of new replacements.

With daylight I got a good look at our surroundings. Only then could I appreciate fully what a desperate, bitter battle the fight for Kunishi Ridge had been—and was continuing to be. The ridge was coral rock, painfully similar to Peleliu's ridges. But Kunishi was not so high nor were the coral formations so jagged and angular as those on Peleliu. Our immediate area was littered with the usual debris of battle including about thirty poncho-covered dead Marines on stretchers.

Some of our riflemen moved eastward along the ridge, while others moved up the slopes. We still didn't set up our mortars: it was strictly a riflemen's fight. We mortarmen stood by to act as stretcher bearers or riflemen.

Snipers were all over the ridge and almost impossible to locate. Men began getting shot one right after another, and the stretcher teams kept on the run. We brought the casualties down to the base of the ridge, to a point where tanks could back in out of the view of snipers on the ridge crest. We tied the wounded onto the stretchers and then tied the stretchers onto the rear deck of the tanks. Walking wounded went inside. Then the tanks took off in a cloud of dust along a coral road to the aid station. As many men as possible fired along the ridge to pin down the snipers, so they couldn't shoot the wounded on the tanks.

Shortly before the company reached the east end of the ridge, we watched a stretcher team make its way up to bring down a casualty. Suddenly four or five mortar shells exploded in quick succession near the team, wounding slightly three of the four bearers. They helped each other back down the ridge, and another stretcher team, of which I was a member, started up to get the casualty. To avoid the enemy mortar observer, we moved up by a slightly different route. We got up the ridge and found the casualty lying above a sheer coral ledge about five feet high. The Marine, Leonard E. Vargo, told us he couldn't move much because he had been shot in both feet. Thus he couldn't lower himself down off the ledge. "You guys be careful. The Nip that shot me twice is still hiding right over there in those rocks." He motioned toward a jumble of boulders not more than twenty yards away.

We reasoned that if the sniper had been able to shoot Vargo in both feet, immobilizing him, he was probably waiting to snipe at anyone who came to the rescue. That meant that anyone who climbed up to help Vargo down would get shot instantly. We stood against the coral rock with our heads about level with Vargo, but out of the line of fire of the sniper, and looked at each other. I found the silence embarrassing. Vargo lay patiently, confident of our aid.

"Somebody's got to get up there and hand him down," I said. My three buddies nodded solemnly and made quiet comments in agreement. I thought to myself that if we fooled around much longer, the sniper might shoot and kill the already painfully wounded and helpless Marine. Then we heard the crash of another 105mm short round farther along the ridge—then another. I was seized with a grim fatalism—it was either be shot by the sniper or have all of us get blown to bits by our own artillery. Feeling ashamed for hesitating so long, I scrambled up beside Vargo.

"Watch out for that Nip," he said again.

As I placed my hands under his shoulders, I glanced over and saw the entrance of the sniper's small cave. It was a black space about three feet in diameter. I expected to see a muzzle flash spurt forth. Strangely, I felt at peace with myself and, oddly, wasn't particularly afraid. But there was no sound or sight of the sniper.

My buddies had Vargo well in hand by then, so for a brief instant I stood up and looked south. I felt a sensation of wild exhilaration. Beyond the smoke of our artillery to the south lay the end of the island and the end of the agony.

"Come on, Sledgehammer. Let's move out!"

With another quick glance at the mouth of the small cave—puzzled over where the sniper was and why he hadn't fired at me—I scrambled back down the rock to the stretcher team. We carried Vargo down Kunishi Ridge without further incident.

After bringing down another casualty, I passed our company CP among some rocks at the foot of the ridge and overheard one of our officers talking confidentially to Hank Boyes. The officer said his nerves were almost shattered by the constant strain, and he didn't think he could carry on much longer. The veteran Boyes talked quietly, trying to calm the officer. The officer sat on his helmet, frantically running his hands through his hair. He was almost sobbing.

I felt compassion for the officer. I'd been in the same forlorn frame of mind more than once, when horror piled on horror seemed too much to bear. The officer also carried a heavy responsibility, which I didn't have.

As I walked past, the officer blurted out in desperation, "What's the matter with those guys up on the ridge? Why the hell don't they move out faster and get this thing over with?"

Compassion aside, my own emotional and physical state was far from good by then. Completely forgetting my lowly rank, I walked right into the CP and said to the officer, "I'll tell you what's the matter with those guys on the ridge. They're gettin' shot right and left, and they can't move any faster!"

He looked up with a dazed expression. Boyes turned around, probably expecting to see the battalion or regimental commander. When he saw me instead, he looked surprised. Then he glared at me the way he did the time I had too much to say to Shadow back on Half Moon. Coming quickly to my senses and remembering that a private's advice to first lieutenants and gunny sergeants wasn't considered standard operating procedure in the Marine Corps, I backed away quietly and got out of there.

Toward afternoon, several of us were resting among some rocks near the crest of the ridge. We had been passing ammo and water up to some men just below the crest. A Japanese machine gun still covered the crest there, and no one dared raise his head. Bullets snapped over the crest and ricochets whined off into the air after striking rocks. The man next to me was a rifleman and a fine Peleliu veteran whom I knew well. He had become unusually quiet and moody during the past hour, but I just assumed he was as tired and as weary with fear and fatigue as I was. Suddenly he began babbling incoherently, grabbed his rifle, and shouted, "Those slant-eyed yellow bastards, they've killed enougha my buddies. I'm goin' after 'em." He jumped up and started for the crest of the ridge.

"Stop!" I yelled and grabbed at his trouser leg. He pulled away.

A sergeant next to him yelled, "Stop, you fool!" The sergeant also grabbed for the frantic man's legs, but his hands slipped. He managed to clutch the toe of one boondocker, however, and gave a jerk. That threw the man off balance, and he sprawled on his back, sobbing like a baby. The front of his trousers was darkened where he had urinated when he lost control of himself. The sergeant and I tried to calm him but also made sure he couldn't get back onto his feet. "Take it easy, Cobber. We'll get you outa here," the NCO said.

We called a corpsman who took the sobbing, trembling man out of the meat grinder to an aid station.

"He's a damn good Marine, Sledgehammer. I'll lower the boom on anybody says he ain't. But he's just had all he can take. That's it. He's just had all he can take."

The sergeant's voice trailed away sadly. We had just seen a brave man crack up completely and lose all control of himself, even to the point of losing his desire to live.

"If you hadn't grabbed his foot and jerked him down before he got to the crest, he'd be dead now, for sure," I said.

"Yeah, the poor guy woulda gotten hit by that goddamn machine gun; no doubt about it," the sergeant said.

By the end of the day, Company K reached the eastern end of Kunishi Ridge and established contact with army units that had gained the high ground on Yuza-Dake and Yaeju-Dake. Mail came up to us along with rations, water, and ammo. Among my letters was one from a Mobile acquaintance of many years. He had joined the Marine Corps and was a member of some rear-echelon unit of service troops stationed on northern Okinawa. He insisted that I write him immediately about the location of my unit. He wrote that when he found out where I was, he would visit me at once. I read his words to some of my buddies, and they got a good laugh out of it.

"Don't that guy know there's a war on? What the hell does he think the First Marine Division is doin' down here anyway?"

Someone else suggested I insist not only that he come to see me at once, but that he stay and be my replacement if he wanted to be a true friend. I never answered the letter.

A small patrol from the 7th Marines came by, and we talked with an old buddy. He said his regiment had been in terrible fighting for the several days it had been on Kunishi Ridge. Then we sat silently, ruefully watching a group of Marines far over to the right get shelled by large-caliber Japanese artillery. Word came along the line about the death earlier in the day of the U.S. Tenth commander, General Buckner.*

Not long after we were relieved on Kunishi Ridge (in the afternoon of 18 June), I asked Gy. Sgt. Hank Boyes how many men we had lost fighting on Yuza-Dake and Kunishi. He told me Company K had lost forty-nine enlisted men and one officer, half of our number of the previous day. Almost all the newly arrived replacements were among the casualties. Now the company consisted of a mere remnant, twenty-one percent of its normal strength of two hundred and thirty-five men. We had been attached to 2/5 for only twenty-two hours and had been on Kunishi Ridge for less time than that.

---

*Gen. Simon Bolivar Buckner, USA, had come up to the front lines to watch the 8th Marine Regiment, 2d Marine Division, in its first combat action on Okinawa. He was observing from between two coral boulders when six Japanese 47mm artillery rounds struck the base of the rocks. Hit in the chest, he died shortly thereafter. Lt. Gen. Roy S. Geiger, USMC, III Amphibious Corps commander, took command of the Tenth Army and carried through to the end of the fighting a few days later. To this date in 1981, Geiger remains the only Marine officer to command a force of army size.

CHAPTER FIFTEEN

End of the Agony

From 11 to 18 June the fierce battle for the Kunishi–Yuza-Yaeju escarpment cost the 1st Marine Division 1,150 casualties. The fight marked the end of organized Japanese resistance on Okinawa.

The battle for the Kunishi escarpment was unforgettable. It reminded many of us of Peleliu's ridges, and we still weren't used to the fact that night attacks by Marines had played a significant role in capturing the difficult objective. Among my friends in the ranks, the biggest surprise was the poor state of readiness and training of our newest Marine replacements, as compared to the more efficient replacements who had come into the company earlier in the campaign (they had received some combat training in the rear areas before joining us). But most of the new men who joined us just before Kunishi Ridge had come straight from the States. Some of them told us they had had only a few weeks training or less after boot camp.

It's no wonder they were so confused and ineffective when first exposed to intense enemy fire. When we had to evacuate a casualty under fire, some of the new men were reluctant to take the chances necessary to save the wounded Marine. This reticence infuriated the veterans, who made such threats against them that the new men finally did their share. They were motivated by greater fear of the veteran Marines than of the Japanese. This isn't to reflect on their bravery; they simply weren't trained and conditioned properly to cope with the shock, violence, and hellish conditions into which they were thrown. The rank and file, usually sympathetic toward new replacements, simply referred to them "as fouled up as Hogan's goat," or some other more profound but profane description.

With a feeling of intense relief, we came down off Kunishi Ridge late in the day of 18 June. After rejoining the other companies of 3/5, we moved in column on a road cut through the ridge. As we wound south, we talked with men of the 8th Marines who were moving along the road with us. We were glad to see a veteran Marine regiment come in to spearhead the final push south. We were exhausted.

The veterans in our ranks scrutinized the men of the 8th Marines with that hard professional stare of old salts sizing up another outfit. Everything we saw brought forth remarks of approval: they looked squared away, and many of them were combat veterans themselves.*

I talked to a 60mm mortarman who was carrying almost an entire cloverleaf of HE shells on a backpack rig. Asking why he was so overloaded, I was told his battalion commander wanted the mortarmen to try the arrangement because they could carry more ammo than in a regular ammo bag. I hoped fervently that none of our officers saw that rig.

I also saw a machine-gun squad with "Nip Nemesis" stenciled neatly on the water jacket of their .30-caliber heavy machine gun. They were a sharp-looking crew.

We passed a large muddy area in the road cut. In it lay the body of a dead Japanese soldier in full uniform and equipment. It was a bizarre sight. He had been mashed down into the mud by tank treads and looked like a giant squashed insect.

Our column moved down into a valley at five-pace intervals, one file on each side of the road. An amtrac came clattering slowly along, headed toward the front farther south. It passed me as I was daydreaming about the delightful possibility that we might not get shelled or shot at anymore. But

*The 8th Marines came up from Saipan to reinforce the 1st Marine Division in the final drive on Okinawa. Among the many streamers on its regimental battle color flew one for Tarawa.

my reverie was terminated rudely and abruptly by *whiz . . . bang! whiz . . . bang!*

"Disperse!" someone yelled. We scattered like a covey of quail. About ten of us jumped into a shallow ditch. The first enemy antitank shell had passed over the top of the amtrac and exploded in a field beyond. But the second shell scored a direct hit on the left side of the amtrac. The machine jolted to a stop and began smoking. We peeped out of the ditch as the driver tried to start the engine. His crewman peered back into the cargo compartment to assess the damage. Two more shells slammed into the side of the disabled amtrac. The two Marines in the cab jumped out, ran over, and flopped down, panting, into the ditch near us.

"What kinda cargo is in there?" I asked.

"We got a full unit of fire for a rifle company—'thirty' ball, grenades, mortar ammo—the works. Boy, she is gonna blow like hell when that fire gets to that ammo. The gas tanks are hit so bad there's no way to put it out." The driver crawled off along the ditch to find a radioman to report that his load of ammo couldn't get through to the front.

Just then a man crawled over next to me and stood upright. I looked up at him in surprise. Every Marine in the area was hugging the deck waiting for the inevitable explosion from the amtrac. The man was clad in clean dungarees with the new sheen still on the cloth, and he displayed the relaxed appearance of a person who could wash up and drink hot coffee at a CP whenever he was in the mood to do so. He carried a portable movie camera with which he began avidly filming the pillow of thick black smoke boiling up from the amtrac. Rifle cartridges began popping in the amtrac as the heat got to them.

"Hey, mate," I said. "You'd better get down! That thing is gonna blow sky high any minute. It's loaded with ammo!"

The man held his camera steady but stopped filming. He turned and looked down at me with a contemptuous stare of utter disdain and disgust. He didn't demean himself to speak to me as I cringed in the ditch, but turned back to his camera eyepiece and continued filming.

At that moment came a flash accompanied by a loud explosion and terrific concussion as the amtrac blew up. The concussion knocked the cameraman completely off his feet. He was uninjured but badly shaken and terribly frightened. He peered wide-eyed and cautious over the ditch bank at the twisted amtrac burning on the road.

I leaned over to him and said pleasantly, "I told you so."

He turned his no longer arrogant face toward me. I grinned at him with the broadest smile I could conjure, "like a mule eatin' briars through a barbed-wire fence," as the Texans would say. Speechless, the cameraman turned quickly and crawled off along the ditch toward the rear.

Four or five Marine tanks were parked close together in the valley downhill from us about one hundred yards away. Their heavily armored fronts faced up the valley to our left. The crewmen had been alerted by the first enemy round fired at the amtrac; we saw them swinging their 75s toward our left and closing their turret hatches. Not a moment too soon. The entire Japanese 47mm gun battery opened rapid fire on the tanks. Too bad the movie cameraman had felt the call of duty summon him to the rear after the amtrac exploded, because he missed a dramatic scene. The enemy guns fired with admirable accuracy. Several of their tracerlike armor-piercing shells hit the turrets of the tanks and ricocheted into the air. The tanks returned fire. In a few minutes, the Japanese guns were knocked out or ceased firing, and everything got quiet. The tanks sustained only minor damage. We went back onto the road and moved on south without further incident.

Until the island was secured on 21 June, we made a series of rapid moves southward, stopping only to fight groups of die-hard Japanese in caves, pillboxes, and ruined villages. The fresh 8th Marines pushed south rapidly. "The Eighth Marines goin' like a bat outa hell," a man said as news drifted back to us.

We were fortunate in not suffering many casualties in the company. The Japanese were beaten, and the hope uppermost in every weary veteran's mind was that his luck would hold out a little longer, until the end of the battle.

We used loudspeakers, captured Japanese soldiers, and Okinawan civilians to persuade the remaining enemy to sur-

render. One sergeant and a Japanese lieutenant who had graduated from an Ivy League college and spoke perfect English
gave themselves up in a road cut. Just after they came out and
surrendered, a sniper opened fire on us. We eight or ten
Marines took cover next to the embankment, but the Japanese
officer and NCO stood in the middle of the road with the bullets kicking up dirt all around them. The sniper obviously was
trying to kill them because they had surrendered.

We looked at the two Japanese standing calmly, and one of
our NCOs said, "Get over here under cover, you dumb bastards."

The enemy officer grinned affably and spoke to his NCO.
They walked calmly over and got down as ordered.

Some Company K men shot the gun crew of a 150mm
howitzer emplaced in the mouth of a well-camouflaged cave.
The Japanese defended their big artillery piece with their rifles and died to the last man. Farther on we tried to get a group
of enemy in a burial vault to surrender, but they refused. Our
lieutenant, Mac, jumped in front of the door and shouted in
Japanese, "Do not be afraid. Come out. I will not harm you."
Then he fired a complete twenty-round magazine from his
submachine gun into the door. We all just shook our heads
and moved on. About a half hour later, the five or six Japanese
rushed out fighting. Some of our Marines behind us killed
them.

Our battalion was one of the first American units to reach
the end of the island. It was a beautiful sight even though
there were still snipers around. We stood on a high hill overlooking the sea. Below to our left we saw army infantry advancing toward us, flushing out and shooting down enemy
soldiers singly and in small groups. Army 81mm mortar fire
kept pace ahead of the troops, and some of our weapons
joined in coordination. We got a bit edgy when the army mortar fire kept getting closer and closer to our positions even after the unit had been apprised of our location. One of our
battalion officers became furious as the big shells came dan-
gerously close. He ordered a radioman to tell the army officer
in charge that if they didn't cease fire immediately, our 81s

would open fire on his troops. The army mortars stopped shooting.

The night of 20 June we made a defensive line on the high ground overlooking the sea. My mortar was dug in near a coral road and was to illuminate or fire HE on the area. Other guns of the section covered the seaward part of the company's sector.

Earlier we had seen and heard some sort of strange-looking rocket fired by the Japanese from over in our army's sector. The projectiles were clearly visible as they went up with a terrible screaming sound. Most of them exploded in the 8th Marines area. The things sounded like bombs exploding. A call came for every available corpsman to help with casualties resulting from those explosions.

The Japanese on Okinawa had a 320mm-spigot-mortar unit equipped to fire a 675-pound shell. Americans first encountered this awesome weapon on Iwo Jima. I don't know whether what we saw fired several times during the last day or two on Okinawa was a spigot mortar, but whatever it was, it was a frightful-sounding weapon that caused great damage.

The night turned into a long series of shooting scrapes with Japanese who prowled all over the place. We heard someone coming along the road, the coral crunching beneath his feet. In the pitch dark, a new replacement fired his carbine twice in that direction and yelled for the password. Somebody laughed, and several enemy started firing in our direction as they ran past us along the road. A bullet zipped by me and hit the hydrogen cylinder of a flamethrower placed on the side of the adjacent foxhole. The punctured cylinder emitted a sharp hissing sound.

"Is that thing gonna blow up?" I asked anxiously.

"Naw, just hit the hydrogen tank. It won't ignite," the flamethrower gunner said.

We could hear the enemy soldiers' hobnailed shoes pounding on the road until a fatal burst of fire from some other Company K Marines sent them sprawling. As we field-stripped them the next morning, I noted that each carried cooked rice in his double-boiler mess gear—all bullet-riddled then.

Other Japanese swam or walked along in the sea just off-shore. We saw them in the flarelight. A line of Marines behind a stone wall on the beach fired at them. One of our men ran up from the wall to get more carbine ammo.

"Come on, Sledgehammer. It's just like Lexington and Concord."

"No thanks. I'm too comfortable in my hole."

He went back down to the wall, and they continued firing throughout the night.

Just before daylight, we heard a couple of enemy grenades explode. Japanese yelled and shouted wildly where one of our 37mm guns was dug in across the road, covering the valley out front. Shots rang out, then desperate shouts and cursing.

"Corspman!"

Then silence. A new corpsman who had joined us recently started toward the call for help, but I said, "Hold it, Doc. I'll go with you."

I wasn't being heroic. I was quite afraid. But knowing the enemy's propensity for treachery, I thought somebody should accompany him.

"As you were, Sledgehammer. Ya might be needed on the gun. Take off, Doc, and be careful," an NCO said. A few minutes later he said, "OK, Sledgehammer, take off if ya wanta."

I grabbed the Tommy and followed the corpsman. He was just finishing bandaging one of the wounded Marines of the 37mm gun crew when I got there. Other Marines were coming over to see if they could help. Several men had been wounded by the firing when two enemy officers crept up the steep slope, threw grenades into the gun emplacement, and jumped in swinging their samurai sabers. One Marine had parried a saber blow with his carbine. His buddy then had shot the Japanese officer, who fell backwards a short distance down the slope. The saber blow had severed a finger and sliced through the mahogany carbine forestock to the metal barrel.

The second Japanese officer lay dead on his back next to the wheel of the 37mm gun. He was in full-dress uniform with white gloves, shiny leather leggings, Sam Browne belt, and campaign ribbons on his chest. Nothing remained of his head from the nose up—just a mass of crushed skull, brains, and bloody pulp. A grimy Marine with a dazed expression stood over the Japanese. With a foot planted firmly on the ground on each side of the enemy officer's body, the Marine held his rifle by the forestock with both hands and slowly and mechanically moved it up and down like a plunger. I winced each time it came down with a sickening sound into the gory mass. Brains and blood were splattered all over the Marine's rifle, boondockers, and canvas leggings, as well as the wheel of the 37mm gun.

The Marine was obviously in a complete state of shock. We gently took him by the arms. One of his uninjured buddies set aside the gore-smeared rifle. "Let's get you outa here, Cobber."

The poor guy responded like a sleepwalker as he was led off with the wounded, who were by then on stretchers. The man who had lost the finger clutched the Japanese saber in his other hand. "I'm gonna keep this bastard for a souvenir."

We dragged the battered enemy officer to the edge of the gun emplacement and rolled him down the hill. Replete with violence, shock, blood, gore, and suffering, this was the type of incident that should be witnessed by anyone who has any delusions about the glory of war. It was as savage and as brutal as though the enemy and we were primitive barbarians rather than civilized men.

Later in the day of 21 June 1945, we learned the high command had declared the island secured. We each received two fresh oranges with the compliments of Admiral Nimitz. So I ate mine, smoked my pipe, and looked out over the beautiful blue sea. The sun danced on the water. After eighty-two days and nights, I couldn't believe Okinawa had finally ended. I was tempted to relax and think that we would board ship immediately for rest and rehabilitation in Hawaii.

"That's what the scuttlebutt is, you guys. Straight dope. We're headed for Waikiki," a grinning buddy said. But long conditioning by the hardships that were our everyday diet in a rifle company made me skeptical. My intuition was borne out shortly.

"Get your gear on; check your weapons. We're moving back north in skirmish line. You people will mop up the area for any Nips still holding out. You will bury all enemy dead. You will salvage U.S. and enemy equipment. All brass above .50 caliber in size will be collected and placed in neat piles. Stand by to move out."

A FINAL CHORE

If this were a novel about war, or if I were a dramatic story-teller, I would find a romantic way to end this account while looking at that fine sunset off the cliffs at the southern end of Okinawa. But that wasn't the reality of what we faced. Company K had one more nasty job to do.

To the battle-weary troops, exhausted after an eighty-two-day campaign, mopping up was grim news. It was a nerve-wracking business at best. The enemy we encountered were the toughest of the diehards, selling their lives as expensively as possible. Fugitives from the law of averages, we were nervous and jittery. A man could survive Gloucester, Peleliu, and Okinawa only to be shot by some fanatical, bypassed Japanese holed up in a cave. It was hard for us to accept the order. But we did—grimly. Burying enemy dead and salvaging brass and equipment on the battlefield, however, was the last straw to our sagging morale.

"By lawd, why the hell we gotta bury them stinkin' bastards after we killed 'em? Let them goddamn rear-echelon people git a whiff of 'em. They didn't hafta fight 'em."

"Jeez, picking up brass; that's the most stupid, dumb jerk of a order I ever did hear of."

Fighting was our duty, but burying enemy dead and cleaning up the battlefield wasn't for infantry troops as we saw it. We complained and griped bitterly. It was the ultimate indignity to men who had fought so hard and so long and had won. We were infuriated and frustrated. For the first time, I saw several of my veteran comrades flatly refuse to obey an order. If some of us hadn't prevailed on them to knock off arguing hotly with an NCO, they would have been severely punished for insubordination.

I'll never forget cajoling, arguing with, and begging two veteran buddies to be quiet and follow orders as I unstrapped my entrenching shovel from my pack. We stood wearily in a trampled cane field beside a bloated Jap corpse. Both buddies were three-campaign men who were outstanding in combat but had reached the end of their ropes. They weren't about to bury any stinking Japanese, no sirree. I prevailed, however, just as Hank Boyes came over grim-faced and yelling at them to turn to.

So we dragged ourselves back north in skirmish line. We cursed every dead enemy we had to bury. (We just spaded dirt over them with our entrenching shovels.) We cursed every cartridge case "above .50 caliber in size" we collected to "place in neat piles." Never before were we more thankful to have the support of our tanks. The flame tanks were particularly effective in burning out troublesome Japanese in caves.* Fortunately, we had few casualties.

In a few days we assembled in an open field and fell out to await further orders. The weather was hot, so we all took off our packs, sat on our helmets, drank some water, and had a smoke. We were to be there for several hours, an NCO said, so we got the order to chow down.

A friend and I went over to a little wooded area near the field to eat our K rations in the shade. We walked into a completely untouched scene that resembled a natural park in a botanical garden: low graceful pines cast dense shade, and ferns and moss grew on the rocks and banks. It was cool, and the odor of fresh pine filled the air. Miraculously, it bore not a single sign of war.

"Boy, this is beautiful, isn't it, Sledgehammer?"

"It looks unreal," I said as I took off my pack and sat down on the soft green moss beside a clump of graceful ferns. We each started heating a canteen cup of water for our instant coffee. I took out the prized can of cured ham I had obtained by trade from a man in the company CP. (He had stolen it

---

*The total number of Japanese killed by the five American divisions during the mop-up was 8,975, a large enough number of enemy to have waged intense guerrilla warfare if they hadn't been annihilated.

from an officer.) We settled back in the cool silence. The war, military discipline, and other unpleasant realities seemed a million miles away. For the first time in months, we began to relax.

"OK, you guys. Move out. Move! Move! Outa here," an NCO said with authority ringing out in every word.

"Is the company moving out already?" my friend asked in surprise.

"No, it isn't, but you guys are."

"Why?"

"Because this is off-limits to enlisted men," the NCO said, turning and pointing to a group of officers munching their rations as they strolled into our newfound sanctuary.

"But we aren't in the way," I said.

"Move out and follow orders."

To his credit, the NCO appeared in sympathy with us and seemed to feel the burden of his distasteful task. We sullenly picked up our half-cooked rations and our gear, went back out into the hot sun, and flopped down in the dusty field.

"Some crap, eh?"

"Yeah," I said, "we weren't even near those officers. The fighting on this goddamn island is over. The officers have started getting chicken again and throwing the crap around. Yesterday while the shootin' was still goin' on, it was all buddy-buddy with the enlisted men."

Our grumblings were interrupted by the sound of a rifle shot. A Marine I knew very well reeled backward and fell to the ground. His buddy dropped his rifle and rushed to him, followed by several others. The boy was dead, shot in the head by his buddy. The other man had thought his rifle was unloaded when his young friend had stood over him and placed his thumb playfully over the muzzle.

"Pull the trigger. I bet it's not loaded."

He pulled the trigger. The loaded rifle fired and set a bullet tearing up through the head of his best friend. Both had violated the cardinal rule:

"Don't point a weapon at anything you don't intend to shoot."

Shock and dismay showed on the man's face from that moment until he left the company a few weeks later. He went, we heard, to stand a general court-martial and a probable prison term. But his worst punishment was living with the horror of having killed his best friend by playing with a loaded weapon.

While the company was still sitting in the field, five or six men and I were told to get our gear and follow an NCO to waiting trucks. We were to go north to a site where our division would make a tent camp after the mop-up in the south was completed. Our job was to unload and guard some company gear.

We were apprehensive about leaving the company, but it turned out to be good duty. During the long and dusty truck ride to the Motobu Peninsula, we rode past some areas we had fought through. By then we could barely recognize them—they were transformed with roads, tent camps, and supply dumps. The number of service troops and the amount of equipment was beyond our belief. Roads that had been muddy tracks or coral-covered paths were highways with vehicles going to and fro and MPs in neat khaki directing traffic. Tent camps, Quonset huts, and huge parks of vehicles lay along our route.

We had come back to civilization. We had climbed up out of the abyss once more. It was exhilarating. We sang and whistled like little boys until our sides were sore. As we went north, the countryside became beautiful. Most of it seemed untouched by the war. Finally our truck turned off into a potato field not far from high rocky cliffs overlooking the sea and a small island, which our driver said was Ie Shima.

The land around our future campsite was undamaged. We unloaded the company gear from the truck. The driver had picked up five-gallon cans of water for us. Plenty of K rations had been issued. We set up a bivouac. Corporal Vincent was in charge, and we were glad of it. He was a great guy and a Company K veteran.

Our little guard detail spent several quiet, carefree days basking in the sun by day and mounting one-sentry guard duty at night. We were like boys on a campout. The fear and terror were behind us.

Our battalion came north a few days later. All hands went to work in earnest to complete the tent camp. Pyramidal tents were set up, drainage ditches were dug, folding cots and bed rolls were brought to us, and a canvas-roofed mess hall was built. Every day old friends returned from the hospitals, some hale and hearty but others showing the effects of only partial recovery from severe wounds. To our disgust, rumors of rehabilitation in Hawaii faded. But our relief that the long Okinawa ordeal was over at last was indescribable.

Very few familiar faces were left. Only twenty-six Peleliu veterans who had landed with the company on 1 April remained. And I doubt there were even ten of the old hands who had escaped being wounded at one time or another on Peleliu or Okinawa. Total American casualties were 7,613 killed and missing and 31,807 wounded in action. Neuropsychiatric, "non-battle," casualties amounted to 26,221—probably higher than in any other previous Pacific Theater battle. This latter high figure is attributed to two causes: The Japanese poured onto U.S. troops the heaviest concentrations of artillery and mortar fire experienced in the Pacific, and the prolonged, close-in fighting with a fanatical enemy.

Marines and attached Naval medical personnel suffered total casualties of 20,020 killed, wounded, and missing.

Japanese casualty figures are hazy. However, 107,539 enemy dead were counted on Okinawa. Approximately 10,000 enemy troops surrendered, and about 20,000 were either sealed in caves or buried by the Japanese themselves. Even lacking an exact accounting, in the final analysis the enemy garrison was, with rare exceptions, annihilated. Unfortunately, approximately 42,000 Okinawan civilians, caught between the two opposing armies, perished from artillery fire and bombing.

The 1st Marine Division suffered heavy casualties on Okinawa. Officially, it lost 7,665 men killed, wounded, and missing. There were also an undetermined number of casualties among the replacements whose names never got on a muster roll. Considering that most of the casualties were in the division's three infantry regiments (about 3,000 strength in each), it's obvious that the rifle companies took the bulk of the beating, just as they had on Peleliu. The division's losses of 6,526 on Peleliu and 7,665 on Okinawa total 14,191. Statistically, the infantry units had suffered over 150 percent losses through the two campaigns. The few men like me who never got hit can claim with justification that we survived the abyss of war as fugitives from the law of averages.*

IT WAS OVER

As we finished building our tent camp, we began trying to unwind from the grueling campaign. Some of the Cape Gloucester veterans rotated home almost immediately, and replacements arrived. Ugly rumors circulated that we would hit Japan next, with an expected casualty figure of one million Americans. No one wanted to talk about that.

On 8 August we heard that the first atomic bomb had been dropped on Japan. Reports abounded for a week about a possible surrender. Then on 15 August 1945 the war ended.

We received the news with quiet disbelief coupled with an indescribable sense of relief. We thought the Japanese would never surrender. Many refused to believe it. Sitting in stunned silence, we remembered our dead. So many dead. So many maimed. So many bright futures consigned to the ashes of the past. So many dreams lost in the madness that had engulfed us. Except for a few widely scattered shouts of joy, the survivors of the abyss sat hollow-eyed and silent, trying to comprehend a world without war.

In September, the 1st Marine Division went to North China on occupation duty, the 5th Marines to the fascinating ancient city of Peking. After about four and a half months there, I rotated Stateside.

My happiness knew no bounds when I learned I was slated to ship home. It was time to say goodbye to old buddies in K/3/5. Severing the ties formed in two campaigns was painful. One of America's finest and most famous elite fighting divisions had been my home during a period of the most

---

*The 1st Marine Division received the Presidential Units Citation for its part in the Okinawa campaign.

extreme adversity. Up there on the line, with nothing between us and the enemy but space (and precious little of that), we'd forged a bond that time would never erase. We were brothers. I left with a sense of loss and sadness, but K/3/5 will always be a part of me.

It's ironic that the record of our company was so outstanding but that so few individuals were decorated for bravery. Uncommon valor was displayed so often it went largely unnoticed. It was expected. But nearly every man in the company was awarded the Purple Heart. My good fortune in being one of the few exceptions continues to amaze me.

War is brutish, inglorious, and a terrible waste. Combat leaves an indelible mark on those who are forced to endure it. The only redeeming factors were my comrades' incredible bravery and their devotion to each other. Marine Corps training taught us to kill efficiently and to try to survive. But it also taught us loyalty to each other—and love. That esprit de corps sustained us.

Until the millenium arrives and countries cease trying to enslave others, it will be necessary to accept one's responsibilities and to be willing to make sacrifices for one's country—as my comrades did. As the troops used to say, "If the country is good enough to live in, it's good enough to fight for." With privilege goes responsibility.

A Roll of Honor
Peleliu Veterans with K/3/5 at the End of Okinawa

1. James Allen
2. Charles Anderson
3. James C. F. Anderson
4. Franklin Batchelor
5. Henry (Hank) Boyes W/NE
6. R. V. Burgin W/R
7. J. T. Burke
8. Guy E. Farrar
9. Peter Fouts
10. G. C. Gear
11. Anton Haas
12. Julius (Frenchy) Labeeuw
13. Les Land
14. Thorkil (Toby) Paulsen
15. Les Porter
16. Bobby Ragan
17. John Redifer
18. D. B. A. Salsby W/R
19. Vincent Santos
20. George Sarrett
21. Henry K. Schaeffer
22. Merriel (Snafu) Shelton S/R
23. E. B. Sledge
24. Myron Tesreau
25. Orly C. Uhls
26. W. F. Vincent

NOTE: W/R—wounded returned to duty; W/NE—wounded not evacuated; S/R—sick returned to duty.

Of the approximately 65 Peleliu veterans who landed with the company on Okinawa, only the above survived death, injury, or illness, and were present at the end of the battle. Many of the above had been wounded on Cape Gloucester or Peleliu.

BIBLIOGRAPHY

The books and documents listed here are not the only accounts and references to the battles of Peleliu and Okinawa, nor should the reader construe them to be suggestions for further reading. My story is personal. It relates what I saw and knew. I used the following references to check my facts for the few pieces of connecting tissue I've included to orient the reader to the larger war that raged around me and to be sure I had the names and places right.

Appleman, Roy E., et al. *Okinawa: The Last Battle.* Washington: Historical Division, Department of the Army, 1948.

Davis, Burke. *Marine! The Life of Lieutenant General Lewis B. (Chesty) Puller.* Boston: Little, Brown and Company, 1962.

Davis, Russell. *Marine at War.* Scholastic Book Services, N.Y., 1961.

Falk, Stanley. *Bloodiest Victory: Palaus.* New York: Ballantine Books, 1974.

Frank, Benis M. *Okinawa: Touchstone to Victory.* New York: Ballantine Books, 1974.

Frank, Benis M. and Henry I. Shaw, Jr. *Victory and Occupation: History of Marine Corps Operations in World War II,* Vol. V. Washington: Historical Branch, G-3 Division, Headquarters, U.S. Marine Corps (hereinafter HQMC), 1968.

Garand, George W. and Truman R. Strobridge. *Western Pacific Operations: History of U.S. Marine Corps Operations in World War II,* Vol. IV. Washington: Historical Division, HQMC, 1971.

Heinl, Robert D., Jr. *Soldiers of the Sea: The United States Marine Corps, 1775–1962.* Annapolis: United States Naval Institute, 1962.

Hough, Maj. Frank O. *The Assault on Peleliu.* Washington: Historical Division, HQMC, 1950.

Hunt, George P. *Coral Comes High.* New York: Harper and Brothers, 1946.

Isley, Jeter A. and Philip Crowl. *The U.S. Marines and Amphibious War.* Princeton, NJ: Princeton University Press, 1951.

James, D. Clayton. *The Years of MacArthur* Vol. II, 1941–45. Boston: Houghton Mifflin, 1975.

Leckie, Robert. *Strong Men Armed: The United States Marines Against Japan.* New York: Random House, 1962.

Mayer, S. L., ed. *The Japanese War Machine.* Secaucus, N.J.: Chartwell Books, 1976.

McMillan, George. *The Old Breed: A History of the First Marine Division in World War II.* Washington: Infantry Journal Press, 1949.

Moran, John A. *Creating a Legend.* Chicago: Publishing Division, Moran/Andrews, Inc., 1973.

Morison, Samuel Eliot. *The Two-Ocean War.* Boston: Little, Brown and Company, 1963.

Moskin, J. Robert. *The U.S. Marine Corps Story.* New York: McGraw-Hill Book Company, 1977.

Muster Roll of Officers and Enlisted Men of the U.S. Marine Corps: Third Battalion, Fifth Marines, First Marine Division, Fleet Marine Force. From 1 September to 30 September, 1944, inclusive; from 1 October to 31 October, 1944, inclusive; from 1 April to 30 April, 1945, inclusive; from 1 May to 31 May, 1945, inclusive; from 1 June to 30 June, 1945, inclusive. Washington: History and Museums Division, HQMC.

Nichols, Charles S., Jr., and Henry I. Shaw, Jr. *Okinawa: Victory in the Pacific.* Rutland, VT: Charles E. Tuttle Company, 1966. Originally published in 1955 by the Historical Branch, G-3 Division, HQMC.

Paige, Mitchell. *A Marine Named Mitch.* New York: Vantage Press, 1975.

Shaw, Henry I., Jr., Bernard C. Nalty, and Edwin T. Turnbladh. *Central Pacific Drive: History of U.S. Marine Corps Operations in World War II,* Vol. III. Washington: Historical Branch, G-3 Division, HQMC, 1966.

Smith, S. E., ed. and comp. *The United States Marine Corps in World War II.* New York: Random House, 1969.

Steinberg, Rafael. *Island Fighting.* Morristown, N.J.: Time-Life Books, 1978.

Stockman, James R. *The First Marine Division on Okinawa: 1 April–30 June 1945.* Washington: Historical Division, HQMC, 1946.

Time Magazine, 9 October 1944, p. 29; and 16 October 1944, p. 38.

Toland, John. *The Rising Sun.* New York: Random House, 1970.

United States 1st Marine Division. Operation Plan 1-44. Annex A, B Serial 0003 over 1990–5–80 over 458/332; dated 15 Aug 1944.

——— Palau Operation, Special Action Report, Serial 0775 over 1990–5–80 over 458/390; dated 13 Sept 1944.

——— Field Order No. 1-44 through 9-44. Serial 1990–5–80 over 458/332; dated 20 Sept, 21 Sept, 22 Sept, 25 Sept, 2 Oct., 5 Oct, 8 Oct, 10 Oct., and 13 Oct 1944.

Index*

"Ack Ack" (*See also* Haldane, Capt.
Andrew A.) 67, 96, 117–18,
150–52
Amtrac (Landing Vehicle Tracked)
23, 59–60, 65, 95, 126, 137,
201, 205–6
Armor-piercing shells, 126
Angaur 113
Army Units, U.S.
Tenth Army 200, 207
XXIV Corps 206, 208
Divisions:
7th Infantry Division 208, 214,
242
27th Infantry Division 208,
214, 223, 231n
77th Infantry Division 208,
242, 300n
81st Infantry Division
(Wildcats) 7, 111, 164, 165n
96th Infantry Division 208,
214
Regiments:
106th Infantry, relief of by 3/5
226–30
321st Infantry 111, 113
Battalions:
2d Battalion, 321st Infantry,
relieves 3/5 164
Asato Gawa (River) 231, 243,
259

Attitudes, Japanese, 140–42,
233–36, 311, 325, 326
On surrender 128, 307–8
Attitudes, Marine:
Attacking at night 322–23
Cleaning up battlefield 338–39
Combat troops toward
noncombatants 52–53,
112–13
Drafted Marines 186–87
Enemy dead 69–70
Mopping up on Okinawa
338–39
Noncombatant souvenir hunters
144–45, 164
Pavuvu 39
Souvenirs 129, 131, 133–34,
166–67
Surrender 127
Toward Japanese 39–40, 160
Toward Japanese POWs 306–8
Unit 106
Value of Peleliu 177, 206
Awacha Pocket (battle of) 244–53,
257–58

Birmingham, USS 241–42
Bishi Gawa (River) 206
Bloody Nose Ridge (*See also*
Umurbrogol) 100, 101, 103,
256

---

*This Index has been prepared as an aid to the general reader. For the sake of
brevity the names of comrades have been omitted except for those directly
involved in the chain of command.

Banzai charge, Marine prediction of
　　　on Peleliu 76
BLT (defined) 198n
Boot Camp 11–16
Bougainville 22
Boyes, Gy. Sgt. Henry A. (Hank)
　　　233, 285–86, 317, 327, 339
Buckner, Lt. Gen. Simon Bolivar,
　　　Jr., USA 208, 223, 329n
Burgin, Cpl. R. V. 123, 124–32
　　　passim, 234n, 237, 255, 267
Burial vaults, Okinawan 309

Camp Elliott 16, 16n, 17–23 *passim*
Camp St. Louis (New Caledonia)
　　　29–33 *passim*
Cates, Gen. Clifton B. 61
Chimu Wan (Bay) 214
Combat stress, Marine preparation
　　　for 13, 170–72
　　During prolonged combat
　　　255–56
　　Effects of 68–69, 77–78, 81–82,
　　　159–60
Corpsmen, USN 336–37
Corsair fighter plane 120, 123, 220

Dake (defined) 321, 321n
Dakeshi Ridge 251–52, 256
Dakeshi Village 231, 251–52,
　　　256–58
del Valle, Maj. Gen. Pedro 184
Discipline, on Pavuvu 46–47
Doherty, Cpl. T. J. (drill instructor)
　　　9–16 *passim*
Douglas, Capt. Paul 96–97, 97n
DUKW (rubber-tired amphibious
　　　truck) 66

Fear:
　　Concern about 22, 26, 75–76,
　　　98–99, 255–56
　　Eve of Okinawa landing 200–1
　　Eve of Peleliu landing 57–58
　　Morning, D day Peleliu 58
　　Of shell fire 78–79, 135–36,
　　　140–41

Okinawa landing 200–4
　　Of ambush 218–19
　　Peleliu landing 64–66
　　Prior to a major attack 236–38
Field sanitation 154–55
Fire discipline, Japanese 94
Franklin, USS 196–97

Geiger, Maj. Gen. Roy S. 61, 103n,
　　　208n, 223, 329n
General Howze, USS 33–34, 36
Goettge Patrol 39n, 40
Great Barrier Reef 28
Guadalcanal 49–51, 188–89
Gustafson, Maj. John H. 110

Haguski 204, 320
Haldane, Capt. Andrew A. (*See also*
　　　"Ack Ack") 45n, 45–46,
　　　114–17, 181, 274
Half Moon Hill 267
Hallucinations, on battlefield
　　　292–93
Halsey, Adm. William F. ("Bull") 60
Higgins Boat, LCVP, (Landing
　　　Craft Vehicle Personnel) 23,
　　　193–94, 197, 204, 205
Hizaonna 214–16
Hodge, Maj. Gen. John R. USA 208
Hope, Bob 41

Immersion foot 288
Infiltration, Japanese (raids) 115–19,
　　　142–44, 275–76, 284–86
Intelligence, Japanese secrecy 266
Iwo Jima 62, 198–99n, 200

Japanese, suicidal tank destroyer
　　　teams 261
Japanese tank attack, D day, Peleliu
　　　74–75
Japanese troop strength, Peleliu 61
Japanese units
　　Divisions:
　　　14th Infantry Division 61
　　　24th Infantry Division 242
　　　62d Infantry Division 242

Batallions:
    2d Battalion, 15th Regiment
        119n
Jones, 1st. Lt. Edward A. ("Hillbilly")
    97–99, 105–11 passim

Kakazu-Nishibaru Ridges. (See
        also Okinawa defense plan)
    200–14, 231n
Kamikaze, function of in Okinawa
        defense strategy 200, 201n,
        241–42
Kunishi Ridge 320–31 passim
    Snipers on 325–29 passim
    Yuza-Dake, Yaeju-Dake Ridge
        (See also Okinawa defense
        plan) 143
Kwantung Army 76
Kyushu 188

Loveday, 1st Lt. George 233n
LST661 (Landing Sky Tank)
    53–59, 104

MacArthur, Gen. Douglas, USA 51,
    60
McCracken, USS 193–95
Marine Units:
    III Amphibious Corps, 7n, 61,
        208, 329n
    Boundary of 259
    Divisions:
        1st Marine Division 7n, 211,
            214–15, 223, 241–42, 251,
            259, 267, 315
        2d Marine Division 22–23, 61
            On Tarawa 208
        3d Marine Division 22, 35n,
            36, 189
        4th Marine Division 189
        5th Marine Division 189, 200
        6th Marine Division 206, 214,
            259, 266–67, 304
            Moves onto right flank of
                southern front 243
            Battle of Oroku Peninsula
                315

Regiments:
    1st Marines 53, 68, 93, 103,
        111, 113, 137, 147, 156,
        240, 241, 259, 320, 323
    5th Marines 53, 68, 82, 93, 96,
        111, 114, 127, 137, 156,
        259, 320, 323
        Approach Dakeshi 244
        In Korea 35n
        In Peking 343
        Regimental decorations
            184
        In Vietnam 35n
        In World War I 8, 35n
    6th Marines in World War I 8
    7th Marines 53, 68, 73, 137,
        138, 147, 156, 177, 259,
        315, 320–23, 329
    8th Marines 329n, 331, 331n,
        333, 335
    11th Marines 53, 114, 183,
        223
Battalions:
    1st Battalion, 1st Marines
        (1/1) 321
    2d Battalion, 1st Marines (2/1)
        84, 93, 102–3
    2d Battalion, 4th Marines (2/4)
        275
    1st Battalion, 5th Marines
        (1/5) 68, 84, 93, 252, 300n
    2d Battalion, 5th Marines (2/5)
        84, 85, 87, 93, 102, 252,
        259–61, 323, 329
    3d Battalion, 5th Marines (3/5)
        68, 71, 84, 85, 87, 93, 102,
        103, 135, 138, 156, 193,
        204, 214, 241, 251, 252,
        259, 267, 270, 300n
        Incomplete history of on
            D day, Peleliu 71, 71n
        Attached to 7th Marines
            140–45
        Reaches east coast D day,
            Peleliu 334
    3d Battalion, 7th Marines (3/7)
        68, 71, 73, 87, 250

Battalions: (cont.)
  1st Marine Tank Battalion 147,
    223
  46th Replacement Battalion
    25, 33
Companies:
  A, 1st Battalion, 5th Marines
    (A/1/5) attack on Shun
    Castle 300
  K, 3rd Battalion, 5th Marines
    (K/3/5) 87
    Author joins 34
    Exposed right flank on
      beachhead, Peleliu 68
    Reaches eastern shore D
      day, Peleliu 72
    Exposed right flank of
      Division D day
      afternoon, Peleliu 72–77
    On division right flank
      Wana Draw, Okinawa
      270–99 passim
    CP at Half Moon Hill 270,
      272–73, 285
    Attack on Shuri 298–305
      passim
    Kunishi Ridge 325–29
  L, 3d Battalion, 5th Marines
    (L/3/5) attack on Shun
    299–300
  K, 3d Battalion, 7th Marines
    (K/3/7) 68, 214, 216–17
Machinato Airfield 224, 231n
Macquitti Bay, Pavuvu 178
Marmet, Sgt. John 64, 150–52,
  161–63
Mississippi, USS 123
Morotai Island 177
Motobu Peninsula 214

Naha 304
Naha-Yonabaru Highway 309
Nakagawa, Col. Kunio 61
Ngardololok area, Peleliu
  137–38
Ngesebus Island 114
Nimitz, Adm. Chester, 337

North China, occupation of by 1st
    Marine Division 343
Noumea, New Caledonia 28–29

Officer Training V-12 program 5, 6
Okinawa Shima 62, 148, 171–72
  Civilians 211–12
  Defense plan ridge systems 200
  Geographic features 199–200
  Horses 213
  Location 187–88
  U.S. invasion plan 206–8
  Terrain 212–13
  Vegetation 213

Palau Island Group 51
Pavuvu
  Coconut work parties 35–37
  Geographic location 36n
  Physical condition of Cape
    Gloucester veterans 37–38
Pay, Marines' monthly 103
President Polk, USS 25–29, 33
  Troops daily routine 26–28
Puller, Col. Lewis B. ("Chesty")
  USMC 53n

Replacements
  Combat readiness 330–31
  Reaction to front line 289–91
Rupertus, Maj. Gen. William H.
  USMC 53n, 56n, 103n
Russell Islands 195

Seabees (Naval Construction
    Battalion) 112, 192–93
Sea Lark Channel (Iron Bottom
    Bay) 193–95
Sea Runner, USS 169, 172, 177–78
Shofner, Lt. Col. Austin C. USMC
  77, 321
Shuri 259, 267, 270, 306, 321
  Defensive plan 200
  Shuri line 244, 258
Stanley, 1st Lt. Thomas J.
  ("Stumpy") 152n, 233n,
  273–74

Star shells (illumination, artillery or
        Naval gun shell) 78

Tactics
    Japanese (*See also* Iwo Jima)
        Changes in 61
        D day on Peleliu 76
        Defense-in-depth 61, 189
        Defense of Okinawa 200
        Infiltration (raids) 88–89,
            142–43, 148–49, 284–85
        On Okinawa 251
        On Saipan 200
        Snipers 148–49
        Tank infantry on Peleliu 76–77
    Marine
        Bypassing enemy troops 101
        Defense against infiltration
            142–43
        Night defense 88
        Passwords 90
        Rifle company deployment
            during attack 100–2
        Rifle squad 17–18, 31–33
        60mm mortar training 19–20
        Tank-infantry teams 147–48
Takabanare Island 222–23
Tanks
    Flame 263, 339
    Japanese 74, 76–77
    U.S. (M-4 "Sherman") 135,
        147–8, 246, 259–60, 263,
        271, 322, 333
Troop strength
    Marine infantry regiment
        342–43
    U.S. ashore D day, Okinawa 208

Ulithi Atoll 196n
    Briefings for Okinawa 197
    Fleet anchorage 195–96
    Mog Mog Islet 197
    Ships in Okinawa invasion fleet
        196
Umurbrogol Ridges (*See also*
        Bloody Nose Ridge) 113,
        139, 165n
Ushijima, Lt. Gen. Mitsuru 200

V-E day, news of 243

Walt, Lt. Col. Lewis, USMC 77,
        77n
Wana Draw 251, 258
    Air strike 261
    Appearance of battlefield
        267–68, 271–99 *passim*
    Battle of 259–67
    Frontline living conditions
        270–304 *passim*
    Japanese utilization of terrain
        259–61
    U.S. bombardment of 262–63
Wana Ridge 251, 259
War dog, Doberman pinscher
        109
Wasp, USS 196n

Yaeju Dake (also Yuza Dake—
        Yaju Dake Escarpment)
        321–22, 328–29
Yontan Airfield 206, 215, 219
Yorktown, USS 196–97n

Zero (Japanese plane) 219–20